Micheal Kazuhiro Nishi

Dedication

This is for my daughter, Yumi Bollag and my friend, Bill Fuller and Lee McGarity. Your sacrifice with joy and selflessness on this book is greatly appreciated. Without you, my dream would never have become a reality. To Daniel, Santi, Alex and Lyla Bollag. To my Mother Sadayo in Japan and in memory of my late Father, Tamotsu. Gracias por todo, mis amigos y amigas de Cuba.

The Last Revolution

Acknowledgements

This story is fictional and is based on my personal experiences while traveling throughout Cuba. In the novel, the history mentioned about Cuba and Japan is based on actual historical events, facts, and people. The main characters in the novel were drawn from my imagination. There are no such persons living in Cuba; the characters are a product of the author's imagination with input from many friends, relatives, and people I've met along this journey

After the completion of this novel, I was driving home from Knoxville, Tennessee, when my daughter phoned to tell me that she was watching *CNN Breaking News*. I drove to the nearest truck stop to find a television. The report said that Fidel Castro had undergone emergency surgery and had handed over temporary power of Cuba to his brother, Raúl. I was stunned. It was as if I were watching the first chapter of my novel unfolding in reality.

I wished for Castro's healthy recovery. Soon after this broadcast, I returned to Cuba to visit old friends. There were no apparent signs of chaos or political unrest due to Fidel's failing health. The Cuban people on a whole were concerned for their leader and expressed genuine sadness over his illness. This was a very different attitude from the Cubans here in the United States who long for Fidel to pass on.

Cuba has not changed much. My friends and acquaintances still continue to live under depressed economic conditions and to deal with the day-to-day hardships of life under Communism and this unusual dictatorship. They still wheel and deal in the black market. They still live in crumbling homes. They still smile and love Cuban music and gatherings.

Nothing ever seems to change much in Cuba. Despite their problems, the people remain peaceful and friendly. They still have nothing but time on this tropical island. Cuba will always remain a beautiful and soulful place where the people are the true treasure. Cuba is a fascinating place and is a dream world that will always hold a special place in my heart. *09-20-06, Trinidad, Sancti-Spiritus, Cuba.*

Micheal Kazuhiro Nishitani

I want to thank all those people who inspired these characters and this story. I want to thank all those who helped me in editing this novel. Thank you for your input, ideas, and valuable research information. This story was made possible by a wealth of people and a collaboration of thoughts and ideas. All have a voice in this novel and have made this story rich and alive. I extend my heartfelt thanks to the following people who made this novel possible:

Original manuscript translator/Creative rewriter, editor:
Yumi Nishitani Bollag

Executive editor
Lee McGarity

Creative literature / editor consultants:
Robin Willcox

Associate editing consultants:
Dwayne Thieme
Ken Nishitani & Ashlee Barker
Kimberly Bolan in Manila Philippines

Proofing/Editing:
Floyd Deal
Rema Murphy
Pamela Rains

Medical consultants:
Jon Katze, PhD
Emmet Bell, MD

Proof reading consultant by:
Bob & Nina Mcvay, Tracy Bollag,
Mary Sciara, Terry Duncan

Advice on technical issues related to computer science:
Daniel Seung Ik Jun, PhD

The Last Revolution

Japanese sake consultant by:
    John Gauntner
    www.Sakeguy.com

Computer technical advices:
    Donnie Sowell
    Carol Thomas

Equipment technical service:
    Dennis Seaton

Military advisors:
    Ed Hickman, Harold McPherson

Mathematical technical advice:
    Nancy & Greek Gates

Cuban culture, Spanish language consorted by:
    Aymee Rodríguez, Elían Bacallao,
    Freddie Díaz, Claro Díaz MD,
    Marieta Vásquez, Habana, Cuba
    Delia Medina, México,
    Lissett & Hiro Ito, Puerto Rico, Japón

Korean culture advisors:
    Ki Won and Lucy Yoo Jeong Chung.

Book Cover Design:
    Kelly Simpson,
    Williams Creative Group Shreveport LA.

Website Created & Maintained by
    Jacqueline High
    www.wsimarketing.com/jhigh

Finally, books Publishing Consultant:
    Bill Fuller
    April Bogdon and Lauren Woolley.

Micheal Kazuhiro Nishitani

The Last Revolution

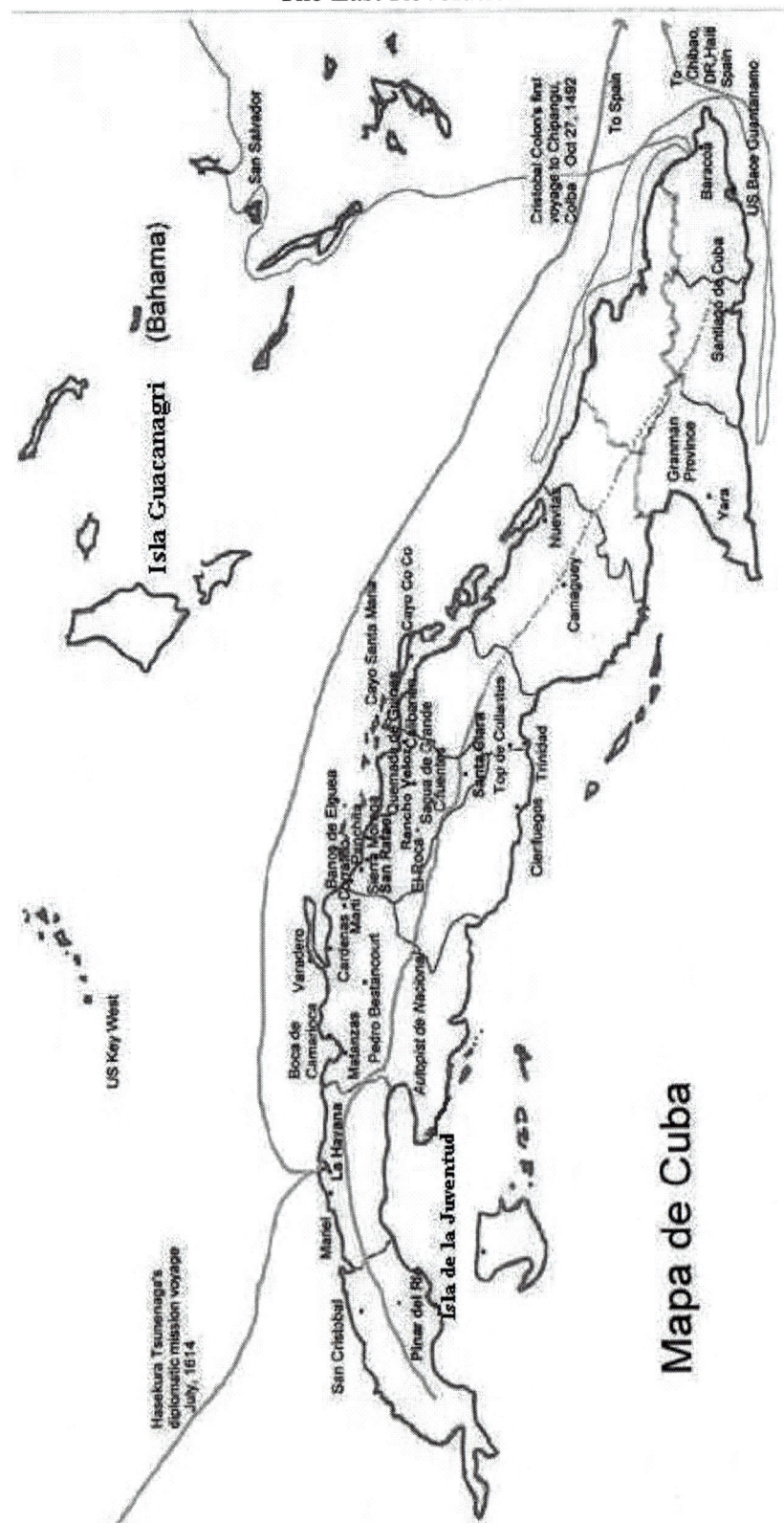

Micheal Kazuhiro Nishitani

The Last Revolution

最後の革命

La Última Revolución.
Лоследняя революция. Die Letzer Revolution.

Written by
Micheal Kazuhiro Nishitani.
ISBN-10: 14196-6774-2
ISBN-13:978-1419667749
http://www.thelastrevolutionnovel.com
ALL RIGHTS RESERVED.
U.S & International Copyright © June 22, 2006.

 ## Chapter 1

July 6, 2008, 8:00 a.m.

CNN Late Breaking News: Broadcasters report that thousands of Cuban-American refugees are fleeing Southern Florida in an attempt to return home to Cuba. The Cuban Navy and Coast Guard have announced that they will shoot to kill any refugees attempting to cross the Cuban coastal boundaries. The Cuban military has requested the support of the US Coast Guard in preventing the return of these refugees and averting further disaster.

Meanwhile in Cuba, mass hysteria mounts as rumors of a revolution are spreading like wildfire. In the streets of San Cristóbal de Habana, enormous frenzied mobs chant, "Viva Cuba! Viva Cuba! Cuba libre!," as they await news. The last twenty-four hours have wrought amazing changes in Cuba.

In the center of the city, at the replica of the US Capitol Building called Capitolio Nacional, hundreds of thousands have gathered—young and old—to celebrate this pivotal moment in Cuba's history. Today their lives will begin anew. Explosive excitement fills the air. From Santiago de Cuba to Pinar Del Rio, all Cuba has rallied together to learn their future. TV and radio broadcast capabilities have been established in all cities and towns across the country to receive the life-changing news coming from Havana's center square.

July 3, 2008
Three days earlier at the Army Corps headquarters in Santa Clara, Province of Villa Clara, Cuba

At 4:30 a.m., Fidel Castro's gigantic presidential Mi-8T helicopter and escorted by eight security choppers neared the heliport. Everything looked normal. The port was on full alert due to the emergency situation. From the heavy assault chopper, the Black Akula KA-50, Commander Lt. Martin Naranjo, contacted the Santa Clara Army communications tower—the first of the helicopters lined up in the air space above the E2 heliport in preparation for landing.

Twelve young, uniformed honor guards and security guards waited for Castro's arrival. At precisely 4:35 a.m., the ground crew directed the helicopter traffic as they normally would. Security was tight. Fidel's team didn't suspect a thing, nor did they seem at all suspicious that anything could be wrong. The situation looked perfectly secure.

Fidel, his brother Raúl Ruiz Castro, and the top General of the Cuban Army, Chief General Hector Elias Garcia, were in the first helicopter to touch down. The eight attack gun ships touched down just after them. The ground crew was on high alert as they waited below. The door opened, and a team of elite and heavily-armed bodyguards rushed out and surrounded Fidel, Raúl and General Garcia as they exited the chopper. Fidel looked old and tired.

The Army ground crew directed the entourage to the lighted red carpet. Fidel always insisted on an official reception. Second-in-command of the Army, General Abelardo González, stood waiting. As Fidel approached him, the general saluted and looked straight into Fidel's eyes. Fidel looked relieved to see his favorite young general. Fidel smiled and saluted him in return.

July 5, 2008, at 9:00 p.m., Havana
As night fell, the people of Havana waited expectedly to confirm the rumors they had been hearing over the last twenty-four hours that the President of Cuba, Fidel Castro, his brother Raúl Castro Ruz, and chief military Army general, Hector Elias Garcia, had been killed in a *coup d'etat*. General Abelardo González now controlled the country.

All of Cuba felt as raw as a finger in a wasp's nest. The very earth seemed to quake. Emotions spilled into the streets. The excitement was uncontrollable. Police could not control the mobs and chaos overtaking the country. The entire infrastructure of Cuba had collapsed. The government, the schools, and all major institutions had completely closed down. In one moment, the heaviest presence in this country had become as weightless and elusive as a ghost. What had seemed posed to last forever was now gone.

The Last Revolution

Pandemonium reigned in the streets. Everyone felt it, and the whole country was alive with the excitement of sharks in a feeding frenzy. Radical new changes and events were about to unfold. Even radio and television announcers, normally so well-schooled in vocal modulation, shouted and screamed over the airwaves. The broadcasters cried, "*Viva Cuba, Sobre*" and "*Cuba libre*" to all who listened. The national newspapers, *El Habanero* and *Tribuna de la Habana*, as well as both national and international newspapers and television stations, flooded the city streets as their crews fought to broadcast the first coverage of this sensational event. News focused on rumors of the assassination of Fidel by General González. The coup was rumored to have taken place in Santa Clara, the central province of Ville Clara. However, at this point, no one knew if freedom was truly at hand.

At the same time that the radio and television broadcasters screamed the news, they were also asking people to remain calm and to obey martial law. The military was enforcing an 8:00 p.m. to 8:00 a.m. curfew. But even this did not stop the people who had gathered outside with their neighbors to learn what was happening. Streets were cleared to make way for army trucks bearing soldiers armed with machine guns. The military was roaming the countryside in an effort to maintain a semblance of control. The military presence was generally appreciated and created a feeling of safety among a populace who had not slept in the last forty-eight hours. The people were wired into events coming to them live and just minutes away. Hysteria and awe prevailed.

July 6, 2008, at 10:30 a.m., Havana

The entire island vibrated with anticipation of long-awaited freedom, and the changes it would make in their lives. Cubans across the country could not believe that the mighty reign of Castro was over. A convoy of Russian-made jeeps and other military vehicles carrying Army General González and assorted military officials rumbled ponderously through the center of Havana Crowds rushed closer to catch a glimpse of the convoy and its passengers. Several hundred police officers forced the locals to make way for the approaching vehicles.

Micheal Kazuhiro Nishitani

The mob chanted and screamed as well-armed soldiers in military vehicles escorted three generals along with their wives and families to a waiting podium. Accompanying them was a distinguished looking, gray-haired Asian man with a beautiful Cuban wife and two children. No one had ever seen this man and his family among the high-ranking Cuban generals. Silence was total at this momentous portal of freedom. Anticipation lit every tear-lined face. Faces all over Cuba's fourteen provinces shared the same emotions visible here in the crowds in Havana. The hearts of all the people were united in this riveting moment as the prestigious group walked along the red carpet to the podium.

By 11:00 a.m. at the Capitolio Nacional, there was a deafening gun volley. A handsome and well-built man in a decorated military uniform was seated at center stage. He was Army General Abelardo González, Fidel's trusted second-in-command from the Army Corps in Santa Clara. González walked up to the microphone. The crowd started chanting, "*Viva Cuba! Viva Cuba! Viva Cuba!*"

The screams and cheers died out as a second volley was fired off. A beaming General González began to speak saying, "Greetings to the people of Cuba, distinguished guests, and the world. How different Cuba looks and feels today!" General González smiled with confidence and humility at the sea of faces and continued, "We have gathered here to celebrate the birth of a new era in our country. Together we weep with joy and thanks for the end of the political, economic, and personal tyranny that has held us captive for too many years."

"Today we are fully alive and awake to witness extraordinary and powerful changes for our country and our way of life. Together we are united in freedom for the first time in many years and in the knowledge that everything is possible. We can finally direct our destiny towards a new and brighter Cuba." The crowd cheered and applauded.

"I want to first introduce a very important man who has been my friend for many years, Dr. Hiroaki Nakagawa." All eyes turn to the gray-haired Japanese man and his beautiful Cuban wife and daughters sitting next to the generals. "He is also a friend to all Cubans. I am permitted to say that he is now a naturalized Cuban citizen. He is the one responsible for creating the events that have lead to Cuba's freedom, your freedom. Dr.

The Last Revolution

Nakagawa has an important message. Please give him your attention." Anticipation and bewilderment filled the crowd as they watched General González walk toward the Japanese man who looked to be in his late fifties. He had a likable face that radiated intelligence. They shook hands and bowed to one another. The man appeared humble as he walked to the microphone and turned toward the crowd.

Nakagawa spoke with quiet power into the sea of silence saying, "I ask you to pause for a moment as we remember the former President of Cuba, Fidel Castro." He waited briefly then said, "Also, please offer a moment of silence for his brother Raúl Castro and for Chief General, Hector Elias Garcia."

After the pause, the Asian man resumed speaking by saying, "My name is Hiroaki Nakagawa. It is a great honor to be here with you. Today we have made history. You are now living in a democratic and free Cuba. From this day forward Cuba belongs to you and not to a handful of political elite. This is your country, and you are now free to choose your own destiny, free to live your dreams. No one will interfere with your freedom. But remember, the gift of freedom comes with a very heavy price. Nothing in life is free, not even freedom itself. The price you must pay is responsibility for your own actions. The profit you will earn is responsibility for your own actions."

"Soon you must elect a law-enforcement agency to protect this great country. You must help create a code of law that will protect us all equitably. You must also agree to respect the laws that you create. When you can respect and obey those self-created laws, then a new Cuba will reap the benefits of true democratic freedom. These are the first steps in launching a free society. Freedom is not simple. On the contrary, it is both complex and elusive. And yet, it is as fundamental as one person. A free society begins with you. You are responsible for your own actions. And your own actions constitute the very foundation of this remarkable country."

"Today marks the end of the Communist regime! That regime died with Fidel Castro. But it will take time to establish a new and better system. For the next twenty-four months, General Abelardo González will oversee a temporary government. Cuba has been at a standstill for so long that it will take at least that much time to start it moving forward again. During that period, we must all help each other. The laws of this temporary government and authority must be respected for peace to prevail, and for a more prosperous and open society to emerge. We are all in this together. Embrace your motherland, for she has always embraced you!"

"Soon, with the whole world watching, you will participate in an open election. This first free election must be monitored by the United Nations. You will have twenty-four months to select and nominate your candidates; candidates chosen by the people. From among these, you will elect your leaders to office. Cuba is in your hands today. This country is yours both to mold and to enjoy. Congratulations to you all. I am deeply honored to be among you today!" The crowd slowly began to absorb the meaning of Nakagawa's address. They muttered, then rumbled, then exploded into chants, shouts, and wordless cries as military guns erupted once, then twice, and then a third and final time in a twenty-one gun salute.

The Japanese man stepped back and joined the three uniformed generals. The Cuban Army band began to play the Cuban National Anthem. On this historic day, July 6, 2008, crowds across Cuba and here in the city square sang along as tears poured down their faces. It was impossible to believe that the rule of Fidel Castro and his Communist regime was finally over. The people were now living in a free society. Freedom! Cuba was finally free!

It was mid-day in Havana. Amid the endless blue skies and the scorching sun, the palm trees swayed gently in the Caribbean breeze that had softly kissed her people for eons. These tropical breezes had caressed indigenous tribes and welcomed fearful slaves. They had touched conquerors and stroked dictators. Like the lullaby of a loving mother to her fretful babe, the rustle of the palms serenaded the city. Cuba continued to celebrate for the next thirty days. The United Nations Council recognized and accepted a new government and democracy. The United States, the European Union, Japan, China, Russia, and many other countries around the world sent their congratulations. The G-8 countries promised to pour financial aid into Havana. The world celebrated this gigantic step for Cuba and looked on in anticipation.

The rebuilding of Cuba as a nation under the new democratic government began slowly and carefully and not without tremendous difficulty for the people of Cuba. They had

The Last Revolution

lived their entire lives under the familiar constraints of Communism, to be sure, but now they trusted that democracy would nurture them. Greatness was theirs for the taking. The question still remained, though, "Could this new democracy remain secure?" Only the fullness of time could provide the answer.

The world continued to look upon the events in Cuba with bewilderment. People around the globe were curious about how these events had come about. How did the enigmatic leader of Cuba, known by so many around the world by his first name alone, really meet his end? There were so many unanswered questions. The experts devoured the facts they were given and still could not connect all the dots. They knew there had to be more to this. However, Hiro and the two generals had made a pact never to reveal the true events that had led to the last revolution. It was their secret, and the world would be left to wonder what had really happened.

Chapter 2

1955 in the mountain prefecture *of Chugoku in Hiroshima, Japan.*

As a middle school student, Hiro was very interested in mathematics and was always at the head of his class. His teachers recognized that he had exceptional abilities in number concepts. People living in this mountain countryside worked hard to earn extra money, and twelve-year-old Hiroaki was no exception. Hiroaki rode to and from middle school on his new blue bicycle. To earn five cents, after school hours Hiro made three trips into town daily carrying firewood on his back to sell. He had been selling wood for the last three years.

Hiroaki Nakagawa was born in Fukuyama, Japan, on August 6, 1942. His father was the first son of an old farmer. His father and mother, first cousins, were married at a very young age. In those days in Japan, people frequently married cousins through arranged marriages in order to keep wealth in the family. The Japanese countryside where Hiro's family lived had not changed much in thousands of years. The people were still very old-fashioned and lived life in the traditional way. The first settlement had started in this location around 1200 A.D. Hiroaki had an honorable farming family history. His lineage could be traced all the way back to 1465.

His father Tamotsu became a skilled construction worker who received special training; ultimately, he became one of the best concrete construction specialists in the country. In 1940, he created a construction business that was awarded many contracts by the Japanese Army and Navy, and work was abundant.

As Japan continued to expand into new territories overseas in Korea, Manchuria, and China, work poured in, and Tamotsu's business boomed. Hospitals were constructed under his watchful eye for the Japanese military as Japan's Imperial Army began to fulfill their goal of controlling the entire Asian mainland. Having government contracts meant great profit, but the work was also very difficult and stressful. Working with the Japanese military added extra pressure to the family's life as Hiro's father was seldom at home, usually returning only one day every few months. His absences were difficult for his family.

Hiroaki was the first born of four children. In Japan, to be the first born son is a very special position within the family. Over the years, he was also the only son, so his father was especially proud of Hiroaki. In his pride, he planned for Hiro to become an ocean freight engineer, a very lucrative and prestigious job. Tamotsu chose this for his son's future career because it would ensure a good life with security and wealth for Hiro.

When Hiroaki was born, Japan was at war with China over territorial expansion. Since the US had a treaty with China, the US became involved in this war causing international relations between the United States and Japan to worsen. Since Japan was devoid of natural resources, such as petroleum and ores, she looked overseas to meet her needs. Before 1939, the US was Japan's major supplier of such natural resources.

The US, in an effort to end Japan's war with China, enforced a strict trade embargo to control Japan's newly created war machine. Ultimately, Japan decided to go to war with the United States over those oil and trade embargoes. Japan's need for war materials meant that it had to set its sights on the Pacific Southeast. Only the US stood in Japan's way.

At the time, Japan's Navy was one of the strongest in the world. The US Pacific fleet located in Pearl Harbor was its only threat. In order to protect Japan's interests in the Pacific, Japanese fighter pilots led a surprise attack on Pearl Harbor on December 7, 1941, paralyzing America's fleet.

Japan's strategy to occupy the Pacific Southeast also included seizing the Philippines, Malaya, Burma, Singapore, and the Dutch and British colonies in Indonesia and the West Indies. Japan looked to the European colonies of the southeast for coveted raw materials and natural resources. By 1942, Japan had succeeded beyond their wildest expectations and severed the American line in the Pacific. However, in the coming months, Japan's lack of radar technology led to a major defeat at the hands of the US military at the Midway Islands, and to similar defeats in the South Pacific. Japan was unable to make up its losses.

Micheal Kazuhiro Nishitani

Growing US airpower made it impossible for Japan to re-supply its forces ashore, so the Japanese troops began to go hungry and were soon on the verge of starvation. Slowly, the US troops regained their control of the Pacific Southeast and moved ever closer to Japan itself with defeats in Luzon, Iwo Jima, and Okinawa. In 1944, the US conducted a strategic bombing campaign on Tokyo, the capital of Japan, and on Hiroshima, its major port city. Hiroshima was pounded as US Air Force B-29 bombers from Titian bombarded the city. Every night the skies were filled with fire. Families were forced to escape by staying in emergency underground bunkers and tunnels for safety.

When Tamotsu returned from constructing hospitals in Korea, he told his wife to go to the mountains in the country for safety. The family had relatives living on a farm there. Hiro's father felt that this remote area would be safe from bomber raids. He knew that the threat of attacks by US B-29 attack on southern Japan would leave much of the city in ashes so no one in or near Hiroshima would be safe. The family had no other choice but to flee their home.

The intense bombing became more and more frequent. In a final all-out effort, the US dropped atomic bombs on Hiroshima on August 6 and on Nagasaki on August 9, 1945. Hundreds of thousands of people burned to death during each bombing. Thousands upon thousands more were severely injured, maimed and disabled for life.

Meanwhile, at sea, Japan was defenseless. Its Air Force was almost depleted, and its cities and populace had been destroyed by the bombing campaign. This destruction meant that the end of the war was near. Hiroaki's family of five survived by remaining safely hidden away in the mountainous countryside.

A visit to them in their rural refuge was the last time Hiroaki and his family would ever see their beloved father. In 1943, he and his Navy construction battalion consisting of 2000 Seabees departed from Japan for the last time from Kure Naval Station just outside Hiroshima and headed to Guam Island to complete emergency military construction work. Hiroaki's father never returned from this deployment.

When Hiroaki was only five years old, his mother received the devastating message from the police. His father had been killed while on military duty in The Mariana Islands.

The Last Revolution

There were over 31,629 members of the Japanese Navy deployed by Japanese on Saipan. Approximately 29,500 Japanese died as a result of the fighting. Only 2,100 Japanese prisoners survived the battle. Tamotsu Nakagawa was not one of them. Hiroaki's mother Sadayo went into a period of intense mourning. Forever afterward, Hiro remembered his mother weeping and crying all the time in her soul-deep sadness over the loss of her husband. As a child, Hiroaki watched his mother mourn, but did not understand what had just happened or what it meant. He wouldn't fully understand the depth of this loss or its unforeseeable consequences until much later in his life.

Despite the feeling that the Nakagawa's life had stilled the moment Tamotsu's heart stopped beating, activity in the world around them marched on. On August 15, 1945, Emperor Hirohito publicly announced Japan's surrender. The war in the Pacific came to an end and a defeated Japan lay in ruins. Hiroaki and his family in the countryside had survived the war intact, but their spirits were defeated. They had lost everything material, and their hearts had been torn out.

After Tamotsu's death, the Nakagawa family's shelter in the mountain village was very poor compared to the small comfortable home they had fled during the war. The five of them lived in a tiny twelve foot by twelve foot room with one small table where the family sat together and worked. This was all they had. By night, they slept in this room on their futons. By day, they rolled-up their futons and moved the table back to create a living room. There was only one light and no windows. Electricity was not installed until Hiro's fourth year of school, when they finally got a single 40 watt light which constituted a sensational event in their lives.

There was no indoor toilet, either. When anyone needed to use the toilet, they had to walk to their uncle's home about fifty yards away. No one wanted to use the bathroom at night as it was a nightmare to walk there in the dark, the cold, or the rain. In this remote village, people still believed ghosts came out at night, so the children especially dreaded the terrifying night treks. During their self-imposed exile, Hiroaki's mother worked as a farmer doing "stoop" labor, cultivating crops by hand. This was back-breaking hard work but it was what she had to do to feed her family of five. And Hiroaki and his three sisters all had to help their mother just for the family to survive.

Micheal Kazuhiro Nishitani

This remote village was so secluded that not much out of the ordinary happened here. It was always peaceful and quiet. The population of the village was about forty people. The mountains were steep. Occasionally, American occupation Army jeeps got lost as they wandered off the country roads. The roads were narrow along the steep mountainside. The Jeeps could barely maneuver along the winding mountain paths. The arrival of a jeep was highly unusual so it caused a lot of excitement when the people saw the Americans.

Most automobiles at that time used wood-burning steam engines because of the high cost of gasoline. Charcoal was less expensive than gasoline. Periodically, businessmen came to buy food from the farmers just after the harvest. This was an important event in the small village because not many visitors came there.

In the countryside, children often farmed. They cultivated the soil and harvested rice and wheat. Rice planting was the worst; All of the children had to help in the rice paddies because the work was so labor-intensive. Since his own family did not have farm land, Hiro tried to help his uncles in any way he could, even though he never liked farming because of the hard physical work. When he did out of necessity go into the paddies, he would work math problems, lost and safe in a world no one else could enter. For Hiro, numbers always held more magic and more mystique than anything else ever could.

When he did farm work, he never had to use his brain much so he just socialized with his relatives and enjoyed the peace. He was quiet and thoughtful. His uncle Takatoshi-san would look at Hiro's math book and say, "What are you doing with that book! You're only twelve years old. You should do fifth grade mathematics like the other kids. You think you can figure out that book?" Everybody always laughed, because everyone knew Hiro was a genius with numbers. Hiro just grinned.

By the time he became a teenager, Hiro knew he did not want to become a freight engineer as his father had hoped. He wanted to do something that would utilize his brain more and be related to his ability in mathematics. And he really did not want to become a teacher. The choice was crucial, because in this part of the country, when you decided on a job, it became your future, and you remained in that career for the rest of your life. This is

The Last Revolution

why students took their studies so seriously. Junior high was every teenager's nightmare as the time to choose a career drew near.

A new era was coming, and with it much opportunity for him. The Sony Corporation of Japan had just introduced the first transistor radio to the United States in March 1957. It was the first time the US had recognized that Japan made high quality items. Prior to this time, "Made in Japan," was synonymous with cheap items. But now, as a new era of technology was being born, Japan was leading the way.

During the winter of 1958, Hiroaki was sixteen years old. The daily entertainment at home consisted of listening to the news being broadcast from an old black radio. Hiroaki always loved to listen to the news, but this day he heard something sensational from the other side of the world. A revolution was developing in the Caribbean. He listened closely as Radio Japan NHK reported live from Havana, Cuba. It was after 8:00 PM when his mother arrived 8 p.m. home exhausted from work. But she cooked rice with wheat and vegetables for her children. Hiro told his mother about the news reports. She listened without comment.

Hiro got out his world map to see where Cuba was located. He didn't know where Cuba was on the New World Map, but when he finally found the country, it looked like Japan to him—a small island on the other side of the world. He looked at the surrounding countries and saw the Dominican Republic. He remembered that his teacher had told the class that one of his school mates had left for the Dominican Republic because his family had immigrated there for rice farming. He remembered the teacher's words.

With each new broadcast, Hiro was transported to the revolution raging in streets a world away. Reporters spoke of Cuban officials, of army generals, and of their staff who had been captured. But in the background of the broadcasts, Hiro heard live gunfire and screams. With each staccato explosion, Hiro jumped. He closed his eyes to block out the horror, but the battle raged on the screens of his eyelids. He was terrified. But he had to listen. Day after day, he listened. And he knew that the cries of the revolution would be imprinted on his memory forever.

Micheal Kazuhiro Nishitani

Since Hiroaki lived in the countryside outside of Hiroshima, he had been sheltered from seeing the destruction and devastation caused by the end of the war. But the war had changed Japan forever, and the destruction and deaths from the bombings were tremendous. The final death toll was over a million people, but Hiro hadn't experienced anything except the peaceful countryside during the war years. Here, it was as if time had stopped, and the family remained isolated and far removed from life in the cities. Now, though, after hearing the radio broadcasts from Cuba, Hiroaki began to have flashbacks even more vibrant. Sometimes he would awaken in the middle of the night screaming, his entire body bathed in sweat. His mother knew Hiro was suffering from terrible nightmares. She wanted to take him to a psychologist. But there was no doctor nearby. There was no money to pay for a visit to a doctor, anyway.

Now he remembered back to WWII when his country was at war. He was young, not yet three years old, and all he could remember were visions of bombs falling from the sky and the sounds of airplanes and explosions in the distance. But because he was so very young when this was happening, his memory was unclear. He actually remembered having a lot of fun inside the emergency tunnel. He used to love to go underground into the bunker. This was like an adventure for a young child who could not understand the reality of the situation. Japan had been devastated by the bombardments and all the cities were in ruins, but here in the countryside Hiroaki and his family were sheltered from seeing this destruction.

Right after the war there were many women who had lost their husbands and had become "war widows". There were also many single Army men who returned and married these women. But Hiro's mother did not want to marry again. Many people tried to introduce her to these men, but each time, she rejected the notion of meeting another husband. She could not forget Tamotsu and his love for her and for their children. She remembered his last words to her, "I ask that you always take good care of my children. Please make sure that my only son goes to the university to become a freight engineer. I want him to have a good career. Make sure that my daughters are well-educated and marry good men."

She remembered these words as if it were yesterday, and she pictured his handsome face, his smile, his strength. That

The Last Revolution

was why she always sat with Hiro as he did his homework. She was determined to make his father's wishes come true.

"Your teacher thinks you can pass the national achievement test in mathematics. If so, then you may have your tuition paid for," she said one evening. "Son, this is a great opportunity for you. All you have to do is to score 95 or higher." She looked at him with her dark, steady gaze. "Do you think you can make that score?"

Hiroaki simply replied, "Mother, I will try."

Hiroaki's mother continued. "Your father wanted you to become a freight engineer, but you know we don't have enough money to pay for you to attend the school in Yokohama. Maybe you can become a mathematics professor at the university instead." She knew that her son's education would secure such an opportunity for him.

Not long after, Mother went to have a discussion with Hiroaki's teacher. She came away from that meeting believing that her son's skills would best be used in the new technology industry. The teacher suggested that his mathematical skills could be used in the development of a new machine called the "computer".

When his mother arrived home, she approached her son with this news. Hiroaki had never heard of a computer. He was curious and asked if one could watch it or listen to it. All that his mother knew was what the teacher had told her. The school teacher had gotten her information from the head school in the city, and there had been much discussion about the news that someone in the United States had received a patent to create this new machine that could calculate numbers on a TV screen.

In Japan this was perceived as a great invention indeed, because it was common knowledge that most Americans had difficulty calculating equations in their minds and used their fingers to solve problems. Therefore, Hiro thought this "computer" held great potential. Hiro asked, "Would the Americans become dependent on this machine?" He remained silent but had many thoughts about the machine's possibilities as he finished his school work.

Chapter 3

In the mountainside, one could witness nature in its most beautiful forms. The water in the streams was so clear you could see the bottom. Many types of fish were plentiful in these fresh streams, but it was a delight to see the Ayu fish swimming and feeding on the algae growing on the rock beds. Hiroaki had spent much of his time fishing there over the years.

Hiroaki loved to fish every chance he got. Hiro fished to provide protein for his family since chicken and fowl were so expensive. The fish were free and abundant except in the winter months. Hiro especially loved the Ayu fishing season in June and July each year. The Ayu fish lived in freshwater and fed on algae built up on the surface of the rocks. Then in the fall, they swam to the ocean and lived between freshwater and saltwater to hatch their eggs. The baby Ayu then swam upstream toward freshwater in the spring. As adults, they returned in the fall as the cycle of life continued. The cycle of the Ayu was similar to the behavior of the salmon. But the Ayu only grew to be six to seven inches long and weighed less than one-eighth of a pound. Although small, they were very tasty fish and were a favorite among the people.

Ayu often appeared in historic Japanese art work on ukioe traditional 18th century woodblock prints. The prints showed old fishermen wearing straw skirts and straw hats. This was the traditional outfit for fishermen to wear in ancient Japan. The woodblocks showed the fishermen with small ropes tied to cormorants' necks so they wouldn't fly away. They put the birds into the water, and the kamo birds dove down and caught the fish and brought them up to the surface. The rope made it so the birds could not swallow these fish. This was the traditional way of catching the Ayu fish not seen anywhere else in the world. It is still practiced today in Japan in the country. At night, the fishermen would use torches to provide light for these unusual fishing expeditions. The Ayu season was very famous in Japan's

The Last Revolution

history.

Hiroaki could not wait for the Ayu fishing season to begin. The habits of the Ayu were not the same as other fish, and good fishermen had to learn and to understand the behavior of the fish. Hiroaki was fascinated by their behavior. In order to catch these special fish, one must have a special license. When one was given the license, the new fisherman was given one single live Ayu fish to use as bait. Having the single Ayu was crucial. This way Ayu fishing was very restricted.

Hiroaki grew up fishing in this way with his friends. When the bait Ayu was put into the water, it fought other fish with its hooked tail. Hiroaki took his fighting Ayu to a clear place in the stream and waited for other Ayu fish to swim near to protect their territory. When the fight began, eventually the other Ayu would get hooked, and then Hiroaki would gather them with a small hand net. This is the way Ayu fish were caught unless the fisherman had traditional cormorant birds. After the bait Ayu caught two or three fish, it began to grow tired. It was then customary to change to a new Ayu. Only a strong fresh Ayu could successfully "hacker" other Ayu.

It was one of the most unique ways of fishing in the world. Hiroaki loved the fishing season and he always caught many fish for his family. His mother cooked a feast with his fresh catch. Tender Ayu and hot rice were his favorite dinner.

Chapter 4

When Hiro finished middle school, he successfully passed the national achievement exam in mathematics with a perfect one-hundred score, which was a very rare and much honored achievement. He thus secured for himself a position at the University of Hiroshima. His perfect score and academic excellence also earned him a full scholarship. His career in mathematical science had begun.

At the university, he was at last introduced to the intriguing new machine called "the computer." It was only in the research stage, and the university didn't even have a fully developed model or prototype yet but Hiroaki became fascinated with the computer and wanted to know as much as possible about it. He soon realized that eventually he must go to the United States for further study. He decided to apply for a scholarship through Fulbright foundation. To become an exchange student, one must be chosen officially and be recommended by the university.

He studied almost eighteen hours a day for four years. He became known for his excellence in mathematical science and for his unwavering determination to receive perfect scores on his exams. He also became a dedicated and innovative research student who was asked to assist many of his professors. He knew he had to do whatever it took to get this Fulbright scholarship. It would be his first and last chance to get close to the best and brightest minds in the United States. This was his golden opportunity.

While many of the other students attended dinners and sports events or socialized throughout the year, Hiro chose to delve ever deeper into his studies and research. His life narrowed to one focus: his studies, his dream. The sacrifice was enormous, but it finally paid off in his senior year when he became the only student ever to receive a perfect score on every exam. It was rare to have a student like Hiroaki .The university honored him with an official recommendation to The Fulbright Foundation,

The Last Revolution

and Hiro learned that he would get a full scholarship to one of the most prestigious universities in the US. With the news of his good fortune, Hiroaki could not help but feel blessed, and he knew that destiny was guiding his steps.

Hiro arranged a special meeting with the Fulbright administrators through their office in Tokyo. To reach the meeting place, Hiro had to take a long train ride on the midnight express named "Aki" which left Hiroshima at 10:30 p.m. and arrived in Tokyo at 7:00 a.m. the next morning. The Tokyo train station had a red tiled roof and a special eighteenth century European style designed by the famous architect, Tatsuno Kingo, the first modern architect of Japan. Originally, he had designed a building in the style of the Momoyama Palace as Japanese influence, but Emperor Meiji requested something foreign in feeling, as it faced the Imperial Palace. This was why it was so different from buildings found anywhere else in Japan.

In the train station, Hiro went to the lavatory and washed his face and brushed his teeth to prepare himself for his important meeting. Then he caught a city bus at the west side of Tokyo station at the bus terminal. He took bus number 42, which went straight to The University of Tokyo campus where the most elite of all Japanese students attended college. The university was very expensive, and Hiroaki couldn't afford a school like that. It was for the rich of the nation. He got off of the bus on the side street near the university campus and walked to the front gate to ask for information from the attending officer.

In the office, Hiro met a young female counselor who was also a Fulbright student who had studied at the University of Michigan and had returned to Japan to represent the organization in Tokyo. Hiroaki was surprised when she began to speak in excellent English saying, "Good Morning, Mr. Nakagawa. My name is Yoko Higashi, and I represent The Fulbright Foundation. I will be interviewing you this morning. Please take a seat, and we will begin." Hiroaki nervously took his seat. He was a very shy boy and was not used to representing himself.

"Please tell me why you requested a meeting with us today?" Hiro was so surprised by her perfect English that his mind went blank. He froze. Then Yoko asked the same question a little more slowly. "Mr. Nakagawa, why have you come to our office today?"

Hiro became red in the face and began to stutter. "Ugh... Ugh... I understand what you are saying, but my English is not very good. I understand more than I can speak," he replied.

Yoko smiled and said, "We can proceed in Japanese if that is more comfortable for you."

Immediately, Hiroaki regained his confidence. "I need some information about which universities I will be able to attend using the scholarship," he asked her. "I want to understand my options. That is why I am here today."

Yoko looked over his paperwork. Then she said, "There are six universities in the US available for you in the area of mathematics."

Hiroaki asked, "What do you think about computer science? I have heard that new research is being conducted in this field of study somewhere in the US, and I am very interested in it."

"Yes, I believe that you are looking for the Massachusetts Institute of Technology—M.I.T. They have created a new computer science department, and that is the only one beginning to work in this new field of study. If you agree, we can submit your application to M.I.T. I didn't see anybody else applying for this school because it is extremely difficult to be admitted, but I think you have a good chance of being accepted with your high scores and recommendations."

Hiro sat in the office and Yoko brought him the paperwork. He had to complete the application in English. This was extremely challenging for him, and he needed assistance. He wanted to express to M.I.T that, although his degree was in mathematics, he was very interested in computer science and wanted to focus his attention in this area of study. He felt uneasy about his weak English, but Yoko was patient and kind to Hiroaki through the entire process.

Hiro took the bus back to the train station, but the train was not scheduled to return to Hiroshima until the next morning. Hiro didn't have enough money to go to a hotel for the night so he decided to sleep on the waiting room floor. He had packed a small obento, or lunch package, that Mother made for him so he would have some food to eat. He was contented that he was finally making progress toward his goal, so he did not mind the inconvenience.

The Last Revolution

Hiro looked around the train station and saw many young Japanese wearing bell-bottomed jeans, side burns, and long hair. This was all new to him. He still wore the school uniform of the university—a black long-sleeved shirt with a high collar, dark pants, and plain dark shoes. He covered his short hair with a university hat. All students wore this uniform. But Hiro's was worn out and faded because he was poor and could not afford two uniforms. He knew in a few weeks that he would abandon this uniform and, with it, this phase of his life.

It was March, and the floor of the train station was chilly. For most people, it would have been intolerable, but Hiroaki didn't mind because his excitement kept his mind focused on his future. His goal was finally coming true. This night at the train station was one of the happiest times of Hiro's life. He knew that anything was possible. Hiro prepared for the night and closed his eyes. There was a smile on his young face as he stretched out on the freezing floor of the Tokyo station. But every time Hiro closed his eyes, he felt the rumblings of approaching trains. He heard their screeches as they neared the station. Instantly, he was a child again, and the skies of Japan were filled with B-29s. He was on the streets of Havana surrounded by gunfire and the screams of the executed. No bomb shelters. No radio. Just guns. Screams. Terror. They would haunt him the rest of his days.

The next morning the train arrived on time. Hiro boarded the train and returned home to Hiroshima. There were steep mountains, and the air was chilly. The wild mountain cherry trees were just beginning to blossom. Spring was coming.

When he got to his mother's house, she was not at home. As Hiro waited for her, he looked around at the one tiny room his immediate family had shared for years and could not believe that he lived here. He could not believe he had grown up in such poverty. Without realizing when it happened, already in his mind he had moved on. The world, his future, beckoned like a siren. Finally, when his mother returned, Hiro began to speak. "Mother, Mother, I have good news. I have just come from Tokyo, and I have sent the application to study abroad in computer science to the US university called M.I.T. It is located in Boston."

Most Japanese do not express their emotions, but Hiro's mother had during and after the war.

Then they hugged each other tightly. She always had shown her love to her children. Hiro was also an exception to this rule when expressing his emotions to her. In the midst of war, with his father gone, and their comfortable home a mere memory, Hiro's world had contracted, then contracted again. In the end, all that remained were his beloved numbers. His science. These could never hurt him—or desert him. His mother, whose love was constant, would never change.

The slogan for the imperial Japanese government was: "Save money; have more babies." The post-war period of the late 40s was all about hand-outs from the US. In the 50s and 60s, Japan was just beginning to exit from this cycle as the country became more independent. The Japanese did not like hand outs and wanted to make their own way.

"Education. Education. Education." Japanese youth heard that word time and time again; after all, they were taught that the mind is the only true resource. Because Japan lacked natural resources and had been a farming country for thousands of years, it had developed a unique culture and traditions. It prided itself on them, pulling them on like a protective cloak in the storms of international relations.

That was why there were few Japanese nationals going to study overseas to the US, and even fewer getting scholarships. Usually, only few businessmen who already had US business contacts traveled abroad. Only a small fraction went for educational purposes. Most stayed at home in Japan to study because the government tried to control spending of the dollar. Japan wanted to save money just like everyone else. And it wanted to save currency for the future.

But as the years after World War II passed, Japan became very uneasy. There was political unrest and a movement for independence from occupation by the United Nations and especially the US. To its unhappy citizens, Japan felt more like a US colony than a sovereign nation. Its pride had been crushed. The youth of the nation, especially, agitated to become completely independent. Under the pressure of this unrest, the Socialist-Communist organization seized the opportunity to exploit the situation and to use the youth as the vehicle to gain political power. Their goal was to convert Japan to Communism like its neighbor, China.

The Last Revolution

This movement began in the 50s and 60s, and his mother always told him, "Communists and Socialists are trying to make trouble, and they preach that everyone should be equal. They are using the students to gain power for their political organization. They even pay the students money to demonstrate. They don't care about the people; they just want to gain control of Japan's parliament."

He remembered when he was young when the Communist group had come to his home. They wanted to give his mother money in exchange for her vote. She took the money, but told Hiro later that she never voted for them. She took the money only because she needed it to survive and to feed the family. Desperate times called for desperate measures. Hiro remembered and knew that the Communists were no good. That was why Hiroaki never wanted to join any of the demonstrations. He didn't believe in marching against the government, and he didn't like what the Communists were doing. He thought they were causing trouble, "stirring the pot."

Chapter 5

In early May 1962, Hiro was staying with his mother in the countryside. A month had passed since his trip to Tokyo. He was reading quietly when he heard the clatter of a bicycle outside. He looked up to see the postman, Yamamoto-san, approaching with a registered letter. The envelope said The Fulbright Foundation. Hands shaking, he opened it. He had been accepted to M.I.T. with a full sponsorship. The first semester began September 15. He had to go to Boston. He jumped up with a shout as he digested the news.

His mother was working on the farm almost three miles away, but Hiro felt as if he could run a hundred miles. Seeing Hiro from a distance, Mother stood up and waited. He rushed her and nearly knocked her to the ground with the force of his hug. He started crying; his face was red. He could not speak. He handed her the letter from Tokyo. She read it and shook her head. Tears streamed down her sunburned cheek as she said, "I knew you would get it."

As they walked home, Mother said, "You know, we need to go to Hiroshima to shop for your trip. You need to look presentable and honorable, like a businessman's son. I want you to look wholesome and decent for your classes and teachers." Then she added, "If your father were alive, he would be so proud of your accomplishments."

Hiroaki countered, "You know if he were here, he wouldn't want me to study in the US because he wanted me to be a freight engineer."

Mother said, "I know. But I can feel him smiling down on us. "

She said no more about it, but reminded him not to mention anything to anyone in the village because news like this would travel quickly, and everyone would know about it within the hour. She wanted him to keep his acceptance a secret. In Japan when something big happened, it was customary to keep a confidence until everything was sure and official. Once home,

The Last Revolution

she told Hiro that they must go to the savings department of the post office. This was a community service of the postal system, and many people used it exclusively for their savings. Hiro's mother was no exception. So the next day very early in the morning, they walked for an hour to the post office. After they withdrew the money, they caught a bus to the train station in Fukuyama. It was almost five p.m. by the time the train bound for Hiroshima arrived.

In Hiroshima, they spent the night in a small and inexpensive room across from the university. The next morning they visited the mathematics department and thanked the faculty for their official recommendation. The president patted him on the head and said, "You are a son of Hiroshima, and we will all depend on your good work. Make us proud!" As they were leaving the campus, Hiro looked around at this place and felt comfortable remembering his life of the past four years. He remembered all the days and nights of studying and preparation. He had many, many memories here but this moment was worth every minute of his hard work. Hiro had come here to say good bye to this place once and for all.

Mother wanted to take Hiro to a wholesale clothing store to buy as many things as possible. He needed nice shirts and pants and shoes. This was the first time he and his mother had ever been shopping together. In fact, it was the first time that they really had ever shopped. It was exciting for them both. Before this, they could not afford clothing in the big city shops so his mother had sewn all of his clothes by hand. At the university, he had worn the same uniform every day and washed and dried it every night.

As they walked along the bustling streets of Hiroshima, they passed Peace Park, a memorial to the victims of the atomic bomb. They stopped there remembering that 80,000 people had instantly disappeared when the atomic bomb had fallen on Hiroshima on the morning of August 6, 1945, at a quarter past eight. It had been a muggy, hot summer morning. The children had just gone to school. They were running and playing on the stone streets, but within seconds they had disappeared leaving only imprints of their shadows on the stones as they were vaporized. Their shadows were all that remained.

Hundreds of thousands of people had been burned when the bomb exploded. Within seconds the whole city was an inferno. One could smell only burning human bodies. Witnesses said that to be in Hiroshima that awful day was "like entering the burning gates of hell." Thousands of people ran in agony to the river Ota-gawa Motoyasu-gawa in the middle of the city. They were on fire. Their skin was melting. They were crazed with thirst. And as soon as they drank the water, they died from radiation shock.

Many fireman and soldiers came to help from nearby towns, but they had never seen horror of this magnitude. The scene was surreal. They were helpless. Everywhere they looked, people ran screaming in pain, the skin from their arms hanging over their fingernails. This was truly hell. Those who didn't die in the blast continued to suffer agonies in the aftermath. Even unborn babies were affected by radiation poisoning, and even today people suffer from what is known as "atomic radiation syndrome." Some infants were born with unspeakable deformities and illnesses. Year after year there are still news reports of those dying from exposure to radiation from the blast of 1945.

Today Hiroshima appeared normal, but there remained a scar on the heart of the land. If this atrocity had happened to a US city, they would have hated Japan forever. But the Japanese never expressed their feelings to others about this tragedy. Instead, they said nothing, but silently screamed the agony which time could never erase. Hiroshima became an industrial town with a focus on its reconstruction. Much progress had been made since the war. The government of Japan continued to provide resources to rebuild the infrastructure, but the people had never forgotten the horrible event that took place that infamous day in 1945. Historians believed that the atomic bomb brought about the end of World War II thus saving thousand of American lives; however, Hiro knew that the US had simply used Japan as a guinea pig.

It was hard to understand how intelligent, sophisticated humans could destroy human life so casually and wipe out an entire population. Hiroaki could not understand the psychology behind the war and how one part of the human race could try to eliminate another. Visiting Peace Park for Hiroaki and his mother was a way of paying tribute and giving honor to those who had lost their lives that day and in the war.

The Last Revolution

Hiroaki and his mother shopped for everything over the next couple of days, buying all the items Hiro needed to attend university in the US. Then they returned to their small village in the mountains where Hiro spent his time Ayu fishing until the end of July. This had been not only his favorite pastime since childhood but also a sacred time for him to connect with nature and meditate on his plans for the future. In the mountains, fishing in this ancient and unique way, he felt serenity all around him; he could think quietly.

Because the mountains in this area were not as steep as other areas of Japan, this Chugoku Mountain region had a 2000 year old history: the Chinese and Koreans periodically had traveled through, leaving behind many tales, and remnants of their own cultures. Some even intermarried with the local Japanese, weaving a unique culture in the countryside. Hiro needed to soak up this atmosphere for the little time he had left in the mountains. He wanted to hang onto "home" as long as possible.

It was difficult to describe, but home lived deep inside his heart like a mirage. His heart was here, but he knew that he must leave; he could not achieve his dreams in the countryside. Even his sisters had had to leave this place for the surrounding cities to work and to marry. Life was a like a circle, and he knew it.

Finally, the end of summer came, and it was time for Hiroaki to leave Japan for the United States. He knew that he owed all his good fortune to Mother and Father. He also knew that his was not a dream just for himself, but for all his family; they all would benefit and prosper through his own efforts and successes. The Japanese believed in honoring their elders and appreciating their accomplishments in life. It was the old way, and Hiro lived by this tradition. Although Japan had been a democratic free nation since 1945, even post-war this old tradition was alive and well. It was ingrained into the Japanese brain and handed down through the family generation after generation. The system of living by the law of the land was like a curse: one had to obey it, even if one did not quite fit the culture.

Mother did not want to go to Tokyo to see Hiro leave Japan. His sisters also did not want to say good bye. It was understandable, and Hiro was sympathetic to their feelings. He held their hands and looked at their faces. Suddenly, he was overcome with a hot flash in his eyes. Tears came streaming

Micheal Kazuhiro Nishitani

down his reddened face, and he could scarcely see his mother standing right in front of him. She was crying because she knew this might be the last time she saw her son for many years. Hiro composed himself and, carrying his small suitcase, left the tiny house in the country. He took his first step over the precipice of the unknown on August 2, 1962.

The next day he arrived at Haneda Airport, the main international airport in Tokyo. He stepped onto the TWA DC-3 prop plane, and as it took off felt fear for first time in his life. But, to fulfill his dreams, he knew he must leave the comfort of home and of the known. At 7:30 pm, Hiroaki Nakagawa's flight landed in Honolulu, Hawaii. From there he traveled on to Los Angeles, and finally to his new home Boston.

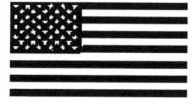

Chapter 6

Hiroaki walked into the scholarship office in Cambridge. An older, very tall gentleman greeted him with a smile. "You must be Hiroaki. I'm Dr. Arthur Smith. We've been looking forward to having you here."

The man was friendly and very gentle. His manner caught Hiroaki's attention because in Japan people were usually serious and almost cold when meeting someone for the first time. And he was so tall...about six feet five inches. Hiro had never seen anyone so big in his life. This was also the first time Hiro had been addressed by his first name in public. In Japan, people addressed others by their last names, never their first names. First names were reserved for close friends and family only.

But Dr. Smith was friendly and spoke very slowly and precisely. He helped Hiro complete all the paperwork easily. Then Dr. Smith stood up and told him, "Congratulations young man. You are officially a student of the Massachusetts Institute of Technology. God bless you." He was also surprised that the man had mentioned God. He had never heard such a thing in Japan. In Japan, religion was a very private matter.

Before they separated, Dr. Smith called his assistant to show Hiroaki to his dormitory. Once they arrived at a building that held a striking resemblance to the Tokyo train station, Hiro was hit by wave after wave of culture shock. He had a room of his own—the very first of his life. To some it might seem spare, but Hiro was overwhelmed by the bed, the chair, the table, and the mini-fridge. For him, the room was like staying in a fancy hotel room. In Japan, a dorm room this size would have housed eight students. He felt lucky and said so to his guide. He could scarcely believe how wonderful his life had suddenly become.

As his mind raced from object to object, he couldn't contain his excitement saying, "This is so nice. Just for me. Even a bed and a fridge. I can't believe this is my very own room." For Hiro, the coup de grace was something that was at first incomprehensible to him. "What are these for?" he asked.

His guide replied, "They're your cafeteria tickets. You get three meals a day, and they're a real smorgasbord."

"Smor-gas-bord? What's that?"

"It means that the cafeteria has a huge variety of foods to choose from daily. You can go at just about any hour of the day, and there will be something interesting on the menu."

Hiro's eyes widened. In Japan, most of his meals were very small and included the typical rice, some pickles, a small piece of fish, and miso soup. To drink, there was always water or green tea, never any variety. Hiro could not wait to visit the cafeteria. It sounded too good to be true. "Anything I want? Are you sure? That is something that I will have to see to believe."

Soon Hiro was overcome by exhaustion after his flight from Japan and from all the excitement. He stretched out in his soft bed, so unlike his hard futon back home, and fell into the deepest sleep of his life.

The next morning arrived, but it seemed more like a dream. Hiro walked to his dorm window and looked out over the campus. The vista was amazing—huge trees that must be hundreds of years old. It was a comfort that he recognized many of them as the same familiar oak trees that grew in Japan. But others looked unfamiliar and offered silent testimony that he had truly come a very long way from home.

A knock on his door pulled Hiro from his reverie. On the doorstep stood four young men with blond hair and blue eyes. They were impressive in their laid back American way, masculinity, and casual dress. And they were so tall. This was Hiro's first encounter with other students in the US, and he was intimidated. The most outgoing one introduced himself saying, "Hi. I'm Jim McCormack. I live next door." He was a surprisingly chubby man with reddish hair and freckles. Hiro stared at him, forgetting to answer, fascinated because he had never met anyone with freckles before.

But Jim had a very friendly way about him and went on gamely saying, "You're in the computer science department with me. We'll be studying together for the next four years." It was not Hiroaki's way to be open with strangers, and he was always reserved and quiet in the correct Japanese manner.

He replied, "Hello, my name is Hiroaki Nakagawa. I am so honored to meet you." It was nice to know that they were all on the same floor and that his neighbor, Jim, was in the computer

The Last Revolution

science department, too. Very soon, Jim and Hiro would be vying for the top spot in the department. The other students told him their names and room numbers and said good bye.

After the students left, Hiro opened his small suitcase and began meticulously to organize his new clothes. Each item had been folded and packed with his mother's love. She had taken great care in packing their purchases. His new friends would not have understood the depth of his feelings when he closed his eyes and tears fell onto his cheeks as he said aloud, "Thank you mother. You are always with me, and I know that I will achieve my goals with your support."

Chapter 7

Four years later Almost before he could imagine it, Hiro's graduation day arrived. As a graduate of the prestigious M.I.T., he naturally received many offers for employment from the business community. Many companies, chief among them IBM, wanted access to his knowledge of computer science. They had all heard about him and his achievements at M.I.T., and the recruiters hounded him mercilessly. But Hiro had always wanted to build an experimental computer based on his own ideas for a new system of computer language.

He understood that the commercial companies were only interested in the bottom line. But Hiro had his own agenda. Machines and numbers were familiar and trusted friends. Business dealings and human feelings were part of an uncharted and suspect wasteland. So, despite aggressive recruiting by the major companies, he decided to move to Los Gatos, California, which was home to many Japanese. Here in this very small mountain community he rented a house on a hillside. Los Gatos was usually very dry, but it reminded him of his country village in Japan when it rained. Besides, Los Gatos was still close enough to Silicon Valley that he could take a taxi to get there when necessary.

Almost immediately, Hiro began working in his garage. Without interruptions or any real obligations, this was a good time for him to explore the new frontier of experimental computer theory and prototype software. His total focus was numbers, math, chips, and codes. He worked like a crazed man, scarcely emerging to bathe or to eat.

As a student, whenever he had the time, Hiro had worked on a computer game based on his own theories. Now he continued his experimentation, although it never occurred to him that the game could be marketed. One day when his old friend Koji was visiting from Hiroshima, Hiro showed him the "The Muncher," a fun game with a moving mouth that ate everything in sight. Hiro had designed it based on his love of dining in the M.I.T. cafeteria.

The Last Revolution

He also showed his friend designs for other games that he had created over the years. Koji had an uncle in Tokyo who was in the gaming and entertainment business. And he thought that his uncle just might be interested in Hiro's game. Koji asked Hiro if he could take a copy to show his uncle. A few weeks later he received a call from Japan. It was Koji and his uncle was indeed very interested in purchasing the rights to Hiro's games. Thus it transpired that Hiro agreed to sell the rights for his computer games to Koji's uncle. Later that company would become one of the leading computer game manufacturers in the world—the Nintendo Corporation.

Several months passed uneventfully. Then Hiro had an unexpected visitor—Jim McCormack, his only friend from the dorm at M.I.T., and his colleague in the computer science department. They had remained good friends over the years. Jim now worked for IBM, and had become quite famous in his field by writing some very successful programs. His innovation and expertise were so highly respected among the executives that he was promoted to finding new talent, and he found himself spending more and more time scouting for brilliant program writers and less time writing code himself.

Jim had come to Hiro to try to convince him to work for IBM. He made Hiro an offer that he could not refuse. It involved substantial amounts of money, and Hiro had to eat. He did, after all, love his American smorgasbord. Up to this point, Hiro had received only a small monthly royalty from the Japanese game company. So Hiro agreed to sell some of his prototype software designs to Jim and IBM.

Soon he successfully created many more products for the company. He also rewrote the first word processing program, making it easier for the average person to use. This program became an overnight sensation. But Hiro was still not motivated by money. He contacted IBM and sold his rights to the software he had developed and got out. Jim seemed to understand that Hiro had some sort of higher calling. He graciously stepped aside, and they did not see each other again for years.

Next Hiro decided to establish his own research company. He named it Brainstorm, LLC. And although he continued to write prototype business software and accounting programs for the masses, Hiro did not enjoy the work because it consisted of simple mathematical calculations that did not challenge his brain in the slightest. How uninteresting. He did it for the money. He hated it. Some time later his old friend Jim came to call once more and tried to convince Hiro to become the head of the research department for the international software division of IBM, but Hiro still wasn't interested in being wealthy or in being a big shot. He couldn't have cared less about position or status. His motivation was and always had been intrinsic satisfaction with his own work.

    His refusal did not faze Jim, who stayed at Hiro's home that night. They stayed up late talking about software systems and computer languages. It was like the old days at M.I.T. Hiro loved telling Jim about his newest research. He loved showing Jim his projects.

    Hiro's work area was a fire waiting to flame up, with papers piled to the ceiling. Jim could not make out a thing. When he reached out to touch one of the models, Hiro said, "Please don't touch anything. If you move it, I'll never be able to find it again." Jim cracked up at that, but put his hand back down. Hiro picked up his newest model, which would go on to change the look of a computer screen forever. The new method consisted of various doors and windows that opened onscreen by using a small hand operated gadget Hiro called Nezumi, the Japanese word for mouse.

    When the Nezumi was clicked, the user could toggle back and forth from one program to another. It was a groundbreaking invention, and Jim stood in shock. He was seeing dollar signs—ones with lots of zeros after them—and he was nervous and excited at the same time. He was witnessing the work of a genius, and he knew it. Jim was already impressed, but was even more so when he found out that Hiro had developed twenty-five other incredibly workable ideas after his graduation from M.I.T. Jim said, "Hiro, you can make a hell of a lot of money with these things. They're all marketable. You're sitting on a gold mine here."

    Hiro looked at his friend and said with a grin, "I don't need a gold mine. If I wanted to, I could make software and a system that could make a perfect reproduction of the US dollar. And no one would know the difference." They both start laughing.

    Hiro offered Jim a Japanese beer called Sapporo Light.

The Last Revolution

Jim looked at it suspiciously and asked, "What the hell is a Sapporo Light?"

Hiro said, "You know Americans get beer bellies and Japanese don't. This will allow you to drink all the beer you want without getting fat."

"Damn Japanese," said Jim, "What're you going to come up with next?"

The evening passed by quickly because they were both having such a good time. Then, perhaps only a bit into his cups, Jim said, "Hiroaki, I've come up with a brilliant idea. Why don't you write the programs, and I'll market them. Forget IBM. We can put together our own ideas and sell them. We could become a wholesale operation, and the companies can put their own labels on our products. I have all the connections. It's time to explore new business ventures, and there are thousands of small companies popping up all over the place. Not just in the States, but globally. What do you think?"

The truth was Hiroaki was very technical and precise, but he only understood machines, computers, and numbers; in fact, he was the perfect person to be doing field research. But over the years he had become disconnected from humans and their feelings for that very reason: he had worked so long with machines and math that he'd had little human interaction during that time.

Jim, on the other hand, was an Irish-American and was an interesting and likable man, more like a salesman than a research analyst. After he popped his question, he shut up and waited.

"I guess we'd make a pretty good team," replied Hiro.

Without any fuss or fanfare, Jim said, "Ok, so let's get started. I even have a name for our company. How about Micron-software, Inc., or just Micro-software?"

Hiro saw that Jim was serious, and they began to discuss their new venture in detail. Jim finally crashed some time around three a.m. After a few hours of fretful sleep, Jim made plans to fly to New York to submit his resignation to IBM. He did not tell anyone of his plans for this new business with Hiroaki. He simply told IBM that he would remain with them until they found his replacement. On February 19, 1972, Hiroaki and Jim founded Micron-software, Inc., in Los Gatos. Jim moved to Los Gatos with his beautiful young wife Tracy, who was quiet and easy to get along with. The couple moved in with Hiro temporarily until they found a home.

Jim spent much time on the phone with the bank and prospective clients setting up lots of meetings. Tracy was in charge of managing the home office for their new corporation. Very few people visited the office, however, because everything was done by phone and computer. In fact, Hiro's new word processing software and his other innovations came in handy for their own use. Jim ultimately decided to go under contract with a chipmaker in Silicon Valley to mass produce chips for Micron-software. Sometimes he felt as though all he did was sign his name; once, he even woke in the middle of the night to see his hand looping in the air, forming his all-too-familiar signature on some phantom document.

Resources were pouring in from every direction—especially from Bank of America. Things went on well for quite some time. But after awhile, Hiro longed once again to focus on his own ideas; he wanted to get out of the business, so Jim and Tracy bought stayed Hiro's shares, and they parted ways amicably. They did, however, remain friends for life and in constant contact. Later, Jim and Tracy decided to move his headquarters to Seattle, becoming the biggest software company in the world, while Hiroaki remained in Los Gatos to do more research.

In the 1990s, Hiroaki remained near the Silicon Valley and focused on research. His think tank was Brainstorm, LLC. He was free from all corporate tentacles. His main function now was to develop unique systems and prototypes for larger corporations that would then mass produce them and sell them to manufacturers or distributors. After the creative process was over, Hiro was finished. His mind moved on at lightning speed to the next idea, the next project, and the next theory. He had no time for loneliness or for regrets. Family never entered his awareness.

Each system he developed was like his own child to Hiro, so in sending it out into the vast world, he would only deal with people that he felt he could trust. He was very careful that his technology did not fall into the wrong hands.

Unfortunately, like a flesh and blood child grown and ready to leave the nest, once a product was gone, he really had no more control over it. Because Hiro's research was almost twenty-five years ahead of what was currently happening in the computer field, his products were profitable for everyone involved. Not only did Hiro work on futuristic ideas but also he continued to conduct research to improve the capacity and capabilities of existing models to implement next generation theory and invention. One of the concepts Hiro puzzled over most involved integrating physics and electrical currents with human physical function.

He focused on researching a new generation of neuro-electronic interfacing system which was an interfacing system between neuron cells and a computer.

Hiro's mind ticked like the proverbial perpetual motion machine toward his quest of constantly finding high-tech solutions to problems the rest of the world did not even know it had. Toward this end, his brilliant skill in performing calculations in his head gave him a huge advantage over less gifted scientists.

It was in 1990 that Hiro discovered a big problem in his software for the very first time. It was a glitch in his program that would erase the entire memory. It was a mathematical virus that was self-destructive and would wipe out everything in its path. He referred to it as mathematical fall-out which was created by siege mathematical dysfunction like fall-out in military terms. It was unexplainable. This siege would form in the hard drive and completely erase the memory.

Within weeks, the computer would no longer function. All computer corporations were experiencing this phenomenon at this time. It was not just unique to Hiro's work. Hiroaki began developing a new system called an "anti-mathematical fall-out antidote" to combat the problem. It was not successful until August of 1991.

This antidote was a landmark creation which successfully blocked the fall-out and all the resultant problems. He finally named it an anti-virus program. Hiro then sold the license to other corporations to wholesale to computer programming companies.

Then another new problem surfaced in the 1990s when computer hackers began to hijack data from various companies. Also, industrial espionage and corporate spying became a huge business which plagued the industry. Many researchers tried to come up with software to combat these modern day pirates, but nothing ever worked successfully. The business industry began to have doubts about banking their information in computer files, and the industry was in an uproar. All the big computer software companies urgently worked on programs to help alleviate the problem as it reached epidemic proportions becoming a national problem. Even the government's own high tech surveillance teams were having problems. Finally, the government stepped in and offered financial aid to corporations and researchers to create something to fix this disgusting problem. Hiro began to play with numbers and calculations trying to find a solution to lock out the thieves.

It was July 1992. Hiroaki was daydreaming on his back patio, thinking about the days of Ayu fishing in Japan. He had made his own computer game based on Ayu Fishing that he called "Hacker," like the Ayu fishermen themselves. The new game was intended only for fun for himself. It was 8:30 a.m, and there was a trace of cool rain in the dry valley of Los Gatos. Rain made him feel peaceful. After a thirty minute downpour, and a fun session of "Hacker," he was totally at ease playing the game always had that effect on him.

During the game, an opposing Ayu fish approached for attack. The object was for your Ayu fish to defend your territory and to attack the intruder. The combat between the two fish was similar to the old Mitsubishi A6 Zero fighters that became the finest shipboard fighters in the world during the first years of World War II in the Pacific. The Ayu fought like the Zero planes—fast and very maneuverable except in the water. It was a thrilling game; one fought to the death. Suddenly, Hiro noticed that one of the Ayu intruders had disappeared. He tried to find it, but it didn't reappear on the screen.

He checked the calculations behind the software down to the very smallest number and discovered something amazing. He found what could only be explained as a mathematical storm that was the cause of the problem. He had found the key he needed to interpret the mathematical chaos. It was like a mirror shield for the user that protected him from the hacker. The hacker could not get through and was bounced back to his own computer, thereby neutralizing the intruder.

Hiro was able to find the pattern by inverting the input in a very raw binary form. He knew that this type of binary communication could theoretically be the foundation for real anti-spy and anti-hacker software. He neutralized the storm and discovered the basis of the program for the nation's problem. He then proceeded to rewrite the program to the highest accuracy over the next three months. The US government was very satisfied with his system and incorporated it into their surveillance department. Because of a clause in the agreement, Hiro was also able to distribute his system through the major computer markets.

It seemed that he should be at the top of his career. After all, he was now well-respected by both his colleagues and the scientific community. Hiro had always thought that the successful completion of his goals would give him a sense of comfort. Somehow, that was not the case. Somehow, he was still not satisfied. For some reason the fire inside had not subsided. He knew there was something else. He was not finished. There was no way to tell where his instincts would take him at this point. Having achieved his life's goal and having been acknowledged as one of the finest instinctual scientific minds of the twentieth century, Hiro should have felt elated and fulfilled. But something was lacking.

It was time to turn the microscope on himself. It was time to find out why, although his train station nightmares were infrequent, they never stopped. It was time to research the virus inside himself, to locate it, identify it, and create his own personal "Shield" against it.

Suddenly Hiro withdrew from the field of computer science. He sold Brainstorm, LLC, to a colleague and simply disappeared from Silicon Valley. No one knew where he had gone, perhaps back to Japan. He was gone but not forgotten. Who could forget his brilliant talent and landmark achievements? He was one of the fathers of computer science. With the entire scientific community searching, Hiroaki Nakagawa disappeared and discovered how to live.

Chapter 8

Hiro did not tell anyone that he was beginning to suffer from violent nightmares about the war in Japan. He had terrible childhood memories of the bombings which had followed him throughout his life. Hiro was able to ignore them during his years as a student at M.I.T. and later as a researcher, but they became worse each year.

After disappearing from the computer community in Silicon Valley, Hiroaki returned home to Hiroshima. He saw many old friends and his family and spent much time Ayu fishing and relaxing in the country. He found serenity. It was a good retreat for him mentally, and home was a place that had never left his heart.

During his visit, Hiro also returned to the University of Hiroshima. He had many friends who still worked there. He became an honored faculty member in the computer science department and spent time teaching mathematics and computer science to other staff members. It was Hiro's way of giving back to the community and the school.

However, there was one big obstacle. Hiro had a difficult time relating to the students because he was not responsive to human feelings. He had worked alone and with machines for so long that he lacked the ability to relate well to others. He could not understand their feelings. Therefore, the students perceived Hiro as an anti-social nerd so he stayed behind the scenes training faculty instead of teaching students.

Hiro began to have flashbacks about the bombing raids in Hiroshima carried out by the US's B-29s and the NHK live broadcasts about the Cuban revolution. He could still hear screams, and his nightmares became so severe that he could not sleep. He woke up screaming and sweating. Hiro was suffering from post-traumatic stress disorder in the form of nightmares and insomnia. Hiro's symptoms were worsening. He was like a zombie in the day due to sleep deprivation. The ravages of war in Japan had been replaced by modern buildings so on the

The Last Revolution

surface one could not see the reminders of war. But a deep scar remained in the minds and hearts of the people. Hiro was no exception. He was plagued by horrible nightmares every time he closed his eyes and tried to sleep. Soon he could not think clearly during the day, and it was becoming debilitating for him. Hiro had to do something.

Hiro decided to visit Dr. Keiichiro Sugihara, a famous seventh generation doctor of Oriental Medicine and acupuncture. His family had treated members of Hiro's family for centuries. Acupuncture dated back to the twelfth century B.C. in the writings of *Huang Di Nei Jing* in the Yellow Emperor Classic Medical Book from China.

Hiro arrived at Dr. Sugihara's office in Hiroshima's central district in the heart of the city near Peace Park. His office was in a very modern four story white building. Dr. Sugihara was very famous, and Hiro's mother and sisters all agreed that he should seek treatment from Dr. Sugihara because there had been a relationship between the families for so many generations. It had been many years since Hiro had received any acupuncture treatments, but Hiro was willing to try anything to get relief and to escape from the agony caused by the flashbacks to his childhood. As Dr. Sugihara began to stimulate the points along the meridians with thin silver needles, Hiro felt his nerves tingle slightly.

Part of acupuncture was the stimulating or sedating of acupuncture points and the central nervous system. The brain was almost able to reprogram itself and turn areas on and off just like a computer. Dr. Sugihara applied mokusa or dried herbs rolled into a small tight cone. These cones were set on fire. After blowing out the fire, he placed the cones on meridian points. Hiro began to feel relief. He continued to receive treatment from Dr. Sugihara. The treatments helped to relieve Hiro's tension temporarily. Finally, the doctor recommended that Hiro actually revisit the war-torn places that haunted him. It would be psychological therapy to ease tension on his brain's memory cells. Dr. Sugihara told Hiro, "Sometimes you must revisit the past to continue with the future."

Chapter 9

It was March 18, 1995. At 8.30
pm, an Aero Caribe Airlines McDonnell Douglas DC-9 flight began its final approach into the Cuban International Airport Jose Martí. Hiroaki laid his head close to the window because he wanted to see the Havana city lights from the night sky. He was so curious about this place. The flight attendant announced that the plane was approaching the airport in its final descent, but Hiro saw no lights. He could see only a trace of what might be streetlights. Hiro was surprised that this was Havana, the capital city of Cuba. He wondered if he were landing at a different airport.

Hiro suddenly became concerned and frightened, but the plane continued its final descent to the runway. It was dark, and Hiro could see a few landing lights at the airport. It was strange.

Why didn't this airport have lights? Hiro could see the outline of buildings, and he noticed Russian airliners and jets, Aeroflot Tupolev-Tu-154s, and USSR-made supersonic Tupolev Tu-144 LLs. He had never seen real ones. He'd only seen pictures of these planes in a magazine. After sighting the Tupelovs, Hiro finally felt liked he was actually in a Communist country. As the airplane landed, several green-uniformed Cuban military officers approached the plane. They didn't carry weapons. Several transport buses followed them. The buses looked old and run down.

Other than Hiro's plane, there were no other airplanes in sight. It was only 8:30 in the evening. If this had been a US airport, Hiro would have seen many planes, workers with carts everywhere, and lights and more lights. It would have been busy and lively, but in Cuba this was not the case. The difference was like night and day. Hiro was shocked and couldn't believe what he was seeing. *Bienvenidos a Cuba*! This was Havana, and it was very dark. The first impression of Havana was scary to this

The Last Revolution

outsider who did not know that Cuba was trying to conserve energy and only burned necessary lights at night.

Hiro was used to the living in the US which had the highest standard in the world. He had almost forgotten what it had been like back in Japan during and after the war. He had grown up poor, but that was so long ago that he had forgotten. Arriving in Havana, he felt like he had come home. Cuba was similar to wartime Japan.

In the airport, Hiro saw many American-Cubans returning home to Cuba as well as American tourists who were traveling illegally to Cuba. Americans had not been allowed to enter Cuba legally since 1965.

In this airport there was a female officer in a green uniform handing out tourist cards and telling people to complete all information requested. She charged $20 per card and asked questions about how long the tourist intended on staying and where. Hiro could not wait to see what would be next.

Everything was so different. People in military uniforms were everywhere, and they were intimidating. Hiro started to fear for his life and became nervous. He thought that he would experience some trouble here and was beginning to question whether it had been a good idea to come.

The uniformed officers assisted people waiting in the immigrations line. Many of the tourists looked like Cuban-Americans who had come to visit relatives. Hiro went to the second booth and an officer assisted him. The plywood booth was old and unkempt. It was dark in the immigrations area and therefore difficult to see. The only light was from a small fluorescent tube.

The immigrations area was plain and shabby, looked old, and was depressing. There were eight similar booths side by side. The officers checked data on outdated computers. These computers resembled some of the early ones that Hiro had used nearly twenty years previously. These types of computers were relics and were obsolete in both Japan and the US. But here in Cuba they were still being used. Hiro was very surprised.

The officers used the computers to check the immigration status and background information on the tourists. The Cuban government took security seriously and was very strict due to threats of overthrowing Castro and anti-government activities. The Cuban officers were harsh and tough with the

American-Cubans who were returning home. This checkpoint was a formidable place.

Hiro was next in line. The immigrations officer spoke Spanish. The officer was in his 30s, looked tense, and had a somber face. Hiro had a red passport issued by the Japanese government. The immigrations officer took a slow, close look at Hiro's passport and said in a stern voice, "What is the purpose of your trip?"

A few weeks before this trip, Hiro had begun to study Spanish. His vocabulary was still limited, but he was comfortable enough to speak with some confidence to the officer. Hiro told him in Spanish, "I am here to tour the country."

The officer then asked, "Do you have a reservation in a hotel? Do you have a voucher?"

Hiro didn't understand the word for voucher, so he told him, "I would like to stay here for four weeks."

The officer repeated the question again. Hiro answered nervously, "A hotel?"

The officer told him, "If you don't have a voucher from a hotel, you will have to pay a fee here. The cost is $45 dollars a day for three weeks."

Hiro answered, "I have a computer printout from a Canadian tourist company. I'm not sure if it is a voucher."

Hiro presented all of his papers to the officer. The officer looked through the paperwork and told him that everything was in order. It was indeed a voucher. The officer showed Hiro that he had a hotel reservation in downtown Havana at the Hotel Inglaterra.

Then the officer looked closely at Hiro's picture comparing the face on the passport to Hiro's real face. He used his hands to signal Hiro to take off his hat. Hiro complied.

The officer told Hiro, "You can stay in Cuba for only twenty-one days on this tourist card. If you want to stay longer, you must go to the immigrations office downtown and file for an extension. We can authorize only twenty-one days here at the airport."

Hiro told him, "I am a Japanese citizen, and I would like to visit the Japanese Embassy during my trip, too."

The officer said, "That is fine, but remember that you are authorized as a tourist only."

Hiro asked, "What do you mean by as a tourist only?"

The Last Revolution

The officer said, "Your visa is just for tourist purposes. You can stay only at a Cuban tourist hotel and only use the Cuban tourist taxis. You cannot stay in a Cuban's home or ride in a personal car. That is the law."

Then the officer asked Hiro, "How much money are you carrying for this trip?"

Hiro answered, "I have enough." Hiro was careful about his answer because he was afraid that the official might confiscate his money. He was afraid and did not trust anyone here. Hiro had $18,000 in cash in his money belt. The Canadian tourist company had told him that he must use cash in Cuba because credit cards and travelers checks were not accepted.

Hiro had never traveled with so much money before in his life. He had brought a lot, because he wanted to stay in Cuba for a couple of months and didn't know how much he would need. The official told him if he ever had trouble and needed more, he could go to the Japanese embassy in Havana.

The officer became noticeably impatient with Hiro and asked him again, "How much money do you have?" Most tourists carried a large amount of cash, but Hiro had a small fortune in his belt. He had never had an official ask how much money he carried.

Hiro answered, "I have $18,000 US dollars." Hiro showed the official his waist pouch. Hiro was extremely uncomfortable at this point. The officer was amazed when he saw Hiro's cash that was all in one-hundred-dollar bills.

The officer said, "Eighteen thousand US dollars in cash?" He couldn't believe this Japanese tourist was carrying that much money. The officer shook his head in disbelief and said, "Wow, that's a lot of money. I've never seen that much before. My monthly salary is only 500 Cuban pesos or about $12 US dollars. Be especially careful!"

Hiro felt bad that this man made such a small amount of money. There was a huge difference in wealth and social economics here as compared to the US or Japan. However, the officer did not ask for any money. He stamped Hiro's paper for his twenty-one day visitor's visa. He didn't stamp Hiro's passport but instead stamped his tourist card.

The official warned Hiro again, "If you want to stay longer than twenty-one days, then you must go to the downtown immigrations office one week in advance of the expiration date on the visa to complete the necessary paperwork. If you don't do this, then you'll be fined and imprisoned. Do you understand me?"

Hiro answered, "Yes, I understand—one week before expiration. Thank you."

The officer was thoroughly professional, and his conduct at this moment showed it. He had been trained to be strict in his job. The officer opened a door to the luggage area, and Hiro left the immigrations interview room.

Hiro's suitcase was waiting for him in the baggage claim area. The luggage was in a big pile on the floor. Since the immigrations process had taken so long, the luggage had arrived much earlier. Everything seemed haphazard to Hiro. Cubans had nothing but time and thus no concept of business efficiency. Hiro realized that he was in a different world here. Hiro needed his claim check to pick up his luggage. The Cubans were strict about this unlike the luggage claim areas in the US. A guard double-checked that the claim ticket number matched the number on his suitcase. Hiro had only a small suitcase and a camera bag.

Then Hiro stood in line waiting for a customs officer to inspect his bags. In front of him, he saw a fat Cuban-American woman place two huge suitcases and one large box on the customs table. The officer opened everything. She had brought many used clothes, shoes, and other items. The customs official weighed the items which totaled 140 pounds.

The officer asked her, "Are these your clothes?"

She answered him, "Everything is mine. No gifts."
Then the officer looked at her and wrote a tax ticket for $1400 dollars with a 50% discount. Therefore, she must pay of $700 in duty taxes plus $150 for a small used television that they had found in the box to take the items out of the customs area. The woman must pay a total of $ 850.

In the states, Hiro figured that this TV bought used only cost around $60. Hiro calculated that the government charged about $20 a pound for things. It must be a way for them to make extra income. He had never heard of such a thing and was happy that he had packed only a small suitcase.

The woman began to cry and told the officers that she didn't have enough money to pay the duty tax. She pleaded with them that these were only her items and to please let her pass. The woman began to argue with the officers. The officers told her that they would give her another 50% off but she had to pay $425 or leave everything with them and pay for storage. Then when she left Cuba, she could take it all back home with her. The woman began to cry uncontrollably becoming hysterical and felling to the floor.

She said that she only had $325 dollars. The officers told her she could pay for storage and take all of it back when she departed the country. They said, "Take it or leave it." The officers were disgusted with her at this point.

Hiro had never seen anyone so upset before. He felt sorry for the woman and told the officers that he would pay the difference. They all looked at this Japanese stranger in shock. Hiro paid the remainder of $100. That made the woman so happy that she grabbed him and kissed him all over his face.

Hiro stepped back, wiping his cheeks with his hands. He didn't know how to react. He was totally caught off guard by this woman's impulsive behavior because in Japan people did not show public displays of affection let alone grab a stranger like this and kiss him. The woman thanked Hiro over and over and took her huge luggage out the door.

Now it was Hiro's turn. He stepped to the table with his bags. The officer asked, "Do you have any friends here?"

Hiro replied, "No. This is my first visit here." The officer told him to go on through when he saw that Hiro had very little luggage.

After leaving the customs area, he found a restroom. It was very unkempt and rundown and looked like it could use a thousand gallons of paint. The bathrooms had old 1950s fixtures. They were antique and beautiful and every piece of hardware looked unique. Its appearance was so different from the modern facilities of the US and the Japanese.

There was a skinny old man cleaning the restroom. He handed Hiro some toilet paper. Beside him was a money jar with some coins in it. Hiro realized that he had to pay for the tissue. He put a one dollar bill in the jar and shook his head. It was unbelievable.

He realized that Cuba had remained back in the 50s standing still while the rest of the world had moved onward. He realized that modernization had not yet occurred here. He left the bathroom and walked to the exit of the airport. As he approached the door to the outside, he smelled a very unpleasant odor. He stepped outside, a tropical breeze hit his face, and he heard many people yelling names and talking all at once. The place was dark, and it was difficult to see but it became clear that there were hundreds of people waiting for friends and relatives to arrive. They had been waiting for hours.

It was about eleven p.m. He had been in immigrations and customs for nearly three hours. He saw people greeting their friends and family with open emotions. Everyone was hugging, kissing, and happy to see each other. Everyone was talking loudly. Hiro was surprised at the different cultures and their greetings.

In Japan, one greeted another person quietly and with little emotion. Many of these people were being reunited with their loved ones after being gone from Cuba for many years. Many were probably refugees who had left long ago. He knew this from their reactions to one another. People still had deep wounds inside them which remained from the Cold war intervention between the US and USSR. He could see it. Havana and the Cuban people were victims of the Cold War, and he was witnessing it in the present.

Instantly, Hiro had a flashback of the live radio broadcasts from the Cuban revolution that he had heard when he was fifteen years old and living in the mountain village in Japan. That was January 1959.

This night it was March 1995.

In front of the airport, there was a small parking lot with many cars from the 1950s. He saw a 57 Chevy, 55 Ford, 50 Ford and 55 olds. There was a 1956 Chevrolet Wagon and so many more. Among the cars, he saw many compact Russian-made cars called Ladas. He had seen these cars in books in the past. It was very unusual to see these vehicles in person. He began to grin because he had almost forgotten how cars had looked back in the 50s. Here they all were, parked in a lot. The old 1940s and 1950s cars that lined the city streets were nicknamed "yank tanks."

It was like Hiro had stepped into a time warp. He hadn't seen cars like this since his youth except in classic car shows. Here in the parking lot, there were many of them, some in very good condition. However, most were worn out with the bumpers falling off, with homemade patches and repairs, and even some with hammered aluminum soft drink cans used in place of real bumpers. He could see that there were plastic sheets and tarps

The Last Revolution

used to replace the missing glass for the windows. Some of the cars were rusty and falling apart. Cuba had stood still for a long time, and this parking lot was a testament to that fact. In forty years, things had remained frozen in time. He knew this, but it really hit him as he stood looking at all the old cars. He smiled and said to himself, "So, this is it. I am really in Cuba. I can't believe I am finally in Havana."

Hiro remembered that according to the law he had to use a tourist-authorized taxi. The taxi business was a hustling and bustling business. There was a sign overhead that said Tourismo. A taxi driver waved his hand at Hiro signaling him to come over, but he did this quietly. The Cuban taxi driver was using a Korean car. When Hiro sat inside, it smelled like pungent Cuban cigars but looked new and clean.

The driver was a young man who was nicely dressed. His clothes were not fancy, but they were nice and clean. The driver was pleasant and polite. Since he was a tourist taxi driver, he had to be a government employee.

The driver asked Hiro, "Where would you like to go?"

Hiro replied, "Please take me to the Hotel Inglaterra."

The driver said, "No problem." And they left the airport and begin to drive down the streets of Havana. There were no streetlights, and it was dark. The streets were run down, and there were many people waiting for buses in the dark. It was unbelievable to see. Old automobiles were passing by, many with bumpers falling off, and some in worse shape. It looked like anything that could move was being driven. Hiro found this very interesting.

He remembered back in the 50s when he was a boy. People said that those were the good old days. But Hiro hadn't enjoyed the 1950s, and those were not the good old days for him because he had spent 100% of his time studying with no leisure time. Hiro had worked so hard to achieve his dream that he hadn't gotten to enjoy his youth. The 1950s had passed Hiro by, but today was the first time he had realized it. Now he had discovered a place that had been frozen in time. He felt like he had stepped into the past.

As the taxi approached the center of the city, he noticed old buildings. They were crumbling, and he saw that there had been no maintenance or repairs. Even in their current state of disrepair, Hiro could see that unique and interesting architecture from the 1800s was still standing. It was a shocking sight to see, but he loved it. It was historical, and yet it had been forgotten for the last forty-five years.

Japan was also an old country, but the 1800s were not so old there. Even his mountain village dated back to the beginning of the eleventh century. But Japan did not have many old buildings from that era still standing because the wood used had not withstood the test of time. Only some castles and temples still survived through regular maintenance. Also, Japan had had severe earthquakes that had destroyed many buildings and structures.

The taxi driver told him, "Here is the Hotel Inglaterra. I will take your luggage inside for you." The hotel porter met the taxi driver and took the luggage.

The porter told Hiro, "Come with me, and I will take you to the front desk for your reservations." Hiro looked at the hotel. It had incredible curved designs along the walls with crown moldings and Italian marble. This was Cuba's oldest hotel and dated back to 1875. It had been declared a national monument and looked as though it had been well-maintained. It was on the *Paseo del Prado* in Old Havana. The *Parque Central* is just across from the hotel. There were views of the park from Hiro's hotel window.

The hotel was three stories high with beautiful facades and balconies. The lobby had huge ornamental wrought iron doors and a chandelier. It was lavishly decorated, and the people working there wore hotel uniforms consisting of black pants, a white shirt, a black jacket, and a vest.

The woman at the reception desk smiled at him and said in a friendly voice, "Hello! What can I do for you?" Hiro turned to her and handed her his voucher and reservation. She smiled and said, "Ah, yes I have your room." She gave him some papers and the hotel log book to sign. She handed him a key which said room 321. "Here is your key, and we have a safe for your passport, money and valuables." Then she gave Hiro some information about the hotel. She was helpful and polite.

The porter returned and picked up his luggage saying, "Right this way." In front of them was a huge old American elevator with a Cuban mahogany frame around it. The date of manufacture read 1952 Dover Corporation Memphis Tennessee USA. The elevator still worked smoothly and took them to the

The Last Revolution

third floor. The porter showed Hiro to room 321. The room faced the street.

Hiro looked out of the room's windows, but he couldn't see Havana because it was too dark. He looked around the room and said, "Wow, this is unbelievable art work." He thanked the porter and gave him a tip.

The room was large with an antique brass bed and an early 1900s sofa. All of the room's furniture was in excellent condition. The bathroom was beautiful and lavish with old brass fixtures and Italian marble tiles and mosaics. Hiro smiled and looked at everything with curiosity. It was past midnight, but he could not sleep. He tossed and turned and his mind filled with all the things that he had just seen and all the people that he had just met. He imagined the kind of life people had in this country.

Hiro thought about the fact that the great democratic leader of the world, the US, had tried unsuccessfully for forty-five years to overthrow Fidel Castro, Cuba's leader. Castro had become the iron-fisted dictator who understood the people of Cuba. Hiro had heard that Fidel Castro was a great dictator, and he thought to himself that being a good dictator was better than being a democratically-elected president because a dictator could do whatever he wanted without opposition.

Hiro didn't understand how Fidel could be a good dictator because tonight he had seen the crumbling buildings, people hitch-hiking in the dark streets by the hundreds, no lights, and people living in shantytowns. A dictator should make things better quickly. Hiro did not have much interest in politics or political ambitions, but he was interested in the people living in this isolated country under a Communist system.

The people of Cuba had chosen Fidel nearly forty years earlier. When Fidel took over Cuba, it was in its heyday and Havana was a glamorous city. Everyone wanted to visit Havana, and it became the playground for the rich and famous. But now, after all these years, Havana was crumbling and seemed doomed. Hiro wondered why the people had chosen this way and Communism. Perhaps they did not know that their choice would become like this. Hiro fell asleep thinking about what might have been.

Hiro slept deeply but awoke screaming and in a panic. He sat up in the bed sweating and breathing hard and fast—another nightmare. Hands shaking, he managed to sip from his bedside water glass and then laid his head gently on his pillow. He finally went back to sleep.

Chapter 10

Suddenly, a loud noise awakened Hiro. It was a car with no muffler. When he looked out of the window, he discovered a bright, sunny morning. From the window he could see many cars from Russia and many from the 1950s. He had almost forgotten that he was in Havana. He dressed and went down to the lobby for breakfast. He was directed to the hotel restaurant facing the front street. There he ordered a coffee. The waitress asked, "Would you like a Cafe Cubano or Cafe Americano?" He ordered the Cafe Cubano. The waitress brought him a tiny white coffee cup filled with dark black coffee. The coffee tasted strong and sweet. It tasted differently than an espresso. He liked it.

Then he ordered breakfast. The items on the menu were like those in the states, and he ordered two eggs over medium with toast. Hiro looked around and saw that half of the guests were European or Canadian tourists. He noticed that some of the people were wearing dirty t-shirts and flip flops—improper clothes to Hiro's way of thinking. He suspected that they were American and that they had come to Cuba via a third country like Hiro had through Mexico. He also saw some Chinese people. His breakfast arrived, and his toast was good. The eggs tasted unfamiliar. Maybe they fed their chickens something different in Cuba because the taste was unusual.

While he ate, Hiro looked through some tourist brochures. He wanted to take it easy today. After breakfast, he took a walk outside the hotel and down the street. He enjoyed people watching. The people called him "Chino" and said hello. Cubans were used to calling all Orientals Chinese. Hiro corrected them immediately and said, "Soy Japone!" He told them that he was Japanese. They just smiled.

In front of the hotel, many people were wearing fashionable clothes, especially the younger people. Hiro was curious about the Coco taxi. These yellow three-wheeled bicycle taxis bearing one or two passengers made Hiro smile. Another oddity was the split-level bus pulled by a semi-truck full of locals called the El

Camello. It resembled a two-humped camel, thus its name. This type of transportation was only for Cubans. Tourists used the main bus, which was called The Viazul. The tourist bus only accepted dollars.

He saw one older man who was poorly dressed and wearing old shoes. Hiro could almost see his toes sticking out of the holes in his shoes. The old man was sweeping the street. Hiro watched him sweep very slowly. It would take him all day to sweep the entire front of the hotel at this pace. Hiro wondered how this old man could survive just sweeping the street. What kind of daily life did these people have?

A young man with fancy Nike shoes approached Hiro and said in broken English, "Hey Chino, you want a woman?" Hiro was surprised to hear him speak English. The young man then said, "I get you sexy Cuban woman for cheap!"

Hiro answered, "Yo no Chino! Soy Japone! No, no I don't need a woman."

The man apologized and then explained that he was a private tourist coordinator for the black market. He said to Hiro, "Anything you want, I can arrange it for you."

Hiro started to relax and said, "I do need something. I would like a local person to be my tour guide and explain things to me in English. Do you have someone who could do this?"

The young man answered, "No problem. My name is Tito."

Tito told Hiro that he would be back in a couple of hours and then he left. Hiro sat on a bench in the front of the hotel, watching people, both young and old. He was curious and wondered what kind of life they had.

While he watched, he had not seen anybody begging for money. The people stared at him more than he looked at them. They were curious about him. Not many Orientals came to Cuba because the country was so isolated. Since Japan was on the opposite side of the earth, it was not easy to get to Cuba. It was not possible to fly directly into Cuba from the US. One had to approach through Mexico or a Latin American country.

Japanese people hardly ever lived in or visited Cuba. Any who did were usually Chinese or Korean businessmen. There were not many Japanese, because they had honored the US embargo against Cuba since 1965. Japan had a trade agreement with the US and they did not want to do anything to anger the

The Last Revolution

US. The Japanese were concerned that their politics would restrict them if they violated the embargo so they did not do much business in Cuba. Other cultures were rare, too. When Fidel came into power, he had kicked out the Jewish people because they controlled most of the businesses in Cuba. He simply told them all to leave and confiscated as many of their assets as he could. Only a few Jews still lived in Cuba.

Hiro had gone up to his hotel room after waiting several hours for Tito to return. Then, not too much later, a porter knocked at his door. He told Hiro that a young man named Tito was looking for him downstairs. Hiro went down to the lobby and found him. Tito said, "I've located a man who can take you around town, and his cousin speaks English. She will translate for you. She speaks English better than I do."

Tito took Hiro out front and introduced him to this man. The man looked to be around thirty years old and had a likable face. He appeared to be tough. He had black hair and was tanned. He was tall with big hands and had a black beard. The man looked like a typical Cuban to Hiro, but he did not look like a city person. When Hiro came closer, the man extended his hand and shook Hiro's hand firmly. Hiro said, "Ouch!" because it hurt. The man was surprised at Hiro's reaction and smiled.

The man started to speak Spanish very slowly because he didn't speak any English. He said, "My cousin speaks English well and can be your translator. I will be happy to drive for you. My name is Pedro Gomez Pelayo, and I will drive you around. We will have a good time."

Hiro asked, "How much will this cost?"

Pedro answers, "You give us any amount you want to pay us, but remember that gas is very expensive here. It costs $4.00 US per gallon."

Hiro answered, "Ok, I will pay you a hundred dollars a day plus gas and three meals on me. Do you think this is enough for both you and your cousin per day?"

Pedro asked, "How many days do you want us to work for you?"

"Well, how about twenty-one days?" replied Hiro.

Pedro was surprised and asked, "Twenty-one days? Of course that will be enough."

Hiro later found out that the average Cuban only earned $10 to $15 US dollars a month. A doctor made roughly $40 a month so the money that Hiro was offering to pay was a huge amount. Hiro tipped Tito with a $20 bill.

Then Hiro invited Pedro and Tito into the hotel bar for a drink. They both agreed to sit at the counter of the beautiful old bar. The bartender asked, "What would you like to drink?"

Hiro answered, "Yes, how about some beer?"

Tito told Hiro, "Hatuey beer is really good." Hiro ordered three beers—one for himself, one for Pedro, and one for Tito. It came in a red can with an Indian's face on it. It was a typical Cuban beer, and Pedro liked it. The three of them sat at the bar and talked about life in Cuba.

Hiro asked them many questions, but they glanced around frequently and looked over their shoulders as they answered many of his questions. It was almost as if they were uncomfortable speaking openly.

Actually, they looked frightened by his questions. Hiro found this peculiar and asked them, "Why do you look frightened?"

Tito answered, "I'm looking for the secret police. They're always around. And, as you've learned, it's illegal for you, a tourist, to be doing business with private Cuban citizens." Hiro realized that this was indeed a Communist country.

Tito began to talk about Cuban activities like fishing, the beaches, women, and social life. He did not talk about work or his goals. He would not talk at all about politics. From the way Tito talked about Cuban life, it seemed as though Cubans had plenty of time. He noticed that Pedro was quiet and said almost nothing. Pedro just listened to the conversation. Hiro enjoyed talking with these strangers for many hours. He felt so comfortable with these two men. It was as if he had known them for many years. They all loved to drink beer, especially Hatuey beer.

Hatuey was a strong beer with an alcohol level of 5.5 % vol which tasted similar to Kirin from Japan or American Budweiser. It was a golden ale which Hiro enjoyed. The Cuban beer was named for a Taínos Indian chief, who was one of the original inhabitants of Cuba before the arrival of the white man.

According to history originally recorded by Father Bartolome de Las Casas which described the fate of the Taínos, Chief Hatuey was from the region of Guababa in Cibao. Today this area is known as the Dominican Republic and Haiti. Hatuey

The Last Revolution

courageously defended his territory against the brutal genocidal colonization by the Spanish. Hatuey fled, made a canoe, and took a few hundred comrades to warn other tribes in Cuba. They landed on the eastern shore of Guantanamo Cuba and told the people that the Spanish were a cruel and evil force who meant to kill and enslave them. He told them the conquistadors wanted gold at all cost. He was successful in setting up a resistance, but most Colban's (Cuban) the original were was disbelieved.

The chief displayed gold and jewels as he gave a famous speech: *"Here is the God the Spanish worship. For these they fight and kill; for these they persecute us and kill us and that is why we have to throw them into the sea.....They tell us, these tyrants, that they adore a God of peace and equality and yet they usurp our land and make us their slaves. They speak to us of an immortal soul, and of their eternal rewards and punishment, and yet they rob our belongings, seduce our women, and violate our daughters. Incapable of matching us in valor, these cowards cover themselves in iron that our weapons cannot break...."*

Hatuey formed a resistance movement and took his loyal fighters to storm the Spanish in a legendary battle. They were successful and pushing the Spanish back to their fort at Baracoa. However, many native Cubans didn't join him in his fight when he needed them. Sadly, three years later he was captured and burned at the stake at a place called Yara which is close to the city of Bayamo, modern day Granma province. Thus the life of Cuba's first freedom fighter ended on February 2, 1512.

In Yara several thousand Colban Taínos welcomed Spaniards they gave them drink and feast, but were immediately wiped out once the feast was over. It was a fiendish set up. Father Bartolome de Las Casas wrote, *"They set upon the Indians, slashing, disemboweling and slaughtering them until their blood ran like a river."* Then the Spaniards sent those that remained to the mines to work as slave labor. They were forced to work beyond their physical means and were tortured. They were harnessed to loads they could not drag; they hacked off their hands and feet and mutilated their bodies beyond description. Besides being the first guerilla-style warrior in Cuba's history, Hatuey was the first martyr in the struggle for Cuba's independence.

The famous story goes that a priest asked Hatuey if he believed in Jesus Christ just before his death. The weary Indian

Chief asked, *"Are there Spaniards in Heaven?"* Of course, the priest told him *"there were many like us."* Hatuey said *"I wanted nothing to do with a God that allowed such inhumane and cruel people, such as the Spanish to perpetrate crimes in his name. If the Spaniards go to heaven, then I certainly do not want to go there, so do not baptize me, I would prefer to go to hell!"*

Hatuey was the first freedom fighter in the New World and was considered to be Cuba's First National Hero. Sadly three hundred thousand pre-Columbian indigenous Taínos-Ciboney Indians were wiped out by the Spanish conquest within twenty years. But four hundred years later, Fidel himself took Hatuey's idea about guerrilla tactics and succeeded.

Hiro and his new friends talked until 5:00 p.m. and then they decided to separate. They shook hands and said that they would return in the morning. Hiro went to his room and stretched out on his bed before dinner because he was tipsy from drinking too much beer. When he drank, it always made him get sleepy. Many Orientals lacked the enzymes to break down the malt and alcohol in the beer. Many Japanese had this problem, so they got drunk easily, and their faces turned red.

The next day Hiro awakened up early. He decided to walk around the hotel property. The Cubans were friendly and genuine and no one gave him any trouble. He enjoyed walking around, and by the time he got back to the hotel, he saw a brown 1956 Ford parked in front. A tall man with a hairy face was standing there.

He looked closer and realized it was Pedro. Hiro said, "How are you doing this morning?"

Pedro answered, "Bien Gracias. Look! This is my cousin Aimee. She speaks English very well." Pedro added in slow Spanish, "She will be your tour guide."

Aimee was in her late 20s with dark straight hair and was about five-feet four-inches tall. She had a big smile and seemed friendly. The three of them sat in Pedro's brown 1956 Ford.

Aimee asked, "Where are your from? Are you Chino or Korean?"

Hiro replied, "I am Japanese. I'm from Hiroshima, Japan."

Both Pedro and Aimee looked at one another, and she

The Last Revolution

said, "Hiroshima! We have never met any Japanese person before!"

Hiro said, "Yes, Hiroshima, Japan, is my home."

Pedro said, "Oh boy, I'm amazed that you are still here. You must be the bionic man. You escaped from the atomic blast. How can people still live there after the bombing?"

Hiro answered, "No, I'm not a bionic man, but I'm young. I was only three years old when the atomic bomb hit my hometown."

Then Aimee said, "I know many people were killed instantly. Is this correct? I also saw a documentary about the bombing and what happened. There are still people who die from atomic radiation. Is this so?"

Hiro answered, "That is true. Every year many people die and continue to suffer from the radiation poisoning resulting from the atomic blast."

Then Pedro said, "The Americans are terrible. They even killed women and children. That was absolutely horrible."

Hiro said, "You know, war is always bad. It doesn't matter which side you are on. Both sides are wrong. I don't judge the US because Japan was involved, too. I think politicians should never lead us to war. They should resolve their differences though talking. This is my theory, but it is a shame that it doesn't work that way." The three agreed.

Pedro started driving. It was amazing that the old Ford still ran so well. It sounded powerful, and the ride was smooth. Pedro was a careful driver, and they took off for a tour around the city.

Then Pedro began to talk about the Cuban revolution. They spoke freely inside the car. Aimee took over the conversation and changed the subject and said, "OK, let's talk about Havana. I will tell you how the city was started." She didn't want to talk about Cuban politics, but Hiroaki didn't understand why.

Aimee explained that Don Cristóbal Colón came to the new world in 1492. He was fascinated with Marco Polo's Far Eastern expedition and daily read journals that Polo had written in 1299. In his writings, Polo described pagodas covered in gold on an island off the coast of Cathay (China) called Cipangu, modern day Japan. A Bahamian native guide named Guacanagari, who was onboard, told many tales of the riches of

Cibao, the island now known as the Dominican Republic and Haiti. Local Indians called the island adjacent to Cibao, *Colba* (currently Cuba). Cristóbal Colón was convinced that he was indeed approaching Cipangu, or Japan, since his expedition sought to discover a new route to the Orient.

Columbus's first voyage landed in *Colba* (Cuba) at Bariay Bay, which he renamed Porto Santo. The bay was near Baracoa in north eastern Cuba. Columbus described Cuba in his logbook as... "*I was enamored with the island's flora and fauna and the wild birds. I thought it was paradise and wished to stay forever.*"

Then he added the following to his log: "*I found humble fishermen and their families who had fled from terrors living near the beach. The used simple objects such as palm, bones, horns, and shells to make their nets, tackle, and fishing hooks. In small rustic huts, these natives lived peacefully together. There were also dogs and domesticated animals. I was touched by the simplicity of their lives and envied their uncomplicated existence.*"

His log also described for the indigenous Taínos-Ciboney Indians saying: "*that both men and women went naked and were unashamed. These simple natives used paint to make markings of color on their faces and bodies using red, white, and yellow dye made of what they found in nature. The men were strong and handsome. They had long hair that was uncut except for bangs on their foreheads. There were many younger men under the age of 30.*"

Then on the fate of the failure indigenous people he wrote: "*The Indians possessed gold. They wore rings in their noses. And they had a king that ruled them in the south. He had much of the shining metal. For these gentle people, the possession of gold marked the beginning of the end for them.*"

"*They made very sturdy canoes out of trees. They were remarkable works that held as many as 45 men. They also made compact canoes for just two or three people. They were highly skilled in their wood working and crafting and were able to paddle at a swift rate.*"

It was October 27, 1492.

Eventually the Spanish conquered the Caribbean; Conquistador Diego Velázquez de Cuéllar founded Havana for Spanish king Ferdinand II of Aragón on August 25, 1515." He

The Last Revolution

named "Villa of San Cristóbal de Havana." It is said that he named the main town Habana, island after he heard about a beautiful daughter of the local Indian chief Habaguanex. but no one knows for sure. Habana became the capital of the New World.

La Havana was divided into three parts: Old Havana, Central Havana, and *Vedado*. Old Havana was the original settlement. Hiro enjoyed seeing the famous Cathedral San Cristóbal. All of the buildings were built in the style of colonial architecture and looked like those in France and Spain. Central Havana was fairly quiet yet many parts were a bit seedy. Vedado was the third section of Havana, and it had more trees and greenery. It was the calmest section of the city, and many of the nice hotels were located there. The John Lennon Park was also in this area. This park was a testament that everyone loved the Beatles, and it contained the only statue of a western musician in the city. Aimee told him that people left round glasses on the statue. Hiro laughed.

Hiro could imagine what Havana must have looked like back in its glory days. It must have been a prosperous and prestigious city with much commerce. There must have been a rich society back in the 1800s and earlier.

Hiro thought about Japan back in the 1500s to 1800s. It was peaceful and controlled by the Shogun warlords. They were strong dictators who dominated all parts of Japanese life, even death. It was similar, in a way, to Cuba. Both countries had all-powerful dictators who controlled life and politics. Hiro began to think about the strong dictator system of Japan and Cuba and its similarities. Until now, he had never compared the two.

Pedro drove slowly and carefully in Old Havana. Many buildings were falling down and were decrepit. Paint was peeling off, and the structures needed much work. Hiro didn't understand why the Cubans did not maintain these old buildings. The streets were shabby and badly in need of repair. He thought to himself that it had been many decades since repair work had been done, and he could not understand this. It seemed that people here had plenty of time, and if the government wanted something done, then it should be easy to accomplish. Hiro started to question why the government did not do anything about the quality of life and the shabbiness of the city. Havana looked dirty and unkempt. The streets looked like slums. Come to think of it, Hiro had never seen anything labeled "Made In Cuba".

Hiro noticed that there were no restaurants, no food stores, no food stands. He thought, "Where are all the cafes?" He was curious about life in Havana. On the one hand, he enjoyed the feeling of life in the 50s, but on the other hand, he questioned why they were still stuck in the 50s and why had Cuba not changed? Why was Cuba in hibernation? His Japanese mind could not comprehend these things. Why had nothing been improved in all this time? He once thought that Cuba must have a great dictator, but now he questioned that as well as the Communist system. From what he had seen here in Havana, it didn't seem like a superior system. Cuba had had a great dictator for a long time, so Hiro wondered why things had gone downhill. Aimee and Pedro knew everything about living in a Communist country. They had both been born after the revolution so they had grown up under the Communist regime. They were a product of Fidel Castro.

Chapter 11

"Hiro!" shouted Aimee, "I just remembered that there is a Japanese samurai statue in Havana harbor. I don't know what I was thinking. That first Samurai came here a long time ago. I remember reading an article in the Cuban newspaper, *Granma International*, about it."

The official newspaper is "Granma". It is published by the Communist Party of Cuba. The other national newspapers are the "Juentud Rebelde" which is put out by The Union of Young Communists and the "Trabajadores" which is published by the Center for Cuban Workers. There are many other regional newspapers.

Hiro replied, "Yes, I know about him. He was from Miyagi Ken, Japan, which is in northern Japan in a place called Sendai. He was the first person to arrive in Cuba from Japan. The statue was donated to the city of Havana by the Sendai Ikue Gakuen Sports Training School and the Japanese historical society."

Pedro thought that was odd and said, "Really? No joke? You must be lying!"

Hiro was adamant and said, "I am serious. It's true! Most Japanese have no knowledge of Hasekura Tsunenaga. He was the first Japanese citizen and samurai to visit La Havana back in July of 1614. He was on a diplomatic mission for Japan."

Hiro asked, "May I explain a little Japanese history to you?"

Both Pedro and Aimee were interested and nodded their heads in agreement that they would like to hear more.

Hiro cleared his throat and began, "About 49 years following Columbus's arrival in 1492 the first Portuguese sailors shipwrecked on the southernmost Japanese island called Tanegashima. Arriving with them were the first primitive European firearms which were similar to a musket."

"Six years later in 1549, a Jesuit missionary, Francis Xavier arrived. After sixteen centuries, estimated 500,000

Japanese had converted to Catholicism. The Japanese referred to the European arrivals as Nanban-jin which meant 'southern barbarian'. They were given this name because they were unsophisticated by Japanese standards."

"After the peaceful Kamakura era in the fourteenth century, Japan's Civil War lasted one hundred years. During this time, military warlords tried to control Japan. After the arrival of the Portuguese at Tanegashima, warlord Oda Nobunaga quickly replicated their firearms using mass production. Possession of superior weapons had a major impact on the outcome of the Civil Wars in which he was involved. Oda Nobunaga controlled Japan from 1573 through 1582. His rule was followed by Toyotomi Hideyoshi who dominated Japan from 1582 through 1598, which was called the Momoyama period. Finally, Tokugawa Shogunate united Japan and stabilized political power. During this era, the capital moved from Kyoto to Edo (modern day Tokyo). Also during this 270 year era, Japanese art, the country's infrastructure, and commerce expanded."

"In 1604, the Japanese Shogun, Ieyasu Tokugawa, ordered an English-style galleon to be built. It was to be an exact replica of the ship that an English man by the name of William Adams used for his voyage to Japan. Adams was actually the very first westerner to become a Samurai in Japan. He and his companions were asked to build an English-style sailing ship at Ito on the east coast of the Izu Peninsula."

"The first vessel completed was only an eighty-ton machine. Then the Shogun ordered a larger one to be constructed. The next galleon was a monstrous 120 tons. It was built by a powerful northern warlord and daimyo, or governor, named Date Masamune, who was a trusted ally of the Shogun. He was from Sendai, and he used lumber from the northern cedar trees of that area to build the ship. With 3000 highly skilled carpenters, it took him only forty-five days to complete. It was built in record time. The ship was named *Date Masamune Maru* later renamed *The San Buena Ventura*."

"The Shogun put his most highly trained admiral in command of the ships. Masamune was also named the official ambassador on a voyage to Spain with the objective of sending a Japanese trade mission to Spain. In turn Masamune ordered his most trusted Samurai, Hasekura Tsunenaga, to be in charge of the mission. Hasekura was sent to discuss trade agreements with the Spanish crown."

"At that time, Spain was a threat to Japan because of its superior firepower. The colony of Spain's far eastern regiment located in The Philippines was waiting for an order to advance on the Shogun. The Shogun felt threatened and feared for his territory. The arrival of the Spanish in Japan would trigger a revolt among the Christian warlords that would overthrow the Shogun's regime."

"In October of 1613, Hasekura undertook a mission with a delegation of twenty-two Japanese. One hundred and eighty men set out for New Spain near Acapulco, Mexico, and continued overland through the Caribbean to Spain."

"After the Christians invaded Japan, the Spanish conquistadors and the Catholic Church tried to control the country using psychological warfare. Japan had a very complex and highly developed culture by that time, as well as a sophisticated society. Some of the Japanese people succumbed to religious conversion during this time, but others were not so easily swayed. The Spanish tried with all their might to control Japan through brainwashing the people with Christian dogma. Many people converted. Even the northern warlord Masamune Date and his commander were converted to the Christian faith."

"These Christianizing endeavors also included a trade agreement between the central governments of Japan and Spain. It was to be a very lucrative agreement and the Shogun Tokugawa sent a special, letter to Pope Paul V in 1615. Tokugawa indicated that he didn't mind Spain making a profit in Japan, but he wouldn't tolerate Christianity being spread in Japan. However, the northern converted warlord Masamune Date wanted to be in charge of the trade mission so he sent his man as ambassador of the delegation. Masamune hoped to bring more priests from Spain to convert more Japanese with the ultimate ambition of overthrowing the Shogun's central government."

"This mission occurred around the same time as the colonists arrived on the American frontier as settlers of Jamestown, Virginia. They suffered such a harsh winter that only 60 of the 500 original settlers survived the winter of 1613. They were forced to resort to cannibalism to survive the American frontier."

"Masamune's plan did not succeed, and after Shogun Ieyoshi died in 1616, his son and successor, the xenophobic and brutal Hidetada, closed the country to outsiders as his father had wished. Hidetada ordered that all Christian priests in Japan be executed in the land of golden pagoda roofs. Hasekura Tsunenaga and his followers were executed because of their Christian beliefs. But historians say he abandoned his belief in the Christian faith and became ill. Although no one knows for sure, it is believed that he spent his last days in sakoku (isolation) in Japan and died on August 7, 1622."

"Soon after Hasekura death, the Shogun murdered his entire family for their secret Christian beliefs. Date Masamune, out of fear of the Shogun, took mild anti-Christian measures to remain the Shogun's ally and to keep his connection with the central government. The Shogun rewarded him by giving him many projects that kept him financially drained so that he had to struggle to survive. This kept his ambition suppressed and under control so he was no longer a threat against them."

"When Masamune died in 1636, his son succeeded him. Masamune's greatest achievement was captaining the first Japanese expedition to sail around the world. This uncharted voyage was one of Japan's only attempts at foreign diplomacy. Masamune showed sympathy to Christian missionaries and traders in Japan. On the other hand, the Shogun already suspected what the outcome would be in Japan. Since the goal of the Spanish was to take over the country, the Shogun knew that he must execute all Christians to save Japan from Spanish rule. The Spanish world map showed clearly, that at that time, Japan was already Spain's territory."

"Unfortunately, prior to this time, Japanese warlords had never funded adventures of this sort. It was probably the first and only successful naval expedition in Japanese history."

"At least five members of the exploration party stayed in Coria, Seville, (Spain) and lived out their lives there to avoid the persecution of the Christian faith in Japan. Six hundred of their descendants still live in Spain today and have the surname Japón from Hasekura of Japan."

"The Christian faith was strictly prohibited, and the Shogun, Hidetada Tokugawa, closed the country to the outside world. The successful Tokugawa shogunate lasted from 1603 until 1868, nearly 270 years. This Shogun saved Japan and left unique and rich culture. Otherwise, Christianity would have erased the culture eventually. That clearly indicated that the Shogun was the superior leader."

Hiro paused for a moment, which interrupted his history lesson. He almost voiced his belief that Fidel would be placed in the Shogun's category, but Hiro decided not to lead the conversation in that direction.

Hiro continued, "The first Japanese immigrants moved voluntarily to Cuba, as well as to other Central and South American countries, in the 1880s. They were looking for work and for better lives. The immigrants had heard about the huge sugar economy that triggered a massive boom to the Cuban economy in late 1800. This created an influx of immigrants. Today descendants of those original Japanese immigrants total about a thousand people."

"Most of the Japanese immigrants returned to Japan after they had saved enough money for their passage home. Some of the immigrants succeeded and got a jump-start on a new life in South America. Especially successful were those who went to Brazil and to the United States. There are large populations of Japanese living in those two countries today."

"The reason few remained in Cuba was due to the politics of World War II. Most of the Japanese who immigrated to Cuba stayed around the Isla de la Juventud or the island of Pinos. They cultivated vegetables for export to the United States. During World War II, a very sad development occurred for those Japanese immigrants. They were sent to a Cuban concentration camp and the government confiscated everything they had including all personal possessions, homes, and farms. When the war ended, they were all set free but their confiscated property was never returned to them by the Cuban government."

"It was a nightmare for those remaining in the Japanese community in the country. Today, there are still a few Japanese who live on Isla de la Juventud, but their number is very small, perhaps less than a hundred. Thus, they made no big contribution to Cuban culture or history."

Hiro took a big pause and looked away to indicate that he had finished lecturing. Aimee and Pedro were surprised at his grasp of history. Aimee, as Hiro's guide, felt challenged to expand his knowledge of the city of Havana, Cuban history, and Cuban government. Aimee was fast to jump in, and said,

"Wow that was interesting. I didn't have any idea that all that happened!"

Hiro hadn't seen any restaurants, grocery stores, markets, or merchants. He saw poorly decorated shops that looked like they had nothing to sell. He compared the commerce of Cuba to Japan and to the US, and he surmised that materials and supplies were very limited in Cuba.

He began to have a flashback about the Cuban revolution, something that he had heard on the radio as a young boy in Japan. During the broadcast, thousands of people were excited and supported Fidel Castro. He remembered hearing the shouts of joy for Fidel Castro, as he became Cuba's new leader. But what had become of Cuba today under his leadership?

In 1950, Cuba was a hundred percent better than Japan. Cuba was prospering while Japan was not. His mind continued to race between comparisons of Japan and Cuba. He could not understand why there was such a limited food supply and why the people did not have many choices. He had never seen a Communist country in real life. He had only read about the system in books or heard information on the theory via news reports. Now that he was actually in a Communist country, he could see first hand that this system was not working. It was unlike the theory of Communism that he had read about. The community was supposed to be protected by Communism, but this was a totalitarian society where few prospered and the masses suffered. There was no even distribution of wealth. Why did Communism fail? In hindsight, it was a real example of trickle down economics, except the Communists were very tidy.

Hiro noticed that although the people looked happy and seemed very friendly, they seemed to have an invisible weight upon them that kept them suppressed. It seemed as though the people were genuinely connected, but in reality they were only interested in their own selfish needs and unable to think ahead. They were beautiful because they were in the moment, but it was certainly no path to success. It seemed to Hiro that still waters would run deep, but when he dipped his toe in, he found it very shallow. It was late in the afternoon, and the tropical sun was scorching hot. It was miserable in the Ford even with all the windows rolled down.

Hiro finally said, "All right, this is enough for today. I would like to return to my hotel." He, Pedro, and Aimee drove to

The Last Revolution

the Hotel Inglaterra and walked into the lobby. Hiro invited them to the restaurant and bar where they ordered some *Hatuey* beer. Aimee said she would like to have some red wine. They all three sat down and enjoyed their drinks. They had not eaten lunch and had made do with some small snacks Pedro had in the car, so Hiro invited them to have dinner with him in the restaurant.

Both Pedro and Aimee were excited about the invitation and accepted. They had never eaten in a fancy hotel restaurant in their lives. In their minds, this place was only for rich tourists. Both were hungry and were eager to be served. As they entered the restaurant and asked for a table, members of the hotel security force entered. They approached Pedro and Aimee and politely asked them to leave. Hiro watched in disbelief and could not understand why Cubans would be asked to leave a public restaurant. They were his guests and his friends, and he was offended. He thought, "How could the government interfere with personal life like this?"

In Cuba, tourists could neither associate with individual Cubans, nor could they ride in a personal car. It was against the law. Hiro now realized what the immigrations officer in the airport had been talking about. Aimee and Pedro could not explain to the guards why they were with Hiro, because they were making money illegally. They were afraid to say anything. They both gave Hiro a look that meant not to say anything about what they had been doing. They looked so scared that Hiro understood that these guards might give them trouble if he protested. Aimee gave Hiro the sign for money by rubbing her fingers together. Hiro didn't really understand that being with Pedro and Aimee was illegal until this moment.

Finally, Hiro said, "I am a guest here in the hotel. These are my friends, and I want them to dine with me." He slipped them a twenty dollar tip to split. The security guards subtly accepted the cash, and said, "It's OK." They left quietly.

Hiro asked Aimee, "Are we in trouble?"

Aimee answered, "The guards were happy to get that money. This happens all the time here and money talks, Hiro." Then they ordered a traditional Cuban meal that consisted of salsa, chicken, black beans, cabbage salad, and local pastries. The food tasted terrific. They drank more *Hatuey* beer and red wine and had a great time.

Aimee and Pedro said, "We always wondered what it was like in here. Wow! The tourists eat so well. We didn't know what we were missing."

After an evening of incredible Cuban cuisine, Aimee ordered one more glass of red wine. Then Pedro remarked with a proud voice, "Hiro, You should try some Cuban rum. The finest Cuban rum is about fifteen years old and has a superb taste." Hiro wasn't a big consumer of alcohol, but since he enjoyed Cuban beer, he thought he might give rum a try. "After all," he pointed out to himself, "rum is famous in Cuba, and not to taste it would be a shame."

Pedro persisted, "Hey, it's your opportunity to taste our Cuban rum." Pedro laughed, "And if you taste *Havana Club,* you probably will never want to drink anything else!" Hiro was amused at Pedro's persistence and decided to order a bottle of the famous fifteen-year-old Havana Club.

The rum was quick to arrive at the table. Pedro lifted his hand, gesturing in the manner of a magician, and said, "I'll show you the way we drink rum here." With great showmanship, he poured a glass of water for himself and Hiro. Hiro thought water was a good start. Pedro continued, "This is your chaser after the rum." Then he poured each of them half a drinking glass of rum and handed one to the Japanese novice. Hiro drank it down all at once, just as Pedro did. He hoped for the best and feared for the worst. Stoically, yet politely, he gently coughed, drank the entire water chaser, and exhaled.

"Woooo!" It tingled and nearly anesthetized his tongue! It had a rich and powerful taste. It was so vivid and bold that it sent a shockwave throughout his entire body. It was premium Cuban rum with a powerful kick. "Woooo!" It kept on kicking.

Aimee told Hiro that Ernest Hemingway's local hangout was the Floridita bar and restaurant on *Obispo* Street. There, Hemingway was a notorious lady's man who watched the girls dance and exchanged stories with friends. He routinely sat in the same chair at the same table and ordered *mojitos* and daiquiris. He was quite a character. Now, tourists flocked to the Floridita to try the famous "Hemingway Special." She made Hiro's mouth water as she described the famous Cuban *mojito*. "You have to try a *mojito,"* said Aimee. "It's like our national drink. It's superbly refreshing and cool with lemon, lime, hand crushed sugar and fresh mint added to the perfect amount of rum. I am going to take you to La Bodequita del Medio for the ultimate *mojitos,*" Aimee mused. *Sangria* was another local favorite alcoholic drink.

But Pedro argued that place was too fancy. He liked to get his drinks at the local bars for practically nothing. As long as the rum was plentiful and cheap, he was happy. He liked his drinks, but he was always smart with his money. Aimee leaned forward to command the conversation and shared a bit of history and sociology with Hiro. "Rum is derived from sugarcane and aged in wooden barrels. It can vary in color and flavor by or by what is added to it. The best Cuban rum is aged for at least fifteen years. The most famous brands of Cuban rum are Havana Club, Bacardi, and Havana Libre."

Before Castro took over the government, the Bacardi family moved its headquarters from Cuba to the Bahamas. They also built a huge facility in Puerto Rico that allowed for business with the US market. When Fidel seized the old Bacardi factory in Cuba and took over the books, the Bacardi family was stunned. They had been huge financial supporters of the rebels against Fidel. Fidel declared that the government had claim to Bacardi's rum and factories as well as those of Cuba Libre and Havana Club. Fidel said they belonged to Cuba and it was a matter of national pride. He said that rum was a landmark product of Cuba. Without Cuban soil and sugarcane, they wouldn't be in business. A bitter dispute followed and those families sued the Cuban government on grounds of international patent trade mark infringement.

Ignoring the Cuban government's decision and position, US courts gave the Bacardi family permission to use the Bacardi trademark. They became a near monopoly throughout the Caribbean, regulating almost all rum trademarks and production. The family made billions. Cuba lost out. Litigation has continued. The Bacardi family's ambitious trademark theft was absolutely a criminal act against the Cuban people. "It made the Cuban people angry that financial giants can crash there card game anytime they wished."

"I'm sure, Hiro, that the more you learn and see, the more you will agree that the Bacardi label—that is to say the Cuban label—must belong to the people of Cuba. They suffer the loss of their greatest national financial resource." Amy leaned back in her chair to indicate that she had finished.

Hiro found this all very interesting, and thought Aimee convincing. Coca-Cola or McDonald's would certainly never give up their trademarks without compensation. Cuba did hold the Bacardi trademarks and patents first. And he had seen such poverty here. Hiro felt lucky to have met Aimee and Pedro through Tito. They enjoyed the evening together and left contented. Hiro appreciated the day's tour and the meal with his new friends. He began to understand the Cuban people, their culture, and the government a little better through Pedro, his cousin Aimee, and this experience.

Hiro had also observed something out of the ordinary about himself. He was amazed that he had not been constantly calculating and planning as usual. In Cuba, at least today, he was a captive of fate and surprisingly comfortable with it. As if predestined, he had met his driver, Pedro, a carpenter from Rancho Veloz, who just happened to be in Havana visiting with his family, which just happened to include a translator, Aimee. Hiro met her only accidentally through her next door neighbor, Tito, who just happened to be the first person Hiro saw outside his hotel. Pedro was randomly asking if anyone needed anything. Who might this new Hiro be? But then he began to deep think again.

Hiro asked Pedro, "Tell me more about Rancho Veloz. Do you have rivers or lakes or mountains there? What is the countryside like?"

Pedro said, "My hometown is very small and remote. It is quiet, and there are nice people there. Almost all of my relatives live near there, and yes, we have both a river and a lake and there is good fishing. There are rolling mountains and wild deer. It's nice." Hiro listened to Pedro's description and knew he would like to visit. It reminded him of the countryside of Hiroshima and fishing.

They drank more beer and wine and soon they were all relaxed and sleepy. Pedro stood up and said, "Thank you, but it is getting very late, and we should go. We'll be back in the morning."

Hiro faced Aimee and said, "Wait a minute. Don't go yet. I was wondering if you could also tutor me in Spanish. I will pay you an extra $25 a day for a two hour daily lesson. I will need materials and books. Do you think you can get these things?"

The Last Revolution

Aimee looked delighted. That was more money than she would earn in years. "Of course, I'll find my old school books for you to use. No problem."

Hiro said, "I have a Spanish dictionary in my room."

Aimee said, "Great. When do you want to start?"

Hiro answered, "My brain works better in the morning. Maybe you could come here two hours earlier, and we can have the lesson before the tour. Also, I would like to treat you both to breakfast every morning." Pedro and Aimee accepted happily.

Hiro's Spanish vocabulary was limited. He knew that he needed many hours of lessons to perfect the accent and to learn to communicate in Spanish like a native. His photographic memory had served him well for the grammar patterns, but he had not devoted enough time to regular vocabulary, idioms or slang. Every day the friendship between Pedro, Aimee and Hiro deepened. For the first time in his life, Hiro was beginning to understand people's feelings and emotions. His nightmares had subsided, and it had been days since an anxiety attack.

Since the first fateful day he had met Tito, Pedro and Aimee, Hiro had begun to live in the moment—the first time in his life. He had always lived, planned for, the future and calculated life years ahead. He noticed a huge difference in himself, and he liked it. Hiro calculated about not calculating: "Is my metamorphosis originating from predestination or from the budding of human emotions and empathy?" His mathematical mind had trouble justifying predestination.

He began to like Fidel Castro's gift to him. He had never had a time in his life without pressure. Aimee began to feel comfortable enough around Hiro to open up and even complain about her life in Cuba. She told him that the government controlled every aspect of daily life. She had attended to the University of Havana and had graduated with a journalism degree. She worked as a journalist for The Cuban Press and as a translator for the government. She knew how everything operated behind the scenes in this country and now she felt like she could share what she knew with Hiro. She trusted him.

As their friendship progressed, Hiro began to appreciate Aimee's intelligence and everything she had shared with him. Aimee was an intellectual. As the days went by, Hiro learned about the Communist structure and more about the Cuban people from her. They discussed many subjects in English everyday when they were together. She felt very comfortable and secure speaking in English because very few Cubans understood the language. Aimee had influenced Hiro's perceptions about daily life. She had also begun to like this strange Japanese man who was so quiet and gentle. He had a kind heart and it showed each day through their friendship. She suspected he was very brilliant from their conversations.

Hiro never talked about his own life and was very humble, but Aimee appreciated his intelligence and quiet nature. They were together all the time, and on occasion, she invited him to her home to have dinner and Cuban coffee with her family. She lived in a two bedroom apartment house that the family had received from a state lottery. It once belonged to a family that had moved to Miami, but the government had given it to her mother. The family had had to wait five years for the accommodations, but the rent was free. Before the lottery, they had lived in a small studio apartment with four people. It was so crowded. Aimee was a twenty' nine' year' old single mother with a sweet, twelve-year-old daughter named Laura. Aimee was highly educated and a modern young Cuban woman. Hiro had never met anyone who talked so much. He was not used to this. In Japan, women were very reserved.

She was very social, knew everybody and had many friends. He began to know her very well over these days and grew closer to her family. On the weekends they invited all their friends and relatives for dinner and Cuban beer. Hiro bought all the groceries and beverages for her and her family at these gatherings. He was unimaginably better off financially than most Cubans, so this was the least he could do. At first they felt bad that he paid for everything, but when he insisted, they gladly accepted. Since there were no stores, Pedro purchased the items on the black market.

Pedro was an easygoing fellow who acted as their watchdog. Every time he came close to a police checkpoint in the street, he told Hiro to duck his head and act as if he were asleep in Aimee's lap. They gave him a baseball cap to cover his face. They wanted to avoid getting caught since it was a crime for a tourist to be riding in a personal car. Hiro thought that sometimes he must be crazy for doing this. He was always scared that they would get caught, but he began to love his friends very much and was willing to take the risk to be with them. He had never done anything illegal in his life, but he felt compelled to be with them. His humanity was returning.

The government of Cuba had a strong and aggressive hold over its citizens, since Fidel had taken control of the island. Fidel didn't need weapons to control the people, because he had created a system like a neighborhood watch where average citizens could turn in political dissidents or those against Fidel and the government. In exchange for this, they received food tickets called *bonos*. They were coupons worth pesos. People were rewarded for information so you could never trust anyone. But Pedro and Aimee took the risk, because Hiro wanted to pay them more money than they could ever make in their entire lifetimes.

They felt they had to take the chance. If they were caught, they might get imprisoned and Pedro's Ford would be impounded. They were taking quite a big risk to associate with Hiro. Pedro and Aimee also knew that the police would take bribes and that Hiro could afford to pay the bribes. They figured it was worth the chance. The Cuban people were like puppets who just blindly obeyed the government and Castro's system. They hibernated from the rest of the world while Castro used the embargo as a means of controlling the people. He told them the embargo was the reason that Cuba had a tough time. He blamed the US when in reality the embargo actually helped Castro control his own country. If the embargo was suddenly dropped, then Castro would have no power over the people.

Fidel enjoyed the embargo since it was the key to his survival. The Communist and Socialist model of government worked well in theory in Latin American countries, because the masses were not educated. Hiro thought that Cuba probably had started out with pure Socialized Communist ideals when Fidel Castro had taken over control of the country. But over the years, Castro had modified his ideals to remain in power. He had such a big ego that he would not step down from office. Ultimately, Cuba had evolved into a totalitarian system that Fidel called Social-Communism, and Cuba was self-destructing slowly because of it. It seemed only a matter of time until Fidel would be deposed.

A couple of weeks passed by and Hiro began to understand why Cuba remained in hibernation. Through Pedro and Aimee and all that he saw, he became quite well-educated about the real Cuba. Hiroaki began to think of his childhood in post-war Japan. At that time, Hiro did not know that he was living in poverty. It was just the way things were. Now that he was in Cuba, he could see that living in Japan back in the 50s was very hard. In fact, the conditions in the 50s in Japan were much worse than in Cuba today. He had lived through worse times. His strong analytical mind knew that there was something wrong with the system, and he began to pinpoint exactly what the problems were.

Back in the 1600s, Japan was isolated and closed to the rest of the world much like Cuba was today. Japan also experienced a hibernation period with a strong dictator system with the Shogunate ruling the island country. Because of its isolation, Cuba, like Japan, had developed a strong and unique culture. But with this system of rule, the weak were dominated by the strong. Hiro began to see that Fidel really didn't care about the individual's life. He cared only about his own vision for Cuba. Feelings didn't have a place in this system. It was actually very similar to the life Hiro had lead up to now. Hiro was all about achievements and reaching his long term visions and goals. But once he was there, he realized that that his system had flaws.

He had reached the top finding that there were no real rewards. Now he was searching for something else. Funny that he had come all the way to Cuba just to realize this. He had been there and done that, so he could recognize it. Fidel was still in-progress while Hiro had already passed that stage. Hiro could relate to Castro in this way, but the people of Cuba could not. They were tired of this system. It was the theory of evolution that only the strongest survive. It wasn't about fairness. Even the mightiest country in the world, the United States, was based on this kind of philosophy. It was the politics of the fittest.

Hiro continued to learn to understand and enjoy Havana. He was fascinated with the Cuban culture, the apathetic people and their daily life. There was no other place like this in the world. The people that he met and befriended continued to complain and whisper about what they didn't have and what they could not do. He saw that they only complained and that they didn't do anything to make their situations better.

Cuba was a culture of people who complained behind closed doors, but remained complacent. They were waiting for someone to hand them their freedom, because they did not want to get their hands dirty. They were not willing to suffer the consequences for freedom now.

Chapter 12

Hiro asked Aimee and Pedro, "So, what are we going to do today? You do have any ideas?"

Aimee said, "Hiro, it's time you had your first cigar. If you haven't had a Cuban cigar, then you are still a virgin!"

She and Pedro began to laugh. Hiro had seen people smoking Cuban cigars since the minute he had walked out of the airport, but he had never smoked in his life. Hiro smiled and said, "I don't know much about smoking cigars, but I'll give it a try."

Aimee laughed said, "No problem my friend, we are going to show you everything you need to know." Aimee and Pedro talked a bit and decided to show Hiro the cigar factories of Havana. They got into Pedro's brown 56 Ford and took off to see one of Aimee's friends, Manuel. He worked at a local factory and they thought he might be able to give them a tour. Manuel worked as a cigar tester. He tested many bootlegged cigars as well as fake cigars from overseas. These fakes usually came from The Dominican Republic or Central America. These bogus cigars cost the Cuban economy millions and millions of dollars in revenue each year. Therefore, Cuba employed official cigar testers. Manuel was one of these. Manuel made good money at his job because he could easily obtain fake cigars to take home and sell in the streets of Cuba at a great profit.

After visiting his home, Manuel gave them a bundle of fake cigars. He said, "Now, these are what I smoke. They are made from the poorer quality leaves and scraps. I don't know if you are going to like them, but some of them come from the Dominican Republic or Central America. They are pretty good but nothing like the real thing. You can give them a try." They thanked Manuel and said good-bye. As he drove away, Aimee gave the bundle to Pedro.

She said, "I'm not going to let Hiro try these. They are not good enough for him. You take them home for you and your brothers. We need to get Hiro something good." Pedro agreed. They explained that these had a poor finish, burned unevenly, and had a rough, hot taste. Aimee said "I take them to my father who loves any kind of cigar!"

Pedro said "OK! That's a good idea. Give me a few and take the rest to him." They were not very good cigars, but this was what many locals smoked because they were cheap and affordable.

Most Cubans never got to smoke a good quality cigar. They only had the opportunity to smoke a good one on special occasions or if someone had stolen some cigars and sold them cheap on the black market. Most stolen cigars got redistributed to the tourists for top dollar, so again most Cubans never had the opportunity to try the good brands. Aimee explained that the nice hotels all had a store which sold cigars. They could also be found in special government shops. These were the only places that tourists could purchase cigars. Then Aimee, Pedro and Hiro drove to a part of Havana that had many stores and souvenir shops.

These shops were government-approved stores and carried all of the good cigar brands of cigars. The average Cuban could not buy cigars here because they were extremely expensive and for tourists only. Even Aimee and Pedro admitted that they had smoked only a few good ones in their whole lives. When they smoked a cigar, it was always the cheap, poor-quality peso cigar. Pedro got a *Montecristo* on his wedding day from his brother and also received one as a gift from friends at the birth of each of his children. Aimee had also tried several over the years at special events and parties related to her work. She could not afford to buy them herself, because they were high priced and considered to be very extravagant.

As they entered the cigar shop, Aimee and Pedro's eyes opened wide. They were like two kids in a candy shop. The shop also sold Cuban coffees, rum and other specialty items. This store carried the best of what Cuba produced, but it was all for tourists. They showed Hiro all the different brands—*Partagas, Montecristo, Romeo y Julieta, Punch, Fonseca* and *Cohiba.* There were many more brands, but these were the few that Aimee showed Hiro. The manager of the store came over to talk to him. Aimee and Pedro got the feeling that they were not welcome and told Hiro to buy what he wanted and to meet them out at the car. Besides, they directed their friend to talk with the manager to get his opinion. The man asked Hiro if he could answer any questions for him.

Hiro asked, "What is the best cigar you have here?"

The man laughed. "Well, that depends on how you like your cigars. Here in Cuba, we have the finest tobacco in the world, and I can tell you what is most popular. I can also show you a few of my favorites."

Hiro replied, "Great, I am new at this, and I have never smoked a cigar in my life."

The man looked surprised and said, "Well, you came to the right place." He pointed to a beautiful box with a picture of an Indian's head on top and gold along the bottom. The name *Cohiba* was on the top of the box. "This cigar company began in 1688, and the cigars were originally for diplomatic use only. They were nicknamed the 'King of the Cubans' because only the finest tobacco leaves are used. They are one of the most popular brands. You may like to try the *Cohiba Siglo's V*. In 1992, the company made the Siglo's series in honor of Columbus's 500th anniversary of discovering the new world."

The manager added, "The *V* and *IV* are personal favorites, although they are all nice. They are powerful, have a fabulous texture, and have a creamy and peppery finish. Also, if money is no object, I highly recommend the *Esplendidos*. They are an older, more refined cigar, but one of the best cigars made by *Cohiba*." Hiro noticed the price of the Esplendidos was $595.00 for a box of 25 cigars. The price of the *Siglo's* was $425.00 for a box of 25. He asked for a box of each. The man had a big smile on his face, "Very good choices sir. Anything else?" Hiro was quite interested in seeing more. The man showed him the brand called *Montecristo*. "This, probably the most famous brand, was started in 1935 by the H. Uppman owners. They were named after a famous novel written in 1844 by Alexander Dumas, *The Count of Monte Cristo*. They are all hand-rolled and medium-bodied. They are excellent. Most cigars are now judged by the standard of the *Montecristo*," he added. "I also recommend the *Especial #2*, pointed in shape like a torpedo, and the Edmundos brand. You will not be sorry."

The clerk showed Hiro several other brands like the *Punch Churchill* named after Winston Churchill. He said, "The finish on this cigar lasts for hours." He also showed him the *Romeo y Julieta* brand. Hiro got the full descriptions of

The Last Revolution

each—some were described as grassy, spicy, chocolaty, velvety, and some even hinted of coffee. The boxes ranged in price from $250 to $650. After the man took him through all the selections, Hiro thought for a moment and pointed to several boxes. He must have pointed to at least seven boxes. The man looked shocked because those boxes contained quite a lot of cigars and were very expensive. The clerk said, "Wow, for someone who doesn't smoke, you are buying many cigars. They must be gifts." Hiro just smiled. The man gave Hiro a special government-issued receipt and told him that if he wanted to clear customs in Mexico with these cigars that he must have this receipt. Without it, the cigars would all be confiscated. He also showed Hiro the special seal on each box that was a top-secret government code.

The government code had to change frequently because there were hackers who tried to duplicate the seals. The seal was in place to protect the real cigars from bootleggers. The man explained to Hiro that there were many fake brand-name cigars being sold on the streets to tourists, and that unless there was a seal on the box, you could not be sure of what you were getting.

Also, the clerk showed Hiro a real *Cohiba* and a fake one. Hiro barely could tell the difference at first, but then the man showed him that the real one used raised gold lettering while the fake one had flat lettering. Also, the width of the fake *Cohiba* label was smaller than that of the real one. The most important difference was that the fakes were poorer quality. Showing Hiro two cigars, the clerk said, "See how the color of the real one is dark chocolate brown while this fake one is lighter with rough markings. It is made with poor quality tobacco." The man added, "Many tourists buy the fake ones at top dollar only to find out later when they smoke them that they are fakes. Bootlegged and fake cigars are popular here and a way for the locals to make good money."

The clerk also told Hiro that he would need to purchase a good humidor for keeping the cigars fresh. He showed him several for sale made by Cuban crafters. Each one was a work of art, made from native Cuban cedar and imported rose wood. They were gorgeous with rich, inlaid rose wood and shined to a piano finish with twelve coats of lacquer. He showed Hiro one that had a cedar interior with a felt-lined drawer. It had cedar aerators, brass inset handles, a humidification system and a lock and key. He also showed Hiro a special propylene glycol solution for the humidor that helped to stabilize the humidity at an optimal 70% and would prevent mold and bacteria from forming. The man explained that a zip-lock baggie or plastic container would not be sufficient for all of these cigars.

The clerk said, "Perhaps for a few, but not for this many. You have made quite an investment with these. You must take care of them and keep them at the right moisture level for your enjoyment in the future." Hiro agreed and listened as the man gave him specific instructions on how much water was needed and where to put it inside the humidor. The man also sold him three cigar cutters and a few special lighters to use as gifts. Hiro thanked the man for his help and walked out of the shop with two big bags and a box with a humidor. Aimee and Pedro were waiting in the car and wondering what Hiro was buying when they saw him walk out of the shop. They couldn't even see Hiro's face behind all of his purchases.

They were surprised and couldn't wait to see what he had bought. Aimee was jumping up and down in the car, clapping her hands and squealing with delight. "Dios Mio! Look at all the stuff Hiro just bought," she muttered to Pedro. Pedro just had a big grin on his face and shook his head in disbelief.

Hiro walked up to them and said, "Well, I think I have enough cigars here to last us a lifetime!"

Aimee and Pedro looked in the bags and picked up the brand new boxes. They ran their hands across the boxes. "Que rico!" Aimee said. She added, "I have never held a whole box in my hand before. I've only seen them in store windows."

Hiro told her, "That is for you Aimee, the whole box." Her jaw dropped open, and her eyes widened. She was in shock for a minute. She kissed the box, and then kissed Hiro.

His face turned bright red, but his reward was the smile on her face. "Thank you Hiro, Thank you so much. I can't believe it. I can't believe this is for me," exclaimed Aimee.

Hiro turned to Pedro, "OK Pedro, your turn. Pick a box for yourself. Which one would you like?" said Hiro. Pedro was speechless; he didn't know what to say. Then after a minute he said, "Hiro, you keep these. These are too expensive"

Hiro immediately said to him, "I have so many boxes here, and I wanted to get you and Aimee each one, too. Please, it

The Last Revolution

is my gift to you. You must take one!" Pedro finally agreed and reached for the box of *Montecristo Edmundos*.

Hiro said, "Oh, you like the super Robusta! Full bodied with a spicy finish." Aimee and Pedro both looked at Hiro. He told them, "The man explained each one to me. I know a little bit about each cigar and brand."

Aimee laughed and replied, "You're going to be a cigar expert soon!"

They decided since it was late that they would teach him about smoking tomorrow. Enjoying a good cigar should not be rushed. Cigars also tasted better with some Cuban rum and a good meal. Besides, Hiro was tired and was ready to return to the hotel. The pair dropped Hiro off at the entrance of his hotel and made a plan to pick him up for a nice breakfast and cigar lessons the next day. Pedro and Aimee both thanked Hiro again for the very generous gifts. Hiro knew that they were overwhelmed to receive them, but he really liked his new friends and wanted to do something special. After all, they had helped him so much. Even though they were earning wages, they had bent over backwards to help him and to see that he was treated well. Hiro was in a generous mood and very happy for the first time in a long time. It was as much fun for him to give the cigars as it was for Pedro and Aimee to receive the cigars.

When Hiro got to his room, he unpacked his brand new cigars and humidor. He did exactly as the clerk had instructed with the humidor, and carefully put the glycol solution in the humidifier. He had intended on going to bed, but he was so excited when he took out his cigar boxes that he decided to smoke his first cigar on his balcony. "Why wait?" He thought.

Hiro opened his first box of Cuban cigars, the *Cohiba Esplendidos*. He was told by the cigar store owner how to cut the top of the cigar off. He slid the cigar through the cutter, only cutting off enough to get a good draw of air through. Too large a cut would make the cigar burn too hot.

Next came the art of lighting a cigar. The clerk had told Hiro to never let the flame touch the end of the cigar. He had told Hiro to hold the cigar just off the tip of the flame, letting it ignite from the steady heat, gently turning the cigar to get an even burn. Hiro puckered his mouth over the cigar, drawing in the air in a succession of puffs to fully light the cigar. Now it was time to enjoy the crown jewel of Cuban cigars.

Micheal Kazuhiro Nishitani

Splendid! This was Hiro's first taste of a Cuban cigar. Hiro sucked in a big inhalation of fine Cuban tobacco. One thing the cigar shop owner did not tell Hiro which was the most important rule of all—never inhale cigar smoke!

The grandeur of this once-in-a-lifetime moment was suddenly transformed into a nightmare of choking and coughing, since Hiro had inhaled the spicy strong smoke. It was as if his lungs were on fire. He felt dizzy and nauseous. His face turned green and he started to gag. Hiro set the cigar from which he had only taken one puff on the table, had a sip of water, and decided to call it a night. Hiro decided to wait until tomorrow to let Aimee and Pedro show him how to really smoke cigars the Cuban way.

The next morning, Hiro was already sitting in the lobby reading tourist brochures. The flyer about Hemingway's Place captured his attention. He had been approached by many hustlers, or jinteros, who offered to show him around the city and to take him on tours. These are known as paladares all across Cuba. Jinteras hit the streets of Havana looking for their next client early. These illegal female prostitutes work the streets targeting tourists who pay for their services with U.S. dollars. Many were married, but had to work to support their families back in the countryside. The money they make in one month in the city would support their family all year. They charged a hefty price so Hiro was glad to be with Pedro and Aimee. He felt he could trust them because they were not going to take advantage of him.

Oslo They were restaurants which were run out of people's homes they decided to have breakfast before going sightseeing. The hotel served an excellent breakfast, but Hiro wanted to try something different. Aimee and Pedro had never eaten a buffet style breakfast before. Hiro was delighted to treat them and asked the receptionist for a restaurant recommendation. She sent them to the Hotel Deauville on the Malecón.

Pedro parked his car across the street and they entered the front of the hotel. The hotel was basic and plain. It seemed very clean, but it was not a very interesting or scenic place. As soon as they entered the lobby, they noticed many tourists. They all were wearing t-shirts and baggie shorts and flip-flops. Right away, he understood that this hotel catered to those on a shoestring budget

The Last Revolution

and backpackers. Pedro and Aimee looked around and were surprised to see how different it was from the Hotel Inglaterra.

The Deauville was built of plain white concrete just like every other modern building in Havana. The hotel had been renovated, but it was still simple with little decor and style, but it was centrally located across from the Havana Malecón and had an excellent view of the sea. It was near the Castillo de los Tress Reyes del Morro, which was near the entrance of the bay of Havana Malecón. This meant that the hotel visitors could walk quickly to *Vedado*. It was nice to have everything nearby. The Hotel Deauville did have all modern facilities, and they asked to see one of the rooms. It was plain but looked comfortable. Each room had a terrace with a view of the sea or of Old Havana. One great feature was that it had a nice rooftop pool.

This was one of its most popular features, because the public could swim for a small fee, and hotel guests could swim at no charge. Aimee asked the front receptionist about the restaurant. The receptionist was very young and cheerful and said, "Well, you came to the right place, but we serve only our hotel guests. If you don't have a room, then I'm sorry, but you cannot dine in our restaurant. The waiter will ask for your hotel key before taking your order." Aimee began to argue that Hiro was a tourist and a guest of the Cuban government. She showed the receptionist his Japanese passport. Finally, the girl went back to the office to speak with her manager. A few minutes later, the hotel manager came out and discussed everything with Aimee. After some persuading, the manager gave special permission for Hiro and his friend to enjoy the buffet.

In the restaurant, Aimee and Pedro's eyes got very big. They were seeing a buffet for the first time and couldn't believe how much food was on it. There were huge serving dishes of foods including all types of fresh fruits, potatoes, polish sausage, bacon, ham, cheese, eggs, pancakes, breads, croissants, sweet rolls, black beans, rice pudding, oatmeal and a variety of cereals. There were even several jams, jellies and honey. It all smelled so wonderful. Pedro and Aimee had never seen anything like it before. Hiro said, "Be my guests!" They all three got in the line and walked to the buffet.

Pedro said, "How much do we take?"

Aimee said, "It looks like you get as much as you want."

Hiro said, "Yes, it is all-you-can-eat, so please help yourself." They all dug in, heaping food on their plates. The buffet displayed many different kinds of foods. Most Cubans had never seen this much food in real life because this hotel catered to the young, shoestring travelers from Europe and Canada. Almost no Americans or Cuban-Americans stayed at this hotel. Pedro and Aimee were shocked to see the huge quantities of food. They could not imagine such a thing; they almost felt guilty eating such a feast. Periodically, they would peek at Hiro while he was eating. He was quiet and enjoyed a huge assortment of fresh fruits. He loved giving his friends the opportunity to have this type of smorgasbord. He also explained that this was typical in America. Buffets were common for breakfast, lunch and dinner in the US.

Most Cubans ate only bread, milk and maybe a little fruit for breakfast. They had never had the chance to eat lavish foods in this quantity. Aimee and Pedro were actually shocked to see most of the hotel guests eating only half of their servings and throwing away the rest. They told Hiro that it was such a waste. They couldn't understand why the foreigners would throw away so much food. The food they threw into the garbage could help feed the poor people in the city.

They ate all of their food, but they couldn't help but think about how different Cuba was from other nations. The tourists took the buffet for granted while Aimee and Pedro were grateful to have enjoyed such an amazing grand feast. To these tourists this was the norm, while for a Cuban this was a magical moment. It highlighted the contrast in cultures. Aimee and Pedro didn't want to waste a drop and ate everything on their plates, there were huge quantities of beautiful fruits, but Hiro noticed that his friends were not interested in eating them.

Hiro asked, "Why don't you eat the fruit?"

Pedro and Aimee said, "Hiro, we can eat fruit anytime, but the other imported items are almost impossible to buy here. These meats, egg dishes, and cheeses are very expensive for us. We simply cannot afford things like this, so we want to eat that stuff!" Hiro understood, and all three smiled as they enjoyed the feast. They went back three different times to get more food. Each time they ate everything on their plates, not wasting one bit. They loved all the variety and enjoyed every morsel.

The Last Revolution

Hiro said, "The lady at the reception desk at the Hotel Inglaterra was right on the button!" They nodded in agreement.

After an hour of feasting, Pedro and Aimee could barely move. The three had eaten so much food that they were stuffed and uncomfortable from overeating. Pedro had to unbutton his pants. Hiro offered them a Cuban coffee, but they both declined. They could not consume one more thing, and they just sat there completely stuffed. Hiro started laughing, "Next time you two need to eat more fruit and not just proteins—maybe just a small quantity. It will be better for your health, and you won't feel so miserable." Pedro and Aimee laughed about how much they had eaten.

Pedro said, "Just let us sit here a little while. We will be fine."

Hiro said, "Look, I brought several Cuban cigars. Let's go someplace to smoke. I want you to show me the Cuban way to smoke correctly."

Pedro said, "Give me a minute to digest all this food then we can go sit at the Malecón. Ma I will show you the Cuban way, no problem." After a while, all three walked along the Caribbean beachfront called Malecón.

It was about half a block down and across the street. Already, the sun was scorching hot. "It's the Caribbean's hot kiss," said Aimee as she put on her sunglasses.

Hiro said to Pedro, "It is too hot to sit on the wall of the Malecón. Let's go someplace cooler so we can enjoy smoking our cigars."

Pedro agreed, as the sun was already making him sweat under his traditional white cotton Guayabera shirt. Pedro said, "Look, just a little way up ahead. They have a refreshment bar with coffee and drinks. They usually have a sun umbrella and chairs right next to sea. It will be cooler there and smells like the ocean. You will like it there at Castillo de los Tress Reyes del Morro. OK, Hiro?" Just ahead about two blocks from the hotel, they found the refreshment stand. There was a young Cuban fellow serving ice cream, snow cones, soft drinks, and Cuban coffee. There were already several young locals sitting under sun umbrellas. They couldn't afford to pay for the treats, so they just sat talking and enjoying the beautiful beachfront of the Havana Malecón. It was gorgeous and fresh by the sea. It was a famous spot in Havana for both tourists and locals alike.

Micheal Kazuhiro Nishitani

They sat down in white plastic chairs under a sun-bleached umbrella beachside. Hiro pulled out a box of premium cigars from his small backpack. Pedro said, "Hiro, let me have one, and I will show you how we here in Cuba smoke a cigar." Hiro gave him one of the torpedo-shaped *Romeo y Julieta Churchill Cigars,* Pedro stood with the cigar using a showing-off gesture of Fidel that made fun of the political situation in Cuba.

Hiro looked at the young college-aged people among them and turned to Aimee and said, "Wait a minute! I have some cigars I got from the tobacco store manager. I would like to give some to these young people if they would like to join us." Aimee thought that would be a good idea. She asked all of them if they wanted to join them in smoking a cigar. There were about six of them between the ages of 18, to 20, years, old. They were just hanging out by the beach, a very popular activity for the youth of Havana on hot days. They were so excited and jumped at the chance. Hiro handed them a couple of cigars to share and although they were young, they lit them up like pros. Hiro saw that they were experienced cigar smokers even at their young ages.

Than Pedro started to speak again, "Look, Hiro, this is great opportunity. I am going to show you how to smoke the correct way!" He got really serious and said with a straight face, "Watch carefully, this is only with premium cigars. OK, Hiro?" Then Pedro said, "First you cut off a small part of the tip opposite the side of which you smoke like here with the end that has the tiny hole already made by the manufacturer. Hiro, make sure you cut the correct end. This cut should be small and straight so the cigar burns slowly and evenly all the way to the finger. Then you lick both ends to get them moist, and then lick the entire cigar. As your tongue licks the cigar you begin to taste the nicotine in your mouth. Then, Hiro, you pull your pants off, put the cigar up your ass and say, 'Thanks, Fidel!'"

Hiro's face went blank. He didn't know what to say. Pedro starting laughing hysterically. Everybody started laughing like crazy. Aimee couldn't believe what her cousin had just said. She began to laugh so hard she was that crying. Then, his mind having translated the slang slowly, Hiro realized that Pedro was joking. He hadn't seen it coming, because normally Pedro was so quiet and serious. Then Pedro stopped joking and said, "Hiro, you must not let the flame touch the end of the cigar. That is the secret. Just leave it about a half a centimeter away from the tip and puff in gently. It will light this way. You must take very slow puffs and never inhale the smoke. Just enjoy the taste of the tobacco."

Pedro added, "A cigar is nature's great gift. Cuban tobacco is not like any other. It is like a drug and almost makes you enter a state of bliss and dreams. You feel euphoric. When you smoke a good cigar, you will experience a feeling of being in a fantasy world. Your head will feel light as if you are floating. Your limbs feel weightless, and you feel so relaxed. You get quiet and calm. There is no other feeling quite like it, and it's addictive! Welcome to Havana!"

Then everybody started to laugh and clap in agreement. One of the girls stood up yelling, "Viva Cuba! Viva Cuba!" and started singing the national anthem. She was joking around because the young people did not agree with the government. Soon the other youngsters started singing and dancing while they smoked the cigars. Hiro couldn't help but laugh to see the sight. They were acting very comical and free and having fun with the cigars.

It was a Cuban moment. Later Aimee told Hiro that it was all very unusual because people usually didn't openly express their political feelings against the government. Hiro said, "It must have been the premium tobacco that did it." Aimee and Hiro laughed.

Chapter 13

Aimee continued to tutor Hiro two hours every morning. He learned very quickly and had already completed the elementary and high school books that Aimee had brought him. He was now on the college level material. Whatever she gave him to learn, he memorized perfectly just like information stored on a computer chip. Within twenty days, he had almost memorized the entire dictionary that consisted of 12,000 words. Because of his photographic memory, he made tremendous progress very quickly. Aimee was astounded by how quickly Hiro retained and memorized everything. She had never met another person like him before. She knew that he was generous. She also realized that he was extraordinarily gifted she was fascinated by him.

One day, after dinner Aimee said, "Hiro do you like music?"

He answered quietly, "I really don't know much about music.
I've never had an opportunity to open up to music, because I never had any leisure time in my life before now."

Aimee said very curiously, "No time? Why is that? You don't need time to listen to music or to enjoy it and relax. Music is just for fun and on some occasions, you can dance to it. Just go with the flow. Would you like to listen to some music and dance with me?" Hiro didn't know how to respond.

Then he said, "Pedro, do you like music and dancing?"

Pedro replied, "Yes. I love Cuban music, but I don't like to dance. I just watch and enjoy the beat. Hey, do you want to go some place to listen to music tonight?" Hiro was still very quiet and somewhat shy about the topic.

Aimee had an idea, "There is a famous salsa club called *Casa de la Music*, but there is also a great disco near the Hotel Havana Libre. It's a happening place for music, and I prefer it. Both locals and tourists go to this disco to enjoy salsa and rumba. It is so much fun!"

The Last Revolution

Pedro added, "That is not too far from here at Calle 23 entre N y O Vedado, yah?"

Aimee said "Maybe—that's right—you remember better then I do."

Then Pedro said to Aimee, "Do you know Casa de Aimee?"

Aimee said, "Yes, that's my house."

Pedro said, "No! I saw an apartment building called *Casa de Aimee*!"

Aimee said, "I didn't know that they had apartments called Aimee. Oh, I'm rich! I own my own apartment building here in Havana. La-de-dah!"

Everybody started laughing with Aimee. Pedro said, "It's true! There are apartments by that name near *Vedado.*" Pedro knew the place well because he had driven all over Havana for years. Pedro tapped Hiro's shoulder, "Hey, don't worry. You don't have to dance. We can just sit and drink beer and enjoy life. If you feel like you want to dance with Aimee, she'll teach you!" Hiro decided it would be fun to listen to Cuban music. Pedro parked the car in the hotel parking lot. Hiro paid the security guard ten dollars to keep an eye on the automobile.

After the country was nationalized in 1960, the Havana Hilton changed its name to Havana Libre Hotel. It was the most popular hotel in Havana. The hotel had an enormous and beautiful garden as well as an attractive, modern reception area. There were also many nice shops and great restaurants to accommodate all the tourists. Just a few blocks walk from the hotel's entrance was a small discotheque.

As they walked into the entrance, a bouncer asked them for identification and made them pay a cover charge. They could hear loud Cuban music in the background. Aimee was already feeling the music and moving her body as the music got louder. Pedro was very cautious and laid back. He looked all around and looked very serious. He didn't look like he was enjoying the evening. Inside, there were about sixty tables with chairs all around. In the middle of the club, there was a huge wooden parquet dance floor.

Aimee said over the music, "Maybe we should sit in front so we can see the dancing." Pedro agreed, and they got a table right in the front. Hiro looked at all the people moving to the music. There was a festive and fun atmosphere all around the club. Everyone was having a good time. As soon as they sat down, a waitress came over asking if they wanted to order drinks. They all ordered *Hatuey* beer. Aimee explained to Hiro, "This is called Afro-Cuban salsa. It has a very fast beat repeated over and over." At first, Hiro didn't like the fast beat. It was too frenetic and made him nervous.

Then the music changed to regular Cuban salsa, and Hiro began to relax and to enjoy it. You could tell by the expression on his face and Aimee said, "Oh yeah! I know you are enjoying this. Look, Afro-Cuban salsa is not for everyone. It's something you must get used to. Give it some time; you will learn to like that music, too."

Hiro leaned over and said, "Maybe so." Pedro sat in the chair with his arms folded tight. He just sat there not moving at all and watching everyone like a watchdog.

Aimee asked Pedro, "Look, do you see Leda over there?" Leda Gonzalez was Aimee's best friend. Leda also worked at the Department of Translations. They were very close friend. When the music stopped, Aimee ran over to see her friend. They both came over to meet Hiro and sat down at their table. Aimee introduced Hiro and Pedro to her friends.

Leda was quite thin, pleasant and a sincere person. She had a ton of gorgeous black ringlets that cascaded down to her waist, making her very sexy. She asked Hiro to dance, but he declined. Leda said coyly, "Hiroaki, please dance with me!" But he was so shy. Hiro was embarrassed and didn't know what to say.

Then Pedro nagged Hiro and told him, "Hiro, go on." Leda grabbed his hand and took him onto the dance floor. Hiro didn't know how to dance. He felt awkward, like he had two left feet. And he felt shy around this woman who was dancing so close to him.

Hiro began to get anxious and he felt like he was going to suffocate. Leda suspected that Hiro was truly uncomfortable from his tense body language. She was very understanding and so she gently said, "Hiroaki, it's OK. Why don't we go back to the table now? Let's listen to the music a little bit. You may enjoy that more than dancing together right now." Hiro grinned and was relieved. He didn't want to be rude. They both sat drinking beer. Leda liked to dance, and after a few songs, she asked Pedro to dance with her. But he declined. It was Leda's unlucky night with these two.

Leda had a meeting with a Canadian business group that she was doing some translating for. They were staying at the Hotel Havana Libre. A few of the young people in the group wanted to go out and drink and dance, so Leda was trying to show them a good time. Leda had a small baby and a husband named Ivan. They lived with her mother in an apartment near the Malecón. She and Aimee were old friends and attended the University of Havana together. They now worked in the same government department. They had been close friends since their college years.

After an hour of listening to Cuban salsa music, Hiro began to lighten up and get into the beat of the happy music. It was quite different from Japanese music. The Cuban people enjoyed being in the moment of life and they expressed their emotions when they danced. They seemed to have no other cares or problems in the world while they were dancing.

Hiro sat in his chair drifting into a dream world mode. It was hard for him to believe that Cuba was a Communist country. The culture and ideology didn't seem to fit. This puzzled him. He could understand a country like Japan becoming Communist because the personality of the culture was a better fit. The Japanese were reserved, serious, and goal-oriented. Cuba, on the other hand, was a laid back, fun loving island culture with a *manana* attitude: no rush, no hurry, do it tomorrow. Hiro thought the principles of the Communist model and the culture of Cuba were a sharp contrast. He began to believe that the way Communism had thrived in Cuba was an accident, but he still thought it was odd. Did the Cuban people really want Communism or had they just accidentally became a Communist country? Hiro's mind continued to ponder this issue. He continued to wonder about the reason.

The volume of the music grew louder. The live band played great traditional *gigu*. The professional musicians were playing their hearts out and moving passionately. When they got into the beat, they acted like they didn't have a care in the world. Through the passionate sounds of the beat and flow, they grooved and swayed without a care in the world.

Aimee explained that salsa music had been born right in Havana around the 1970s. It was a blend of the Latin rumba and reggae that came together in the creation of this distinctly Cuban music. Added to this was the beat that Africans, as slaves for the sugar plantations, had brought with them. The beat later mixed with the salsa and became Afro-Cuban salsa music. Afro-Cuban salsa combined with other Latin musical forms like the mambo and the rumba from Brazil. Afro-Cuban music had a faster-paced beat than Cuban salsa. Salsa was about feelings and passion and about life in general. Contemporary Cuban salsa music had become one of the most popular types of music throughout Latin America and the world.

Unfortunately, many of the top Cuban artists were exiled. Those musicians had always associated with the anti-Castro movement. Hiro thought that music was art to be enjoyed by all and he was saddened that music had been used as a tool for political debate. Within a few hours, Hiro began to feel the passion. He liked the salsa, and he had never felt so happy. His body swayed to the beat and his feet were tapping on the floor. Hiro finally understood what being in the moment with the music was all about. It was a wonderful experience to think of nothing else and just let your mind go free and move to the passionate rhythms and percussion sounds. Hiro was used to Japanese music. That was what he had grown up with. The two types of music were complete opposites. In Japanese music, the lyrics were primary to understanding what the music was about, why it was constructed as it was, and what was going through performers' minds when they played it. For the Japanese, there had to be a meaning and explanation for everything. Forget about being in the moment with the flow of the music. It didn't exist in Japanese music.

Hiro preferred the Cuban music to Japanese music because you didn't have to try to understand its meaning. Cuban music was simple and all about freedom. It was about not being restrained. For him to step away from his mind and thoughts would be a mystical wish come true. He needed so much not to think about anything. He wanted to explore the feelings and passions that he felt when he heard the Cuban music. He had never had this kind of opportunity in his life. He smiled and breathed in the air. It was an amazing feeling. Hiro began to love Cuban salsa.

For Hiro, relaxing and getting out of his thoughts was a very difficult task. His entire life he had been a victim of intense

The Last Revolution

mental focus. As his feelings began to surface and when he opened up his soul to other people, he felt out of control, stupid and crazy. From an Oriental standpoint, it was a very difficult thing to be freely flowing with life for a whole evening. It felt so amazing. It was almost like therapy. There were moments when he felt very childish and shy. It felt awkward to just hang loose. That feeling didn't come naturally to Hiro, but thanks to Aimee and Leda, he began to enjoy himself more and more.

Pedro just sat listening to the music. He didn't move. He just drank beer and watched the people. Hiro said to Aimee, "Your cousin doesn't like Cuban music." Aimee said, "No, he likes it, but he has not shown his emotions since his uncle was executed in Santa Clara. We understand him. Actually, he likes Cuban music more than we do. He just has trouble showing his passion." Hiro understood this, because Pedro was a very sincere person. He looked very tough, strong and contrary on the outside; but on the inside, he was a sincere, sensitive and intelligent man. He also had an excellent mind and Hiro respected him tremendously.

Hiro began to feel something inside his heart and for the first time he felt passion coming to the surface, little by little. It felt great. He had never used these feelings in the computer science world or for his work with precise mathematical calculations and measures. He was so pragmatic that he never had shown his feelings, except to his immediate Japanese family. He taught himself how to suppress them. But now, here in Havana, he began to open his heart and mind. He felt something warm inside his heart. He felt alive for the first time.

Three weeks had passed by. In just this short time in Havana, Hiro had formed a strong bond with Aimee and Pedro and had met many new people and learned so much. And thanks to Aimee, he had also learned first hand about Fidel's regime. On many occasions, Aimee confided in Hiro about what she had learned being a journalist as well as a translator. She received a lot of information that the average Cuban didn't have access to because of her jobs. They had often discussed Fidel Castro's philosophy and political tactics over the years.

Hiro believed that Fidel was a master game player. He actually admired Fidel's control methods that enabled his vision to survive. Hiro remembered a school project that he had created back in the 60s at MIT. It was a computer game called Chase

Man, based on a similar system. The goal was for the player to control everything in his path. Fidel was doing this exact same thing. Hiro began to unravel Fidel's system by what he saw, heard and experienced around him. He already understood the players in Fidel's game and understood how it worked. His mind quickly analyzed the situation to find a solution. This was an automatic response for him. Hiro wanted to know what made Fidel tick.

One day while going to the vegetable market, Aimee asked, "How long do you get to stay in Cuba with your papers? Isn't it for 21 days?"

Hiro says, "Yes, I have 21 days, but I am thinking that I need to get an extension and stay a little longer."

Aimee told Hiro that they should go to the immigrations office first thing tomorrow morning. "Yes, let's go tomorrow," said Hiro.

Aimee then told him with a laugh, "I am supposed to go to the doctor's office tomorrow."

Hiro asked, "Are you sick?" She told him that she was pretending to be sick to get time off from work. Pedro looked at them and began to laugh.

Hiro asked, "Is something funny?"

Pedro said, "No, she just needs to get a paper from the doctor's office so she can stay home." Hiro did not understand exactly.

Aimee liked to be around with this unfamiliar Japanese man who was so curious and also for whom money was no object. In the days that they had spent together taking Spanish lessons and touring, Aimee had made several years salary. For any Cuban, this was extraordinary money. Besides, she was in the process of changing positions at work. She was going to be a press coordinator instead of a translator, so she could take some time off with no problems.

She said to Hiro, "You don't need to worry about me. You are only here for a short time and I will be here forever." Aimee was laughing and always smiling. She was upbeat all the time. She never seemed to have any problems.

In the marketplace in Havana, there were many good fruits and vegetables available. They were abundant and cheap and the merchants accepted only Cuban pesos as payment. This place was for locals and unknown to tourists. According to

The Last Revolution

Aimee, the prices were expensive for Cubans. She bought cabbage, broccoli, green beans, celery, rice, pork, chicken and eggs. The meat was hanging from the ceiling at the butcher's stand. He sold the pork by the pound and cut the meat into very thin slices. Hiro was fascinated by how the butcher could cut the meat wafer thin and watched with much curiosity.

There were also lunch plates for sale in paper boxes in the market. The price was twenty Cuban pesos or about sixty cents. They bought lunch. When they opened the box, it contained a type of fried rice and a small piece of fresh cabbage sliced thin like slaw with salt and lemon juice. There was also a small portion of fried pork.

The only thing that Hiro didn't like here, other than everybody calling him Chino instead of Japone, was that there were flies everywhere. The locals didn't care, but it bothered him greatly.

But he liked being at the marketplace because it made him feel like he was experiencing a part of normal life that most outsiders didn't explore.

He felt comfortable mingling with the locals and having direct contact with them. Aimee observed Hiro as he watched the people. She saw his tremendous interest in them. She noticed that he tried hard to understand the conversations because he always had many questions. He had so many questions that even she could not answer them all.

Chapter 14

The next morning, Hiro woke to the sound of the telephone ringing. He hadn't had any nightmares in many days. The front desk was calling to tell him that he had visitors. He quickly got dressed and went to the reception area. Aimee and Pedro were smiling and waiting for him. She said, "Did you forget that we were going to immigrations, in *Vedado* today?"

Hiro answered, "Oh yeah, I almost forgot. Thanks for reminding me." He rushed back to his room to get his passport and paperwork to take to the immigration office. *Vedado* was an area of downtown Havana, a few miles drive from the hotel.

They arrived at a big white building that looked like it had not been painted in decades. All the paint was peeling and many water stains were clearly visible. As soon as they entered the front door, security guards approached them. They asked Aimee to leave because it was for foreigners only. No Cubans were allowed. Aimee quickly told them that she was a department translator and that she was here to translate for this tourist. She showed her identification card to them and they permitted her to pass with Hiro. He understood that Aimee was lying, but he knew he might need her help. He felt insecure going to this government office since he had been touring the country illegally. He didn't want any trouble. Aimee wanted to be present in case he ran into any problems. She felt protective of Hiro and she didn't want anything to happen to him. Besides, she wanted Hiro to stay in Cuba longer. She was getting emotionally attached to this man.

In the immigration office as Hiro applied for an extension to his visa, the officer asked, "What reason do you have for staying longer?"

Although Hiro clearly understood, Aimee translated.

Hiro answered in English, "I want to extend my visa for another 21 days because I want to travel to other parts of Cuba."

Once again, Amy translated to prove she was on official duty. Then the officer asked, "What type of business do you do in Japan?"

The Last Revolution

With translation, Hiro answered, "I am a professor in Japan. I teach mathematics at The University of Hiroshima."

The officer asked, "How long have you been teaching?" Hiro answered, "I have been teaching since I was twenty-six years old."

The man asked, "Would you like to visit a university here and a mathematics class?"

Aimee translated once more and Hiro answered, "That would be very interesting, but maybe next time. On this trip, I am interested in seeing the countryside of Cuba."

The officer said, "That is fine." She stamped the extension for 21 days on Hiro's passport. He paid eighty-five dollars and left the immigrations office.

Suddenly, an older security guard called to them to come back to the office. Hiro and Aimee looked at each other with concern. They wondered what was wrong. Had the immigrations officer had become suspicious about why this Japanese tourist wanted to visit the Villa Clara province?

The immigration officer instructed them, "Please take a seat. Your translator can stay, too."

Then she quickly changed her mind and said, "No, I want you to come back in one hour. It is fine if you want to wait here."

Aimee asked, "Is there a problem?" The officer didn't say anything and took Hiro's passport. The official left the room.

Hiro asked Aimee, "What do you think is going on in?"

Aimee replied, "I have no idea."

They were both surprised about this sudden turn of events. It was 11:00 a.m. and Hiro said, "Let's go someplace near here for lunch."

Aimee said, "We are close to the hotel, remember?"

Hiro answered saying, "But I would like to go to a Cuban restaurant around here. Is there one that you know of?"

Aimee replied, "There aren't any. Cubans don't eat lunch in restaurants. They are only for tourists." She insisted that they go back to the hotel to eat.

Pedro countered, "OK, I know a place where we can grab a bite to eat." They drove to a little shop near the bus stop. It was a sandwich shop. There was a woman who appeared to be about forty years old working in the shop. She was heavy, friendly and talkative.

Suddenly, they forgot what might be waiting for them in

the immigration department. They were enjoying their conversation with the woman. Pedro said, "These are typical Cuban sandwiches." There were hot dogs and bologna sandwiches served with fried bananas and a drink. The way she was cooking was so greasy. Hiro thought it was very unhealthy food.

Pedro saw Hiro's face and said, "You said you wanted local food. It's not the hotel kind, but it's better than nothing. No tourists come to these dives. They accept only pesos here and they are not allowed by law to serve tourists. But she will because you are with us and I am buying. If you came here alone, she would not serve you. The exchange rate on the black market is 48 Cuban pesos to one US dollar. But tourists don't have any use for pesos because one must have a Cuban identification card before paying with pesos. This keeps tourists out of places for locals only. There are some small, private operations, but not many."

This was the first time that Hiro had eaten this type of greasy food. Pedro always ate sandwiches similar to these, which were made with Cuban bread. The bread was cut from a long loaf, which had been made with lard instead of oil. It made the bread extra moist and gave it a rich flavor. He usually ate his sandwich with cold sliced pork or ham or fried fish. There was only a little butter to accompany it. Aimee liked eggs of all kinds. She often ordered Huevos a la Habanera or fried eggs with rice and fried bananas. She also like Tortilla de papa, a potato omelet. She didn't like the fatty meats and sandwiches. Now Hiro knew why she wanted to eat at the hotel.

The conversation returned to why immigration suspected him of something. Aimee thought about other people who had been in this same scenario. Her uncle had had problems here. They thought he worked for the CIA. When the officials asked him for all his paperwork from birth records to the present and he couldn't produce them, they put him in jail to wait until all the paperwork had arrived. He was charged $25 dollars a day, as well. He stayed in jail for two weeks and had to pay $350 before it was all settled. Pedro also heard of a person who came back from Miami who had forgotten his green card. Immigration put him in jail until the green card arrived. They talked about many scenarios, but they didn't understand how Hiro could get into any trouble because he was a Japanese citizen with a Japanese passport.

The Cuban people loved Asians because they were against the American imperial government. They loved them for becoming mighty industrial giants, and they knew their products were of good quality--from TVs to cars. Pedro and Aimee continued to discuss the situation. As Hiro listened to everything they said, he grew more concerned and worried. They ate and returned to the immigration office within the hour.

When they arrived, a young immigration officer greeted them, "Please proceed to the back of the building to the waiting room."

Aimee asked, "In the back?"

He said, "Yes, there is a big waiting room there, and you must stay there until we call you." They went to the large room in the back where there were forty people waiting. There were several policemen with weapons guarding the room. They politely told Hiro and Aimee to have a seat. Hiro was uncomfortable seeing the weapons.

She questioned the police, "Are these people here in trouble?"

The policeman replied, "Yes, some of them are here illegally without an extension visa. Some probably will go to jail."

When she looked around the room, she saw a few Chinese people and many American- Cubans. They were all waiting very quietly. She explained, "This man has an extension, but the official had a question and took his passport."

The police man said, "I don't know why there is a problem, but you will have to wait until you are called. Please take a seat." Hiro and Aimee sat down in uncomfortable wooden chairs. Aimee whispered to Hiro what the policeman had just told her. Hiro was silent. Sometimes government red tape was very frustrating.

He had experienced this before in the past in immigration offices in the states when he was at MIT. They always questioned him thinking he might be an illegal immigrant from the poor country of Japan. He didn't like that he was stopped and questioned just because he looked different. He suspected that the same thing was happening here, so he wasn't completely worried. Aimee was frustrated and upset. She was Cuban and knew that something was not right. Her guilt about working for

Hiro made her feel very scared. But how could they know? Time passed slowly. Three hours later, there was still no word.

Aimee finally went back to talk to the policeman. She wanted an explanation. They directed her back inside to immigrations with her questions. There, another official told her to wait about thirty more minutes. They gave her no other explanation and sent her back. She returned to Hiro and told him they would still have to wait. With this announcement, Aimee became more panicked. Hiro still wasn't too worried, though. Hiro closed his eyes. It was about 5:30 p.m., when a young female officer asked Hiro and Aimee to please come to her booth. Aimee was scared.

As they entered the room, they saw a man who appeared to be about sixty years old. He was thin and tall and looked very intelligent. He sat next to the female officer. Hiro and Aimee both sat down in the remaining chairs. Aimee started to panic and said nervously, "What is the problem? Is there something wrong with his passport?"

The female immigration officer didn't answer and just put several pieces of paper and a pencil down on the desk in front of Hiro. She said, "We want Mr. Nakagawa to do some math problems. Is he willing to cooperate?" Aimee translated to Hiro because that was her supposed reason for being with him.

Hiro answered, "Si." The young female officer then introduced the older gentleman to Hiro as Professor Hector Sanchez. He was a professor of mathematics at the University of Havana.

Aimee was shocked to see that they had brought in a real mathematics professor to test Hiro's skills. Instantly, Aimee started to freeze and thought that they were caught in a lie. In all this time, Hiro hadn't told Aimee his past history. She knew he was smart, but that was all. Aimee thought Hiro had been lying when he had told the immigration officer that he was a math professor back in Japan. Now he was going to get in big trouble. She was very nervous. She has to hold herself back from peeing her pants. The paper the professor gave him contained several extremely advanced and difficult problems. Professor Sanchez told Hiro to take his time to figure out the six problems correctly. Hiro looked at each problem and began to mumble. Hiro looked very serious. He recorded the answers without doing any calculations.

1. Evaluate $\dfrac{\sin\left(\tan^{-1}(e)-\cos^{-1}\left(\dfrac{\sqrt{5}}{8}\right)\right)}{\sec\left(2\cot^{-1}\left(\dfrac{5}{7}\right)\right)}$.

   Ans: $\dfrac{5\sqrt{5}e-5\sqrt{59}}{48\sqrt{1+e^2}}$

2. Evaluate: $\displaystyle\lim_{n\to\infty}\sum_{i=1}^{n}\dfrac{3}{n}\left[\left(1+\dfrac{3i}{n}\right)^3-2\left(1+\dfrac{3i}{n}\right)\right]$

   Ans: **48.75**

Prove that $\begin{vmatrix} 1 & x_1 & \cdots & x_1^{n-1} \\ 1 & x_2 & \cdots & x_2^{n-1} \\ \cdots \\ 1 & x_n & \cdots & x_n^{n-1} \end{vmatrix} = \prod_{i<j}(x_j-x_i)$.

(The proof is too long for the space.)

Let $F(x,y,z)=(3x^2yz)\vec{i}+(x^3z-3x)\vec{j}+(x^3y+2z)\vec{k}$

.

110

3. Evaluate $\int_C F \cdot dx$ where C is the curve with inner initial point (0, 0, 2) and terminal point (0, 3, 0) shown in the figure.

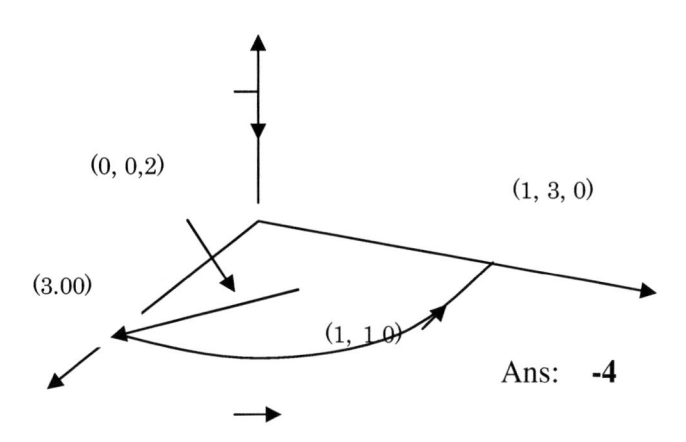

(0, 0, 2)

(1, 3, 0)

(3.00)

(1, 1, 0)

Ans: -4

4. Find the orthogonal trajectories of the family of curves $(x - C)^2 + y^2 = C^2$.

Ans: $\dfrac{3}{2}x^2 + y^2 = D$

5. A point P is located inside the unit square $ABCD$ with $A(0, 0)$, $B(0, 1)$, $C(1, 1)$, and $D(1, 0)$. Let Q be the midpoint of $\overline{AP}$, R be the midpoint of $\overline{BQ}$, S be the midpoint of $\overline{CR}$, and T be the midpoint of $\overline{DS}$. If point T is the same as P, compute the slope of $\overline{AP}$.

Ans: $\dfrac{1}{2}$

6. Evaluate: $\displaystyle\int_0^1 \int_{\sqrt{y}}^1 \int_0^y xy\, dz\, dx\, dy$.   Ans: $\dfrac{1}{24}$

Hiro did this very quickly and with ease, although these math problems were higher than college level and solving them would take an average university mathematician at least ten minutes per problem. It took Hiro only a few minutes to do them all.

Hiro asked, "OK, is this it?"

The professor was so surprised. He said, "Impossible!" He looked over Hiro's answers and they were all correct.

Professor Sanchez was astonished that this Japanese man hadn't even needed to write down the calculations. He had never seen anything like it. He stood up and shook Hiro's hand and said, "I am so proud to meet you. You must be a very famous professor in your country. I can tell this by your work." Hiro shook his hand, but didn't know what to say. The interrogation was over in less than ten minutes.

The female immigration officer smiled, "Well, that's it." She now became friendly toward them. Before the demonstration, she had been serious and almost scary looking. She explained that they had thought that Hiro might be lying on his application. They thought he looked younger than his age. His passport said that he was fifty-three, but he only looked around forty. They had thought his job description didn't match his age. She explained that Professor Sanchez was a math expert, as well as her father. She had called him in to test Hiro's skills to be sure. Now that Hiro had proved his ability, they knew he was not lying. She was also glad that her father had met another mathematics professor, especially one from Japan. Aimee waited patiently throughout the whole incident. She had worried that Hiro would fail the test and suffer the consequences. She also would have been jailed if this had been the case. She was so relieved.

Another female officer named Louisa, handed Hiro his passport and told them to have a good time in Cuba. Just as they left, the professor ran up to them, "I have forgotten to ask you something. I would like you to come as my guest to the mathematics science department at The University of Havana. I am so glad to have met you." He shook Hiro's and Aimee's hands and gave them his business card with his phone number. He continued, "Please stop by anytime that is convenient for you, or call me, and I will meet you and show you around the department. I know my daughter and the other officers here at immigrations had some suspicions about you, but please understand that they were only doing their jobs. I have always heard about the Japanese being highly intelligent, but now I know this is true."

The professor told them all about the University math department and his work there. Hiro and Aimee just listened. Aimee continued to translate. Aimee told the professor that she promised to bring Hiro to the University. They decided that they could meet on a more personal basis there and exchange information about the latest on the mathematics frontier. Hiro, Aimee and Professor Sanchez shook hands and said good-bye.

Pedro was still waiting across the street from the immigration office. He was sound asleep in his Ford. He had had insomnia for several nights because he had been concerned about the health of his grandmother and also about his carpentry business back home. Every evening after he finished driving for Hiro, he searched on the black market for medicine for his sick grandmother. Medicine was hard to come by but easier to get in the city than the countryside where Pedro lived. He had checked many places and hadn't had any luck. Pedro needed to find the medicine soon. Hiro approached the car and slammed his hand on the roof of the car. Pedro being a very tall, woke up and hit his head on the ceiling of the car making a big noise. Hiro and Aimee were laughing. Hiro said, "Are you OK?"

Pedro realized who it was, and he was surprised. Pedro said, "Yes, I'm fine."

Aimee explained in fast Cuban slang to Pedro what had just happened in the immigration office and why it had taken so long. Hiro was fascinated by this colloquial speech. Pedro said, "Dios Mio! I was worried about you guys. That took so long, I just fell asleep. I am glad things are fine."

They all went back to the hotel. Hiro wanted to have a special dinner to celebrate. The front desk gave him a message from Japan. He suspected that something was wrong. He tried to call the number on the message, but no one answered due to the time difference between Cuba and Japan. Hiro decided to try again later.

The three of them went to the restaurant bar and relaxed after the stressful events of the day. They were exhausted and they hardly said anything while they ate. They had a quiet evening, enjoyed a hearty meal with drinks and called it a night.

The Last Revolution

Hiro went to his room and called Japan. It was now 2:00 p.m. next day in there. He reached his mother and found that she had just called him to see how he was doing. The family had been concerned that they had not heard from him since he went to Cuba. She told him that she was glad that everything was going well. Hiro told his mother that he was staying another 21 days and would call them in three weeks.

The next morning Pedro, Aimee and Hiro met for breakfast. Aimee told Hiro, "You know, I really must get back to work. I have a new position now as coordinator for the Cuban Press in *Vedado*, and it is a better position than I had before. I will have more access to information and a raise, of course. I also have many things to do in my house and with my daughter. I have really enjoyed getting to know you and becoming friends."

Hiro said, "Thank you so much for helping me. I now know Cuba inside and out thanks to you and my Spanish has improved. I am so happy. I will never forget you and all of our time together." Hiro thought this was the last time they would see each other.

She said, "Just wait a minute. We are going to see each other again, aren't we?"

He said, "Of course we will."

Aimee smiled and kissed his cheek. Pedro said, "This has been great, but I have to return to my home in the country and take care of things there. I have stayed in Havana longer than I had planned."

Hiro said, "I'm going to miss both of you. I'm probably going to stay around in Havana just a few more days and then go somewhere else."

Hiro looked at Pedro and asked, "When are you coming back to Havana?"

Pedro responded, "I don't know yet. It depends if people need me to drive them here again. I won't know until I return home." Pedro looked at Hiro with an idea. "Hey, would you like to come see the country?"

Hiro said, "How many hours is it to Rancho Veloz? Is there a place I can go fishing?"

Pedro answered, "Yes, we have a river and a huge lake called Saqua. It has a big dam with a lot of fish. We also have a small lake, but where I live, it is not like Havana. It is the countryside with rolling green hills and palm trees. It is farm land and ranches with sugarcane fields and very few people."

Hiro began to imagine what it was like there and it sounded like a great place to visit.
Hiro began to fall into his daydream.

Pedro slapped him on the shoulder and said, "Look Hiro, if you want, you can come home with me. Let's go."

Hiro smiled and he looked very excited and replied, "Ok, I would like to go. I can't believe it. Thank you for inviting me."

They give one another a big bear hug and shook hands and laughed. Aimee smiled and was happy that Hiro was going home with her cousin. The two men had become great friends over the past three weeks of touring Havana. Although Pedro looked tough on the outside, he was very kind and thoughtful on the inside. He was also sincere, and he liked Hiro very much. They both respected each other and had formed a strong bond. Aimee smiled and said, "Hey, *maricon*!" and started laughing. *Maricon* was slang for homosexual. She was just kidding them.
Hiro said, "When are you planning to leave for Rancho Veloz?"

Pedro said, "Well, if you are coming with me. the best time to leave is about 11:00 at night."

Hiro looked puzzled and said, "11:00 p.m.? That's an odd time to leave. How many hours does it take to get there?"

Pedro explained that it was about four and a half hours away if they didn't have any car trouble. Aimee interrupted and said jokingly, "You know you might not have to cover your head with a baseball cap and pretend to be asleep on the floor of the car like here."

They both started laughing and Hiro shook his head and said, "I'm afraid I don't understand."

Pedro said, "Look, there are not too many police out at that time of night, and besides, it's very cool and pleasant and comfortable then. Because you have a tourist visa and you are Japanese you stick out like a sore thumb in Cuba. My ass will get in trouble. I don't want to lose my car. Do you understand?" Pedro looked at Aimee and she agreed.

Hiro said, "I need to pay you two for your time." Pedro and Aimee didn't want to receive the money in public.

Pedro told Hiro, "Let's go outside."

All three walked to the Ford and sat inside. Then Pedro said, "Look Hiro, I was uncomfortable discussing money outside because we are illegally touring you around here. It is considered a crime and Fidel doesn't like it."

Pedro and Aimee were OK inside the car because there was no one around. Hiro understood. Hiro asked Pedro, "What is the fee for the last three weeks?" Pedro answered, "Whatever we agreed on is fine with me. I think that was $100 a day at 21 days, so $2100."

Hiro gave the cash to Pedro, and Pedro divided it with Aimee. Hiro said to Aimee, "I also need to pay you for the Spanish lessons. We agreed on $25 a day."

Aimee interrupted Hiro and said, "Just give me a tip. I don't want to charge you for that part. That was out of friendship and on-the-house."

Hiro smiled and he asked, "Isn't there something special for your home that you have been wanting?"

Aimee said in surprise, "What?"

Hiro asked again, "I want to buy you a special gift for your home to remember me by like a TV or something."

Aimee replied ecstatically, "Oh yes, I need a TV very badly."

Her neighbor who had left for Miami two years ago had given the family a present of an old black and white Russian-made TV. It was probably twenty years old, and it didn't work well. They had to move the antenna all around to get reception. The image on the screen wasn't clear anymore. Hiro remembered seeing that old set now that she mentioned it. Aimee started to squeal like a little girl and bounced up and down in the car clapping her hands together. "I can't believe you are going to buy me a new TV!" She was bubbling with delight and people on the street started to look at her, because she was making a scene. She didn't care at that point because she was so excited.

Then Hiro gave Pedro a $400 tip. "Thank you so much, my friend. I appreciate your looking out for me. Go buy some new tires for this old thing!" Pedro smiled and gave him a firm bear hug. Pedro was grateful. Both Aimee and Pedro froze when they saw all the cash in their hands. They both were uncomfortable, but very excited at the same time. They had never handled so much cash before. It was like winning the lottery. Hiro felt very good about the exchange and knew that his money would be going for good things for their families. Pedro told

Hiro that they should go to *Le Tienda Pan-American* to buy some things before they left. The three hopped into the 1956 Ford and took off for the store.

The Pan-American stores is state owned corporation CIMEX, had popped up everywhere in Cuba since the 1990s right after the Cold War when the Russian economy collapsed and Cuba no longer received Russian financial aid. The Pan-American stores were introduced as a new concept by the Cuban government to collect US dollars and foreign currency. American relatives could send money to their families back in Cuba and their families could spend these dollars in the store to get much needed items. Also, tourists and anyone with US dollars could shop there. The merchandise was often of poor quality and expensive, but there were no other stores in the country. They had no choice but to shop here. Cuban Pesos were not accepted at the Pan-American stores. Stores that accepted pesos did not carry the same merchandise. They charged inflated in price and were money traps.

The Pan-American stores were very efficient and had items that the Cubans needed for daily life. As the three approached the front door, a security guard asked them to stop. The guards locked the door. They were monitoring how many people were inside shopping. They were controlling the crowd and preventing shoplifting by limiting the number of people shopping. Most people stayed for a long time spending most of their time window-shopping because they didn't have much money to spend.

While they were standing in the line waiting their turn to enter. Hiro began to daydream about his childhood. He remembered going to a small country store trying to buy soy sauce. Another family was there buying their children *ramune*, a drink that had a small marble-sized ball on top. When the ball was pushed, it opened the drink, which had a nice refreshing flavor similar to the US Sprite. He remembered those children getting *ramune*. Hiro's mother had very little money and she could only buy the soy sauce. Hiro watched the other children drinking this and wished he had a drink, too.

Suddenly the security guard opened the doors, and they rushed in with a few other people. Then the guards shut the door again. Hiro saw five different TV sets. Four were from China but the fifth one was made Japan. It was a 27-inch Sharp TV. Aimee

The Last Revolution

said she liked that TV more than the others. The price was $1200. That was more than double the price that would have been charged for a similar TV in the Japan or US.

Hiro said, "Wow, they are stealing my money." But he knew there was no other choice. Aimee was as excited as a little child. She could not hide it and she was on top of the world. The store workers helped them to carry the TV to Pedro's car, but it wouldn't fit. It was too big so they put a rope around it and tied it safely to the trunk. They told her it wouldn't fall off, but she was unsure about it.

As they drove away, Aimee yelled every time they hit a bump, and she made Pedro stop so she could get out of the car to check on it. Then, as they reached her apartment house, Pedro honked the horn so her family would come out to see what was going on. They saw Aimee yelling and screaming, and they didn't know what to think. Aimee felt so rich owning this big new TV. She had never believed that she would have a TV like this in her entire life. Only the wealthiest government people in Cuba had TVs like this one. All the people living in the apartment building came outside to see what the drama was about. Hiro really enjoyed seeing Aimee so excited over his generosity.

When he was a young boy, Hiro would have had the same reaction if someone had given his family a nice gift like this. Aimee's father Eduardo, her mother Delia and her daughter Laura came out to help take this new gift inside the apartment. Everybody was thrilled with Hiro's gift. For him it was almost like watching a movie.

In the house, Aimee made Cuban coffee. Her hands were still shaking from the excitement. Pedro told Hiro and Aimee that he had to go and that he needed to take Hiro back to the hotel. Later, when he dropped Hiro off he told him that he would return to pick Hiro up at 11:00 that night so they could leave for the countryside. Hiro decided to pack his small suitcase. He had brought very little so it only took him an hour to pack. He found his family photo and thought about his family back in Hiroshima. He missed them. Hiro decided to take a nap and tried to rest since it would be late when they departed.

At 7:00 p.m., Hiro was awakened by the sound of someone knocking on the door. It was a hotel security guard telling him that he had a visitor at the front desk. Hiro awakened and went down stairs. Tito was waiting to see him. Hiro said, "Where have you been? I haven't seen you in a long time."

Tito said, "I have been at home in the country, but I saw Aimee today. She told me that you are leaving tonight for Rancho Veloz with Pedro." Hiro took Tito to the bar they and each ordered a *Hatuey* beer. Tito told Hiro that his home was close to Rancho Veloz but on the other side of the island. It was a place called *Cienfegos*. Tito said it was a beautiful port and industrial town. "If you ever visit the city of Santa Clara, it is near by. Please visit my family there," said Tito. "Pedro knows where my parents live."

Hiro says, "I would love to visit your home. I would like to see *Cienfegos*, too."

Then Tito gave him five homemade salamis and several loaves of French bread. Tito said, "This is a gift for you, since you are driving at night and there are no places to stop for food on the way."

Hiro said, "Thank you for your thoughtfulness and friendship. Without you I would have never met Aimee and Pedro." Without Tito's connections, Hiro would not have met his new friends because he was a stranger on this remote island so far away from his home. Tito and Hiro shook hands and wished each other good luck. Tito left, and Hiro decided to walk around the streets in front of the hotel one last time.

This once beautiful building with colonial architecture was now crumbling. These once busy streets were now empty and run down. Hiro saw only a few people walking in the street and very few cars passing by.

Hiro walked along the Malecón or the ocean front street. The sun was just setting due west and he took in the cool, refreshing Caribbean breeze along the oceanfront. Both young and old walked along the Malecón. They has nothing but time. It was quiet and peaceful and there were very few lights along the street. Buildings were crumbling away everywhere he looked. Havana was a dying city.

In his mind, Hiro could imagine what these buildings had once looked like. He could compose computer graphics in his head to generate the restored version of the original. He could see in his mind's eye Havana back in its glory days when it was a romantic seaside city. Havana back then, was a romantic city made up of gorgeous buildings and flower-lined streets with bright lights everywhere. It was *the* place for the beautiful people to be seen.

Hiro had been in Havana for more than twenty-one days. Here he had met such good people and made nice friends. They were the children of the revolution. He was thinking to himself, "Because of my new friends, I have more of a connection with human feelings now than to machines." Hiro's nightmares and flashbacks had diminished and his mind felt easy as he learned to relax. Hiro thought about what was happening and compared himself to a computer. As a computer disk gained more space with a defragmenter, his brain had grown new space. Passion was surfacing in his heart. He had forgotten what it was like to feel so lighthearted and refreshed

The tropical sun had set into the Caribbean Sea and it had begun to get dark. Night was covering the dirty and decrepit things in Havana. It was a beautiful time of day and Hiro wished it were 1958 again here in the city.

Hiro paid his hotel bill and checked out. As time passed Hiro became quite anxious to travel to the country side. He hadn't seen anything but the city.

At 10:45 that evening, Pedro drove up in the Ford. He said, "Hey, are you ready to go? Where is your luggage?"

Hiro ran upstairs, got his two small pieces of luggage and came back down. "This is it," said Hiro, "I'm ready for a new adventure."

Chapter 15

Pedro and Hiro got into the car and took off. The engine purred because Pedro took good care of his car. It was very dark. The 1956 Ford had dim headlights so it was difficult to see the street. At first, Hiro was scared because he saw many people roaming and hitchhiking rides in the dark. They headed to the *Autopista National,* the Cuban freeway. Pedro was concerned about the people on the street and he scanned the streets to look for police. Pedro knew exactly where the police checkpoints were so he frequently changed streets to avoid the police as he left the central part of the city and headed south. This southern part of town was the industrial area. It was very dark and similar to a ghetto town.

Suddenly Pedro said, "Hiro, Quick! Go to sleep on the floor. I see a police check point!" Pedro remained very calm on the outside, but inside he was very frightened. He started sweating because he was scared. Four policemen came to check the car. There were four cars in front of Pedro's car. One of the young police officers headed back to Pedro's Ford. Hiro had a baseball cap over his head and looked like he was in a deep sleep. The policeman asked for Pedro's ID and car registration papers. A young officer carefully checked his ID and asked, "Where are you going?"

Pedro answered, "I am going to my uncle's home across the next street *Carreterra Central.* Then on to *Catarina de Quines.* My uncle lives there. I am visiting here from the country for three days."

The policeman said, "OK," and let him pass. The officer was only interested in seeing Pedro's ID. Since he knew the street where Pedro's uncle lived, he let them pass. Pedro took off slowly and headed east toward the freeway.

Finally, Pedro reached the freeway Cuban called Autopista National. It was in fairly good condition, but not compared to most modern freeway in the world. It was inefficient because there were no lines painted to designate lanes. It was just blacktopped. There were trees growing on the side of the road. In some places, grass was taking over the road. There had been no maintenance of the highways in a long time, but they were good enough to drive on. The freeway was supposed to have been completed from the east to the west of the island in late 1980, but at the present, it was only fifty percent finished. Pedro said that it might never be finished completely. Since Russian financial aid had been withdrawn from Cuba, there were many other projects that had priority over highway construction.

The most important project in Cuba was to feed the people. Rice, beans and a staple food supply for Cuban citizens were the focus. If the government defaulted on supplying food, then they would risk an uprising very quickly. The government knew this very well. Therefore, the government had to keep the people fed and happy. The primary objective was to have good food resources and a welfare system in place. Almost a hundred percent of supplies were imported from the Far East. The government bartered with countries in the Far East using Cuban sugar as a commodity. Unfortunately, Cuban sugar production had continued to decline for the last decade due to lack of adequate funding. And nickel, sugar, and tobacco were the three top exports. The country now heavily relied on tourism and nickel exports to survive. China invested in the nickel industry.

The loss of Russian support had affected everyone in Cuba. Previously, each month the Cuban people were given a book of food ration coupons. Each family was given staples, such as beans, rice, corn, meat, eggs, bread and spices according to the number of members in the family. Before the Russians withdrew, bankrupt Cubans received a thirty-day supply of these staples. This month's supply of food cost about 35 pesos which equaled less than 75 cents per person for a month of food. This was a highly effective system.

Since the withdrawal of Russian financial aid to Cuba in 1985, the system had suffered huge set backs. The thirty-day food supply allocation had been trimmed down to only a fifteen-day supply. At that time, the black market had started to grow strong and popped up everywhere to help supplement the reduced food supply. Cubans had to stretch their fifteen day food supply over the month so they were forced to find alternatives on the black market.

High-ranking government officers stole from the government warehouses and sold to intermediaries who delivered the stolen foods directly to the black market. It was similar to capitalism except that it was based on stolen goods instead of purchased goods. The government was aware that the thefts were going on, but they were forced to look the other way because their hands were tied. The black market had to continue as an alternative food source or the people would starve. This illegal activity was built into the system and was a spoke in the wheel of Cuba.

When the government caught political dissidents from time to time, they used the charge of theft for supplying the black market as a reason to jail them. As Pedro and Hiro continued to drive along the dark freeway, Hiro was surprised to see hundreds of people walking. They were all over the road, not just on the sides. They were hitchhiking and yelled at Hiro and Pedro as they drove by. Hiro asked Pedro, "Why do these people do this?"

Pedro said, "Well, they need to get back home and there are no buses available so they have to try to hitch a ride or walk." Hiro saw big government trucks with large truck beds stopping and picking up people. There were many people jam-packed into the back of the truck beds and people were piled up high.

People were screaming at the trucks to stop, hoping to catch a ride. It was a mad house and everyone was running toward the trucks in the darkness. Pedro told Hiro that this was very routine for the people, but for Hiro it was a strange sight. Pedro explained to Hiro that he didn't want to stop because many people would try to jump into his Ford and it would be chaos. Also, the Ford wouldn't be able to handle the load. It would be too risky because Pedro's car was his livelihood. Therefore, while Pedro felt sorry for the people, he couldn't take the chance.

The asphalt surface of the road was not smooth but was in fairly good condition. The signs were few and far between. Occasionally, there was a small sign with the name of the town and the number of miles to that town on it. Periodically, Hiro saw small fires in painted cans along the road which looked like fires on the highway.

Hiro asked, "What is that fire?"

Pedro looked at the fires and answered, "Oh, those are to indicate big pot holes on the highway. The cans of fire are signaling a detour." Hiro was amazed because it was all so haphazardly done without signs. The speed limit was 55 mph, but most cars were going faster and passed the Ford. Pedro obeyed the speed limit because it was better for his car. He took very good care of his jewel and he could not afford to have a problem on the highway. Pedro and Hiro discussed many subjects on their way to the country. He had many questions for Pedro. Hiro thought about his home in the countryside of Japan and compared it with life in rural Cuba. About by one, They had traveled a distance of about forty five miles when Pedro took a small detour road. It was a country road near the small town of *Jaguey Grande*. The streets were narrow and there were few lights.

The town was so small that they drove through it in a matter of minutes. The homes were made of concrete and they all looked like they were still under construction. Each house looked like a lifetime project, and the front porches sat right on the road. There were no signs of life. It looked like a ghost town to Hiro.

As they drove past, they entered an area of sugarcane farms that were controlled by government co-ops. They passed miles and miles of sugarcane. Hiro knew that the sugar industry had been suffering tremendous financial difficulties for the past few decades. The sugarcane fields were flat with a few hills. There was a cool Caribbean breeze as the ocean was only about twenty miles away. Even though they were inland, Hiro knew that the ocean was nearby because of the tropical breeze and the smell. It made the night air cool and fresh. Pedro knew this highway very well. Now Hiro knew why Pedro had wanted to travel home at night.

The next town was called *Martí*. Pedro said that *Rancho Veloz* was about an hour and a half away. On this remote country highway, the moon was shining down, and it seemed to be the only light guiding them in the darkness. The cool breeze was very pleasant and smelled like the ocean and sugar cane. It was fresh and warm this evening. Hiro could see many small country villages and pueblos on the way to *Rancho Veloz*. There were run-down looking shacks and people were out in the streets. He wondered who they were and what they did there. After a while, They came to a sign that read, "Welcome to Martí."

Hiro asked, "I remember this name. Is this the same as Jose Martí International Airport in Havana?"

Pedro answered, "Yep, he was born right here. Later he moved to Havana. He was a famous Cuban in the independence movement. He is considered a local hero."

Hiro said, "No way, Pedro. Jose Martí was born in Havana 1853. I saw an article in a tourist book. Are you telling me the truth?"

Pedro started laughing and replied, "You got me. I was just bullshitting you. I think that article is right. I was pulling your leg."

Hiro laughed, "I almost believed you. You are a big *minteroso*." They both laughed. That was one of the great things about Pedro. He was calm and easy going and always had a good sense of humor. He liked to have fun and was playful with his friends and family. His positive nature was refreshing to be around.

Normally, Hiro was surrounded by serious academic minds. He preferred to laugh and be light-hearted. Pedro was a simple man, but for Hiro, he was a breath of fresh air and as good-natured and genuine as they came. Then Hiro found a mini flashlight and opened the tourist book that he had brought along with him and started to read.

It said: "Jose Julian Martí was a writer and patriot who lived most of his life in exile. He was one of the great political and literary figures of the 19th century, whose death in battle made him the martyred symbol of Cuban aspirations to independence. He was born on January 28, 1853, in Havana where he received his primary education. At the age of sixteen he was imprisoned as a revolutionary in Cuba, and then at seventeen, José Martí was exiled to Spain for his hostility toward colonial decree. He graduated with a law degree from the University of Saragossa in Spain in 1874. Then he moved to Guatemala and Mexico where he began his literary career. Later he traveled to the United States where he stayed a year. Then he left for Venezuela. Martí had hoped to make his home in Venezuela, but the dictatorship in the country forced him to leave so he moved back to the US and lived in New York City for twelve years."

"In New York, Martí organized the Cuban independence movement. Martí believed in justice, liberty, and absolute freedom. Later he reached Cuba, along with the independence hero General Máximo Gómez y Báez. Martí was killed a month later May 19, 1895, during a battle with Spanish troops at

The Last Revolution

Dos Rios. As a writer, Martí was a precursor of modernism in Spanish letters; he was noted for his simple, fluent style and his personal, vivid imagery. He in no way accepted the abuse of the human spirit; Martí taught instead that each individual was entitled to total freedom, total self-realization. To that end, he maintained that any totalitarian form of government, especially dictatorships, abused human rights, and constituted egotism and ego-centrism at their worst. Dictatorships, in his view, always legislated against the individual in favor of the acquisitive empowerment of the dictator in question."

Pedro sat spellbound as Hiro read out loud. After a quiet pause, Hiro continued reading: "Martí also criticized the lack of spirituality inherent in the creed of any totalitarian rule. Martí published his thoughts on these matters, and spoke out in public about them every chance he got. Basically, he espoused the ideals of democracy, saying that in freedom there is always greater personal security."

Hiro glanced over at Pedro, who sat still, silent and motionless, caught up in his own thoughts, obviously in agreement with Martí. Hiro now voiced, "I don't know what happened to Cuba. Everything he supported was the exact opposite of the reality of Cuban life under Castro. How did we get here? With Martí as a role model, how did we end up living under control of the world's most total dictatorship? How could this have happened?"

Then Pedro said, "Hey! Where did you get this? You understand José Martí better than a native Cuban! I can tell you that Fidel hijacked Cuba for himself! But I don't feel like discussing politics. I am sick and tired of politics!"

Then Pedro stopped talking and became very quiet. Hiro peeked at Pedro's face. His silence was disturbing. They had been driving for almost three hours. It was about three in the morning. Pedro stopped next to a small village called *Joya Colorado*. They were on the outskirts of town and they drove to a small house that had a light burning. It was the only light on in the town at this time of morning.

Pedro said, "We have been driving for nearly three hours, and we need to rest a little while and get something to drink. I can see that my friend is up."

Hiro said, "Your friend?"

Pedro replied, "Yes, My friend Lorenzo lives there. He is a mechanic. If you drive in the country, you have to get to know people who are mechanics or who have equipment so you are prepared when you need help. There are no service stations here. This guy has fixed my engine before and he has car parts for many late model 1950s American cars."

Pedro explained that Lorenzo worked at night because he liked to work when it was cool so he could sleep during the daytime. Pedro added, "Lorenzo works from seven to three normally. It is good business to have the shop open at night because many people drive after dark when it is cooler."

They stopped and went around to the back of the shop. They saw two men working in the garage. Lorenzo saw Pedro and said, "Hey, what's up?"

Pedro answered, "Nothing much. I am driving back home and just stopped by to say hello. Say, do you have any coffee?"

Lorenzo and the other mechanic were very friendly and very dirty. Lorenzo said, "Hell no! I don't have any coffee, but I do have some home-made rum." It was moonshine rum, Cuban called 'chispa de tren.'

Pedro introduced Hiro to the other men. They all toasted with the rum and passed the bottle around taking sips. Hiro took one sip and almost choked. He didn't want to drink anymore because it was too strong for his system. The Hiro, tasted like gasoline. The men laughed. They enjoyed drinking moonshine and it was quite common in the country. For Pedro this was a social visit to see his friend in this remote country town. They talked for a while. This was the only time Hiro had seen Pedro really talk a lot. Pedro and the mechanics talked about cars and how to fix this and that.

Hiro went to sit in Pedro's 1956 Ford while he waited for Pedro to finish visiting. Hiro looked up in the sky and saw many sparkling stars. It was wide-open country with no outside lights. There were millions of stars shining in the clear sky above. It was a breathtaking, dramatic view. Hiro had never seen anything like it. Even his village in Japan did not have such a sight as this at night. Hiro sat looking north to south and east to west. Everywhere he looked he saw millions of stars. Hiro imagined that he was in a dream world.

Then Hiro's brain took over. He knew that the anatomy of a computer's memory was like stars or fireworks. He

The Last Revolution

imagined the electrical current in the hard drive coming from the chip with millions of electrical currents sparking to become memory. He could not help but think and imagine everything that he saw through the eyes of a computer scientist. It had become second nature. Hiro enjoyed letting his imagination wander. Pedro returned and Hiro said, "Where is *Rancho Veloz*?"

Pedro replied, "The next town is *Corralillo* which is about thirty minutes away. Then thirty minutes farther is *Rancho Veloz*. We will probably get there around four. Is that OK? Are you getting tired of riding in the car so long?"

Hiro said, "No, I am not tired. I am just anxious to see your village."

"Well," said Pedro, "the town is so small that if you blink your eyes you might miss it." They started laughing. Pedro asked, "Do you have many *negritos* living in Japan?"

Hiro answered, "Yes, some American GIs. Many women like them and think they are beautiful and strong. Correct?"

Pedro said, "They are very strong physically and in the past they were slaves. But now they are all the same as everyone because of the 1959 revolution here in Cuba. They are great at baseball and basketball."

Hiro started to remember that when he had lived in the US, he had seen reports on the news about African-Americans with many socio-economic problems. Pedro said, "Some black people here are very aggressive. I don't trust them for business." He hesitated, "What is wrong? Why are you so quiet?" Hiro didn't want to discuss racial problems. He didn't understand why the races were separated. Hiro had always been told by his mother not to talk about people of other races using racial slurs or bad names. Japan had similar problems with the Koreans and Chinese. Hiro never had any friends from other cultures to allow him to understand firsthand cultural differences firsthand.

Hiro remembered when he was at The University of Hiroshima in the late 50s that there had been a young Japanese teenage boy in love with a Chinese girl whose family didn't approve of their courtship. They had loved each other very much and did not want to be apart so they went to a mountaintop in Kyoto. There they tied themselves together and committed suicide by cutting their wrists with a knife. They left this life so they could be together in the next life. It was tragic news when Hiro was at The University of Hiroshima. Hiro was silent thinking about this sad event. Then Pedro said, "Hiro, Hiro, what is the matter with you?"

Hiro answered, "Oh, I am just remembering when I was younger when a Japanese teenager fell in love with a girl of a different race. When the parents found out, they were totally against the relationship and forbade them to be together. The kids ended up committing suicide over it all."

Pedro said, "Oh no! That is impossible. There is no need to die for love. Dying is only a last resort. God decides when it's your time to go, and besides when it comes to love, if it doesn't work out with one woman, there is always another one waiting. I would never even think of killing myself over love. I guess that is just the Cuban way." Hiro began to think about the Japanese culture and how the concept of death was so different from other cultures.

In Japan, it was considered good to die in an honorable way. This concept came from the ancient ways of the *Bushido*, an unwritten creed of the Shogun, which said that death was better than disgrace or dishonor. The Cubans wouldn't understand *seppuku* or *hara-kiri*. Pedro continued to talk about the story of the teenage suicides in Japan. He said, "Cubans could not believe it was possible to die for love. We love life too much. You know we love to live, dance and have a good time. Life is short and we want to enjoy each moment. Sometimes things don't work out in love, so you just find someone else to love. You cannot talk about love and suicide at the same time." Pedro's voice became louder and louder because he liked to talk about love, and the rum was working.

Then Hiro started to think that maybe suicide didn't exist in Cuba. As they were driving on the country highway, Pedro pointed to the north side of the highway on his left. "Hiro, there is a hot spring over there and a hotel with hot spring waters. This place is well known for helping people with physical problems. The hotel is called *El Elquea*. It is a good place to relax, and many tourists come here. Look, Hiro! The next town we come to will be *Corralillo*. It is the capital of my county. It is a little smaller than *Rancho Veloz*, but tourists visit there because of the hot springs. No tourists visit *Rancho Veloz*. Then they entered the town of *Corralillo*. Within three minutes, the town disappeared. Several other shantytowns appeared and disappeared.

The Last Revolution

Then Hiro saw a huge communication tower. Pedro said, "Look, we are getting closer to my home." The lights on the communication tower were red and white and sparkling in the night sky. Then, they passed several tiny grass huts. It looked like the town was starting. Hiro saw an old blue weathered metal sign that read, "*Bienvenidos Rancho Veloz!*" This was Pedro's hometown.

Before they entered the town, they turned left onto a dirt road. They barely could see because it was dark and very bumpy and poorly built. They drove slowly over the bumps and holes. In the darkness, Hiro could see some small crumbling homes on both sides of the road. It looked like a shantytown and it was quite different from the way Hiro had imagined the town to be.

About fifty yards away, he could see several homes that were still under construction. They drove toward one home that looked unfinished. Pedro said, "This is my home." He parked in front of a big metal drum tank. Hiro's mouth dropped open in disbelief when he saw where Pedro lived. Hiro now knew why Pedro had been so uncomfortable at the *Hotel Inglaterra* and many other places they had visited in Havana. Hiro could see a small dim fluorescent light mounted on a wooden base. Pedro carried the luggage and all of the things he had bought in Havana inside the house.

A beautiful and very friendly woman welcomed them at the door. She had dark eyes, dark hair, and a lovely smile. She extended her hand and said, "Hi, I'm Madeline. Welcome to our home. Pedro mentioned to me that he had made a Japanese friend in Havana. I am glad you came here with my husband."

When Hiro walked into the room, he saw that it was divided into two parts. There was an unfinished concrete floor with a four foot high concrete block partition. On the other side of the partition was a kitchen and bathroom. There were few furnishings, but it was very clean. Hiro saw only one bed. Pedro said, "Hiro, this is your bed."

Hiro asked, "Where are you going to sleep?"

Pedro answered, "Don't worry about me; this bed is for you!" Madeline brought them some sweet hot coffee. It was delicious and very strong.

It was five in the morning. Madeline smiled and looked curiously at Hiro. She had never met an Oriental person before and she could not help but stare at this strange man. She thought he was short but nice looking. She noticed that his eyes and skin looked different from hers. He wore shorts and only tourists wore shorts. But overall, he looked likeable and quiet. Pedro said, "My wife used to be a school teacher, but she only made 350 Cuban pesos per month—about $10. It's better for her just to stay home and take care of the kids and the house." Madeline had a little five-year-old girl from a previous marriage. Hiro thought that Madeline appeared to be in her late 20s. She seemed very gentle and easy-going. Madeline had very white skin and dark hair. She was a white Cuban and looked strong and healthy. After they talked for a while, the sun rose. Pedro decided to go to sleep beside his step little girl on a sponge mattress on the floor. They had no blankets or sheets, just a foam mattress pad.

  Madeline asked, "Would you like to go to sleep, too, Hiro?" Hiro felt bad to be offered the only bed, but Madeline insisted and said, "Go ahead. You are our guest. Please sleep here." Hiro was so tired and sleepy that he stretched out fully-dressed and fell asleep immediately. He was out like a light within minutes. They all slept like logs.

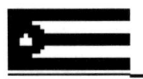

Chapter 16

After several hours, Hiro awakened to ear-splitting noises. As he opened his eyes, it was already midday. Pedro was still asleep on the floor. He was exhausted from driving all night. Hiro got out of bed and found Madeline in the kitchen. She said, "Good morning. Did you sleep well?"

Hiro replied, "Yes, I slept very well, but I still want to sleep some more."

She laughed and smiled at Hiro. "After you eat and drink something, you can go back to bed and relax today."

Hiro answered, "Maybe, but what is that noise? It sounds like wood being cut."

Madeline said, "Oh, that is my father-in-law doing carpentry work."

Hiro remembered that Pedro had said that his family did carpentry work. She gave Hiro a cup of coffee and Hiro peeked through some home-made blinds. He noticed that the side window didn't have any glass, only wooden blinds. When the blinds were open, the outdoors was exposed. Through the open blinds, Hiro saw a workshop next door between the two houses where several people were making something. This is where the noise was coming from.

Madeline began to cook breakfast, or an early lunch, since it was already mid-day. She fried fish, which smelled good. Hiro hadn't eaten any fish since he had been in Cuba. He had eaten only chicken or pork. Hiro loved fish and could eat it any time of the day. Hiro asked, "Where did you get that fish?"

Madeline answered, "From *Ponchita*. It is a fishing port about ten minutes from here. You can see the ocean from here." She opened the window and pointed north. Hiro could see the ocean because Rancho Veloz faced north toward the Bahamas. She explained that there were many small islands called keys off Cuba. The keys were not livable however, because when the tide came in, the keys were completely covered with water. When the tide receded, the land turned into little islands covered with salt vegetation. There were hundreds of small keys in the Bay of Villa Clara. Panchita was known as a fishing village. It was like a shanty town, small and very poor. When hurricanes hit about every ten years, everything in the village was wiped out.

About this time, Pedro woke up and came into the kitchen. He looked tired, because he had been driving all night. Pedro started to make conversation over coffee. He told Hiro about the area and the province of Villa Clara and Santa Clara. It was the fourth largest city in Cuba and was famous because of Fidel's revolution in 1958. It was the location of the last battle for Commander Camilo Cienfuegos Gorriarán and Ernesto Guevara de la Serna Cubans called him Che Guevara or el Che. Che entered the city, but it took him several weeks to take it over from Fulgencio Batista y Zaldìvar's troops. Many buildings still bore bullet holes and marks of revolution. The battle was an important part of history.

The Spanish had founded Santa Clara as an escape from ocean pirates in the 16th century and had built the city with long narrow streets. The surrounding area was home to Chief Colban and the Taino-Arawak Indians. This chief controlled the whole area in the early 15th century. However, today there were no archeological sites because the Taino Indians only slept in grass huts and lived off the land. Therefore, no traces of their existence remained.

Pedro said, "What would you like to do today?"

Hiro answered, "Whatever you want to do is fine with me."

Pedro replied, "Hey look, whatever you want to do today, just ask." Pedro smiled and patted Hiro's shoulder.

Hiro smiled back and said, "Ok, after you rest a little more, I would like to see the town of Rancho Veloz. I want you to explain it to me." Pedro and Madeline began to laugh hard.

Hiro looked at them and said, "What is so funny?"

Pedro answered, "Remember I told you this village is small. There is nothing here. You are looking at the town right here." Pedro finally went back to bed for a while. Hiro also went back to bed to read his tourist book, *Lonely Planet*. He had purchased the book in Japan before he left for Cuba. Hiro fell back asleep after reading a short time.

The Last Revolution

It was late afternoon when Hiro and Pedro woke up again. Finally, they felt refreshed and decided to walk around the town together. Pedro explained the pueblo and showed him the school. The town had approximately 3000 people and was a farming community. Most of the people worked for the government-run sugar industry. Cuban soil produced the finest sugar in the world, and Cuba was dependant on bartering sugar for trade. This town was one of many small rural communities that had been built around sugar agriculture since the Spanish arrived. There was still a small fort standing on the hilltop overlooking the town.

In the center of town, there was a small park. There was a huge oak tree growing there. Its roots had grown under the concrete, buckling the street. Hiro could see that the tree was very old. Pedro explained that no one knew how old this oak was for sure, but he had heard that it was planted by the first Spanish settlers who arrived in Cuba. The main road that ran though the town was called *Independencia*. It was a small road paved with concrete that had many potholes. The road, like the rest of Cuba, had not been maintained.

Next to the park there was a huge Catholic church which was painted white and had a red tile roof. It was built using Spanish-style architecture. Even though the church was practically falling down, it was still used for community service. Next to the church, there was a bus stop. Many small peso stores that looked deserted lined the main road. There was also a small government vegetable market with very little produce to sell.

One crumbling bar was across the street. It was a very poor town, but people congregated in this part of town to listen to news and to exchange information. It was a meeting place and the social hub where people checked in with each other. Pedro knew everybody and greeted them by saying "Hay, Pedrey!" to all the people as they walked by. Hiro thought that Pedro knew the whole town. He remembered his little country village back in Japan. This place was much larger. The homes here were poor and crumbling. Pedro explained that many of them had been stores before and during the revolution when people left for Miami. These former stores were now homes.

The main street of Independencia connected to five lesser streets. There was a small primary school and a tiny secondary school. There were flags waving in the schoolyard and children were playing outside. Surprisingly, there was even a dentist's office and a medical clinic. Hiro was impressed to learn that there were five doctors here. There was one doctor for every 250 people. The medical system in Cuba was socialized. While the equipment and medicine were free, there was a lack of supplies. The clinic was poorly equipped and the quality of medicine was not adequate due to the blockade. But for a town of this size, the care was adequate. On the surface, people seemed very friendly. Forty-five percent were white Cubans, ten percent were Negritos and forty –five percent were mulatto—mixed black and white.

There were many coconut and palm trees swaying in the breeze. It was a sleepy, but beautiful village. Hiro imagined in his mind that this once was a thriving town. There was very little business, since people were just waiting for the government to change. Life in the town had remained at a complete standstill. The streets and buildings were unkempt and it looked as if nothing had been fixed for decades. The streets smelled like hogs, because many families raised hogs in their backyards for food. The hogs ate leftovers and garbage. The stench was horrible in the hot weather.

Pedro showed Hiro a small police station next to a 1950s gasoline stand. The gas station hadn't been used since the 1950s. It was rusted and deserted. There were five policemen in the town so it was a very safe place. Many houses were run down. Most people didn't care about maintaining their homes. They were concerned only about getting food for daily survival. Since the government gave them the houses, they didn't care about taking good care of them or improving them. Hiro believed that this was human nature. In his experience, if people didn't earn something, they didn't take care of it. They just existed.

As Hiro got used to the town, he discovered many different things. Almost all of the Cubans dealt with the black market for daily survival. Every item was stolen by those who worked for government institutions. The government knew about the black market but looked the other way. If the government had taken notice, then the people wouldn't have had daily necessities. Hiro saw that the locals lived with very few creature comforts, such as furniture and material items in their homes. The people seemed happy with this arrangement.

However, the simple life looked good to Hiro. But it seemed peculiar that such poor people wore new clothes. In the

The Last Revolution

U S, he saw many affluent people wearing junky clothes with holes and rips. Here the fashion was neat and clean. Pedro explained that this was Cuban style. Pedro shared that Cubans admired high fashion and they wanted to look good when they went out in public. The women wore high heels and carried purses. The men had on hats and watches. Men did not wear shorts in public, only in their homes. Hiro was wearing shorts because it was hot, but apparently, only tourists wore them in the streets. For a poor country, Hiro was puzzled to see all of this. They cared more about clothing than their homes.

As he got more acquainted with the small town, Hiro found there was a seamstress, one tiny fish market with no fish, a shoe repair shop and several shoe shine chairs along the street. There were a few cigarette lighter refill stands dotting the street as well as junky little shops with rice and very few food items on the shelves. There was also a small, ragged restaurant with poorly prepared food which served one item daily based on whatever was available. The cost of the plate lunch was sixty Cuban pesos which was about twenty cents per plate. Across the main street, there was a bus stop with the roof caving in. Several wooden benches were provided for people waiting for the bus. Hiro saw a handwritten schedule on a board which indicated that one bus ran in the morning and another bus ran in the afternoon from Santa Clara to Corralillo. Sagua was a town about twenty-five miles away. All of these tired businesses and shops were government- controlled and licensed.

Pedro told Hiro that there were very few privately-owned businesses. However, Pedro's family owned their own carpentry shop. The family had to report their income to the government twice a year, but they never told the truth about how much they earned. Every small private business owner had to lie in order to survive. Purchases were usually made in cash or were bartered, so it was easy to hide the profits.

From a tourist's viewpoint, Hiro didn't see evidence of the black market, but there were many venues, and the locals knew where to find what they needed. These black market businesses flourished. This was truly the Cuban economy and the way they participated in a free market system. Communism functioned only on the surface. Hidden below the facade of Communism, capitalism existed in the busy black market system. It was all about supply and demand and Cuba could not exist without it. When Hiro first arrived in this sleepy town, he couldn't imagine how people actually survived and how the town functioned because Rancho Veloz looked like a ghost town. But he soon found out that there was always something going on behind the scenes. One just had to be attuned to the local level to witness and experience it. One had to know where to look. Although the standard of life here was poor, it appeared to Hiro that the people were very happy and had a very good life.

Rancho Veloz was a small community. Everyone knew everyone else in the community and helped each other. This was quite different from the way Hiro had grown up in Japan. Japanese people did not reach out to help each other often. If they did, they made a big deal out of it, which often escalated into a family or community dispute. The Japanese were more solitary and independent. Even in poor villages this was the Japanese way. Hiro could not remember a time when his mother had asked for help. The only assistance had come from family members and even this was kept very private.

On the surface the Japanese were very quiet and gentle, smiled frequently and seemed easy-going. But from Hiro's experiences, he thought that the majority of Japanese were actually very calculating and suspicious of each other. The Cubans had a much more open society and were closer to their friends, neighbors and family. This intimacy created a support system that made life thrive. The only thing the Cuban people seemed suspicious of was the government police.

Most Cubans were carefree and enjoyed life. Their biggest concern was having enough money for daily survival and food for their families. Hiro had never heard people talking about education. Mainly only white Cubans cared about higher learning; few minorities seemed to care about it. Although education was free in Cuba, no one seemed very interested. To Hiro this was very curious. Hiro discovered that the people who climbed the ladder of success and joined the Communist Party did so because of their family connections. If a Cuban wanted to become a doctor, lawyer, or professional, that person had to join the Communist Party. Very few people were interested.

Pedro knew many people in town and they respected his family and his carpentry skills. But his family had not been blessed since the revolution because they were outspoken and very critical of Fidel's Communist regime. Many of his family

The Last Revolution

members had been executed because they dared to speak out against Fidel Castro and his politics.

The government had zero tolerance for dissidents. Anyone who spoke out or tried to work against the Communist Party was imprisoned or murdered. For Pedro, politics caused nothing but heartache. It was all nonsense and Pedro was tired of all the pain and suffering. Pedro, like so many Cubans, was still wounded from the revolution and the government's totalitarianism. They were not free to speak their minds and the nail that stuck out got hammered down one way or another. They had learned not to talk about politics or about their own beliefs.

Chapter 17

As Hiro and Pedro spent more time together in Rancho Veloz, they began to discuss their families' histories.

Pedro could trace his ancestors from Spain nearly 200 years back. They were originally from the Basque region of northern Spain near France. His ancestors had fled Spain to escape persecution by the Spanish and French. The Basque region was culturally different from both Spain and France and still maintained its own language and way of life. This small region in the north of Spain had been in turmoil for hundreds of years and the Basques' fight for separatism continued today. Pedro's descendants settled in the French colony of Haiti until the Haitians became independent. The whites in Haiti were despised by the black Haitians. To escape further problems in Haiti, Pedro's ancestors fled to central Cuba.

Later, Pedro's descendants moved to Santa Clara, and his father came to Rancho Veloz for work. Pedro's father had beautiful white hair and blue eyes. He was a quiet, gentle man who had learned the carpentry trade from his father. Likewise, Pedro's father had learned his craft from his grandfather. Pedro told Hiro about the work traditions that had been passed down through several generations. Pedro had been born in Rancho Veloz. He had three sisters and three brothers. Many of his relatives in this part of the country were very critical of Castro's Communist-Socialist government. Many were jailed, killed, or had immigrated to the United States seeking political asylum from the US government. It had been a difficult road for Pedro's family. Those family members who were still alive, but lived elsewhere, were greatly missed.

Those who had emigrated to the U S could not return while Castro was in power. If they returned, they risked not only their lives but also the lives of their family members. It was a very painful subject for Pedro to talk about because it had caused much hardship for the entire clan. Those who remained in Cuba lived around the Santa Clara and Rancho Veloz area and they remained close. Since Castro had come into power, families were not allowed vote, have free speech, or move freely from one town to another so it was common to see extended families living in the same house with their parents and their grandparents. The family bond had become even more important since the revolution.

Hiro could see that Pedro's family worked together and helped each other tremendously. It was very touching how they greeted and shared with each other. To Hiro there was nothing more beautiful than this gift of human kindness among the family members. This was also true in the country in Japan. Within the family, one member helped another one on every occasion. It was traditional to even marry a family member to sustain the family's wealth. This was the case with Hiro's own father and mother. He understood first hand this culture of a strong, family-based society.

He was fascinated to watch the small, cute lizards called Logavtijo that eat insect and live around the house while watching, the worries and concerns of the rest of the world seemed to melt away.

The people were happy and friendly and it was a place to relax and live in the present. He also began to form close relationships with these people and a society that he had never known before. Hiro and Pedro seemed like old friends in a short time. A special bond of true friendship and trust had developed between Hiro and Pedro's family. This was food for Hiro's heart and soul. Pedro also introduced Hiro to many of his close friends in the neighborhood, and spent much time showing Hiro around Rancho Veloz and the Villa Clara province. There was much to see even in this small town. Everything fascinated Hiro, and he was enjoying his experiences while getting to know the Cuban countryside.

Hiro especially loved the Calbarien and the keys of Santa Maria. This area was tropical with beautiful clear blue waters and ocean as far as the eye could see. Many keys dotted the Cuban coast and it was a lovely area. There was a nice hotel there, but Pedro couldn't enter it because Cubans were not allowed. Many nice places were off limits to Cuban citizens. The Cuban government built the resorts for tourist use only to draw foreign currency. The government depended on this currency for the country's survival. Hiro slowly began to get used to this. Each time Hiro was shocked that he could enter, but his friend could not.

Santa Clara was the capital of the province. The second largest city was Sagua la Grande. It was a small, old city with few shops and poorly built roads and buildings. Like most Cuban cities, Sagua la Grande was in a state of deterioration. There was a beautiful train station that had been built in the early 1900s, and the streets were paved with cobblestones. However, some of these old streets had been converted to modern asphalt. It was nice to see that there were horse and buggy carts still in operation. Hiro loved the sight. Pedro and Hiro spent time roaming the city. It was quiet and quaint and the people were friendly everywhere they went.

The city of Santa Clara was the capital of the Villa Clara province and the population was nearly 200,000. It was a decent-sized town with much industry. The older part of town had very narrow streets made of cobblestones. It got very hot in Santa Clara because the town was located inland and thus was far ways from both coasts. In the summer, it was especially unbearable due to the heat. But since there was much industry and commerce, Santa Clara had more to offer in the way of amenities. There were many government factories in Santa Clara and it remained an important area for the Cuban economy. There was a well-maintained two lane highway in Santa Clara. As cars passed by, the people waved and yelled greetings.

In the 1950s back in Hiroshima, Hiro remembered that the country people were also very friendly and stopped to chat and say hello. Hiro could relate to his neighbors and he loved it. He found that Cuba today was much like the Japan of his childhood and he found himself always comparing them both. Hiro also found that he missed communicating with people because of his years of isolation in the field of research. Now Hiro had rediscovered this important connection and it was changing him daily. He could feel a difference which was exciting. For so many years, Hiro thought he had lost this ability to connect, but here in Cuba, he had rediscovered himself. Because of this restoration of the human bond, Hiro found inner peace.

As a result, Hiro's dreaded nightmares were almost completely gone. Not only did he sleep more deeply but also he had good dreams again. It had been a long time since he had enjoyed peaceful sleep. He spent time rejuvenating here in the countryside of rural Cuba and it did him much good. The Japanese doctor had been right after all. The doctor had suggested that Hiro come to this place to heal his mental scars. All these years, he had only known the terror and screams that he had heard on the live radio broadcasts as a child about the revolution. This had haunted Hiro's nights. Now he had come to Cuba to make peace with this terrible memory. It was only by understanding the country and its people through adult eyes and through real human experiences that this transition was possible. To come to this war-torn country was the only way Hiro arrived at closure.

Hiro had never spent much time studying world politics due to his intense focus on computer science and his personal goals. From time to time, Hiro would hear or read something about them, but he could never understand the problems that existed between the US and Cuba. It had never made any sense to him. But now, after this visit, Hiro's interest in politics had grown much.

By spending time in Cuba, Hiro learned first hand from the people how politics had affected them and their country. It had been such a great source of information and a truly eye-opening revelation. Being here in person was better than any book he could have read.

Also after befriending so many Cubans, Hiro had begun to feel their problems as if they were his own. Living among them, he had gotten close to the people. Hiro now believed that the U S was abusing Cubans by their blockade in the name of freedom. The people were suffering. Hiro knew that Americans were kind and open and the first ones to want to help others, but the U S government was not on the same page. It was as if the government was doing the exact opposite of what most American citizens would do, if they only knew what was happening here behind the scenes. Hiro believed that the U.S. citizens would want to help the Cuban people and stop the unnecessary hardships placed on the people. Instead, the U.S. government called Cuba their enemy. Why?

Recently, the U.S. had established free trade exclusively with China. Now trade had also been extended to Vietnam. The companies who participated stood to make huge profits. However, Cuba, so physically close to the US, was not even recognized as a country. The US continued to support a complete trade embargo and blockade against them. Many Cuban-Americans were suffering because they wanted to return home, but could not. Hiro thought that Cuba was a victim of the Cold War between the U.S. and the U.S.S.R. Due to the Cuban missile crisis, the U.S. had never forgiven Cuba and Cuba was still paying a heavy price.

Hiro believed that the U.S. wanted to punish Fidel Castro, but the people were suffering the most. America was always known as the land of the free and the home of the brave. He had always looked up to these values, but he wondered where the famous kindness and aid was. The U.S. had a big heart, but not for Fidel Castro, and so the whole country of Cuba suffered the consequences. Cuba unfortunately was just another victim of American bureaucracy.

Another great thing about this visit for Hiro was the inter-relatedness of Cuba and old Japan. Often he remembered his childhood home in Japan. Hiro came from a farming lineage and farming community. People there farmed generation after generation. Land and farms were handed down through these generations. It was a tradition that was part of the Japanese social structure.

Before the revolution, Cuba had the same system where property changed hands within the family for generations. The original inhabitants of Cuba were the Taino-Arawak Indians. Their land was stolen from them in the name of Christianity. Under the Communist government, ninety present of the property was confiscated from the farmers and the private sector and declared government property. Fidel Castro told the people that the confiscated land would be divided equally among everyone, both poor and rich. Fidel wanted to equalize the population. The rich lost everything and the poor gained and had a better life in Cuba. Hiro thought this was a good philosophy, but the truth was that this was good only in theory.

In reality, it was not working. Hiro believed it was because human nature was selfish at the core. The Cuban people were ultimately concerned with themselves and what they could gain. Fidel underestimated the power of the selfish nature of humans. This greed was the beginning of the downfall of Cuba and Fidel's system. Before Fidel took over, Cuba was five times richer than Japan. It also had a higher standard of living than

The Last Revolution

most European countries. After the takeover, the standard went completely downhill within three years. Cuba needed the U.S. dollar to sustain its quality of life. Without it the whole economy took a nose dive.

Here in this remote country village, Hiro found that the people were happy and lived in a unique culture. Through Pedro, Hiro met many nice people. Pedro had shown him many parts of the beautiful countryside of the Villa Clara province. Pedro's family had been carpenters for several generations. Now, his three brothers and his father worked together in a 20 by 15-foot woodworking shop built with leftover wood. It was a makeshift operation and worse than a shack, but it worked for them.

Hiro found it unique because everything in their shop was home-made, even the equipment. Pedro and his family had invented their own home-made tools, even electrical tools. They had to use what they had because they didn't have a lot of money and besides no equipment was available for purchase. Hiro was really interested and very impressed with their inventions. He was impressed with their thoughtful design and creativity. Their home-made inventions worked as well or better than most tools and equipment that he had seen in the U.S. or Japan. The shop was very efficient and functional. They had a lot of work orders, and there was even a three month waiting list for items.

Pedro's family bartered their goods or received some cash. Although they could make just about anything, they mainly produced rocking chairs, kitchen tables, dressers, bed frames, and cabinets. They made bookshelves and decorative items, too. The most popular items were the rocking chairs and kitchen table sets. They usually made a rocking chair and a table set once a week. The family had good workmanship and mechanical skills and each piece was of good quality. Most of the furniture was left natural, but they did some painting and finishing work.

All their wood and materials for the workshop were purchased from the black market and were very inexpensive. If they waited on the government, they would never get anything done. They bought their supplies on the black market. There were no receipts. Once or twice a year, the government came to inspect the family carpentry business to see pad the receipts for their supplies. When word spread that an inspector was coming, they stop work and disappear until the coast was clear. Every time Hiro saw this, he laughed.

After selling an item, Pedro paid the utility bill and any other costs. Then they divided the remaining profit between the brothers and their father. For example, Pedro told Hiro that they sold one set of rocking chairs for 4000 Cuban pesos (about $220). Therefore, after the bills were paid, each worker received about $25 a week. The average Cuban only made about the equivalent of $12 a month. A schoolteacher made around $15 a month while a doctor made about $40 per month. So, Pedro and his family did very well and always saved their money.

The workshop was a free enterprise so Pedro's family was a living example of the capitalist principle in this Communist nation. Hiro recognized this and found it fascinating. Hiro thought back to his own career and achievements over the past thirty years. He had worked to get to the top of his field only to find that his accomplishments didn't fulfill him. Hiro had discovered that what he once considered so important, what he sacrificed everything for, didn't matter to him any more. What mattered now was that he was really happy and he felt that he had found lightness in his heart again. Hiro was no longer concerned with the future and was enjoying living in the today. It was the first time in many years that he felt at peace and truly content. In a strange way, Hiro owed some thanks to Fidel Castro. Without Fidel, the Cuba that Hiro had discovered would not exist. Some good had come from Fidel's failed vision. Hiro loved Cuba and the life he found there.

Hiro liked Pedro's family very much because they were really nice to him. They treated him like a family member. The family had never known an Oriental person before Hiro's arrival. They enjoyed his company and became close friends. As the days passed by, Hiro became more and more familiar with the Cuban family structure, social life and government structure. He saw how the government interfered with daily life.

On the outside, people were easy going and friendly; but as one got to know the culture, it became evident that the people were always worried about something. They were afraid of the government. There were always government spies around, which was threatening. The CDR was the neighborhood watchdog. There was a person in every neighborhood that had to report to the government. Everyone knew who this person was so they tried to avoid him. When this person was around, people had to put on a face showing that everything was great. They did not discuss the government or politics in the watchdog's presence. As soon as this person left, the people could resume their discussions and voice their real complaints about the system. No one discussed government issues outdoors because of their fear of getting in trouble and going to jail. There was no freedom of speech in Cuba.

Hiro had never had a hobby as an adult, so he asked Pedro to teach him about woodworking. Hiro began to love this craft as he worked side by daily with Pedro's family. Hiro surprised himself that he could learn this craft so quickly and besides, he loved Pedro's company. Before, Hiro had always used his brain when working. Now he found that working with his hands was enjoyable. It was meditative. Hiro was a quiet and patient worker and remembered everything that Pedro told him. He was a great student, and Pedro could use the extra hands. Pedro could see that Hiro was more open and relaxed than when they had first met back in Havana. Pedro was happy that Hiro had decided to come to Rancho Veloz to be part of his world. Life in the county was quite different from life in the big city of Havana.

As they worked together in the shop, Hiro remembered that one of his neighbors back in Hiroshima was also a carpenter. When he was little, Hiro had enjoyed watching him work. Hiro had been fascinated by the way the man was able to make furniture out of plain wood using hand tools. Pedro was making many different useful items. His specialty was designing the graphics for beautiful woodcarvings with an artistic flare. One of his workers named Mandy would then carve out the designs.

The finished products were unique and elegant. Mandy was well-known for his designs including hummingbirds, old Spanish- styled carvings, dolphins, whales, and flowers. Whatever the people wanted, Pedro could design. He was very creative and loved his craft. Hiro learned by watching others work. Hiro could not believe that in Cuba he was doing carpentry work like he had seen as a child in Japan.

Life was good and Hiro had no worries here. He hadn't even thought about his company, Brainstorm, or the computer science world. Here, his head seemed clearer and he could relax and decompress. This made him very happy, and it was as if he were getting a chance to begin his life over again. This was a different way of living that he had never known existed. Even though work was busy, Pedro made time to show Hiro the area. Pedro knew that Hiro loved to fish. Pedro decided to take Hiro to the Rio San Pedro reservoir which was a small agricultural dam the government had constructed near a fresh water spring which pumped hundreds of thousands of gallons of water per minute. It was cool, clear water and the reservoir provided a source of drinking water for Rancho Veloz and the surrounding area. There were plenty of fresh water fish in the reservoir also. The reservoir was about the size of a five acre lake and was located about thirty minutes from Rancho Veloz.

The fishing area was near the town of Corralillo, due south on the highway to Santa Clara. Just before Corralillo, there was a right turn on a dirt road leading to a small pueblo called Rio San Pedro. The population was about forty five people with one small building, like a community center, in between twelve houses. Those were the only buildings in the small town. Just past this area and down the road were the river and the reservoir. There was a beautiful waterfall with a fifty foot drop. It was scenic and the water was clean and cool. Many people came here to swim because it stayed cool and fresh during the hot summer weather. As many as a hundred people came on the hottest days of summer. It was always hot at the beach during the summer season so many local people preferred swimming in the reservoir instead.

As soon as they arrived at the freshwater dam, Hiro immediately began to fish. The minute his line hit the water, he got a bite. Hiro was very excited. Pedro started screaming because he had never seen anyone catch a fish before. Pedro rushed over to watch Hiro wrestle the fish on his line. Pedro was fascinated at Hiro's fishing rod and reel and how it all worked. At the end of Hiro's rod was a large mouth bass. It took some time for Hiro to reel it in. Pedro now understood why Hiro loved to fish so much and Pedro could see that Hiro was a very good fisherman. Not many people here fished because they lacked the needed gear. A crowd had gathered around to watch Hiro. The children came running to see this strange Oriental man fishing. It was a sight for them. The large mouth bass weighed about two pounds. As time went on, most all of the children living in the village came to see Hiro fish. Hiro became an instant celebrity. These kids had never seen fishing done with a rod and reel and

The Last Revolution

an artificial lure. Hiro had brought these items to Cuba in his luggage.

The Cuban people fished the old-fashioned way using no fishing poles. They held the line with their bare hands and just pulled it in when they felt a fish bite. They used earthworms and their method of fishing was very rudimentary and simple. Hiro gave the fish away to one of the children and they went crazy. The children could not believe this man had just given them a free fish. They were happy and felt special. Hiro enjoyed seeing the children smile. Pedro observed quietly. Pedro didn't want to fish, but enjoyed watching the spectacle. Hiro thoroughly enjoyed his day fishing. As the afternoon approached, they decided to drive to Panchita which was a small fishing village near the ocean. They wanted to purchase some fish to cook because Hiro had given all of his fish away to the children. Pedro and Hiro preferred to eat saltwater fish over freshwater fish.

The population of Panchita was about a one thousand, and the poorly built houses lined both sides of the highway. Hiro noticed a terrible smell. It was an open sewer line in a ditch along the beach. It was unhealthy and smelled terrible. The beach looked more like dirt than sand. The locals lived in wooden shacks built all along the beach. During the summer months, the locals rented out their shacks for 150 Cuban pesos ($5) a day which was a great way for them to make extra money Hiro and Pedro approached a huge wooden pier. They saw several wooden fishing boats tied to the pier and people gathered nearby. Pedro told Hiro that those were government-owned boats and that the fish they would buy here were not actually caught by the locals. Instead, the fish for sale came from these government fishing boats whose nets were cast into the Caribbean. Pedro told Hiro that even though Cuba was surrounded by water, few Cubans had private boats. Those who did had to have special government licenses.

When Hiro asked why, Pedro explained that if people had boats, they could escape from Cuba and go to Jamaica or Florida or to another Caribbean nation. Many Cubans wanted to leave the country and a boat was one of the only ways out for many people. Pedro told Hiro that many people had escaped in small canoes and home-made boats since the revolution. Many had died at sea. Pedro explained that the government strictly controlled boating and fishing which was why the locals could not fish in the open sea. That seemed curious to Hiro. Cuba was surrounded entirely by a beautiful ocean, but Cubans could not go out into it. It was like a beautiful prison island.

As they drove past the small harbor, they saw people on the street. Pedro greeted the people walking along the road who said, "Hey, Pedrey! What's up?" Pedro knew almost everyone in town. It was a very friendly and warm atmosphere. Pedro stopped by several houses to say hello to his friends and to see if they had any fresh fish. They told him where to go and who had good fish for sale that day. This was, of course, all black markets' supplied. People who worked for the government took their fish to families in Corralillo who sold them to the locals for money. Then in turn, the locals would sell to individuals. Every one knew who had the fish supply and where. It was one big circle. The government knew, but pretended not to see. They had to turn a blind eye to this because it was how the country maintained an economic balance. The fish were very expensive but were fresh and good. There were usually a couple of choices of local Caribbean fish for sale, but red snapper, called *Pargo,* was the most common.

Pedro finally found a man who was selling fish. He had five huge red snappers for sale for 600 Cuban pesos. That was equal to one month's wages for people who worked for the government. It was an outrageous price for Cuban, so Pedro started to negotiate a reasonable price. Hiro wanted to have good fish for dinner and he had the money, so buying these beauties was no problem. But for the average person, this price would be too high. Therefore, these were considered a real treat and Pedro was excited to bring them home for dinner. Pedro already had a sack ready for them. The fish were heavy and altogether Hiro had purchased about eighty pounds of fish. Pedro said, "I imagine that if you caught a freshwater fish this big that you would enjoy ocean fishing more than freshwater fishing." Pedro's interest in fishing was about eating, while Hiro enjoyed the technical aspect of the sport. This highlighted two different opinions about fishing. When Hiro was younger, his fishing skills had provided food for his family, but this was many years ago.

As they returned from Corralillo, they visited Pedro's baby sister. There was a man standing in the street yelling and screaming for Pedro to stop. It was an older man in his 70s with a

The Last Revolution

white beard and Pedro pulled the Ford over to see what was going on. He had seen this man before, but Pedro didn't really know him well. The old man told Pedro that he had just heard that his granddaughter had been in a car accident near Sierra Morena. Since he didn't have any transportation, the white haired man had to hitchhike to the clinic in nearby Corralillo and was quite upset. Pedro told him to jump into the car and quickly rushed back to Corralillo.

The man told Hiro and Pedro what had happened in Sierra Morena. His granddaughter had been playing in front of her house in the dark. The approaching car couldn't see her because there were no streetlights and older cars had dim headlights. The car accidentally hit the girl while she was riding her bike. The man who had hit her said that by the time he saw her, it was too late and his brakes wouldn't stop fast enough. It was a bad accident. Pedro drove as fast as he could and they reached the Corralillo medical clinic within thirty minutes.

The man told Pedro to come with him inside the clinic. They told Hiro to stay inside the car. The medical clinic looked to be fairly good-sized. It was a concrete building two stories high with a beautiful front yard with many roses and flowers in a garden. Right next door was the local Corralillo schoolhouse. After about twenty minutes, Pedro returned telling Hiro what had happened to the little girl. She was not seriously hurt, but she had broken her left leg and left arm. Other than that, she looked all right according to her doctor. She would have to wear casts and walk using crutches for a few months. Pedro told Hiro that it was very painful to see such a young girl hurting so badly. She was crying and scared. Her grandfather came out and told Pedro how grateful he was for his help. The old man tried to give Pedro money for gasoline, but Pedro wouldn't accept it. Gasoline was hard to come by in Cuba so the older man wanted to give Pedro money for helping. Pedro told the man to buy crayons for his granddaughter. Hiro knew from his observations that Pedro was a good-hearted and decent man. He was a kind person who would help anyone in need.

By the time they returned home, Madeline had already finished cooking dinner and she asked, "I thought you had car trouble on the way home. It is past midnight. Where have you been? I was expecting you two hours ago." She was very concerned.

Pedro explained to her about the man and the accident and having to drive back to the Corralillo clinic. She was very shocked to hear the sad news because she knew the little girl. She was the daughter of her friend from Wendy's school. Pedro's daughter Wendy also knew the girl as they were about a year apart in age. Wendy decided to go and visit the little girl the next day at the clinic. They wanted to check on her.

The next morning, they all drove back to the clinic in Corralillo to visit the girl. They brought her flowers, white paper, crayons, and candies. The girl was there with her family and she was very happy to have visitors. Her grandfather was also there and he thanked Pedro and Hiro again for their kindness the previous night. The little girl already had a thick cast on her leg and another on her arm. She was resting in a clinic bed and seemed like she was doing better. They had given her some medicine for her pain so she was quite comfortable. The inside of the clinic was fairly simple. It was small and old and didn't have much in the way of modern equipment. Hiro could see that they had to make do with what they were given and they didn't have many supplies and medicines like clinics in the States or Japan.

The doctor at the clinic was professional and friendly. The girl's mother told them that her daughter was doing much better and that she had only broken bones and had no serious internal injuries. The doctor had watched her overnight to be sure. The little girl would have to stay there another day and then she could return home. She would have to wear the casts for ten weeks and then the casts could be removed. Wendy talked with her friend for a long time. Both Hiro and Pedro were glad to see that she was doing fine. After a while, they all said good-bye and headed back to Rancho Veloz.

Several days passed by, and Hiro started to relax more and more. He felt at home in this remote little country town. He was really interested in carpentry work and wanted to learn all he could from Pedro. He enjoyed learning about the beautiful wood grain that came out naturally in each piece. Each kind of wood, whether it was oak, pine, or cypress, had a different grain and Pedro spent a lot of time teaching Hiro about working with the grain. Pedro's years of experience and good skills increased his Oriental student's enjoyment of the craft, teaching Hiro to appreciate that which already existed in nature. Nature made

The Last Revolution

different forms and patterns in the wood and Hiro began to really appreciate the uniqueness of each piece.

It was a carpenter's job to see where the design could enhance nature's beauty. It was completely the opposite from the unnatural inventions of the computer science world. Working with the conceptual rather than the natural world had been Hiro's job for many years. Therefore, carpentry work was very therapeutic for him. Also, working with Pedro's joyful family was also so good for Hiro.

Hiro felt a bond with Pedro's family and found that he actually preferred working with people to working with machines. Hiro began to see how decent and kind these people were. They were simple people, but warm and gracious. They were extremely hard-working, and Hiro was very impressed with their small wood working operation. The family also had many friends who would stop by and say hello and talk. Hiro got to know all of the family's friends and vice versa. They all loved meeting the curious oriental visitor. They were all intrigued by him when they came by to visit.

People were not in a hurry and the attitude was that they had nothing but time. This was wonderful to experience. Hiro loved enjoying each moment. He had never really known this kind of life. Hiro's life had been about hard work, studying to achieve his goals, and pushing to succeed in everything he did. He was like a mouse in a wheel always trying to get ahead, but here in this little country town he began to discover himself as well as the art of living in the moment and appreciating the simple things in life. Hiro thought that he had found gold here in Cuba and that no other country on the planet was quite like this one.

Life in Cuba was unique and special and he was grateful to have this opportunity to be here and to live among the locals. He was recapturing lost time and it was as if he had stepped back into the 1950s.

Life in Rancho Veloz was quiet, slow-paced, and in Hiro's mind, good. People had plenty of time to mingle and interact with each other. They had time to share and connect with each other. Hiro had never experienced anything quite like it before. For Hiro, he was always thinking ten years ahead about his accomplishments and goals and now he didn't have any future planning hanging over his head. Hiro thought that one good thing Fidel had done was to give him this wonderful place. Hiro appreciated what he had received from being in Cuba.

At first, Hiro hadn't known what to do with his time when he arrived to Cuba. It was a difficult adjustment period because he didn't know how to enjoy time. He had never lived like this before. When one had time, it could seem boring because it was not always appreciated. But Hiro realized now that having time was actually a luxury. He had had to readjust to this way of living and thinking. What he found out is that to enjoy time, one must connect with others. Otherwise, life was lonely. Hiro realized that the connection between people was an important element in enjoying time. Hiro had never had so many friends.

Whatever Hiro needed, Pedro was there and ready to help him. They had become good friends and they respected each other. For Pedro, it was also a special friendship because he had never met or had the opportunity to know an oriental person before. Hiro was extremely intelligent, and Pedro had learned many things by just being with him. But Hiro still hadn't shared his personal background with Pedro. Pedro only knew that Hiro was a professor at a university in Japan. Hiro trusted Pedro but he didn't want to get anyone in trouble or to have problems so he had kept his computer background a secret.

Pedro introduced Hiro to one of his favorite places. It was a hot spring named Elquea. There was a decent hotel with about 80 rooms near the springs. The hotel also had a nice restaurant, bar and convention room attached. But it was very empty because few people visited Elquea. Not many tourists visited this remote area. It was about five miles west of the town of Corralillo. They had hot mud baths, steam baths and hot mineral water springs. The mud was rich with minerals, such as bromide, chloride, sodium, and sulfur. Hiro loved coming to this place to relax and heal his mental wounds. It was a nice place to relax both body and mind. Hiro thought many Japanese tourists would love to visit here, but they didn't know it existed. The spring and hotel were not commercialized like those in Japan.

The Elquea was quiet and simple, and the minerals very healing. Hiro found serenity here. Hiro's mother loved the hot springs in Japan and he wished he could bring her here one day. He knew she would be delighted with this place. But it was such a remote spot that no Japanese tourists ever came. The one thing that the Japanese wouldn't like about this place was the mosquitoes. The pests loved Hiro's Asian blood. The swampy area attracted many mosquitoes. The locals weren't bothered, but Hiro found it very irritating.

Periodically, Hiro was seen running away from the mosquitoes that flocked to him as it got dark. The number of mosquitoes worsened as it got closer to dusk. The hotel was fortunately equipped with a large machine that fumigated for this very problem. When the employees heard and saw Hiro yelling from his mosquito bites, they rushed to help him and gave him attention right away. Even though the mosquitoes were troublesome, Hiro visited the hotel and springs quite often. The healing waters and serenity kept calling him back and reminded him of his visits to hot springs in Japan.

The hotel employees got to know Hiro very well because he was the only Japanese person in the area. They had never had another Japanese guest before so he was a novelty. They were intrigued by him and got to know him better with each visit. Hiro was always very courteous and kind and stopped to talk to people. He also left the staff tips that were much appreciated. The staff nicknamed him *el Japone*.

The hotel was located in the lowlands facing the bay of Villa Clara where there were thousands of small keys. The mosquitoes were dense in this area because the water around the keys was closed in like a swamp and was a perfect breeding area for these pests.

The only positive thing to be said about the mosquitoes was that they attracted small fish that in turn attracted big fish making this a good fishing spot. For Hiro, this spot was very scenic and beautiful. Interestingly enough it was also the only underground volcano site on this tropical island. Thus the spring had arisen from the underground volcanic activity.

Anytime Pedro and Hiro had the chance to come to Corralillo, they stopped by Elquea to relax in the hot springs baths. The springs were medicinal and made the mind and body feel light and refreshed. Hiro was also grateful to find a local doctor of natural medicine here. His name was Dr. Andy Hector Garcia. He was very well known in the area and was associated with the Institution of Cuban Medicine. Dr. Garcia offered many treatments including a therapeutic massage which helped to move stagnation in the body. His treatments were similar in a way to the acupuncture done by Dr. Sugihara in Japan. Later, Hiro found out that Dr. Garcia had studied at the University of Guangzhou, a Chinese Oriental Medicine institution. Hiro enjoyed these treatments tremendously and visited the springs and Dr. Garcia regularly.

The employees at the hotel were nice and helpful. Hiro instantly connected with these people and they made him feel welcome and at home. This was only a tourist hotel and no locals came here. Locals were only permitted to take a steam bath or to use the swimming pool and restaurant. Cubans never spent the night in the hotel. Hiro treated Pedro to the baths and meals and then they drove back to Pedro's home. Hiro wished that he could treat Pedro and his wife to an overnight stay, but the hotel would not permit it. It was the law which Hiro thought was unfortunate.

The Cubans could not enjoy their own hotels and vacation spots freely. At the hotel there was a wonderful restaurant which served tasty fish dishes. Fish caught at the bay of Villa Clara were prepared Cuban style. The restaurant staff was extremely friendly and helpful. They always recognized and welcomed them back. Hiro always enjoy the nice dinner, but Pedro was shy and uncomfortable because he knew that this was a tourist place which usually did not allow locals. Under Fidel's government system, Cubans always had to be cautious and not invite trouble.

Back in Rancho Veloz, Hiro continued to work in the carpentry workshop every day. Hiro's skills were progressing, and his woodwork was getting better and better. He enjoyed spending time learning this new skill and meeting the many nice friends who visited the shop. He had already learned how to choose the wood, make a design, cut the wood, and make legs or a base with a lathe. Finally, he learned to shave the wood and use a chisel. Surprisingly, there were no nails used in their work, only wood glue. Hiro could not believe that they did not use nails. It was a sign of real craftsmanship to make something so sturdy and well without a single nail. Pedro always reminded Hiro not to rush and to take time to enjoy the process. Pedro always complemented Hiro and told him that he was doing good work. Pedro and his family were good teachers and they enjoyed their workday together. They were always laughing, talking, and having a good time. Hiro worked from nine in the morning until noon almost every day.

The Last Revolution

Since there was no real schedule, Hiro could do whatever he pleased, but he enjoyed coming to the workshop daily and learning all he could while he was in Rancho Veloz. He knew that he would have to leave one day, so he'd better get it all in while he could. And Hiro really enjoyed everything about this workshop, especially the fact that there were many family and friends dropping in. They congregated around the workshop to talk. It was a real social hub. Hiro listened to the people talking about daily life and news. They also loved to gossip which was fascinating to Hiro. He found it very entertaining.

Hiro had never had the opportunity to enjoy daily life and simple living. As long as he could remember, he had always studied and worked diligently toward his goal. Hiro had felt a tremendous pressure to succeed and to achieve at the highest level possible. And he did.

Hiro had poured his heart and soul into reaching his goals and he spent all of his life figuring out mathematical phenomena, computer science calculations, computer languages and systems and new inventions in the field. He dreamed of being the best and worked until that was accomplished, but he had never truly enjoyed the spoils of his hard work. Satisfaction and enjoyment had never really entered his mind until now.

He could see that he had become more connected to machines than human beings during those years. The machines were ultimately extensions of his mathematical equations, logical mathematical systems and codes and computer science inventions. They were complex, but they were finite. Once they were created and finished, that was it. These computers and their hardware were no longer complicated at that point. Human beings on the other hand were just the opposite. They seemed simple in many ways, but they could never really be figured out because they were always growing and changing. People were dynamic and infinite. Hiro was discovering how much he had missed all these years.

Therefore, Hiro was delighted to be in this new phase of his life. His life was coming full circle. What was once missing in his life was now here in abundance and he was grateful.

Hiro had a difficult time dealing with people and feelings. He knew he owed many thanks for the great advice from Dr. Sugihara, his Doctor of Oriental Medicine in Hiroshima, Japan. At last, emotions that Hiro had buried deep had resurfaced. In

Micheal Kazuhiro Nishitani

Cuba, Hiro connected with life. Finally, he knew what he had missed. Because of this monumental change, Hiro decided to stay longer in this remote village. He believed it would rid him once and for all of the terrible nightmares and mental flashbacks that had haunted him throughout his life. Hiro wanted to relax and rejuvenate in this ideal place. Pedro also wanted him to stay on longer. They had grown to be great friends.

Chapter 18

As much as Hiro was enjoying his visit with Pedro in Rancho Veloz, he realized that he had to return to the real world. Hiro mentioned to Pedro that he needed to revisit the immigration office. Hiro said, "I only have a week before my visa expires and I need to go back to the immigration office in Havana. Can you take me?"

Pedro asked, "Extension visa in Havana?" Hiro nodded.

Pedro thought for a minute and answered, "Look Hiro, I think Varadero has an immigration office because so many tourists go there. And I know for sure that there is one in Santa Clara which is about a two hour drive from here. Why don't we go down there and check it out to see what they can do for you? Havana is such a long drive."

Hiro looked happily surprised and asked, "Great! Could we go tomorrow morning?" They both agreed to go to the Santa Clara immigration office first thing in the morning. After visiting the immigration office they planned to stay a few extra days because Pedro wanted to buy some carpentry supplies and materials on the black market in town.

Pedro also had an aunt who lived there and it had been quite some time since Pedro's mother had seen her sister. Pedro asked, "Do you mind if my mother comes with us? She would love to see her sister."

"No, I don't mind," answered Hiro. The two then finalized their plans and went to sleep.

Early the next morning they left for Santa Clara by driving through Sagua La Grande and over the viaduct of the Autopista headed south. They passed many rural communities, there were abundant sugar fields as far as the eye could see and peaceful countryside. It was a nice drive and the weather was pleasant at that time of the morning.

Just before reaching Santa Clara there were many houses and some high-rise apartment buildings on the outskirts of town. Pedro turned down a side road. This was where Pedro's aunt lived. The house was small with white paint and concrete. There was only dirt in the front yard with no grass. Hiro could see that there were many banana trees in the back yard. This was a typical middle class Cuban home. Here in Santa Clara the homes were a lot better than the homes in Rancho Veloz. These homes and neighborhoods had been built before the revolution.

There were many cars parked on the street. As they pulled into the driveway, Pedro's aunt came outside to greet them. She was happy to see them and gave each of them a big hug. They introduced Hiro to her. Pedro's mother was glad to see her sister and they all agreed to meet later that day. They waved good bye as Pedro and Hiro pulled out of the driveway. As Hiro and Pedro drove a bit farther toward town, there was a big metal sign that read, "Welcome to Santa Clara!"

Hiro noticed that suddenly there was a lot of traffic in the town comprised of old cars, buses, horses and buggies, and motorbikes. The streets were crowded with people. Pedro made a left turn onto a main street where the immigration office was located. They parked along the street in front of an old, colonial-style building. As they approached the front door, a security man approached them and said, "Excuse me, are you here for immigrations?" They answered yes. He pointed and motioned outside saying, "The immigration offices have been moved to Carretera Central and Colon on the other side of Central Park."

They drove to the new location and waited a few minutes for a parking space. It was crowded in this town and there were many cars. As they arrived at the new location and walked up to the building, they approached an information desk. The office was small and had only a few chairs for waiting. The man at the front desk looked very familiar to Pedro. Pedro, who was normally very quiet said, "You look very familiar to me. Are you related to Christina Alvares from Las Tunas?"

The man looked shocked and answered, "Why yes? That's my mother! It's a small world. Who are you?"

Pedro laughed and said, "I knew you looked familiar to me. We are cousins! I am Ana Maria Pelayo's son from Rancho Veloz." They had not seen each other for many years and began to talk.

Eduardo had been only a young boy when they had seen each last so he could hardly remember Pedro. But the more they

The Last Revolution

looked at each other the more they could see the family resemblance. They talked briefly about the family. Eduardo had just graduated from The University of Las Tunas with a degree in political science. Originally, he had been hired by the interrogations department in Santiago de Cuba located on the far eastern side of the island. But he had just returned to Santa Clara to work at this office. It was just a coincidence that they had run into each other today.

It was Hiro's lucky day. Pedro said, "Eduardo, this is my friend Hiroaki Nakagawa from Japan, and he needs an extension on his visitors' visa. He would like a twelve month visa because he would like to receive treatments at Hotel Elquea."

Eduardo answered, "Just a moment, I need to talk to my supervisor." A few moments later Eduardo introduced them to an intelligent looking man in his fifties. He was formal and very professional but seemed to have a gentle way about him. The man smiled as he approached them. Eduardo took a moment and explained the situation to his supervisor. The immigration chief looked at Hiro with much interest and curiosity. Hiro didn't know what to think. Would there be another test like the one in Havana?

The chief asked Hiro to come into his office at once. Pedro came along with him. They were both uncertain about what was coming next. The man took them to a small office with a desk and a couple of chairs. The man motioned for Hiro and Pedro to take a seat. Then, quite nicely, the immigration chief made a quick introduction to Pedro in Spanish and shook his hand and then suddenly he turned to Hiro and changed from speaking Spanish to Japanese. He shook hands with Hiro. Hiro was stunned. This Cuban was speaking excellent Japanese.

The official said, "My name is Fredric Lalvarez Díaz. Call me Freddie. I am the Deputy Minister of the Interior in Havana. I am working here at this office temporarily conducting some inspections for the department. I guess that makes me in charge here. Are you surprised to hear me speak Japanese? And just call me Freddie."

Hiro was almost speechless but he managed an answer, "Yes, your Japanese is very good. It is very nice to meet you."

Freddie Díaz said, "I will have my assistant help you fill out the proper paper work and to explain the details. When you are finished, please come back so we can talk some more. I have to make a phone call now. Please excuse me."

Then Freddie called for his assistant. She was a very nice young lady in her thirties. Freddie gave her specific instructions to take care of Hiro and to help him file the extension application. Hiro and Pedro went with her to her desk. The assistant was very efficient and friendly and it was quite different from his other experience with immigration back in Havana, where he had had a difficult and scary experience.

The young female officer told him she unfortunately could not issue him a one year visa. She said they only had the authority to grant him a three month visa extension at this office. For a one year visa he would have to go to Havana and there was a lot of red tape involved. It required many documents from Japan and it would take a couple of months to process the paperwork. The documents also must be legalized by the Cuban Embassy in Tokyo.

She told Hiro that she could only permit a ninety day visa, and he would need to pay a $135 processing fee. Hiro agreed and it was all done very quick and easily. Hiro was so relieved that everyone here was courteous and polite. The atmosphere at this office was wonderful. He told Pedro what a good idea it had been to come to the Santa Clara office. Pedro looked pleased, too, and he remained quiet the whole time, observing. Pedro also talked to his relative Eduardo while Hiro was busy. Hiro completed the minimal paperwork and paid the fee.

The most impressive thing to Hiro was that he had met a Cuban who actually spoke Japanese. It was unexpected and Hiro wanted to speak with this man again. After the visa was granted, Hiro and Pedro went back to visit Fredric Lalvarez Diaz's office. Freddie was just ending a phone call and motioned them for them to come into his office. After he finished his call, he told Pedro that he was going to speak in Japanese to Hiroaki. Pedro said that was fine.

Freddie mentioned that he had studied economics at The University of Matanzas and then had gone to work with the Department of Economic Development. The department had sent Freddie to Tokyo for an extended study at The Sophia Jo-chi University and he worked with the Cuban embassy's immigration office in Shibuya in Tokyo. He was twenty-eight

The Last Revolution

years old at the time and had ended up spending ten years in Japan at the Cuban Embassy. Freddie told Hiro that he loved the Japanese people, the culture, and the food, and was especially impressed with their technology and industry. He found the people to be very intelligent and bright.

As Hiro listened to Freddie, he thought to himself that the Japanese were not any different than Cubans, except that the Japanese people knew that Japan needed success in technology and business as a national goal, so they all worked toward that. The Cubans did not work together for a common goal, except for small groups escaping to Miami.

Hiro was surprised because there were few Japanese tourists in this area. When he was in Havana at the immigration office, he had seen a few there, but in Santa Clara there were no Oriental tourists. Freddie enjoyed reminiscing about his past in Japan. He also enjoyed practicing his Japanese with Hiro. Freddie was interested in Hiro because he reminded him of his times in Japan and he felt an automatic connection to him, besides he rarely had the opportunity to meet and talk with a Japanese person.

Hiro told Freddie what he had experienced in the immigration office in Havana previously and that he had been worried about returning there. But Hiro was also cautious about what he told Freddie, because he didn't know him. They both spoke very formally to one another because this was their first meeting. Hiro admitted to Freddie that he had worried about coming to this office in Santa Clara.

Freddie smiled and said, "From now on if you go to immigrations, please call me and I will arrange for someone whom I know to interview you. This way you won't have any problems." That was a great idea because Hiro didn't understand how the Cuban government's institutions worked and needed a connection. He thanked Freddie for his offer. Hiro never had completely understood Cuban politics, the immigration office, or the government's criteria. Hiro was not sure what they were looking for. Freddie explained that security played a major role in the function of the immigration office.

Hiro thought Freddie was very intelligent and well-educated. He was interested in different cultures. Freddie continued to ask Hiro many questions about Japanese news and current events. Freddie enjoyed getting an update on all the latest news from Japan. He asked Pedro where they would be staying while in Santa Clara. Pedro told him that he had an aunt who lived just outside of town and they would stay there. Pedro told Freddie that they would stay for several days to take care of some business. Hiro was happy that he had meet Freddie. He found him very friendly and helpful. He was glad that he had had such a good experience at this immigration office.

After they returned to Pedro's aunt's home, they relaxed and visited with the family. Pedro and his mother had not seen each other for quite some time. When Hiro saw Pedro's mother and aunt, they reminded him of his two sisters in Japan. There was something similar about them. The families in Santa Clara were exceptionally hospitable and warm. Later in the afternoon many family members came by to visit. It became a big party and everyone brought a dish of food and something to drink. It was great to see everyone bonding and joining together. Hiro really enjoyed Pedro's big family gathering. They played salsa music and everyone was laughing and joking around. There were about twenty people in the house so it was quite a large group.

At the party they served delicious local dishes. Croquetas were small fried cylinders of fish, ham, and beef covered in dough and breadcrumbs. Hot papas rellenas, fried potato balls with beef in the center, were passed around. There was a favorite of Hiro's called Bacalao. It was a fried, salted cod and very tasty. A typical dish that was very Cuban was called Picadillo a la Habanera. It was grilled beef covered in a mixture of olives, raisins, and capers served over hot rice. It had an unusual sweet and sour flavor. Although, Hiro did not eat many sweets, he did enjoy the island's fruits. The desserts were always made with tropical fruits. There was Dulce de Coco, or ground coconut, and guayaba fruit with brown sugar. Banana-based cakes with guava and mango marmalades and coconut milk rice puddings were always plentiful.

Pedro had a big family, and they liked to talk about family news and to exchange stories from Cuba and the US. Hiro watched all of this with delight and thought that it was very different from Japan. The Japanese people weren't so open and few relatives gathered together like this because of time and money. In Japan, the gatherings were usually small. Large groups only assembled for very special occasions such as weddings or funerals. But in Cuba the system allowed people to have a lot of time to get together. It was very common for people to gather like this often. They played dominoes while laughing and carrying on and dancing to the music. It was a fun atmosphere and very free and happy. In Japan, people were not as free and open in public, even among family. They didn't dance or listen to loud music like this or laugh and tell jokes with one another. Hiro couldn't help but compare the two cultures. They were so opposite.

About 7:00 p.m., a new white Russian-made car called a Lada pulled into the driveway. Eduardo and Freddie Diaz got out of the vehicle and came to the front door. They were immediately welcomed inside because Eduardo was part of the family. Freddie asked to see Hiro and Pedro. They had just left a work meeting and Eduardo had told Freddie about the party and invited him to join them. As soon as he began to shake hands with Hiro, Freddie began to speak Japanese. Everyone was amazed and became quiet. They couldn't believe that the Cuban Immigration Chief spoke fluent Japanese. They all paused to listen to this peculiar language.

Freddie told Hiro about the time he was in Roppongi in Tokyo in the late sixties. Hiro listened to all the interesting place and experience that Freddie had had while in Japan. Hiro thought about where he was in the late sixties. Hiro had been in the US. Studying electromagnetic currents in the computer science department at MIT. As Hiro listened, he remembered how much Japan had changed over the decades. Even for Hiro, every time he returned home for a visit he was so surprised at the changes. Japan had a rapidly changing economy and culture. It had gone from being very old-fashioned to ultra modern very quickly because the Japanese were masters at copying others and adapting.

After the war, Japan caught up with popular culture around the world and became a trend setter, especially in the area of technology. The Japanese were always ten years ahead of the rest of the world. Pedro asked Freddie about an event that had taken place in the sixties in Japan. It was the tragic love story of the two teenagers who couldn't be together because they were from different cultures: China and Japan. The couple had committed suicide on a mountaintop in Kyoto. Pedro hadn't believed that story when Hiro had first told him about it. Freddie acknowledged that this story was indeed true. He told Pedro that it was very difficult for Cubans to understand this suicide mentality over love. In Japan it was considered tragically beautiful.

Freddie also informed Pedro of another example of this: a whole family had committed suicide together when the father made a huge mistake in the workplace and lost the company's money. The man took his life and let his entire family take their lives to atone for the dishonor. It was a completely different cultural view of death and honor. It was very difficult for Cubans to understand the Japanese Bushido mentality. Their conversation continued onto topics such as technology, modern industry, education, and popular culture; and all of the people at the party were fascinated. Freddie also translated his Japanese back into Spanish so that everyone listening could understand.

For them, this conversation comparing the Cuban and Japanese viewpoints was about the most interesting conversation they had ever heard. Hiro knew that Freddie appreciated the Japanese culture very much and that he had a real insider's perspective from living there for ten years. Freddie understood the Japanese culture which was unusual for an outsider, especially a Cuban. Normally, you had to have been born in Japan or had to have grown up there to understand the Japanese culture. Hiro was very grateful to have become acquainted with someone who understood the Japanese culture and who was also a person in a position to help him with many things if he decided to stay in Cuba.

The next day Pedro searched for the needed carpentry materials through his black market contacts, and he went downtown to check out what they had in the way of supplies and to see what was going on around town and with the people. Hiro and Pedro always enjoyed each other's company. Together they went all over Santa Clara and Hiro got to know many things. Driving in Santa Clara was easy, and Pedro knew his way around pretty well. They enjoyed the day. It was all new for Hiro.

The Santa Clara policemen were relaxed and easy-going compared to the officers in Havana. Pedro was familiar with most of the policemen. Periodically, the police stopped in the middle of the street to chat with Pedro. Hiro just observed and remained quiet. Hiro didn't have to worry that they would get in trouble for riding in Pedro's car. Pedro seemed to have many friends here in Santa Clara through his business. Most people he

The Last Revolution

saw were from the black market business. One could get just about anything if one knew whom to see about it. It was a good and efficient system thriving in the underground. Hiro thought this system must be similar to the underground drug market in America. Santa Clara was not an exception. Every city in Cuba was woven into a black market web.

Santa Clara was a bustling city and people were very nice and helpful. They were very open about everything. Pedro gathered many items that he needed for his woodworking business. On every occasion when he had come to the big city, he had always brought Hiro. Because Pedro was very familiar with the surroundings, the city, and its people, he felt comfortable taking Hiro along on these excursions. After three days of buying on the black market, attending to business, and running around, Pedro finally decided to say good bye to his Santa Clara relatives and to return home.

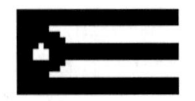

Chapter 19

They left around three in the afternoon for Ranch Veloz. Before returning home, they decided to stop on the outskirts of the city at a huge agriculture and produce market which had many fresh vegetables and fruits for sale. Hiro wanted to stop and buy produce because he loved vegetables. Pedro wasn't too excited about it because he didn't like vegetables very much. Most Cubans had little use for vegetables in their diet and were not accustomed to eating a large variety of them. They ate mainly pork and rice and a few fresh vegetables and fruits. This government operated and controlled the vegetable cultivation and the prices were good. Hiro compared the prices to those in the states, and they were less than one-tenth of the price of US produce. Pedro joked that vegetables were so cheap that Cubans fed them to their goats.

They were glad to return home. Pedro had missed his wife and daughter. They had fun together the evening they returned home. Pedro's mother was happy to have had the opportunity to see and stay with her sister for a few days in Santa Clara. Pedro's father and brothers appreciated that Pedro had gone to the trouble of getting so many great supplies. They welcomed them back with smiles and laughter in the woodshop. Hiro continued to enjoy his woodworking lessons every day because he was serious about this new craft. Little by little Hiro made steady progress and developed new techniques and good skills. Pedro was a good mentor and teacher, who gently guided Hiro.

One day, Pedro told Hiro that the next morning he would be leaving for Corralillo at ten to take his sister to Sagua la Grande Hospital. Pedro tempted Hiro, "If you would like to go fishing in Rio San Pedro we can go tomorrow!"

Hiro jumped up and shouted, "Yes, I want to go!" Pedro could see that Hiro was happy about the suggestion. Hiro enjoyed the calming effect of fishing and wanted to go every chance he could get. Pedro knew this well, but he still didn't understand why Hiro enjoyed fishing without eating what he caught. Pedro always wondered what Hiro saw in it.

The Last Revolution

Pedro's sister had had baby a few weeks before, but since the birth she had been bleeding so the clinic in Corralillo had advised her to see another doctor at the Sagua la Grande Hospital. Pedro thought he could kill two birds with one stone by taking his sister to the hospital and Hiro to the reservoir. The plan was that Pedro and Hiro would go fishing and then pick up his sister in time to drive her to her ten o'clock appointment. It was only an hour's drive from her home. So, early the next morning, the two left home and drove through the outskirts of Corralillo. Then they turned right and drove south to the reservoir.

At this time of morning it was cool and misty. It looked like the fish would bite well because it was quiet and serene. No one seemed to be around and this was good for fishing. Hiro started fishing. He used some top bait which hovered at the surface of the water. Top bait didn't sink and was good for this type of water. Hiro cast out several times. Somehow Hiro found it strange that he hadn't caught a single fish in over an hour. Before, when they had fished here it had taken only minutes before the fish took the bait. Pedro watched and said, "Hiro, what's the matter with you? By now, you should have caught four or five fish already!" Pedro was laughing and kidding. He yelled to Hiro, "You've lost your touch because you haven't fished for over a week."

Hiro replied, "No! The fish are still asleep in the deeper water. I don't know how to wake them. Can you help me out Pedro? Tell me how you wake them up the Cuban way?" Pedro laughed and smiled. He loved joking around with Hiro.

Then Pedro's friend Condera, who lived in the town of Rio San Pedro, brought them some hot Cuban coffee. It tasted terrific and they were happy to have it. Hot Cuban coffee and fishing were two of Hiro's favorite things. Condera had known Pedro very well for many years because he brought him sand from the Rio San Pedro River. Condera stole the sand from the reservoir and sold it on the black market. Pedro used the sand to mix cement for construction. When Hiro and Pedro passed Condera's house on the way there, he had seen Pedro and Hiro and had waved good morning saying he would bring them some coffee because he wanted to chat. Hiro hadn't caught any fish and it was already eight in the morning. Pedro told Hiro that they must leave soon to get to his sister's home on time. Hiro said,

"All right, let's go. I don't know how to wake up the fish. They don't understand my Japanese." Pedro and Condera started laughing so hard that they almost dropped their coffee cups. But even though Hiro didn't have good luck catching any fish, he still enjoyed coming to the reservoir for the serenity. It was a beautiful and peaceful spot like something one would see on a post card.

On the way down to Corralillo there was a magnificent ocean view. There were hundreds of miles of ocean as far as the eye could see. There were palm trees swaying in the breeze and cattle ranches all around. There were many cows grazing in the pastures. It was the country side of Cuba and it was utterly timeless. Hiro admired the view very much. He wished he could have a house on the top of the hill with a window looking out over this gorgeous view. Hiro could see himself living in a home here and even having a Cuban wife one day. Hiro said to Pedro, "What would you think if one day I decided to move here and build a small house on the hill to live in happily ever after? Maybe I could even have a Cuban woman. What do you think about that idea?"

Pedro answered, "I'd love to see you with a Cuban woman. And you'd be a very happy man if you married one because they are the hottest lovers in the world. Did you know this, Hiro?" Hiro didn't say anything and just remained quiet.

Soon they arrived at Corralillo and Hiro could see the vegetable market up on the hill on the left. There was a white apartment house about six stories tall. Pedro's sister, Belgis, lived on the bottom floor in apartment number 2. They knocked on the door and her mother-in-law came out and greeted them. Belgis lived in a small two bedroom government apartment. Pedro told him that an apartment of this size cost about 100 pesos a month, which was about $2.50 US per month. The rent sounded reasonable, but this amount was about a quarter of her husband's salary. Belgis was the younger of Pedro's two sisters. She was twenty-six years old and she was very easy-going and soft-spoken with dark hair and beautiful dark eyes. For Hiro, he always remembered her because the first time they had met at Pedro's house, she had made him a Cuban coconut pie. She was a sweet young lady and Pedro was very close to her. Belgis was dressed nicely and waiting to go. Her mother-in-law was there to take care of the baby until she

The Last Revolution

returned. The baby girl was doing fine and was in good health. Belgis, her husband Georber, Hiro, and Pedro hopped into the Pedro's old Ford and headed to the hospital.

On the way to Sagua la Grande, Belgis didn't feel well and was very weak and pale. She looked quite ill and Georber became worried about her. He was a good husband and always ready to help her. Hiro could see how much Georber cared for her and how painful it was to see Belgis in this shape. They rushed as fast as they could to the hospital. When they arrived about an hour later, Pedro parked in the front of the hospital. Belgis and Georber had a 10:00 appointment. Pedro told them that he and Hiro would return in a couple of hours to check on them. Pedro didn't like hospitals. He chauffeured people there a couple of times a month because besides being a carpenter he also had a taxi license so he could drive people when they needed a ride. However, it was a funny situation because he could not afford to be a taxi driver. Since gasoline cost so much, most people could not afford to hire him. A gallon of gas cost around 360 Cuban pesos and people only made about 400 pesos a month, so gas was outrageously expensive. Because the price was so high he usually lost money being a taxi driver, so he only did this when there was an emergency or when someone really needed his help. Then he took some money in exchange, but usually it was only a fraction of what the gas cost. Pedro was a very kind person and always wanted to help other people.

Pedro told Hiro, "You know—you always have a friend here in Cuba. Never forget it!" Whatever Hiro wanted to do, Pedro was always there to help him. Hiro appreciated Pedro very much and had never had a friendship like theirs before. People always wanted money and money made good friends. Even in Cuba, money talked. Hiro often wondered why this was because Cuba was a Socialist country where everyone was supposed to be equal. Even in the schools they taught the children that money was evil—capitalism was evil. But in Hiro's experience the complete opposite was true. The Cuban people wanted money more than anything. Hiro still had many questions about how Communism worked in Cuba and this Socialist system. Things just didn't add up.

Chapter 20

Hiro joked to Pedro saying, "Here in Cuba, you don't need any money." But today Pedro was very serious and looked around turning his head nearly 180 degrees because he was worried that other people on the street might hear them.

Pedro said to Hiro, "Yeah, you know we don't need any money because we are living in a Communist country. That's right!" His voice got louder and louder. Then finally he said to Hiro, "The theory is correct and it sounds beautiful in the books—like an ideal society, but in reality life is shit! Shit, shit!" Hiro looked shocked. It was the very first time Pedro had mentioned his real feelings about politics to him. Until now Pedro had never mentioned politics. Even the children of the revolution like Pedro had second thoughts about the system and their own opposing opinions. Hiro thought to himself. "How can the people complain over and over about Cuban life and yet not do anything about it? Why not take a collective risk for change?" But Hiro knew the answer to his own question. The Cubans did not try to make their lives better because they were afraid of speaking out due to the severe consequences.

To risk speaking out put them in danger so they became more like pets to Fidel. Whatever he said, they did. Those who had been brave enough to stand up had been imprisoned or executed. Fidel was not kind to political dissidents. Those who had had enough of Fidel and his politics escaped. There was the mentality that if you had guts, then you'd jump into the water and go to Florida and protest from Miami instead of Havana. Hiro knew that going to Florida or escaping was not what they needed and it certainly wasn't going to solve any problems. What they needed was to rise up and overthrow Fidel.

There was a huge cultural difference between the Japanese and the Cubans. The Japanese were willing to lose their freedom and even their lives for a cause while the Cubans were not. They had sold their souls to Fidel in exchange for precious little. They believed they were receiving free things from Fidel and the government, but they had lost their dignity in the process

The Last Revolution

of accepting the system as is. They had become powerless and voiceless. They had become selfish, scared, and didn't want to stand up because of the consequences. They didn't want to harm themselves so instead of helping themselves, they were actually helping Fidel stay in power.

Fidel was very brilliant in the way he controlled the Cuban people. He did this without guns, without soldiers and without physical involvement. But he had a strong grip over the people. Fidel had his own vision for Cuba and he had been able to maintain it through fear. The biggest loser in all of this was the soul of the Cuban people. Fidel gave the people free education, free medical care, free housing, and almost free food and clothing. He even offered free birthday cakes for children less than five years of age. The people started to get into this welfare mentality and, one after another, lost individual will and became complainers. They lost their motivation. Hiro knew that the Japanese would never do this. They would kill themselves before of losing their dignity. With all the free stuff, the less free they became. It was a vicious cycle. When they accepted Fidel's free goodies, they also accepted his reign of power. They then gave up their own personal pride and dignity. This worked well for Fidel. The people were afraid, and so they remained lab rats in Fidel's grand experiment of Communism.

Unfortunately, the people neither understood the whole matter nor did they see their part in it. They did not see that they were the glue holding the whole thing together. They could make changes if gathered together in solidarity, but that was just not the case. They had accepted Fidel's system of rule and Communism blindly. The people even loved Fidel, but they hated him at the same time. That is why this regime had lasted this long. Fidel knew how to manipulate the people and the Communist system with fear, control, and his own designs. He was the master puppeteer leading the show.

Hiro respected Fidel's ideas and philosophy. Fidel was doing his own thing and Hiro admired this. He could understand what it took to see a vision to its end and to succeed. Hiro had lived this all his life and so there was something he could identify with in Fidel Castro. Of course, Hiro did see the negative and did not condone these acts. But nevertheless, it was the dictator's mind and his plan that Hiro was interested in. He knew it had taken a brilliant mind to achieve all of this. Fidel was probably the only dictator in the world who controlled his people without machine guns. There were no signs of weapons or armed guards in sight on this tropical island. He knew Fidel was exceptionally intelligent and his mental capacity was that of a genius to have created this system and see it to fruition. Fidel had out lived eight US presidents and yet he was still a strong and virulent ruler. His Cuban vision had worked well for him.

Hiro respected Fidel's philosophy and he wanted to meet him someday. For example, when Fidel gave a speech he spoke for several hours, even in the scorching hot tropical sun. He continued to speak without the words of professional speech writers. He remained passionate about his vision. He occupied two national TV channels for nearly five hours or longer to have his speech televised. This was probably the longest speech ever presented by a head of government in any part of world.

Hiro remembered Japan's Shoguns. They were the supreme dictators in the 16th century in Japan. The whole country was controlled by many warlords. Among these powerful warlords and dictators were: Oda Nobunaga, Tokugawa Ieyoshi and Toyotomi Hideyoshi. They were three brilliant military philosophers, excellent strategists, and strong men who controlled Japan. Each had their own individual and unique philosophy and theory of tactics.

Hiro remembered an old story from childhood which told what each of the three mighty supreme dictators would do about a songbird that doesn't sing.

Nobunaga said, "If the songbird doesn't sing, then I will kill the bird." Nobunaga controlled Japan only for nine years.

Then, Toyotomi Hideyuki said, "If the songbird doesn't sing, I will make the bird sing." Toyotomi Hideyuki controlled Japan for sixteen years.

Then Tokugawa Ieyoshi said, "If the songbird doesn't sing, I will wait until she sings." And Tokugawa Ieyoshi and his family controlled Japan for almost three centuries."

This was a story that showed a great comparison between each warlord and their different personalities. The last one, Tokugawa controlled after a bitter battle with rebellion that lasted for many years. Finally, he controlled the entire island nation of Japan and united the island with a strong iron fist and absolute power. After he changed the capitol from Kyoto to Tokyo, Tokugawa made a brilliant new system. Each district's

The Last Revolution

warlord must keep some family in Tokyo and visit them and the Shogun castle in Tokyo every year. In those days people had to travel by foot. These district war lords came with an entourage consisting of hundreds of people traveling tremendous distances. It was such an expensive journey for many of these warlords that they used up their resources making the journey, and it made them poor. It was Tokugawa's plan so they wouldn't have resources left to fight or to overthrow him. He also made them remain loyal to this plan with a mandate that if they didn't make the pilgrimage once a year, then he would cut off their heads and kill their entire families.

This brilliant system kept every warlord poor and under his control. This became a great system of survival and no one could go against the central government. It had nothing to do with fairness; it was just a system of survival. This system kept the peace for nearly 300 years until the Americans came to the shores off Yokohama in March of 1854. Until then, Japan remained closed to the rest of the world and entirely self-sufficient.

Commodore Matthew Perry led this entry into Japan by the US. He became the first successful foreigner to open up Japan after its 270 year isolation period. He succeeded due to his diplomatic skills, presentation style, and the gift of a locomotive train.

The timing was perfect for the US, because the Shoguns' power had begun to disintegrate. They became weak due to the long span of dictatorship. They lost the ability to foresee the future, and they were not active in the world economy because they had been isolated for too long. Tokugawa governed Japan with and such a firm hand with absolute power that he abused the system and kept people fearful for their lives. This abuse weakened him over time and with the decreasing economy due to the isolationism of Japan, it was time for change. Finally, Japan decided to open the country and enter into a treaty with the United States

Chapter 21

Hiro didn't understand much about political systems, but he respected Fidel Castro's philosophy. All Hiro knew was that he loved Cuba today and it had been a gift for him to spend time in this island nation. Hiro wasn't sure whether or not the people were abusing the system. To Hiro this was an individual choice. Many Cubans might disagree on whether or not they actually liked the system. Hiro thought that the Japanese descendants who lived under Tokugawa's rule for nearly 300 years might have been in the same position. It was anyone's guess whether or not they loved or hated the system that they lived under. On the other hand, Japan became one of the most beautiful and peaceful cultures ever to exist during Tokugawa's rule.

On this trip to Cuba, Hiro had learned more and more each day, and he was beginning to understand more about Fidel Castro and his dictatorship. As Hiro compared Japan to Cuba, he believed that the Japanese Shoguns were far superior to the dictatorship of Castro. It was because they were never dependent on anyone else. Fidel depended on outsiders for financial support. Hiro saw that there were some similarities between Fidel and the Shoguns.

They both believed in keeping their people financially poor so they didn't have the resources to revolt. Both the Shogun and Castro believed in ruling with an iron fist. They also both admired and supported the arts and education of their people. And, they both wanted peace within the country so both strictly enforced the law.

Fidel had controlled Cuba for less than fifty years. Now there were signs of dissatisfaction. Fidel couldn't support his vision of Cuba without help from the outside because of the huge Cuban welfare system. Castro couldn't support his own weight, especially after the withdrawal of Soviet support in the 1990s. Fidel had always had to look for resources from other countries; therefore the Cuban economy had continued to decline.

The Last Revolution

There were many problems within Cuba including a rising poverty level, growing class and regional inequalities due to lack of economic opportunities for citizens, and inequitable access to public services. Cuba was not set up to be self-sufficient and this would ultimately be the cause of its downfall. Both Japan and Cuba were almost the same size, but Cuban living space and cultivation space was about 100 times greater than Japan's. Japan had only 20 percent usable land good for cultivation because the majority was rocky mountains. This small percentage of arable land was helped by monsoons that provided the necessary rain for growing crops.

Again Hiro into deep flashback thought about Japanese history.

Of all the Japanese minds, the Shoguns were the saviors. They kept Japan from falling into the hands of European colonists. Because of the Shoguns and their vision, Tokugawa definitely prevented Japan's colonization under Christianity. The Europeans used religion as a weapon to try and gain control over Japan. Tokugawa was wise and could foresee what the Europeans had in mind for Japan's future. Tokugawa was a shrewd strategist and very intelligent and was always ten steps ahead of the Europeans.

The Europeans tried to place their feet on the shores of the southern island Nagasaki called *de-gima*. At that time Japan had a sluggish economy due to a one hundred year civil war, was vulnerable, and already occupied by Christianity. The Spanish and Portuguese used religion to put the fear of God into people. In a short time, they took control of Japan using psychological warfare in the name of religion.

When Tokugawa became Shogun, he already knew their ambitions. He was a brilliant man and had long suspected that the Spanish planned to usurp the Japanese people and culture for their own profit and for gold.

The Spanish had no other ambitions for this island nation. In fact, they came to Japan looking for gold because of what Marco Polo had written in his diaries of 1272. The travels of Marco Polo told about an island off the coast of China which he described as the "forbidden island nation Cipangu, or Jipangu" that was covered with a pagodas made of gold. Marco Polo never made it to Japan because of problems with a Mongol assault in 1274.

Micheal Kazuhiro Nishitani

The Mongol Kublai Khan's Grand son first attempt to invade Japan involved 23,000 and troops and 900 ships, most of which were destroyed by a typhoon. Again, in the summer of 1281, Kublai Khan attempted to invade Japan with 4000 ships. The Mongols reached northern Kyushu Island and again a typhoon destroyed half the force. Ever since that event, the Japanese have called a typhoon Kamikaze-God-wind-Japan's protector from outside invaders.

In 1633, Tokugawa decided to close Japan's doors to all foreigners. He had to act fiercely and quickly and killed all the Christians and their priests who were occupying Japan. He left no stone unturned and even destroyed all the churches. He believed in the total annihilation of Christians in his country. He closed Japanese society to the outside world.

This was called sakoku. Even those Japanese who lived outside the country could not return, and no one could exit. If a person left Japan, then that person's family and his entire village were executed. Tokugawa family ruled Japan with absolute power for nearly 270 years. Good or bad, he saved Japanese dignity from crumbling at the hands of foreigners. But saving dignity wasn't easy, and everyone had to pay a price. There was no denying that Tokugawa did the right thing in the minds of Japanese people today. Without Tokugawa's ambition, Japan would not have become such a motivated nation. The Japanese people believe to this day that their 270 year sacrifice gained them a better future. Japan had one of the most beautiful and peaceful cultures ever built in this era.

Cubans would never even think of this type of scenario. They wouldn't imagine closing their doors to all foreigners and killing everyone and their families and the whole villages of those who tried to exit Cuba. Hiro thought that there was just no way Cuba could survive for 270 years on its own. He knew it was completely dependent on help from the outside. Besides, the Cuban people liked to complain too much. They would never make it. Castro had to play political games with outside nations to survive, because the world had become much smaller in the last 400 years.

This was a key difference between Shogun Tokugawa and Castro. On the one hand, the Shogun Tokugawa had a stronger vision and never needed outside resources for survival. He cherished the culture and wanted Japan to be self-sufficient.

The Last Revolution

His rule lasted for nearly three centuries. But if Japan hadn't had Tokugawa as its Shogun at that crucial juncture in its history and instead had had something like the Cuban culture, then there would have been a completely different history.

Perhaps the Spanish would have taken control of Japan. Today Hiro's name could have been Jorge, and the whole culture would have been completely different. Tokyo would have had a different name and the entire Japanese culture could as we know it, have been lost forever. There would be no more Buddhism or Shinto religion and no spiritual life with Zen or Bushido. The famous art, music, food, and fine culture of the Edo Period would have been lost. Hiro thought about Japan's flourishing art and culture that had developed during this most unique period. Without Tokugawa, it might have been wiped from existence. The Japanese might have become like the Cuban Taíno-Arawak Indians and become extinct.

Hiro reflected on the distinct personality of the Japanese people. It was born out of this era of isolation. After the country was opened to the rest of the world, it had to catch up. The Japanese placed much attention on advancing to a higher level though higher education, and put great emphasis on high mental capacity and intelligence.

They never to be isolated again. The Japanese understood that their survival depended on exchange with the outside world. Japan had been hibernating for so long that they had to play catch up with the west.

Japan today understood that it needs to build a foundation for future generations and how important it was to look to the future. Hiro knew that what the Japanese did today affected future generations, and that the society worked together for the greater good of the collective whole. Japanese enjoyed believed that without this, they would not have the powerful industrialization and growth that Japan enjoys today. Hiro was no exception to this opinion and was a product of his culture.

Chapter 22

Hiro and Pedro returned

to the hospital around two in the afternoon to check on Pedro's sister, Belgis. She and her husband Georber were sitting in the waiting room. Pedro asked, "Have you been waiting a long time?"

Georber replied, "No, only about fifteen minutes." He explained what the doctor had said to his wife. Belgis just needed to eat certain kinds of food and get more rest. She would be fine as she was just worn out being a new mother. They were all glad that there was nothing seriously wrong. After a brief conversation, the four decided to return to home to Corralillo. When they arrived, Georber's mother had dinner prepared.

When the group reached Corralillo, it had started to rain. It was a tropical thundershower which could sometimes turn violent. The rain could pour down for a couple of hours and then suddenly rain stop become full clear view. Pedro said, "When the thundershower stops, we must go back home. It's getting late." Within thirty minutes the rain subsided, and Pedro and Hiro said goodbye and left for Rancho Veloz. The streets were flooded in some places, so Pedro had to drive very slowly. They passed many dinky houses along the road to Sierra Morena.

Suddenly they heard a loud noise like an explosion. "Shit! Bombs! Mother!" shouted Hiro. Quickly, Pedro slammed on the brakes. The car skidded out of control and plowed into a sugarcane field. A quick check revealed that they were OK, and Pedro climbed out of the car to check on the damage. The rain had begun to pour down again.

The tropical storm continued to pound on the car. It was almost pitch black outside, so Pedro couldn't change the tire. He added, "We'll have to wait inside the car until the storm passes. It may take thirty minutes to an hour."

It was not a good idea to get soaked so Hiro agreed that they would wait inside the car. In the close quarters, they started to talk about how and where to buy a tire in Cuba. Pedro said, "We have to go to a government store and purchase the tire with

The Last Revolution

US dollars. Since they're expensive, most people wait until someone steals some tires to get a better price."

Hiro asked Pedro questions covering a wide range of topics ranging from the weather to carpentry work, from culture to women. The rain continued, the conversation stopped, and the pounding on the hood of the old Ford was loud. It didn't seem as if it would ever end. It was unusual to have such rain in this part of Cuba.

Hiro had plenty of time to think about his reaction to the loud noise. Why did the sound of the blow out cause him to become so upset? When he thought about the tire explosion, his mind raced back to the moment of his childhood when the American B-29 fire bombs hit his city. He thought back to when he was three years old and hiding in the bomb shelter with his family.

But today as a grown man, he was still reliving that instant. He felt embarrassed and thought to himself, "I hear a bang and automatically I think I'm being bombed." Hiro chuckled about his fear. "It's so illogical that it's funny." He laughed at himself. Then he had a revelation. He turned pale, stared wildly through the rain, and gasped out loud. Pedro didn't know what was going on. Hiro was unsure, but it felt as if he had challenged an angry goddess. "I just laughed at my nightmares! I just laughed at my nightmares!" shouted Hiro, both scared and overjoyed.

Normally the rain stopped within an hour, but tonight it had already been over three hours, and it was still raining very hard. The men had become restless waiting. They were tired, and it was late. They were wet, and the temperature dropped. Hiro began to shiver. Pedro noticed Hiro's discomfort and started the engine to try to keep the car warm, but there was no heater. Hiro started to laugh apologetically and said, "You think that engine will make it warm inside?"

Pedro grinned and answered, "Maybe. We will see."

Hiro replied, "You need to stop the engine because gasoline costs too much." Pedro agreed and stopped the engine. They remained quiet for a while longer listening to the hard pounding of the rain on Pedro's Ford. There was no sign of the rain stopping.

Chapter 23

Pedro finally said, "I know somebody who lives about 75 yards up the hill. It may rain all night, so maybe it's a better idea to go there and wait until the storm passes. What do you think?" It was pitch dark outside and they could not see five feet in front of the car.

Hiro answered, "It's so dark. How are we going to find the road?" Then Hiro remembered that he had a flash light in his pouch. It was small but worked well.

Pedro said, "Well, I think it's better than staying in this damp car all night." They mutually decided to take a chance and go up the hill to the home of Pedro's friends.

They used some nylon that Pedro kept in the car as an umbrella. The rain continued to pour down as Hiro and Pedro walked together under the nylon tarp with the mini-flashlight lighting their way up the little road. They still got soaked, because the rain was torrential. The water was like a small flood over the dirt road. Hiro was amazed because it looked like a stream. Once at the top of the hill there were some grass huts with wooden siding. They were typical Cuban country homes, poor and shabby. As they approached, a dog started barking like crazy in the dark, and they heard a man inside yelling at the dog to stop. they could see a door open.

Pedro shouted "Hey! I'm Pedro Gómez Pelayo from Rancho Veloz!" A person was standing in the doorway of the shack.

He yelled "Hurry up! Come on in!" The door opened wide and a skinny man with a mustache greeted them. He was friendly, and it seemed that he knew Pedro. Hiro and Pedro entered the house. There were two kerosene lamps shining inside the room. Hiro saw eight eyes staring at him. He figured that there were four people in the house, but it was so dark that he could see only the whites of their eyes, not their faces.

He heard the friendly voice of a woman saying with a laugh, "Oh boy! What are you men doing out in that rain, Pedrey? You must be soaking wet. Please use the bathroom and

The Last Revolution

change to some dry clothes." She told her oldest daughter to bring them a dry towel and a change of clothes.

Pedro said, "Don't worry. There is no need for the clothes. I think we just need to dry off and then our clothes will dry OK." But the daughter brought clothing for them to change into. The woman insisted that they go to the bathroom and change. Hiro and Pedro used the towel to dry themselves. Then they changed into the assortment of dry clothing. It felt a whole lot better than their soaking wet clothes.

By that time Hiro's eyes had gotten used to the dark. He could see the family and the rooms better. The man's name was Pepe and the woman's name was Isabel, people called her Isa. Isabel was friendly and warm. Hiro had never met anyone who laughed so much. It was welcoming. During their entire conversation, she laughed and was bubbly. Hiro could feel by her personality and body language that she was a happy person. She was large and fat and very kind to them. Even though it was about midnight, she acted happy to see them. Hiro was surprised at the warm reception. Pepe was quiet.

As soon as Hiro's eyes got used to the light from the kerosene lamp, he could see three girls staring at him. Two girls appeared to be about six and eight. A beautiful older daughter was around eighteen years old. They had never seen an Oriental person before. They acted like their mother and giggled at the sight of him. This made Hiro smile and he thought they must be a happy family. Isabel insisted, "Pedrey, you and your friend must sit at the table. I have plenty of soup left over from dinner. I will just warm it up for you two."

By that time, they were both starving and shivering from the damp cold. They were grateful for the hospitality and the warm food. Pepe joined them at the table and offered them Cuban rum. Pedro took a sip and passed the bottle to Hiro. He took a swig and immediately started coughing and coughing. Pedro, Pepe, and everyone in the house looked at Hiro with worried faces because he was coughing so much. This homemade Cuban rum tasted like gasoline to Hiro, and it hurt to swallow. Pedro turned to Hiro saying, "Are you all right?"

Hiro nodded yes, and whispered, "OK, I'm OK. Don't worry." Finally, Hiro stopped coughing. The homemade Cuban rum burned his throat when he swallowed. Homemade rum was typical out in the country because alcohol cost too much to buy.

Hiro thought of this rum as Cuban moonshine, Cubans call homemade rum "chispa de tren (great sound of hissing steam from train)." Everyone shared the alcohol from the communal bottle around.

By now, everyone in the house was laughing at Hiro's reaction to the rum. To them, seeing this Japanese man almost choking on their daddy's homemade brew was funny. The youngest girls started laughing and giggling so much that they couldn't stop. Their mother told the children to be quiet, but they simply could not. Then the oldest daughter tried to intervene and calm the girls down. Hiro smiled and realized that he was the entertainment for this evening.

Hiro looked around and saw that there was little furniture in this country home—only a homemade wooden kitchen table and several wooden benches. There was one homemade rocking chair with a hand-made steel bar which the family offered Hiro. It was hard and uncomfortable and his seat hurt after a little while. Isabel noticed that Hiro was uncomfortable so she brought him a pillow from the bedroom. There was a small black and-white Russian made TV.

Other than these items, there was nothing else in the room. However, there were many children's drawings tacked onto the wall with rusty nails. The drawings were artistic and made the house seem homey. Hiro saw several plastic buckets on the floor collecting water from the leaking roof. This family was very poor, but friendly and inviting. They laughed and giggled like nothing bothered them. It was such a contrast for Hiro to see people who were so poor yet so happy. He was touched by their generosity. They had giving him warm clothes and food when they had so little themselves.

He thought that few people in rich countries would have helped strangers coming out of the rain so late at night. Isabel brought hot Cuban soup called caldoza. It smelled good and had a delicious flavor. There were big chunks of corn, meat, and yucca in the soup which was typical. They used whatever they had. As Hiro and Pedro started to eat, Hiro asked, "What kind of meat is in this soup?" Pedro didn't know and asked Isabel. She said it was mundongo. Pedro explained that they were eating pigs' intestines. Hiro had never eaten any kind of intestines, but it tasted good. Hiro enjoyed his bowl of Cuban country caldoza soup.

The Last Revolution

He ate the noodle soup the Japanese way. The normal and polite way was to pick up the soup bowl with the left hand and bring the bowl close to the mouth. Then with the chopsticks or spoon, he slurped the soup and made the biggest noise when eating from taking in big breaths of air along with the broth and noodles. As he did this, the entire family stopped eating to observe him. They couldn't believe it and were so surprised to witness his strange eating habits. The girls began to laugh hysterically. Their mom had to quiet them. Hiro realized they were laughing at the way he ate and became self-conscious. He realized that they ate their caldoza soup very quietly and kept the bowl on the table. This was one of many cultural differences Hiro would meet along this journey.

Pretty soon Hiro's glasses fogged up. He had to take them off and put them on the table. The kids started laughing and giggling again. It seemed that these kids would laugh at anything Hiro did. He seemed like an alien to them. Isabel continued to talk about the tropical rainstorm. It had been pouring for nearly five hours, which was an unusually long time. Pepe commented that it was wonderful for their vegetable garden because they hadn't had any rain for nearly two weeks. Isabel continued to smile and to joke around. Hiro felt comfortable and at home with this extremely friendly family. He had met a lot of people while visiting Cuba, but none like this family. Pepe was a gentleman and reserved. He smiled through the dark as he sipped his "chispa de tren" moonshine rum.

By the time, everyone got more comfortable and used to each other, Isabel asked Pedro, "Is this gentleman Chinese? Where is he from? I have not seen him around here before"

Pedro answered, "No, he is Japone, and we met in Havana. He is visiting me and is interested in learning carpentry."

Isabel commented, "Japone?" Hiro took over the conversation. Everyone was surprised that he could speak excellent Spanish. He told them that he was from Hiroshima, Japan, and worked at the University there. Isabel asked, "Are you a professor?"

Hiro answered, "Yes, I am a professor of mathematics." They were very surprised because he looked so young.

As soon as he mentioned Hiroshima, the oldest daughter said, "Hiroshima? I know about Hiroshima. I learned about it in school—about how many people were killed by the atomic bomb during the Second World War. I learned about this in my high school and it was so terrible. Also, I saw a film about it in class." She was concerned about his family and asked how they were. Hiro explained to them exactly what had taken place on August 6th, 1945.

Isabel suddenly became silent. She listened to the details of the awful event that had happened to this Oriental gentleman and the people in his hometown. She looked very concerned and became upset. She said, "I don't like Yankee gringos. Look what they did to Japan. Fidel is always telling us that gringos are bad. He has been telling us so for many years. Now I know he is speaking the truth." Isabel was a loyal supporter of the Cuban Social-Communist Party. Her generation had received much more social welfare through Fidel's government than her mother's and grandmother's generations had.

Pepe and Pedro quietly sipped their rum while listening to this conversation. For nearly thirty minutes, Hiro, Isabel, and her oldest daughter, Dania, were in a deep conversation. Then it was time for the two younger children to sleep because they had to go to school early the next morning. She asked her oldest daughter to help her prepare the bed. First they put nylon on the floor and then placed a sponge mattress over the nylon. They made extra beds for Pedro and Hiro. Dania liked the first Oriental man that she had ever met. He was intelligent and interesting; and because he was quiet and reserved, she wanted to know more about him.

Isabel told Pedro, "You two stay the night and then tomorrow morning you can fix the tire. It is too late to fix it tonight, and it's still raining outside."

Pedro said, "No, thank you. We need to go. Don't worry about us. We can make it." Isabel continued to insist that they stay overnight due to the bad weather.

Finally Pedro gave up the argument, looked to Hiro, and said, "Is this OK with you, Hiro?"

Hiro answered, "It's OK with me." They both agreed to stay because it was late. It was now one in the morning and they were both very tired. Pedro and Hiro stretched out on a sponge bed covered with mosquito netting. It was comfortable and the blanket kept them warm, but it smelled like dirt. Hiro started thinking about his old school camp. He also remembered his mountain village near Hiroshima. Their living conditions then

The Last Revolution

were a lot worse than this little house. This home was about five times bigger than that old country home in Japan where Hiro had grown up. This house even had a bathroom and kitchen, and the family members all wore nice tennis shoes.

Hiro remembered that when he was in the fourth grade, the Americans who occupied Japan following the war sent dozens of new tennis shoes to the school. Shoes were divided among each classroom and the teachers devised a lottery to distribute the shoes. Only one out of sixty-six students were in the lottery for the new shoes because they were not free. They cost 200 Yen, which was equal to 75 cents. Hiro was the lucky winner. He couldn't believe it when he was the winner on one glorious spring day. They were black, American tennis shoes. Hiro was crazy with excitement because he had never owed a pair of good quality shoes in his entire life. In the countryside, they always wore flip-flop-type shoes or a type of homemade shoes.

Hiro kept looking at his new shoes and couldn't believe they were all his. He felt so lucky. When Hiro returned home that day wearing his new American shoes, he asked his mother for the fee. But to his disappointment she told Hiro that she didn't have the money to pay for them. He pleaded with her because the shoes were so beautiful and cost 200 Yen. (75 cents) that was her hard day-wage back then. His mother told Hiro that food was more important than shoes. Hiro didn't say anything as he took the new tennis shoes off. He knew that he had to return them the next day. For Hiro, this was a terrible moment. He wished he had never even won the lottery. It was like a bad joke. The next day he took the shoes back to school and explained to his teacher that he couldn't keep them.

The teacher accepted the shoes and chose another winner. The new winner happened to be Hiro's cousin. He was mean and had always competed with Hiro in everything he did. Hiro's heart sank. Hiro didn't like that his cousin Kazuyuki had won his shoes. His cousin made sure that he showed the shoes to Hiro every chance he got over that school year. Hiro's cousin was a smug boy who liked to show off. Every time Hiro saw them, he thought, "Those shoes should have been mine." Hiro never forgot this incident. Hiro continued to remember his sweet old home in Hiroshima. His mind was eight thousand miles away, and it seemed like it was just yesterday when he was a boy and living in that old country home. Within a short time, he heard loud snoring from the four corners of the house. Soon Hiro, too, fell into a deep slumber.

A few hours later, Hiro began to dream. His hands were tied with rope and there was a white hood on his head. There were twelve Cuban officers in a firing squad armed with AK47s standing in front of him. He was about to be executed for overthrowing the government. He had been arrested and was waiting to die. A Cuban lieutenant said, "Ready! And Aim! One! Two! Three! And fire!" With a jolt, Hiro woke up screaming. His entire body was dripping with sweat and he was as white as a ghost. Hiro looked around and realized that he was having a nightmare.

By that time, the whole family and Pedro had awakened and were very concerned about this strange Oriental man. Hiro was surprised and embarrassed when he found everyone standing in his room. Hiro was breathing hard and tried to compose himself in front of the group.

Pedro said, "Hiro, I think you must have had a nightmare, and from the sound of it, it must have been a bad one."

Isabel joined in, "A nightmare? I was so scared. I didn't know what was going on. I wondered what had happened to Hiro."

Pedro asked Hiro, "What were you dreaming about?"

Hiro was still breathing hard and was sweating profusely. Pedro asked Isabel for a cool towel for Hiro's face because he was so sweaty. Hiro finally opened his eyes and managed to answer Pedro. "Oh, my God!" Hiro answered, "I was being executed." His eyes were wide open and his expression was frightening. Hiro had to look around to be sure that he had indeed been dreaming. His nightmare had seemed so real. Then Hiro added, "I was standing in front of a twelve-man firing squad and Fidel's officers were preparing to execute me."

Pedro looked concerned and asked "Fidel? He tried to kill you?"

Hiro said, "Yes, I collaborated against the government and they were about to execute me."

Isabel said "Oh! Yes. You had a nightmare. I understand now. My daughter has terrible nightmares, too. Sometimes she wakes up crying and screaming. I always get scared." Then she started laughing and everyone relaxed and things returned to normal. Her oldest daughter was surprised about what had happened to this strange Oriental man.

Since his arrival in Cuba, Hiro's nightmares had lessened, but occasionally he had one. This was the first since Hiro had come to the countryside. Hiro had hopes that one day his nightmares would disappear altogether, since something about the Cuban way of life made Hiro feel relaxed. He wouldn't think about the future; he instead would learn to live like any other Cuban, thinking only about the moment instead of the future. In this carefree lifestyle he would overcome these nightmares.

Early in the morning, Hiro heard people laughing in the kitchen, and he could smell Cuban coffee brewing. Pedro was talking to Isabel and Pepe. Isabel had been up since five making a country Cuban breakfast before anyone else awakened. Hiro was still sleepy and had trouble opening his eyes, but he had to get up to help Pedro fix the tire on the Ford.

Isabel noticed Hiro. As she remembered Hiro's violent nightmare, she said, "Good morning, Hiro! How are you this morning? Are you still sleepy? Come here, I have hot coffee for you!" She brought him a small Cuban coffee cup. Hiro loved the smell of this special coffee. It tasted incredibly strong and sweet. The coffee had a good punch and was always smooth to the taste. It was the best way to start the morning. There was nothing like this Cuban coffee elsewhere in the world.

Sadly, Aimee in Havana had explained that Cuban coffee production was declining due to lack of funding. The restaurants they visited had introduced Hiro to the various coffee brands and types. There were several brands of special Cuban coffees from which to choose. Hiro loved tasting each of the dark, rich brews. His favorite was Cubita, grown in Trinidad, Sancti-Spiritus, Cuba. It was full-bodied, mountain-grown, and rich in flavor—a very expensive brand. But here in the countryside of Rancho Veloz, black market coffee beans were dark in color and the people liked it better than Cubita.

Black marketers measured out the coffee beans in beer cans. A can full of beans cost eight Cuban pesos or about twenty cents US. Sale of these beans was prohibited to tourists. Therefore, these darker beans were only for Cuban consumption. For coffee lovers, tasting good, strong Cuban coffee is a distinctive experience, consumed cappuccino-style or espresso-style with sugar and milk. Hiro observed most Cubans drinking it without milk but instead with a generous amount of sugar. They drank their coffee like a shot of alcohol, and they loved to drink coffee anytime. Even in the evening, he would see people having a shot of coffee. For him, there was nothing better than the taste of it, and he became addicted immediately.

Pedro was already eating the breakfast that Isabel so graciously had prepared when Hiro awakened. The meal consisted of scrambled eggs, a country sausage called *salchicha,* papaya, and Cuban bread which was crusty and hard on the outside but soft on the inside. The breakfast smelled great and was just what they needed this morning. Hiro joined Pedro and Pepe at the table. After they finished, they cleaned up after themselves and thanked Isabel and Pepe for the warm reception, the clothes, and the great food. It had not been raining for quite some time, but it was still dark outside. It was only 5:45.

About 6:00, as they walked to the car, they saw the sun coming up. On the road they could see many areas that looked washed away. Debris had collected in the washed-out places. Pepe wanted to assist in changing the tire in exchange for a ride about a half mile down the road where an eighteen-wheeler truck came to pick up workers for the sugarcane farms and fields. Hiro and Pedro were grateful for Pepe's help. They changed the tire and dropped Pepe off at his stop. They said good-bye and drove away.

At Rancho Veloz, Madeline was waiting for Pedro and Hiro. As soon as they arrived she said, "I was wondering if you might have stayed at your sister's apartment last night. It was raining so hard that I knew you couldn't drive safely. I heard today that the road was washed out in many places. The news said it was a hard tropical storm. I was worried and hoped you were safe."

Pedro explained what had happened last night in San Rafael outside of Sierra Morena. Madeline was smiling and said, "Oh, good. You stayed at Isa's home. She's such a nice person, and I know she has a heart as big as a mountain." Hiro smiled because he agreed completely with the assessment. Hiro had never met anyone as friendly as Isabel. What a kind woman!

The next morning Pedro and Hiro started their carpentry work. They began making the legs of a table. After a while Madeline called to Pedro and Hiro saying, "Come back to the kitchen. You have a visitor from last night! It is Isabel's oldest

The Last Revolution

daughter, Dania Hernandez." they was happy to see her and thank her for last night's hospitality.

Hiro said, "Thank you so much for everything last night. I really enjoyed being at your home and with your mother and family." Dania replied with a smile, "No need to thank me. You're welcome any time! We all really enjoyed your visit."

Dania smiled at Hiro. She had brought vegetables for him in a nylon rice sack. "These are from my mother. She wants you to have them. She remembered that you said you loved vegetables. These are from our home garden."

Hiro was so surprised that Dania had traveled so far to bring him a gift. He looked down on the kitchen floor and saw two big sacks of vegetables. The sacks contained greens, carrots, cabbages, onions, and radishes. Hiro said, "Did you carry this all by yourself? This is so heavy!" He was surprised because she had walked a long way from her house.

Dania answered, "I had to walk half of the way. Then I was lucky, because one of the sugarcane trucks stopped for me. They drove me just one block from here."

Hiro appreciated this gift, and he saw that Dania had a beautiful smile. He had not noticed until now. Her hair was also beautiful, dark and curly, and she looked different from Japanese women. She had smooth olive skin; and Hiro found her very attractive. Last night he had not really seen how beautiful she was, but now in the light of day as she stood close by, he admired her good looks. Pedro asked, "So, what's up Dania. Where are you going next? You look dressed up."

She said, "You know, I'm going to Cienfuegos because I need to see my uncle. I'm picking up two sacks of toothpaste to sell on the black market."

Chapter 24

For many people when they finished high school, they began selling items on the black market. Government jobs did not pay much, so it was better for Dania to work on the black market. She made about 3200 pesos every two weeks and split it with her aunts. This was good money for any Cuban. It helped her family to survive because they had several mouths to feed.

Dania had been selling things on the black market since finishing high school. She visited her uncle to obtain damaged goods that he could dispose of with legal authority. Dania collected the damaged goods, cleaned, repacked, and resold the items for a profit. She made one hundred times more than Pepe made in a month working in the sugarcane fields. The family depended on her income for survival. Dania was also a friendly and likable person so many people were fond of her and bought goods from her. Even the police liked her. The items that she sold, such as toothpaste, were much cheaper than items sold in a store, and were things that everyone needed. She had built a market for these items and sold everything she collected within a two week period of time. Dania made this trip twice a month and she was quite adept at it. Most of her customers didn't have the money to purchase commercial items, so Dania bartered the goods in exchange for other items her family needed, such as goat meat. Pedro knew Dania very well. Pedro and his family were one of her customers.

She had to take a three-stage bus trip to Sagua la Grande through Santa Clara and onward to Cienfuegos. Traveling to the factory took all day and was time-consuming because of the slow speed of Cuban transportation. Dania had decided to drop off the vegetables while on her way to her uncle's factory.

Madeline had just finished cooking. She invited Dania to join them for lunch and all four of them sat together at the table. They continued their conversation about life in Cienfuegos and their friends and family. Hiro listened and observed.

This was the first time Hiro had heard Dania carry on a conversation. He was fascinated and liked the way she spoke.

The Last Revolution

She was good-natured and had a beautiful smile. Hiro could not stop staring at her. She was an interesting and attractive young woman. Every time he looked at her, he was overcome with emotion. His heart fluttered and he felt giddy with happiness. Dania's presence made him feel warm and energetic. His heart was beating fast. But Hiro tried to remain clam and composed and listen politely while watching her every move. Hiro had never had time for dating or romance in his early years. Later he was so consumed with his work that he repressed any urges and kept his work goals at the forefront of his mind. He had not allowed himself to even think of a social life, because it would have distracted him from his inventions and goals. Instead, he had chosen to pour his heart and soul into his machines and mathematical systems rather than relationships with people. For the first time in his life he felt a deep attraction to a woman. It was wonderful.

Dania's mother, Isabel was a descendant of the Yoruba tribe from the southwest part of Nigeria in Africa. Members of the tribe had been shipped to the Caribbean by Spanish slave traders for hundreds of years until the last slave ship arrived in Cuba in 1866. There were many black Cubans whose ancestry originated from the slaves that had been brought to the islands.

Dania's real father had died when she was only twelve years old. Her mother had later married Pepe who had been a good stepfather to Dania and had raised her as if she were one of his own children. Dania's real father had been white and he had never married her mother. Isabel had been only his mistress. Dania didn't know a whole lot about her father except that he had come to visit them several times a month before he died. Dania's father had worked for the government tobacco industry as a chief district manager for tobacco production in Santa Clara.

He and Isabel had grown up together near Sierra Morena. He had grown up in a white middle class family not friendly to her because she was black and from an inferior family on the social ladder. They had always liked each other, but had remained just friends until many years later. Dania's father was stuck in an unhappy marriage.

Hiro was interested in listening to her family history. They talked and enjoyed lunch together. After lunch, Dania said her good-byes. Hiro shook her hand and said, "I would like to come visit you and your family again sometime."

Dania replied, "We'd like that. Please come by anytime. We'll be waiting."

Hiro's face turned red and Pedro noticed this. Pedro knew from Hiro's body language that he was interested in Dania, but he didn't want to embarrass Hiro so he didn't mention anything.

After Dania left, they went back to work in the woodshop. As Hiro worked silently on his table in the workshop, he thought about Dania and remembered their conversation. He smoothed and polished the table and continued to work quietly. Normally he and Pedro talked or Hiro asked questions about the work, but today they worked in complete silence. Pedro knew that Hiro must have something important on his mind. Pedro thought it might have something to do with Dania's visit, but he didn't want to pry. Pedro just observed his friend's unusual silence.

For Hiro this was the first time he had ever had feelings for a woman. He had liked Aimee in Havana, but it was a friendship, not a real attraction. Aimee was nice looking, interesting and intelligent. But Hiro didn't feel anything for her. There was not the instant chemistry like he was experiencing with Dania. He just couldn't stop thinking about her. He wondered when he would see her again. This was all new to him and he was not sure how to approach the whole situation. All he knew was that he must see her again and soon. Hiro thought about how he had found himself here in Cuba—this place frozen in time. He had rediscovered parts of himself that had been lost. Here he had regained his connection with people and feelings, and it was healing him. The worlds of computer science and mathematics were analytical and exact, and he had been so consumed with his work that he had become a robot. He hadn't developed the emotional part of himself and was more at home with his computers and inventions.

Hiro had been living in such a repressed state that it was like being in a thick steel box. It had become his sanctuary, but also it had kept him from connecting with people. No one was ever able to influence him in this place that he had created for himself. Here he had felt safe and secure for nearly forty-five years dealing only with mathematics and computer science. It was all he had had to think about, other than his nightmares. Hiro was suffering in his sanctuary. Thanks to the suggestion of his doctor in Japan, he had found a door out. Here in Cuba he had found himself. He felt alive, content, and peaceful for the first time in his entire life.

After meeting this beautiful young woman he felt so wonderfully strange. Thoughts of her were invading his sanctuary where he once had felt secure. Now he was beginning to feel afraid. He felt helpless. Thoughts of her almost consumed him.

Suddenly he felt like he must escape to the gray area once again. Hiro started to feel a tremendous threat to the security of his personal sanctuary. His brain was trying to operate as it had previously, using computer and mathematical ways of dealing with the intruder. He thought about defragmenting and adding new software to his emotional development to create new spaces in his brain chambers.

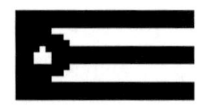

Chapter 25

By the age of eighteen, most people reach an emotional and sexual peak, and eventually marry. However, Hiro, in his early fifty's, had not experienced any of this. His memory stick, which should have stored and defined love for him, was totally empty.

Day by miserable day, he worked to define and understand his strange new feelings. While they germinated in his brain, he isolated himself, trying to learn what to do with his new and foreign emotions, Hiro knew that nature must take its course in this process, but Pedro and Madeline became more and more upset watching him lie in bed staring at the ceiling, or searching the dictionary for definitions that weren't there. Hiro had eaten almost nothing for three days, so Pedro turned to Madeline, who had some idea what was tormenting Hiro. Because she understood, she smiled at Pedro and said, "I think I have just the medicine for Hiro! Come, I want you to take me someplace." They left immediately. Madeline smiled at Pedro, who frowned in confusion on their way to Sierra Morena. She said, "Pedrey, remember when Dania was on the way to Cienfuegos? Remember? Hiro acted strange. I think he's infatuated with her."

Then Pedro's face lit with a slow grin, "Now I understand, but why are we going to her house?" She replied, "Because tonight at eight in the town square there's a fiesta with music and dancing. Just go along with me tonight, Pedro, OK?" Pedro nodded.

As soon as Pedro drove up to Dania's house and parked the car next to the sugarcane field with a view to a hill in the distance, Madeline could see Isabel and the children sitting on the front porch. Isabel jumped up and shouted, "Que pasa?"

Madeline said, "Nothing much. But you and I have to talk." After a round of hugs, Pedro went into the house, talking to Dania, while Isabel and Madeline strolled off to inspect the vegetable garden. The children were ordered to stay with Pedro and Dania. Madeline began, "Look, Isabel, I think Hiro is

The Last Revolution

infatuated with Dania. And I think it's pretty serious because for the last three days he isolated himself and has barely eaten. I think this is the first time Hiro has ever felt this way, and it's real. So we're asking permission for him to see Dania, maybe to date. I know he's older, but, look they're having a fiesta in town tonight, and I would really love for Dania to come to town for the festival and spend some time with him." Laughing happily, Isabel agreed, and they continued to talk about the budding relationship between Hiro and Dania as they inspected the garden.

Isabel felt encouraged that Dania might have a good man in her life. She had been such a good daughter for so long. And Isabel knew that Dania liked Hiro, because ever since she had met him, she had talked about Japanese culture. She found books in the school library on Japanese history. Now Isabel understood and began giggling in the vegetable garden with Madeline. Dania glanced outside and said to Pedro, "Look! What're they doing?"

Pedro just shrugged. "I don't know. Maybe they're crazy." Out in the vegetables, Madeline and Isabel were laughing harder and harder and grabbing each other's arms just to remain standing.

The two women returned to the house, where Dania had made coffee. Its homey odor mixed with the strong fumes from the kerosene stove and the cars parked just outside. Pedro asked, "Where's Pepe's rum?"

Isabel had hidden it in the closet. She said, "If I don't hide his bottle, he'll get drunk and never do his work. The first time my sister introduced me to him, she told me she had to control his drinking because he couldn't. Other than that, he's a good man."

Madeline invited Dania to her house that afternoon after Pedro had gone to get goats from his uncle. "We'll probably get back in an hour or two. There's going to be a big party," said Madeline. "We understand that Hiro really needs company," Madeline suggested, looking at Dania, whose face glowed with excitement and a big smile. Unable to hide her feelings, Dania said, "I really like that man. He's interesting and intelligent. I love that he knows all his country's history. But more than that, he's gentle and quiet." Dania became quiet as her mother became excited. Soon, Pedro and Madeline left to go to his uncle's home on the other side of Corralillo.

"They won't be back for a couple of hours," Isabel added. While Dania was taking a long time under a cold shower, her mother looked for a dress and shoes for her. She was concerned, because Dania really had nothing to wear. Then she quickly scribbled a note on a scrap of paper and sent her second daughter Lillian on a quest to the neighbor's. Julissa was a good friend, and almost identical in size to Dania. She also had more dresses.

By the time Dania emerged from the shower screaming for her mother, panicked that she had nothing to wear, Isabel was prepared. "Look," she smiled as she held up her hands.

"Thank you, Mami." They hugged each other tight and kissed in shared delight. Isa, such a good mother, was almost as excited as Dania. It had been a very long time since Isa had primped like this to go to a party with men, but she hadn't forgotten how it felt.

She said, "I used to be thin and sexy like you. Your Papi and I used to go dancing all the time in Sagua la Grande when we were first dating. It was wonderful—the happiest time of my life." Then they giggled and chatted, playing make-up with Liana and Lillian while Isabel ironed Julissa's dress. It was a nice dress—red flowers on a purple background. There were also some black shoes and a small, neat purse to complete the outfit.

Dania wanted Mami to tie her long frizzy hair in a ponytail so it would look straighter. But Mami said, "No, Dania. Let me take care of your hair. I know what men like." She chuckled to herself as she pushed Dania's hair this way and that. Finally, she nodded to herself in satisfaction as she added setting lotion and twirled locks into fat, sexy ringlets that cascaded down to her shoulders. Dania had never fixed her hair like this before. Mami said, "Men like women's hair long and loose like this." But Dania wasn't happy with the way she looked. Big, silent tears rolled down her cheeks. Isabel gently patted her shoulder, saying, "Dania, you look pretty. Really. You have to wear your hair like this tonight. Please—trust me." She kissed her over and over, her mother's joy building until she was once again giggling.

Dania allowed her mood to be lightened by her mother's, and as time passed, she got more comfortable with her softer, sexier hair-do. Her entire life she had hated her frizzy hair, so she had always pulled it back or up in an effort to tame it. She always thought God had made a mistake with it. She dreamed of straight, shiny hair. Understanding, Mami Isabel said, "People never like what they have. Hiro's hair is straight. I'm certain he likes what he doesn't have, too. That means he will love your curly, frizzy hair. The first time your father and I dated, he told me he loved my hair, and it's just like yours."

The truth of this gently eased Dania's pain, and within an hour she had accepted mother's choice. Isabel laughed once more as she kissed Dania, saying, "My darling, you look so beautiful. I was and just was your age when your father and I met. And look what happened!" Dania had quieted down, but when Pedro returned with the goats, she panicked all over again. "What if he doesn't like my hair?" And over again, Isabel assured her. "Don't worry. Everything will be fine. You'll have a wonderful time. And God will be with you." Then she kissed her. With that, Lillian ran in screaming that someone was coming. Dania's panic hitched up a notch as her mother went outside to check. It was just Pepe returning from work. "What are you two doing? Where are you going?"

Isabel said, "I'm not going anywhere. Madeline and Pedro invited Dania to the town square for the music festival tonight. They want her to spend some time with that Japanese man Hiro. Remember?" Pepe smiled in happiness for his stepdaughter. She'd never dated before. She was always taking care of the family. When they heard the sound of Pedro's car on the road, Lillian and Liana ran to meet him and Madeline.

Dania walked at a more sedate pace down the hill. Catching sight of her for the first time, Pedro gave a low whistle. "You look great!" Dania jumped into the 1956 Ford and off they went to Rancho Veloz. At the house, some family members were cooking yucca and rice with vegetables for the party, but Pedro didn't see Hiro anywhere. He asked his mother Ana, "Where's Hiro?"

She said, "I think he's inside. He was still sleeping the last time I saw him." When Pedro entered, Hiro was still in bed. He said, "Hiro, we're going to have a party with lots of friends and family tonight. It might be better if you changed into some clean pants instead of those ratty shorts for a change."

Hiro asked, "A party?"

Pedro was quick to respond, "Yes, with singers in the town square. We can drink pipa and maybe dance. Want to come?"

Sitting up, Hiro said, "I'd like that." Pedro didn't mention Dania, or that she was at his mother's home. Instead, he just waited as Hiro changed clothes and ran a comb through his hair. Then they took off driving the car to the town square with a five gallon bucket to fill with pipa for the night. Hordes of people roamed the square. One corner held a bread shop outside of which stood a huge refrigerated case filled with pipa, a beer produced in huge quantities by the government and distributed to the villages often on special occasions such as this. Purchased by cup or can, it cost only six pesos Cuban, twelve cents, to fill a five-gallon bucket. Pipa was a great sweet beer that tasted wonderful cold, but if consumed in large quantities, could produce a severe headache the next day. For the Cuban peasant, it was better than nothing. Hiro loved pipa. The first drink was as smooth as Japanese Sapporo beer, with a pleasant sweet taste that lingered on the tongue. But he always drank slowly and moderately, because he knew, from sad and painful personal experience, the possible consequences.

By the time, the old Ford returned with the buckets of pipa, the house was overflowing with friends who spilled onto the patio and even into the yard. Everybody was greeting, joking, and shaking hands when Madeline and Dania came out. Hiro was the first to notice, saying, "I didn't know you were here."

She looked down and blushed a bit. "Yes, so I can talk with you again." She smiled and he gave her a chair, happy to realize that it was only six in the evening.

Meanwhile, Pedro and his brother Jorge killed the goats and were dressing the meat for a Cuban-style barbecue with loads of spices and tomatoes. Pedro loved to barbecue like this. The goats usually sold for around five hundred pesos--$13--from a private farmer, almost one month's wages for a Cuban worker. The financial burdens on the average Cuban were unimaginable from an American or Japanese viewpoint. It was like the government got 99.5 percent from everyone's income. Hiro justified this, as he understood the exchanges made—housing and food at two cents on the dollar, free parks, free medical care, and free education, up to and including graduate school. What he didn't understand was why so few Cubans took advantage of the free higher education available to them. And whenever he posed this question, the answer was always the same: a dismissive shrug and a muttered, "What for?"

The Last Revolution

Hiro brought out another small chair from the workshop since there were not enough for everyone. Many of their friends were standing around drinking pipa and just enjoying the evening. Hiro, too, was enjoying himself more and more—mostly because of Dania. Every time he looked at her, she sent him her biggest smile. And every time they talked, she wanted to know more about Japanese history or to discuss Cuban culture. Sitting out here like this in folding chairs on the patio with Dania in the soft night air, with the sounds of friendly Logavtijo-Lizards and conversation swirling around them their relationship developed Hiro opened up, he softened. He found himself talking to her about Japan, and fishing, about work and farming vegetables and rice. They talked and talked, barely aware of the party around them. They were so eager to get to know more about each other.

Pedro was just finishing his barbecue, and the aromas were tantalizing. He had been laboring for over two hours, starting with a huge steel pot into which he dumped the meat, sugarcane chunks, and his own special blend of spices. This mixture was then cooked over what looked like a campfire, taking all Pedro's attention and skill. But the result was worth the work and the wait: incredibly juicy, tasty meat that separated from the bone effortlessly. Compared to the best American barbecue, it was very different, but every bit as good.

Hiro liked to tease Pedro that he should enter some big American barbecue contest, because he would win. And Pedro would always laugh and say, "If I get the chance, I will. But I'd never come back to Cuba." But they both knew that he would never leave his country, or his warm, large family. Many Cubans stayed for this same reason. They loved their customs and traditions that had come down to them through so many generations, and sensed that if they emigrated, they would lose this great richness. After the fabulous feast of pipa and goat, everybody was mellow. Just to ensure total happiness, though, Pedro's youngest brother Fred brought back another five gallon bucket.

There was a crowd of about thirty friends and neighbors with Hiro at the center, answering questions about the newest industry and technology in Japan, and especially about life in Japan. The serial novel "Oshin" on Cuban national TV, produced by Japanese TV-NHK, had piqued their interest. It was also guided by a general understanding that Japan was second only to the United States as an industrial giant. And they were fascinated by the idea that Cuba and Japan were identically-sized island nations at opposite ends of the earth. Since Hiro spoke excellent Spanish, good conversation about a myriad of stimulating topics abounded throughout the long, pleasant night. Dania was sitting with Madeline, enjoying people's conversations with Hiro. At eight, the sounds of salsa coming from the town square began to drift over to them, as the festival got underway. They were in for a long, loud, happy night, because Cuban people, young and old, loved music and dancing. The music would carry them well into the early morning, bolstered by the abundant rum and pipa.

Isabel and Pepe were arriving just as Lillian and Liana blew in, giggling and talking up a storm. Isabel said, "We just couldn't stand waiting to hear how much fun Dania had with all of you." She laughed her delight. Pepe, always reserved, didn't add anything. Pedro said, "We just finished with the barbecue. There's a little left. Would you like something?"

Madeline agreed. "It's not much, but there's some yucca and a few other things." So they put together some plates of goat, yucca, and other vegetables for the newcomers.

"That's plenty. Thanks. It smells so good." Then they carried the laden plates to the kitchen table where Lillian and Liana began eating with enthusiasm. Dania had to tell them to slow down, and then asked if they wanted water. Isabel said, "After you all left, we sat on the patio for a long time, just chatting and thinking about the fiesta. It's been maybe ten years since Pepe and I have been dancing. So we decided to join you!" She said the last with a huge grin on her face, and the joy she felt spilled over into her voice.

Pedro answered, "Finish eating. Then we'll all walk down to the town square. It's only about three blocks." So the plan was set.

On the north side of the town square, hundreds of people had gathered where a huge stage had been erected. All the streets had been blocked off, and a wild, swinging salsa beat, combined with the effects of the pipa and rum, had folks dancing, laughing, and moving around enthusiastically. Hiro loved to watch the dancers as they swirled and waved happily, hips undulating to the sensuous Latin rhythms. Being with Dania just added to his enjoyment. Soon Dania and her two sisters Lillian and Liana were dancing. Then Madeline's daughter Wendy joined in. They needed lessons from no one; their natural talent just took over automatically as they stepped onto the dance floor.

It was almost a cultural imperative for Cubans to express their strongest feelings outwardly from the heart through the body in the movements of dance. So Isabel and her family urged Hiro to join them, and Lillian gently undertook to teach him. Hiro let himself be led onto the dance floor, where he laughed and shook his best. The family laughed in delight that he had joined them. Hiro had never really danced before, had never developed any feelings he might have exposed through the rhythms, certainly no romantic feelings. But tonight was different. By just watching Dania dancing he felt romantic. He felt sexy.

The salsa music got louder and louder, and as time passed, the townspeople and those from the surrounding villages, old and young, gathered in ever-greater numbers, just enjoying themselves, forgetting every problem they might have. Pedro and Madeline stood there unmoving, just watching. As the dancing grew more frenzied and the noise level increased almost to a scream, they just stood watching. In great contrast to most Cubans, and ever since Hiro had known him, Pedro had always been reserved and on-guard, like a watchdog. His mother told Hiro that he had been this way ever since his uncle Camello was executed in Santa Clara for having organized an anti-Castro campaign in the early 1980's. He was captured by government police and later executed by a firing squad. Pedro was very attached to his uncle, who had taught him all he knew about auto mechanics under the Alamo tree in his backyard. Ever since then, Pedro hated the government police, and was rabidly anti-Castro. He never expressed these emotions aloud, hiding them behind an external reserve. And there were many others who did the same.

The wilder the dancing became—the louder the music screamed—the more Pedro and Madeline longed to return home and relax. In contrast, Isabel and her family were relaxing through the music, which to them was in itself a form of therapy. Even Pepe, normally a quiet man, had been dancing nonstop for over four hours, fueled by frequent sips of rum. The music soothed. The music was life.

Micheal Kazuhiro Nishitani

In Cuba, life seemed simpler, yet, below the surface, the traditional system had been crushed and had become dysfunctional. Even among the elite white Cubans, life was rigid and difficult. Pedro's family was always uneasy, trying not to be politically involved, existing almost exclusively within their tight family unit—a strong support system they felt comfortable with.

Pedro, so sensitive to the ever-present political dangers, hid himself in his comfort zone. Tonight was no exception, but Pedro did enjoy himself, mingling happily with family and friends all evening. Hiro, too, enjoyed himself, especially since in his bliss he had no idea that Pedro suspected his love for Dania. Tonight Hiro had come to the end of a long, lonely road. He had come to what appeared to be an intersection in his suffering and emotional dysfunctions, starting down a new path of love, joy, family, and belonging. It had been a great evening for the people in Rancho Veloz. The rhythm of life, the swirling emotions, and the sheer enjoyment: this was the most wonderful night Hiro could ever remember.

Back home in Hiroshima, they had never had events such as this, with old and young enjoying themselves together well into the night. The old customs, developed through religious practice, dictated that people enjoy themselves in solitude, not in groups. The Oriental way was to hide one's emotional enjoyment from the eyes of others. Always, understanding what was left to be guessed at. Even the Japanese language lacks direct words to express feelings.

At the end of the long, lovely night, Hiro asked Pedro to take Dania and her family to Sierra Morena. But because the distance was too great by foot, and he had drunk so much, Pedro suggested that everyone spend the rest of the night with them. Madeline agreed, immediately making pallets of foam mattresses, one for the men, and the other for the women. Then she got extra T-shirts for everyone to sleep in. Almost before their heads were settled on the pillows, everyone was asleep. What a great evening.

Chapter 26

After the night of the dance in the town square, Hiro and Dania continued their courtship. They liked and respected each other the solid nature of their growing relationship. They were together almost constantly, as he spent most of his time at Isabel's house. It was a time of awakening for both of them. They found the country side interesting and extravagant in its own special way.

The only TV was a small black-and-white, and the only decorations were broken cast-offs from family. Isabel was a big, likeable, talkative woman who loved to cook for and feast with her children. She made this humble house a home.

Isabel was in her mid forties and heavy but healthy, giggling and laughing all the time. She had lived in this house, since she was a baby and except for when she went to Santa Clara on an academic sports scholarship, achieving the highest honors in high school. Dania was also an athletic, especially successful in volleyball. The family in this house was extremely happy. They didn't require much as long as there was plenty to eat. They worked hard for the basic necessities.

Hiro wanted to help the family, so first he purchased a nineteen inch TV from the Pan-American store. Next, he bought a refrigerator. The house was secluded, too, inconvenient both for bringing in goods or visitors. Therefore, the only visitors were neighbors, with whom Isabel was close. Within a few hundred yards, ten families lived almost as one in this secluded, small village. The house had been Isabel's grandfather's, and had passed to her from her mother. It wasn't much really, just a roof to keep out the rain.

Suddenly Hiro had a great inspiration. He talked with Pedro about buying wood and cement for a bit of remodeling: the kitchen was falling apart, because the incredible ants, seeking the cooking grease that had seeped into the very structure, had eaten almost everything, including some of the concrete. In truth, the kitchen needed to be torn down and rebuilt from the ground up.

Pedro suggested that it would probably be best to change the floor to concrete as well, not just in the kitchen, but also in the living room and the two bedrooms. He wanted to add another bedroom, too. Isabel was thrilled beyond imagining. Never had she dreamed of having anything so grand. She told Hiro that anything he wanted to do was fine with her.

Suddenly, this was a big project. Hiro was excited, heading off to scout up the needed materials in Santa Clara. The problem was that there was almost nothing to be bought, except on the black market. Now Hiro would have to deal with the underground free enterprise system, whether he wanted to or not.

Hiro started to sketch and reckon the cost of purchasing construction material. Even during all the excitement of the remodeling project, Dania continued her usual bi-weekly visits to Cienfuegos to visit her uncle Pablo, the younger brother of her deceased father Jorge. Pablo was well-placed in Cuban industry. This time, Hiro went with her, and Pedro and Madeline went along for an impromptu outing. Madeline planned to visit her aunts there, as well as other family. Arriving in town in the 1956 Ford, they went their separate ways. Pedro and Hiro hunted up building materials while Madeline and Dania looked for household goods, barely daring even to glance at the beautiful clothes offered because they couldn't afford such luxuries. But they did love to window shop. Pedro knew many contacts for the building materials, and Hiro couldn't wait to see what they could find. The answer was not much. The selection was very limited, and the white cement he was hoping for was simply impossible to obtain.

When he went to Cienfuegos, Pedro always liked to rent from a friend, a pleasant guest house with a small kitchen, a living room, two bedrooms, and a bathroom. Before, when she had come alone, Dania had always stayed one night with her uncle. But now, with four people in the group, and a planned stay of three days or more, they opted for the rented guest house. Hiro liked the arrangements for the privacy because it gave him good thinking time for his big project. Usually, since Dania made the trip to her uncle's alone, she could manage to carry back only one or two sacks of the broken toothpaste tubes with which she made her living. But with Pedro's car, she could manage four full sacks, which Pablo always saved for her family and for his other sisters living in Corralillo. Whenever she visited her uncle, Dania

The Last Revolution

was all smiles, because Pablo was a kind, gentle man who had taken care of his brother's family ever since he died. He had promised to.

In Cienfuegos, there were many more contacts for building materials than in Rancho Veloz. Even so, Pedro was totally surprised when one of them insisted that he had all the cement needed, and that he would take it to Rancho Veloz, no problem, for 50 percent down and 50 percent upon delivery. And because they had done business together many times before, Pedro told him lunch would be waiting when he got there.

Now, Cuban people never bought anything in such large lots at one time. And Hiro was officially a tourist who was supposed to stay in a tourist hotel and not mingle with the locals. In this remote area, though, no one cared, not even the police, who were friendly, too. Everyone called him Chino. Hiro didn't like this, and always insisted, "No Chino! Japanese!" But no one seemed to learn.

Since days of his visit having passed, Hiro needed to get to the Japanese embassy to receive his money and have some documents from Hiroshima sent to the Department of Foreign Affairs. He asked Pedro to go to Havana with him again to the immigration office to get another visa. This time he was applying to observe Cuban mathematics and science classes at The University of Havana. He thought he had a good chance of getting a one-year visa, with an optional two-year extension.

Pedro agreed to go with him and help set up the necessary meetings. Meanwhile, he contacted Aimee in Havana for information, asking her to contact the professor at The University of Havana. He also visited Freddie at the Santa Clara immigrations office to get some pointers on how to proceed in obtaining the visa. Freddie knew very well Professor Hector Sanchez and his daughter Louisa. At the Department of Foreign Affairs, they discussed the special arrangements given to delegates from other nations.

Freddie told Pedro and Hiro, "Don't worry. I'll call ahead to Havana and tell them you're coming." The two felt relaxed for the tough interview to come. Freddie also gave them lots of detailed advice. He told Hiro that first he needed to have a meeting with the professor at The University of Havana to tell him of his interest and ask the school to sponsor his training for cultural exchange work and to help him obtain a special educational visa. Hector's daughter Luisa, talking with Freddie by phone, was convinced from an educational standpoint that Hiro needed to stay at least one to two years. Since there were many more contacts in Havana who had more influence, they decided to go to the capital city next Monday evening and stay two weeks until everything could be settled.

  Madeline thought it might be a good idea for Dania to go along with them for the company. But Pedro vetoed this, saying they had no idea what might happen. If things went well, they would return home in a week, but if not, they could be away much longer. Madeline and Dania, understanding how tricky and frustrating it was to deal with the government agreed. And they knew Hiro was on the spot: his four-month visa was due to expire in just fifteen days. He had to get that extension. The next day, July 1, 1995, at 8:00 p.m., Pedro and Hiro left once again for Havana in the battered brown 1956 Ford.

Chapter 27

On the way to Havana,

Pedro wanted to visit his cousin in Santa Martha, so he drove through Varadero. At 12:30, he reached the town of Cardenas, where two buses and two passenger cars were parked on the left side of the highway. It was a police checkpoint, and many people were standing around, waiting. Pedro didn't know what to do. Hiro was lying in the back seat, sleeping. Within ten minutes, a man who looked like a farmer approached Pedro, asking for ID. He was an undercover Federal police officer.

They had just gotten a tip that someone on the highway was transporting a large haul of marijuana. He insisted on inspecting the truck and the entire luggage. Once he was satisfied, he asked, "Who's that sleeping in back?"

Pedro replied that he was on his way to his cousin's and that Hiro was a Japanese man he had found hitchhiking just before Cardenas.

"Japanese? I've never seen a Japanese person in my life!" Under the pretext of needing to check Hiro's passport, he made Pedro wake him. "Japanese! Where are you from?" He glanced at Hiro's passport. "Hiroshima? OK. Have a great time in our country." Then he told a shocked and relieved Pedro to go on. As they drove away, Hiro glanced at Pedro and saw that he was covered in sweat. His shorts were soaked.

Pedro explained that he sometimes saw government police, but never in disguise. This was a first for him. "Lucky night for me!" He said, "Between here and Matanzas there's a toll booth. There might be more police. Go back to sleep." Hiro just swore, "Shit." But the toll booth was empty when they got there, so they continued on to the airport, where many foreign visitors landed for a visit to Varadero beach.

At two in the morning, the streets of Matanzas were deserted. And entering Havana had been easy, with no police in sight. Next to the house was a huge gated parking area, which Pedro used. He didn't like parking his car on the street if he could avoid it. If he had to, he slept in the car. Uncle Willie and his wife woke up and greeted them, offering a small bedroom upstairs. After carrying in their belongings, they all went to sleep.

The next morning, Aimee arrived and said how much she'd missed Hiro since he went to Rancho Veloz. She went to the university and talked with Professor Sanchez about having Hiro offer a seminar to the mathematics faculty. When he heard the specifics of the proposed lectures, Sanchez was delighted, saying they had not had any updated instruction in modern mathematical science for over fifteen years. Hiro's help was badly needed.

Dr. Sanchez agreed to talk with the director, suggesting they present him with Hiro's resumes and a syllabus of the material he planned to present. Aimee reminded him of the urgency of the situation because of the imminent expiration of Hiro's documents. She suggested that Hiro's status might fall under the category of cultural exchange, if that could speed the process along. Sanchez understood, suggesting that Aimee meet him at three o'clock that afternoon. He said he would have all the paperwork ready by then. He was polite and understanding.

Aimee told Hiro that he should come to her apartment so they could work on his resume and syllabus. They would probably need several hours, and it was already ten a.m. Pedro drove through Plaza de la Revolution where the huge statue of Jose Martí and Che Guevara adorned the front of the Ministry of Interior. Che Guevara's statue was on the ten story building on the northwest corner of the Plaza. Then they passed the center with its enormous revolutionary memorial monument tower. At Avnida 20 de Mayo, he turned left where he dropped Aimee and Hiro off saying he would return at one o'clock.

Inside the apartment, Hiro sat on the couch and asked Aimee to give him fifteen minutes, then closed his eyes and reclined. In the meantime, Aimee made some of the strong Cuban coffee that Hiro loved and got out her laptop. In precisely fifteen minutes, he sat up and saw the computer. "Where did you get that?"

"From work. It's Government Issue. You know, officially I'm a reporter for the government. But I co-ordinate with the foreign press daily, and I report to the Central Office every week." She was proud to have access to this computer, and to

The Last Revolution

other informational gadgets not available to the general population.

"Aimee, do you have Internet?"

"No! Only the Cuban government internal website Cuba Si. We can only access e-mail, no internet website because the Cuban government doesn't trust Microsoft or any other Gringo's system." Hiro just shook his head. With the aid of the computer and some exceptional typing skills, Aimee and Hiro created a resume and syllabus in record time. Hiro included his Japanese education and career as a professor at The University of Hiroshima, but was careful to exclude his background in computer science at MIT. Because the United States considered Cuba as enemy territory, he never discussed anything about the US with anyone here. He also made certain to use a Japanese passport.

In fact, Hiro hadn't discussed computer science with anyone since he'd arrived in Cuba, because computer technology was such a sensitive area of Cuban intelligence. Plus, he didn't want to confuse people with the details of his specialty. No one in the entire country could probably understand it anyway; they'd just misinterpret what he said and create problems. It would be better, he decided, to offer the mathematics lectures he was planning.

At one, Pedro knocked on the door. Aimee let him in and showed him the resume and outline she and Hiro had prepared. Pedro was stunned. He said, "I had no idea Hiro was this smart. This stuff is way over my head. Why he'd bother with me, I can't imagine. I'm just a carpenter."

But Hiro just laughed, "This is just a bunch of bull. It may look intelligent, but it's nothing."

Pedro asked, "Does the Cuban government buy this stuff?"

Aimee answered him: "Yes. It looks very official. These are just the kinds of documents the immigration office and the university need." At precisely 3:00 p.m, Dr. Hector Sanchez was waiting in his office with the long-time director of the university, Jorge González. About sixty years old, Gonzalez had come here from his previous post at The University of Santiago de Cuba, east of Havana.

When Aimee and Hiro arrived, everyone shook hands and Aimee explained her presence as interpreter. González started by saying that the university had been looking for someone who could give seminars to the faculty for some time, adding that this was a great opportunity for the school. He gestured toward the already-completed documents Hiro would need for immigration, and said he would like Hiro to begin as soon as possible. In truth, both Sanchez and González were extremely pleased to accept this tremendous offer. At the conclusion of the meeting, Hiro invited everyone to dinner at the Hotel Inglaterra, probably the best restaurant in the entire city.

Because he had once lived in Havana for over a month, Hiro felt at home. He knew that the hotel was in wonderful condition, other than that its generator made lots of noise. Sitting between Paseo de Martí and Agramonte, it still drew many foreign businessmen on extended stays. The *mojitos* served street-side were probably the best in town, and the food was excellent, especially the seafood. Not liking the generator noise, Aimee urged him to change to the Seville on the other side of the central park. She reminded him that many members of the press stayed there, as she did when on government business. She liked to swim in the pool there, too, which the public could use for a small fee. Aimee insisted that they go to the ninth floor rooftop restaurant of the Seville, the Roof Garden, where the night view was magnificent. Everyone finally agreed.

When the congenial meeting ended, it was five. After the university visit, Aimee wanted to go back to her apartment to rest for a while before going out that night. Pedro and Hiro returned to Uncle Willie's. As soon as he opened the door, he started firing questions at them: "Did everything go OK? What happened? Did you get the papers?"

Pedro told him how well the meeting went. Willie said, "I thought things would work out. The university always needs good people."

At seven, Pedro returned to pick up Aimee, and then drove on to the hotel, where he pulled in to the ground level parking lot and received a parking ticket. He looked around carefully for a safe place to leave his car. He noticed that in the hotel lot, most of the cars were late model Korean and Japanese imports. There were almost no other 50's models like his. The security guard had a funny look on his face, like maybe average Cubans didn't park here. Aimee explained that they were meeting the director of the university for dinner. Finally satisfied, the guard allowed them to pass. Pedro parked close to the guardhouse as Hiro observed grim-faced. Pedro was always cautious about his car. The security guard continued to watch them carefully, since this hotel was for foreign visitors, not Cuban citizens. Every time he saw the guard watching them, Pedro swore, "Shit!"

As soon as they entered the lobby, Aimee checked at the front counter to see if their guests from The University of Havana had arrived yet. The smiling desk clerk told her they were already on the rooftop. As Aimee, Pedro and Hiro waited at the elevator, they looked around at the bright, open lobby. It was such a contrast to the Hotel Inglaterra, which was built in the early 1900's. This was a first visit for both men. Pedro looked all around cautiously, unsmiling. Aimee always laughed at his watchdog mode. But she knew that before his uncle was executed by the government, he hadn't been like this at all.

Dining on the rooftop was pleasant. Cuban cuisine was a fusion of Spanish, African, and Caribbean cuisines. The soft sea breeze whispered past them as they entered, and to the north one could see the incredible Caribbean vista up to the beachfront at Malecón, almost through the entire city of Havana. The sun still shone, highlighting the huge white gazebo that served as a bar in the middle of the rooftop. That was where Dr. Sanchez, his daughter Louisa and Dr. González sat waiting. They both rose to greet the newcomers. Then everyone moved to a grouping of patio chairs.

The waiter took Pedro and Hiro's order for Hatuey, their favorite Cuban beer. Aimee asked for red wine. While they waited for the waiter to return, Jorge turned to Hiro and started asking him more questions about The University of Hiroshima. Hiro gave him a history of the school from the past to the present, explaining the courses he taught there and their main focus. Hector asked about the new mathematics, and Hiro responded with details about the Mathematical physics, and concept of Computational complexity theory experiments that constituted from his own calculations of an algebraic.

Aimee and Pedro sat there listening quietly, pretty much dumbfounded. The level of conversation was way over their heads, so they turned to one another and chatted generally as the other men remained immersed in their science. After about thirty minutes, the waiter returned them to their dinner table. Louisa told Jorge that she had already talked with the head of immigration and Freddie Diaz at the Santa Clara immigrations office. Freddie had phoned her just before she left this evening. According to what he said, Hiro shouldn't have any problems since the director of the university signed all documents for faculty for continuing education. Hiro and Aimee were delighted to hear this news. Jorge and Hector shook hands over the success of the new project.

Everyone was thrilled; they sat around until one in the morning sharing more *Hatuey* and wine, smug and pleased with themselves for finding a way to best the immigration regulations. Aimee assured Hiro that the visa process would go smoothly, telling him of his special appointment at two the next day. She told him how lucky he was to have so many important connections in Havana to help him. His reply was that he was lucky to have met so many nice people, and that the longer he was in Cuba, the more he loved it. She nodded her complete understanding. Because he was always relaxed here and slept so well, Hiro had almost no nightmares or flashbacks anymore. In fact, in the last few months, he hadn't had any. He learned to think only of today, and never to worry about tomorrow. His life had changed 180 degrees.

When he awoke and went downstairs the next morning, Hiro heard Pedro talking with his relatives, catching up on family news. Particularly because Cubans always enjoyed a good, long conversation, Cuba's bad telephone service from ETESCA, made it difficult to communicate around the island. In Havana it wasn't so bad because a Canadian company had rebuilt the system in 1995, but rural service was another matter with poor connections that often made it difficult to hear. Worse than that, people worried that the government listened in on their conversations. That was why they never discussed politics over the phone. And that was why it was so important to exchange family news face to face. Hiro asked when Pedro wanted to leave, and he told him they could leave in about forty-five minutes to get Aimee. She was taking several days off, supposedly to help with Hiro's visa. But she had another motive: she was getting more and more interested in him, and wanted to spend more time with him.

It was 2:00 p.m., and they were in the now-familiar immigrations office. Aimee and Hiro asked which department they needed, and the receptionist told them to wait a few minutes

The Last Revolution

to be called. Finally, after about fifty minutes of waiting, they were directed to Room 6. Louisa was supposed to conduct the interview but had been detained elsewhere. In her place, ten minutes later, a woman with the biggest hips Hiro had ever seen entered to take her place. She told Hiro that Louisa was going to meet them as soon as she could get free, and meanwhile she had told Hiro to sign four documents, which he did. She said, "Congratulations. You are now the proud owner of a three-year cultural exchange visa. And don't worry you don't have to stay the whole time. You can come and go, as you like. But when you stay longer than twelve months you must register your residence. In this case, that's Santa Clara, right?"

Hiro smiled, "Yes, Rancho Veloz."

"That's it for today," she explained. "Your passport has been stamped." Hiro was thinking how simple and quick the entire process had been—just one day, thanks to Freddie and Dr. Sanchez.

All this time Pedro was waiting close-by on the street, anxiously checking his view of the city, where he was always uneasy. When Hiro and Aimee came out, he waited till they got to the car to speak. He said, "That was fast. I wasn't expecting you so soon. What happened?" Hiro held out his passport with the visa stamp. "Did it cost a lot?" Pedro asked.

Hiro admitted, "Yes, but I can stay in Cuba three years, and anytime I want I can leave and return. No problems. Now you don't have to worry when we see the police."

"That's great!" Pedro responded. He gave a relieved high-five to Hiro, then Aimee. Pedro said, "You know, Hiro, you're a very lucky man."

"Thanks to you and Aimee. Without you, I probably never would have gotten this visa," said Hiro.

After a quick group hug, Pedro said, "I have to get back to the house to take care of some family stuff. We invited Aimee and her family tonight for a celebration feast. I'll call my uncle and go to the farmers' market to buy some pork."

Aimee chimed in, "Let's go right now and get us a nice fat pig."

They hopped into the brown 56 Ford to go to the market closest to the house. There were markets all around Havana, as part of a free enterprise system supplying fresh meat and produce for the locals. They were bustling and exciting, but also expensive, especially for Cubans. Hiro insisted on paying the tab, but Pedro said he would. Hiro clinched the argument by saying he had the money and that he wanted to do something nice for his family because they had helped him so much. Finally, Pedro and Aimee agreed.

At the Agro market, Aimee bought lots of good fresh vegetables including squash and broccoli, round onions and green onions, cucumbers and string beans, and a rainbow of fruit: mangoes and papayas, bananas and pineapples. She had to buy three empty rice bags just to carry it all. Pedro found a guy who had a whole fresh pig he would sell for 3000 pesos (US $120). Pedro countered for 2500 pesos (US $ 65), and off they went, arguing back and forth on the price. Pedro loved this! He always said that being Cuban, this kind of haggling was in his blood.

In Japan, Hiro knew, this kind of price negotiation was impossible. People would think you were crazy. In Cuba, you'd be crazy not to haggle. At the home of Pedro's Uncle Willie, conversations were swirling among the relatives already gathered, and when Hiro and Pedro arrived, several of them jumped up to help carry in the one hundred fifty pound pig. Willie started the fire in the pit while Pedro got out the garlic and other spices they needed.

Aimee decided to go home, take a shower, relax for a while, and return later. She knew it would take Pedro and Willie at least four hours to fix the food, which it did. The whole time it was cooking, the neighbors were sniffing hungrily and wishing the feast was theirs. That's why Willie watched the grill with an eagle eye: sometimes people stole the meat and ran with it. Stealing was easy in Cuba. By 7:30, the house was jam-packed with more than thirty people. Everyone had brought food and drink. Willie's wife, Eduvijes, set up space in the kitchen to serve it all. Most of the rum and wine was homemade.

Pedro's mother Anna had a large extended family scattered all over Havana, but his closest relations lived mainly in central Cuba. Everyone in Pedro's family was friendly, homey, and thoughtful. Hiro always enjoyed them, because they treated him as one of their own. Aimee brought her father and her daughter to the impromptu reunion to see distant relatives from Pinar del Rio, some of whom she'd never met before. Aimee brought a special Cuban apple pie that she had made after shopping at the Agro market. As she made room for the huge pie

The Last Revolution

on the overflowing table, she said, "I'm not much of a cook, but I know this is good because it's my mother's recipe." Her father just looked on and beamed and nodded his approval. Time progressed and the gathering, as usually happens on these freewheeling and friendly occasions, broke into small groups scattered all around the house and grounds. Hiro was with Uncle Willie, who was talking non-stop about being a lieutenant in the Cuban army when Fidel sent troops into Angola to help the Communists.

Hiro was fascinated by his experiences. Soviets and Cubans shared the primary objective. Castro assisted pro-Soviet forces by sending troops to Angola, Ethiopia, and Mozambique in the 70s and 80s to support Marxist guerrillas. Angola was a major battleground in the cold war between the United States and the Soviet Union. The US backed the United Nations' troops which fought until 2002 with military advisors and weapons while the Soviet Union provided the same support for the Angolan army. Augustino Neto had become Angola's president upon its declaration of independence from Portugal on November 11, 1975.

The first Cuban military contingent was sent to Angola at the request of Neto, leader of the leftist rebel group called the Popular Movement for the Liberation of Angola (MPLA). Castro sent his first 5000 Cuban troops to Angola on November 4, 1975. They were tasked to protect the capital city of Luanda. The arrival of Cuban troops was considered decisive in preventing Luanda, the Angolan capital, from falling into the hands of the UNIT guerillas backed by the South African government and financed by the US. Between 1975 and 1988, some 350,000 Cubans took part in the Civil War in the South African nation. This was the last time Cuba's military forces were involved in an armed conflict.

The aftermath left emotional and psychological scarring, and post-traumatic stress syndrome among the troops. The guerillas fighting the Cuban army were no match for them because, although the guerillas (UNIT) had highly modernized weapons supplied by the United States, they were ill' trained. Furthermore, it was difficult for the guerillas to advance to the interior because the generals did not support them. The goal that everyone was fighting for was independence from the colonialist Portuguese.

In reality, the war in Angola was a heated conflict between the United States and the Soviet Union in their Cold War. The United States supported the UNIT troops, while the Soviet Union supported the Angolan army. As a lieutenant commander in the third infantry, Willie Muro served six years in Angola. He explained that his units were supposed to serve as trained observers. He observed that the war was a stupid one with the blood of young, innocent Cubans fertilizing the soil of Angola. His regiments were trainers from the Santa Clara Army base, where every unit had specific assignments. His unit was assigned to observe the fighting tactics of the rebel army and to assist the Angolan army

The United States and the Soviet Union were very interested in ending the conflict without involving Cuba because of the potential for an explosion of international involvement. To avoid the conflagration, untold millions of dollars exchanged hands, never to be totally accounted for. Its hot, dry sands had absorbed Namibia by the time Cuba was able to withdraw its troops fully from Angola in 1997.

So many young lives lost for no reason. Every time Willie thought about the war in Namibia, he thought what a mistake it was and what a waste for Cuba to have been involved. Cuba had been the underdog and had been given absolutely no credit in the worldview. Instead, it was dismissed out of hand in the welter of US politics. "The guerillas were backed by South African troops in the capital city of Luanda," Willie said as tears came to his eyes. He went on: "In intense fighting over three weeks, we lost sixty-seven, out of one hundred twenty of our boys, one third of them. They were all bright, young boys." Willie always wondered how much money passed between the US and the Soviet Union, but no one would ever know for sure.

Willie continued his nightmarish account into the wee hours of the night, often with tears in his eyes. Hiro and Pedro sat silently, unmoving on the concrete steps, listening to the incredible story of how the human brain and body dealt with the harshness that was Angola at war. Willie repeated his litany of loss: "So many young Cuban men gone, just disintegrated in the dust. No purpose. They just disappeared." He recounted the story of a young soldier from Havana who found a baby monkey only six inches high. It was sitting in mud on its dead mother's body. The soldier rescued it, keeping it in his pocket, nurturing it and training it always to stay in his front pocket all through the war. When the Cuban troops were withdrawn and ordered home, the soldier requested to take the monkey home with him, but was ordered to leave it behind. Somehow, that soldier and his pet monkey had come to symbolize to Uncle Willie everything wrong with the war: the senseless death, the barbarism, the uselessness.

As Uncle Willie talked on, it became clear that he was voicing the same thoughts shared and understood by most Cubans: the deep, destructive emotions generated by this war that affected them all. These emotions mirrored almost exactly the criticism Americans expressed about their involvement in Vietnam. It was successful for Fidel's strategy of spreading Communism in poor African nations, and that achievement was recognized as good moral intervention in the Cold War era. Cuba was not exactly considered a puppet of the Soviet Union.

After the long emotional night, Hiro and Pedro slept until almost ten. Hiro had been fascinated by the complex account of Cuban politics and war in Africa, and was still ruminating about all he had learned when Pedro derailed the train of his thoughts: "Today we'll go find some of the stuff we need for the house project—some hardware for the doors and cabinets. I'll be ready to leave around noon. We'll go to the industrial section of town. Willie gave me the names of some black market friends who can help us." They spent the rest of the day rounding up all the supplies they could find to take back with them.

Later that afternoon, Aimee stopped by after work and stayed for dinner. Pedro ran out for *Hatuey* and wine and everyone decided to stay in at Willie's and just hang out. Pedro asked Willie for a tape player and they put on some new salsa tapes Pedro had bought. Despite its being so foreign to a Japanese ear—or maybe because of that—Hiro loved salsa. It made him happy, it made him forget everything.

For Hiro, it was the ultimate relaxation to be there with his friends, listening to this new Cuban music. Everyone relaxed. Pedro and Aimee danced and urged Hiro to join them, but he just smiled his pleasure, watching and remembering another night of dancing in the town square with Dania and her family. The music was different then, but the feeling of pleasure was the same. This was the first time he had ever seen Pedro dance because normally he was reserved in front of others. He loved to dance, but usually felt reluctant to. But here, among friends, he could dance with his cousin and free his emotions.

They had only danced for a short time, though, when Pedro decided to go down stairs and talk to Willie. Aimee and Hiro stayed put, drinking some more and listening to the compelling music. Aimee started feeling more than relaxed—she started feeling amorous. Hiro, though, was oblivious. He was just chatting, drinking, and enjoying her company, when suddenly she began to touch him and kiss him. He didn't stop her. Aimee whispered how much she liked Hiro, how much she loved him. He just listened, reaching for his Hatuey, and sipping as she talked on. The more she talked, the quieter he got. He popped another *Hatuey* and took in slow deep draughts as Aimee touched his hair, his face.

She whispered, "Hiro, I love you so much, and I missed you. Don't you have anything to say to me? That you love me? You missed me, too? Can't you tell me?"

She kissed his neck, his jaw, her feelings overflowing. Hiro stayed emotionless and still. But Aimee didn't seem to notice. She kept murmuring, "Hiro. I love you so much. You smell so good. Your skin is so soft." She feathered him with dozens of tiny kisses, stroked his shoulders and his arms. Her hands wandered farther, but her mind remained fixed. "Say something!"

"Aimee, Listen! Do you want some more wine? We need to talk," Hiro said. He stood up, wandered toward the window and gazed out. Aimee just followed, and grasped his hand, saying, "Please, darling, come and sit with me."

But Hiro remained where he was, and she sat back down on the couch and slowly sipped her wine, her face suffused with the gentle look of the deep love that was just now beginning to unfold. From where he stood, Hiro began, "Please listen. I'm going to tell you some very important things tonight. I'm speaking with total honesty, and I need you to understand what I say." Aimee nodded, smiling. "Aimee, I met a girl in the country, and I'm just now beginning to realize that I have special feelings for her. I never felt this way before. You remember. I told you a long time ago that I never had any real feelings for people. But now! Now I can understand what other people were telling me." He paused, repeated almost to himself, "I never felt this way before."

Aimee's face grew serious, almost as still as Hiro's had been. "Girl? What girl?" she asked. Hiro started to answer then stopped. How could he explain to her what he didn't understand himself? Aimee asked again, "What girl, Hiro?"

He began again, "Look, I love you as my special friend, and nothing can change that. But I think I may really love this girl I met. I don't know what love is, but I know it's a very serious matter to me. I need to find out what this is between us,"

Aimee looked at Hiro, saying nothing. She digested what he said, serious and curious at the same time, because never had she heard Hiro so much as mention his feelings. That he did so now showed her the importance of the little he said. She was caught off guard, but beyond the pangs of hurt she felt for a love lost before it was ever truly found, she also felt happiness for this quiet man she had grown to love. She was gracious and humble.

Now she smiled for another reason. "Tell me about her." Hiro talked and talked, explaining how he met Dania. He talked about dancing in the town square in Rancho Veloz. He talked about Dania's family and about their life in the country. Aimee just listened, her face impassive, all her attention on what he had to say, and how he said it. When he finally finished, Aimee quietly hugged him as she confessed, "Hiro, I'm so jealous. But I'm very happy for you. I think maybe you've found the perfect woman for you. I wondered why you were gone so long. I was worried." Then she began a barrage of questions: How old was Dania? What did she look like? What did she do?

They were sitting on the couch again, sipping more wine and filling in the details when they heard a sound on the stairs. It was Pedro, and he wanted to know what they were up to. "Am I interrupting anything?" he asked.

"No. Hiro was just telling me that he has a girlfriend and I'm jealous," she smiled. "What do you think about our Hiro?"

Pedro joked, "You know! I didn't do anything when I saw it happening because I was happy for him. I don't see how a man can live without a woman. So I'm grateful Hiro found someone. Hey, she is Murata...a hot lover. Only now he'll probably just be a big beraco!" They both laughed. Beraco was Cuban slang for a full-grown male hog that looks to mate every minute that it's not eating. When Cubans joke, they describe their friends in these crude but loving animal terms.

Micheal Kazuhiro Nishitani

Although Aimee was sorry Hiro wasn't in love with her, she was glad he was in love. She knew how hard it was for him to feel anything at all, and how much harder it was for him to express what he did feel. Normally, he hid everything deep inside, rendering him quiet and serious. She recalled going with him to a disco in Havana, and how shy he'd been barely talking to anyone. But he'd observed, and locked his observations deep inside the dark vault of his heart. Hiro leaned over and impulsively kissed Aimee's cheek. "Seriously, I don't even know what to think about me! I'll be better soon," Hiro sighed.

Pedro just looked funny asking, "Aimee, you don't love him, too?"

She confessed, "Yes, but I'll get over it. I'm just happy he's found Dania and real love." Pedro joked with her about being one step too late. Somebody was just quicker than she was. "I'm sorry. I know how much you care about him," whispered Pedro. Then he hugged her.

After that eventful night, Hiro and Pedro spent another four days in Havana, collecting all the carpenter's supplies they could get their hands on. The section of Havana they canvassed was filled with architecture dating back to the shell out seventeenth and nineteenth centuries, with large areas preserved much as they had been in those days. For nearly fifty years since Fidel's rise to power, development had come almost to a standstill. Yes, he had cleaned out the corruption of the old regime and restructured social programs, not entirely copying the pattern established by the Russian Communists. But when he took over, almost 90 percent of the Cuban brain trust was exiled, so he reorganized the education system and set in motion a plan to educate as many medical personnel as possible in a ten year period.

Almost overnight, the Cuban population became one of the best educated in Latin America. Yet, Castro still had to feed them and find a way to keep them satisfied—no small undertaking for a single politician. And all that had to be conducted under the shadow of the superpower next door. He had survived against these incredible odds for nearly forty-five years. Hiro had always admired Castro for his great ambition and his achievements with the Cuban people. It seemed he thrived on crisis; the more difficult the problems, the better he came out. The more problems he had, the more he flourished, the stronger

The Last Revolution

his position became. Because he could be overthrown at any moment by brilliant army generals conspiring against him, he always had to be ten steps ahead. And because he always seemed to be embroiled in one international crisis or another, he had to be a brilliant player in that arena as well. On every occasion, he beat the odds and survived, even thrived.

Then Hiro into deep flashback mode went thinking about Castro this way led Hiro's thoughts to another brilliant politician, the ultimate warlord, Tokugawa Ieyoshi. In the seventeenth century, he didn't play international politics. He simply demolished an entire population of Christian faithful as invaders. He was brutal, like Castro, but his brilliance ensured the survival of Japan for the next four hundred years. Tokugawa's scheme was to keep every opposing daimiyo, or warlord, financially weak. He did this, in effect, by holding each warlord's family hostage in Tokyo.

Furthermore, he decreed that each daimiyo must then visit his family there once a year or forfeit his life. This sound simple, but was in truth a diabolically clever plan, because no warlord could or would ever travel alone or even in a small party. He had hundreds of followers—warriors, bodyguards, cooks, house staff and the like—who all had to travel with him, at enormous personal expense to the daimiyo. Every year these enormous entourages swarmed toward Tokyo to save their lives and their positions like so many bees returning to protect their hive. The Shogun's plan was elegant and deceptively simple.

By executing it to perfection, he was able to rule all of Japan without a single mistake during his entire reign. He didn't need to worry about international crises; he simply discarded surgical removal any potential threat from Japanese soil. He was the ultimate player and the ultimate ruler.

Chapter 28

When he returned to Rancho Veloz, Hiro's first order of business was to get Pedro to hire some government workers to bring in a backhoe to convert the old unmanageable dirt road to a gravel one so the building materials could be driven up to the door instead of being carried laboriously up a hundred yard incline. Within six months, they were pours the concrete floor and had set the exterior concrete blocks. They installed windows where mosquito net had once sufficed. Through all the work, Hiro sported one of the local guano grass hats he loved. It protected him from the scorching sun and cooled him in the absence of air-conditioning as it had for the Taino-Arawak Indians many centuries before.

He and Pedro remodeled all the kitchen cabinets to be Cuban mahogany aided by Dania's cousin Pipo, her mother's sister's first son.

Pipo was thirty-one year's old. He worked at a government-owned dairy farm, where for only three hundred pesos (about $9) a month, he was responsible for the health and welfare of all the cows. Pipo was very tall and skinny, with size-15 feet which were the butt of many good-natured jibes. All his life it had been close to impossible for him to find shoes that fit, and as a result he was obsessed about taking care of them. At home, he always went barefoot inside, putting on the shoes only when he went out. He was a great help to Hiro and the entire family always pitching in with whatever jobs needed doing.

Hiro was enjoying the house project. As he worked, he used much of the existing structure, with the exception of the bathroom. He built an extension right next to the bedroom and set an extra big pipe for the sewer system and for a real Japanese hot bath with solar power. It wasn't easy to find all the materials he needed for that part of the revamp, but Pedro scrounged enough to create a series of small thin water tanks on a concrete platform.

He also built a new twenty-five foot by twenty foot bedroom for his privacy. His and Dania's—he hoped. He laughed in quiet delight thinking, "I'm going to turn into the biggest beraco ever." It had taken him and the others only about six months to do what it would have taken other Cubans ten years to accomplish—remodeling an entire house. But, financially secure because of his past ventures, he had resources far beyond those of the average Cuban, and more than he ever mentioned. He had used those resources and his status as a foreigner who could pay top dollar on the black market, to push the project through to completion. Of course, Pedro had been extremely helpful.

From the outside, his house looked like a typical Cuban country house with bare white concrete blocks and a guano grass roof. But inside, it was completely modernized and refreshed, built entirely of Cuban materials. What they couldn't find, the ever resourceful Hiro had invented and Pedro had made using his clever talents and his mechanical skills. When house was completed at last, Hiro invited everybody for some of the barbecued goat he loved so much. He was truly pleased at what they had accomplished in six short months.

One day not too long afterward, Hiro was sleeping in his new bedroom when he was awakened by an incredible din: screaming, shouting and the increasing noise of a Cuban drum being beaten louder and louder. Immediately, more people began screaming and shouting. Jumping up to see what was going on, Hiro saw an incredibly scary looking woman with a fierce wig waving a stick, dancing in circles to the increasingly frenzied beat of the African drum. It was Dania's cousin Dounia. Her eyes were watery, and she looked like a ghost dancing around and around, unaware of her environment and unable to respond to it. She was in a trance state, pointing her stick at whatever person she was in front of. Hiro had never seen anything like this before. Very quietly, he asked Dania, "What's going on?" When she remained still, he repeated, "Dania, what is this?"

She whispered, "Mi amorsote, our people in Santeria, the Way of the Saints. We believe the spirits are using her mouth to speak to us." He was witnessing a ritual of Santeria, an African religion that had been transplanted here when slaves were brought to the New World to work on the sugar plantations hundreds of years ago. It soon became clear that this crazy-looking creature was no longer Dounia but was now some demented alter ego dancing to the overpowering beat and sound of the drum. Dania watched and clapped, singing along with the others as the one-not-Dounia dribbled saliva, caught in her own trance.

Later, Hiro questioned Isabel further about Santeria. He learned that it was an age-old religion, a fusion of the Yoruban culture of Africa and the Christianity that had been forced upon the slaves when they got to Cuba, combining elements of both Roman Catholicism and their ancient African beliefs. The religion was based on belief in the creator, along with several other deities that represented the various forces of nature, such as rain or principles such as war or love. Chief among them was *Olodumare,* the Owner of Heaven, Owner of All Destinies, the source and owner of creation itself. Because *Olodumare* represent the ultimate mystery, and is himself unknowable to man, he is represented on earth by Orishas. These deities are often compared to the Saints of Catholicism and during slavery in Cuba, worship of the Orishas was often disguised as prayer to the saints.

In fact, many Cubans still referred to some Orishas by the names of Saints. Specific Orishas often required sacrifices, such as the blood of chickens, goats, turtles or pigs. They rule over every element of human life, and could be petitioned through the correct application of prayer, rituals and trances. Also important was foods, colors, numbers and dance. In other words, Santeria employed something specific to represent each possible object, idea, group, or quality of life in an allegorical way. Isabel finished her explanation with a final caveat: she warned Hiro that, although many outsiders automatically associated Santeria with black magic and evil, it was neither magic nor evil, but rather a rich and mysterious religion.

An Orishas also often required an individual representing him to dance into a state of apparent semi-consciousness in order for its spirit to enter the representative's body. The male and female priests, the *Babalochas* or *Santerios*, often participated in this way. Some highly secret rituals that had originated mainly in Nigeria had been handed down from generation to generation, sending deep roots into every aspect of Afro-Cuban life. Hiro was amazed to witness a human being actually going into a cataleptic state in a ritual setting such as this. Immediately, his scientist's mind took over, analyzing and puzzling over something he couldn't understand, because he had never researched the brain. For the moment, the only solution he could offer himself was the idea that there had to be some sort of abnormal brain function at work.

After the Santeria ceremony, Hiro and Dania's relationship seemed to go into overdrive and they decided to get married legally with a Cuban wedding at her family home. This was to be a traditional Yoruban ceremony which was quite involved and beautiful in its loving application of ancient sacraments. The morning of the wedding, the bride bathed, and then was dressed lovingly by her aunts. Afterwards, she returned to her mother, her face now decorated with white-striped tribal make-up. She carried a traditional wedding basket woven of sugarcane from the nearby fields, crusted with multitudes of beautiful iridescent pink and white shells that represented abundance, wealth, and great blessings for the couple. Her mother wept as she gently whipped her from head to toe with banana leaves for purification and to celebrate this, the bride's first official farewell from the home of her youth.

For the remainder of the day Dania stayed quietly in her room with her two sisters while the rest of the household danced and feasted into the early evening. From their seclusion, they could hear the Afro-Cuban music that drummed the beat of their hearts, of the very soul of their culture. Finally, her stepfather Pepe, as the man of the house, called Dania to join everyone and to greet the guests and family. Meanwhile, Hiro, who had been sequestered, was also summoned. She joined him, and finally Dania and Hiro were announced to the gathering as man and wife by the Santeria priest wearing traditional grass skirts. The white-striped painting of his entire body was the tribe's symbol that announced Dania and Hiro to the gathering as man and wife.

As a final blessing, each guest took a banana leaf from a pile created for just this purpose, and proceeded to whip the bride and groom top to bottom, literally bombarding them with wishes for love, health and wealth. Afterwards, the leaves were put into a stack once again and burned, the smoke they created now forming the final prayer that wafted straight to heaven for the well-being of the newly married couple. The conga drums beat strongly as Hiro and Dania and their family and friends ate, laughed and danced the night away, not once thinking of the bleak history that had brought them to this wonderful moment. The food they feasted on now was the result of the famine of centuries earlier and the laughter they shared here was based on the tears of their forefathers.

Hiro's and Dania's ceremony, filled as it was with the richness of ancient tradition, was a direct reflection of her family's history. While they gazed into each other's eyes, smiling, the conga beat and the age-old Yoruba chanting swirled around them, echoing through time the story of this colorful culture. Only a twist of fate had led them here, for when the Spanish took the Yorubas as prisoners for pay, they kept tribes and families intact. This one fact left them with hope, with heart. They had survived, and then thrived in their new environment, and today their soul shone as the joy of this new marriage, another colorful thread in the tapestry of this glorious people.

Hiro and Dania began their marriage in the home of her family, living happily along with Dania's parents and two younger sisters. For Hiro, his new life was beyond a dream come true, because in his previous emotionless existence he could never even have conceived of such warmth and belonging. Each day was like a new blossom unfolding in a bouquet of beautiful todays—today's love, today's tasks, today's traditions.

Chapter 29

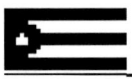

San Rafael, a tiny village

between the towns of Sierra Morena and Rancho Veloz, became home for Hiro. His roots were growing deep and strong in the rich Cuban soil. Soon after the marriage, Freddie, from the immigrations office in Santa Clara, let Hiro know that as the husband of a Cuban citizen, he could remain in residence indefinitely and that he could visit other countries whenever he wished.

Meanwhile, his life here was totally foreign to the insular, unemotional Japanese ways. But Hiro was enjoying the most peaceful, most wonderful time of his life, and the agonizing nightmares seemed to have disappeared. He was so comfortable and relaxed that sometimes he and Dania slept peacefully as late as ten, and were teased mercilessly for being in bed so long. Pedro's friendship was another source of joy for Hiro; they fished long days together or went for the hot baths at the Hotel Elquea. Pedro continued mentoring him with his carpentry, so that over time both Hiro's proficiency and their friendship became unassailable facts.

Freddie had become a great source of official information for Hiro, as well as a friend. Periodically, they saw one another either in Santa Clara or at Rancho Veloz. Through Pedro, Hiro now had a family, a large circle of good friends, and an authentic, simple life that suited him perfectly. He had no thought or desire to return to Japan—ever. He felt no pull to his former academic life, relishing instead the humbler, more meaningful tasks of carpentry and vegetable gardening. The life was simple, with few material objects and only minimal financial demands or rewards, but peaceful—graceful in some strange way. He could not fathom why so many Cubans were putting their lives in danger clinging to flotation devices, trying to get to Florida.

Hiro began to think they were crazy, and that they didn't understand the value of the basic human happiness and the gift of sanctuary afforded them by Fidel's social reforms. Certainly, Hiro enjoyed Fidel's great gifts, but every time he tried to discuss politics, especially Castro's, all his friends in Rancho Veloz laughed at him. Eventually, they simply refused to discuss politics with him at all. From Hiro's perspective, Castro's system was a good one that had worked well for nearly forty-five years: Cubans, as he saw them, were kept poor but happy, and well-provided with the basics of life. He understood that it was not a perfect system and that it was not politically ambitious, but that it did create an atmosphere of peace that was rare in the world. Fidel created a sort of a dream world.

Unfortunately, the people of Cuba cast their gaze out into the wide world beyond them and found their lives lacking the material and financial gain open to people living elsewhere. They wanted their share. Many Cuban citizens were upset living under Fidel's yoke. But they kept their disquiet to themselves.

Hiro understood their dislikes and their reticence; nonetheless, he lived among them in contentment, satisfied with every aspect of his life. He still thought Cuba was benefiting greatly from Fidel's vision. He felt that, although Fidel was indeed a dictator, he was one of the world's most brilliant, and dwelt on the peaceful existence available to each individual. Hiro focused on the great relationships he now had, on the happiness and lack of stress in his family life. He awoke whenever he wanted, and spent as much time with his family as he wished. He loved his newly acquired carpentry skills and making furniture. The time, the happiness, the relationships, the lack of emphasis on the material—Hiro could conceive of no better mode of living. Until Hiro met his Cuban wife, he had never felt this way. His former life was full of academic achievements and professional growth. But it was devoid of emotion. Now, as he saw it, he was enjoying the true sweet fruit of Communist philosophy—and he loved it.

In the next eight years he fished with friends, built furniture with Pedro, gardened in the yard, and fathered two wonderful daughters, Masako Adriana and Yumiko Alexandra. Yumiko and Masako loved *Batidos*, or milk shakes, made with fresh *mango, banana, papaya, mamey, and cherimoya*. Sipping one was like drinking a dessert. Hiro and Dania took the girls to get one every weekend. They girls added even more layers to his happiness here, and Hiro thought it would be impossible ever to experience greater feelings of abundance and delight.

The Last Revolution

His time in Japan and the United States had led him to the material view: everywhere he looked, he saw stressed, unhappy people trying to ease their pain with more and more wealth, or through dangerous drugs, both legal and illicit. He too, fell victim to the more-is-more philosophy, seeking to use his great intelligence to gain financial security. Along the way, he sacrificed whatever happiness he might have gained through loving relationships.

Hiro unbalanced his life in the direction of work, often spending eighteen hour days with his machines, in pursuit of his elusive vision. He understood machines. He understood ambition. In this understanding, Hiro was merely following the imperative of his native Japanese background and culture. He became a victim of the highly moralized, regimented social culture of his country. Thus, as his successes and advancement in research grew, bringing with them all the recognition and rewards he could have asked for, his simple, authentic life diminished in inverse proportion. But at the time, he was quite satisfied with the order of his life. The truth was, he basically had no relationships other than a few distant ones with co-workers. But he didn't feel lonely, mainly because he didn't feel. He rather liked living his isolated existence in the small cubicle where he worked on his machines. Other than the mental challenges he constantly faced, the only real problem was the tremendous anguish caused by his recurring nightmares.

That bleak time was over, though. Its emptiness had been filled to the brim with every good human feeling and Hiro reveled in every single one. His life was complete. He didn't even have to abandon his intellectual side in Cuba, because, true to his original agreement with the university, he offered classes on a regular basis, gaining once again the recognition of the academic community. His intelligence, especially in the field of higher mathematics, was cause for wonder and amazement. Freddie Diaz was always there with his help and support for Hiro in this arena, drawing on his elevated rank in the Cuban government and his important political contacts to smooth the way for him. He too, enjoyed favor in the rarefied atmosphere of academia. He lectured several days a month in the fields of economics and the industrial revolution in the Far East. This intellectual common ground was a major element in cementing the friendship between Hiro and Freddie.

Despite that friendship, though, and because he still feared having his knowledge put to ill use, Hiro never revealed to anyone—not even Dania—his other special skill as a computer science engineer and researcher in the software industry in the United States. As far as everyone was concerned, he was a professor of mathematics from Hiroshima, Japan. Period.

At one of Hiro's lectures to the faculty of The University of Matanzas, he met Fidel Castro in October 1999. His initial impression was of the man's overwhelming charisma—of his great height, his excellent build, his glowing olive skin, his serious demeanor. As they shook hands, Hiro's smaller one was engulfed in the leader's huge powerful grip, and he felt a shock of power surge up his arm and strike his psyche. He was still reeling from his reaction when Castro launched into a barrage of questions about mathematics.

Finally, he told Hiro, "I'm no math professor who can follow what you're saying, but I'm very grateful to you for the work you're doing here." He knew Hiro's science was beyond his own understanding, but, for the sake of the Cuban people and their education, the depth of his interest was vast. Castro then posed many questions about Hiroshima and the infamous attack that almost destroyed it in 1945. Next, he asked about technological advancements and the industrial growth of Japan after World War II.

Soon, Hiro realized that Castro's own intellect, and his curiosity about virtually everything, were both immense. He had often thought about Fidel's vision, about his dreams for his island nation. He asked himself how anyone could have conceived, let alone have implemented, a plan with such complex notions. And beyond that, how does one man sustain for over forty-five years the culture he has created? Now he had his answer. Intellect conceives, charisma drives and sheer power sustains. All of these attributes together defined the sum of Fidel's parts and together they formed a whole that was indeed greater than their sum. Hiro enjoyed his conversation with the dictator tremendously, all the while reflecting on the power of his vision and intent. Castro assured Hiro of continued support and gratitude. Hiro still remembered shaking Fidel's hand—the strong grip of a sincere man.

He remembered watching Cuban TV in 2000 at the center of a heated controversy as the story of little Elian Gonzales

The Last Revolution

unfolded to a rapt world audience. Elian had been aboard a small vessel that sank off the coast of Florida. Everyone, including his desperate mother, had perished—but six-year-old Elian clung to life in an inner tube floating on the ocean, and was finally rescued after more than ten hours by some Florida fishermen. But, instead of bringing an end to the drama, the rescue began another one of even greater proportions—pitting the US government against Cuba for custody of the tiny, terrified boy. Finally, after a heartbreaking humanitarian ordeal, he was returned to Cardenas near Varadero to his father, and to Fidel. Hiro remembered Fidel's political victory clearly. He also knew that the boy needed his father.

In Fidel, Hiro saw a shrewd card player who always seemed to have one more ace. In the complex game of world politics, he appeared relaxed, ready. This was a man who was not only capable, but who relished the challenges and the complexity of interaction. He did not shrink from the confrontation with the U.S., but met it head-on with the fervor of moral conviction. Fidel had played these games since 1959, had enjoyed them and intended to play many more—and win.

Also, Elian, like anyone in Cuba, could get a great education, going as far as he wished, for free. For this, Fidel didn't ask much; just be a member of the Communist Party, and pass a government examination, which wasn't hard for a determined student. More than any other world leader, Castro offered superior education to his countrymen. In Hiro's opinion, the boy would have a much better life in Cuba. As he saw it, social life was a hundred times better here than in the US or Japan. It would never become the kind of life Hiro remembered in his youth in Japan—full of stress, empty of warmth. Hiro thought the U.S. and Japan had a lot to learn from Fidel.

But all this largesse came with a definite price. The free education had to be paid back by working for the government and the individual had no real career choices. So, if you were a person with ambition and the desire for personal advancement and wealth, it was a given that you would never be happy living and working in this isolated island nation.

Sooner or later, you would have to jump the water in search of personal choice, freedom, and self-satisfaction. That was why most estimates claimed that should the Cuban borders be opened for emigration; fully ninety percent of the educated elite—the doctors, lawyers, and Engineers—would exit en masse, leaving only the uneducated peasantry in place. That was why Fidel worked so hard to prevent the borders from opening.

For Cubans, escaping was ultimately about personal economic gain, as far as Hiro was concerned. But one important objective they never seemed willing to confront was the effort to restore such personal freedoms on their own island, in the true vision of Jose Martí. Maybe it was the difference in culture.

Maybe leaving was just easier. Alternatively, maybe the Cubans were just apathetic. Hiro really could not understand their thinking on this. He shrugged, and life went on. The quiet, simple life he lived in Cuba allowed a sort of natural wisdom to develop and this wisdom brought with it a kind of fulfillment he had never sought because he had never known of its existence. It grew from his marriage to Dania, from his friendships within her family and from fatherhood. Family life had become the center of Hiro's universe and life was good beyond measure. He now called this tropical island home, and in the secret recesses of his own mind he thought of it as a sanctuary. Hiro's most fervent wish was simply for this idyllic existence to go on forever.

Eight years had passed,
since Hiro had first stepped onto his new island home. He continued to feel blessed by the simple, contented life he was able to have here, by the wisdom he felt growing within, and by the emotional progress he knew he'd made. It was the best life he could ask for.

Why, then, did he have to keep reminding himself that his life was idyllic? He tried to think and live totally as the Cubans around him did, but his identity was not Cuban. He was Japanese. He tried to forget his birth identity, but found to his dismay that the Oriental mentality could not be expunged at will. Little by little, and against his own wishes, Hiro felt his identity as a scientist re-emerging. He began to ponder the future of computer science in Cuba. He didn't come up with any ideas at first, but was determined to study and research the problem.

And now that he had committed himself to the project, Hiro realized that he had another problem to overcome, as well: during these last eight years, he had isolated himself from the flow of current information in computer technology. Because of the nature of computer work, for all intents and purposes, his

The Last Revolution

knowledge was obsolete. In fact, in any given twenty-four hour period, some new concept could be released, and all that went before would be rendered virtually obsolete. Knowing and understanding the nature of computer science, Hiro understood the challenge he now faced.

Chapter 30

With new ideas in mind, Hiro approached Pedro. "Where do you think I can get a computer?"

Pedro said, "Maybe Havana. I'm not sure. I never really looked for one before. I might have seen one in Santa Clara. We can go take a look if you want. Maybe Freddie Diaz will know something." So the next day, the two of them took off to Santa Clara in the '56 Ford. They went directly to Freddie's office at immigrations and asked him about a computer. Freddie sent them to a sort of dollar store, La Tienda Pan-Americana. He said, "Once in a while you'll see one there. Go to Maximo Gomez Street, turn right on Second Street, and you'll see a big store on the left. Ask for Luis. He's a friend of mine, a district manager. We've been friends since Havana. If they can get you a computer, he'll know."

Now that they had an idea where to go and what to look for, Hiro and Pedro were men on a mission. Hiro drove through the blistering streets of Santa Clara. It was February, a comfortable month in Rancho Veloz, but here in this inland city, the air had nowhere to go, and it became hot and uncomfortable. On top of that, the streets were swarming with pedestrians; Pedro had to be careful not to hit anyone with the car. The walkers were fearless, and left the lookout to the hapless drivers.

As Hiro and Pedro entered the store, they had to pause for a moment in the relative cool to allow their eyes to adjust to the darkness of the interior. Then, they began to take in the veritable sea of cheap Chinese-manufactured goods that crowded the aisles and shelves, imported by the government in exchange for sugar. They spied loads of new cheap electrical products, rows of washing machines and ranks of refrigerators. The main purpose of the store was not so much to trade goods, but rather to collect as much money as possible from the Cuban-American relatives of the local population. It was a clever way indeed to gain US dollars for the local economy, because the US dollar was worthless in all other Cuban stores except La Tienda Pan-Americana.

The Last Revolution

Pedro stopped the first clerk that he saw working in the store and asked for Luis. She directed them to go to the back of the store to the right, and to look for the white door. That was where his office was, and that was where Luis would be found. On their way, Hiro noticed how many people were shopping there, willing to pay clearly inflated prices for obviously cheap goods. In Japan, things were expensive, but not this expensive. But, for the items even to be available, they had to be imported, and the Cuban government charged import taxes of almost two hundred percent.

For the locals there was no choice: either pay the price or do without. Most of them understood that without this source of revenue, without the influx of foreign currency, Cuba would starve. To them, this situation was normal. Only foreigners like Hiro seemed to notice anything amiss with the system. Pedro knocked at the white door, which was promptly opened by a secretarial-looking young woman in a navy blue dress. She gestured them in, and immediately Hiro's eyes were drawn to a bank of sixteen new-looking computers. Recently, the government had reformed the entire business web of the nation with a new system, and what they were seeing now was part of that system. Santa Clara was the main hub for central Cuba. Pedro and Hiro were both excited by what they saw.

Luis came out to greet them, a nice-looking man in his late 40s with curly blond hair and blue eyes. He smiled as he held out his hand, first to Hiro, then to Pedro, for a warm handshake. "Freddie told me his Japanese friend was coming, so I was expecting you. What can I do for you?" Pedro told him they wanted to know where Hiro could buy a computer. Luis shrugged a bit sheepishly, "Really, I don't think you can find a new one anywhere in Cuba. But I can get you a used one, no problem.

The government is practically giving them away to citizens for their homes. You just have to register at the police station and get a special permit." Hiro, understanding the government's desire to educate its citizens, was delighted with the information. Hiro and Pedro listened as Luis went on, explaining to them that there was another store in the Santa Clara area, and six more in Havana where all the used computers from government offices were sold. He exuded friendliness as he walked them around the store with pride, explaining to Hiro that

Freddie had arranged for him to receive a 50% discount on his purchases.

Finally, the men left, driving again on the busy streets toward the south side of town to a remote industrial section Luis had directed them to. In a small, unbelievably crowded store, they found a veritable treasure trove of used goods. There were the requisite refrigerators, of course, but also every conceivable office item, including computers, printers, keyboards, and all the peripherals a computer user could ask for. Pedro was delighted. "Hiro, this place is great. I bet you can find everything you need here. Look. Some of these computers look new." But Hiro had gotten serious, and he'd lost his smile. Standing still, he let his gaze cover the room. Pedro, uncomprehending, saw his frustration nevertheless. "Hiro, what's wrong?" Hiro just stood and looked. "Hiro?" Slowly, he walked around the entire store, still silent. "What's wrong with you?"

Hiro exploded, "Pedro, these computers are obsolete. This one is almost twenty years old. I can't use this thing. It's worthless! These computers are all too old. They don't have enough capacity or speed and they aren't compatible with the new ones on the market. They only have 1.5 MB of memory. They're only good for really simple stuff, and you can't use them at all for Internet research."

Pedro said, "Well, I don't really know anything about computers. Most Cubans don't. Besides, you're Japanese, and the Japanese know all about high-tech stuff. You invented most of it." He kept muttering on, but Hiro tuned him out, lost in his own dismal thoughts. He understood that Pedro's opinion reflected the Cuban view of things, but that didn't help him any. There were very few customers in the computer store, so he went up to a salesgirl and asked for the manager, only to learn he was out for the day.

He decided to take a shot: "Do you have any new computers for sale?"

"No," he heard, "I don't think there are any in Santa Clara. Everything here is about the same, because everything comes from Havana." Both men were disappointed. They decided they needed to get back in touch with Freddie, who knew lots of high-ranking government officials. If there was a new computer to be had in Cuba, Freddie could track it down for them. They arrived at immigration, excited that they might be making headway, only to be stopped cold; Freddie was tied up in negotiations with Canadian businessmen trying to work in Santa Clara. There were many Spanish and Canadian businesses with offices in Santa Clara because it was near a great shipping port in Cienfuegos where many tourist hotels were under construction in the area—a great stopping off point for the Calibiren and Cayo Santa Maria.

Pedro and Hiro sat waiting in the car parked under a huge Alamo tree, cool and sheltered from the scorching sun. Hiro was still brooding about the sad selection of computers in the store, and didn't want to entertain even the slightest thought of going into another store, he was so depressed. Pedro, always the concerned friend, offered an alternative, "Maybe Freddie can find a computer for you. Or maybe you can call Japan and get one—Sony, maybe, or Hitachi. It might take some time to get here, but at least you'd have one." Pedro's suggestions got Hiro searching for other options, too. They discussed the many difficulties of living in Cuba and how frustrating it was to function without basics, especially for people from other countries.

Pedro observed, "We just live without. A computer is the last thing we need. We just look for something to eat this week. That's all we think about because what is available is just shit anyway!" He was telling the truth, and Hiro knew it, because he had lived the same truth for the last eight years. He was still quite content with his life here and with his family and friends. That hadn't changed. But he was beginning to chafe under the business and political constraints that limited his actions and choices.

Finally, after more than an hour, the security guard from the immigration office called Hiro and Pedro back to Freddie's office. When they got there, he shook their hands and asked if they had found a computer. Hiro told him yes, they had found computers, but they were unusable for his purposes. He explained that he wanted to use the internet and that he needed a much more up-to-date unit for that. Once more, he repeated his request for a new computer.

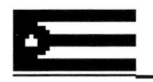

Chapter 31

Freddie listened quietly and then responded, "Hiro, you forget you're living in a Communist social system here; the Cuban government does not permit us to have computers for personal use. Not even if they're gifts. It doesn't allow us access to the outside world through the Internet and only limited e-mail access, if we're involved directly in international business regulated by the government. And of course, even then every move we make on the Internet is watched; in Havana there's a surveillance center that keeps track of everything we do."

So Hiro asked, "What if my friends or family in Japan can ship me a computer or satellite dish?"

Freddie just shook his head. "I'm telling you straight! There is no access for the general public to computers, satellite dishes, or the Internet. If anyone did send any of those things to you, customs would confiscate them. There is absolutely no way for you to have these items in Cuba. Even I can't help you. It's just impossible for you to get them."

He shook his head again for emphasis. It wasn't hard to see that Freddie disagreed with his government's policies controlling all media and news from the outside world. He went on, "If you did manage somehow to get hold of a new computer, you still would be prohibited from accessing the internet. And if the government ever found out, the computer would be confiscated, and you would have to pay a huge fine, probably even go to jail for a year, because having the computer and using the Internet are both crimes."

Hiro was shocked. "I can't believe it!" Hiro looked at Pedro and shook his head no. That just couldn't be true. He and Pedro both thought they knew the Cuban system, but in this area they clearly had been wrong. For Hiro, it was the most painful news he'd gotten in the eight years he'd been here. In all those years, he had not sought material gain. He had just cultivated and relished his peace and happiness. And he'd been grateful for every blessing. But now, he faced a huge obstacle. He faced the government of Cuba.

The Last Revolution

Hiro tried an end run: "If I have international business, can I have a computer?"

"Yes, but you can't bullshit the government, Hiro. You have to have permits, licenses. And that's not easy because, for all intents and purposes, you're a Cuban citizen. You get the same treatment as anyone else. It is simply impossible for you to have a computer with Internet access. It's as simple as that."

Freddie fell quiet. He truly felt sympathy for Hiro, but there was nothing he could do. He couldn't get him items that were forbidden to ordinary citizens. Defeated, Hiro and Pedro left for Rancho Veloz. The drive home seemed very long. Even the talkative Pedro fell silent. He was out of ideas. Because of the government restrictions, Hiro was clear that his dream of researching with a new computer was an impossible one. He also knew that to try to overcome those restrictions and actually obtain a computer was a dangerous game. Slowly, an idea began to form in his head, almost against his own will. He really didn't want to get in trouble, because he didn't want to face the consequences.

Lost in thought, both men remained quiet. They didn't even notice the small towns or the people going about their business in the streets, because all they could think about was what Freddie had said to them in Santa Clara. Suddenly, Hiro decided that he'd just have to forget the computer. He was afraid about what Freddie had said. If he bought one and was discovered, since he was a non-Cuban, Hiro would be extradited to Japan. As long as the Communist regime existed, he would never see his wife or children again. It wasn't worth it.

Back home on the outskirts of Sierra Morena, Dania was unaware of the obstacles Hiro and Pedro had encountered. Blissful in her ignorance, she waited excitedly for good news and for a new computer. She ran out to the car with a big smile on her face, but it slowly faded as she took in the men's grim countenances, and the unnatural stillness of their movements. Neither spoke; Hiro just walked past her, went directly to their bedroom, and shut the door. Silence. The family gathered but didn't try to talk to Hiro. They knew something was wrong, and that was enough. Even the little girls, usually so giggly and wiggly, echoed the solemnity of their elders. Everyone figured when the time was right, Hiro would tell them what had happened. Isabel, Pepe and Dania all stood ready to support him, no matter what. That was the way of family. As for Hiro, he needed the night to think. He needed time to examine his options.

But after a few hours, Dania had had enough. She couldn't wait anymore so she knocked gently on the door. When Hiro said, "Come in," she went directly to him and sat on the edge of the chenille spread right next to him. Gently, she put her hand on his arm, and leaned over to kiss his cheek and then his lips. Friend and lover, she put her arms around his shoulders and hugged him in silence.

Finally, so quietly, she asked, "Hiro, what happened in Santa Clara? Weren't there any computers?" While she listened without comment, Hiro told her everything that had happened. Understanding far more than her words implied, she asked, "What do you want to do next? You'll think of something. Let's leave it be for a week or two. Then we can talk again after we've had time to think."

Hiro was touched beyond words. She understood, she supported him, she loved him. All he said was, "Good idea. Be sure to tell your mother everything. I just don't want to talk about it for a while."

While Hiro brooded, Dania went to Panchita and bought three huge red snappers for him because he loved fish dinners. Isabel cooked them Creole style, his favorite, with fresh lime juice over the fish, and sliced cabbage and turnip greens on the side. The family was smiling again, even Hiro. "Woo!" he told Isabel , "That was fantastic—my favorite meal in Cuba! I'm a happy man." And he was. He gazed around the table, seeing each of his family members. Conversation ebbed and flowed easily, its rhythm the rhythm of life, of love, of belonging. Always thoughtful, Isabel mentioned nothing about Santa Clara.

That same night, Pepe approached Hiro about a problem of his own. "Hiro, can you check the water pump tomorrow? Something isn't right. The water pressure isn't as strong as it should be."

Hiro said. "OK. I'll get Pedro to help me. I want to go fishing near dawn. Pedro will probably meet me, and we can check the pump then." Early the next morning, Pedro went to pick up Hiro for their fishing excursion to the Rio San Pedro. Even at dawn, there were kids waiting at the lake, ready to lounge against Pedro's car as they watched Hiro prepare his great fishing gear—artificial worms and beautifully decorated tackle.

The Last Revolution

The children loved to watch Hiro prepare and loved to watch him fish. As for Hiro, he appreciated having them as an audience and felt obligated to come up with a decent catch so they wouldn't be disappointed. Pedro added to the festive atmosphere, always joking and kidding with the children.

Hiro fished for quite a while with no luck at all. It was a beautiful, misty morning and it had rained during the night. He couldn't figure out why the fish weren't biting, but he knew that he couldn't win every time. Finally, he decided to call it quits. But Pedro wouldn't hear of it. "Hey! We've got lots of time. I want to see a big fish. Where's my big fish?" Pedro joked.

Pedro just kept on, "Where's my fish? What will I eat for dinner?" Both of them were laughing by then.

Pedro finally relented. "OK. I have to go by my uncle's house anyway. I'm supposed to get a goat so you and your family can come over tonight. Madeline wants to feed everyone."

"Everyone?" asked Hiro.

Pedro just shrugged, "Why not?" There was a one beat pause. First, Hiro cracked up and then Pedro burst out laughing. Finally, they exchanged adolescent high fives.

Pedro's Uncle Lodo lived about five miles from Rio San Pedro on a private cattle ranch. Even though he owned the ranch, it did not mean he could kill any of the cattle because to kill cattle for food was a criminal offence carrying a thirty-six month jail penalty working hard labor as a sugarcane cutter. Prisoners were given very little to eat and were forced to work like mules. When men returned they were lean, buff, and strong—perfect models of health. Hiro knew several very healthy men.

The government had come down hard on slaughtering cattle because if it hadn't, there probably would not have been any cattle left in Cuba. People loved their beef—particularly if it came almost free through theft. So the cattle belonged to the state, and the people could use them for dairy production, or as beasts of burden, but not for meat.

The Cuban people were so desperate for protein that sometimes dogs or cats disappeared. After all, they were roaming the streets, they were free, and they were easy targets. Purchasing meat, when it was available, was prohibitively expensive, even with government subsidies. That was why stealing had become a way of life for many, and a bane to others. The farmers had to struggle vigilantly to protect their farms from night predators of the two-legged kind. Potatoes, onions and yuccas were targeted along with the meat. Many visiting harvesters were caught and sent to jail. But for those not caught, the meat was free for the taking. And if it all could not be hauled away at once, the thieves ingeniously dug enormous holes in the ground, salted the carcasses liberally to prevent rot, and returned later to reap the benefits of their enterprise.

People in other countries might well criticize a regime that created a system of deprivation like the one in Cuba, and then crushed its citizens when they attempted to supply themselves with the basics of life they were deprived of. They might, like the US, have imposed embargoes in the name of humanitarian concerns. But the truth was that the blockades hurt the very people they were intended to help, and in an ironic twist, they actually served the purposes of the government at fault. And even more ironically, the Cuban public, so severely restricted and punished in so many ways, actually enjoyed more peace and order in their daily lives than those in the US, where the laws were unequally enforced, leading to anger and unrest.

In one famous speech, Fidel railed that the US treated him like a cockroach. But Fidel, a brilliant dictator and strategist, always waited quietly for conditions to develop in his favor. He used every opportunity that came along for his benefit, always adapting, always surviving. Maybe he treated Cuba as a cockroach. Maybe Fidel was the cockroach.

Cuba was a product of the Cold War with the United States, and if the US were to lift its sanctions against it, the Cuban Communist system would quickly be carried away in a flood of commerce. A free society would bring abundant opportunity for the Cuban people, who actually practiced their own brand of free enterprise every day. If they had any guts at all, they wouldn't be jumping into the ocean to swim away to Miami; they'd stay in Cuba and work from there. That was their best chance of helping Cuba to become a truly free society. But Cubans were apathetic people, and those who did make it to Miami would rather scream and carry on from the safety of distance than take any meaningful action.

As for their Miami demonstrations, in Hiro's mind they served no real purpose; certainly nothing back home in Cuba ever improved as a result. Hiro always hated to see his adopted countrymen lose their dignity by demonstrating uselessly on the

The Last Revolution

streets of Miami; he thought they should remain on the island and stand ready to sacrifice their lives if necessary for the good of their motherland instead of waiting around for some nameless someone to do some unknowable something to help them. In Japan, people never surrendered their own ideologies. Before they would let that happen, they would commit suicide.

Hiro remembered Jose Martí, whose statue was in every village, and whose name was on streets and schools in every town in Cuba. Martí had been a true hero in the earlier cause of independence from Spain. He had worked from within the country and from without, but had never surrendered his vision of an independent Cuba. Marti had dedicated his entire life to this cause and had ultimately lost that life to it. What Hiro couldn't understand was that the same people who named airports and buildings for Martí, who espoused his philosophy verbally, and who claimed they admired his actions, still took the easy way out. They dove into the nearest waves hoping to be carried away. Hiro knew this scenario because most Cubans never did anything but complain.

When they reached Lodo's ranch, Pedro noticed that Hiro was daydreaming. Pedro screamed, "Hiroaki!"

Hiro jumped and exclaimed, "What? What is happening?"

Hiro was jumpy and Pedro said, "I knew you were deep in thought. What were you thinking about?"

Hiro was a little shy and took time to compose himself before he spoke, "Oh well, I was just thinking about my home in Hiroshima." Pedro understood Hiro very well and knew that he was getting homesick.

As soon as Lodo and his entire family came out, Lodo told a funny Cuban joke and everyone cracked up. However, Hiro had difficulty understanding the joke because it was related to Cuban culture and history. Then Pedro wanted to purchase the biggest goat he could find, but his uncle only sold him a small male because the biggest goats were kept to breed stock for a healthy herd.

Pedro paid for 450 pesos ($12), tied its four legs together, and then threw it into the trunk of his car. When he and Hiro got home, Madeline wanted to know where Dania was because she was counting on her help with all the cooking. Hiro replied that she was planning to be there around six and that they were leaving right away to go get her. Madeline was satisfied with that because she was planning to feed more than twenty-five people, friends, and relatives. Soon, Dania and Isabel arrived with bushels of vegetables to add to the feast and the three women set about their preparations in an atmosphere of shared gaiety.

Pedro did one of his famous goat barbeques, Cuban-style, which Hiro never tired of. He had tried many times to duplicate the perfection of spices that Pedro had mastered, but much to his chagrin, he had never come close. Despite his own culinary inadequacies, Hiro was thoroughly enjoying himself because he loved being among his adopted family and the silly chatter. As his teeth tore off succulent bits of tender meat, he secretly chewed more on his computer problem. But he and Pedro kept quiet about his computer search. He didn't want it to become food for common gossip.

Chapter 32

A few months passed uneventfully, and Hiro and Pedro decided to start a new project—an entertainment center made of Cuban mahogany, complete with drawers for cassettes and tapes. Nobody around here had ever seen anything like it; Hiro got the idea from a cabinet his sister owned. His version would be a detailed, unique piece. He was thoroughly relishing his woodworking when a white Russian Lada drove up and Freddie from Santa Clara got out and asked, "What's going on?"

The two men paused in their work to shake hands with their friend. "Nothing much. We just started this new piece. Hiro designed an entertainment center last week. We started it today. It should be done in about two weeks." Freddie examined it with interest. It reminded him of furniture he had seen when he lived in Japan. It was a simple design with clean lines, yet still retained an Oriental flair.

Pedro and Hiro were truly happy to see Freddie; they enjoyed his company for his intelligence and pleasant disposition. Having lived abroad for so many years, and being familiar with different cultures, he was more cosmopolitan than most Cubans were, and he had loads of interesting experiences to share. Pedro felt a further kinship with him because his nephew and Freddie were both alumni of The University of Matanzas. Not only did Pedro's nephew Eduardo work for Freddie but also he was a very close friend of Pedro's Uncle Willie.

Hiro asked Freddie how long he planned to stay. Freddie said, "I'm visiting my wife's family in Corralillo, and I have several things to take care of in Rancho Veloz. We might spend the night in Corralillo, then we'll probably go home tomorrow afternoon."

Hiro offered, "I'd love for you to come visit us at my home tonight, if you can. There are some things I'd like to discuss with you in person. If you come by, I can promise some great Creole cooking. My wife is a terrific cook, just like her mother." Freddie agreed, saying that if his wife agreed with the plan, they'd be there around seven. Hiro thought that sounded fine. He promised fish, saying with a private laugh that Pedro had a source for some big fish.

Freddie left and Pedro and Hiro set their woodworking aside, deciding they needed to make a run to Panchita. When they returned an hour later, they found Dania and Isabel cleaning the porch. The men parked in front of the house and opened the trunk, hauling out four huge red snapper caught last night by a government fishing boat. Dania and her mother screeched in unison at sight of the expensive surprise. Dania said, "That's a lot of fish! We're only cooking one tonight, right? And we'll save the others for later."

But Hiro told her delightedly, "No. We'll probably have around fifteen people to feed tonight. Freddie and his wife Yorina and Julissa and Laline are coming. Pedro, Madeline and Wendy, too. You'll just have to figure out how to spread the food around to feed everybody."

Dania was not to be flustered. "Fine, I'll come up with something special." Isabel stood aside watching this exchange with growing delight and an air of I've-been-there. Slowly, a grin graced her face, soon to morph into a full-fledged belly laugh. Watching her, the children all started laughing, too. Doubled over, she told them to stop. But they didn't hear her because recalled that somehow, uncharacteristically, Dania had managed to burn the fish the last time they had it.

Isabel told Dania straight-faced that she would help cook them this time—just to be sure they didn't poison their important guests. At that, everyone in the house laughed, first Isabel, then Dania, until the room was awash in good tears. When one finally managed to catch his breath, someone else would start up again, double over, and off they all went again. There wasn't a dry eye in the place, and every cheek was happy-sore from the outburst. Dania, trying for stern, told everybody to shut up. But that just made Hiro laugh, and he gently touched her shoulder and kissed her ear. Kissing her ear was his secret tender-love sign to her and it always thrilled her.

Hiro, ever the good host, realized they probably needed some liquor. So off he went with Pedro to see Pedro's friend Guico, who was responsible for the local park and activities, and

The Last Revolution

who usually, had a supply of beer. Pedro knocked at his office door in the park. Guico, a huge man, filled the doorway, asking what they needed. "You have any beer?" asked Pedro.

"Yeah," Guico answered, "but all I have is Mayobe. Perhaps 5 six-packs. Nothing else."

It wasn't *Hatuey*, but it had a smooth enough taste. Guico got it from his home in Holguin to sell. It came from a small brewing company there in the eastern part of the island. Hiro didn't like Mayobe because its taste was almost too smooth, like sweet water, he thought. But many women liked it for that very reason.

Hiro inquired, "Do you have any rum?"

"Yeah, but only by the gallon. I can give you a good price, though. Wanna make a deal?" Guico challenged.

Guico was always wheeling and dealing like this with his friends. He'd order more than he needed, then sell it on the black market. Hiro became friends with him through Pedro, but he'd never bought anything from him before. Guico sold only to friends of long-standing, people he trusted, and Hiro had become trusted. They made a deal on the beer and a good quality rum, and went back to the party.

When they returned, Pepe was still eating Hiro, Pedro joint with him and all the others were sitting in rocking chairs, drinking rum and beer, their stomachs and hearts full. Hiro started talking, "Freddie, I have some things I want to talk over with you. I think I'm going to Havana. I want to talk to Fidel. It's time someone changed his mind about freedom."

"Freedom?" Freddie quizzed.

Hiro replied, "Yes. I want to talk to him about computers, and the Internet and satellite dishes for entertainment. And I think everyone in Cuba is ready for information on the newest technology and getting access to it. I think the government should ease the restrictions in all these areas. More openness would educate the people better. After more than ten years, don't you think Cuba is ready to grow?" As he talked, Hiro grew more and more excited. He was feeling frustrated, and the progressive loudness of his voice reflected that. "Give me your honest opinion," he insisted. The entire gathering grew silent, and there was a collective drawing in of breath. They all had their own ideas about the government, but waited to hear what Freddie would say.

"Hiro, I'd like to help. But, you're talking about totally prohibited items. The government is not going to change its regulations under any circumstances. And if I even tried to help you, I'd lose my position as head of immigrations and director of development of Cayo Coco. That means I wouldn't be able to help you anymore, either. I think you should just let this idea go," Freddie advised.

Still, no one said anything, but they exhaled, and their bodies lost just a bit of tension. Shoulders relaxed. Freddie knew what he was talking about. Surely, Hiro would back off now. Freddie continued, "You'd probably get nothing but loads of trouble. I strongly recommend you stop thinking about this stuff. Stop complaining. Don't even think about going to Fidel. It's simple: Castro took his chances and beat the odds. He is totally in control. I don't understand much about politics, but, believe me, his position is strong. No one's going to change the system while he's in charge." Hiro listened. Freddie continued, "You asked for my honest opinion. I'll give it to you. If you so much as try to see Fidel and say what you want to say, what will happen is your name will end up on a black list, at the very least. Or, the government will find some excuse to throw you in jail. At the worst, you'll just disappear in an unfortunate accident. I might disappear, too. There aren't many options here. Either Fidel kills you, or you kill Fidel. Or—you do nothing."

Freddie looked around suspiciously. He was feeling the fright every Cuban felt every day. His voice dampened to a whisper, "Hiro, you are not Cuban. You have a permanent visa only because you're married to Dania. So they might deport only you to Japan. But it would be permanent. You'd never be able to return as long as Cuba was under Communist control. How much of a hardship would it be for you never to see Dania or the girls again? If you don't stay in line, that might be the consequence."

The silence was total—the concentration absolute. Fear was on the rise as everyone considered the consequences of not obeying the government unquestioningly. Freddie began again, voicing into the silence the truth they all knew: "No matter what we do, nothing will change. Things have been this way for fifty years, and they're not going to change any time soon. It may sound like it, but I'm not against the government. I have a good job with it. I make a decent living. It's not that I love Communism, but I do love Cuba. This is where my heart is. I'm sorry, Hiro, really. You're my best friend from Japan, and I'd like to help you. But what you're asking—it's impossible. It's crazy. Please, just forget it. It's a disastrous idea."

Usually it was the children who suffered from generalized fear, but this was the opposite. All the adults sat unmoving, not talking. Each in their own mind was repeating a litany of anxiety and frustration, especially Hiro and Freddie. Because of their heated conversation, they felt awkward, uneasy. Hiro was realizing that nothing could be done. He was seeing with brutal clarity the impossibility of his situation. He began to apologize to Freddie, saying how grateful he was for his honesty and great friendship.

Freddie chose to ignore the unpleasantness, and changed the subject by saying, "OK, Hiro. We need to talk about those seminars in Camaguey and Holguin—before summer session at the university in Havana starts. We need to discuss the details. Did you know over 200 professors have already signed up?" The group seemed to let out its collective breath as normal conversation started up again, and topics came and went on whim. But Hiro was still caught up in his thoughts.

Pedro said something he didn't hear, several times. Finally, he tapped Hiro's shoulder. "Hey! Are we going to work on the cabinet tomorrow? We need to finish it soon. We might need to get some more wood. Maybe we can go get it tomorrow and do some fishing, too."

Hiro let go of his lingering frustration and grinned, "Why don't we go see that friend of yours? Maybe he'll have the wood." Pedro agreed. Soon everybody was drinking and gossiping as usual, and the soiree lasted until well past midnight. It broke up when Freddie said he and Yorina had to get back to Corralillo. Everyone hugged warmly, silently reassuring one another that the bonds of friendship were still strong. They gathered up the children who were sound sleep in Masako and Yumiko's room and carried them off into the night.

But when everyone was gone, Hiro began to brood again. He sat almost motionless, sipping his *Hatuey*. Dania watched from the kitchen, knowing something serious was happening, because ever since she had met him eight years earlier, until tonight, he had always been gentle and easy going. She loved him because he was so different from the men she'd known all her life. And she loved his intelligence. She felt so proud of his accomplishments in mathematics. Ironically, she knew nothing of his even greater genius in the field of computers, as he had never mentioned it to anyone.

Usually when Hiro was quiet and withdrawn like this, she left him alone. But tonight she sensed that something else was called for, so she went to him and put her hands on his shoulder, then in his hair. "Let's go to bed, and think about all this tomorrow." She kissed his forehead.

"Are the girls OK?" Hiro wondered.

Dania stated reassuringly, "They're fine. They really enjoyed all the company, but they're exhausted now. They're sound asleep."

Dania looked at him, one brow raised, a grin on her face. Hiro laughed softly as he took her hand and led her to their bedroom. When they were cuddled softly against each other, their tiredness transformed into a kind of comfortable, wordless need. This came from years of living and loving together. With soft and gentle sighs, they joined, not just bodies, but souls.

As soon as Dania was deeply asleep, though, Hiro carefully eased out of bed and returned to the patio, where he sat thinking and thinking. What should he do? Would he be killed or would he kill Fidel? His mind was a torment of turbulent thought. He was a scientist and mathematician, not a ninja. The longer he thought, a fewer number of ideas seemed to come to him. All he knew with certainty was that he didn't want any harm to come to Dania and the girls. He kept searching, using his brain like the computers he knew so well. The right answer had to be in there. He just had to input accurate data and program the right variables. He searched some more, but nothing came to him.

At six, Dania turned over lazily, reaching out to cuddle Hiro. But he wasn't there. She got up and went to the window facing the patio to look out. She wondered, "My God! What's he doing out there?" She threw on her robe and went to him. "Hiro, are you all right? Have you been out here all night?" Hiro didn't answer. He looked serious, and strangely emotionless. Dania felt a fist to her gut, but asked calmly, "Is something wrong? What's wrong?" She hugged him tight, kissed his head. Silence was the only reply. No movement. No emotion. Hiro looked like a ghost of himself. Dania ran inside, panic consuming her. She banged on Isabel's door. "Mother, get up! Something's wrong with

The Last Revolution

Hiro." She banged again. "Mother, I need help. I think Hiro's sick! Please!"

It seemed like an eternity, but Isabel opened her door almost immediately and shouted, "What's wrong?"

Dania struggled to say, "Come see. Something's wrong with Hiro. He won't move. He won't talk!" Her throat constricted her tears and fear took away her ability to speak.

Isa went to Hiro and called his name twice. He still didn't move. He was sitting on the concrete patio. Dania knelt in front of him and reached out to touch his lips. She took his hands in hers and rubbed them, hard. No response. Isa ran to the kitchen for a towel of icy water to wipe his face. Even she, who was usually so calm, felt panic. Her hand shook as she handed Dania the towel. Dania's fear was absolute as she shook Hiro over and over. "What's the matter with you? Tell me! I love you!" she nearly screamed.

Finally, finally, Hiro spoke, in the quietest of whispers. Dania had to kneel and lean in close, almost reading his lips to hear what he said: "Must be left alone. Thinking.. of a solution. Don't tell Pedro. Just wait. Please, Dania." This brief speech drained him, and again he lapsed into the ghostly trance of before.

But Dania was elated. "I promise. Just tell me what's going on."

"Leave me alone," he managed to say. Then Hiro closed his eyes and went away inside his thoughts.

Despite continuing concern, Dania and her mother were relieved that Hiro was responding at least minimally to them. Isa made some coffee and gave it to him. As he sipped, Isabel said she'd make breakfast, but Hiro only wanted some fruit. Dania told Hiro to lie down in their room, and he agreed. Once there, his body stilled while his mind went into overdrive. Soon it was overwhelmed by flashbacks of his childhood. Dania brought freshly sliced papaya arranged beautifully on a plate. But Hiro barely nibbled one piece. Dania sat next to him, watching. She kissed his face, trying to coax him to eat even a tiny bit more.

Hiro seemed oblivious to her ministrations, though. He whispered, "Fidel is going to kill me, or I have to kill him." Dania stiffened in shock. She had thought that discussion had ended last night. Without a word, she got up and closed the windows and the door. This was not a conversation that could be overheard.

"Fidel isn't going to kill you. And besides, you've always liked him so much, I know you're not going to kill him!" Dania said. "Hiro, before Fidel, we had nothing. My grandmother always talked about how much he helped the poor of Cuba. Without him, the rich white Cubans would return from Miami and take everything we have. We'd be slaves again. Fidel is good, Hiro." She paused and continued to express her thoughts, "I know you, Hiro. You're a kind, gentle man. You can't want to murder our president." Hiro said nothing.

She began again, "Hiro, you're making things difficult for yourself. And if you make a mistake, you could destroy the entire family, all for a stupid computer or the stupid Internet. Those things aren't even important in our lives! Why all of a sudden do you care so much about this stuff? Tell me, Hiro, because I don't get it." Hiro said nothing. Dania added, "I think you're too tired. You need to rest."

Hiro didn't budge. Not for two weeks. He ate almost nothing. He didn't change his clothes. He slept very little. All he did was stare and think. Dania watched and worried. He was so isolated. But the worst was his lack of emotion. It felt as though she were watching a man in mourning, or even a dead man. When she tried to get him to eat or bathe, she got no response. Hiro was alone in a universe of his own making.

Pedro began to worry, too. He hadn't seen Hiro for nearly two weeks, which was quite unusual for them. There was no fishing, no carpentry. He just stared at the untouched wood and wondered when Hiro would get back on track. Friends stopped by and asked where Hiro was. He always shrugged his shoulder carelessly and muttered something about Hiro being home, or busy. He decided to go find out for himself what was going on. Maybe Hiro was sick. At about ten the next morning, Pedro and Madeline arrived. Isabel ran up to Pedro and put her hand on his arm, explaining quietly what had been happening. Pedro thought they should take Hiro to the hospital, but Isabel told him that Hiro was quiet and didn't want visitors. She explained how worried she was, "I've never seen anyone act like this before. It's scary."

As soon as he stepped into the house, Dania came up to him and started whispering, "Pedro, I don't know what's

The Last Revolution

happening to Hiro. I've tried everything, but nothing works. He's lost so much weight. He won't take anything except milk." She began to cry, ignoring the tears that covered her cheeks. While Madeline and Isabel stayed on the patio Dania took Pedro to Hiro.

Chapter 33

In spite of the warnings, when Pedro entered the room, he was shocked to see Hiro sitting absolutely still on the floor. His body was emaciated, his face white. He had the face of a ghost or a dead man. In fact, it could have been a death mask he was so emotionless. Pedro lowered himself to the floor next to his friend. "Hiro, what's going on?" But once again, Hiro retreated by simply closing his eyes. Pedro decided that Hiro needed to go to a hospital regardless of his wishes. Pedro called Dania and gently gathered his friend into his arms to carry Hiro to the car. Pedro and Dania observed the silent Hiro. They turned to exit, but Hiro opened his eyes and said in a flat monotone, "Pedro, I'm not sick, really. I just need to be alone to think about what I am and who I was. Please, let me be alone."

Hiro closed his eyes and returned to his trance on the cool concrete floor. Pedro understood what Hiro needed and escorted the others from the room. In the living room he explained to Dania, Isabel and Madeline that Oriental people meditated sometimes when they needed guidance or answers. He said that it could take many days to cleanse the soul and to wash the brain and have it reprogram itself like a computer. Sometimes it took longer. Pedro remembered when Freddie had explained all of this to him at his aunt's house when Freddie had returned from duty in Japan.

"Don't worry," Pedro reassured, "when he has everything figured out, he'll come back again."

But Madeline was still dubious and demanded, "Tell me why you think you're right about this, and why Hiro is on the floor." So Pedro explained that several years ago, when he was at a party in Santa Clara with Hiro, Freddie had talked with them about the custom of Zen-Buddhist monks and of many older Japanese people who sat on the floor in absolute stillness and meditated. Through meditation, they hoped to gain a deeper understanding of themselves and to refresh their minds.

The Last Revolution

Pedro urged the others to leave Hiro alone but to watch him closely while he went to Santa Clara to talk with Freddie. He estimated that Hiro could remain in his strange and disturbing state for another ten days or so if he remembered correctly about deep meditation. When he left, Dania and Isabel felt greatly relieved. Freddie's little lecture on Japanese customs explained things that they had never heard before and gave them hope that Hiro's state was explainable. The explanation made the situation less threatening than they'd feared.

Meanwhile, as soon as Pedro left San Rafael he headed straight for Freddie's place in Santa Clara. Freddie's daughter Julissa answered the door when he knocked. She called her dad, but it was several minutes before he emerged from his shower. The minute he saw Pedro's face Freddie stopped in his tracks and asked what was wrong. Pedro poured out his concern for Hiro. Even though he felt sure he'd told the truth to Dania and Isa. Now he was the one who needed reassurance. Freddie listened to Pedro's outpouring in shocked silence. Then he said, "Describe his condition to me." Pedro answered.

Freddie continued, "I'm not sure what he's doing. Maybe it is harmful to his health or maybe he's just practicing Zen Buddhism."

Pedro asked, "Explain this Buddhism to me. Why would the Japanese torture their bodies that way? If he is meditating, what will he gain from it? I don't understand."

Freddie replied that in meditation people might look as if they were thinking but really they were erasing all thought. In creating an absolute blank, they were able to tap into their own destinies or even into the universal mind. No one else could enter one's meditative secret inner world. Freddie said it was extremely difficult to explain the concepts to Cubans because the cultures were so different.

Oriental customs were thousands of years old, and age alone created a culture gap that was almost insurmountable between the two. As a result, there existed a huge difference in mentality. Abruptly, Freddie shifted focus and returned to Hiro's plight. "I'm very concerned about Hiro's health," he told Pedro. "I'm going to get my doctor to go with me to see him tomorrow." Pedro didn't argue.

The next morning a white Lada pulled up in front of Pedro's workshop and Freddie emerged with a gray-haired older man. Pedro smiled in welcome as he opened his door. "Que pasa?"

Freddie smiled back and introduced his guest, "Pedro, this is my dear friend Dr. Andres Josie Sanchez, a psychiatrist from The University of Santa Clara medical school." He turned to Dr. Sanchez adding, "And this is Pedro, a good friend of the family and Hiro's best friend.

As the men shook hands, Dr. Sanchez asked gravely how long Hiroaki had been withdrawn. Pedro told him that it had been about two and a half weeks and that during that time Hiro had eaten almost nothing. "We've tried to give him goat's milk and water, but he's refused just about everything. He just sits on the floor emotionless. That's the hardest part--he shows absolutely no emotion."

Dr. Sanchez said, "I think I may be able to diagnose Hiro's symptoms, but first I'll have to examine him." Madeline came in with a tray of Cuban coffee, and everyone sat in rockers in the living room to discuss Hiro's crisis. Pedro couldn't understand how anyone could go into such a deep and severe withdrawal.

Dr. Sanchez explained that right after medical school, before Fidel's revolution, he had been a medical assistant to the military in Santiago de Cuba. After December of 1959 many medical doctors had fled to the US and other countries so Fidel had lost almost ninety percent of the medical community within a few years. Then he was asked by his superior commander to begin medical training at The University of Havana.

"For four years we had trained many new doctors, nurses, and medical technicians, and had staffed many cities' main hospitals. I was interested in psychology so my superiors sent me to Chunking, China. Twelve of us studied there for five years. When we returned, we became professors of medicine in universities all over Cuba,"

Dr. Sanchez reminisced. "What we learned there really made us question our western concepts of medicine. In the Orient, they had been controlling brain activity for thousands of years through meditation and other unfamiliar techniques."

He digressed a bit, "You know, even here in Cuba, long before the Spanish came, there were the Taino and Caribe tribes here who had some similar practices to those of the Orientals. They meditated for the general welfare of their communities.

The Last Revolution

They had medicine men who participated in special meditations for death and marriage. They would spend days in meditation thanking God for food, water, or any other good that befell them. These were very important ceremonies for them until the Spanish destroyed their cultures."

"What I observed in China wasn't exactly the same as what went on here, but it was a similar way of controlling the brain's chemical activity. In effect, they were reprogramming the brain by defragmenting its cells. I personally watched many Buddhist monks do this. They had such complete control of the brain that they could undergo operations without any anesthesia whatsoever. They actually conducted normal surgical procedures. It was amazing to the Western mind because what they were doing was almost incomprehensible."

Chapter 34

In San Rafael, Isabel and Pepe were sitting on the front porch with the children when the white Lada stopped in front of their house. Isabel heart leapt at the thought that someone might be able to help Hiro. After everyone exchanged greetings, they all sat down in the living room to talk out their strategy. Dania came out and was introduced to Dr. Sanchez, who wasted no time in seeking details regarding Hiro's condition.

Dania reported, "Well, he was on the floor, without moving, for almost forty-eight hours. This morning around ten I finally forced him to go to bed because he was getting so weak." She paused. "I know something inside him is changing. I can almost feel it. Sometimes his eyes open and he almost looks normal. He might go to the bathroom. So I help him or I bathe him with warm towels. He did drink some water. Then he wanted to sleep so I helped him to bed. I've been checking on him every fifteen minutes. I think he needs medical assistance. Can you help?"

"Yes, I believe I can," suggested the doctor, "but I'd like to examine him first."

Because she feared that Hiro needed the sleep more than anything else, Dania hesitated, but finally she led Dr. Sanchez into the bedroom where Hiro was. Pedro and Freddie followed. Hiro's deep sleep and wasted look shocked everyone. His body was burning up, and his face was sweaty. His arms and legs thrashed restlessly, and the bedding was as knotted and bunched as his thoughts. Dr. Sanchez managed to dodge his flailing limbs long enough to take Hiro's pulse and to check his heart. He looked up and smiled, "Everything seems normal."

Hearing this, Pedro reached over and squeezed Dania's shoulder softly in shared relief. But after watching Hiro for another fifteen minutes, they saw that, although he still slept, he was becoming more agitated. Dania asked the doctor if she should get him a moist towel, but he told her to wait.

The Last Revolution

Suddenly, Hiro sat straight up in bed and let out a blood-curdling scream. Sweat poured down his face, and his bedclothes were soaked through. His breath came rough and his voice rasped. With eyes wide open, he scanned the room without seeing, all the while breathing as hard as if he'd run a marathon. Intermittently, he seemed to stop breathing. Then he drew in a long, labored breath to get enough air into his cheated lungs.

Fear and shock stalked the room like clawed and snarling beasts. Even Dr. Sanchez, who was usually so calm, shot out of his chair and rushed to Hiro. But Dania was already there on the side of the bed shouting, "Hiro! Hiro! Are you OK?" Tears coursed down her cheeks unheeded, and her hands shook even as they efficiently ministered to the man she loved. Pedro and Freddie sat immobile--fright denying them speech and action. What the hell could be haunting Hiro?

Once again, Dr. Sanchez checked Hiro's pulse. This time, it was racing. And his sweat was a stream, no-- a river. Sanchez requested a bucket of water and towels which were applied on all of Hiro's pulse points to cool his body as rapidly as possible. So intent were Dania and the doctor that they didn't notice at first that Hiro was again among them looking around owl-like in sudden recognition of his friends and loved ones. He spoke softly, "I had a bad dream."   All eyes were riveted on his face.

"What kind of dream?"

"Hiroshima." The word was more of a whisper.

"Hiroshima? You mean the atomic bomb?"

"No, B-29s."

"What?"

But Hiro was done. He closed his eyes and left them again. Dr. Sanchez checked him over quickly, and satisfied himself that all was basically well. "He just needs to rest.   Later, we'll get some bland food into him.   Food and rest are what he needs right now."

Back in the living room, everyone started talking at once:

"B-29s--weren't those American planes?"

"Yeah, a B-29 was a huge bomber."

". . . World War II . . ."

". . . over Japan for two years . . ."

". . . a B-29 dropped the atomic bomb . . ."

". . . on Hiroshima . . ."

". . . What Hiro's seeing in his nightmares . . .?"

Dr. Sanchez explained solemnly that often, when children with quieter, gentler personalities suffered trauma, they carried the image, the horror, with them for years, even decades. Unacknowledged and untreated, it could haunt them into adulthood and destroy their peace. "Has Hiro been acting like this for very long?"

Dania answered, "Yes, when I first met him he had terrible nightmares. But ever since we got married--and that's been eight years now--I've never seen him have a single nightmare. How could he have had this problem for years, like you said, without my knowing?"

"Sometimes one's memory is hidden away, festering. It doesn't always manifest in an outward way. And not always violently," the doctor lectured.

"Is there any medicine that could help?" she wondered out loud.

"Yes, there are all sorts of medications we might use, but they're expensive and we don't have access to them like they do in the US or Europe. We'll just have to wait and observe Hiro a bit longer," Dr. Sanchez apologized.

Everyone else went out onto the patio while Dania returned to lie beside Hiro, her lover, her life. Exhausted, she dozed to the reassuring even rhythm of Hiro's breathing and the gentle distant murmur of her friends outside. Dr. Sanchez voiced his prognosis, "I'm encouraged by Hiro's general health although we'll have to continue to feed and hydrate him carefully. Hiro's childhood trauma is curable with lots of difficult and time-consuming therapy, but the man's agony cannot be ignored.

Chapter 35

Freddie wondered aloud if Hiro could ever be normal if he had indeed suffered war trauma. And Pedro wanted to know what the doctor thought they could expect of him. But Sanchez refused to voice with an opinion. Only time would reveal the answers. "Let's give it two or three days. See what progress he makes. I'll stay here, if Isabel will have me." The doctor stayed, and the next morning everyone was up early, asking about Hiro's condition. Drawn by the tantalizing aroma of fresh coffee, they gathered together once more. On this warm and perfect morning, they silently seated themselves on a mattress on the floor in Hiro's room and kept watch over their friend.

Around 8:30, Hiro began to stir with slow, small movements at first. Then, he opened his eyes fully for the first time in weeks. Dania leaned over quietly and kissed his cheek. "How are you?"

"I think I'm OK. What's everybody doing in my bedroom?"

"We've been worried. You've been sick for a long time," answered Dania.

Dr. Sanchez stepped up to Hiro to examine him, but Hiro pulled back in surprise. Freddie urged, "Just relax. Dr. Sanchez is the best."

Days passed, then a week, and each day brought a bit more color to Hiro's cheeks, a bit more energy to his steps. The old Hiro was being renewed. He felt so much better that several weeks later he suggested a celebration. He wanted to go with Dania and her family to the Hotel Elguea. They'd never stayed there before because it was so close to their house, but Madeline loved the swimming pool, and Hiro and Pedro loved the mud baths and steam baths whose rich sulfurous smells and abundant minerals created the perfect spot for relaxation.

The baths had been a favorite restorative in these parts since 1860, when a local sugar mill owner named Don Elguea allowed one of his slaves to use the mud on a skin infection he feared would spread to other slaves. When the slave returned completely cured, the mud baths became famous. By the early 1900s, the first hotel dedicated to the baths had been built--located to take advantage of the only thermal springs in Cuba. Other draws were, then and now, the perfectly cooked fish in the hotel restaurant, and the welcoming, homey atmosphere. Pedro recognized many friends and acquaintances, and Hiro was greeted by one and all. How nice it was to relax in this friendly, quiet retreat. Hiro blossomed in the healthful atmosphere.

Hiro loved it here, except for one small problem: everywhere he went, clouds of mosquitoes, veritable storms of them, swarmed around him to sample his sweet Oriental blood. He'd run off screaming to escape them as the hotel crew arrived with the foggers to save him. Pedro, Dania and Madeline were never touched. Hiro joked that they had strong body-odor so the mosquitoes wouldn't touch them.

Meanwhile, despite his evident return to health and his levity with the others, Hiro had not returned to normal yet. Whenever he closed his eyes, his thoughts flew back ten years. But he mentioned nothing. He thought. He pondered the problem. He ran the probabilities, considered the permutations. And what he saw inside his head took on the appearance of a secret code. A computer code few, if any, could break. He attacked the problem again

"?????????????0110000101100010011000111100100110 0101011001100110011100001000101000101100100011001010 1 10011001100111000010001010 0010 0001111001001100101011001100 1100111.???????????????"

It was no accident, then, that ultimately Hiro did solve the problem he had set for himself. The solution was a fiendishly complex and elegantly structured computer game that would accomplish everything he wanted. This one game, of which he was the sole architect, was the culmination of Hiro's studies, of a lifetime of work in the areas of mathematics and computers.

After almost eight years living as a simple carpenter in rural Cuba, he was now using his enormous intellect to design an entirely new artificial language for the computer to recognize in order to execute his plan for Cuba. Hiro knew he needed to write new software, but he had absolutely no idea how to make it influence human behavior in real time. And that was his goal. He must learn more about brain function, about the anatomy of brain activity. Here in Cuba, he knew, there was no meaningful research being conducted in cutting-edge medicine. Furthermore, he wanted no one to suspect that he was researching. And certainly not what he was researching.

Feeling guilty, Hiro deceived Dania and their friends and told them that he needed to return to Japan to seek the mental therapy they had discussed. They all agreed that it would probably be best for him to return to the familiar culture of his childhood to deal with his trauma head-on. Dr. Sanchez kindly suggested several possible approaches to his therapy. But more importantly, he suggested introducing Hiro to his old friend Hector Ortiz, who was now Cuba's ambassador to Japan. Ortiz spoke fluent Japanese, and was an expert in Japanese history and culture. Hiro had isolated himself in rural Cuba for eight years; now he was finally ready to go home. He was emotionally ready for this journey.

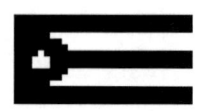

Chapter 36

Hiro left Cuba for Cancun, Mexico, on Aero Caribe Airlines on June 10, 2004. Dania and Pedro were among the crowd of friends who came to say farewell. Hiro was leaving Cuba for the first time in eight years, and it was the first time he and Dania had been separated. Dania was crying and tears were falling on her cheeks. She could not stop crying and was very emotional. Dania gave Hiro a big hug, kisses, and said, *"Cuidate Mi Amor!* As Hiro departed, a part of Dania's love left, too. Hiro remained quiet and said his good-byes to everyone. He didn't say much, but he was emotional. He always hid his emotions.

They had been flying only ninety minutes when Hiro saw the horizon of the Mexican coast from his window. Although Cancun and Havana were close geographically, to Hiro, they seemed ever so far apart. It was like another world. Cuba was the largest island in the Caribbean and was located only ninety miles off the shore of the US. Cancun was a modern tourist destination while Havana seemed like a city forgotten, frozen in time.

Cuba was unique and different from any other country in the world. That was the reason Hiro loved Cuba so deeply. He appreciated finding his true happiness in Cuba. Hiro remembered his experiences in Cuba and held them dear in his heart. Hiro could not compare Mexico and Cuba on a material level. The beauty and special quality of Cuba existed deep within the souls of the people. A rich culture existed below the surface.

Hiro heard the announcement, "This is our final approach to Cancun International Airport." As the flight attendant made her landing announcement, Hiro was filled with anticipation at rejoining the modern world. He had been living in the 1950s for so long. When he had left Cancun many years ago, the airport was old and not yet updated. It was now completely renovated

The Last Revolution

and had been Americanized, because US tourists flocked there by the thousands each day for vacation. He could see that many US dollars had been spent on modernizing the airport terminal.

It was modern and sleek, and Hiro hardly recognized it. It looked like any other modern terminal that he had seen in the US. It had lost its Mexican flavor which was sad to see. The old stores and its original look had been replaced by Starbucks and t-shirt shops. Americans were everywhere with their funny, casual tourist clothes and hats. By Hiro's estimation, ninety percent of the people coming into the airport were American tourists headed to the beach. It made Hiro sad because the modernization had erased the old, unique Mexican culture that had been so exciting to see. He had not seen any police presence and airport security appeared to be lax. This was a different experience from Havana where the police were everywhere. Back in the modern world, Hiro hesitated for a minute. He suddenly missed Cuba and yearned to return immediately, but he could not.

Hiro went to the Mexicana counter and said, "I have a round trip ticket from Havana to Cancun, but I need to ask about a flight."

The young lady at the counter asked, "Where do you want to go?"

Hiro replied, "Is it possible to purchase a ticket to Boston, Massachusetts, in the United States?"

She answered, "Yes, may I see your passport, please?" Hiro presented his passport. She said, "Just one minute. When would you like to return to Cancun, Mexico?"

Hiro answered, "I really don't know when--maybe just one way with an open date?"

She said, "It is better to purchase a round trip ticket and just not use the other portion. You'll save a lot of money."

Hiro was grateful for her honesty. Not every airline employee was interested in helping the customer. He said, "OK, but can we make the return portion for a date several months ahead in case I want to change the date and actually use the return ticket?"

The clerk answered pleasantly, "Yes, let me see what I can do for you." She was very helpful and checked the computer for him. Finally, she told Hiro, "All right. I booked the return flight for twelve months from today to give you a big cushion for changing this date. It is a non-refundable ticket at the price of $740 and you can change the date of return for a $75 penalty."

Hiro said, "Great, I'll take it." The clerk printed out the ticket, and Hiro gave her a cash payment in Cuban tourist money.

She said, "No, we can't accept Cuban dollars as payment. These are Convertible Cuban pesos, and we don't honor this currency. Do
you have American dollars?"

Hiro replied, "Sorry." Hiro had almost forgotten the US monetary system. Hiro had $1000 cash in his wallet, but he handed her his black American Express card. He had received this honorary card for being a lifetime member which meant he had an unlimited charge status. The black card came with special privileges although Hiro had not often used them. Hiro knew that the card automatically drafted funds from his account with the Bank of Hiroshima in Japan.

The clerk took the card with a surprised look. She stared at Hiro and said, "I have to check on something with my supervisor. I'll be right back."

A few minutes later she came back with a smile and said, "Well, Mr. Nakagawa you should have shown me this sooner. You have special Centurion status with this card and automatically get a first class reservation. I've never seen a black AMEX card before, but now I know about it." She gave the card back to Hiro and jokingly replied, "You hang on to this. It's black gold." They both laughed. The clerk upgraded his reservation, gave him instructions on his seating and handed him the return portion of the ticket. The clerk explained that Hiro would be flying from Cancun to Miami and then on to Boston. The return flight would follow the same route. She also repeated her instructions regarding his ticket. Hiro thanked her for her assistance and was on his way to Boston. Hiro felt excited to return to his old stomping ground at MIT. He wondered how his friends in the department and his old teachers were doing. He waited in the airport lounge reflecting on those old days until he boarded his flight. Dania and Cuba were also in his thoughts.

The flight to Boston was long so he tried to rest on the plane. As soon as Hiro arrived in Boston, he checked into a small hotel near the college and contacted his old dorm neighbor in Cambridge. Jon Katze was now part of the computer science faculty at MIT. Jon had a Ph.D. in microbiology and computer

The Last Revolution

science and was well-known in his field. He and Hiro had been great friends, and they decided to meet the next morning in Jon's office. Jon's specialty was researching artificial electrical currents. He had graduated with honors and later had become a professor at MIT. Jon was two years older than Hiro and had always looked after Hiro in the dorm and in the department. Jon had also studied computer digital imaging an innovative area of study.

Hiro loved seeing his old university. It really hadn't changed much since he had left in the 1960's. Hiro remembered that there was a computer science center in the faculty administrative center. The location of the computer science faculty office hadn't changed since Hiro's college days so Hiro headed to his friend's office. A young lady in the office asked, "May I help you?"

Hiro answered, "Yes, I am looking for Dr. Jon Katz." She smiled and answered, "Just one minute." She went into the back office and returned with Jon. Jon looked a lot older, but his face and features were still the same. His hair was almost all white, but he still had that wonderful smile. Jon had always been outgoing and personable. Hiro thought highly of him because Jon was extremely intelligent and had studied a variety of subjects. Hiro remembered how much Jon had loved to help others. Hiro had thought in their college days that Jon would make a great professor, so he was happy to learn that he had continued in the field of teaching. How wonderful it was to teach what you loved and to transform the minds of young students.

"Hiro! Wow, it's been a really long time!" Jon walked over to Hiro and gave him a huge hug and a firm handshake. It was a great moment for Hiro, and he felt joy at being reunited with his old friend again. Jon was very excited and said, "I wondered what had happened to you. The last time I heard you had returned to Japan to become a professor at The University of Hiroshima. Then you disappeared from the computer science world. What have you been doing? Where have you been living?"

Before he arrived in the US, Hiro had decided that he would keep his existence in Cuba a secret so as not to jeopardize his life or the lives of his Cuban family. He had decided to tell everyone, for political reasons, that he was living in The Dominican Republic. Hiro knew that he must be careful. Hiro answered, "Yes, all that is true, but I am married with two children and living in The Dominican Republic"

Jon said, "The Dominican Republic?   Oh, wow!"

Hiro asked, "What about you? You had a girlfriend who was a nurse."

Jon smiled and said, "Yes, you remember Kathy. We've been married almost thirty-five years now and we have one daughter and three beautiful grandchildren!"

Hiro was surprised, "Great!" They both were happy to see each other. Jon showed Hiro into his office where they had a wonderful time chatting about the many things that had happened in their lives over the years. The pair laughed and had a good time catching up. Hiro had known Jon for many years, but they normally chatted about computer science and work-related topics, not personal events. Now, Hiro was able to connect with Jon on a personal level. This change was possible because of Hiro's time and experiences in Cuba. Hiro had returned to the US a different person, a well rounded individual.

Jon was impressed and enjoyed seeing Hiro again. He said, "Would you like to go lunch with me? We have a lot to talk about, and I have some free time this afternoon."

Hiro said, "That's perfect. I'd love to." They continued to talk about many things as they left Jon's office. In fact, they talked the whole time as they drove near the Charles River in Jon's car.

Hiro asked, "Is that restaurant called No Name still here? Do you remember that place? We used to go there many years ago."

Jon said, "Yes. That seafood shanty's been owned by the same family since 1917. It's still considered a local secret. Do you remember their New England-style seafood and that seafood platter with fried clams, scallops, shrimp, and scrod? It was excellent. Do you remember Hiro?"

Remembering broiled fish and lobster plates, Hiro said, "Oh, yes! I remember it like yesterday."

Then Jon said, "No Name is still on the pier."

They looked at each other for a moment, and then chimed together, "Let's go!"

They drove to the bay area of Boston where many fishing boats were in the harbor. Jon parked his car nearby. The area looked about the same as Hiro remembered it. There were a few

The Last Revolution

minor changes, but not too many. Some of the light fixtures inside the restaurant had not changed since the 1960s. The No Name was packed with a big lunch crowd, and the food smelled good. It smelled like Boston. They got a table overlooking the pier. The restaurant was busy since many business people were enjoying their lunches and the beautiful weather. Jon wanted to know everything about Hiro's life. Hiro wanted to know all about the computer science world.

Hiro told Jon how he had isolated himself. During that time, many changes had occurred in the computer world. Hiro was eager to receive an update. Computer operating systems had changed rapidly. Hiro began to think that his knowledge might be obsolete by now. It was easy to feel out of the loop, and that was what had happened to Hiro over the course of eight years. Hiro was fascinated and just listened. Jon gave him all the latest news from the computer world. Jon was a good teacher, and he quickly brought Hiro up to speed by explaining the different aspects of the computer science industry and scientific frontier.

Hiro had been isolated, but his mind had dulled. Hiro listened intently and understood the fine details and technological advances that Jon spoke of. Hiro could almost visualize all that had progressed since he had left and many advances he had thought about before going to Cuba had come to pass. Many innovations that Hiro had once dreamt of were now possible or were realities. It was all very interesting and Hiro relished hearing every detail, but at the same time, he missed his life in quiet and peaceful Cuba. For a quick second, all he could think about was Dania and the children. His heart was with his family and with Cuba. He thought to himself, I made the right decision. I don't miss all of this. Hiro then turned his full attention to Jon's explanations.

After a couple of hours giving updates, Jon asked Hiro, "How about The Dominican Republic?"

Hiro answered him, "Well, there's nothing there as far as computer science. They're in the Stone Age as far as technological advances. However, the flip side is that they have plenty of time to relax and to enjoy life. The people are friendly and I really enjoy living there. You know, I spent my whole life chasing a smoking dragon, and I found out that it didn't exist. I worked with computers, machines, and equations for so long that I almost forgot about being human. But I finally found myself again there. I feel lucky to have found another way of life and I have a happy family. I really don't miss the world of computers very much. Can you believe it?"

Jon laughed and smiled, "I know what you're talking about, Hiro, because I'm still chasing the dragon--always have and always will. My wife wants me to retire, but I'm not ready."

Hiro told Jon, "My wife and I have two daughters. The youngest one is four and our older daughter is seven. I gave them Japanese names, Yumiko and Masako. They are cute and very intelligent."

John started to smile, "Of course with a dad like you they would have to be." They both smiled and continued talking and enjoying each other's company. Jon and Hiro enjoyed a great meal of seafood chowder and fish and chips. It was all very tasty, and they enjoyed talking on the pier and watching the harbor activity. It was a sunny day and the air smelled fresh. Hiro loved being in Boston. It was like old times, and it felt good.

Jon asked, "What're you doing here in Boston and the United States?"

Hiro answered, "I'm here for a short visit to try and understand something that I'm researching. I'm looking for some information."

Jon asked, "What kind of information. How can I help?"

Hiro replied, "I need to find a top-notch research scientist in neurology."

"Neurology?" Jon asked.

Hiro explained specifically what he was looking for. Jon thought a minute and said, "I have an old friend who is head of the Neurology Department at Johns Hopkins Medical School. He and I met at Cal Tech. My friend is terrific. He is one of top researchers in neurology in the United States." Jon added, "I can put you two in touch. No problem. My friend thinks like you did in computer science and sees what'll be possible nearly twenty-five to fifty years ahead. He's impressive. He's also extremely imaginative, and he has successfully transplanted the brain of one mouse into another mouse. It was a big step even though the mouse only lived fifteen minutes. He's known to be controversial due to this innovation, and some don't approve of his work. But I think he's a genius and he's kept his work quiet since that incident. Only a few people in the scientific and medical community know of his work. It is amazing what we can

The Last Revolution

do in the field of science and medicine. We need more researchers like him."

Hiro was shocked to hear of this experiment. He had trouble believing that someone could transplant an entire brain. Hiro knew this was the right person with whom to discuss his research and questions. Jon asked, "What is it that you're actually looking for?"

Hiro told him, "I'm looking for some fundamental interactions between neural cells. I want to be able to understand their relationship and transpose the connection into computer code."

Jon said, "Well, you haven't changed that much as far as I can see. You may be a laid-back family man now, but you're still cutting edge, Hiro. Where do you come up with these ideas? You always amazed me and our friends. Hell, I'm only a computer scientist, not a neurologist. It's over my head. You should definitely meet my friend. Maybe he knows what you're looking for." Hiro agreed.

Jon thought for a moment as he looked out over the view. "You know, I've been postponing some business at Hopkins. Why don't we go together so I can personally introduce you to him?"

Hiro said, 'That would be perfect. Thank you! You just made my life easier. I thought it would take several weeks of digging to get anywhere. But now you've come to my rescue."

Jon laughed and said, "You know you came to right place. MIT is the best scientific community there is, and we can find out almost anything. You have a lot of friends here. We're called old farts and dreamers. But hey, it works!" They both laughed at Jon's comment and finished their lunch.

Jon asked Hiro, "Would you like to come to my home? We can sit down and talk some more. I need to put some documents together for tomorrow for my visit to Hopkins. It should take me about thirty minutes. As a matter of fact, I probably need to call my office and have my secretary put some things together for me, too." Jon proceeded to call his office using his cellular phone.

While Jon was giving directions to his secretary, Hiro began to daydream about how Cuban people might cope with being thrust suddenly into the modern world and the age of technology.

Would modern day civilization keep these people happy? How would they change? What if the Cuban government suddenly changed tomorrow? Would the Cuban people starve to death? Would the nations of the world come to Cuba's aid?

Hiro thought about the possibilities for change and wondered which system would be better for the people. While Castro's system was brilliant and idealistic in theory, it was not so perfect in reality. There were so many holes in Castro's system that Hiro hadn't accounted for, and the Cuban people were the ones suffering for it. But Hiro still saw the best parts through the hearts of the people. Perhaps their simple lives and few choices had kept many of them pure and good. Perhaps the greed of capitalism would change them. Who knew what the outcomes would be?

But, for better or worse, since 1959, Cuba had been in the hands of Castro and a Communist-Socialist system. And for better or worse, Hiro had come to love the Cuban people. Hiro continued to ponder on the politics of Cuba.

What if Cuba were to change to a Democratic system of government? Would the people benefit from living in a free society?

Perhaps, they would or perhaps they would only be miserable and come to hate it. From living in the US and observing their democratic system, Hiro knew that it was all about the survival of the fittest in many ways. This was true for most political systems, but especially in a democracy. One had to work hard for success and for rewards. Survival of the fittest could be seen in the animal kingdom as well as within the social system. It ran the whole gamut. Some people thrived while others were left behind. This is how it was in Cuba before the revolution of 1959.

At that time, many groups living under the Batista regime were dissatisfied and supported Fidel Castro as their savior for change. When Castro successfully overthrew Batista's regime, he gave special favors to those who were loyal and who had supported him. Yet, the educated elite of Cuba became frustrated. They wanted to escape to Florida when they saw their heads were on the chopping block. The government was confiscating everything they had worked for. Castro wanted to equalize the wealth of the country and give land to the peasants. He sought to break up the class system, but for the rich and elite this was agony. They had to leave Cuba for there was little room for their way of life. They needed to leave quickly while they had some wealth left.

Many people fled Cuba then and also in the early in 1990s. Hiro thought that it would benefit Cuba to educate the people to stay and to give them some incentive to remain in Cuba. This might cost the government a tremendous amount in resources for education, but it would be profitable for Cuba. Castro believed in education, and that is why it was free to all Cuban citizens. The problem was that the people didn't take advantage of this opportunity because there was no possibility of upward mobility. Why should they study if they could make more money on the black market? University graduates working in tourist hotels made one-hundred percent more than they could earn working for the government. Hiro thought that, sadly, it all boiled down to economics.

Hiro continued to daydream and ponder the possibilities for Cuba and its people. Castro could have created and developed a brilliant think tank among the people through education if he had done it differently. It was similar to the phenomenon in Japan where youth were encouraged and rewarded to study and to achieve.

"Hiro!" He heard someone calling his name. It was Jon. "Hiro. You've been lost in thought for several minutes. What have you been daydreaming about?" Jon began to laugh. Hiro was embarrassed. He knew that he had drifted off inside his thoughts as he sometime did.

Hiro answered with a smile, "Well, I was thinking about my family and home. I guess I'm missing them right now."

Jon said, "Well, I certainly can understand that, my friend. Why don't I take you back to your hotel so you can get some rest for tomorrow? We have a big day ahead of us." Hiro felt tired and agreed. He had had a long day full of excitement. It was quite a lot to take in, and he needed to get some sleep.

The next day the pair left Boston early in the morning while it was still dark. The drive to Hopkins in Baltimore took several hours. On the way, Jon and Hiro talked and admired the beautiful scenery. Coming from Cuba, Hiro had almost forgotten how well-maintained the interstate system was. It was an efficient system that mobilized citizens and was good for the US economy. Being able to travel was a reward of living in the states that most Cubans couldn't imagine. Travel was suppressed and difficult in Cuba and few Cubans could afford gas for a car, even if they had one. Hiro thought about Pedro. He was one of the lucky mobile Cubans. Hiro thought about all the people who were stuck out in the country.

Many people were already traveling this morning. Hiro thought about where all these people were going and what they might be doing. They were working in the big wheel of the US economy. This freeway was like the heart of money and material wealth in the modern world.

It was a smart and efficient way of life. People had access to everything. Hiro amused himself by counting how many different styles and makes of cars and trucks he saw. It was the first time he had done that. In Cuba, he could count them on one hand. In Rancho Veloz there were only old junky cars. He asked Jon, "How the hell do you choose which car you want? So far, I've seen a hundred and sixteen different types of cars in the last few minutes!" Hiro enjoyed mulling this over on the drive to Maryland.

When the pair arrived at the Department of Neurology, they were expected and warmly received, as per instructions from Jon's friend. The assistant showed them to a waiting room, gave them coffee and politely asked them to wait there. Fifteen minutes later, a man with over-sized, thick glasses and white, wavy hair entered the room. He was dressed smartly and looked professional. He struck Hiro as distinguished and interesting. In addition, there was something kind about the man's presence. Jon stood up, shook the man's hand, and gave him a big hug. They were obviously good friends and very open with one another. This helped Hiro feel comfortable right away. A good friend of Jon must be a good man.

The man said gingerly, "How are you two doing? Did you have a good drive? " Hiro was quiet and nodded yes. He immediately liked the sound of the man's voice. Jon was happy to see his friend and was all smiles. On the drive, he had told Hiro that they had been friends since high school in Los Angeles.

Hiro stood watching the two men. For a moment, he thought to himself, "What a beautiful thing." He admired them because it was a true friendship from time spent together in their youth and not based on work or financial reasons. Unfortunately, this was most often not the case. He remembered from his time living in the US that some friendships were built around money, and he had always distrusted those. But in Cuba and Japan, he had found friendships like this one between Jon and his childhood friend. Their friendship was solid and pure.

Jon immediately introduced Hiro to his friend, "Hiro, I want you to meet my old friend, Dr. Emmett Bell. I think he can help you with your questions." Hiro and Dr. Bell shook hands.

Dr. Bell said, "Dr. Nakagawa, it is an honor to meet you. I certainly already know about you and your work. Your reputation precedes you. Every day I use programs originally created by you. I couldn't do my work without your innovations. You have been a life saver!" They both laughed.

Hiro said, "Any friend of Jon's is a friend of mine. Please call me Hiro. Thank you so much for seeing me today. I really appreciate your time and assistance." Hiro and Emmett had a lot to talk about.

Jon interjected, "Hiro is interested in some specific areas of neurobiology. Is there any way you can assist him in finding what he is looking for?"

Emmett said, "I'll try. What particular areas?"

Hiro remained calm even though he was eager to see if Emmett could help him. "I'm trying to find a neurological bridge between computer language and the human brain. I'd like to see if the neurons of the brain could be compatible with an artificial computer code so they can function together. More precisely, I'm interested in triggering complex human neurological responses and activities by introducing specific computer science commands and codes."

Hiro continued, "I am interested in writing a computer language and system, let's call it *Sonic Brain*. It would be compatible with the human brain. It would be possible for this system to duplicate the human brain so that when the human dies the system could recapture and actually store that person's memory, thoughts, and history in real time for future research and study."

"The program would then act as a copy of a person's brain and could be accessed later. For instance, a great-grandson would be able to communicate with his great-grandfather using the *Sonic Brain software* in real time. They could communicate in real time although they might not be able to understand one another well because of the cultural and generational time gap."

"The applications are endless, and it would be like a human time machine as far as communications are concerned. A further advanced application that I have thought about, let's call it *Cyclone Sonic,* could be implanted into actual human neurons thus triggering the part of the human brain that controls motor sensors and movement of the body. *Cyclone Sonic* would be a super code and system to be integrated with a human subject's brain to dictate movements in real time."

"It could all be controlled by the use of low level frequency laser beams. This could be used through a remote computer monitor to control the brain activity of the subject. Brain neurons and movements could potentially be manipulated by this remote-controlled source with *Cyclone Sonic*. Do you think this is possible or is this all nonsense?"

Emmett was silent for a moment, deep in thought. Finally, he took a sip of coffee and spoke, "Hiro, I don't know whether to think you're a madman or a genius. But I like the way you think. Honestly, with today's technology, it doesn't seem possible; but knowing your background, you may be just the person to develop this code." He took a look at some of Hiro's notes and research and said, "It is amazing how much you understand about neurology and your research is most impressive. I think you're onto something here. I certainly can assist you in further research. I have several manuscripts you may want to take a look at. Fortunately, my expertise is in synthetic brain chemistry."

Emmett added, "I may eat my words later, but I think your idea of a computer technology that could duplicate brain memory cells, enabling memory to be accessed, like hacking into a computer, may be possible. It may be a good idea to utilize computer science in this way. I know that no research has been done in this area yet."

"The anatomy of the human brain is an amazing world, and a most complicated system. The brain has fascinated man since ancient times, yet, for the most part, it still remains an enigma. As a science, we still are finding out that we know very little. Perhaps, coming from a computer science background you can see things differently and help us in developing a new system for understanding the brain. The memory code of the brain's neurons, how they talk to one another, is, at present, almost a black box. We still have a long way to go in our studies."

The Last Revolution

"First we must find a way to trigger sensory feedback. Then we may be able to interface with memory and eventually learn the memory code. Finally, we may be able not only to access but also to manipulate memory. We could even control human movement. Unfortunately, these ideas are closer to science fiction than realistic near-term goals--say the next twenty years or so. We still have a great deal of research to do before this can occur."

"An important goal in our field has been the creation of artificial brain tissue. It's a complicated matter to fabricate the tissues of the brain; and so far, no one has done it. If, however, we were able to make synthetic brain computer software and integrate it with neurons, this would be an artificial brain. The method to control the neurons to elicit neuronal compliance has already been created, although it's still in a primitive stage. The medical community is aware of these advances and is anxious to be able to apply them in many diverse ways. Among them is the utilization of binary language to interpret brain activity through direct contact with a physical device which, in turn, remotely controls robotics to do whatever tasks are needed. For instance, a robot might be guided through thought to enter a building engulfed in fire. Another greatly anticipated use, as you may well imagine, is to help people with limbs afflicted by paralysis to use those limbs naturally once more."

"Over the last few years, my colleagues and I have been studying a new brain wave related to human emotion. It has been explored in the form of bio-feedback, which uses various systems of light, sound, electro-magnetic force and physical vibration to stimulate and trigger the brain. You might even say it is re-booting the brain. These stimuli can in turn be synchronized with external codes or signals to create regular neuron firing where it is needed: in breathing, the heartbeat and such. These involuntary activities can be triggered or stopped by the brain, but normally they cannot be regulated in this way. Now, we are able to stimulate synthetic waves in the brain to create essential bio-feedback among these fundamental body functions."

Hiro and Jon were fascinated and listened intently as Emmett continued, "Our brain wave frequencies trigger and control our memories. If adult brain cells are erased, there is no way to get them back. New ones cannot grow in their place, and the memory cannot be retrieved. Some neurologists are studying what happens when individual neurons within the brain are corrupted, and the memory is erased similar to the way a computer erases data. When that happens, the injured person will never recover because he is no longer living in real time."

"Do you remember the woman in Florida who was in a vegetative state for years? Her memory was destroyed, and her husband wanted to pull the plug on her. If her memory had been duplicated before her accident occurred, then her memory could have been carried in a hard drive the way an ipod carries tunes. Using the externally stored data, her memory could then have been duplicated and totally restored. It may soon be possible to carry out such functions with the direction technology is going. We just don't know?"

"Maybe one day we'll develop a method to replace these dysfunctional cells. Imagine the gift that would be to mankind! We do know that neurons can regenerate themselves, but new ones cannot grow in their place. Right now that's not possible—but ongoing stem cell research may change that." Hiro could see the excitement in Emmett's eyes as he spoke about the future of neurobiology.

Emmett continued, "A recent study by a biological engineer at MIT used two-photon imaging to trigger specific neurons. Over a period of several weeks, he tested the surface layer of the visual cortex in animal studies. He focused on specific neurons that cluster in a pyramidal form that house interferon, the chemical gel-like protein that controls the neuron system and much more. Also, as a result of the startling new imaging technology, we can now monitor the neuronal structure in living human brain tissue. There is evidence that the brain can restructure itself, but it has yet to be proven."

Emmett spoke to Hiro, "I have all the documentation on our research; and if you would like to take notes, you are welcome to be our guest. The only string attached is that you must sign a compliance and legal agreement not to copy any of the content. The information is also not to be used in any form of publication and only used to study, help in research, and in understanding neurology further. If you uncover any new evidence in this area of research, this agreement gives us access to a copy of your work. We believe in sharing our scientific information and expect the same from others. We must share in the consequences for the betterment of society and mankind. It is for all of our futures."

The Last Revolution

      Emmett showed Hiro those documents that he felt were most applicable to his interests. He suggested that he begin at the elementary brain anatomy and then go on to more advanced areas. He told Hiro that he could find all the information he was seeking on a set of CD-ROMs, but that it would take a year, or possibly two, to study and assimilate it all. Emmett added, "Hiro, you can come to my office and make it your home base while you begin to learn something about neurobiology. It will probably take at least ten days. Then you'll be better able to choose areas of special focus. You won't understand every aspect of the field, but this initial investment of time will be well worth it. Accumulated here is about thirty years' worth of information." Hiro was very pleased but didn't quite know what to say. Emmett was being so generous to him, including the use of his office. Hiro knew that Emmett was offering him exactly what he needed. He had hit a gold mine.

      Hiro smiled and shook Emmett's hand, "Emmett, I don't know how to thank you. I appreciate your concern for my studies and feel that you have just what I am looking for right here. I would very much like to come to your office for ten days to examine your documents."

      Emmett replied, "Well then, it's decided. You can begin whenever you like and stay for as long as you like. You are my honored guest. Please make yourself at home and let me know what else I can do to assist you." Emmett had another appointment and said good-bye to Jon and Hiro.

Chapter 37

Hiro and Jon needed a place to stay. Hiro had never been to Baltimore. Jon suggested that they stay somewhere quiet and relaxing. He took Hiro to the Clarion Peabody Court Ritz-Carlton Hotel in the heart of downtown, in the lovely and historic Mt. Vernon area. The hotel was upscale with elegant accommodations. Hiro remembered staying in places like this before living in Cuba.

He had forgotten how nice five-star hotels were. Everything was new and modern. The lobby was sleek and elegant, and the guests were all well-dressed. After living in Cuba for so long, this place seemed like a palace. The luxury of the facilities and the accommodations for one person were unbelievable. He thought to himself, "Only in America." He had forgotten what money could buy in the U.S., and the high standards that Americans expected

Jon wanted Hiro to stay here because he knew this hotel well. Jon had stayed at The Clarion many times. Jon had suggested it because of its proximity to the medical school, and he knew the service would be excellent and that Hiro would have a peaceful environment for his studies. In Hiro's opinion, it was too luxurious. He told Jon that he would feel more at home at a small hotel that he had seen nearby. Jon insisted that Hiro should stay at the Clarion. Jon was convincing and told him that he should enjoy living in style while he was in the US. He didn't know Baltimore, so he trusted Jon's judgment. Jon told him it would be convenient and a perfect environment for temporary living.

The two checked into the Penthouse suite, with separate rooms and parted company for the evening. Jon had to prepare for a morning meeting at the medical school. Hiro was pleased with his spacious room which was free from noise and crowds. The location was perfect, because he could see many nearby restaurants. He would be able to catch a taxi going in any direction easily. Hiro was exhausted and needed to sleep. He was still digesting the information that Dr. Bell had shared with him. He fell asleep pondering the incredible possibilities.

The next day Hiro caught a taxi to the medical school campus. Emmett helped him get a temporary security pass to the main faculty facility, so that he could come and go as he pleased. Then, Emmett showed him to a desk with a laptop. Emmett had designated an exclusive workspace for Hiro in the library area of his own office. Emmett walked Hiro quickly through the computer's security code clearance and showed him how to access his personal files and those of the medical libraries. He could access all the information he needed by computer and he knew that he would absorb the material and research at a startling pace.

Hiro had developed this skill as a student back in Japan where pressure to excel was high and competition was fierce. He had not lost his touch. He was fascinated by all the information available, and wanted to learn as much as possible in the short time that he would be in Baltimore. He studied daily from eight in the morning until ten at night taking only short breaks for food and personal needs. Hiro found that he was able to hack into data from a national scientific and medical database from Dr. Bell's computer. The possibilities for information were astounding, and he knew he had to act fast since he was in a time crunch.

Hiro showed Emmett how he could tap into this rich storage of information with some hacking know-how. Emmett was amazed at Hiro's unconventional methods of research. He also admired his complete dedication to the research. Hiro and Emmett forged a strong respect for one another and a warm friendship grew. It wasn't just a one-sided relationship—they were both learning and exchanging information.

Within ten days, Hiro had memorized an astounding amount of information. It was as if he had completed graduate and postgraduate courses in neurobiology in just ten days. He was completely focused on absorbing all the knowledge he could, and his photographic memory helped him retain almost everything. He found the information stimulating. These were totally new concepts for Hiro in a fascinating new field, and he concentrated on those new frontiers of neurobiology that would help in the project he had in mind. Most importantly, Hiro came upon precisely what he had been looking for.

Emmett was astonished that Hiro had finished his research within the ten-day period. It was an impossible task to read and process all those documents and computer files. Emmett decided to ask his friend Jon to help test Hiro on how effectively he had accomplished this task. Jon would be returning to Baltimore tomorrow, because he had been invited to give a seminar the following day in the Computer Science Department. He and Hiro planned to meet at Emmett's office so that they could walk together to the seminar.

Even better, as far as Hiro was concerned, was a phone call that he received from Jon that afternoon: Jon and Kathy would be coming to Baltimore. They would be staying at the Clarion for two days and they wanted to meet Hiro for dinner.

Hiro was happy to get the call. He hadn't seen Jon's wife, Kathy, in many years. She had always been a warm and interesting person. Back in his graduate school days, they had been great friends. Hiro was looking forward to the great company, a good meal, and a stimulating discussion. He had so much to tell them about his successful research.

Hiro returned to the hotel at four in the afternoon. There was a message for Hiro at the front desk saying that his company had arrived and what their room number was. He quickly went to his suite, changed clothes, and freshened up. Hiro called Jon and Kathy's room, and they decided to meet in the lobby at five. Kathy had been short and slender with long dark brown hair thirty years ago. He wondered what she was like now.

As Hiro exited the elevator into the lobby, he saw Jon and Kathy. They gave him hugs and warm greetings. It was a wonderful reunion of old friends. Kathy said, "Well, Hiro. I've gotten old, haven't I?"

Hiro said, "We all have, but you look great." She was now in her mid-50s and a bit heavier, but still attractive. Her long brown hair was now short and red. The haircut and color really made a big difference in her appearance, but he could still see that same great smile. Hiro remembered that, despite being shy, she had possessed a wonderful sense of humor. They reminisced about the good times and laughs they had had when the two men were attending graduate school.

Kathy grabbed Hiro's hands and said, "You've hardly changed at all. Your hair is gray, but otherwise you look the same. It's those good Japanese genes you have!" They all

The Last Revolution

laughed. Kathy said, "Jon told me that you were staying at The Clarion. I've always wanted to come here with him. This is quite a fancy place. Jon has been here for work several times while I was stuck in Boston, but not this time." She laughed, "Besides, I have been dying to see you. When you came to Boston, I was at my sister's in Florida and missed seeing you by a week. I hope you don't mind that I invited myself along on this trip."

Hiro replied, "Not at all. I'm happy that you came. Jon has helped me so much, and my research with Dr. Bell has been astounding. It has been the best trip for me! And now, it's even better because of seeing you. I've been looking forward to it all day. Please come to my suite. I've ordered some wine and refreshments from room service for us to share. Please be my guests." They took the elevator to the executive floor where Hiro's suite was located.

Kathy loved Hiro's suite. There was the nice-sized sitting room with plenty of seating for everyone. The view overlooking the downtown area was gorgeous. Kathy joked, "I'm moving to your suite, Hiro! This is elegant and so spacious." Room Service arrived delivering a bottle of wine and a tray of assorted appetizers. Jon said, "Wow, what a spread! You didn't have to do this, Hiro."

Hiro said, "Please, you're my guests tonight. I also want to celebrate the conclusion of my research here at Johns Hopkins. I'm finally finished and I got just want I needed here. Without your help, Jon, I would never have found it."

Hiro poured each of them a glass of wine, and they raised their glasses in a toast. Hiro said, "To good friends." They all smiled, toasted, and tasted the wine. The wine was delicious. He invited the pair to sit down and enjoy some refreshments. They talked and enjoyed the time together. He had asked Jon to bring Kathy with him for his seminar. Having Kathy join them in Baltimore had been Hiro's idea.

After the wine and some catching up, they were all three relaxed and looking forward to a good meal at the Clarion's seafood restaurant, a lively place with wonderful views of the city. They all loved seafood and perused the extensive menu with delight. Jon and Kathy ate a lot of seafood in Boston, but they never grew tired of it.

Kathy was especially excited because she saw that the chef was French, and that many of the dishes used classic French recipes. She had visited France many times with Jon when he had attended different meetings over the years. Besides, her mother was from Paris. Both of her parents were brilliant scientists. Kathy's father had received his doctorate in chemistry from MIT.

    Kathy loved the taste and special flavors of French Cuisine. She ordered the *Coquilles Saint Jacque Parisian,* sautéed jumbo scallops in a cream sauce. Jon had orange roughly with tarragon—simple, but delicious. Hiro chose *bouillabaisse.* He ate every bit of this traditional French seafood dish with shellfish and golden saffron. They drank more wine and talked all night. Hiro told them about some of his research and they were deep in discussion all evening. After dinner, they had a delicious dessert of vanilla crème brulée and a warm berry tart with chocolate sorbet. It was a delicious meal with great company and equally great conversation.

Chapter 38

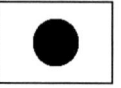

The next morning, Jon and Hiro met Emmett at his office. They began chatting about Jon's upcoming lecture. They sat on the office sofa while Dr. Bell's secretary served them coffee. Emmett told Hiro that although it might seem a little like a parlor trick, they would like to know how much Hiro remembered from his studies over the past ten days. Hiro explained he had mastered the material. However, Emmett had trouble believing that Hiro had been able to do this so quickly. Jon asked Hiro, "May we test your memory?"

Hiro sipped his coffee, closed his eyes, and remained silent for a moment as he began to access his neuron-encoded, compressed bio-memory of the documents that he had studied:
"??????????01110001110?????1100110011001110110110010110000101100010011000110110010001100101011001100110011101101001011011000110111001100100110010001110001100101100100011100?"

Emmett began, "What is the occipital lobe and what is its function?"

Hiro sipped his coffee and became silent again. Then, he answered calmly, "From your documentation on Microsoft CD ram segment 5, page 16, and second column from the left: Then Hiro recalled from his memory bank the photographic digital image of the research describing the central nervous system.
Emmett and Jon checked and found this exact paragraph on CD ram segment 5, page 16 the second column on the left. Jon said, "It's written just as he has said. He's correct." Emmett understood photographic memory, but had never known anyone with the capacity that Hiro had demonstrated. He said, "It is a great gift you have, Hiro." Emmett added, "I want to continue with another question. Immune cells help to maintain cognition and cell renewal. What is neurological process?"

This time Hiro stood as he drank his coffee. He was calm as he walked toward the window and looked up at the sky. Then he began: "This is found on CD ram segment 8 pages 42, column 3, which contains information from a team of researchers at Neurobiology Department."

Using his eidetic memory, Hiroaki repeated word for word the section of the research paper which described the specific areas of the adult brain which have the ability to sustain the function of cell renewal throughout a person's life. These findings have possible implications for delaying and slowing down diseases, such as Alzheimer's or Parkinson's.

Jon and Emmett checked CD segment 8, page 42, and column 3. "Incredible! It's amazing. Hiro got it exactly right." Jon had not known that his good friend had this ability. He had known Hiro for a long time and had known that he was brilliant, but this was beyond anything he had ever imagined. Hiro was almost savant. Jon had trouble believing that a human could memorize this much information. Jon and Emmett were in awe as they witnessed Hiro's demonstration.

Emmett shook his head, "Hiro, I know about photographic memory, but you have the highest capacity I've even seen. I wish you could stay here and let us examine your brain. I promise it won't hurt. You have an incredible ability."

Then Emmett said "Hiro just watch this very carefully." Emmett picked up and twisted a Rubik's Cube 24 times. As he handed the cube back to Hiro, he said, "What is this combination and what are all of the possible rotations?"

As Hiro twisted the cube, he replied, "You are asking me something impossible to answer. This may be the greatest mystery puzzle of all time. I can recognize more than forty-eight combinations, but actually all there are 43,252,003,274,489,856,000 possible combinations. It would take a modern computer nearly twenty-five years working day and night to find each arrangement."

Emmett shook his head and stated, "I'm afraid he is correct. Hiro's memory is based on mathematical layout. I have never met anyone who has a brain like his." Even as a young boy, Hiro was able to read something and know it by heart. Then as a student, this ability came in handy. He could study and access the material instantly for his exams. It was just something that came naturally to him. Emmett turned toward Hiro, "I presume you will be continuing this new interest, the combination of computer science with neurobiology?"

The Last Revolution

Hiro answered, "Yes, and it's possible that Jon and I might work together in the future on this." Everyone smiled in agreement.

After the meeting was finished, they walked, together with some other faculty members, to the Computer Science Department to hear Jon's seminar. Kathy was already there waiting for Hiro and they sat together during the lecture. Kathy was proud of her husband. Jon gave an insightful and interesting discourse on computer biotechnology—a new area of interest for Jon and his colleagues at MIT.

Before the lecture, Hiro invited Emmett to a thank-you and farewell dinner with Jon and Kathy. They had a reservation at Trattoria Alberto, a local Italian favorite recommended by Emmett. The restaurant had a lively atmosphere and enticing aromas filled the air.

Hiro, Kathy, and Jon dined on fresh tomato bruchette, arugula salad with figs and shaved parmesan, homemade spinach ravioli, and wonderful grilled halibut in white wine sauce. Emmett had capriccio with a lemon and olive oil marinade followed by osso-bucco. He ordered a round of lemon cello liqueur for all to sip.

Emmett, Jon, and Kathy reminisced about the old days and laughed over stories from their past. Hiro enjoyed hearing these tales as he enjoyed the rich flavors of the food. There were no Italian restaurants in Cuba, and Hiro had not had Italian food in many years, so this meal with his friends was a special treat. They drank two bottles of red wine.

During the dinner, Emmett and Jon didn't mention Hiro's photographic memory. They had decided to keep Hiro's skill confidential. After dinner, they sipped on port and shared a tiramisu and a chocolate hazelnut torte. They were full but managed a few more bites. It had been a most enjoyable evening for them all.

The group said their goodbyes. Shaking Emmett's hand, Hiro said, "I couldn't have done this research without your help. I hope that one day I can return this favor. Thank you so much. I appreciate everything!"

Emmett smiled and patted Hiro on the back. "Hiro, it was an honor to work with you. Please keep in touch. Let me know how your research project pans out. I'm very interested in seeing the final results. Come and visit me anytime. And thank you for letting me test you today. I am still speechless over your demonstration!"

After Emmett left, the three took a taxi back to the hotel. Jon and Kathy, who had to get up early for their return to Cambridge, said goodbye to their good friend. Hiro, too, was leaving the next day, to see his family in Japan. They all hugged and promised to stay in touch. Jon and Hiro both felt they would be working together in the near future and looked forward to that day.

Kathy had tears in her eyes as she gave Hiro a big hug and kiss. She said, "Take care, and next time I want to see those cute children of yours. Have a safe trip to Japan." It was always difficult to say goodbye to friends, especially ones who went back as far as they did and who had such big hearts. Hiro, exhausted from his marathon research, a little tipsy, and full of good food and friendship, slept deeply that night.

| ● |

Chapter 39

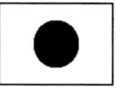

The next evening, Hiro left Boston for Tokyo, Japan. He wanted to see his family. His younger sister, Mariko lived in one of Tokyo's suburbs called Saitama. She was the youngest of the four siblings. Mariko was beautiful and sweet and had two daughters and a baby boy. She was married to a kind man who was the CEO of a Japanese toothpaste company. They were happy to see Hiro after being apart for so many years. Hiro stayed at their tiny, but comfortable home.

For dinner, Mariko prepared some of Hiro's favorites, such as tempura, pickles, and salad, along with the standard *miso soup* and hot white rice. Hiro loved these foods; he had grown up eating them. They ate together sitting at a small table on the floor. The kids were real cute and giggled a lot. Mariko and Hiro chatted during the entire meal, catching up on everything.

Mariko's husband and Hiro did not discuss business. They just enjoyed the family and talked about what everyone was doing. Mariko and her husband were supportive and helped take care of their elderly mother in Hiroshima. She always reported their mother's status to Hiro through letters. Hiro relaxed with his sister and her family for ten days.

Hiro planned to travel to Hiroshima on the Japanese express train which was called Shinkansen. He loved riding this train because it was the product of twenty-first-century technology. It was the world's fastest train and traveled between 135 and 165 mph. The Japanese were also developing the next generation of Shinkansen that was supposed to travel up to 350 mph. Unbelievable! The Japanese were tops in the high tech field and the many branches of the industry. Hiro loved how the Japanese could adopt modern technology so quickly. By Shinkansen, it took four hours to travel from Tokyo to Hiroshima. The Shinkansen was a magnificent model of modern technology which functioned efficiently. The Japanese could not live without this invention. It was the main method of transportation for most business people and for millions of daily commuters. It linked the entire island.

Every time Hiro returned to Japan, he remembered his youth in the 1950s and became nostalgic. It was the country of his origin and ancestry. He remembered his dreams of reaching the upper echelon of education in mathematics and then in computer science. He had been a humble young man back then. Hiro had come a long way. He remembered that he and his three sisters had been reared to obey and honor their mother's wishes in anything she wanted them to do. His mother had always encouraged her children to aim high. For Hiro, his mother was always in his heart, but he had not seen her in nearly eight years.

It was now monsoon season in Hiroshima. It was the time when the farmers finished planting the rice paddies. Hiro was able to see Mount Fuji on this train trip from Tokyo to Hiroshima. It was always a favorite site for him. Mount Fuji, a dormant volcano beloved by the Japanese, was the subject of much art, photography, and silk screens since ancient times. But today, on the tail end of monsoon season, it was almost impossible to see the peak through the rain and fog.

Anytime Hiro arrived at the Hiroshima train station, he would go to the food court, so he headed there immediately. His favorite meal was a traditional, regional favorite called *Okonomiyaki*. It was prepared with various chopped vegetables, chicken, and shrimp which were mixed into a pancake-like batter and fried on a hot steel grill. Hiro loved the sweet and salty ginger sauce poured over the top. The dish was nicknamed Japanese pizza by foreigners, but it was more like a lunch pancake. The famous recipe had been handed down from many generations, and was still the basis of thriving businesses in Hiroshima.

Kure was only thirty minutes away by train which was where Hiro's mother and sister lived. At the station in Kure, Hiro hailed a taxi. At 1:00 p.m., the taxi arrived at the house of his mother. Hiro pushed the doorbell, and she came running out to greet him. It had been so long since they had last seen each other. Hiro's mother had tears of joy in her eyes. They were both overjoyed to see one another. Sadayo had prepared a special meal called *"Chimaki"* for her special son. She was so excited that she couldn't stop talking. She told him all the latest news and chatted for nearly two hours until his sister returned home

The Last Revolution

from working at her own small store in the downtown area. Kure was the formal Japanese Naval headquarters, and there were many shipbuilding businesses in the area. Kure was an area of heavy industry, housing companies such as Kawasaki and Mitsubishi.

Kure had been a robust area for many years, but because of the high cost of wages for Japanese workers, much of the business recently had moved to China and Korea. Japan had been suffering from an economic slump for nearly fifteen years and was in an economic depression. The structure of the city had changed because of the low Japanese birthrate which was only 1.3 children per family. That meant smaller families, because times were harder and there were not enough incentives for couples to have bigger families. It just meant more mouths to feed from fewer resources so, consequently, there were not enough workers. Industry suffered tremendously.

Hiro enjoyed visiting his family and returned to The University of Hiroshima to meet with all his old friends. He felt comfortable there. It was like a docking station for his brain. He also enjoyed helping the younger professors and chatting about the latest in science and mathematics. It was just like the old days. Hiro always had helped the faculty of the departments of mathematics and computer science. The professors were honored to have him back and also to have his help with their research questions. He was a local legend, and he felt proud and honored to be back. Hiro also liked giving lectures to both the professors and the students. The university asked him to do this, and Hiro was receptive. Hiro spoke almost every night after the professors finished their classes and work. The lecture hall was always packed with people wanting to hear Hiro speak and to ask him questions.

Hiro returned to his mother's home around midnight. Even though it was late, she was waiting up for him. His older sister waited with her. They were a very sincere family, although they didn't have the same happy-go-lucky attitude as his Cuban family in Sierra Morena. It was the difference in cultures and the past. Nevertheless, Hiro enjoyed being with his family. Although it had been so long since he had seen them, nothing much had changed.

Ayu fishing season always began on the first day of July. Hiro stayed in Hiroshima until the last week of June, looking forward to going fishing in the secluded, countryside Chugoku mountain village called Ueno where he had grown up. It was his favorite pastime, and he couldn't wait. He had been dreaming about Ayu fishing for years. Hiro still had several cousins who lived in Ueno whom he was excited to see. He planned to stay at one cousin's house that had been in the family for nearly 400 years. It was a traditional country village home with a thatched roof and big rooms, but it was comfortable and Hiro liked it. A typhoon had hit this area; and although his cousin's home and the village were fine, the fishing spot hasn't had changed a lot since Hiro was last there. Some areas had been destroyed, and trees had fallen into the stream. The whole mountain stream looked completely unchanged and river was so small from back in the old days, but the fishing was still good.

Hiro went Ayu fishing every day during his visit in Ueno; he was in heaven. There was a real art to this particular type of fishing, and Hiro had to regain his skill level. It was like riding a bike in that he regained his skills quickly. Hiro was joyous during his time on the mountainside, spending most of his time fishing by himself. The mountains were green and majestic. Back in the days of his youth, there were rice paddies built along the ridges as far as the eye could see. Hiro remembered planting rice by hand in his childhood with his mother. It was hard, stoop labor, but there was a certain joy and simplicity in it. Hiro had played alongside his mother while she had worked.

All that had changed. Today, there were only a few cultivated rice fields, and many of the old farmhouses were abandoned. The days of country farms had long died out and very few families continued their ancestral work. Hiro knew that even in his own family that after his cousin's death, there would be no one else to take over the family property. The children had moved to the cities for jobs. Few people wanted to live in this remote village anymore.

Even though it had been neglected by age, the countryside was a unique and special place which held a great ancient history. Hiro thought about all the families that had lived off the land here. Rice farming had been the heart of this area for many centuries. People had come from the towns to fish every July. Although his family had possessed limited material things while Hiro was growing up, they had felt good and safe. Now, even fishing was not so popular anymore in the age of

The Last Revolution

technology. Everyone headed to the bigger cities for other jobs and spent their time in the modern world. But Hiro knew the difference and appreciated being there. He thought it was sad that it was a dying culture and that the young people wouldn't get to experience the serenity of the countryside.

While Hiro fished, the Japanese mountain monkeys came and stole his lunch. It happened all the time and was quite funny. Hiro didn't mind, although he was a little hungry. Lunch was a small obento with onigiri, which were rice balls wrapped in salty dried seaweed with sour plums in the center. The monkeys amused Hiro.

Hiro admired the beautiful waterfalls and rising water. It was so fresh and clean here. There was not a hint of industry, and it was amazing. The green lush mountain filled with tall trees was a beautiful sanctuary. It was a place from his past that he could still enjoy today. For Hiro, there was nothing quite like it.

Hiro remained there for another week, and then planned to return home to Cuba. He missed his wife and children. He had stayed in Japan for as long as he could. Hiro had wanted to take a nice long trip because he knew it would be a few years before he could return again. Saying good-bye to his mother and sisters was the most difficult thing. He hated being so far from them, but his life and destiny were in Cuba. He longed to rejoin his love, Dania, and to live the simple life with his children in Rancho Veloz.

Hiro departed Tokyo and headed back to Boston. From Boston he traveled on to Cancun. Here, he began the last leg of his trip back to his final destination of Havana. Although Hiro had spoken weekly to his Cuban family by phone, it had been almost four months since he had left Cuba, and he couldn't wait to get back to his wife and children.

Hiro arrived in Cuba with many gifts for Dania, their children and his friends but he had to hide the gifts so they wouldn't be confiscated by Cuban customs. Hiro had many goods and fabricated materials that he had obtained for his computer. They were materials he had gotten from his connections in Hiroshima. As well, Hiro had purchased many items for his friends, such as materials for making computer chips and many small electrical tools. Hiro needed these items for the second phase of his computer science research in Cuba: the creation of a new generation of neuroelectronic interfacing

Micheal Kazuhiro Nishitani

systems between neurons and high-powered computer memory to explore and clarify the nature of human memory function.

Chapter 40

Hiro arrived in Cancun

by Aero Caribe operated by Mexicana Airlines. It was a day filled with beautiful, tropical Caribbean weather. Hiro could see hundreds of miles of beautiful, lush green fields and palm trees. He couldn't wait to smell the fresh scent of the tropics and to see coconut trees. It was a sunny day, and Hiro knew quite well that with the scorching tropical sun overhead it would be hot when he landed in Cuba. Hiro would soon disembark in Havana. He thought, "Now I know Cuba is my home." He felt good. Hiro was excited about returning to his beloved family, and he envisioned their happy faces. He had missed them so much. Over the past four months, Hiro had accomplished a tremendous amount of research toward his new plan. He would be the architect of a great, new invention in computer science technology. His invention would revolutionize the world.

Before he knew it, his plane, an Aero Caribe DC-9, touched down at Jose Martí International Airport in Havana. He was glad to be back in Cuba. It was 10:30 in the morning, September 28, 2004. It was quite different from the original airport where Hiro had first arrived in Havana all those years ago. A Canadian construction firm had rebuilt the airport in 1997. Today it was a facility of contemporary architecture.

Many things had changed since the Communist block had weakened. The Communists' departure had left Cuba with a huge financial burden. Therefore, Cuba had turned quickly to a tourist-dependent economy. The government also had deemed US currency to be the main currency circulated in Cuba. American dollars were used to purchase many badly needed items that were necessary for the survival of the Cuban family as well as for the Cuban government. For Hiro, it was sad to see the old culture of Cuba disappearing.

For the first time since the Communists had overtaken the country, there was a huge disparity between the rich and poor. Communism had brought more equalization but now there was a rising class difference. This shift was due to the influx of the strong U.S. dollar. Those with access to US money had an easy life. Those who were limited to Cuban pesos struggled. It was a difficult situation. It was the same as in a free-enterprise government system. The few rich just got richer while the many poor just stayed poor. Cuba was a living example of a true Communist social government, but because of Fidel's ambition to stay in supreme power for life, Cuba hadn't achieved true success.

Many citizens were frustrated with Castro's leadership. Fidel lived in fear for his life and had to move around in secret. No one knew where he was at any time. Fidel lived this way because he feared that the citizens might take revenge against him, so he always kept himself one step ahead in his political strategy and rule of Cuba. This had created much international criticism about Castro during the years.

In theory, Social Communism was a beautiful, perfect system. But in reality it didn't work. The life of the average Cuban citizen was a poor and difficult one, stumbling through life on the tropical island and barely getting by. Hiro loved the resilience and spirit of the people, but he also felt their pain and suffering. The only commodity that the Cuban people had in abundance was time with their families—the Cuban people had nothing but time. With the economic depression, the people were restless and conditions were getting worse. Fidel had to work quickly while he still had a card to play in his hand. Hiro knew that Castro was a shrewd political player, but the stakes were now high, and the game was becoming increasingly more challenging. In the past when the chips were down, Fidel had always come back, using every trouble or problem to his advantage. He was a magnificent spin-doctor.

Fidel was a great politician who had pulled off many difficult schemes over the years, but Hiro wondered if he could do it again. It was time for Fidel to come up with a new plan for Cuba. Otherwise, his days were numbered. Fidel Castro was nearly 79 years old. He had always possessed a strong charisma and had been a passionate leader who had remained so since the early days of the 1959 revolution.

Fidel loved to speak to the Cuban people, and the people loved to listen to his rhetoric. Even at his advanced age, he still continued to give speeches. Castro could begin speaking and continue for five more hours. He was a marathon speaker, and Cuban TV channels and radio stations would air the entire thing. For Fidel, staying connected with his people was a key component of his strategy.

However, in recent months, the European Union had been critical of the human rights abuses committed by the Cuban government. Fidel was under scrutiny for his brand of politics which had resulted in declining tourism. Castro had had to import petroleum from Iraq and Iran. Petroleum was high at the time that Fidel's political platform changed, and he had shifted to adjust to the new changes in the economy and international market. Then Castro turned his focus toward Venezuela. President Chavez of Venezuela favored a social government, and he had tried to persuade the politicos of other South American countries this way. Chavez was also very anti-American, like Castro.

Hiro understood that people in Latin American countries needed a strong social-democratic government to enforce the law and to exert control over the rising population. The poor supported the socialized government, while the rich were more in favor of a democratic, capitalist-based government. Hiro wondered if some new sort of economic compromises could help, or if nature's path through agony and misery might be best.

Chapter 41

At long last, Hiro's retreat to the Far East and the U.S. was over, and he was finally back in Cuba. He was also back at the infamous Cuban immigration security checkpoint at the airport. But to his surprise the process went very smoothly. All the luggage was x-rayed but not inspected, thanks to Freddie. Before Hiro had left Japan, he had sent an E-mail to his friend in Santa Clara, asking him for a favor. Freddie had received the information from Hiroshima and was happy to help Hiro. He was smart and knew what to do to allow Hiro to avoid the rigorous luggage inspection at customs. Freddie also personally spoke with the head of airport security to make the arrangements before Hiro left Japan. Luckily, the head of airport security was an old friend of Freddie's. Without assistance from Freddie, Hiro could not have brought anything related to technology from overseas unless it had been inspected first by Cuban customs authorities.

Freddie had pulled some strings so Hiro received preferential treatment. He prearranged for him to have special foreign diplomat envoy status. In order to receive this status, Hiro had to use his Japanese passport to enter with special documents from Hector Ortiz, the Cuban Ambassador to Japan. He was able to bypass all customs inspections which normally would have been a nightmare and a very frustrating ordeal. Hiro was relieved because he was carrying many things that would have been confiscated without this special treatment. The Cuban immigrations officer treated him like someone with diplomatic status. Freddie was a great friend who always looked after Hiro's safety and welfare. Hiro was grateful for the smooth arrival courtesy of his good friend.

Just as Hiro was leaving the customs area he heard, "Papi! Papi!" Hiro was delighted to hear the precious voices of his two daughters, Yumiko and Masako. They had been waiting just outside the customs office for hours. They ran to Hiro and jumped into his arms. Such sweet hugs and kisses they gave him. They were overjoyed to see their father.

The Last Revolution

Then Hiro saw Dania. He felt like he was in a dream. His lovely wife was there beside him again, and she was smiling with tears in her eyes. She embraced him with all her might and cried into his shoulder. "Welcome back, my love," she whispered through her tears. They stood embracing for a long time.

Hiro knew he had missed his family, but it wasn't until this moment that he realized just how much. There was nothing better than being with his family, and he knew he had been away too long. As Hiro stood there hugging his two young daughters and his wife, they all cried tears of joy. At last, the feelings of peace and serenity filled his heart once more. It was being back at home and with his family that made him feel complete again. For the past four months, he had been operating on autopilot—doing what he had to for the sake of research, but paying a heavy price for being parted from his family.

Dania dried her tears and touched his hair and face saying, "Hiro! Hiro! I love you! I missed you so much. I just can't live without you. You are my life, and the most important thing to me. My heart is yours!" Then she began crying very hard. It was a cry from her heart, and Hiro was overcome with emotion. Tears streamed down his cheeks.

Hiro whispered into Dania's ear, "I love you, too. I'm sorry I've been away so long... never again." Hiro had just left Japan where he said good-bye to his mother and sisters. His family had been composed and calm during his departure.

In Japan, one would never witness a scene in an airport like Hiro's family reunion. The Japanese were taught to hide their emotions in public and there were never big public displays of affection. But here in Cuba, Hiro was able to be his new self and to express his emotions with his wife and children openly. Their reunion was a beautiful moment.

Hiro looked at his cute treasures and said softly, "Hey, Masako and Yumiko. I missed you so much. I love you both very much. Papi will never go away like this again. I promise." All three hugged and kissed.

Then out of the corner of his eye Hiro noticed his old friend Pedro walking toward him. Pedro approached smiling saying, "Hola, Hiro, What's up? "

Hiro answered, "Good to be back in Cuba. What's up with you?"

Pedro replied in his usual tone, "Hell, Nothing much." The both smiled and Pedro gave him a strong bear hug. Pedro was so strong that his hug made Hiro's body ache, but it was a welcome ache. Dania and the girls laughed. Then everybody started to laugh.

Then Pedro's wife Madeline approached Hiro and gave him a hug and kissed his cheek. "We all missed you here," said Madeline. Hiro's happiness was so evident and genuine that everyone thought his supposed therapy in Japan had gone splendidly, but nobody mentioned it. The air outside of the airport smelled very Cuban. It was a blend of the tropical breeze and the smells of Havana. The hot sun was high overhead which made Hiro sweat like a Cuban kiss. He thought to himself, "I'm really back in *Colba*-Cipangu. This is my home." Hiro's emotions were high, and he felt elated. At last, he was rejoined with love's well, quenching his spiritual thirst and immersing his soul.

In the US and in Japan, he felt like a lonely traveler just passing through. But here, in his heart, he was not. Here on this island in the Caribbean he was at peace with his lovely family and felt alive. Today he knew that Cuba was his true home. Hiro thought, "I was born Japanese. Then I was a Japanese-American. Now I'm a true *Cipangu-Colban.*"

Hiro's mind took in sights and sounds like an ever-changing kaleidoscope. He was filled with joy, happiness, and excitement all at once. He was in the most upbeat period of his life. This was what life was all about. "This is really it," he thought.

Most of Cuba was living a full life without money—no money, no status. But money and status no longer meant anything to Hiro. He always had wanted to achieve and have money as a child, and had accomplished that in the US, but in Cuba he had found what he was really looking for. Hiro realized that he had found love in a Communist-ruled system, and it was the greatest gift.

The Cuban people might not agree, but Hiro knew better. He had suffered all his life from haunting flashbacks of the 1959 Cuban revolution and from the war in Japan. Now he felt immune to the flashbacks because of his new life here.

His career as a computer scientist dealing with the technology frontier was also not an easy task. Hiro thought about

The Last Revolution

Fidel and how he also had to look ahead to the future. What Hiro did today would pave the way for the future. He had to be prepared with a strong plan of action. If not, there would always be someone to take over and succeed in his spot. The Social-Darwinist philosophy of survival of the fittest applied here, especially to dictators.

Hiro had done his part, and now he wanted to enjoy what was left of his life with his loved ones. He thought about what mattered most to him. It was the love of his family. But he knew so many others who were caught up in the rat race. They were focused on money, position and status, which made them miserable. Hiro knew he had it best. That other life was not acceptable for him any longer. It all seemed so empty now that he had real love, real friendships, and a real family. He might be living a simple life, but to him it was the life of a king. Now it was time to enjoy his happiness and unity with his special family. He took a deep breath and thought, "I have everything I love in Cuba! I love my home in *Colba*-Cipangu"

Pedro helped Hiro carry his luggage. He had quite a bit and every piece had a red sticker indicating that the bags were part of a special envoy for a special foreign visitor. Freddie had called his boss and arranged this treatment for Hiro. Freddie had paved Hiro's way for two reasons. First, because Freddie wanted to make the hassle at customs easier for Hiro, and second, because he knew Hiro would bring back many gifts for his friends and family. All the gifts were fine with Freddie, but would not be with the government. Freddie knew Hiro was generous and would be bringing things that people needed in their everyday lives, not lavish items, but items which were difficult to get in Cuba.

Thanks to Freddie, Hiro didn't experience any problems in customs and his many pieces of luggage were intact. Hiro had smuggled in some important supplies and information for his computer science project. He also had hidden a Sony laptop computer which the customs officials had not found. Hiro knew he was taking a big risk, but he knew that Freddie was covering his back. It was worth the risk, because possession of a laptop in Cuba was unheard of. Hiro needed the laptop to carry out his plan.

Chapter 42

It was almost midday in Cuba and the scorching Caribbean sun burned Hiro's face and cheeks. Hiro liked to feel the hot rays on his face. That was Cuba. A cool ocean breeze kept them comfortable on the drive north along the coast through Varadero to Rancho Veloz. It was a long drive which took nearly four hours on the old unkempt highway. Hiro was a little uneasy because today there were many police present on the highway. Hiro asked Pedro, "Do you think we need to worry about the police?"

Pedro answered, "Hell no! The police will think you're tourists. Look here at all your luggage." Hiro had a huge, overstuffed suitcase tied on the top of the luggage rack. "Only Cuban-American tourists would bring that much stuff. Don't worry," said Pedro.

Then Pedro pointed to a gaping hole in the highway pavement. Hiro pondered out loud to Pedro, "When is the government going to fix this highway?"

Pedro answered, "Look, what do you expect? People need to eat more than they need a new highway. It's about survival. Besides, no one complains except the tourists. They don't care about us. They're only trying to take a cheap vacation here."

Pedro continued driving through Matanzs and the northern coast of Cuba. It was a beautiful scene filled with peaceful countryside views. Hiro could see shanty houses and a few people. They all looked like they were living in slow motion. No one seemed to be in a rush; they were just taking their time. Hiro liked people and observed that everybody helped everybody else.

In the car, Pedro asked about the highways in Japan. He wanted to know more about them. He was also interested in Japanese cars and electrical technology. Hiro explained everything. The passengers listened and imagined what life in Japan was like. Dania asked about his family in Japan and Hiro told them about his mother, sisters, and cousins.

Hiro's girls were giggling and full of questions, too. Hiro

The Last Revolution

told them everything they wanted to know which helped to pass the time during the long drive. Hiro told them about Ayu fishing and how he had caught many fish. He also had purchased a video camera and had filmed much of his trip. Everyone was looking forward to getting home to see what Hiro had been talking about.

Between the towns of Matanzs and Varadero, there was a small fishing village called Boca de Camarioca. It was a tiny village that had a great roadside grill which served wonderful fresh fish Cuban style. The fish served there always had an incredible taste which Hiro loved. Hiro was feeling hungry and asked Pedro to stop at the food stand when they noticed two police officers beside the grill. Pedro just kept driving.

Hiro yelled, "Pedro, stop! Why did you bypass the grill?"

Pedro said, "I hate those two policemen back there. They're no good." On another trip, when Pedro had been returning from Havana, he had received a ticket from them because he had lost his official ID and had only a temporary Carnet de Identidad. The policemen presumed he had illegally forged the ID card even after he explained the situation to them. The policemen had taken him to jail. Fortunately, Pedro had been able to call the Rancho Veloz Police Capitan Henry Perez to explain the situation to them. Finally, Pedro had been released from jail, but he still hated the police in Boca de Camarioca with a passion.

Hiro remembered his first year in Cuba when he had been hassled by the government security guards and the police. Now Hiro didn't need to worry about being arrested because he could act as any other Cuban would, because the Cuban government was good to foreigners who married Cuban women. They treated the foreign spouses as Cubans. But Hiro remembered when he and Dania had been walking together on the street near a town frequented by tourists. Every time they walked there together, government undercover agents harassed Dania. So as not to upset Hiro, Dania always gave him a signal that everything would be OK.

Dania quickly presented her Cuban marriage ID to the agents. Any Cuban married to a foreigner had to have an ID card called "Carnet de Identidad Matrimonio con extranjero." When an undercover policeman saw a foreigner and a Cuban woman together, they immediately suspected that she might be prostitute. Hiro always shook his head and kidded

Dania saying, "So I am with a prostitute?" Dania flashed Hiro a big grin and winked at him. Without getting married, it was very difficult to get a resident visa in Cuba. Hiro was lucky because he had fallen in love with Dania and had decided to stay in Cuba to marry her.

Hiro said, "Look, I'm a permanent resident of Cuba now, and I also have a document identifying me as a professor at The University of Havana." Hiro was hungry and his impatience was getting the best of him.

Pedro said, "Stupid police! OK, you win." And he turned the car around and drove back to the grilled fish food stand.

At the grill, Pedro and Madeline sat together. Hiro, Dania, and the children sat across from them at the table on the patio. The employees knew Pedro and Hiro because they stopped there every time they passed this way coming or going to Havana. Hiro also gave the workers a big tip of $20 which was equal to six hundred Cuban pesos. This amount was equivalent to one month's salary for many Cubans so everybody knew Hiro at this little south-side grill in Boca de Camarioca. The owners immediately came over to greet the party and to chat. They all sat at the patio table watching a young mentally handicapped girl dance beautifully to the music of a local guitarist. The guitar player played his harmonica at same time, just like Bob Dylan. The guitarist was short, and since he was shy about his baldness, he always wore a homemade Cuban hat.

The entertainment was delightful. Hiro always gave the dancer chocolate or chewing gum. She loved seeing Hiro. The little girl danced merrily when Hiro gave her the treats. She was about ten-years-old but acted more like a two- or three-year-old. Everyone loved her, and she was very innocent and sweet. She just loved to dance to the music. Pedro and Madeline also liked her and always gave her twenty pesos. But the youngster didn't have any concept about money. She was just as happy as possible, lost in her own world. Hiro thought, "What a lucky girl. She'll probably be happy her entire life."

Changing the subject, Pedro said, "Hiro, I've stopped smoking cigarettes."

Hiro was surprised and his face suddenly turned serious as he said, "I can't believe it. I really can't believe that you have actually stopped. That's great. We have been discussing this for many years. Tell me, how do you feel?"

The Last Revolution

Pedro said, "I actually feel much better."

Hiro said playfully, "Well, I almost told you that you looked like you had gained weight. Now I am glad I didn't mention it."

Pedro patted his belly and said, "Yeah, when I stopped smoking, I started eating a lot more. I've put on fifteen pounds over the four months you've been gone!"

Hiro looked surprised and said, "Well, now you need to exercise-- maybe some jogging around Rancho Velloz?"

Pedro just grinned. Hiro asked Pedro, "Have you seen Freddie or Dr. Sanchez lately?"

Pedro nodded his head in answer, "Yeah, I saw them in Santa Clara when I was visiting my aunt. They came for dinner. We chatted a bit and they're both doing OK. They asked about you and your health. They hoped your therapy trip to Japan had helped." This was the only mention of his breakdown.

Hiro smiled, "I miss them a lot. They are so nice, and I consider them my good friends for life!"

Pedro said, "Well, buddy, how about me?"

They both started smiling and exchanged a high five. Hiro said, "Pedro, you are like a brother to me!"

And Pedro added, "Hell, I hope I'm not as ugly as you are!" Everyone started laughing at his joke.

Dania kissed Hiro and held his hand. He gently kissed her on the shoulder and whispered, "I love you so much." Dania kissed him some more. The children were laughing and playing. They were so happy to be together as a family again. The children played with their father. Everyone felt relaxed and happy together. They enjoyed the food and the music.

Suddenly, a police officer appeared and asked for Hiro's ID card. Hiro looked surprised and said, "Look, I'm not a tourist. I'm Cuban-Japanese."

The policeman said, "What is Cuban-Japanese? Is there such a thing?"

The officer looked at Hiro's passport and at his government ID. Hiro's papers proved that he was a professor of mathematics at The University of Havana. Then the officer changed his tone and said right away, "Sorry to disturb you, sir. Have a wonderful lunch with your family."

The officer was quite polite. There were very few like him. Pedro told them that the officer was one of the good ones, but shuddered in relief when he left.

Hiro said, "Pedro, I know you love policemen. Maybe you can kiss his ass since he was nice!"

Everybody started laughing, and Pedro had a grin on his face. It was peaceful at the roadside grill, and the fish feast was wonderful. Hiro loved fish, but this dish prepared in the Cuban style was one of his favorites. Everyone enjoyed the meal.

They were still two hours from home when they got back on the road. Pedro wanted to stop for a minute to see his cousin in Santa Marta near Varadero. He asked Hiro and Dania if that would be OK with them. Everyone was fine with it. Hiro knew Pedro's cousin had many goats and that Pedro wanted to get some of the goats for a feast in Rancho Veloz. Dania asked, "How will you take the goats home? We have too much luggage. Where are you going to put them anyway?"

Pedro said, "Well, we can put the meat in the floor someplace. My cousin has a huge freezer full of goat meat. It'll be fine until we get home. We'd better get it now if we want it. I don't know where I can get goat meat anywhere else. I checked around before Hiro came back and no one has any near home. But if you'd rather we didn't stop, we don't have to." Dania and Hiro loved barbecued goat meat. It was Hiro's favorite Cuban dish. They both agreed to stop to get meat.

As they entered the Varadero Peninsula, Pedro turned left on the second street and drove until he hit a pasture. His cousin's house was there. The whole place smelled like goats. The odor was pungent and strong. Hiro's daughters and the other women in the car held their noses and said "Wheeeew! It stinks here." Pedro's cousin had at least forty goats in a pen front of the house.

Pedro said, "He sells the meat on the black market to the hotels in Varadero. They purchase goat meat for the tourists. My cousin exchanges the meat for food, alcohol, and stolen goods from the hotel's restaurant employees. They steal whatever they can from the hotel's supply closets and put the stolen goods into a community pot. Then they share the profit in an equal amount. It is a matter of survival and much-needed income to support their families."

Pedro went on to explain that they stole to survive because they had to. It was all about survival and nothing more. If the government cracked down on the black market and enforced the law on those who stole, then it would create a huge

The Last Revolution

political problem. The government knew this and was forced to look the other away. But in certain circumstances, they used stealing as an excuse to arrest people they didn't like. The black market had to exist; otherwise Communist Cuba wouldn't have survived since 1959.

Pedro asked, "Where is the best place to put the meat?"

Dania said, "How about you put it inside the trunk next to the tire? Make sure to protect his souvenir from Japan so blood won't ruin it."

Madeline agreed saying, "Last time we did this there was blood all over, and it got all over my dress."

Dania made a face in disgust and said, "Pedro, how about tying down the meat with rope outside on the door latch?"

Pedro said, "Door latch? Well! I don't know about that. We've never done that before."

Dania said, "Maybe you can put the meat at the very bottom of the door so the blood won't spread out everywhere."

Pedro said, "Maybe. We'll see. He successfully tied the frozen meat to the door latch on the side of his door. "It'll be secure," he announced.

"It's really funny looking driving on the country highway like this," Madeline said.

Pedro said, "Well, it looks like that is the only place we can put the meat. My Ford is a tough car, and I know we'll make it back home."

All of the luggage was on the top of car, and the trunk was full of more stuff. There were nylons pack hanging down and goat meat on the door latch, and it looked ridiculous. Hiro thought, "Only in Cuba!" Everyone could see the funny site from a mile away

Chapter 43

Back at home in San Rafael,

near Sierra Morena, Isabel and Pepe couldn't wait for Hiro to arrive. They had missed him very much. It had been four months since Hiro had left, and they were eager to see him. Isabel had been cooking and preparing a vegetable and pork dish. Pepe killed his big pig for the feast tonight because Hiro's return was such a special occasion. The couple wanted to give Hiro a big welcome home feast.

Pepe and Isabel started early preparing everything and had been busy all day long. After the pig was killed, Pepe hung the meat in front of the kitchen door. He was making chicharon, pork sausage, which produced lots of grease from the pork fat. Pepe and Isabel prepared Creole-style pork barbecue because they knew that Hiro loved it.

There were three different ways to make barbecue in Cuba. Because they were descendants of the African Yoruba tribe which cooked in a Creole-style, the type of barbecue prepared by Pepe and Isabel was quite different from Pedro's. First, Pepe dug a ground pit and placed many banana leaves in the center of it. He also placed a big can in the pit to collect grease and used what he collected to baste the entire pig. The pig was then stuffed with natural ingredients including lemon, garlic, oil, comino, onion, tomato, many herbs and papaya skins. The stuffed pig was then covered with many layers of banana leaves. Gravel was placed over the leaves, and a huge fire was set. The pig was cooked anywhere from four hours to all day long, depending on the size of the pig. This method of cooking sealed the flavors of the spices into the meat. Periodically, Isabel poked a sharp knife into the pig to check the temperature.

Her uncle Duenio in Sierra Morena cooked barbecue differently. He made a huge ground pit filled with Cuban hard wood arranged like a camp fire. He hung a two foot by five foot piece of mesh over the fire. Then he placed the pig on top of the mesh. Many natural spices were spread over the entire pig which was then covered with many layers of banana leaves. The cooking continued all afternoon. Isabel's uncle Duenio periodically adjusted the banana leaves to control the temperature. He watched the fire carefully to keep the temperature at a consistent level. Occasionally, he added some herbs for flavor. Isabel's uncle enjoyed drinking Cuban chispa de tren, moon shine rum, while cooking. Dania always said that when he becomes drunk the barbecue was ready to eat. The barbecue was served with Cuban side dishes including rice, yucca, black beans, desserts, fresh Cuban fruits, and of course, Cuban beverages, such as beer and rum.

Since Hiro had moved into this house, pork grease was not used for cooking any more. Hiro wanted them to use vegetable oil which he bought at the Pan-Americana store. Hiro explained to them how unhealthful the pork fat and grease was for them. Hiro couldn't bring himself to eat it. But today, Pepe wanted to use it because he loved the flavor and could sell the grease to his neighbors. The neighbors always wanted to buy pork fat and grease. It was popular in the Cuban diet. Sometimes Hiro saw people pouring pork grease on top of their rice topped with a little salt. Hiro knew how unhealthy that practice was, but people didn't care and did it all the time here. Hiro never let anybody do such a thing in his house.

Pepe sold much of the grease to his neighbors and friends that day. With some of his earnings, he bought some supplies for making his own rum. In Cuba, it wasn't a party without good home-made chispa de tren.

Late in the warm afternoon, they heard the sound of Pedro's 1956 Ford coming down the dirt road below. They were finally home. Pepe and Isabel ran out to greet them. As soon as Pedro parked his car, Hiro's family jumped out, and everybody started screaming for joy that they were finally home. As Hiro stood smiling in front of the house, he daydreamed about a new project.

Hiro planned to create a satellite dish to receive signals for his internet connection. That was still a long way off yet, but he had to get internet access for his idea to work. Hiro would have to reconstruct the house to hide the satellite dish and internet hook-up cables completely. It would have to be hidden from the inside and from the outside because it was a crime against the government to have such things. He knew he had to plan very carefully. Just having a big antenna meant a huge fine and the risk of the government tearing it down eventually. That had happened to another VHF antenna that the government had said was receiving US signals. Whomever owned the VHF antenna had to pay a fine amounting to $100 USD to the government, and the antenna was torn down. A satellite dish would mean far worse consequences for the whole family. Hiro's new project must involve careful planning and precision.

Isabel and Pepe were ecstatic to see Hiro. They hugged and kissed him and welcomed him home. Isabel wanted only the family and Pedro, his wife and his daughter Wendy to join them for tonight's special dinner. She wanted to keep this first evening at home private. Then, in a few days, they would have a huge welcome home feast attended by many friends and family. They had already invited everyone for this big party at Pedro's home.

Hiro felt good to be back in his happy little home. It was quite different from the Ritz-Carlton, but he was happy to be there with his family. It looked like any other Cuban country home with a straw roof and walls made of unfinished concrete blocks. From the outside, no one would think it was a functional house. No one accustomed to a middle class American lifestyle could get used to it, but because Hiro had grown up so poor and in far worse accommodations back in the countryside of Japan, this home was more then adequate. From the looks of the small home, it was hard to imagine that inside three generations lived in harmony.

Actually, on the inside of the home, everything was modern and contained most of the same things that every American home had. The difference was that most of the items in this home had been made by hand. Cubans had to make things from the materials that were available. They also had to be creative. But Hiro intended to change the little house quite a lot. To hide his internet equipment, he had a unique architectural design planned.

Hiro sat on the patio next to the kitchen. He thought about many new ideas for the next phase of the construction project. Pedro asked, "Hiro, what are you thinking about?"

Hiro grinned and said, "I'm just thinking about some ideas for my future home project."

Pedro looked curious, "Oh, like what? I'd like to know."

Hiro answered, "I'll put together a plan very soon, and we can talk about it later. I'd like your feedback and you can give me some ideas. It's a very important project."

The Last Revolution

Pedro said, "Great, I'm excited to help you. When you were gone, we finished my house. The upstairs now has two bathrooms, two big bedrooms, and one small room for my office. There's an upstairs patio which gets a nice breeze from Panchita. It's like your house. Now during the summer heat we catch cool breezes from the Caribbean!"

Hiro smiled, "I can't wait see your new addition. You collected all of the materials for years, and then you sold me most of them so I could work on this house. I know it was very difficult to find additional materials. But, I see you did it."

Before he had left for his trip overseas, Hiro had bought some of Pedro's materials and paid him handsomely. Because Hiro had used almost everything Pedro had stockpiled, he knew he would have to compensate Pedro well. He knew Pedro needed American dollars to replace the material so Hiro gave him a large sum. Hiro also asked Pedro to get extra materials for future construction for his own house while he was at it. Hiro had a plan, and he knew the Cuban system pretty well by now. Pedro also had great connections in the black market.

Meanwhile, Hiro asked Dania to sort though his luggage and find the gifts for Pedro and Madeline and their daughter. For Pedro, he had purchased a Makita portable electric wood sander. Pedro was very surprised at this wonderful present. He turned to Hiro and said, "Well, this is something else! I've always wanted one of these, but they are very expensive here and very hard to find. I really need it, and it will be a wonderful tool for my work. Thank you, Hiro." He had bought a beautiful Seiko watch for Madeline. She almost cried when she opened it. She had never owned an expensive watch before, and this was a treasure. For Wendy, he had purchased a trendy portable Sony Walkman and a Nintendo Game Boy with many games. She was so happy and surprised that she actually did started to cry from sheer excitement. Hiro loved seeing the look of true pleasure on his friends' faces. That was thanks enough.

Pedro and Madeline acted like children on Christmas saying, "Wow! Look what I got! This Japanese watch is beautiful! I never thought I'd ever own such a wonderful watch." Hiro pointed out that Japan had the best technology in the world. Madeline smiled in delight.

Wendy added, "Cool, I love this gift. It's very small, and I can use it every day. Thank you, Hiro."

They all showed their excitement, and then Hiro's daughters screamed, "Papi! Papi! What did you get for us?" They couldn't believe they hadn't received anything yet, and they were concerned about their gifts.

Hiro whispered something to Dania. She took her daughters to another room and said quietly, "Papi didn't give you your presents yet because he got you more things than he got for Wendy. He thinks it would be best to wait until after they are gone to give you yours. We don't want to make Wendy jealous or for her to feel disappointed about her gift. Just hush about it until they leave." Masako and Yumiko finally understood that Papi had better things for them. They said they could wait.

After the gift exchange, they all relaxed and enjoyed a feast of pork roast cooked Creole-style. It had been cooking almost half the day. It was juicy and tender and melted in Hiro's mouth. Pepe happily sipped on his homemade rum. Hiro really enjoyed the evening. Pedro had gotten a smooth beer. Pedro passed one to Hiro.

Hiro said, "Cristal?   Hatuey?"

Pedro said, "You know, Hiro, I can't find the Hatuey brand anymore. Someone told me they were having an international patent dispute in Miami because the Bacardi Empire's the Cuban company couldn't use the name anymore."

Hiro said, "I didn't know that. So that's why people don't carry Hatuey anymore. I only see Cristal. I've been wondering about that."

Pedro said, "Yes, that's the reason why. I looked all over for Hatuey, but nobody had any."

Hiro added, "Well, it's better than nothing. Maybe we should start brewing our own beer at home and call it chispa de Pipa"   Everyone started to laugh at his joking.

Pedro said, "Yeah, it's possible. I don't think it would be too difficult. Maybe we could get help from Pepe." Pepe joined in the discussion about how to make alcohol at home. They discussed some ideas about how to do it.

Hiro wondered why there were not more brands of beer available. Pedro told him that due to government restrictions there were only two national brands of beer: Bucanero, the dark lager, and Cristal, a light brew.   Hatuey, made by the Santiago Brewing Company, was Hiro and Pedro's favorite, but the original beer was no longer available. A locally-produced beer with the same name had replaced it. Whenever it was available, Pedro always ordered it.

As the night progressed, everyone had a great time. The whole evening was smooth and relaxing. Hiro felt peaceful and he thought to himself several times, "This is one of the happiest times in my life." It was all about love and happiness. Being with his friends and family in Cuba was true happiness. All of his life Hiro had searched for true happiness, but he had never known it actually existed or where he would find it. The last place he suspected to find happiness was in Cuba.

Now, so many years later he was grateful that his path had led him to this place. He appreciated the Japanese doctor's suggestion that he visit Cuba to rid himself of his nightmares. It was the best advice he had ever received. Coming to Cuba had changed his life forever for the better. This place and these people were his ultimate destiny, and he couldn't ask for more. Hiro finally felt complete. Hiro didn't want anything more, except a little freedom for his work.

At 9:30 that night, Pedro and his family decided to retire for the evening. They all said their good byes and prepared for bed. It had been a long and exciting day. Pedro asked, "Hiro, I'd like to get together with Freddie and Dr. Sanchez and my family in Rancho Velloz. Would this be OK with you for this weekend? I think it would be best because Freddie and Dr. Sanchez and their children are free from school. What do you think?"

Hiro stood up and said, "It is fine with me--your home or ours?"

Pedro said, "My home. Remember we finished the upstairs while you were away. We want to celebrate with family and friends."

"It is a good time to invite your friends in Santa Clara," said Hiro. "Whatever you want to do is OK with us. Please let me know for sure and don't hesitate to ask me anything. I want to help."

Pedro said, "No problem." Then they both gave each other a high five and said good bye. Dania and Madeline smiled. Pedro said, "Hey, don't forget to come see my new addition tomorrow afternoon. I'll pick you up, and we can eat dinner together if that's all right with you." Everybody agreed and they left Hiro's home.

Hiro and his family were excited because now it was time

for distributing the gifts from Japan and the United States. The girls were hardly able to control their glee. The house became like Christmas morning. Hiro had brought them many things. He knew they would love the souvenirs from Japan. While he was away, Hiro had dreamt of this moment and now it was a reality. He had brought the girls beautiful hand-painted Japanese dolls with big black eyes and delicate red-painted lips.

The girls instantly loved these wonderful dolls. Hiro's mother, the girls' grandmother, had sent them each a soft cotton yukata or summer kimono to wear. Masako's had a red and white cherry blossom pattern while Yumiko's was purple and blue with white iris flowers. They were unique and gorgeous. The girls put them on immediately and showed Hiro how beautiful they looked in the robes. Neither had ever owned such interesting looking robes before and they loved them. Hiro also brought them many small trinkets like good luck charms, jeweled hairpins, Japanese comic books, tiny crayon and colored pencil sets, and many cute mini-sized Japanese toys.

Hiro also gave them each a Japanese Walkman with headphones and a pocket-sized electronic Game Boy and ipod. The biggest gift for his daughters was a prototype newest super Nintendo Wii and Game boy DS Lite, gift by his old friend Koji, and a Sony Play Station 3 to share with Dania's two sisters, Lillian and Liana. Hiro wanted his daughters to determine which game they liked the most before Hiro gave the other game and the Sony Play Station 3 and Game boy to Freddie's daughter, Judi Lalin.

Hiro's mother had sent a hand-made yukata and a small hand-made purse she had sewn especially for Dania. Dania was touched to receive this gift. Hiro also brought her a Seiko watch, a beautiful gold necklace with a heart charm and matching earrings, as well as clothes, tennis shoes, and perfume from the US. They loved their gifts and ran around the house admiring their new possessions. The home was noisy and filled with laughter until midnight.

For himself, Hiro had brought back the laptop computer and many accessories and a computer chip supply for his invention. He also had brought back various tools. He kept these items confidential from everyone including friends and family. The only person that he told was Dania. He told her that he had a plan and that he was inventing something for future technology.

The Last Revolution

He put his things away. Hiro was very pleased with what he had purchased in Japan and was especially happy with some new computer supplies from his friends at The University of Hiroshima. A young computer science professor had many new supplies from underground computer suppliers. He was glad to have these specialty items.

Chapter 44

Dania had promised Hiro that she wouldn't open her mouth to anyone about this arrangement because she was scared that it would cause not only Hiro's life to be in danger but also the lives of their family. Therefore, Hiro took all the necessary precautions and told his wife to trust him. Dania told Hiro that she would have faith in him, but she was scared that something bad would occur that might separate them, or worse, break their entire family into pieces. Dania was very serious because she knew what the government was capable of and how tough the penalties could be. Sometimes people just disappeared, which frightened her. The couple decided never to mention the special arrangements to anyone, and she had to convince herself that everything would turn out all right in the end.

It was difficult for Dania to completely let these anxious thoughts go. She knew that if Hiro were caught, he would pay a heavy penalty that could destroy their entire family structure. Dania had seen many cases like this, even in her small, isolated village. There were no exceptions to the punishment for crimes of this nature.

Dania and Hiro hugged one another tightly. As they lay together in each other's arms, they became one. It was past midnight. The moment was tender, and they were both aroused.

All was quiet and peaceful in their home. There was no noise except the sounds of the small lagartijas-lizards communicating with each other. The cool tropical breeze was relaxing, cool, and romantic. Hiro and Dania kissed each other tenderly. The touch of Dania's hair and skin was like heaven. To Hiro, she smelled like tropical flowers and vanilla. He had missed her and had ached for her. Their lovemaking was perfect and beautiful. After they were sated, they fell into a deep sleep in each other's arms until the morning.

That weekend Pedro had planned to have a party in his home in Rancho Veloz. Many people had been invited and were planning to attend. Word spread quickly and Pedro found out through his family that many more people were coming. They all wondered if the party was getting too big. Hiro was there during the discussion and suggested renting a hotel with more space, but Pedro wanted to have everyone at his house to show them his remodeling project. After some thought, Pedro agreed that his house was just too small to host so many people. Pedro decided he would have a smaller dinner party for his close friends at another time and agreed that renting a larger space would be a good idea.

Everyone was excited just thinking about the big celebration. Since he had become a Cuban permanent resident, it was impossible for Pedro to rent a tourist hotel room himself; but as they talked they thought of the perfect place to have the party. It was called El Roca and was located between Qemado de Guines and Sagua la Grande. It was a gorgeous spot high up on top of the mountain about 250 feet above sea level. El Roca was a stunning old hotel that had served as a retreat for Cubans.

The hotel was once the beautiful estate of a wealthy sugar plantation owner back in the late eighteenth century. After the revolution, the wealthy owner escaped to Miami, and the Communist government confiscated the estate and turned it into a camp facility for Cubans. The main house became a hotel and a bar was located near the entrance. There were sixty-five small cottages facilities for guests which were equipped with electric fans run by a generator. A restaurant was available, and there was a big swimming pool and garden area.

The most incredible attraction of this special place was the view. There was a magnificent, 360 degree panoramic view from the top of the mountain. It was stunning. The first time Hiro had gone there, he felt he could see almost a hundred miles in all directions. The view seemed endless, and Hiro could see the Embalse Alacranes and the Sagua Lake in the distance. The weather was also comfortable because of a year round, cool mountain breeze. Hiro always joked with Pedro and said, "One day I'll build my home here, and I'll be living in a retreat every day!" Pedro and Dania always laughed about Hiro's dream site because this place belonged to the government.

They decided to call Freddie to help them reserve the hotel from Friday to Sunday for their big party. Freddie made a few calls and told them that it was all taken care of. Hiro had to assist with the rent, of course, but he had the funds and wanted to splurge on his friends and family for a big celebration. Hiro told Pedro and his brothers to spread the word to all their friends about the change in venue. Everyone at El Roca was excited about the big event.

Friday night came quickly. Everything was perfect. Many people arrived, and it seemed as if the entire town was attending the party. Both young and old were there. The partygoers enjoyed salsa music and danced all night in the open air patio. The beat went on and on that night. It was fun and festive out on the verandah. All who came to the party brought their own alcohol and drinks to share so Cuban rum and beer flowed freely. Everyone was laughing and smiling. Dania's favorite drink was the refreshing Mojitos.

The smell of Cuban cigar smoke was also in the air as Hiro and Freddie smoked a Cohiba together. Hiro loved the taste of a good Cuban cigar. As soon as the aroma hit the air, many women asked for a cigar. Freddie insisted that his friend Luis open a huge box which contained many types of Cuban cigars. All of the choices were made from first class Cuban premium brand tobacco.

Hiro asked Freddie, "Why did you bring so many expensive cigars? This is a very expensive gift. Who got them for you? They smell so great!"

Freddie pointed to Dania's uncle, Pablo Hernandez, who had connections with the central tobacco industry in Santa Clara. Pablo had donated the cigars for Hiro's welcome back party. He was willing to be so generous because he knew how much support Hiro had given to the Cuban mathematics departments at the universities throughout Cuba. He hugged Pablo to show his appreciation not only for this wonderful gift but also for their great friendship.

Uncle Pablo began a condensed lecture on cigars, saying to Hiro, "In Cuba, there are many famous tobacco brands Hiro, but no two cigars of the same brand are ever exactly alike. They may look the same, but no two are ever identical. Take for instance the Grands Crus. The taste of these cigars varies from year-to-year because the tobacco comes from different farms. Depending on the soil, the tobacco leaves, the factory, and the weather, each crop is different. Thus, the flavor is different. The most important thing is harmony which is the key word used by connoisseurs who demand from cigars a harmonious realization of many factors."

"Also, the occasion, mood, environment, beverage, gender of the company, and other such external factors play a part in the enjoyment of the cigar. To enjoy a Cuban cigar properly, one should take slow gentle puffs. It's a sensory experience and a delight to discover the truly superb details of the world of Cuban tobacco. It's a treat like nothing else; and sometimes when one smokes a great cigar, one feels on top of the world."

"Hiro, very few Cubans can actually afford to smoke good cigars. It's a big luxury to enjoy one of them. They're an export item which translates into money for the Cuban government. Cuban people smoke tobacco that costs around three Cuban pesos per cigar. Cubans smoke cigars made from leftovers found on the floor of the tobacco factories. It's against the law to sell cheap cigars to tourists. Anyone caught doing that pays a heavy penalty and suffers the consequences of breaking the law."

"For the cheap cigars, the tobacco workers gather the leaves. Then they put twenty-four leaves into a bundle for sale strictly to Cubans only. This tobacco is very strong and has a bad taste. These leftovers are of poor quality. But even a poor quality cigar is better than nothing. This is the only type of tobacco that the average Cuban can afford to buy. The cheap cigars are also small. Most Cubans have only drawn a few puffs from a top notch, brand name cigar in their entire lives, we got fucked" Hiro grinned because he had heard this so many times.

Uncle Pablo finished his lecture by opening the boxes of cigars. As soon as they were opened, everybody came to see them. Then Pablo yelled for everyone's attention, "Attention! Attention! There's only one cigar per person to enjoy on this special occasion. I want you each to have one cigar. Even if you don't smoke, you can take it home for your loved ones. The ladies should take one, too."

Pablo continued, "Then whatever is left over, we can enjoy here at El Roca. Let's give a big salute to Hiro, sing the Cuban national anthem, and enjoy smoking these first class cigars." It was a huge treat for a Cuban to enjoy one of these hand-rolled, first class export items.

Pedro always said, "The tourists get premium, and we get

shit."

The fact of the matter was that the monetary system was unfair. It would take nearly thirty months' pay for a Cuban to buy a box of $380-$450 Cohiba cigars while wealthy tourists could afford them. The cost of a box for a tourist was only about half a week's salary which was equal to three years of income for a Cuban citizen.

All of the party-goers got in line to receive their special cigars. Some smoked theirs right away while others put their cigars away to take home. These premium cigars were like treasures, and the aroma of sweet tobacco filled the night air. It was like a dream for them.

A grand party like this could last all night. Isabel, Pepe, and the children had the time of their lives. It was a tremendous treat for everyone.

The hotel had a huge, old swimming pool, but it had not been maintained, so green algae had formed on the surface. To Hiro's surprise, people didn't care and they jumped in and enjoyed swimming. Hiro turned to Dania who was having a fantastic time. He hugged her and said, "This is so wonderful. It doesn't get much better than this!"

She held up her drink to toast, "Magnifico Mi amorsote. It's all for you!"

Many of Pedro's family were from Trinidad and Cienfuegos. Dania had several relatives who were from Cienfuegos. Pedro's family were Spanish descendents from San Sebastian who had immigrated to Haiti. The African Negritos had overthrown the French and became independent. Soon after, they wreaked revenge on the white sugar plantation landowners. Many of them were brutally murdered. The Spanish escaped to the Dominican Republic and Cuba. Pedro's family settled in Trinidad. Many of his family members still lived there.

When Freddie arrived at the celebration, Hiro greeted him with a big smile and a warm embrace. He said, "Thank you, Freddie, for everything. This is all possible because of you, my friend."

Freddie said, "Anything for you Hiro. You are a good man, and I was happy to help." Freddie introduced Hiro to a couple of friends he had brought along. Hiro got them drinks right away and they chatted all night.

Freddie made a special surprise request to have beef

The Last Revolution

served at the restaurant for Hiro. He had made special arrangements to kill a huge bull for Hiro's party because Hiro was considered foreign and not a Cuban citizen. Besides, many Cubans also enjoyed the special meat which was rarely available. The government of Cuba prohibited individuals from killing cattle even if they owned the cattle.

But Hiro was a well-known mathematics professor and lecturer for the faculty in various Cuban universities. Laws were sometimes bent for special individuals on special occasions. Normally, it was almost impossible to have such a treat, but Freddie had connections. The restaurant prepared the meat using several traditional Cuban recipes. It was tasty and delicious. The beef melted in everyone's mouth. Hiro asked Freddie's friend Luis, who was head of La Tienda Pan-Americana, if he would like a second glass of Cuban beer, rum, or pipa. They all enjoyed a sumptuous feast of beef and several drinks together.

Freddie was interested in the Japanese economy and the politics of the Far East. He had accurate and current information because he specialized in Far Eastern affairs for the Cuban government, but he was always eager to hear information first hand from Hiro. Hiro always made sure to soak up current events related to politics, international affairs, and the state of the economy for Freddie because Hiro knew he wanted as much information as possible. Hiro had some connections in different departments at The University of Hiroshima as well as friends at the Tokyo stock exchange and the statistics bureau. Hiro made sure that he got the latest information on international trade relations and new laws that had come into effect recently.

Freddie also wanted better information on education in Japan. They discussed the latest in the field of computers and the high tech industry. Freddie was impressed with the Japanese mentality, and felt Japan's knowledge in the areas of mathematics, computers, and technology information was superior to any other country's. Hiro quickly brought Freddie up-to-speed about the latest in these three areas.

They also talked about their families and about what was happening in the Cuban government. Freddie trusted Hiro implicitly and a strong friendship had grown between them over the years. Hiro and Freddie sat in rocking chairs and spent most of the evening drinking pipa. Pedro joined them, and although he hadn't had any formal education, he was very smart and always wanted to learn more. Hiro and Freddie always included Pedro in their talks. For Pedro, the Japanese culture was fascinating because it was so different from his own.

The weekend celebration and retreat were finally over. Everyone who partied at El Roca had enjoyed a weekend to remember. Hiro, Dania and their daughters, along with Isabel, Pepe and Pedro, Madeline and Wendy, remained until the last guests left. They thanked everyone for coming and enjoyed a wonderful lunch together before taking off. They admired the beautiful views one last time. The resort was quiet and empty by then. Few foreigners visited this hotel because of its so remote location. Few people were familiar with this place except for the people in Villa Clara.

Chapter 45

Although life back in San Rafael,

Rancho Veloz was still as peaceful as ever, Hiro's mind was functioning digitally at an abnormally high rate during this period of inventive thinking. In this mode his brain could work faster than a calculator and he always switched into this high gear when starting a new project.

He was constantly focused on his goal of making access to the internet possible by satellite signal. He had come up with a new design for the house to hide the satellite dish while allowing it to function properly. Pedro and Pipo helped with the construction. First, he modified the roof and installed a homemade water storage tank. It was 25 ft. above the ground and made with rail steel fabric. The home made satellite dish was safely contained inside and could receive a good signal. It was ingeniously connected to an old VCR as the receiver. While in Japan, he collected his supplies from a friend in Hiroshima who also help modify each item just so. The VCR was modified to receive a satellite signal thought the DMCA commercial satellite.

It was difficult to keep the same signal for a long span of time, because the original source was constantly changing. This was done by original-source mainframe software to scramble signals as anti-hacker protection. The ultimate surveillance security software constantly changed, scrambling signals to prevent hacking, because the signals emitted by commercial satellites changed frequently.

But this anti-hacker technique was no match for Hiro's skills. Hiro pirated the satellite's signal in a very short time. The satellite signal was simple technology that enabled Hiro to gain access onto the U.S. DMCA, commercial satellite signal. This could be used safely for short periods of time. With help from Pedro and Pepe, they successfully installed he dish and got a stabilized signal.

Hiro was a hacking genius. For him it was like unraveling a Rubik's cube, a challenge, but completely possible. He was able to hack into several US corporate business accounts and obtain their dish codes and synchronize to their system's computer connection. He was also able to hack into various corporate internet accounts and create his own access codes. It took him nearly a month without proper materials or already made parts. He had to do everything creatively and with what was on hand, so it was tedious and time-consuming. But he was set on achieving his task no matter how long it took. It was nearly a month before it was all fully functional.

It used bandwidth or the internet to link it to these digital images. The files all needed direct input to other servers. Instead of putting them on a synchronized dish code as their local servers, they simply blocked their transmission time, while the bandwidth is overloading. This causes stress for the system and it becomes disbanded temporarily. This period of malfunction is the perfect time to hijack onto the connection and synchronize a new access code. And this was Hiro's ticket online into the highway of modern information technology.

The next step was to modify his laptop computer that he had purchased in Japan as a home computer. For a man like Hiro, the new Sony laptop was a slow and primitive processor, equipped with 2,791 MHz. The average home computer had only 2000 MHz. Hiro had to modify his CPU's capacity to reach over 25,000 MHz, in order to achieve his new phase of computer software he had named the Sonic Cyclone.

For this phase, Hiro would need a highly sensitive chip. He had a good idea and the material on hand, but there was no facility or laboratory in which to build it. However, where there was a will there was a way so Hiro turned his small closet into a workshop. Within a month, he had successfully fabricated a new computer chip. It was a Tamotsu chip with 49,999 MHz. It was the ultimate in chips. Hiro had replicated a perfect copy based on his previous studies on a DNA-based computer chip from 1990. It produced no heat and was one-fourth the size of the original. With it, his processor's capability became one hundred percent faster than the Intel-Nakajima JPX008. He named it the Colbana-Tamotsu-JPX008. It was quite an invention.

While in the second phase of modifying his new chip, Hiro stumbled onto a new theory. It was called Thermal Physics. It was direct conduction through the oxygen molecule, made of two oxygen atoms. The molecules contained dry air, nitrogen, oxygen, and argon. This thermal conductor made communications travel faster than the speed of light. This meant that he had direct chip-to-chip communication and could bypass any wireless facility. This new system could prevent cyberspace crime because it was able to give the users a direct connection. There was no need for a middleman or a wireless company to make the connection for the user. It also utilized the Earth's energy as a power source. It would make the battery a dinosaur.

    Hiro also mastered a low frequency laser beam that could manipulate a person's memory. It manipulated the memory cells using a micro-electronic interface system. It was compatible with any system, and Hiro synchronized his theory and programmed the digital molecules though the air. It was amazing. By using this system he could instantaneously connect browser.

    This chip's capability was beyond anyone's imagination; even Hiro was not sure which way this discovery was headed because of its many applications. It had a big future, and Hiro would go down in history as its inventor. However, he was not interested in this for profit. Hiro's only interest was in researching the next generation of computer technology here in Cuba. But he knew it would become an overnight sensation.

    After hijacking internet communication through global commercial satellite signals, he spent as much as eighteen hours a day at his computer researching the history of computer science throughout the world. Hiro's surfing enabled him to recapture what he had lost during his eight-year absence from the world of technology. Hiro indulged in his hobby of making furniture by visiting Pedro's woodshop and fishing at least once a week. However, during his visits with Pedro, he never discussed anything related to computers or to the internet. No one but Pedro was aware of his secret studies. He had not told even his wife about the research.

    Hiro's room was off-limits to all family members. Dania explained to the family that Dr. Sanchez ordered that Hiro needed private quiet time more than ever, because of his health. Often Hiro was closeted in his makeshift lab all day, surfing the internet to recover what he had missed from the world of technology. Hiro was surprised that computer technology hadn't changed much during his missing years. There had been little advancement, but many enhancements, such as everything becoming simpler, smaller and more complex. Many of the current products were based on his studies from nearly 35 years earlier. Each time he saw a website marketing a digital audio player, he would smile knowing that its existence was based on his 1966 studies.

His seeing the contributions that his research had brought to the were still based in California, still beating their brains out. He liked to memorize new research and invention schematics. Hiro began to reorganize his brain capacity like a computer defragmenter, but still could not come up with any profound new ideas. He was a natural inventor and creative thinker, so he kept searching. World made Hiro very happy. He found that many computer scientists

Chapter 46

Early one morning about six months later, Pedro picked up Hiro to go fishing in Rio San Pedro. They decided to buy goats afterwards at Pedro's Uncle Lodo's home. The fishing was great—they were biting like crazy. Within two hours, the friends had caught fifteen fish. Some were two-pounders. Hiro gave all the fish to the children who watched in awe as they reeled in trophy after trophy.

It was a spectacular site for the children. They loved Hiro. Every time he caught a fish, the children screamed and laughed. After a while, Hiro had finally had enough, so he and Pedro left to drive to Pedro's uncle's house in search of goats. Many Cubans owned sheep, but only a few farmers raised goats. Uncle Lodo was well-known in the area for his goat herd. Hiro always enjoyed chatting with Pedro's uncle each time they traveled in the direction of Rio San Pedro. He always made Hiro feel welcome.

Before noon, the pair returned home to Sierra Morena. As they neared the main highway, they noticed several unfamiliar cars. As they neared Hiro's home, Pedro and Hiro wondered what was going on—something didn't feel right. Hiro got a sinking feeling in his gut and began to worry. Hiro and Pedro raced out of the car toward the front door of the house. Usually one of Hiro's daughters or someone else came out to meet them, but not today.

As soon as Pedro and Hiro entered the living room, two men with pistols grabbed them. Then two other men rushed forward and pushed them down to the floor and handcuffed them. One of the middle-aged men flashed his government ID at Pedro and Hiro. The ID indicated that the man was a federal secret agent. He said harshly, "I am Cuban FBI Captain Luiz Vasquez. You are under arrest for crimes against the government of Cuba. Under federal guidelines, you are both traitors! You are enemies of Cuba."

Hiro and Pedro were both stunned and very scared. Hiro said, "What is going on? What is the problem, officers?"

The agent answered, "Chino look, we received a tip that you have a computer with internet access to the outside world. Do you know this is a federal crime?"

Hiro replied, "I am not Chino I am Japone, Did you find a computer? Can you prove this?"

The agent said, "Oh Yes Chino, we have evidence and we are going to take you to Santa Clara for further investigation by federal law enforcement specialists. Save your explanations until then." Hiro and Pedro looked at one another. They didn't know what evidence the federal agents had, but a grim look passed between them.

Pedro yelled, "Hiro isn't Cuban, and he didn't do anything bad. You cannot take him to jail!"

One of the younger officers stepped toward Pedro and yelled, "Quiet!" The officer punched Pedro several times in the mouth. Pedro started bleeding and the officers knocked him to the concrete floor kicking him with their boots. Hiro screamed, "Please stop! Please stop!" as the younger officer continued to kick Pedro. Finally, the captain made the younger agent stop. At this point, Hiro and Pedro were both scared and worried.

Hiro saw that the older captain was more reasonable, so he looked at him and said, "Please calm your men down. We are cooperating and we will obey whatever you want us to do. We will go with you peacefully and sort this all out. Could you please take off these handcuffs so I can help my friend?"

By this time Pedro's nose was bleeding pretty badly. Another short, young agent in his mid-twenties tossed Pedro a towel. The captain told the agent to uncuff them. He warned Pedro and Hiro "Don't be stupid. Do you understand?" Pedro nodded his head and agreed not to move. His nose was bleeding so badly that he had to lie down to make it stop. Hiro sat quietly next to Pedro. Hiro could hear his daughters, Yumiko and Masako, crying. Their cries were coming from the back bedroom.

Hiro yelled out. "What are you doing to my family? I want to see my family!"

The captain said, "No chino, you cannot move from here. If you do, we will hurt you. So far your family is unharmed."

Hiro said, "I just need to see that my family is all right; I'm not going to do anything. Let me see my wife and daughters."

The Last Revolution

The other agent shoved Hiro in the chest and said, "Be quiet," as he waved his shotgun. The agent walked up to Hiro, stuck the gun barrel to his head, and said, "If you make a move, you know what will happen, so be still!" Pedro flashed Hiro a look. His eyes communicated, "Stay put!"

In the master bedroom, Dania was screaming and making lots of noise. Her screams got louder, and she was crying hysterically. At that moment, Hiro felt like killing all of the agents. He had never in his life reacted with violence, but he couldn't stand to hear the cries of his wife and daughters. It was tearing him up inside and he felt powerless.

A sense of rage came over Hiro. He could hear his family's captors doing something in the bedroom. After a few minutes, the cries stopped. It became too quiet. Hiro's heart was pounding, and his head was spinning. He couldn't imagine what was happening to his family. Hiro took a deep breath to get composed. He knew he had to remain calm, but he also knew that he had to act quickly.

Hiro glanced around and saw that there were twelve agents in his house. Several were gathered around something similar to a computer and satellite receiver. Then the captain entered the main living room again. Then Hiro calmly asked the captain, "May I please see my family? If you let me, I will go with you peacefully. I'll stay calm, and won't try to run away. Look, you must understand that I need to see that my wife and children are unharmed. You have a family. I know you can understand. I'll obey your orders. Please let me see my family; I'll be silent after that."

The captain had no compassion and said, "No. Chino after your buddy's nose stops bleeding, we're moving. We're taking you to the Santa Clara federal jail!" Then the captain went to the patio area of the next bedroom. He talked to several agents and tried to calm everyone down.

After several minutes, he returned and said to Hiro, "Chino I want you to come with me." And he took Hiro to the bedroom. It seemed like a tornado had struck in his bedroom. Everything was broken or opened and strewn all over the floor. His bed was broken and sagging. Every drawer was open, and his all clothes were on the floor. All the boxes of luggage were open, and the closet door had been kicked in. Everything in the bedroom had been destroyed. Hiro was angry and filled with rage, but he was thinking about only one thing.

In a deadly serious yet calm voice Hiro asked, "Captain, where is my family?" He couldn't see them, and he knew they had been in the bedroom. He looked the agent in the eye and said again, "What have you done with my family? Where are they?"

Then the captain finally said, "Chino your family is inside the bathroom." He opened the door and told them all to come out. Yumiko and Masako walked out crying. Then Isabel and Pepe exited, too. They were are all shaking and crying. The agents trained their guns on Hiro's family. Hiro was relieved to see that they were unharmed. He hugged his daughters and they held him tight. The agents quickly separated Hiro from his daughters and put the girls with Isabel and Pepe into the corner. Hiro was worried and asked, "Where is Dania?

Hiro was scared and his heart was pumping hard. He screamed, "Dania! Where are you?" A minute later he heard her call to him in a weak voice. He could hear that she was crying. Hiro broke away from the agent and the captain allowed Hiro to enter the bathroom. Dania was sitting on the commode, shaking and scared out of her mind. Hiro gently placed her on the floor and he hugged and kissed her. They reconfirmed their love for one another and were relieved to see that they were both OK. Dania wiped her face with a towel so Hiro could not see that anything was wrong. Dania didn't want to let the towel go, but Hiro gently removed it and was shocked to see that Dania's face was swollen and bruised. Blood was flowing from her nose.

Suddenly Hiro stood and ran from the bathroom screaming like a mad man, "You Pigs! You didn't have to beat a woman. She is a good woman. How could you hit a defenseless woman?" Hiro grabbed the young secret agent, and they fell to the floor wrestling and punching each other. Than a gun blast made them freeze as the captain fired a warning shot. He had aimed his gun at the windows.

Then four other agents swarmed into room. The officers checked out the situation. The captain nodded to them, and then the two agents cuffed Hiro's hands behind his back. They didn't take kindly to Hiro's outburst and slammed him to the floor, kicking him with their boots over and over. Each kick was like a hammer hitting his body. The pain was wrenching. Hiro closed his eyes tightly. Not only was each blow agonizing, but it also he

The Last Revolution

felt as if he were going to vomit. One kick hit Hiro directly in the mouth. The next one on to his nose. One caused him to see stars. His head became like a computer hard drive with the electric current sparkling in the integrated memory. Hiro also heard a high-pitched hum. Then he was kicked one more time in his stomach. He vomited. The beating was the most painful thing that had ever happened to him. Hiro was not used to violence. His nose was gushing warm blood which covered his clothes.

Dania screamed and tried to cover Hiro with her body to shield him from the kicks of the two agents. She was also getting kicked, but she would not move away from Hiro. She screamed and shouted "Oh My God! Help me! God! Where are you?" Dania pleaded with the agents to stop. When Dania's mother Isabel heard the cries coming from her daughter, she tried to run to the front room to help. Then the other young agents armed with shotguns secured the door and pushed Isabel.

One of them shouted, "If you move, we'll hurt you, too. Don't take another step old woman! Do you understand?"

Isabel became silent. One of the agents yelled at her again, "Do you hear me, old woman?" Isabel began to cry like a baby and began to pray to the Yoruba tribe's Saint Ogun of the Santeria Afro religion. Isabel shouted and screamed for her saint to help her in her time of need. She became crazier and crazier and was almost out of control. Her body was sweating so much that it looked as if she had just taken a shower. The agents didn't know what to do; they just looked on disturbed.

Pepe tried to calm Isabel, but she was out of control. Although she didn't move, Isabel screamed and beat her fists against the wall. The youngest agent tried to calm her down. Isabel was hiding a sharp kitchen knife. Suddenly she turned and stabbed the agent several times. The officer fell to the floor—bleeding and severely injured. Instantly, there were several shotgun gun blasts. Another agent shot Isabel and Pepe at close range. Isabel collapsed, falling to the floor. Pepe fell to the ground reaching for Isabel. Pepe's and Isabel's blood intermingled as he embraced her.

Pepe was crying, "Isabel! Isabel!" He, too, was seriously injured from the gunshot. Isabel's blood spread all over on the floor. She kicked her legs several times; then she became still. There was no sign of movement and everything was silent. Isabel's eyes were wide open in death.

The entire house erupted in chaotic screaming and yelling. Yumiko and Masako huddled together in the corner of the room behind a chair crying and screaming. Everyone screamed and yelled as the agents scrambled to see what had just occurred in the next room. Hiro knew that something terrible had happened.

A wave of panic overcame him. Hiro was still on the floor with Dania as the two agents pointed a shotgun barrel pointed at him. Dania was sobbing and calling to her mother. The situation in the small house had disintegrated. Agents ran around in chaos, but all Hiro and Dania could do was to lie there and wait while the agents pointed their guns at them. Hiro was in much pain, but his thoughts were focused on what might have happened in the other room. Even though Hiro was in agony, his mind was on the safety of his family. He felt helpless lying there on the ground, covered in his own blood. As he lay there, he knew what had happened, but he didn't want to face reality. He closed his eyes as tears poured down his face.

By that time, the bedroom had become very quiet. The yelling and chaos, except for whimpering from the children, had ended and the situation was nearly under control again. Finally the captain yelled, "Listen up everybody. This is enough! We don't want any more violence or accidents. Enough is enough. Do all of you understand me?" He was losing control of himself.

Pepe was lying on the floor embracing Isabel's lifeless body. He was crying and talking to her. Pepe was consumed with grief, covered in blood and badly hurt. One of the agents put a blindfold on Hiro and led both Hiro and Pedro outside. The pair was shoved into the back seat of a black unmarked car. They were being transported to Santa Clara federal jail as political prisoners. For Hiro and Pedro, this was the first time they had ever been in trouble with the federal authorities in Cuba. These agents were very aggressive and similar to US federal agents. Pedro remembered the terrible things that had happened to members of his own family in the past.

Chapter 47

Upon their arrival at the jail, the jailer ripped off their clothes and led them to a shower area. He told the pair to clean off the blood covering their bodies. The showers were dirty and smelly. The water was cold, and neither soap nor towels were provided. As they stepped from the shower, they were handed a set of blue work clothes. Then Hiro and Pedro were checked by medical personnel. The staff was stern and cold to them, and silent. Hiro thought he had been sent to hell, because the jail was unsanitary, dark and depressing. The facility was old and the prisoners were held under terrible conditions. Hiro could see how the other prisoners lived, and he thought that farm animals had better lives than these Cuban prisoners.

That first night in federal jail Hiro and Pedro were placed in different cells. Hiro was put in a cell with four other prisoners. He was scared as he entered the cell and didn't say a word. The cell had four wooden benches and no mattresses. There was only one small light so it was dark inside the cell. There was a urinal in the corner which was dirty and smelled terrible. That night it was difficult to see much either inside or outside the cell, but Hiro knew that the guards walked past about every thirty minutes doing security checks. This facility had limited space and little concern for the welfare of the prisoners. However, the security guards in the jail seemed decent. The guards hadn't talked much and they didn't seem as if they were interested in harassing anybody.

As Hiro sat with the four other prisoners, they marveled to see an Oriental person in their jail cell. They stared at him. Hiro wondered if he would be safe, but then he began to think of what had just happened and he didn't care about himself anymore. One older prisoner said, "Hey, Chino! What are you charged with?" Hiro was quiet and didn't answer. Hiro was visibly shaken up. Hiro glanced at the old prisoner with a blank face and then looked away. The old man repeated the question,

"Chino! I'm talking to you! What're you charged with? What happened? Do you speak Spanish?" Soon the old man gave up.

Hiro looked down at the floor and remained quiet. He didn't want to say anything, and he couldn't have answered even if he had wanted to. Hiro's hands were trembling and he stretched out on the hard wooden bench bed. Being in prison was surreal. It seemed like a bad nightmare. The events of the ordeal that had just taken place ran repeatedly through his mind. The screams and shouts and the sound of gunfire echoed in his ears. Hiro thought over and over, "How could I have let this happen? I knew I was taking a risk, but I miscalculated the aggressive brutality of the Cuban authority."

His crime was a simple internet connection to a personal computer. Now Isabel was dead and Pepe was seriously hurt. How could this be? Hiro shivered and thought about Dania and the girls. He wondered if they were OK. Hiro became petrified and anxious and wanted to scream. As he lay on the hard bench, his whole body ached and hurt. Hiro was badly bruised and swollen from the beating. His body was shaking from the trauma; however, the medical examiner said that Hiro was lucky because he had no broken bones. As he lay on the bench, Hiro closed his eyes and saw images of Pepe and Isabel when she was alive. He felt sick and deeply regretted his actions. Hiro knew that he had just destroyed the happiest family he had ever known. Because of him, Isabel was dead. A few moments later, Hiro passed out from exhaustion and guilt.

The next day as he awoke, Hiro realized that this nightmare was real. He was still in shock and had a difficult time getting his bearings. His entire body was sore and he ached terribly. Hiro could barely move his arms, and he felt off-balance and woozy. As morning arrived, Hiro looked around the jail and noticed that many of the prisoners had terrible scars on their bodies, like they had been beaten to within an inch of their lives. Hiro knew that Cuban prisoners were sometimes beaten and even tortured. He remembered what his old friend Aimee had told him. She had said that political prisoners against Fidel were beaten repeatedly until they passed out and then they were moved to small four-foot-by-four-foot cages for isolation. Aimee had known people who were released from jail and had witnessed the abuse first-hand. To ensure their submission, they were kept hungry—only one meal a day.

The Last Revolution

The conditions were inhumane. Sometimes prisoners with life sentences would stay in these horrible conditions for as long as thirty years. Aimee had told Hiro that during the decade between 1960 and 1970; nearly 500,000 people had been imprisoned for political crimes. They were sentenced to prison and hard labor. Over 1200 people had been executed for crimes against government policy or for being critical of Fidel. Castro acted harshly because he wanted to make examples of people who were subversive or who spoke against him. Fidel ruled Cuba with an iron first.

When Hiro had first arrived in Cuba, he remembered Aimee educating him and Pedro about the Cuban jails. Aimee said that jail conditions had improved since the 1960s, but Cuban jails were still below average third-world standards. Many political dissidents were released after pressure from human rights organizations, some of whom had been serving more than 20 years. Many of the prisoners simply had voiced criticism of the government, Communism, the revolution or Castro.

This all passed through Hiro's mind as he sat in the jail cell. He thought about how many people had come and gone though this hell. Hiro couldn't believe that he was now imprisoned himself. He thought about his family and the terrible incident at his house. He thought about poor Isabel and Pepe and bowed his head low in shame. Hiro and Pedro were both being held in cells for temporary prisoners until a verdict was decided. If they were found guilty, they would be moved to another type of jail, depending on the severity of their crimes. Some of the potential new locations were where beatings and torture occurred.

Chapter 48

Seven long days passed. The warden and Freddie came to the jail and a security guard opened the cell door. He said, "Dr. Hiroaki Nakagawa, Please come forward. You have a visitor." His face, still swollen and badly bruised, Hiro slowly emerged from the jail compartment.

Freddie looked very concerned and gently shook his hand. "Hiro, are you all right? Come with me. It's going to be OK." Hiro was visibly upset and just shook his head. They took him to an interrogation room.

There was a wooden table and six chairs. Pedro was already sitting in one of the chairs waiting. He looked as tired and distraught as Hiro. They didn't say a word, but just looked at one another. Pedro and Hiro were seated across from each other and then two men entered the room. One was a representative from the Japanese embassy and the other a Cuban government official. Freddie introduced them both to Hiro and Pedro. "This is your embassy First Secretary, Mr. Ichiro Iida." Speaking in Japanese, he said "Everything is OK. We already settled your case. But we're still very concerned."

Then a distinguished, heavyset man, Ubaldo de la Guardia from the Cuban department of foreign affairs introduced himself and said, "Dr. Nakagawa. I'm very sorry and deeply apologize for the inconvenience." Then Freddie interrupted, "Dr. Nakagawa, everything has been carefully reviewed and our findings show that this was a government mistake. The only crime you have committed was stealing an American satellite signal. However, we've discussed the issue with a representative of the Canadian satellite company and my higher commander in Havana. Since you are not a Cuban citizen, you are legally able to get satellite service for the cost of $150 a month. You were not technically authorized to have satellite signal, however, we'll overlook it this time and allow you to sign up for this monitored service; and the crime can be forgiven."

"Your crime of theft can then be dismissed and all charges dropped. And the government will recognize and permit you to own one computer in your home. But you may not have access to internet. This is only possible if you have an international business and you get a legal government permit. If not, you may do like the tourists and get it through the telephone company or tourist hotel. They have a facility and access to internet that's costly, but it's only a possibility."

Freddie was behind Hiro as Hiro started to respond, "Uh . . ." Suddenly, Freddie pinched his back. It was a signal not to say anything. Hiro quickly closed his mouth.

The government representative Ubaldo de la Guardia said, "The government promises to give compensation for the loss of the two people and any property damage. The Cuban government is deeply sorry and apologizes for these losses. Dr. Hiroaki Nakagawa, please sign this paper." Hiro did not hear anything the official said after the words 'loss of two people.' Hiro's mind choked: "Two . . . two . . . two? Pepe died! Pepe is dead, too!" And then he silently and humbly pleaded for forgiveness: "Oh, Dania".

Pedro gently tapped Hiro's back. "This is an official release for Mr. Pedro Gomez Pelayo and Dr. Hiroaki Nakagawa," the warden said. He handed Hiro and Pedro the release papers to sign. They both signed and a guard brought their old clothes, which were clean. Someone had washed them. Then the guard told them to change their clothes inside the next room. Hiro and Pedro changed quietly with the guard standing there and then returned to the interrogation room.

Mr. Ichiro Iida said, "This was a terrible mistake. We informed you before that you must register and give us your information about where you live and if there are any political problems you have. You must contact the Japanese embassy immediately. It's your duty and we can help you right away. This time you were lucky because you had an influential high-ranking Cuban government friend. We've known him very well for many years. He's helped the Japanese government tremendously."

He continued to explain about the Japanese authority and how they work in Cuba. He wanted Hiro to talk more, but Hiro wasn't feeling well and apologized and asked to be excused. Mr. Iida handed Hiro the Japanese government document to sign in Japanese, stamp with his thumbprint and mark with his Japanese name. Hiro complied and handed the paper to the representative of the Japanese embassy.

Hiro and Pedro just wanted to leave and go see their families. The last seven days had been like an eternity and they were never so glad to leave a place in their lives. Freddie shook hands with the warden and his government friends. Hiro and Pedro gave them a handshake quietly good-bye.

Finally, they exited the jailhouse.

They didn't say a word until they were safe to speak. In the car, Hiro was furious and upset about the loss of Isabel and Pepe. He started screaming, "They say it was a government mistake? Two in my family are dead, because I had simple internet and satellite? Unbelievable! Damn them!" Pedro told Hiro to calm down. Hiro was distraught, but listened, visibly twitching with anger.

Finally, Freddie said, "Hiro, Hiro! Listen to me just a minute! I'm just as mad that this tragedy occurred. I don't have any words for the loss of Isabel and Pepe. It was a tragic and damnable incident. I'm going to investigate it right away. Dania and Madeline came to my office that afternoon and told me everything. I was shocked, and I know the government very well. I encouraged Dania and Madeline not to stay in Santa Clara, because it would be a long time before they would be permitted to see you. I asked them to go home and let me work on getting you two released. I promised them that I would get you out of jail as soon as I could. They both went crazy. They didn't want to go home; they wanted to see the two of you, but I told them to trust me and to leave town. I really had to work to convince Dania and Madeline to return home."

Freddie became silent. Then he said respectfully, "A funeral has already been held for Isabel and Pepe. It was conducted on the second day. Pepe's body went to the family cemetery at Cienfuegos and Isabel's body was buried in Sierra Morena next to her father and mother." Hiro's heart sank, "Oh, Dania!" Hiro and Pedro started crying. This news was crushing, and the sadness was painful. They both had loved Isabel and Pepe deeply.

Freddie continued speaking, "Here's how it all happened. That afternoon the federal secret agent's office in Santa Clara received information from Havana. They received an arrest warrant for you, Hiro, for having an illegal computer with internet access. The government suspected you were spying on them and used this as grounds for your arrest. That's the only

The Last Revolution

information that they had. I went to see the chief of the department—I went straight to the top man in Havana and he gave me all the information."

"According to his documentation, one of the girls living down below your CDR neighbor is an informant. She checked on you for several weeks and reported to authorities in the Rancho Veloz area. Then they called in the Santa Clara Federal Investigation Bureau. Since the investigation involved a well-known professor, they reported you to Central Intelligence in Havana. They generated an order for your arrest. Pedro was just in the wrong place at the wrong time. There was nothing about you in the papers, Pedro."

Freddie continued, "But Hiro is a different case. Under a new law, non-Cuban citizens must register their computers. I didn't know the law had changed until I was at the Central Intelligence office last week. Anyway, since you created a satellite receiver, they suspected you were accessing the internet and spying threat to national Security. Your computer is with me; they couldn't hack into it. They think your computer is destroyed inside—both the hard drive and the processor. It is broken. I'm very sorry. I have it in the trunk of my car."

Hiro said, "I definitely want it returned to me. What did you do with all of my other stuff?"

Freddie said, "They gave it all back to me and it's all in a big box in my house. I got it from the Santa Clara Federal Intelligence Office. They said that the computer technicians in Havana didn't understand how to use the stuff in the box, so they returned everything intact. They were just interested in your computer." Hiro was quiet and didn't say a word.

Then Freddie continued, "I'm so sorry about Isabel and Pepe. I hate to even tell you this part, but the government is claiming that they're not responsible for Isabel and Pepe's deaths. They insist that their deaths were self-defense on the part of the officers. This came from the top. The government will compensate their two children 80 Cuban pesos—$4.00--a month until they reach the age of eighteen. That is the only information I got from the chief."

Hiro said, "Only 80 Cuban peso ($4.00)--a month?"

They all paused in silence. Then Freddie continued, "If you decide to have another computer and to get a paid satellite dish, they can install it for you. You must order installation from a company in Varadero. It's a Canadian company based in Havana and they have an office in Varadero. Equipment installation will cost $250, and the service $150 a month. You must pay the entire fee for one year in advance." Hiro agreed to pay for the installation and service.

Hiro asked Freddie, "Where is my family now?"

Freddie said, "Well, Dania and Madeline are waiting at my house. I thought it would be better for all of us. This has been a tremendous strain on Dania. She has lost two of the most important people in her life. She is going through a difficult time and I'm so very sorry." Then Freddie became silent.

Hiro asked, "Is Dania OK? How are her sisters and my children?"

Pedro was quiet as Freddie answered, "Yes, everyone's all right. They are shaken up, but they are OK. Dania's cousin, Pipo, is living in the house with them now for security."

Freddie said, "Let me see, I need to stop at the La Tienda Pan-Americana to get some wine and beer for us. Let's go to my house. Everybody's waiting. It's just my wife, Dania and Madeline. My wife's cooking some lunch. You two need to rest and relax." He stopped and bought several cases of beer and three bottles of wine. After a fifteen minute drive, they reached Freddie's home.

As soon as Freddie parked his car in the front of house, the three women rushed out to see their men. Madeline and Dania ran to Hiro and Pedro, kissed and greeted them. Both women were crying so hard that they couldn't stop. Everyone began to cry. No could speak. They all just hugged and wept.

Finally Freddie said, "Let's go inside and relax!" Everyone sat on the comfortable patio chairs. Dania wouldn't let Hiro out of her sight. She sat in his lap like a child. There were a few meek and relieved smiles beginning to appear. Yorina, Freddie's wife, was a kind woman and a gracious and sensitive hostess. She brought out wine glasses and poured the women some wine. She also brought cold mugs of beer for the men. Then, Hiro and Pedro looked around and made a funny face to one another and sniffing with their noses. Freddie asked, "What is it? Is something wrong?"

Hiro asked, "Do I smell goat barbecue? Maybe one of your neighbors is cooking goat. I wish I knew them." Everybody started to smile. This lightened the somber mood everyone was

The Last Revolution

in. Dania tried to be polite and even smiled a little, but the whole time she sat with Hiro. She was so relieved that Hiro was safe and that they were back together again. It was very apparent to everyone.

Then, Freddie's wife brought out big plates of goat barbecue and placed them in front of Hiro's face. He said, "Oh, my goodness! Wow!" He was smiling and he grabbed small piece, shoved it into his mouth, and mumbled, "Nothing can beat this treat!" Everybody was smiling. Inwardly, everyone was still traumatized. Hiro said in Japanese, "Freddie and Yorina, thank you so much for your hospitality. I'm glad to be here with you, and with my friends and wife. This means so much to me. Thank you for being my friend." He nearly cried.

Freddie answered "Do itasimashite. Anata wa watasi no ichiban nakano ii tomodachi desu." Everyone was surprised and Pedro inquired," Freddie, what did you say to Hiro?"

Freddie smiled, "I just said you're welcome and that we are, indeed, good friends. That's all."

Pedro was curious and said, "It sounded to me like you said a lot more than that. Is Japanese that long?"

Freddie said, "No, Japanese uses a different system and is quite different from Spanish or English. We say things directly, but the Japanese use passive sentences because they try to be polite to the other party."

During this casual small conversation, they had started to relax, and the tension of the whole ordeal began to lift a bit from their minds for a moment. They were finally smiling in each other's good company now that Hiro and Pedro were free and out of that horrible place. They couldn't pretend that the deaths hadn't happened, but out of respect to Dania they couldn't talk about it. She had been through enough and Dania was very private when it came to her family. They took her lead and didn't discuss the death of her parents or anything that had occurred. Dania was understandably quiet on this topic and they respected her silence.

As a surprise, and to celebrate Hiro's and Pedro's release, Freddie had asked his wife's nephew, Rico, who was an excellent cook, if he would barbecue goat for them. Rico wanted to cook for Hiro and Dania and had gotten up very early to deliver the meat to Freddie's house. Rico lived in Cifuentes which was almost 30 minutes from Santa Clara. It was Freddie's idea to have the BBQ. And it was a good one.

Everyone drank alcohol, ate a good meal, and became relaxed. Goat barbecue was a special meal and even Dania ate a little. For a moment, they forgot their sadness. Hiro understood well that he couldn't live in Cuba without Freddie's friendship and assistance. Freddie always rescued Hiro from troubles. Hiro appreciated having a guardian angel and a friend in Cuba, far away from Japan. It made all the difference in the world. Hiro knew that one day he would repay all of Freddie's help somehow. He didn't know how or with what, but he knew that one day he would give back to the friends that were always there for him—especially Freddie and Pedro.

Freddie's guests stayed until evening. Freddie suggested that they all stay the night in Santa Clara and then go home the next morning, since they had been drinking. Hiro wanted to see his daughters, but he was also tired and wanted a night alone with Dania. Pedro, Hiro, Dania and Madeline discussed what to do and they decided to stay at Freddie's home that night. The children were in good hands and they telephoned to let them know their change in plans. Hearing Hiro's voice was comforting to the children, and they innocently giggled their love to their Papi. They didn't understand all that had happened that horrible night, and sounded just like the two happy little girls from before. Hiro was touched and held back tears.

Freddie was happy that they all could stay and said, "All right, we'll need more beverages. I'll call my friend and he'll deliver some." Then Freddie said, "I have a better idea. How about if I take us all out for a drink at the hotel Santa Clara Libre? It'll do us all some good to listen to some good Cuban music while we have a drink and relax. What do all of you think?"

Hiro talked with Dania and she didn't seem to mind. Hiro thought, "Maybe that's a good idea. It might cheer us up same." However, due to their recent experiences, none of them was ready for a lot of people or noise.

Then Freddie's wife suggested they go to some place more private. She knew of a place called *Parade Bodequita Del Centro.* She added that they had a private room behind a patio that was very quiet with a charming atmosphere. She had been there before with friends. Freddie agreed and they all went there

The Last Revolution

to have a cocktail. They talked a little, but they stayed only an hour, because they could see that Dania wanted to spend time alone with Hiro. Everyone understood her feelings and needs and they all were quite tired. It had been a long day for everyone. They were glad to be together and made a toast to friendship in the warm breeze before they called it a night.

Chapter 49

The next morning everyone got up early. Freddie drove them to Rancho Velloz. Hiro and Dania were anxious to see their daughters. Dania was quiet and kept Hiro in her embrace during the entire trip home. Dania was glued to Hiro. Wherever he went, she held his hand or touched his shoulder. As Dania leaned over to kiss Hiro, she began to cry. Tears poured down her cheeks; and in response to Dania's crying, Hiro's eyes formed tears. He thought of Isabel, Pepe and the many memories they had shared. His tears continued to flow. Dania and Hiro gazed out of the car window looking at the sugarcane. The white blooms showed on the tip top of the cane. The cane plants waved in the gentle Caribbean breeze, but all Hiro and Dania could think of was Pepe who used to work in those fields and Isabel who was such a happy soul. They both were thinking: "May they rest in peace."

At home, Pipo was busy cleaning everything. The entire house was mess. Isabel's and Pepe's bedroom especially needed attention. Dania wanted their belongings placed in big boxes, sealed and stored in the attic. Someday when she was ready, Dania would open the boxes filled with memories. Pepe's belongings included a huge homemade rum-making machine sent by his family in Cienfuegos. All of Isabel's clothing and personal items were carefully wrapped and put in boxes for safekeeping.

Dania planned to refurbish her sister's new bedroom and the old bedroom would now become Pipo's. These changes were emotional for the family, but they had to move forward. Pepe and Isabel would have wanted it that way. These changes were the most difficult for Dania and her sisters. The tragedy had happened without warning. The mother and father they had once loved and who had been there for them forever, were now gone. It was a sudden and harsh blow. They felt as if the rug had been pulled out from under them and their hearts ached. They all needed time to heal their emotional wounds. Isabel's legacy would live on. Her daughters would remember how she had laughed and joked. They would remember quiet Pepe who

The Last Revolution

worked hard and loved to sip homemade rum. No one would ever forget them. Without her mother and Pepe, Dania had a difficult time coping with everyday activities, such as cooking and tending the vegetable garden. Dania had always depended on them for everything and now they were gone. She suddenly had to restructure her whole concept of the family unit. Everything had to change.

Dania now became the center of the household and the major responsibilities rested on her shoulders. She became stronger as each day passed. Dania thought of Isabel and Pepe constantly and remembered little things they had done that she had taken for granted when they were alive. In death, they were still a part of that house and the land. She missed them terribly.

Dania's two younger sisters now came to Dania for guidance. Dania became the mother figure for them, as they were much younger than she. Dania felt that she now had four daughters, instead of two. But she never complained and held her head high. She knew she must carry on and remain strong for everyone. When Dania felt exhausted or like a failure, she pictured her mother's face and felt as if her mother were beside her again. Dania thought she could hear her mother saying, "You can do this. You will get through this. When you feel tired, just laugh and hug everyone and know that I am with you always."

Dania slowly adjusted to the changes. But it took a long time, and each day was a struggle. Dania depended on Hiro for a lot of moral support and relied on his reassurances that they would be OK. Hiro's strong love supported her. She found strength knowing that Hiro depended on her, too. Hiro was always close to Dania. They were together almost twenty-four hours a day. When Hiro had to go out, he was quick about it or took Dania with him.

Within four months, Dania had adjusted to being a full-time homemaker. She emulated her mother Isabel, and many friends and family noticed that Dania had become more and more like her. Dania had matured because of the tragedy and was busy taking care of the children and her two younger sisters. However, life was never the same without Isabel and Pepe. They tried to fill the huge hole left by Isabel's and Pepe's absence with the routine activities of daily life. Hiro was proud of Dania and their relationship grew even more solid after the terrible tragedy.

Dania's cousin Pipo lived with them permanently now. He took charge of the home's security. He was a tall, slender man. Although Pipo had a skinny body, he was solid and muscular. He had been in the army for ten years and had been discharged because he had developed a bad case of gout. Sometimes Pipo's gout was extremely painful, but Hiro was able to secure medicine from Japan that helped alleviate his pain.

Hiro and Pipo got along well. Pipo was a comical person. He was thirty-one years old and was Isabel's brother's only son. Isabel had taken care of Pipo since her brother had been killed in Angola in 1989. Pipo was a good man who got along well with the entire family. He made a great addition to their home and family.

Since their family had expanded, Hiro purchased property rights to the house next door. The owner had left for Miami, and no one besides Hiro was interested in buying the property. The government would confiscate it if no one wanted it, so Hiro and Dania decided to buy. Dania wanted to purchase the property because she hoped that someday someone in her family would build a home there. They thought that maybe Pipo might build his home there, bit by bit, like every other Cuban approached homebuilding.

Several months after the tragedy, Hiro installed a satellite system from the Canadian company dish network Bell ExpressVu are licensed by the CRTC, based in Varadero with Freddie's help. The entire family thoroughly enjoyed the programs they were able to access. Actually, Hiro's and Dania's home was in San Rafael about ten miles south of Sierra Morena, but everyone referred to it as Rancho Veloz because all Cubans were familiar with that town. Their doors were always open, and neighbors and friends dropped by to visit frequently. Their visitors also enjoyed watching the satellite channels because they were unable to afford satellite systems. However, the family didn't have much privacy because of the neighbors' enjoyment of the Spanish channels.

Cuban state television was called ICRT which stood for the Cuban Institute of Radio and Television. Hiro thought the content of programs was far better than U.S. and Japanese programs and there were only advertisement; Fidel's revolution. There had been only two channels when he first arrived in Cuba, but now as many as five stations were available. ICRT is known

The Last Revolution

for its excellent programming and all Cubans are glued to the tubes.

To accommodate his visitors, Hiro decided to build an open, guano-grass hut on a concrete patio he would pour in front of his house next to a huge mango tree. Within a few weeks, it became an attractive place with the help of Pedro and Pipo. The patio-hut had a concrete floor about 25 by 35 feet in size. Four huge rail steel columns supported the guano leaves that made the roof. The patio was cool and breezy in the scorching Caribbean sun.

Hiro asked Pedro to build ten benches which could seat four people each so that all their neighbors and friends could watch movies every night. Pipo was responsible for overseeing this tropical screening room. Hiro ordered a 52-inch Mitsubishi LCD flat screen televisions from Mexico which mad the patio seem like an outdoor movie theater. Everyone loved the improvised theater because their friends and neighbors hadn't had any opportunity to see movies or special shows. Most didn't own a television, so this outdoor theater was a big deal in the small, rural town.

People in this little village usually went to bed early in the evening because there was nothing else for them to do. Pedro and his family came to Hiro's house at least three or four nights a week to watch movies and to enjoy the Spanish Latino Channel. Hiro did not want to show any CNN News Espanol, because he didn't want to hear any disturbing news from around the world. The news channels seemed to be obsessed with sad or horrible events. Instead of being uplifting and showing human potential, the channels focused on fear-promoting events which was a real downer for everyone. Hiro wanted to keep the atmosphere light and happy in his home, especially after the tragedy.

The reason Hiro decided to build a separate entertainment hut was that many people dropped by nightly. He also built a steel cage around the TV screen and equipment. Only people to whom he had given permission could access the key to enter the hut. Pipo was in charge of overseeing the hut and making sure that no one bothered the equipment. He was also in charge of making sure that people used it only on weekend nights between 7:00 and 1:00. This way Hiro and Dania could still have their privacy.

They loved having company and enjoyed giving others the chance to see the films and shows, but they also valued their privacy and wanted to be left completely alone in the main house. All their friends understood and respected this request. Hiro also wanted Pipo to be sure that only movie and sports channels were played on the TV. Pipo did an excellent job supervising the use of the hut. The responsibility made Pipo feel important.

After the theater was established, Hiro asked Freddie to assist in getting his computer legally registered with the government. Freddie asked, "Is your computer still broken? You need a new one?"

Hiro said, "Actually, my computer is working!"

Freddie was amazed and said, "Really? My top computer technician in Havana told me it had malfunctioned so wildly that the CPU was completely destroyed."

Hiro smiled and answered, "I've been working on it, and everything's OK. I'd like you to register it so we won't get into any more trouble. Can you help me?" He added bitterly, and he was serious, "I don't want to lose any more family members."

Freddie agreed and sent Hiro's documents through Santa Clara's federal office to the Department of the Interior in Havana. When the paperwork was finally cleared, Freddie shared the news with Hiro saying, "Good news. Your computer is finally legal. You won't have any further problems from the Cuban government. Here are your documents."

Hiro looked at the papers and announced; "Now, I'm official!"

Freddie said, "By the way, I didn't know you worked on computers. You seem to know a lot about how they work. Maybe you could help me when my computer has trouble. I'm always frustrated when I try to find someone who can fix it." Then they smiled at one another. Hiro was glad that he could always count on Freddie.

Hiro really didn't have to reconstruct his computer, because he had installed a special device which programmed the computer to go into an artificial sleep mode when he used a special code. Hiro had added this precaution in the event that his laptop was confiscated. To re-awaken his computer, Hiro had also programmed a special device that was triggered by finger vibration and his DNA mark input on the keyboard. The vibration would restore the computer to full working capacity. Hiro used this unique modification to keep his computer and files strictly confidential.

    Hiro obviously had not lost his touch. Even a top-notch computer technician like the one working for the Cuban government could not detect this device. Hiro had made it almost impossible for anyone to reboot his computer. To anyone examining it, it appeared to be completely broken and a lost cause. Hiro had used a tiny microchip to interrupt the computer biocode. Once synchronized, it would temporarily compress and erase the information stored in its memory. The computer would stay in hibernation until further notice from Hiro by way of a DNA mark sensor. After his return from Japan, he had developed this sensor from an idea which had been floating around in his head for many years.

    Hiro used biometric identification to activate his computer. Hiro could not gamble on anyone being able to access data on his computer. He knew it was a matter of grave importance to keep the contents hidden and completely protected. The information on his hard drive could cost him his family and all the happiness he had in the world, so he had to create a foolproof security program. Since Hiro had a photographic memory, he seldom left too much information on his computer anyway. He always memorized what he needed and deleted it from his memo pod. He was careful and watched his every step, obscuring his preparations so that nothing could be traced back to him.

    Hiro had been working on something special. He continued to develop his ideas. As each day passed, he got more and more quiet and serious. He was deep in thought while concentrating on his new idea. Once again, Hiro began to isolate himself from his family. Dania was stronger now emotionally and didn't need him by her side every minute. The girls were busy with their studies and friends. Hiro stayed in his bedroom almost twelve hours a day working on his project.

    Dania become concerned about him. She didn't know what Hiro was up to and became very concerned. She trusted him, but she decided to discuss his seclusion before it got out of hand. One day, Dania went to his room. She knocked gently on the door, "Hiro, I need to talk to you. It's very important."

Hiro said, "Come in. What is it that you want to discuss?" He stroked her shoulder softly and could see the concern on her face. "Please tell me why you look so serious." Dania sat on the bed next to Hiro.

She kissed his face everywhere and said, "Darling, tell me what you have been working on in here everyday. I'm concerned, because we have only each other and you must tell me everything. I'm afraid something bad will happen again." Then she shuddered, and started sobbing. Tears came pouring down her face. Hiro hadn't expected this reaction, but he felt a deep sympathy toward her. She said though her tears, "Hiro, I love you so much. I have only you and the girls. I miss my mother and Pepe so much. Hiro, please tell me what's going on and what you're planning. I'm worried that something has happened to you. You stay in here all day long and you don't tell me what's on your mind anymore."

Hiro became quiet and whispered to her, "I'm planning to neutralize Fidel." Dania's face was shocked, and she became quiet. She kissed Hiro and hugged him, and then she whispered, "Hiro, I want you to do it! He killed my mother and Pepe. They trusted Fidel so much their entire lives!" She cried. Hiro wiped the tears from her cheeks.

He said, "I know I can eliminate him. I'm convinced that it's the only solution for Cuba." Hiro didn't know how to finish this job himself, but he was determined to find a way. The moment Isabel and Pepe had been shot; Hiro determined that he was going to come up with a foolproof retaliation scheme. But in the midst of that horrible chaos, he was unable to observe that his amazing, digital mind had instantly patterned and stored a complete and perfect plan. However, like an undiscovered ancient mosaic, it was hiding and awaiting slow and careful excavation from beneath Hiro's emotional rubble.

Hiro thought that Fidel should have called an end to his reign ten years after the revolution. If Castro had resigned then, he would have been a hero forever. The people would have changed the name of Havana to Castro or something similar. Fidel had been good once and was perhaps a hero for all Cubans, but he had stayed in power too long and the Cuban people were all paying the price. Dania hugged Hiro tightly and whispered into his ear; "I won't ask you any more questions. Just promise me now that you will not put yourself, me or the family in any danger in your quest to eliminate Fidel." Hiro looked her in the eyes and said sincerely, "I promise. You know that I keep my promises."

Freddie and Hiro began visiting one another often. Hiro asked many political questions, and each time he spoke, he did so in Japanese. Both men felt comfortable talking in Japanese, because no one anywhere would be able to understand what they were saying. Freddie was a high-ranking officer, so he felt he could criticize the government and Castro only in Japanese.

After many years of knowing each other, Hiro and Freddie knew that they could talk openly, because they trusted each other completely. Since Hiro had had access to the internet, he had researched the available information on Cuba's dictator, but he still had many questions for Freddie.

Hiro discovered that Fidel's vision was not what the Cuban people wanted. It was only Fidel's selfishness and ego that had led him to hijack the island for himself. Castro had forced his ideas about Cuba's future on other people and had demanded strict control of the country. Fidel's vision sounded good in theory, but in reality, he had no idea what was going on with the people and with this beautiful island. Hiro noticed that the people were always scared and that they felt that nothing in life was guaranteed. They just existed.

The Cuban people had only the present and that's why they couldn't see much of a future for themselves. Fidel wouldn't let them. Hiro thought, "It is a perfect country to live in—if you don't want do anything with your life." In Fidel's Cuba, it was almost impossible to live out your dreams. Whatever goals or aspirations one had, the odds of achieving them were low. There were no incentives to achieve anything.

Chapter 50

Hiro began to research extensively on the internet the topic of Fidel Castro. He wanted to know everything about him. What Hiro found was shocking. Hiro couldn't believe the role this dictator had played in Cuba's history. But, Hiro soon found out that most of the Internet web sites were propaganda maintained by Cuban-Americans. The sites contained information about what had happened from 1958 to the present which Hiro had a difficult time believing. Even if a quarter of it was true, it was still an astonishing record.

Hiro always trusted the articles he accessed on the United Nations web site. Also, the Cuban Affairs site and the Japanese government site reported accurate accounts of Cuba's history and were trustworthy sources. Hiro thought that the US government's website on Cuba was inaccurate and tainted by the Cuban-American influence. Therefore, Hiro relied on the content of the United Nations site and that of the Japanese government to be unbiased and the most reliable.

One article that Hiro found particularly damaging, and the one that he strongly disagreed with, indicated that Fidel had been a criminal since his college years. It stated that Fidel had attempted to murder a fellow student named Leonel Gomez by shooting him in the throat, but Gomez survived the murder attempt. Gomez had been Fidel's rival and a student leader at The University of Havana.

The article also mentioned that later, a campus security guard had testified that Fidel shot Fernandez Caral point blank while Caral was babysitting his son at home on July 7, 1948. The article went on to say that Fidel continued to threaten or physically eliminate any opponents or government officials who stood in his way. Hiro understood that dictators always had competition. Tyrants were at the top of the pyramid, and the competition rose from the bottom. It was a case of survival of the fittest. But Hiro wanted evidence that Fidel had actually murdered people while gaining power. In 1958, members of Castro's movement hijacked three different Cubana airliners at gunpoint. These were the first airplane hijackings in history,

The Last Revolution

making Fidel a pioneer in 20th century terrorism. Hiro decided to ask Freddie for the truth about Fidel.

Freddie didn't really wish to share his opinion, but he trusted Hiro and knew that he was a sincere and honest person. Eventually, Freddie decided to tell Hiro the truth about Fidel's history. Freddie acknowledged the fact that Fidel had once been a terrorist against the Cuban government. At the time, Batista was Cuba's dictator and Fidel simply ignored him and ultimately sought revenge against him. Fidel actually lost his credibility with the U.S. soon after he emerged the victor of the revolution. Freddie also told Hiro that Fidel had tried to brainwash the president of Venezuela, Romero Betancourt, to adopt his vision.

When Betancourt refused to exchange oil, Fidel attempted to have Betancourt assassinated. Fifty years later, Castro finally succeeded in implementing his original master plan to retaliate against gringo-ism. Venezuela's new president, Hugo Chavez, supported massive crude oil aid to Cuba. Nearly 160,000 barrels of oil were sent daily to Cuba. The refineries were not capable of processing such massive quantities, so Cuba resold the excess oil to other nations for profit. Nearly $2 billion dollars went into Fidel's pocket. Fidel had no choice but to turn to Hugo Chavez for economic support. Since 2000, Cuba has subsidized Venezuelan oil for in exchange; he gave Venezuela professional education, technical assistance in the area of agriculture and military training.

Latin American countries, including Cuba, had always seen The United States as a tyrant. Fidel stated openly that he hated the U.S. and would do anything to seek revenge on the US as well as anything related to the gringo mentality. Fidel openly promoted the use of terrorist tactics by creating training camps and exporting terrorists to other countries. Fidel knew the CIA was also sponsoring terrorists, but that the United States would never see themselves as terrorists in other countries. Fidel was totally against the US and wanted revenge on them for supporting the anti-Cuban terrorists known as freedom fighters.

Hiro always knew that the US had strong ideological views on democracy and sought to force these beliefs on other countries. Hiro thought this was the same mentality that the Spanish used during the Inquisition. They justified demolishing the New World with the excuse of spreading Christianity. Now, the US was using the same excuse in modern times by wanting to be the "great protectors of Democracy" by spreading the concept of social equality to everyone. But not all countries wanted to adopt a democratic form of government. This is the reason that the US had had such a difficult time in Vietnam and in Iraq. The US had to learn that they must respect the cultures in other countries because the world had shrunk in the last 500 years. Also, the CIA had a long record of assassination attempts on Fidel. At last count, they had tried to finish him off an astonishing 658 times. Surprisingly, all attempts had failed. Fidel was like a cat with nine lives who always knew how to survive.

In Fidel's most famous speech in 1953 he says, "History will absolve me..." which was later in a book of Fidel's life and exploits. Hiro had this book and read it every chance he got. He was fascinated.

But Politics seemed complicated and were difficult for Hiro to understand. Computer science and mathematics were much more natural to him. But through his research and talks with Freddie, Hiro became disillusioned with Fidel Castro. When he got a good look at the man, he didn't like what he saw. Hiro had once believed that Fidel was a savior of the people, but now he had discovered that Fidel had simply hijacked the entire island for his own selfish vision. In doing this, Fidel had destroyed many people's lives and the happiness of many families.

Records indicated that the government had executed more than 1200 people who were against Fidel. When anyone stood against Fidel or criticized his vision, Fidel simply assassinated them. He eliminated his entire opposition with this tactic. This made Fidel a monster in Hiro's eyes. And after talking with Freddie, he knew that the article saying that Fidel had shot his student rival at The University of Havana all those years ago was true. Fidel was a criminal who placed no value on human life.

Freddie understood the Cuban culture and politics. He believed that Fidel has stayed in power so long because of his thug mentality and the stupidity and ignorance of the populace. They followed him blindly, so Fidel had implemented his plan of psychological warfare successfully. Fidel had enjoyed success, while the Cuban people had become his pets. Fidel controlled the Cuban people and they obeyed him like a dog obeys a cruel master. Hiro began to see the true picture of what had happened to Cuba. For the first time, he thought how sad it all was. Cubans were apathetic and would make no effort to improve their lives. They just waited for someone else to resolve the problem of Castro for them.

Hiro thought about capitalism and democracy. He thought about the flaws in the U.S. system of government. Hiro remembered that African-Americans didn't have equal rights in the US until recently. But even with its flaws, at least people in the U.S. were free and could achieve their dreams. Here in Cuba, people were scared to speak out or to give their opinions, people had no rights and people couldn't achieve their dreams because the government wouldn't allow them to do so. Hiro began to understand Fidel's distorted vision for Cuba and he suddenly felt guilty for enjoying his life in Cuba so much.

Finally, Hiro understood what Pedro and Aimee had complained about when he had first arrived in Cuba. He thought about all those people he had talked to who complained about their lives. It was now clear to him what they meant. Before, Hiro hadn't had been able to relate to them because he had found so much happiness on this tropical island. His extensive research and Freddie's conversations led Hiro to discover the truth about what was really going on, which was disguised as Fidel's nationalism.

Now, after Hiro and his family had suffered the loss of Isabel and Pepe for nothing, Hiro knew what he had to do. Hiro was going to annihilate Fidel Castro for destroying his family and for all the lives that he had taken throughout the years. It was time for Cuba to be liberated from this thug. Hiro's digital mind, cleared by time of much of its emotional baggage, began to reveal the plan to eliminate Fidel that had formed and hidden itself at the moment Isabel was shot. But he had to keep it to himself, if there were any chance of success. It was a long shot, but Hiro had to take it. He had his mind set on it.

Freddie spoke in Japanese during these private discussions. He did this in order to cover up the controversial topics he and Hiro discussed about the Cuban government and Fidel's politics. It was an extremely trustworthy friendship and Freddie felt safe in sharing and in being truthful with Hiro. Perhaps it was a way to relieve his conscience. It was a way to speak the truth to another man without fear that the person would turn him in as a traitor. Freddie and Hiro had an intellectual bond as well as an understanding. They both enjoyed their discussions and talked freely. Hiro began to understand Fidel's true nature and the way that he ruled Cuba using psychology, fear and terror. Hiro appreciated Freddie's friendship and his opinion. Hiro reassured Freddie that he wouldn't push the issue any further. Hiro made up his mind that Fidel had to be terminated and Freddie had confirmed the ugly truth.

Daily, Hiro searched for the answer. He thought about Isabel and Pepe and used them as his inspiration to devise a plan. He had never thought about trying to kill anyone before, so for Hiro this was new and difficult. It didn't come naturally, but he cleared his mind of everything else and focused on his goal while continuing to research his ideas.

Hiro remembered stories of ancient Japan during the days of the ninja. As a young boy, he had been fascinated about ninjas and had studied their mysterious ways. During the 15th century, the ninja had acted as spies and assassins for hire to the feudal lords and samurai. However, he wasn't a ninja. Hiro was only a scientist.

During this time, Hiro asked Dania to give him space and to allow him private time for his research. He said to her, "I need to concentrate and come up with a good idea." Dania hugged him and thought of her parents. She knew that Hiro was the man to avenge them. She saw that he was serious and tried to lighten things up. She said, "Maybe you need a machinegun or long knife like a Japanese samurai sword." She laughed and kissed him.

Hiro admonished Dania saying, "Look, I'm not an assassin. I'm a scientist. This isn't a joke and it's dangerous business. But I'm getting an idea. I'm on to something here." In reality he was about to discover the plan that he had formed instantly at Isabel's death—the plan that his mind had hidden under the emotions of tragedy. It was a plan so unnatural to him, that he didn't know that all he had to do was to excavate it from his memories of that terrible and confusing night.

Dania hugged Hiro and answered softly, "I know, I apologize for joking around. I know you're on the verge of something big. I promise to leave you alone to your work. I won't say anything, and I won't ask you any questions." They nodded to one another, and Dania.

Chapter 51

Hiro had always known that Cuba needed a very different political system. He knew that in Cuba, Communism wouldn't work and neither would capitalism. Hiro researched the Spanish conquest and how it had violated and destroyed the Latin American cultures.

When Europeans began arriving in the New World, they brought a rich culture with them. They spread their art, music, architecture, and politics throughout Latin America and the western hemisphere including the ancient world of the Indians and native peoples. The tribal culture of the natives was a mix of very rich traditions. It was a unique culture unlike any other in world.

The goal of the Europeans was to indoctrinate the people of Latin America with Christianity and to educate the Indians to be more civilized. The Europeans wanted the people of Latin America to be more like them so they destroyed Indian culture. Sadly, much of the Indian culture disappeared from the earth forever. The Indians were tortured and endured hard labor under the brutal hands of the Europeans. The native peoples lived in a state of chaos for many years, and the Europeans never understood or respected these unique indigenous people.

There were many problems with political stability in the different regions in regard to the forming of states and the balance of power. The Spanish conquistadors stole from the native cultures and took what remained of their deep roots. They were bent on exploiting the native peoples and changing them. There had been wide-spread corruption within the governments' high-ranking officers since 1492. These powerful individuals abused the system for their own benefit. They had no regard for the natives or the collective masses they were leading and were concerned only with their own personal finances and social gain. Over many years, power struggles and the formation of divided factions within the governments led to overthrows and brutal dictatorships. These were a frequent occurrence in Latin and South America.

These early settlers had many problems with the system of free democratic enterprise because power was constantly being abused. That was a part of Latin America's history and perhaps is part of the culture today. They had a history of struggling to survive, shifting government regimes, *coup de etat* and dictatorships, and a balance of power. They have always struggled under a democratic free republic. Cuba was all too familiar with this struggle for power in government and society. Hiro learned all he could about the Cuban culture and history and determined that they needed social-democratic development similar to what had taken place during the American occupation of Japan

After WWII. American General Douglas MacArthur, the US supreme Pacific commander, led the way in setting up a social-democratic government in Japan. It worked wonderfully and was far superior to any other system that could have been imposed. Hiro understood this firsthand because he had grown up under this transitional government in Japan. MacArthur was a very strong dictator in a modern democratic government.

General Douglas MacArthur's military career was astonishing. He became the supreme commander of the occupational military. As such, he ordered an end to the Japanese state religions, such as Shinto; and he reformed the entire Japanese system of government by drafting a new constitution which banned the god-like worship of Emperor Hirohito.

Additionally, MacArthur disarmed the Japanese military and made new guidelines for economic reconstruction with a strong and workable plan. He used benevolent judgment and absolute power to resolve Japanese public disagreements. Additionally, MacArthur completely dismantled the *zaibatsu* system that, at the time, controlled economic development and land reform.

He also dismantled the entire class system and divided land and wealth evenly among the people that better then Fidel's system. General MacArthur provided an iron hand for the Japanese people from 1945 to 1950 by imposing a true democratic system. Then in 1949, MacArthur withdrew as dictator and military commander turning over the responsibility to the general Japanese population.

The Last Revolution

MacArthur set many examples of how the Japanese could live in harmony with their neighbors. Japan experienced political turbulence on the way to learning to live within the new democratic free system, but they achieved it successfully within ten years. It was a gift from MacArthur who was called the old soldier who faded away. He was the ruler of Japan for only ten years, but his achievements were amazing. He was a very strong person with an impressive military career. He was fair and never unkind or power hungry. He was still appreciated by the Japanese as a great warrior sixty years after WWII. Disagreement about MacArthur's ambition and his independence caused President Truman to force the general into retirement in 1951.

Based on Hiro's experiences in Cuba and his research going back to the Batista era, he thought that many poor Cubans should have better lives under Castro's reign than under American capitalism. Hiro remembered a quote on the Internet that said, "The Cuban poor are far better off than the American poor." From his experience, Hiro thought this was absolutely true. The poor might not have much in the way of tangible goods here in Cuba, but no one was starving to death. The people had the basic necessities. Hiro had witnessed this truth from living with Pedro and later with Dania and her family.

They were poor, but they always had enough. The government guaranteed to provide basic needs equally to all Cubans.

Hiro recalled a conversation when he had first settled in Rancho Veloz. When Hiro was mingling with people in the street, he met a guy from Enrique who spoke broken English. The man told Hiro his story. The man had lived in New Orleans right after the 1980s. He had been a prisoner in Cuba when Fidel released him and had been part of the Mariel Harbor massive boat lift that ended up in New Orleans.

The man was uneducated, but he struggled to meet the high standards of American life. In Cuba he was a prisoner in jail; in the US he had been a prisoner of money. The man had been a schoolmate of Isabel's. She had described him as always involved in stealing and dealing in agriculture products. That was the reason he had been imprisoned.

The man repeatly explained to Hiro how he had been miserable in the free society of the US. There he had been isolated and poor. The man finally decided to return to his family in Cuba, but he had no money to buy an airline ticket so he ended up hijacking an airliner bound to Chicago and forced the jet to land in Havana.

When he got to the Havana international airport, Cuban soldiers were waiting and the man was escorted at gunpoint to jail where he was required to serve a three year sentence. He spent the years working hard in the sugarcane fields. After he was released for good behavior, he returned to Rancho Veloz where his family lived. The Cuban government enforced the law very forcibly.

Although poor, Enrique was very happy living with his family, but the family had very few material things. He lived with his two brothers and mother in a house with a dirt floor and only owned one light bulb. Domestic cattle in the US lived better than Enrique and his family. Enrique told Hiro over and over that living in the US looked great on the surface, but underneath the veneer, the US was missing many things.

Enrique had said something more important than money. Living in Cuba was stress free and allowed abundant time for family living. Enrique loved Cuba. He loved the freedom of living in a Communist society where most of his needs were provided for. As long as he stayed away from politics, Enrique thought Cuba was the perfect place to live. He still felt this way even though he had been imprisoned in jail many times.

Not long after their last conversation, Hiro heard that the man had been returned to jail for killing cattle. Hiro did not see the man for three years. Then Hiro saw him the year before he left Cuba.

Hiro began to think of the all the pros and cons of the political systems. Dania's entire family was comfortable living under the Communist system. He thought that if Cuba changed suddenly to a democratic free Cuba, they might suffer or it could potentially devastate their entire family structure. It was a risk. Under Fidel's system, they had no incentive for higher education, and they lived for what life brought them. This is why they enjoyed the moment; they didn't look too far ahead.

If the government changed to capitalism tomorrow, they would never receive the positive benefits of a free society. It would offer only hard work, and they would struggle just trying to make ends meet. Perhaps their lives would become agonizing. At least under the Cuban-Communist government, they had a house with no house note, low utility bills, free medical and dental care, some medicine available at a low cost, and the opportunity for free education. Hiro liked that education in Cuba was free.

But Hiro knew that many people didn't take advantage of the opportunity to receive a free education because of low incentives. Why study hard when there were no financial rewards? Unfortunately, many people in Cuba felt this way. For example, there was no cost to become a medical doctor in Cuba. The government even paid students a salary while they attended the university. The Cuban education system was far more advanced than the education system in the US. Cuba's system was even more advanced than Japan's system.

Everyone was fed. They received food rations for fifteen days and had to look for supplies on the black market for another fifteen days. Before Russia had pulled financial aid out of Cuba, the people received food rations for a full month. To Hiro, this was still reasonable and only a minimal discomfort. Although, it might not be a lavish life style, least people were not starving to death, and the rations could sustain life.

Hiro thought about his childhood in the countryside of Japan following WWII. The poor of Cuba were much better off than he and his family had been in those days. Hiro heard the people say many times, "We get shit." But what did they expect? Free was free. When people had to work hard, they appreciated what they got. When things came at no cost, they were rarely appreciated.

Hiro felt selfish because he wanted Cuba to stay exactly the same. For him, life was peaceful, laid-back, and unique. Hiro loved it this way and wished to be left alone for just a little longer in Fidel's dream world.

Hiro wondered if Castro had made a huge mistake in bringing Communism to this beautiful, carefree tropical island. Hiro remembered a famous speech that a Black activist had made in the mid-1960s. In the address, he said, "For white Americans, they landed on Plymouth Rock seeking opportunity in the future to come; but for Black people, Plymouth Rock landed on them and took away all of their freedom and made them slaves." Hiro did not think that Communism was a good fit with the Cuban culture. Maybe Communism had had the same effect on the Cuban people.

Hiro was torn between what he had here in Cuba and what the people wanted and needed for the future. For Hiro, it was very difficult to decide which government system was better and which would benefit Cuba the most. He thought: "The Cuban people must decide their own destiny. I am not Cuban, but I love this country." Hiro saw that the people wanted change and that they needed to have choices. The people were tired of living in fear, and they had no real freedom to speak of. They were prisoners here on the island. Within a week of serious thought and contemplation, Hiro finally made his mind up.

He made a firm decision; he must help free the people of Cuba from Fidel's rule once and for all. Since the people were too frightened to act against Fidel, Hiro must take action. Fidel would not stop by himself and no one was willing to take the risk to go against him to make the necessary changes.

Hiro thought, "I must help him become willing to step aside. But how?"

It was the most complicated puzzle he had ever faced encounter because human factors were involved. It would have been easier for him to work a Rubik's Cube than to work on something with a human dimension.

Periodically, Pedro stopped by to check on Hiro. Dania and Hiro were very cautious and did not tell Pedro about Hiro's plans. Pedro suspected something good was happening to Hiro. He had watched Hiro closely from the time they had first met in Havana, and he knew that Hiro was up to something. When he stopped by, Hiro was alone is his room and hard at work conducting research. Pedro knew that this meant Hiro was deep in thought.

Pedro also knew that Hiro was no ordinary mathematics professor. He knew that he had far-reaching capacities beyond what most people had, and he knew what Hiro was working on was computer-related, but Pedro just kept his thoughts to himself and didn't ask questions. He just stopped by for social visits and to see how everyone was doing.

Meanwhile, Dania asked Pipo to keep an eye on the main house. No one was allowed to get close to Hiro's bedroom. Dania never forgot Isabel and Pepe, so Pipo was focused on Hiro's security twenty-four hours a day.

The Last Revolution

Hiro seemed to be alone in hibernation in his room all the time. He was in fifth gear, and his brain activity became abnormally active. He began to focus on the structural features of his vision. His mind was continually developing ideas at a rapid pace like the beat of a percussion instrument—firing ideas one after the other. When his brain was in this highly active state, he was like a human calculator adding up the various options and eliminating the ones he couldn't use. He was creating a new venture using his brilliant mathematical ideas and his knowledge of computer science and neuroscience. He began secretly writing a new script of his war game.

He named it, "The Last Revolution."

It took Hiro nearly thirty-eight days to complete the script. When he finished, Hiro memorized the entire script and deleted it from his computer. It had to remain "top secret". Now, that the work was done, Hiro began to relax and became like his old self again.

He told Dania, "I need to find a person who works in the Cuban army now. Do you know anyone?"

Dania thought for a moment, "Well, my cousin who lives in Calibrien, you remember Piyo? He used to work in the Cuban army when he was living in Sagua. Now he is in charge of the construction of a new base in Calibrien for the Cuban Coast Guard and the development of new tourist hotels. You've seen it before, Hiro. He's just helping with constructing the new base while still a captain in the Army."

Hiro breathed in a deep breath, thought quietly, and then replied, "Oh yes, isn't Freddie responsible for that development? Right?"

Dania nodded her head, "*Si* that is correct."

Hiro asked, "Do you think Piyo can give me some information about the Cuban army. Just tell him I am curious because I don't know anything about the Cuban military. Can you ask him to explain some things to me?"

Dania said, "I'll try. I'll talk to him this weekend. I'll ask him to come to our house. Probably you need to give him some money. He'll do it for some money because his family is very poor, and I know he really needs it. He only makes about 500 Cuban pesos ($20 USD) per month. It will help him and his wife. I think he'll do it for me if I ask."

Hiro replied, "The money is fine. That's an excellent idea. See what you can do. I want to talk to him as soon as possible."

Dania had never asked any questions since that day they had had the conversation in their room. She trusted Hiro. She invited her cousin Piyo and his family over that weekend. She told them to come for a get together, and they would grill Creole fish at her home in San Rafael near Sierra Morena. She wanted to keep it all private, so she didn't invite anyone else. Dania figured Hiro needed a good amount of time with Piyo.

Piyo's family arrived early in the afternoon. Piyo had two sons from a previous marriage. He had sent his younger son to the University of Matanzas, and the older son was serving in the army. Piyo had remarried an older, white Cuban woman named Teresa. They were happy but lived in poverty. The family lived in a very small home and had few possessions. Dania knew from talking to Piyo that Teresa's health was declining. One of Teresa's sons by her first marriage had left Cuba for the US and was now living in New York. He sent some money from time to time but not much because living in New York was very expensive. Teresa's son sent what he could enclosed in his letters to his mother.

Nevertheless, Piyo was a captain in the army, and he was very intelligent. He spoke French fluently. Piyo had served in army intelligence during the war in Angola where he was stationed in the capital city of *Bangui,* a former French colony. Piyo monitored American intelligence as a native African because he looked like a native. His skin was a blue-black color, and he had kinky hair which looked like a black helmet. Piyo had strong facial features and looked more African than Cuban. No one would have guessed that he was Cuban so he made a great spy. Piyo served there nearly ten years.

Meanwhile, back at home his first wife had found someone else and had divorced Piyo and was remarried by the time he returned from Angola. The news caused heartache for Piyo and was an ordeal for the entire family.

When Dania had a moment alone with Piyo, she asked if he would answer some questions for Hiro. At first, he refused to divulge any military information, but then Dania handed him $200 American dollars. Piyo couldn't refuse the money and agreed to give precise information to Hiro but stipulated that

The Last Revolution

their discussions should remain strictly confidential. Everyone agreed.

Chapter 52

As soon as Piyo arrived, he wanted to start the meeting with Hiro. Hiro was already set up at his desk in his bedroom. On the desktop, Hiro had a Cuban map opened up.

Right away, Piyo closed the door and all the windows. He pulled up a chair next to Hiro. He ask Hiro with a cautious voice, "What do you want from me? What is it that you would like to know?" He was very stiff and looked very uncomfortable. He was very serious yet he looked frightened.

Then Hiro said, "Piyo, please trust me. This will remain completely confidential. It is just for my own knowledge. I don't know anything about the Cuban army and the Cuban military format. Could you please explain to me how the Cuban army functions and what their objective is?

Piyo was very quiet at first. He looked at Hiro with hesitation; then he began to explain the military structure using detailed data and facts. Hiro listened carefully while taking mental notes on the information. It was like he was creating a spreadsheet in his mind.

Next Hiro asked Piyo about specific units, brigades, and weaponry. When Piyo hesitated, Hiro immediately slipped him $200 dollars more. Hiro did not like bribing Piyo, but he had to have the information. Although he was nervous and sweating, Piyo accepted the money without blinking an eye. Piyo proceeded to provide Hiro with a specific list of equipment maintained by the Army, Navy, and Air Defense.

Then Piyo arose from the chair and said, "Look Hiro, the Cuban military has three branches: the Army, the Navy, and the Army's Air Force. Fidel Castro commands all three branches, and his brother, Raúl, is his right hand. Together they have total authority over the military."

"We also have a few medium-range missiles and several short-range missiles that can target the mainland of the United States. The exact numbers are unknown because it is top-secret information. I'm not sure about the progress, but I've heard rumors that the missiles were only for defense purposes except

The Last Revolution

when special expeditionary forces were sent into Africa. That was the first time in our military history that Cuba supported human rights through armed conflict in - Angola and Ethiopia. We were proud and felt that Cubans did a superb job."

"I was one of the soldiers who spent time Bangui in the Central African Republic. I was there for almost ten years, and it was not easy. But we achieved our goal, and Fidel did the right thing. I definitely supported him. All the generals did an incredible job, and even the Russian generals were shocked to see how highly-trained our forces were."

"As you know, the Cuban military is well-trained and very aggressive. When we demonstrated our strength in Angola, the whole world watched in surprise. Also, we were equipped with Russian weapons and standard AK-47's. We had the same weapons as the Russian Army only we didn't have heavy tanks. We had small tanks because Cuba had never needed to use the heavier equipment."

Hiro broke in saying, "Piyo, I don't need any more details. All I need to know is the structure of the Cuban army."

Piyo was looking more comfortable now and said, "Oh that is very easy. The Cuban army is divided into three sections, and three generals control this island. The Navy and Air Force are under the control General of Army General Hector Elias Garcia in Havana. Fidel's brother, Raúl, is the main Chief of Staff of the Army, and Fidel is the top Commander and Chief of all the military's forces."

"From the east, General Juan Carlos Corona, who is about fifty-five years old and very aggressive, has been a main general since the war in Ethiopia. He was a lieutenant Commander in the 1980's and now has the rank of a general. As general, he was the architect of the strategy used by the Cuban Army in Africa. There he demonstrated and showed his intelligence and excellent strategic mind to Fidel."

"The expeditionary forces were under General Ochoa Sanchez's control. He was tough and highly-trained. But Juan Carlos Corona got credit for the success in Africa, and he became a four-star general. After Corona's promotion, General Amodo Ochoa Sanchez was executed in 1989."

"Next is the central Corps of the Cuban Army which is home to the headquarters of the Army's intelligence division. General Abelardo González is a brilliant man and the youngest general in the army. He is only forty-two years old and is the general most trusted by Fidel and his brother Raúl. Most people call him the high-tech general, because he's an expert in computer science and technology and have added and trained a new unit of technology surveillance intelligence. This new phase of technology in the Army has been a tremendous benefit. The central commander and chief, General Hector Elias Garcia, controls the entire Cuban army. He is the chief general under Raúl. Fidel controls every part of the military."

"In the Western region of Pinar del Rio, former western army, now there is Air Force General Enrique Hurtado Rodríguez who has had a wide variety of experiences in air combats. Rodríguez is fifty-seven years old and was trained by the Russian Air Force. He also trained with the North Vietnamese as a pilot during the Vietnam War in air combat and as a dogfighter in the Chinese Air Force based in Chung King, China. He became an expert dog fighter with the MIG-21 and was a major when he was only twenty-years-old. He is brilliant and speaks multiple languages including English, Russian, Chinese, and Vietnamese. He is credited with the high-tech training of his unit. He joined the task force with Major General Abelardo González in Africa with their high-tech surveillance unit with the Army's Air Force. Rodríguez was promoted from a lieutenant to a major in Africa. Now, he controls the entire Cuban Army's Air Force."

"As the man in charge of the Air Force, he controls 145 MIGs including: 46 Russian MIGs, 23 fighter jets, 45 MIG-29/UB Fulcrums, and 23 MIG-23M/23/BN/u/Floggers. The MIG-29s are the most sophisticated in design and equal to the US's F-15 Eagles. They are designed to be defense invaders and are not to be used for offense. Also, they have many Russian Naval MIG-19s and MIG-21s, most of which are obsolete for modern air combat missions. They are still operational but are mainly used for training purposes."

"Recently, the Bahamian Coast Guard seized a Cuban fishing boat. The Cuban Army retaliated using our MIG-19s and MIG-21s to attack and sink the Bahamian Coast Guard's boat. There were casualties. Fidel claimed that the Cuban fishing boat was in international waters at the time it was seized, but the Bahamians later proved that the Bahamian's Coast Guard boat was destroyed inside Bahamian territory. An international

The Last Revolution

dispute ensued. Later the Cuban government had to pay six million in compensation and offer an official apology to the government of the Bahamas."

Piyo continued with his explanation, "You probably remember in 1998 when Cuba attacked two American Cessnas. We shot them down using our three MIG-23s because the Cessnas had invaded Cuban air space. American-Cuban terrorists have invaded Cuba many times unlawfully. Our government warned them time after time, but they still didn't stop. Finally, we had to resort to the use of force and that's the reason the Cessnas were shot down. We believe that our borders must be respected and protected by international law. Our government was exercising their right to use force."

Hiro replied, "I didn't know about any of this. I was living in Rancho Veloz, and we didn't hear the news. I guess I didn't notice because I wasn't listening to much television and news at the time."

Piyo said, "As for our Navy, Admiral Gustavo Pedro Terre is the main Admiral and controls the Cuban Navy. The Coast Guard headquarters is located on Santiago de Cuba and is thorough and efficient. There are 46 stations throughout Cuba housing as many as 280 ships, many of which are small gunboats. Cuba does not own an aircraft carrier."

"The Cuban military is only for defense, but its soldiers are well-trained and have demonstrated that they are tough fighters. All the armed forces are loyal to Fidel Castro. Also, there are several submarines, Frigates and war ships leased from the Russians. The exact number is unknown."

Hiro asked, "Does Cuba have long and medium-range missile capability? Could they potentially aim and hit the United States with these missiles? Does Cuba have nuclear bombs?"

Piyo looked very uncomfortable and hesitated to answer, but finally he said Hiro, "We do not possess nuclear weapons, but we do have medium-range missiles. There are a few in operational condition located at a base close to *Sagua la Grande* and others in western *San Cristóbal*."

Hiro pushed on," Are they ready to develop more missiles?"

Piyo replied, "I don't think so because resources are limited. Fidel doesn't want another big crisis. As far as I'm concerned, Cuba has the strongest army in Latin America, but it is only for defense purposes. We sent troops to Angola because they needed our help, and our government decided to support them for humanitarian purposes. But that was the only exception in our history that we sent troops abroad."

"We are an island nation and no other country will invade us except the United States. The US has tried to control us many times before because of our strategic location in the Caribbean. We are in the middle between North America and South America and the US still occupies a naval base in *Guantanamo* that belongs to our country. The US and Cuba have constantly fought each other throughout history."

"The Cuban Army's research laboratory is working on virus and chemical warfare in Santa Clara. I don't have any information to explain this further, but my boss was telling me that our military scientists are developing a secret arsenal of biological warfare to be used against the United States. I don't have any updated information because it is top-secret research and I am not cleared for it."

"Also, the central Corps of our Army base in Santa Clara has been dealing with a high-tech surveillance unit. It's equipped with a Chinese-made computer and uses Russian KGB top secret software to monitor US spy satellite information. They call it Mi-Cuba Watch.

"I understand General Abelardo González is extremely talented in high-tech technology. He is probably better educated than most American computer scientists are. He is in charge of operating an incredible army surveillance secret unit at his base; also he trains his own staff personally. Hiro, Remember, he is the most sophisticated General in the Cuban army. And he is extremely trusted by Fidel and Raúl Castro. He is next in line to be Cuban Army Chef General under the Communist government and he is a very impressive individual."

Piyo continued to explain how tough the Cuban army was and more. Hiro looked down at this watch and noticed that they had been talking for almost three hours. It was just getting interesting and he became more and more curious, but he had almost extracted all the information for his research."

Hiro said, "We are almost finished. Just a couple more questions. Tell me more about this General Abelardo González. Do you have any description of him?"

The Last Revolution

Piyo said, "I know that General González graduated from the University of Matanzs with a degree in computer science. Later, he attended the military academy, and since then he has been in uniform. He is considered a top-notch, high-tech computer technology wizard with combat experience. He was deployed to Angola in 1989 to help run high-tech surveillance with air force General Alvares Ortiz. They ran a persistent bombing campaign throughout Angola against the South Africans by our air force. Probably he is the highest ranked high-tech person in the Cuban army, and is considered the most intelligent and highly respected man in our force. When he returned from Africa, he also became the youngest general in Cuban history".

Hiro asked, "Tell me about the Air Force General Enrique Hurtado Rodríguez."

"The general was a major in the air force that time and he worked with Major Abelardo González. They both were promoted upon their return from Angola. Both were major in the Army. But General Alvares Ortiz retired five years ago and Abelardo González became his successor at the young age of 33."

Hiro inquired, "How is their relationship the last five years?"

Piyo said, "Both of them have enjoyed their military careers and high-tech training, and they constantly exchange updated information."

Hiro was moving right along because he didn't want to keep questioning Piyo too much longer. "Tell me about who is in charge at the Coast Guard base at Santiago de Cuba."

Piyo answered, "That is Navy Admiral Gustavo Pedro Terre. He is head of the Cuban Navy Coast Guard base on Santiago de Cuba he was also deployed in Angola as the Vice Admiral. He headed a huge victory when he destroyed three South African supply ships with only a frigate smaller than a destroyer and six small gunboats. It was a big triumph; he made Cuban naval history and became Admiral."

Piyo said, "There are many sad stories in Cuba due to the war. There were 2,077 casualties and as many as 11,000 wounded. A deep scar was left after this war. Nearly 250,000 people participated in Angola and many suffered loss and tragedy. But we must give Fidel Castro credit for showing the world that Cuba was a superior force in this humanitarian mission. And our Armed Forces demonstrated their might to the rest of the world. We may be a small island, but we are a mighty people."

Hiro was fascinated. He continued to listen to Piyo.

Finally, Piyo was direct and asked Hiro, "Why are you so interested in the Cuban military? What are you going to do with this information?"

Hiro said, "Well, Piyo, I've always been interested in the Cuban military structure, because Fidel has controlled the country for nearly 50 years successfully. They asked me to help with some security calculations at The University of Havana, but they never give us quite enough information. No one knows how he has the military set up, and I always wished I could know what he was thinking, to help me with my calculations, that's all. I am only a scientist, just a mathematics professor. And since I'm Japanese I don't think like a Cuban. That's why I need this knowledge."

Hiro and Piyo had talked enough and shook hands as they stood up. Piyo's handshake was firm and his large, rough hand was twice the size of Hiro's. When Hiro thought it was time to release his grip, Piyo held the handshake and squeezed a bit firmer. It was uncomfortable for Hiro, but he didn't say anything. Piyo looked very serious and said firmly as he stared into Hiro's eyes, "You can never repeat what I have said to anyone and remember you didn't hear anything from me. You are only my cousin's husband we are here tonight for dinner. It's just a family gathering and nothing more. It's unlikely that you'll see me again anytime soon. I don't want to be associated with anything you may be involved in. No one even knows I'm here tonight, and I want to keep it that way."

Then Piyo released the handshake. His serious expression slowly turned into a smile and he added, "And thanks you for the money."

Hiro nodded his head and added, "I didn't hear anything tonight. This conversation never happened. That money is a gift because you are family—that's all." Then they opened the door to the patio and left the room together.

Chapter 53

Dania looked very beautiful this evening.
She was wearing a white sun dress which looked lovely against her tanned skin. Hiro loved Dania's skin, hair, and her big brown eyes. When Dania smiled, the smile reached her eyes. She radiated warmth across the room to Hiro. She said coyly, "Oh, here they are! Come on over here, you two. Teresa and I have been having a little girl talk. Sit down, and I'll get your drinks. Hiro and Piyo both smiled and sat down in the patio chairs. Dania brought some good rum for Piyo and a beer for Hiro.

Hiro asked, "Hatuey?"

Dania said, "No joke! Honey, only Cristal was what you expected?"

Dania laughed, "Hey, it's better than nothing!" Everybody laughed and began to enjoy their evening together. It was a warm night, not too muggy. Dania was always a warm and friendly hostess. She took after her mother in that way. She was a gracious and attentive hostess, similar to Isabel. Dania even had the same laugh as her mother had. Dania made everyone feel special. She had such a kindness about her.

Dania had worked all day to prepare the food. She served everyone a hardy dinner of fresh fish with lemon and pepper. There was also *cerviche*, rice, beans, potato salad, fresh *guayaba* fruit, and sweet milk custard for dessert. There was so much food that Piyo's and his wife's eyes widened just at the sight of it. Dania said, "I made too much food. I am going to send the leftovers home with you two." Piyo and Teresa replied in unison, "Great!"

The group enjoyed plenty of rum and beer, and they all relaxed together over a good meal and conversation. Teresa had dressed in a nice outfit and fixed her hair, but her efforts still couldn't hide the dark circles under her eyes. She was pale and looked very tired. But tonight she enjoyed herself. Teresa rarely got to socialize due to her health so this outing was a big treat for her. Teresa laughed and had a good time talking to Hiro and Dania. It was a special evening for all of them.

Hiro was eager to get down to business now that he had more information to work with. He told Dania it was crunch time and that he needed even more time alone to concentrate on his work. Dania took the girls to visit friends and family daily while Hiro worked intensely. This way the girls did not miss their father so much.

When Hiro worked like this he couldn't be interrupted; but he always ate dinner with the family, read to the girls, and told them good-night stories before he tucked them into bed. He often told them about ancient Japan, the samurai, geisha girl and the Shogunate.

The girls loved the old Japanese children's stories like Momo-Taro, Urashima-Taro, Peach Boy, or stories about the traditional kite-making festival for children held in Japan each year. He would tell them about the beautiful kimonos the women wore, and the way they walked in their painful wooden shoes. Sometimes he would tell them about the countryside where he had grown up and about Ayu fishing. He also liked to tell them make-believe stories about two girls who lived inside a computer world who could travel to different places through computer links. The girls went on safari in Africa, explored in the Amazon, or dog sledded across Alaska. They loved this adventure series and couldn't wait to hear more. It was Hiro's nightly ritual with them.

Sometimes Yumiko and Masako would ask, "Papi, what are you working on all day?"

Hiro would smile and hug them saying, "Big guy stuff. I am trying to find out how to grow rainbows and use starlight in the day. Maybe I can even create a car that runs on air. My latest research is a bicycle that can fly to moon."

They would just giggle and say, "Really, Papi?"

Hiro would kiss them and say, "Maybe, it is possible. Dream about it for me. Sweet dreams." He never again involved them in anything work-related. He knew that they had endured enough with the terrible incident involving Pepe and Isabel. He always sugarcoated his work so they would not worry. Total immersion into his research was the way Hiro had trained himself to accomplish his academic goals since he was a boy. He locked himself into his room and was in deep in thought with his ideas and plans. He was developing strategies. Hiro had to narrow things down to specific details.

The Last Revolution

He researched everyday for nearly four weeks. It was exhausting work, but Hiro knew he was close to a final plan. Everything had to be perfect. He knew there was only one chance for success with a plan like this, so he couldn't afford any mistakes. The monotony of analyzing large amounts of military information was tedious. Hiro was attempting to combine genetic and neurological research with complex scientific data. He visited an endless number of international research and doctoral level libraries on-line.

Hiro left no stone unturned when it came to his work. He also had to update and revamp his earlier war game. It needed tweaking. Finally, at the end of his self-imposed hibernation of research, study, and brain-storming, Dania became concerned. Hiro was detached from her and the girls for so long. It was almost as if she were living with a different man when he was like this. Dania needed to talk to someone. She went to Pedro to see if he would visit Hiro and check on him.

Pedro was like a brother to Hiro and said, "Don't worry, Dania. I'll keep an eye on him. I always do." Periodically, Pedro stopped by and checked on Hiro. Dania was always relieved to see him. She knew that Hiro needed support from Pedro. She didn't know how or what was going to happen, but Hiro needed some help. Hiro was sitting in a chair on the patio when Pedro dropped by. Pedro was surprised to see Hiro outside enjoying the sun. Every time in the past few days when Pedro had dropped by, Hiro was inside working on his project and studying.

Pedro sat down next to him and asked, "What's up, Hiro?"

Hiro was happy to see his friend, and answered, "Oh nothing much, I feel good about my research and wanted to take the day off. Dania and the girls have gone to see her cousin.

Do you want to go fishing today?" Pedro was pleasantly surprised to hear Hiro ask about fishing. It had been quite a while since they had fished together. "Well, it's not so early in the day anymore. You always like to go early. Do you think you can still catch some fish?"

Hiro grinned and said, "Look, I always catch fish because I am a great fisherman. I have a technique like no one else has. Right?" They both began laughing.

Pedro said, "OK, Let's go fishing!" They got their gear, hopped into the brown 1956 Ford, and headed to their fishing spot in Rio San Pedro.

The Cuban countryside was a pleasant sight for Hiro. The Rio San Pedro reservoir was a good-sized lake. There was a marsh growing around the lake. Sometimes Hiro could see water birds and migratory birds from Canada visiting these waters. The water was very cold because it came from a natural underground water system. As many as 20,000 gallons per minute pumped out from the cold spring during the summer months. In the summer there was more water than in winter, and sometimes that water burst over the dam creating a huge waterfall. It was beautiful and refreshing.

There were several species of Cuban tropical fish, similar to Japanese carp, and many small sunfish. Hiro knew that decent-sized rainbow big-mouth bass were there, the Cuban's called *Turuche* in the lake. But that no one had ever caught one, because they required special tackle and a technique that the Cubans were not aquatinted with. The Cubans fished the old-fashioned way.

The reservoir formed a small stream down the river to the north. It was used for irrigation for the sugarcane fields and for tap water for several small towns including Rancho Velloz, Sierra Morena, and Corralillo.

Since he had arrived in Cuba, Hiro had noticed that the country's geography showed few rivers. Cuba had subtropical weather trends that made the land very dry, because the annual rainfall was small. Cactus grew in many open fields. It was almost impossible to plant rice because of the lack of rainfall. Much of Cuba received only 800 to 2200 milliliters of rain. The trade winds tended to bring precipitation to the western and east-central parts of the island.

In the Santa Clara area, conditions were much drier. If the people living in this area cultivated anything, they had to build a good irrigation system. Next to the Rio San Pedro reservoir where Hiro and Pedro liked to fish, there was a small rice farm. Every time Hiro went there, he noticed it. Seeing the farm triggered childhood memories of his remote mountain village in Hiroshima.

Chapter 54

On the way to their fishing spot, Hiro's thoughts were on the project. He asked Pedro, "Do you know of General Abelardo González?"

Pedro scratched his head and said, "Yap, I've heard about him, but I don't know a whole lot about the Cuban military.

Hiro answered in a straight forward way, "I want to meet him in person."

At first, Pedro didn't know what to say. Hiro's request had caught him off guard. "Hiro, that man is a very high-ranking Cuban general! It is almost impossible to meet someone like him in person. Besides, he is always surrounded by an elite security force so no one would dare to get close to him. It is impossible to become friends with someone like him."

Hiro said, "Even so, I want to see him."

Pedro asked, "Why him?"

Hiro looked out the car window and answered, "I am just interested in him. I heard that he is a computer science high-tech general. Maybe we can talk computer science since that is my area of mathematic expertise."

Then Pedro said, "Well, I didn't tell you everything I know. I have actually seen General González a few times before. Perhaps there is a way you could cross paths with him. He eats at the restaurant on the top of the Santa Clara Libre Hotel often."

Hiro turned his attention to Pedro, "Are you serious? How do you know this? You mast bullshit me?"

Pedro said rather casually, "My cousin's best friend works at the hotel's restaurant. I was at a party there last year, and this friend mentioned that he sees the general almost every week. I didn't think too much about it, but I can ask and see if he still goes there to eat."

Hiro said emphatically, "I would like for you to find this out for me. That is perfect!"

Pedro said, "Hiro, there is another simple solution. You can mention it to Freddie. I'm sure he knows General González well. Maybe he could introduce you."

Hiro shook his head, "No, not yet. I want to meet the general accidentally. That way he won't think that I have an agenda or a strong desire to talk to him. It is better that way, pretending like I don't know anything about him, period." Rio San Pedro was just up ahead. Pedro made Hiro discontinue the conversation completely. Pedro didn't dare discuss government matters while other people were around.

The people in the village waved as they drove by in the old Ford. People in this area were very friendly and knew the pair. Pedro parked, and they headed to the fishing spot. As soon as Hiro started fishing, twelve children ran over to see them. It became a spectacle with all the children laughing and watching Hiro fish. Hiro gave his fish away so the children were always waiting for him. Hiro had become a kind of local legend here. When the people saw Pedro's old Ford, they knew that they would have fresh fish for dinner.

Pedro was all smiles. Just as usual on their fishing trips, Pedro stayed in his car near the shade. His friend Condera soon brought hot coffee to the car. As they sipped the coffee, the two men talked about work and the black market.

Many of the locals also wandered by to say hello. Hiro didn't talk much. He just waved and said hello as he continued to fish. He loved to fish and that was evident by his concentration. Fishing was a way to relax and escape from his thoughts for a moment. When he was fishing, Hiro focused on the water, casting out his line and using his special dragging and bobbing technique with his bait. Then it was a waiting game. He had to be patient and wait for a tug. But Hiro was ready when the fish tried to take the bait. Within a couple of hours, Hiro had caught six small fish. Hiro enjoyed entertaining the kids, and when he showed them his fishing technique the children were always delighted.

On their way home, Hiro continued the conversation again about meeting the general, "Well, Freddie knows General González, but I want to do this my way, OK? I really want you to find out if the general eats at the hotel regularly and what night I might be able to catch him there. I am going to go to that restaurant. I want to plan this immediately."

The Last Revolution

Pedro knew that Hiro wouldn't ask for his help unless it was very important. He also had known Hiro long enough to trust him and to cooperate without asking questions. Pedro said, "OK, first of all I need to find out exactly when he goes to the restaurant or to the hotel. After I drop you off at home, I'll go to Santa Clara alone. OK?"

Hiro replied, "That's fine with me. That information is going to help me a lot!"

Pedro shook Hiro's hand saying, "Hiro, you know you come with a whole lot of trouble, problems and danger. If I didn't love so much, I'd say I was crazy to get involved in your schemes!" They both laughed, and then Pedro dropped Hiro off at his home. Pedro went straight to Santa Clara.

Chapter 55

Early the next morning, Hiro was in his room working. Dania knocked on the door, "Hey, Pedrey and Madeline are here looking for you."

Hiro replied, "OK. Tell Pedrey to come in and see me." Hiro was eager to hear news.

Pedro entered and calmly told Hiro, "I found out about the general. He eats at the restaurant a couple of times a week with several associates. There are many security guards with them, about eight to ten and every one comes up there to check IDs and to do body searches. Almost every Monday he comes in for dinner at seven. In addition, some weeks he comes in on either Wednesday or Thursday for lunch. The general always brings along many friends and associates so your best bet for a meeting is on a Monday night."

Hiro nodded his head in agreement. "Good work, Pedrey! Let's start next week beginning on Monday. Our kids are off from school then. I want to take both of our families on a vacation to Santa Clara for week. I will make all of the arrangements. Can you guys join us?"

Pedro looked worried for a moment, "Are you thinking about getting our kids involved with this?"

Hiro said "No. Not at all. But when I meet General González I want it to be seen as a random meeting. If we are vacationing with our families, then it will seem like a chance meeting. The general must not suspect anything, and he must know me only as a family man with a happy Cuban family. Otherwise, I am going to be an outsider or a foreigner to him with no Cuban connection. This way he will know that I am married to a Cuban woman with Cuban kids. OK?"

Pedro agreed and said, "That's good thinking." Madeline and Dania both understood that they shouldn't ask questions and didn't want to be involved in Hiro's plan anyway. What had happened to Isabel and Pepe was never far from their thoughts.

The Last Revolution

When the women were asked about spending a weeks in Santa Clara for a mini-vacation, they were surprised. Hiro told them they would visit Pedro's aunt and family, stay at the Hotel Santa Clara Libre, relax by the pool, eat at their favorite restaurant, and just spend some time together. Both Madeline and Dania were suspicious right away, but Hiro eased their minds, "Let's just go and enjoy ourselves. Our families can have fun together. Whatever I do there, it will be my business. We all need a vacation and some fun! Is this OK with you?" Both women became excited and started to laugh and hug each other. Also, Dania's sisters Lillian and Liana were invited and were so happy to go with then. Hiro always included them in whatever they did.

On Monday, Madeline, Wendy arrived to pick up Hiro and his family. The children were excited to be going to Santa Clara. They were dressed in their best clothes and chatted together about the trip. Pedro and Hiro remained serious and didn't speak in the car. Hiro was deep in thought, but Dania and Madeline were relaxed and talked all the way to Santa Clara.

They arrived at the Hotel Santa Clara Libre and checked into their rooms which were located just down the hall from each other. Pedro and his family planned to visit his aunt that evening so the two families decided to meet in the morning for breakfast.

Pedro told Hiro that his friend's son Ricardo was working that night in the restaurant and knew to seat the general near them if he happened to come for dinner. Pedro had paid him a big tip. It had all been arranged.

Hiro worked in his room until dinnertime, while Dania and the girls swam in the pool. He had told Dania to pack their best clothes for the trip. He wanted them to look nice at all the meals. The girls and two sisters had even gotten new dresses.

That evening, they went to *The Baritone*, a popular restaurant on the rooftop of the hotel. Ricardo greeted them and talked to Hiro for a moment. Hiro gave him a huge tip for his help. Ricardo was thrilled and very discreet. They were about twenty-five people already seated for dinner. The restaurant was not crowded for a weekday. There were many business people eating and socializing. Hiro, Dania and the girls sat at a table and ordered drinks. Dania ordered red wine for herself and beer for Hiro. The girls enjoyed sodas with tropical fruit decorating the rims of their glasses. The girls were very excited to be staying at this fancy hotel.

The Cuban *Creole grilled chicken* and fish was a specialty for this restaurant. Hiro, Dania and her two sisters ordered it as their entrées. The girls requested fish and potatoes. Dania loved that they were all together and having a wonderful family meal. Everything about the evening seemed perfect.

As soon as their meals arrived, General Abelardo González and his entourage entered and were seated at the table just across from Hiro and his family. The general and his aides were secluded from the other guests. Five security people were stationed around the restaurant, and three were positioned near the table. Hiro got the nod from Ricardo. Hiro knew that he had to get noticed, but his timing had to perfect. Hiro focused on his food and family and waited for the right moment.

The general and his friends were talking animatedly about something that appeared to be interesting and funny. It must have been something good, because they were all laughing. When General González ordered a second drink from the waiter, he noticed the Asian man with a Cuban woman and two children eating across from him. They caught his attention because it was very unusual to see an Asian in this part of Cuba. Very few Asian tourists visited Santa Clara. But the general noticed that the couple wore wedding rings, and then he noted that the girls had some Asian features. The general also observed that the family was well-dressed and that they were having a nice conversation as they enjoyed a family dinner. They were a very striking family. As the general glanced at Hiro, Hiro looked up at that precise moment. They acknowledged each other with a nod. Hiro was calm and played it cool.

Hiro, Dania and the girls devoured a wonderful meal and he wanted the girls to have ice cream. It was Yumiko and Masako's favorite. The restaurant served it garnished with fruit and a cookie. The girls loved the special treatment. When they had finished dinner, the family left the restaurant, and Hiro made sure to pass within eyesight of the general once again as they exited. This time Hiro didn't look at him.

After they left, the general asked his aide, "Who was that man? Do you know him? Please check him out for me." The aide went to the restaurant office and returned quickly with information. The aide whispered to the general, "Sir, his name is Dr. Hiroaki Nakagawa. He is a professor in Havana, and he lives close to Rancho Veloz. He must be visiting someone here."

The Last Revolution

Hiro was extremely pleased with what had happened. The timing couldn't have been better. It was the first time Hiro and the general had actually seen each other. And—what good luck—they didn't meet or speak. How subtle! He knew the general had taken notice of him. He was thrilled that his plan was in motion.

The next day he explained it all to Pedro. Hiro said he also wanted to return to the restaurant on both Wednesday and Thursday for lunch. Pedro said, "You are determined to meet with him. Look, he is a high-ranking Cuban general. Just remember that it's probably very difficult to approach him or even to get near him physically unless he wants to meet you. I'm afraid you don't have a chance. I think the best way is to let Freddie handle this entire affair because that's what he does."

Hiro smiled and responded, "Look, Pedro, I am sure Freddie can arrange a meeting but let me handle it. I know what I am doing. I have a plan." Pedro listened in silence. What else could he say?

Chapter 56

When General González returned
to his office the next morning, he remembered the Asian man at the restaurant. He asked his staff to check the computer file for Dr. Hiroaki Nakagawa. If there was anything on him, the general wanted the file on his desk immediately. Within five minutes, an officer handed him a print-out. The general looked over the papers, and a smile appeared on his face as he read the details.

He read aloud, "Dr. Hiroaki Nakagawa, born in Hiroshima, Japan, is a professor of mathematics at The University of Hiroshima and has been living in Cuba since March 18, 1995. Looks OK." General González also checked entries on Hiro in the federal agents' secret files. He continued reading his file and learned that Dr. Nakagawa forged a satellite signal and modified a VCR to scramble signals. For this, he spent seven days in federal jail. No charges were filed against him and he was released because he wasn't a Cuban citizen.

The file also provided additional information. "Dr. Nakagawa's immigration status was for twenty-one days with a tourist visa in 1995. His visa was extended for three-months. He applied for an international cultural exchange visa for three years. That was in October 12, 1995. Within six-months, he married a Cuban woman, Dania Altamirano Hernandez, of San Rafael in Rancho Veloz. He then obtained a permanent visa in May 12, 1998. He currently conducts lectures for all Cuban university teachers for training purposes. The general smiled and ordered the officer to place a call to Freddie Diaz in immigration.

Meanwhile at the immigration office in Santa Clara, the secretary said, "Senor Diaz, you have a very important phone call from General Abelardo González on line one."

Freddie picked up the phone and said, "Hello, General! What can I do for you?"

The general cleared his throat and answered, "I saw a Japanese professor yesterday whose name is Dr. Hiroaki Nakagawa. Do you know of him?"

The Last Revolution

Freddie was caught off guard but answered, "I met him almost ten years ago, and we have been friends ever since. He is very intelligent and a nice person."

The general replied, "Well, I want to meet him personally because I'm interested in Japanese new technology."

Freddie said, "If you want me to, I can arrange a meeting for you. By the way, I ran into Dr. Nakagawa's friend Pedro today, and he invited me to join them for dinner at the restaurant at the Santa Clara Libre Hotel tomorrow. Apparently, they are vacationing at the hotel for a week. Would you like to meet us there so I can introduce you in person?"

The general seemed pleased with the arrangement and answered, "That is perfectly fine with me I will cancel the other plane. Anyway, I need to see you to discuss army corps engineer construction matters regarding the causeway to Cayo Coco, Cayo Santa Maria.

Freddie said, "All right then, I will see you at the hotel restaurant. Let's say about 7 p.m. tomorrow." They both agreed.

Pedro was glad to have run into Freddie while in Santa Clara. Pedro was eager to get back to the hotel and inform Hiro of the news that Freddie would be joining them for dinner tomorrow evening. Pedro had hoped that it might help Hiro get closer to the general.

It was a gorgeous, sunny day. Hiro was sitting near the pool watching the children and Dania, her sisters and Madelaine swim. He was smiling and laughing at the sight of them playing in the water with the children. The girls splashed, because the women didn't want to get their hair wet. Lillian and Liana watched as Wendy, Masako and Yumiko giggled and continued to splash. Soon the girls had gotten their mothers soaking wet. Pedro walked up, "Hey there, what's up?"

Hiro smiled, "Nothing much, these girls are having some fun. Did you see your black market people in Santa Clara?"

Pedro answered, "Yep. I also ran into Freddie. I hope you don't mind, but I asked him to come over and join us for dinner here tomorrow night."

Hiro said "Excellent. How is he doing? I was going to visit him later this week. I'm glad you invited him to dinner with all of us."

The Hotel Santa Clara Libre was a large facility with 145 air-conditioned rooms. It was a luxury hotel by Cuban standards with features like international dialing, medical services, cable TV, a rooftop bar, a restaurant, and a recreation hall. The *mojitos* at the roof-top bar were wonderful. The restaurant, located on the top floor, offered delicious Cuban fare and afforded a beautiful view of the city. This ten-story hotel located in front of *Vidal Park* was the only official hotel right in Santa Clara. It was almost always full. Cubans couldn't afford to come to a beautiful hotel like this so Pedro and his wife had only come to the roof-top restaurant for a beer and to split an appetizer in the past. Since Pedro's cousin's son Ricardo worked there, they dropped by to see him on occasion, but they had never had the opportunity to dine there.

Most Cuban people couldn't dine here unless it was for a very special occasion, because dinner would cost almost four months salary. The Cuban monetary system made it nearly impossible for regular Cubans to eat out anywhere. Occasionally, people saved up and found a way, but it was rare. So Pedro's family felt like movie stars the whole week long. Hiro loved Pedro and his family and enjoyed treating them to things they enjoyed. Hiro told them it was a gift for always helping him with everything.

After all, Pedro had been there helping him since the beginning. Hiro didn't want to make Pedro feel like he was getting a hand out, though. Hiro just wanted to show Pedro that he appreciated them and their assistance and friendship over the years. This way they could truly enjoy the whole vacation without feeling guilty.

Madelaine appreciated the restaurant the most. She loved to have some one else doing the cooking for a change. And the flavors and meals were always so incredible. Madelaine really enjoyed cooking and got many new ideas from the dishes served at the hotel's restaurant and the special ways in which they were prepared. Ricardo was working and seated them at the same table where they had sat on Monday. He and Pedro talked together for a while. Hiro ordered beer while the ladies got 21-year-old Special Reserve Cuba Libre. The children sipped their orange sodas with fruit garnish. They all looked nice, dressed in their best clothes, and they chatted the whole time. Hiro took a moment to savor the wonderful friendship between their two families. He felt they were more like family than just friends.

The Last Revolution

About that time, General Abelardo González and Freddie along with six aides and several security guards entered the restaurant. Hiro and Pedro both looked up in surprise. They exchanged glances and Hiro knew the moment had arrived when he would meet the general. Hiro let out a deep, slow breath to calm himself.

Freddie approached them immediately saying hello to everyone and kissing the children and wives in the customary greeting. He shook hands with Pedro and Hiro. He quickly explained to Hiro that the general had wanted to meet him.

Hiro and Pedro walked with Freddie to the table where the general had been seated. The general stood as they approached his table. Then the security staff surrounded the general to protect him. The general said to the guards, "No, everything is fine." The guards stepped aside and Freddie introduced Hiro and Pedro to the general. It was all very official at first. Everyone was smiling and making polite conversation. Then Hiro introduced the wives and children to the general. Everyone shook hands. They were all shocked to meet the general and were wary, but the general was very personable. The general commented on how cute the girls were. They were thrilled by the complement from this important man.

Then General González greeted Hiro saying, "I'm very happy to meet you. If you don't mind, I'd like to talk to you and Freddie privately for a moment. Let us have a table for three." Ricardo seated them at a table in the far left corner away from the crowd of people. Freddie ordered beverages for all. Within minutes Ricardo brought them three ice-cold beers.

Then Freddie said, "Hiro, the general is interested in Japanese technology and he has acknowledge of high-tech gadgets."

The general asked, "Dr. Nakagawa, how do you like it here in Cuba?"

Hiro replied, "Please, call me Hiro. Cuba is my home now and I like it very much. Before, I didn't know how to enjoy life, but living in Cuba has taught me that. I am regaining my happiness with love!"

Freddie smiled and added, "Hiro is a lucky guy. He has a terrific wife and two wonderful children. They are such a sociable family."

General smiled back, "Well, I'm glad you're enjoying our island. Please tell me about Hiroshima, Japan. I'm curious to know how the people and land are fifty-nine years after the atomic explosion."

Hiro said, "Of course, there is still a high concentration of contaminates and occasionally a baby becomes infected with atomic radiation *in utero* through the water or soil. But those are isolated cases. The radiation does not affect the general population anymore."

The general looked at Hiro thoughtfully, "I am deeply sorry that an atomic bomb was dropped in your hometown. Tell me what the general population of Japan thinks about United States. I am sure that all Japanese hate America," said the General.

Hiro said, "Well no Japanese hate the U.S. now for what happened during the war. All Japanese know that the war in the Pacific was stupid. What we lost during the war can never be replaced." "Nevertheless," added Hiro, "the Japanese people know that they must now live in harmony and respect other cultures because the world is shrinking. We must live peacefully and help each other, and nations must work together for the good of mankind." The general nodded in agreement.

Chapter 57

Then the General directed

the conversation to a different subject. "Hiro have you heard of the Nakajima-JPX 008?"

Hiro said, "Of course, I know about it."

The General was delighted and said, "Please, tell me more."

Hiro was happy to do so, and began his explanation saying, "Well, it is the ultimate, new generation of computer chips. The Intel Company in the US is disputing the international patent rights. The Americans maintain that the chip was developed and patented by Intel in 2003. The Intel research department claims that one of its scientists committed industrial espionage, stole the experimental chip and sold it to the Japanese company, Nakajima Technology, in Gifu, Japan. The Japanese supposedly duplicated the chip. It will be a long time before the chip is produced and released, because Nakajima claims that they developed it before Intel did."

The general asked, "Is there any possibility we could get our hands on those chips?" Hiro became very quiet, thinking for a moment as he slowly sipped his beer.

Then he asked seriously, "You mean, you actually want to have that chip yourself."

The general answered, "That is the idea."

Hiro said, "I don't know if I could get access of the actual chip, but I can find out. I have access to a secret underground supplier in Japan. They will know whether this is possible."

The general nodded his head saying, "Hiro, that is great news! I'd like to be informed as soon as possible."

Hiro said, "I'll research the feasibility right away. As soon as I know, I'll contact you."

The general was fascinated and extremely happy to hear this from Hiro. Hiro told the general everything he knew about the new technology.

The Nakajima JPX008 was a new computer system theory chip which performed almost 100 percent faster than the present electrical magnetic circuit system and code. The new chip recognized the fingerprint of incoming signals. The chip was a sensational discovery because it could prevent illegal activities such as hacking and piracy.

In 1986, when Hiro was researching for IBM using DOS, he accidentally discovered how to count molecules in code which allowed the computer to detect human DNA .

This clever chip had the ability to be compatible with the current electrical magnetic base system and to attach to medical equipment. It could also monitor any remote computer, detect DNA and use medical devices. For instance, if a person in Havana had a doctor in Tokyo, the doctor could examine his physical condition using Nakajima-JPX008. This chip had been designed to be used by the public. It had the capacity to work 100 times faster than a standard computer's CPU. For example, it could download entire videos and movies within a few minutes.

Hiro said, "General, as you know, your government prohibits the Internet access to the outside world. I have only a laptop computer for my mathematics calculations and for my studies. This is very frustrating for a man like me not to be able to use the Internet freely and have the ability to communicate with other scientists. Technologically speaking, it's crippling!"

The general agreed and answered his complaint, "Hiro, this is our policy as mandated by the Cuban government at the highest authority from Fidel Castro himself. It doesn't reflect the opinion of all of us, but we must comply. The purpose is to protect the system Castro established."

"Furthermore, it prevents Cuban citizens from seeing what's out there in the world and confusing them with the information. As you know, we have many enemies nearby who could brainwash our masses and wreak havoc on the current system."

Freddie agreed and added, "Hiro that is why our government cannot permit one citizen to have Internet access. It would create frustration for others who did not receive permission. If the government allows one person access, then everyone must be allowed the same privileges. Everything here is equal. It's best that the government not permit any new technology information to be used by the people."

Hiro said, "Maybe you believe that your government has this authority, but for me it is unacceptable for the government to interfere with an individual's rights. I find it a disgrace!" Then

The Last Revolution

Hiro got very frustrated and shouted, "Damn it! The ban on information technology is what killed two of my families' most cherished members. They were killed by your secret agents!"

Freddie immediately interrupted, "Hiro please, do not bring up this subject. Calm down. We cannot do anything about it now and it will only lead to more anger and frustration." Hiro became very quiet.

The general looked at Hiro and said, "I can understand your frustration, but if we allow open use of technology, then we cannot function as we are. Just one individual system could alter and threaten the government's regulations. We must strictly control this access even if this means that our people are being isolated from the modern age of computers and technology. We must apply the government's laws to all citizens equally."

Hiro replied, "Well, it may be good in theory, but not in real life."

Freddie said sharply, "Hiro that is enough! It is best not to discuss this with us because we work for the government. We cannot change anything. This is the way it is here. This is not the time for a political discussion."

Then the general began to speak openly, "Hiro, I think I can speak for Freddie and myself. We personally agree with what you are saying, but our hands are tied on the issue of personal Internet access and technology for the masses. It is not under our control and we will not even discuss it further. As for you Hiro, you are another matter all together. I can make it possible to bend the restrictions for your Internet use because you can help us find some information that will be most helpful for the government from your source in Japan. It is a national security matter, not an individual concern." The general looked at Freddie and asked, "Am I correct?"

Freddie said, "Yes, General! I will inform Havana and tell them that this is your recommendation."

The General smiled and nodded in agreement, "Of course, and anyone who has questions should contact my office."

Freddie said, "I will contact the office in Havana. We will see."

Hiro couldn't believe it. It seemed that he would get Internet access with the help of the general and Freddie.

The men began chatting about Japan and Cuba and all the differences between the two countries. They discussed many topics including the Japanese heavy industry of electrical engineering and the whole Japanese take-over of this field. It was almost midnight, and they were still drinking and talking.

Then the general asked Hiro, "How long will you be staying here in Santa Clara?"

Hiro answered, "Well, we will probably be here for another four days. We won't be leaving until Sunday morning."

The General looked up at Freddie; "I am thinking that maybe Hiro should come to my office at headquarters. I'd like to show him something. Can you join us?"

Freddie agreed and said he would arrange the meeting. As they continued discussing options, Freddie and Hiro agreed to meet the general in his office tomorrow. The general added, "1300 hours would be better for me. I have some free time then." Everyone agreed to meet at that time.

Chapter 58

As Freddie and Hiro arrived

at the front gate of the army base; soldiers were waiting in a Russian Jeep to escort them to the general's office. As they entered General González's private office, two well-armed soldiers saluted. An aide jumped to his feet and welcomed Freddie and Hiro to the Army Corps headquarters.

The general rose from his chair and shook hands with his two visitors. He showed them to a sofa in a sitting room adjacent to his office. There the general briefed the pair about the activities of the Army Corps. After the briefing, the general escorted Freddie and Hiro to the far end of the building which looked as if it had been built in recent years.

The door to this area of the building was secured by an armed guard. The guard saluted as the general entered the building. Beyond the point of entry, Freddie and Hiro could see several additional doors. The general went to the third door on the right. The aide entered the security code, and the door opened to reveal an underground concrete bunker containing modern computer equipment.

The area looked like a computer operations division one would see in any business in a western country. However, upon taking a closer look, Hiro noticed that the equipment was obsolete. He was surprised that Castro's government did not have sophisticated equipment, but he remained silent and listened as the general explained briefly that this was his Cuban technology department.

The general said, "Dr. Nakagawa, this is our surveillance unit and the technology area for the army. It was originally built by Cuban intelligence in 1991. It was a highly restricted project undertaken by a group within the military intelligence unit. The director of the group was initially instructed to obtain information to develop a computer virus to infect the civilian computers in the United States. The group spent nearly $45,000 to buy open-source data on computer networks, computer viruses, SATCOM, and related communications technology."

The general continued, "These initial efforts have expanded to a much larger scale. The project was until recently under the direction of Major Guillermo Bello and his wife Colonel Sara Maria Jordan. Both are in the Ministry of the Interior's operation, Mi Cuba. They have acquired the capacity to conduct cyber terrorism. Under their leadership, Cuba represents a serious threat to the security of the United States in the arena of cyber warfare terrorism. This threat has increased enormously since 2000, through cooperation between Cuba and Soviet intelligence."

"However, I'm unsatisfied with the results of the operation Mi Cuba, so I halted the effort and completely overhauled the entire operation. We purchased a state-of-the-art system through a Chinese consultant and resumed the operation." From the looks of the equipment, Hiro felt that they had been sold crap.

Hiro was not impressed with the general's explanation of using cyber terrorism to disrupt American civilian communications traffic. Hiro considered this idea carefully. What connection did the disruption of American civilian computer traffic have to do with modern surveillance?

The technology that the general had purchased was almost a decade behind technology readily available in Japan and the United States. Hiro figured that Cuba's isolation had retarded their technological advances. No matter how much the Cubans improved their system, if they didn't have the knowledge, then they were limited. These limitations were very frustrating to the general.

This was just another sign of the weakness that was beginning to surface in the Cuban government policy. Cuba had fallen behind in technology which was a costly area in which to be lagging.

The General continued, "We've been monitoring US spy satellites for quite some time using Russian technology, but we're very disappointed in the system. We badly need to improve our surveillance technology. This is why I brought you here today. As you can see, we could bring our system up to par with the rest of the world if we could get our hands on the Intel-Nakajima chip. The chip would improve our capabilities in

The Last Revolution

every application including research and surveillance." Hiro nodded in agreement and promised to help find a source for the needed chip.

While they were visiting the general, Freddie made a call to the head of The Ministry of the Interior because General González wanted the government to grant permission for Hiro to have Internet access. Havana quickly granted special permission for Hiro's Internet access because a high-ranking official like the general requested it. After the briefing, the general excused himself for a moment for a quick briefing with one of his staff, Army Intelligence Brigade General Oswaldo Ramon. General González ordered Ramon to arrange a detailed briefing with Hiro. Hiro insisted that Freddie be at his side during the briefing, and the general gave special permission for Freddie to be present during the discussion.

The briefing lasted all afternoon. After the lengthy talk, everyone concluded that Hiro would have Internet access so that he could assist them.

After the briefing, the men shook hands and Freddie and Hiro were escorted back to their car. Freddie laughed and said to Hiro, "Now you are part of the Communist government's spy covert operation."

Hiro answered, "I hope not."

While Ramon had been briefing Freddie and Hiro, General González had been busy briefing Chief of Staff Raúl Castro Ruiz about the Intel-Nakajima chip operation and asked him for approval of the operation. Raúl then met privately with Fidel and received the official OK.

Meanwhile, Brigade General Oswaldo Ramon set up special Internet access for Hiro through Cuban-DSL. This enabled Hiro to access the web and to be able to communicate with his colleagues at The University of Hiroshima.

Nevertheless, as soon as the Internet was installed, Hiro noticed some activity in his Internet connection. The government was trying to outsmart Hiro by monitoring his Internet activity with a traffic-monitoring device. They were suspicious of Hiro's activity, but Hiro played along with them. The government didn't have any idea of the brilliance of the man they were dealing with here.

Hiro asked for authorization to receive new computer hardware, and the government gave him a new home computer as a gift. He altered the entire system for his protection and used it to communicate by the government's rules. That was its specific purpose. Hiro did not use this PC for anything else. He did not connect his own laptop computer to Cuban-DSL in order to keep its contents strictly secure.

From his own laptop, Hiro again hijacked into the US's commercial satellite broadband VSAT Internet signal. He did this carefully through wireless modified Wi-Fi electrical currents with minimal low frequency using as little as 1.25-042 mbps with a hi-gain antenna. It reached a very short distance. At its widest, it was about a two foot signal which gave Hiro capability for his laptop. No one could detect that Hiro had the signal especially since he already had a satellite dish in his home. Hiro also had a satellite receiver so there were no problems this time around. Even with surveillance it would be impossible to detect. This was a perfect set up since Hiro had government permission to have the satellite dish. How he got a signal didn't matter because the Cuban authorities had no idea about his real motives.

General González was pleased with Hiro's cooperation with the government. He began to trust Hiro and became more and more comfortable with him. In addition, the government credited Freddie for his work with the operation.

But Hiro wasn't happy, because he didn't like military presence in his home or neighborhood. Hiro preferred to be left alone. Hiro's project for the general was top-secret, so the general sent security to monitor the operation. Hiro also knew that his friends and family were probably being monitored as well. Therefore, Hiro was careful and didn't invite friends or family over. This solitude didn't set well with Dania. She was worried all the time and couldn't talk to Hiro about her feelings. Hiro had isolated himself from everyone while he worked on the government project.

Due to the military presence, most people stayed away; even Pedro kept his distance. Everyone was scared of the military. Dania and the girls visited friends and family in nearby Corralillo for a couple of weeks. When they were together as a family, neither Dania nor the girls uttered a word about the government. And no one asked any questions. Even at night when everyone had gone to bed, they didn't whisper. They were all paranoid that they might be overheard. Dania knew what was at stake, so she kept her mouth tightly closed.

The Last Revolution

Living under military surveillance was uncomfortable for Hiro and his family. Hiro complained to Freddie privately on many occasions, but Freddie insisted that it was necessary until he dismantled the operation.

However, Hiro did not trust the Cuban authorities and became more anxious as each day passed. He knew he was in deep water. His every move was being watched. He seriously thought about moving his family away from Cuba temporarily, but he had to wait for just the right moment.

Even though stress was interfering with Hiro's life and that of his family, he decided to push ahead with his own politics. Hiro had many e-mail conversations with his source and friend from the computer science department at The University of Hiroshima. They didn't want to authorize a copy of the chip to be made and sent to Hiro, but he persuaded them through many e-mails. Hiro had been a large contributor to the university in both money and teaching time over the years and was well respected.

Therefore, the university couldn't say no to Hiro. They decided to make this one time exception for him, but the copy of the chip was only on loan for thirty days.

General González was ecstatic to hear the news. Obtaining this technology would be the ultimate achievement in his career and have a great impact on the future of Cuba. Since this was such a critical moment for him, the general arranged to send three of his own personnel, along with the Cuban Ambassador in Tokyo, to the computer science department at The University of Hiroshima to collect this treasure.

Cuba's future rested on this tiny chip. The general's emissaries hand delivered the chip to him in Santa Clara. When he received it in his own hands, the general was speechless.

After the arrival of the chip, Hiro was picked up by a security team and escorted to the general's office. Hiro was asked to duplicate the chip within a very short time. He had to use computer graphics to do this. Hiro was the only person capable of making the complicated mathematic calculations diagram needed to duplicate the chip.

After the chip had been duplicated successfully, the general thanked Hiro and said, "Hiro, I am indebted to you for this most important project and step in my career. The Cuban

Army and the government thank you. I want to give you a gift. You name it."

Hiro smiled and said, "I want the military presence removed from my house and my neighborhood, and I want to be with my family and left alone like before. I love Cuba because here I can be a relaxed family man. This would be the greatest gift I could ever receive." The general was surprised by Hiro's humble request, and Freddie who was standing nearby smiled because he understood and knew who Hiro really was. Hiro was just a good-hearted and honest person.

The general said, "Hiro, no problem. You are easy to please. I will call off the dogs this instant. Go and be with your family. I am going to be busy anyway so you might not hear from me for a while. Now I must call Raúl Castro Ruiz for a briefing. Our leaders will want to hear this good news immediately." The general shook Hiro's hand and excused himself.

Then the original chip was put into a secure box and returned to Hiroshima by the general's personal staff once again. The chip was returned to the university within the thirty day period, so all was well.

After the chip's return to Japan, Hiro did not see General González for quite some time. The general had discontinued his communications with Hiro in order to give Hiro a complete break from military involvement. The general honored Hiro's request to be left alone and there was no military presence in or around his home in San Rafael near Sierra Morena. However, Hiro was still suspicious and politics were not mentioned in his home.

Dania and the girls were very pleased with this return to normalcy. Hiro didn't isolate himself in his room any longer. He took a break and watched movies on the patio room with his family. Once again, Hiro found serenity and a new appreciation of the simple things in life.

One afternoon, Pedro stopped by to see Hiro. Pedro was a welcome visitor. Hiro really missed seeing his good friend and their talks. Pedro dropped by to see if Hiro wanted to go fishing. Pedro was hoping that the entire family could go fishing and to the Hotel Elquea for a retreat. Hiro wanted to get away and jumped at the opportunity.

The Last Revolution

When Hiro told Freddie of his plans to get away for a few days, Freddie asked if his family could join them. Hiro and Pedro were happy to have all three families together. Freddie's family drove from Santa Clara to join them for the fishing trip. Hiro and Dania had really needed this time away, and they had a joyful and romantic time.

The whole family relaxed and enjoyed the healing hot springs, and the kids especially enjoyed the swimming pool. The women talked and drank wine in the dining room after their day in the springs. The restaurant served special sea foods for the group.

Since Freddie was a high-ranking officer in the government, he got many perks and special treatment. It was a glorious vacation. At the end, Freddie secretly paid the entire bill. Hiro asked why, and Freddie said, "The general wanted to pay for this one. This is a government perk." They all had a great time at the government's expense.

Since Hiro had helped to obtain the computer chip for the government, fewer restrictions were placed on his activities, especially since Freddie was always present. Nevertheless, Pedro was not comfortable. He remained cautious, and he advised Hiro to be on guard at all times. Pedro reminded Hiro, "Remember, when you dance with a bull, you may get stabbed with the horns." Hiro laughed, but he knew exactly what Pedro meant.

Their stay at the Hotel Elquea had been a grand get away and they returned home feeling rejuvenated and peaceful. But Hiro knew that the clock was ticking for his plan.

Chapter 59

A few months passed but life in San Rafael and Rancho Veloz had not changed much. It was quiet and peaceful and Hiro spent as much as time as possible with his family. He was very content. To liven things up, Pedro and Hiro decided to try their hands at making some homebrew.

In the past, Pepe had helped Hiro and Pedro brew beer. Without Pepe's guidance, it took much longer than expected, but finally they succeeded in producing a fine product, even tastier than Pepe's, and well worth the wait. But making the beer had brought back memories of Pepe and Isabel to Hiro, which made his heart hurt deep inside.

As Pedro and Hiro were chatting, while drinking the fruits of their labor, Dania shouted from the inside the house, "Hiro, you have phone call from Santa Clara. It's Freddie." Hiro had not been expecting a phone call and wondered why Freddie was calling.

When Hiro took the call, Freddie's voice sounded serious, "Hiro! There is an emergency!" Hiro was stunned and listened intently. According to Freddie there had been an accident near the military hospital in Santa Clara.

Freddie added, "The Cuban military has been conducting research in germ warfare. A few days ago, a monkey infected with the deadly Ebola virus escaped from the lab and ended up in a residential park where some kids were playing baseball. The monkey attacked the children, biting two boys and a girl. Their lives are in jeopardy. Oh, Hiro, I know these children. We are desperate for your help!"

"They most likely will lose their lives. The Ebola virus' incubation period is 15 to 25 days. The symptoms begin like the regular flu with high fever; the normal blood clotting mechanism is inhibited and, within three weeks, four out of five infected die of multiple organ failure, often with internal and external bleeding. There is no cure. Our doctors only have standard antibiotics—useless against Ebola—to treat them with."

The Last Revolution

"A Cuban virologist told us about a study being conducted in Japan, at The National Institute for Infectious Diseases, in Tokyo. They have a drug that has cured Ebola infections in animals. There were few side effects. It has not been tried on humans, but it is the only hope for these children." Freddie paused and caught his breath. He had been talking fast. Hiro listened very carefully to every word while thinking that this could have happened to his own children. "Hiro! We need you to help us obtain enough of this drug to treat these children."

Hiro answered, "Look, I know nothing about have a lot of contacts in the medical community, but I will try my best to find out how to do it through my sources. How much time do I have?"

Freddie said, "We only have ten days. Also, you should know that one of the victims is the oldest son of Ishmael Velasquez, one of our chief secret agents. Another victim is the second son of General González, Freddie's distant cousin's granddaughter. The general wanted me to relay to you that he urgently needs your help."

"Hiro, I am calling from a military helicopter that is headed to Sierra Morena right now to pick you up. I don't want to shock you, but I will be at your house in less than an hour."

Hiro instantly logged onto the Internet and sent an urgent message to his sources in Japan to see if they would contact the appropriate people at the National Institute for Infectious Diseases. It was still early in the morning there—too early for anyone to be on the Internet or even awake. It would be at least four hours before he could make contact via an international phone call. Soon, Hiro heard the whirling propellers of Freddie's helicopter overhead as it circled and touched down near the highway just below his house

Freddie jumped out, accompanied by two armed soldiers. They ran toward Hiro's house. Freddie entered the house quickly and asked Pedro to take everyone to his house, until this business with Hiro was finished. Hiro and Dania were caught off guard by this order. They didn't want to separate, but Freddie explained quickly that this was urgent government business which required their 100% cooperation.

Hiro hugged Dania and the girls and told them to pack their things. He told them that he would see them in a couple of days. Dania was worried, but Hiro grabbed her hand and told her that everything was fine. He gently reassured her that he would see them soon. Then Pedro escorted the girls to the car and drove off toward his home.

The next twenty-four hours were tense, but Hiro's contacts gave him a direct connection to Dr. Takeshi Nishimura, the Institute's president and chief of operations. "We recently determined the three dimensional structure of an Ebola virus protein, VP30, which is necessary for virus reproduction. This structure identified a unique pocket that is necessary for the protein's activity and, thus, a viral infection. More importantly, this pocket also is a potential target for a small molecule to serve as a specific anti-Ebola drug. It has taken two years and thirty scientists to identify such a molecule for the Ebola-Zaire strain, the same virus strain being studied in Cuba. This molecule was tested on Ebola infected rhesus macaques. Of 12 animals treated with the drug, 12 survived. There were no survivors in 12 untreated animals. It works!"

Dr. Nishimura, however, refused to release doses of the experimental anti-Ebola drug. He explained that it was unfortunate, but the Institute was legally unable to release the drug because it was in an early stage of development and had not been tested on humans. Much more research would be necessary before it would be safe to use on humans. Besides, it was a long shot and there might be terrible side effects.

At this point, Hiro insisted that Freddie contact the Cuban government for more help. Cuban leaders were going to have to negotiate with the Japanese Prime Minister, Mr. Oizumi, through the Cuban Embassy in Tokyo to get the institute to release the test drug.

Hiro was just one individual, and it was almost impossible to negotiate with the government in Japan. He believed that Fidel had to be involved to request a political favor. No other person could get results at this point. Hiro also urged Freddie to persuade the Cuban government sources to stop all germ warfare research before more people became infected. With no time to waste, Freddie made the call to General González. The general briefed Raúl and Fidel in person and begged them to start negotiations with Japan.

The Cuban Embassy in Tokyo was directed to contact the Prime Minister of Japan in order to set up a conference call with Fidel Castro. It was all top secret, but the US Keyhole series spy

The Last Revolution

Lacrosse satellites and taps within the Cuban Embassy in Japan picked up word of the outbreak. Within hours the United Nations and the US government became involved because of the threat of biological warfare. WIDO (The World Community of Infectious Disease Organization) lodged a complaint against the Cuban government and their use of biological warfare. The US and the United Nations demanded that Cuba dismantle their research facility and hand over the study to UN authorities.

The Cubans had been experimenting with biological warfare since the 1980s, during the war in Angola. Fidel's brother, Raúl Castro Ruiz, who was Chief of Staff, requested that the research continue. Raúl even went so far as to request research related to implanting germs into medium range missiles that could reach as far as Chicago. Raúl and Fidel wanted to have the capability to attack the US using biological warfare. This threat was now being revealed to the world.

If the Cuban research on Ebola had been successful and the virus had been mass- produced, then the world would have been in jeopardy of infection. This was very serious news, and it spread throughout the international media like wildfire. The threat of Cuba using biological warfare made headlines overnight. It would mean tremendous destruction for the American general population, and the U.S. roared against Cuba. It would have been a brilliant military tactic by this poor island nation against the giant, United States, but the accident at the Santa Clara military hospital had become an international incident instead.

Fidel Castro continued to negotiate with Japan and refused to comply with requests from the U.S. and the United Nations. Fidel hated the U.S.

The Japanese Federal Health Authority continued to refuse to release an experimental drug to this communist country. But after three days of talks and much pressure, Fidel agreed to discontinue research into biological terrorism. The Japanese Prime Minister then directed the government to release the drug to be used on the children under strict orders that Japanese scientists would administer it. Japan, the United States, and the UN would have strict authority to oversee its administration and monitor the results. Cuban scientists could only observe. Fidel agreed and negotiations were concluded.

Six days had passed from the time the children had been bitten and the time that the drugs and researchers were granted permission to enter Cuba. The children's chances of survival were decreasing daily, but soon the drugs could be administered. Hopefully, the children would be saved.

The world watched and waited. Floods of international reporters rushed to Japan and Cuba to cover the results. Finally, the experimental drug arrived, accompanied by teams of scientists from the United Nations, Japan, and the US. They all set up camp at the Santa Clara army hospital and a nearby lab facility where the three children were administered the drug by the Japanese scientists.

After two weeks of intensive testing, the three teams were able to report that the test drug had worked. The children would survive. The children would be closely monitored over the next several months as their recovery would be a slow process.

Droves of Cubans chanted outside the hospital and celebrated the news that the children were going to live. Everyone around the world celebrated the good news. Reporters around the world talked about the successful Ebola antiviral that would hopefully be available around the world in the few years. Hiro was relieved. He couldn't believe the events of the past days, but he was glad that it was finally over and that the children would be all right.

The Cuban government agreed to cease its biological research and to comply with US and United Nations sanctions. Teams from the United Nations would be allowed to dismantle the research facility and to receive full disclosure about what the Cuban researchers had been working on. When the UN team arrived at the facility in the military hospital Santa Clara, everything had been completely neutralized and the Cubans were only allowed to observe. It was an international agreement for the sake of humanity.

Three months passed, and the children who had been infected with Ebola were recovering. The teams from Japan, the U.S. and the UN were satisfied with the progress and the outcome of the experimental drug. There was no doubt that it had saved lives.

At last, a cure for Ebola had been found. The children's parents were grateful and the children would soon be able to return to their normal lives. Hiro was also very pleased with the

The Last Revolution

results. A potential disaster had brought forth a miracle. Not only had the children been saved but Cuba had been forced to stop their biological research for now.

A few days later, General Abelard González and the chief federal agent, Ishmael Velázquez, came to thank Hiro personally. They visited his home with Freddie and expressed their gratitude for his help in saving their children.

Senor Velázquez was moved to tears as he embraced Hiro and thanked him, "Roberto is doing well now. From all of our family, thank you for helping to save him." He then handed Hiro a box of Cohiba special-edition cigars. Hiro was astounded by this gift and said, "This is too much. I cannot accept this." Senor Velázquez replied, "Freddie told us that you like Cuban cigars. These are the best. Please, it is a gift of thanks from our family."

Freddie's distant cousin, Adelaide Valdés y Sierra, was overwhelmed by Hiro's kindness. When she tried to thank him, she broke down. Freddie took over for her saying, "Adelaide's daughter Estelle and her family are doing well. All of us appreciate your help."

Adelaide recovered her composure and added, "Freddy told me that your favorite Cuban cigar was a *Romeo y Julieta*. This is from us."

General González shook Hiro's hand and added, "My son, Ja Juan, is doing well. He and my family also send their gratitude to you. Ja Juan asked me to give you this."

He handed Hiro a photo of the two boys and girl who had been infected. They had signed their names and the date with their thanks. The general had framed the photo. The photo would be a reminder of the fragility of life. In the photo, the children were smiling and looked totally normal. Hiro bowed his head and said, "Please thank the children for this gift. I will display it here in my office." Hiro led the men to the patio where they sat and smoked the Cohibas and drank some of the homemade brew. It was a wonderful afternoon.

Chapter 60

After the successful outcome of the potential Ebola tragedy, Hiro and General González became very close friends. The general now fully trusted Hiro. They met frequently to talk and to exchange views on all kinds of intellectual ideas and cultural subjects.

Since the general was into technology and computers, they both enjoyed deep conversations about the technical aspects of computer science. The general had many questions and Hiro taught him a lot. Even though he knew Hiro as a professor of mathematics, the general knew Hiro would be able to modify his VCR to become a satellite receiver. He knew Hiro was a brilliant man with superior knowledge of computers as well. Following one of these discussions, the general invited Hiro, Dania and their daughters to his personal residence near the outskirts of Santa Clara to introduce them to his family.

Freddie and Pedro were excited that Hiro and the general were getting to know each other on a personal basis. However, Pedro was the only one who expressed his concern. He told Hiro to always watch his back and to be careful about what he said to General González. Hiro had always appreciated Pedro's friendship and took his words of advice seriously.

Hiro told Pedro, "I will be careful. Remember, I have a plan and I will see it through. I am always aware of what I am doing. I'll be all right." This was comforting for Pedro to hear.

The general had a nice home. It was much larger than the average Cuban house and had a beautiful flower garden in the front. The general had two sons, Alejandro and Ja Juan. His wife, Marisa, was quite beautiful. She had short black hair and dressed smartly. She was highly educated and sophisticated. She was five years younger than the general. Marisa and the general had grown up in the same neighborhood in Nuevitas, a small city in Camaguey on the northern coast of central Cuba. Nuevitas was a small industrial city that had a sugar port and little else.

The general had been born in 1964, and was the only son of school teachers. His father, Jorge, and his mother, Norma,

The Last Revolution

were both strong supporters of Fidel and believed in the socialist party and government. Jorge even joined the revolutionary army in 1957, Infighting Street in Santa Clara and participated in the march to Havana on the historical day of January 1, 1959.

On this day in 1959, Che Guevara and Camilo Cienfuegos lead the rebels into the capital. At 2 a.m., revolutionary forces took control of Cuba, and Batista and his family and their closest associates boarded a plane and left the island. This signaled that the revolution was over.

Following the revolution, Jorge returned to Camaguey and taught middle school. He later became the principal while his wife continued to teach elementary school. They were both retired from the school system now and lived with their son and his family. The general had added extra living quarters to his home for them to live in.

Dania was quite nervous about the visit at first, but the general's family was welcoming and warm and she began to enjoy the visit. Dania got along well with Marisa and enjoyed talking to the general's parents. They had more in common than she thought.

Dania had an aunt who lived just on the outskirts of Nuevitas. When she was in middle school, she visited her aunt Dorita and stayed with her for a couple of weeks every summer. Thus, Dania was familiar with Nuevitas and knew some of the same people that the González family knew.

Dania fondly remembered a special beach called, *Playa Quatro Vientos* that she had visited often that summer in Nuevitas when she fell in love for the first time with a young local boy. She always remembered that special summer on the beach.

Dania's young daughters, Yumiko and Masako, liked the general's two sons. Everyone enjoyed their weekend together.

The general was extremely interested in Japanese technology and heavy industry, such as ship-building, high tech bolt train, railroads systems, and the automobile industry. He wanted to visit Japan one day; it would be his dream vacation. The general wanted to understand how Japan had become the industrial giant it was today and how Cuba could learn from the Japanese. It was mind boggling to him that this small island nation in the Pacific that had lost WWII and had its economy fall to nothing had risen from its ashes to become one of the great industrial powers of the modern world.

After much discussion, the general showed Hiro his personal computer room upstairs. His office was just next to his bedroom. It was not only an office but also a hobby shop. The general had many new home computers. The general proudly showed his technical ability to Hiro. He had just rebuilt a home CPU with a new copy of the Intel-Nakajima-JPX008 processor chip. The general enjoyed showing off his knowledge of computers.

The general didn't know anything about Hiro's brilliant computer science career or background. All he knew was that Hiro was a professor of mathematics at The University of Hiroshima who lectured on occasion at The University of Havana. The general didn't suspect the depth of Hiro's knowledge. It made sense that Hiro probably had a lot of computer expertise because the field of mathematics was so closely linked to computers.

Hiro asked, "How many copies of the chip do you have?"

The general answered, "So far, fourteen chips. I need them for further study here at my home. I plan to research them and make adjustments on my computer. I still don't know that much about the chip."

Hiro offered to help him. He took the chips and showed the general how to make the necessary adjustments as he quickly re-programmed the driver. Hiro made several diagrams to explain things more clearly to the general. Within two hours, the computer was enhanced and operational. With the new adjustments, the computer functioned very well.

Hiro explained that the chips worked together "multiple in line" which chip worked like an AC-DC converter series on a battery, to become in theory like a supercomputer. He taught the general specifically how the fourteen chips worked and drew diagrams illustrating the process. Hiro also set up and made adjustments to the general's CPU main board and re-programmed the bio input boot commuter. It took Hiro nearly two hours to connect all fourteen chips. But soon they were uniform and functioning efficiently. Now the general had a modified computer that worked as a multiple system. This was a tremendous advantage as far as speed was concerned.

The Last Revolution

The Intel-Nakajima JPX008 chip had been originally developed to eliminate hackers by using its built-in fingerprint identity security feature. Its sole purpose was to prevent illegal computer traffic activity. But Hiro had already modified the new chip by removing this security feature and combining it with a new generation micro-electronic, neuro-electronic system which interfaced between neuron cells and the computer. He renamed it the Tamotsu-Colbana JPX008, and he kept the prototype for his own future research.

The general was astounded at how much Hiro knew about computers. Hiro's knowledge was far beyond the average tech-savvy person. The general chalked it up to Hiro's mathematical brilliance, but he was puzzled at his abilities. He imagined that a doctoral degree in mathematics made learning about computer science much easier, but Hiro's knowledge was advanced.

As the general pondered Hiro's background, he thought to himself, "After all, mathematics is the language of computers. It's possible."

But the general knew that Hiro was not your normal individual. He was exceptionally intelligent and possessed much information on a variety of topics. When the general questioned Hiro, Hiro insisted that computers were a hobby and his favorite past time. Hiro confessed that his mathematical background gave him a huge advantage. Hiro also told the general that his friends were all computer scientists who had taught him a great deal over the years. The general bought Hiro's explanation and was no longer suspicious of Hiro.

Hiro and the general worked as a team on the general's computer. Hiro said, "You got a supercomputer cheap! I think you should name this system "Cyber Space Station Ciboney-Colbana" Ciboney meant precious pearl in the original indigenous language of the Cuban Indians. She will perform 1400 times faster than the average home computer. You still need many adjustments; however, you will have to tweak them as you go along. Now, the whole concept for your unit is that it will perform as a mini-supercomputer. You have the ability to explode into the cyberspace world with this gadget. You will see how fast and quickly you can download. You will be able to operate so efficiently. It is like you have fourteen computers working together. This is a dream machine, and you will be a super engineer with your new invention."

The general's computer was operational and functioning. Moreover, the general liked the new computer chip because it was ultra-efficient and fast. Its speed was quick like a finger snap.

The general thought it odd that this gentle Oriental mathematician understood cyber space as well as any professional computer scientist. But the general was thrilled and could not hide his excitement over his new creation. Hiro, as usual, was very calm and silent and methodically explained every detail of the elaborate layout.

Next the general showed Hiro his collection of Nintendo war games with a next-generation super dual-screen Nintendo DS Browser and stealth super station Wii system. His latest acquisitions were "Ninja Infantry" and "Ninja Frog." Both games used Japanese swords against the modern weapons of their enemies. When the general played, he became like a child enjoying a new toy. The new computer chip made everything work extremely fast which made the war games much more realistic. Hiro had not played a Nintendo game for many years. In fact, he couldn't remember the last time he had played games like this.

Hiro knew that Nintendo games were based on a simple mathematical system and theories. He enjoyed watching the plays and he remembered when he had invented the original concept so many years ago during his days at MIT.

The general's games were the newest evolution which had come a long way from the original "Chaser Man." The technology had vastly improved and now used three-dimensional graphics, but the system was still based on the same theory as Hiro's original creation.

The general stopped playing the game for a moment and said, "I have heard that there are hackers in America. I would like to know how a hacker is able to steal documents from other computers." Hiro just smiled. Then the general said, "Since computer technology is man-made, then it would be possible to break into this system. Correct?" The general was serious and wondered if Hiro knew how to hack, but Hiro remained silent and just listened.

Chapter 61

Finally Hiro asked the general, "Why do you want to know about hacking?"
The general answered, "I want to find U.S. intelligence information on Cuba—the real top secret jewels. Fidel would love to obtain this information." General González smiled at Hiro, "And I have wondered if it's possible to break into the CIA's or the Pentagon's computers?" Hiro's eyes opened wide, and he shook his head in disagreement, "General, it is impossible to break into such agencies. Besides, it is illegal and a crime in both Japan and the US. They have the most secure computer technology in the world. No one would ever have the chance to enter their front door." The general was excited about the idea: "A computer is only a man-made creation. It cannot be impossible. There is always a flaw in the system. Some genius should be able to crack into it." The general laughed at his idea and added, "How much chance do you think I have? You are the mathematician. What are my odds?"

Hiro took the general's comments seriously and did the math. He smiled back and shook his head, "Honestly, you have one in a 205 million chance. Those big mainframe supercomputers have a capacity of thirty-five trillion operations per second. Besides, the coding relies on one of 72-quadrillion (followed by 15 zeros) keys. It is impossible to crack into a coded system like this. It would take an enormous amount of time to find the exact key." The general listened closely. He was fascinated by Hiro's knowledge.

Hiro went on, "If you know the base system on this magnetic supercomputer, then it could be possible to hack in because the entire key is to enter the opposite of the key code. This is your back door. Nearly 250,000 invaders try this each year, and only a couple get close. And mathematically speaking, 99% of the time the supercomputer recognizes the invader and relocates. Then it comes right back to your computer and has the capability to recognize the thief's identity and content. There are specially-made, 468 IBM, high-end, big-frame processors that link together to become like one. It would take 80,000 million humans brains to calculate this manually in a 24-hour day. That is 100 trillion calculations per second." The general was in awe.

Then Hiro said, "Watch this." Hiro took over the computer and began typing. He entered the CIA website and began typing codes quickly. His fingers were on fire. The computer asked for instrumental binary code and execution modes to dynamically trace, connect and link him into the system. Hiro entered a series of zeros and ones and abbreviated symbols at lightening speed while the general looked on in amazement. He used special sigma tracing by over-writing the programming, changing the security parameters dynamically. There were blue lights flashing which asked for a final stage key. Hiro had to input several key codes within seconds. He raced and entered the last key code. Then the monitor displayed access to the CIA's supercomputer.

"Bingo!" Hiro shouted. He was in. He had successfully entered their system.

The general yelled, "My God, Hiro. What have you done? This is incredible! You're in! You're in!" To hide his identity, Hiro had to exit within 6 seconds. Hiro was silent because it was a very tense moment, but he remained calm.

Meanwhile, back in the United States, at CIA headquarters in Langley, Virginia, computer operators' station received the security alert. Someone was trying to invade the CIA's magnetic supercomputer. They immediately scrambled to find the hacker, and the chase began. But Hiro had exited before they could trace him to the general's computer. Hiro struck with lightning speed and accuracy. The general looked on and knew that Hiro had vast knowledge of the supercomputer system.

Hiro was copying the supercomputer's Bio-system. He quickly dismissed the connection within the six second window. Hiro was always one step ahead.

This system was based on his earlier research studies of 1990. Some companies had modified and re-coded the system several times since then, but it was still basically the same root system. That core part was not interchangeable.

Hiro mumbled as he rubbed his hands together, "If they change to a new generation of DNA-based computer technology, no one will ever be able to access their supercomputer. The

The Last Revolution

artificial intelligence surveillance device would be nearly 1082-dimensional. When that happens, there will be no crack in the door."

Within this current system, Hiro was one of the few people in the world who could enter through the back door, but it was difficult even for him. Years ago, before he had left Silicon Valley, Hiro had invented this last and most important system. At that time, though, it was not fully operational and existed only in theory. But it was a giant breakthrough in computer science technology and now the CIA and the US government were using it.

As soon as Hiro checked his copy, he quickly re-coded and modified it. He put it back into the computer and entered the CIA's mainframe supercomputer once again. The computer asked for several codes. Hiro quickly entered a special encrypted code to scramble the surveillance. Hiro then bypassed buffer overflows and used all of the keys to find the information that the general had only dreamed of finding. Additionally, Hiro accessed the CIA's newest top secret documents on Cuba and Fidel Castro. Hiro was fast and efficient typing in rapid fire succession enabling him to download the binary code. In a matter of seconds, Hiro had disabled the connection.

Back at the computer room at CIA headquarters in Langley, the security agents once again were alerted that the hacker was trying to breach their files. Everyone was working on high alert to track the invader. All agents and techs scrambled to find out who was attempting to hack into the system and to discover what they were looking for. The technicians were frustrated and very disappointed when they were unable to track down the hacker. They were dumbfounded. They couldn't recognize any trace of the hacker, but they found the file that was taken. They saw that it was the latest top-secret documents on Cuba called "operation cockroach".

The top technicians briefed the CIA's chief of computer intelligence that the suspected source came from somewhere in Cuba. They all knew that no one in Cuba had this kind of technology or the knowledge to hack at this level.

The CIA chief was stunned and said, "From Cuba? It's impossible to access top-secret files from Cuba. Our intelligence already knows that their computer technology is obsolete. They've never been updated. They couldn't hack into a system like ours. It's impossible! I can't believe this is possible! Get me the file on Cuba, STAT."

By then the CIA chief had lost his composure, and his voice was raised a few decibels. He had to brief and explain this to his boss who was not pleased, of course. The director said in a cool demeanor, "I am ordering a full investigation of all technical aspects here. Have your techs work over time and trace that hacker. I want a full report on the incident on my desk by 0800 hours. I want this taken care of as soon as possible or it's your job. It is a disgrace that the Cubans with their obsolete technology could crack our top-secret files!" The director was visibly angry.

Meanwhile, back in Santa Clara, Hiro made a copy of the top-secret file from the CIA. With the general looking in disbelief, he pulled up the screen to verify that the file was complete. The general was shocked, staring at the screen. He could not believe that he was actually looking at this file. The general was speechless; his hands shook with excitement. But all the while, Hiro remained very calm and quiet. He knew he had to do this to get closer to the general. He just smiled his Cheshire-cat grin at the general.

After taking a closer look at the CIA's file, the general asked, "How do you know how to hack like this? I don't know what to say. I am amazed at how much knowledge you have about computers. I'd be crazy if I didn't ask, so, can you teach me your techniques?"

Hiro said, "General! We are friends, but you'd have to keep this under the strictest confidence. Also, the process is very complicated, but I can teach you some things. Hacking on this level is almost too difficult to explain. I have to calculate with each second, and it is often just in my brain. It's not something I can easily explain."

The general stood up and paced in a circle in the small computer room. He started laughing at the thought of learning this miraculous information. For him, it was like finding the Holy Grail. He yelled, "Thank you, Hiro! Trust me I'll keep it all confidential. I didn't see anything tonight! We were just playing Nintendo games. Correct?" Hiro and the general shook hands. The general was as excited as a little boy who gets the dream Christmas gift. Then, Hiro deleted all the documents on his desktop. It was as if it never happened.

The Last Revolution

It was already midnight when Hiro and the general came downstairs to rejoin the family. The youngsters were still playing Nintendo games in the children's' quarters while Dania and Marisa were sitting on the patio drinking wine. The wives enjoyed the evening together and seemed to be comfortable with each other. The children, on the other hand, were having too much fun playing the video games. They were vocal and loud.
The general and Hiro headed to the patio and kissed their wives' cheeks just as Pedro arrived to pick up Hiro and his family. Pedro joined the group on the patio while Wendy, Pedro's daughter, joined the children playing games.

Madeline, Pedro's wife, joined the adults on the patio and announced to the group, "Well, the children seem to be living it up in there. They are on spring break. Maybe we should just stay until they get ready to conk out for the evening." The adults agreed as they wanted to sit, drink, and chat some more. The ladies sipped red wine while the men enjoyed cold Cuban beer.

It was a good time for everyone and they all stayed up very late at the general's home in Santa Clara. It was a beautiful spring evening in March of 2006. They weather was gorgeous—not too hot—and the mosquitoes were not out in droves yet. It was the perfect time of year to kick back outdoors.

Chapter 62

Military camp and training was a few months away for the general, so he decided to take some well-deserved vacation time. Unless there were a big emergency in Havana, the general would have a break for several weeks.

The general asked Hiro if he had time to teach him how to be a hacker. To mix business with pleasure, Hiro and the general agreed to take their families to the Hotel Elquea for a few days, which would give Hiro time to teach the general the basics of hacking. Hiro decided to teach the general just like a student in one of his college-level classes. Hiro called the class "Multi-variable Mathematical Systems with Computer Theory." It would be a legitimate, but private, advanced seminar. Freddie received permission from the Army Chief Commander to book a private suite at the hotel to use as a classroom.

The general had studied computer science at The University of Matanzas before attending the military academy in Havana. He was knowledgeable about components, applications, and system languages. But, even as advanced as the general's knowledge was, his expertise was not even close to Hiro's.

Hiro's class began with a review of computer theory, language and engineering. The instruction was detailed and Hiro used hands-on teaching methods. What the general didn't know was that Hiro was working simultaneously on his own plan. Hiro taught in English and used some Spanish. He lectured on Micro/Nano processing, nonlinear programming, networks and databases, bandwidth, algorithms, micro-electronic devices, circuits and devices, cluster computing, high speed interconnects, Linuz clusters, and electro-magnetic applications. It was an exhausting course of study, but Hiro had to cover this material to bring the general up to speed in advanced programming and computer science.

Freddie and the secret agents attending the class were lost most of the time. The instruction was way over their heads. As Hiro taught, Freddie and the other secret agents fell behind.

The Last Revolution

Hiro's plan was working. Hiro now went full throttle with the lessons knowing that the others' interest would not last much longer.

Hiro went full speed ahead and began to review Window's operational system's computer languages. They covered and reviewed many of the programming languages, such as programming language B, GCC, C#, FORTRAN, Objective-C, Cp-M, Tel/TK, Perl, Java2, Ruby, Delphi and Python. The general struggled, but each day he was amazed that he could actually retain most of what he had learned from Hiro. Each day the general strained to digest everything about computer culture, to learn operation systems for Window NT, Mac-OS, OS/2, OS, and Linux as well as all of the languages of computer culture he thought he already knew. The general mastered the information in the time it would take a person to snap his fingers.

After the first two weeks, the general said to Hiro, "My brain is working on overdrive. I even dream in binary code. My brain almost hurts sometimes. You were not kidding when you said this would not be easy. This has been more difficult than anything I have ever attempted in my life."

Hiro said, "You must master many computer systems and become a master linguist in computer languages. You are a fast learner, and I know you will master all that you need to know soon. However, we need more time together to work on this. You have a great foundation, and now you must expand your knowledge."

The general worked with Hiro for fourteen hours each day. They ate dinner with their families, but they worked and studied the remainder of the time. The general found Hiro's style of teaching fast-paced and intense. He had to be in front of the computer screen all day while Hiro stood over him supervising his every move.

It was exhausting for the general, but he persevered. Three weeks had passed and he was just beginning to digest the massive amount of information. The general was becoming mentally fatigued. This was an intensive course of study and the general knew that Hiro was his only ticket to learning it. It was now or never for the general.

The next week was spent cracking security password and learning abstract theory. This instruction was designed not to harm or interrupt the targeted operation system. Its purpose was to help the general learn and understand as much as possible about the psychological makeup and motives of the developers of the programs being illicitly entered. The pair had to explore ways to exploit computer systems. The general was motivated to work hard because of his desire to penetrate the most secure computer systems in the world.

Hiro showed the general how to stimulate curiosity in the human brain simply by adding different numbers and letters. He showed the general his tricks on getting into the architecture of programs using special syntax, keywords, multiple letters of the alphabet, and public key infrastructure systems. Hiro also showed him how to input the entire dictionary with thousands of names and words, alphabets from several languages, number recognition to one billion, and the complex binary codes that were most often used. He taught the general cryptanalysis and about ciphers.

Additionally, Hiro taught him how to input and program in nanoseconds the information needed to help bypass the codes. Some turned out to be simplistic, like words and letters while others were complex using computer signs, syntax, and abbreviated codes. Many security passwords were built on playing crossword puzzles and number games until the right combination popped up-Often the right combination was found by playing around with common knowledge. Such as social security numbers and birth dates, the complexity of passwords was the most difficult problem encountered. Cracking the password depended on how complicated the programmer decided to make it for hackers. Knowledge was the key.

Hiro knew more than most programmers in the world, so he was always in the lead. The general struggled but he was learning quickly with Hiro's help. Sometimes it took the general days to figure out how to crack the codes. Hiro gave him real life applications for practice and the general began by hacking into ten different computer codes set up by Hiro. At first, this exercise was a nightmare for the general. He was continuously locked out even after he had tried every avenue he could think of. But Hiro showed him his errors and eventually, the general could correct his own errors.

After the general mastered simple code-cracking, he moved on to more complex codes. Hiro gave him student records

The Last Revolution

from universities, bank account codes, and PIN numbers for special accounts through brokerage firms in the U.S. Each time the general struggled to get in and to get out without being recognized or detected. Hiro watched over the general's shoulder to assist him when there was the possibility of a security risk. Hiro ensured that their identity would not be uncovered. He continually monitored the last binary number in the general's brain to assure adequate ability and skill at understanding the various computer codes encountered.

After hacking into an account successfully, they exited. They never disturbed any private information. The exercise was for practice only. Besides, the general was a man who was concerned only with military security and espionage. Within days, the pair hacked into Dell's mainframe, the Chilean government's security database, and the EU Stock Exchange. The general was exhilarated and amazed. He was grateful for the knowledge but realized that he still had much to learn from this brilliant Asian man.

Unless the general learned to dismantle systems altogether, which involved another level of knowledge, he had to perfectly bypass keys with passwords and codes. Even after four weeks this undertaking was difficult for him, but like Hiro said, "It will take much time and practice. Hacking comes only with much comprehensive experience."

Hiro also told the general, "You have good instincts and you are quick and calm. You retain information well which is a huge part of this type of learning."

The general was hard-working and meticulous about details. He had patience and did not become frustrated easily. Additionally, the general was extremely respectful to Hiro. He was also very intelligent and possessed an abundance of self-discipline. Hiro now understood why the general was one of the top officers in the Cuba Army. But the general was a sitting duck in Hiro's plan while he was being observed and manipulated daily without his knowledge.

Hiro moved forward with his plan by teaching the general about the CIA's computer. The magnetic supercomputer was different from the PC. The magnetic Matrix mainframe computer operated with the system Cp-M (control program of Microcomputer). It was a modified variation of the earlier IBM operating system and was a custom program with a quantum neutral network system in its own custom-built window. To get in, one must get a duplicate of the program and bypass all keys to enter the computer containing all the primary information. It would be a nightmare if these steps were omitted.

Then Hiro lectured the general about computer bio-codes which controlled the computer's operating system and IP address as remote control binary computer language. The general must master the computer language and access the target system to implant micro digital devices or "micro digital imaging" from a remote location. These were known as stealth spy cameras.

Hiro told González, "You'll have the ability to crack every key and password because you actually have a real-time image of the passwords so you can see what's happening in the program as photos, set every minute. This way you'll be able to see what is happening before them. It's quite remarkable and that's how you can beat them every time."

But Hiro was more excited about his latest invention and the effect it was having on the general while he was studying.

Hiro was reprogramming the general's brain without raising the general's suspicion. Hiro began to calculate and use special neural codes on the general's computer screen display from the beginning of the seminar. Hiro's months of research while at Johns Hopkins' Neurology department combined with his years of computer science experience was coming together in this perfect mind-control program and his secret weapon "cyclone sonic." Then Hiro used special binary codes to display and measure the general's brain neuron activity and duplicated his entire memory system.

This duplication was done through electrical magnetic circuit heat sensors placed in the general's monitor and screen along with laser beams. Hiro continued to invade the general's brain, manipulating and measuring activity. Using the neuro-electronic interfacing system on his laptop, which was an interfacing system between neuron cells and the computer which was equipped with "cyclone sonic" software, Hiro helped the general retain complex information by synchronizing the minute signals from the computer with the receptors in the general's brain.

Normally learning everything in a few weeks was impossible, but with Hiro's memory transplanting device, it was possible. Hiro did this while he taught the general the technical

The Last Revolution

aspects of being a hacker. The general thought his success was due to his intensive studying. He continued to digest and understand the material extremely well. The general had no idea that Hiro was working on his brain while they were together. Hiro had other motives, and no one had a clue about what was really happening.

Chapter 63

By that time, Freddie had dropped out of the class and left for Santa Clara because he didn't see any reason to stay. Freddie did not understand half of the information that Hiro was presenting. The security agents positioned at the doors were unaware of what was happening. They had tuned out and were bored with Hiro's academia. This was exactly what Hiro had wanted to happen. He needed the one-on-one time with the general to finish programming the general's brain with his secret weapon. Hiro intended to implant his newest war game.

As the neuron coding and programming increased, Hiro tested its success. He watched for signs that the general had begun reacting with the codes through the computer screen. Hiro made adjustments and bypassed human emotions with entrapped neurons and memory cells. Little by little, Hiro made progress. Within five weeks, the general's brain neurons were accepting high levels of programmed information.

As Hiro's tests progressed so did the general's responses. The new system was MP00X. Hiro modified the system with a combination of WAV MP3.MP4 and digital sound waves. This new format was operational only with secret codes. Implanting the program was time-consuming; nevertheless, it was working. Hiro sent signals to the general's neurons and received reactions in real-time. The modified "MP00X" format that Hiro used worked only to compress documents through a sound card. It eliminated electrical sound waves and used only synchronized low frequency waves that were compressed 1/1000 times smaller than the digital wave called echolocation response. This was similar to the way dolphins navigate, communicate with each other.

To be compatible, the user must have the Tamotsu-Colbana JPX009 DNA-based computer processor chip. Otherwise, it would not function properly because today's computer was electro-magnetically based in design so the compressed code would come out only as noise. It had taken

The Last Revolution

Hiro two months of research to find out why they were not compatible.

The compressed code was so fast that it could accelerate to one million bites a second. It was an incredible machine. For instance, a DVD could be sent instantly and downloaded within seconds. It could compress a file into a mini-kb. The Intel-Nakajima chip was compatible with this system, while most others were not.

The Intel-Nakajima chips were superior in every way. The only disadvantage was that the user's fingerprint could be traced instantly. However, the user was the only one who could access personal data.

Hiro upgraded his computer and modified the original Intel-Nakajima chip. Since he had been the creator of the original theory years ago, Hiro was one of the only people who could modify it. He added a device to the Colbana-Nakajima-JPX008 to alter the format slightly. He enabled the computer to disarm the fingerprint identification and tracing code.

Hiro named this altered chip the Tamotsu-Colbana JPX009 chip. It was extremely small, almost 1/10 in size and weight compared to the modern model produce no heart. He also designed it to process at speed capacities higher than the original Intel-Nakajima-chip.

The Tamotsu-Colbana JPX009 DNA-based computer system performed nearly five times faster than present IBM supercomputer processors' quantum neutral network system. Hiro's recent invention of a molecule-based system could alter the function of many devices, including heat sensor monitors, low-frequency laser beams and DNA molecule-calculating diagnostic devices. Hiro was interested only in accessing a specific part of the human brain – the memory neurons.

Hiro's plan was to monitor and to surgically imprint his game into the memory of the general. There was no other purpose for it. This was his only motive.

Hiro also used a low frequency laser beam projected through a hidden device within the computer display and monitor that the general used daily. Hiro had installed the device before the course began and had used it all along to manipulate the general's memory. Hiro was able to help the general retain more information than normal with his system.

Each day Hiro used the low frequency laser beam, along with the special neuron codes, to implant the war game program into the general's brain. A secret lens within the monitor projector worked like a laser printer on the general's brain neurons. It worked like a laser beam used to remove cataracts from the human eye in reverse. The low laser beam got stronger and stronger. It multiplied as soon as it hit the display monitor.

The laser had an extremely low frequency which could not be felt by humans. It did not damage human molecules yet it could slice an entire object down to minimal molecules, similar to a CT scan concept. It then implemented programs through human neurons through a device that triggered neurons to accept a new secret code. When stressed or confused, the neuron was easily entered - creating the perfect time to duplicate memory or to implant new information.

But it could not replace memory that had been lost or was obsolete. However, a person who already had duplicate neurons could download and add to previous working memory cells. But it could not replace old ones; it could only add to existing ones. He used this as a tool to monitor the brain's entire activity which then reprogrammed itself with existing intelligent memory.

Also, Hiro could manipulate the general's memory in the future to erase what he had learned about hacking. Hiro knew that hacking at this level could be too destructive for anyone to know about, especially anyone in the military. Hiro knew that one day the knowledge that General González gained through hacking could be used to start a war or worse, so he had to be strictly monitored. Hiro wanted the general to learn it using his short wave memory cells and then lose the information. This way the information would remain safe with Hiro.

Through the low frequency laser beams, anything that passed in front of the screen within a distance of five feet could be monitored. Also, the memory of any person within that range could be manipulated. In other words, this Tamotsu-Colbana JPX009 chip was equipped to calculate the molecules in the computer system using a low frequency laser beam. Combined, they replicated the memory found in a human brain.

Hiro call this method "la violación de la mente," meaning a mental rip without any physical involvement. It had huge commercial value. For instance, this invention could revolutionize the medical community. Patients would no longer

The Last Revolution

need to visit a doctor at a medical office or clinic. All doctors' appointments and visits could be done through a personal computer from home. Everything a physician needed to know would be accessible through the monitor. The computer could break down blood molecules, detect viruses and infections, and analyze and diagnose problems within the human body. The applications were endless. Labs would no longer be needed because the lab reports would be available to medical personnel within seconds. The guess work could be eliminated altogether. The Tamotsu-Colbana JPX009 system could change the world for good or for evil, so Hiro had to be sure it was secure.

Now Hiro needed only a remote computer to manipulate and enable his game to be downloaded to the general's neurons. It was a time consuming project with many adjustments. Hiro needed to bypass core human instincts and feelings while he input and downloaded the computer game. Hiro researched real time neuron activity from the beginning, but the general never suspected anything. He had no idea that he was a lab rat for Hiro's experiment. The general did feel very tired because his brain was in overload, but he thought it was because of the intensity of Hiro's instruction and a lack of sleep.

The hot springs were a favorable place to conduct such an intense seminar. After the long hours of instruction, General González and Hiro joined their families at the hot springs or pool to relax. The hot springs were therapeutic and restored their souls. The men joined their families for a late dinner following their soak.

Finally, Hiro completed his successful replication of the general's brain. Hiro was satisfied with his experiment and was able to implant the war game as planned. Now it was only a matter of waiting.

The seminar concluded, and the general was thrilled to be finished. General González returned to his headquarters and worked with army intelligence computer scientists to replace their old technology with the controversial Nakajima-JPX008 chip. The 120 processor chip linked the computers. This system was missing only the new software upgrades; otherwise it was complete.

The general and Freddie were summoned to attend a briefing on using technology to gather intelligence with Fidel Castro, himself, and his brother Raúl. The Chief General of the

Army, Hector Elias Garcia, was also invited to Santa Clara to dedicate the new Cuban supercomputer. Fidel wanted to create more new technology with Hiro. Fidel recognized that this could be an extremely lucrative commercial venture for Cuba.

    Hiro declined to attend the briefing because he had begun to feel a little uneasy. Hiro had no interest in meeting Fidel.

Chapter 64

Meanwhile, a sensational news development occurred in Santa Clara. The General informed Hiro that two North Korean intelligence agents had tried to marry two Cuban women with substantial resources, who had inside connections to the Cuban army's computer research surveillance unit located in Santa Clara. The Cuban central intelligence agency told General González about the North Korean spies' plot to steal the new technology. The spies were trying to obtain the new chip because Cuba had an exclusive contract with the Chinese main frame suppler Jie-Xu Computer, based in Guangzhou Kwang-tung province in South Central China.

Cuba had just duplicated the Japanese Nakajima chip. Possession of this chip would mean huge profits for the North Koreans.

Hiro was surprised that the North Koreans were so motivated. He had always thought that Communist North Korea had possessed only homegrown computer technology. Nevertheless, Kim Jong himself was known to love cyberspace and technology.

According to South Korean intelligence, Kim Jong supervised young North Koreans and granted access to cyberspace technology. North Korea was catching up and making rapid progress in 2003 and 2004 in the area of technology. They began right after 2000, when U.S. Secretary of State Madelyne Albright visited North Korea. Her visit triggered a revolution in information technology. From that kick start, a new era began.

Additionally, Kim Jong visited China and encouraged cooperation between the high tech industries in China and North Korea with Chinese software companies located in ZhongGuanCun. This area was China's Silicon Valley where several hundred computer companies sold software and hardware.

Kim Jong needed technical support, so in April of 2002, North Korea started duplicating all the computer technology they could get their hands on. Also, Kim Jong negotiated an agreement with the German corporation, Portel, to set up a joint Internet venture to make Internet access possible in North Korea.

Since all computers in North Korea were imported from China, the price was beyond the reach of most North Koreans. For example, the price of Internet access for thirty minutes cost almost $50 for a foreign company.

North Korean dictator, Kim Jong, had studied and watched the Soviet Union disintegrate at the end of the 1980's. Therefore, he would not allow his country to walk down the same destructive political path.

The Jie-Xu Computer LTD had been exclusively under contract with the Cuban government for all computer parts and supplies. But the Chinese plotted with the North Korean government by working on a covert espionage operation. Instead of sending twelve Chinese computer technicians to Cuba, they made a switch and sent twelve highly-educated North Korean computer scientists to Cuba. These scientists acted as spies for the North Korean government.

They wanted to acquire the chip using any means. Dr. Ki Won Chung was the architect of this industrial espionage mission even though he remained back in North Korea. He was the most highly-educated computer scientist in North Korea. He had studied computer science at the University of Taipei in Taiwan. His wife, Yoo Jeong Choi, was also a high-tech computer technician in the North Korean army's intelligence unit and a Sojang, or a Brigadier General. She was the one responsible for breaking U.S. and South Korean Army intelligence codes.

Yoo Jeong Choi had received her computer science technical education at Beijing University. The couple headed up the North Korean army intelligence unit and were also responsible for creating eleven university computer science departments in North Korea. The pair had an astonishing career record and were at the top of the computer field in North Korea. Yoo Jeong Choi had strong ties with Chinese computer scientists and she also worked closely with Chinese army intelligence.

Shortly after the North Koreans had begun trying to expand the limits of their technology, Kim Jong sent this team of spies to Cuba to pirate the new technology and get their hands on

The Last Revolution

the Japanese chip. They had been working with the Chinese government's spy agency to obtain a completed copy of the Japanese chip which had been duplicated by the Cubans. Their ambition was to develop a new commercial computer chip in North Korea. They had been under international pressure to dismantle their nuclear arsenal.

President Kim Jong Yong wanted to revamp his country's industrial and technological sectors to become modern and profitable. North Korea was in dire straits financially. He wanted the City Sinuijus in southwestern North Korea, near the Chinese border, to become the center of this new technological industry. Because of its proximity to China, Sinuijus had excellent access to Chinese suppliers and goods transport. This was the perfect solution to his problems.

Meanwhile, Cuban intelligence arrested a Cuban computer scientist and a North Korean spy for espionage. Fidel Castro ordered them to be immediately executed by a firing squad. This was a controversial move by Castro, because few foreigners were ever executed in Cuba without a trial. The Cuban female scientist was executed for being a collaborator.

Then Fidel placed the ten other members of the North Korean scientific espionage unit working inside Cuba under arrest. The government of Cuba demonstrated their power. The North Korean Embassy in Havana had their communications with the outside world terminated.

The North Korean government retaliated. They expelled all Cuban Embassy personnel in Pyongyang, North Korea. Both countries forged ahead with a heated political dispute. By that time, of course, international media frenzy had developed. The Chinese government intervened to try to negotiate and mediate between Cuba and North Korea. The North Koreans asked for huge compensation from Cuba for the execution of a North Korean citizen in Cuba.

Fidel manipulated politics as usual. Finally, President Kim Jong Yong sent a special envoy to Havana. They started negotiations with a diplomatic channel of the Cuban government for the Colbana-Nakajima -JPX 008 chip in exchange for a nuclear bomb with Taepo Dong or a highly sophisticated chemical and biological weapons program.

The Chinese government apologized to the Cuban government. The Korean computer scientists had been employed as temporary workers by China to fill a gap because Chinese technicians were in short supply. Staff in the Chinese Embassy in Havana claimed that it was just an isolated incident.

But prior information proved otherwise. The North Korean Embassy in Caracas, Venezuela, had opened diplomatic relations with President Hugo Chavez. They intercepted information that the Chinese government had been assisting the North Koreans with industrial espionage. Fidel finally decided to offer an official apology and compensate North Korea with sugar.

The Last Revolution

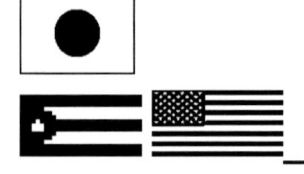

Chapter 65

Back in the United States

CIA technology room in Langley, Virginia, they were working on who invaded their supercomputer. They were having difficulty solving this question, but top analysts believed the hacker to be from somewhere in Cuba using the new unreleased Nakajima-JPX008 technology serial number # JPX008N-UOH-247948.

They knew it left some trace like a finger print and was under research by the distinguished manufacturers Nakajima of Gifu, Japan. The Japanese company was still trying to market it while the Intel Corporation filed a sensational international lawsuit against Nakajima.

The product would not be marketable until this legal settlement was finished. This international patent dispute could take forever. The CIA agent traced an alternate source of the chip to a University in Japan.

T.I.T or The Tokyo Institute of Technology Science as well as the technology departments of the University of Kyoto and the University of Hiroshima. But it was under strict supervision by the university. There was the highest security, but the CIA agent was able to trace the chip's serial number which was a match to the # JPX008N -UOH-247948 to this computer science department at the University of Hiroshima.

Quickly they did a search of faculty past and present of the computer science department and ran a cross search with Cuban flights. Finally a technician keyed in on the name, "Dr. Hiroaki Nakagawa." A brief biographical sketch of Dr. Nakagawa was immediately requested.

Name
  Dr. Hiroaki Nakagawa
General Information
  Born in 1942 in Fukuyama in the Hiroshima Prefecture of Japan.   Known as father of computer science.

Micheal Kazuhiro Nishitani

Discontinued his research in 1995 and returned to his native Japan.

Education
   B.A. in 1962 from University Hiroshima (Japan)
   Master's and Ph.D. in 1966 from MIT (US)

Areas of Expertise
   Specializes in understanding the language of calculating electromagnetic mathematics.

   Expert in hardware and software.

Research topics led to development of:
   Artificial intelligence used to create memory chips
   Internet
   Computer games (Nintendo)
   Mouse and window operation system
   Anti-virus software
   Digital images (digital camera and digital audio player)
   Neuro-electronic interface system (currently theory)

The agent yelled to his higher commander, "I think we've found our hacker." He motioned for him to come and see this information on Dr. Nakagawa. The CIA commander read the screen. "Oh yes, him. Looks like he could be the source. It says he is one of the fathers of computer science. Do we have any evidence that could link him directly?" The technician researched more information.

He said, "Sir, we don't have any further information on him after he left the Silicon Valley. Our files only indicate that he was a faculty member at The University of Hiroshima."

The commander ordered the technician to access secret Japanese States Department files. They were intercontinental files from the government of Japan. But the technician was unable to gain access to these files. The system refused to let him enter. Because of his Japanese celebrity status, officials made it difficult to charge an international cyber crime against him.

Finally, the commander gave up and ordered an internal investigation. They would have to hire 10 special American professional hackers under contract by CIA to break into these

The Last Revolution

Japanese secret documents. These guys were the best and brightest hackers available, but even then, they would have an extremely difficult time cracking the Japanese supercomputer because they were using Japanese passwords as keys. This supercomputer had been modified by the Fujitsu conglomerate and was a heavy-duty industrial electrical mainframe. It was considered a computer giant, and it had the highest security with the most secure architecture in the world. It was designed and built with the latest Japanese technology with an anti-hacker key in place, a combination of 144 keys constantly changing. It took the CIA nearly a month with the best U.S. government contracted hackers working day and night before they were able to enter the system. Finally they were able to break the key and enter.

In the CIA computer technical room, they dismantled the Japanese secret document. It had taken over a month with so many on the job, and it was finally up on the screen.

The commander looked at it and nearly fell out of his chair as the computer displayed the information. Then he said, "Oh, my God." The computer printed out his photo ID. It went on to display his biographical sketch. The scrolled down until they got the just the information they had been searching for. It read,

"Since he left the Silicone Valley in 1995, he returned to Hiroshima where he became an honorary professor. Then on March 18, 1995, he left Hiroshima for Havana Cuba. He stayed on a cultural exchange visa as a visiting professor of mathematical science for The University of Havana where he conducted seminars for staff. He lived in near Villa Clara, Cuba and married Dania Altamirano Hernandez in October 1996. They had two children born in 1997 and 1998. Then in June 2004, he entered the U.S. port of Boston. He stayed four weeks, then traveled to Hiroshima, Japan. He stayed three months in Japan and then returned to Cuba, where he remains.

The commander was speechless for a while. He looked at his team and said, "We don't have proof, but he's our man. Definitely! He fits the bill and is probably one of the only people in the world capable of this kind of brilliance. Now all we need is some type of evidence." He scratched his head and thought to himself. Now they had all the information on him except the connection between Cuba, Hiroshima and the Nakajima-JPX008 chip.

The commander asked, "How did he get his hands on the NakajimaJPX008? Dr. Nakagawa wasn't in Japan at the time the chip was in news? He was living in Cuba for nearly eight years. The information is old news now. How did he get it?" The commander ordered all of the CIA agents living inside Cuba to work on getting this new information as soon as possible. The Commander had a top-secret briefing with the CIA chief Greek Gates. They discussed whether or not to go ahead with the assassination on Dr. Nakagawa. The chief said, "We could kill him now, but we're going to wait for a better time. For now, I'm going to call it off until further notice."

The chief Gates ordered that a proposed contract on his life be postponed indefinitely. He was considered an international celebrity figure as a renowned scientist. The press and media coverage could hurt them. Besides, they needed to locate him first.

Within a week's time, the CIA agents in Havana found some new information as requested. Dr. Hiroaki Nakagawa was living in the Rancho Veloz area. But, his home in Sierra Morena had been completely secured by an army intelligent unit around the clock. There were boots on the ground. It would be almost impossible to assassinate him in Cuba. And the CIA still had no solid evidence to pin on him. He was their number one suspect, but they still needed proof. The Nakajima-JPX008 chip was still at the University and there was no sign of transport to Cuba. They had to find out how he got it from point A to point B.

The CIA also intercepted all communications in Cuba. They were concerned about Cuba's intentions. They knew that Fidel wanted to annihilate them. Fidel had stated this many times over the years and had even trained terrorists to this aim. Cyberspace crime in the hands of the Cubans could have a detrimental impact on U.S. security. Therefore, the CIA's Chief Commissioner Greek Gate had ordered the assassination of Dr. Hiroaki Nakagawa and this covert operation was to be led by Commander Patrick Davis. The plot was to eliminate a top-notch computer scientist whose genius was a direct threat to U.S. national security.

The Last Revolution

The CIA acquired a top-secret document from Costa Rica reporting that Dr. Hiroaki Nakagawa had purchased four commercial airline tickets on Taca, the Costa Rican airlines. Hiro and his family were flying from Havana to Toronto, then on to Tokyo. This gave the United States a perfect opportunity to assassinate Hiro in US air space while en route to his destination in Japan.

The U.S. Government's Department of Homeland Security had other plans. They only wanted to capture and arrest Hiro while he was flying over US air space. They informed the White House and then the Pentagon that they planned to snatch Hiro by sending a US fighter aloft to force the Taca jet liner to make an emergency landing at a US airport. There, he could be arrested. The United States Navy was ordered to send a squadron led by Brigadier General Russell Wiener, based in Pensacola, Florida. Wiener was ready for the operation and waited at the base with four U.S. the F/A-18 Hornet in preparation for the mission.

Meanwhile, Japanese spy satellites intercepted the plan for arresting Hiro. Japanese intelligence had advanced IGS, or Information Gathering Satellites, developed by Mitsubishi. The Japanese government had funded nearly $2.3 billion in research and development of these controversial eyes in the sky. In 1998, soon after the North Koreans sent a missile, Taepo Dong, over Japanese territory, the Japanese government had purchased a global missile defense system from the United States. The Japanese rapidly developed this and the highly sophisticated global-watch surveillance techniques. This technology was managed by a group of computer scientists.

Therefore, the Japanese Surveillance Agency was able to intercept the CIA's satellite signals. This is when the Japanese discovered the United State's motive to hijack a Japanese scientist while flying over U.S. air space. The government of Japan sent an urgent and top secret message to the Japanese embassy in Washington to be delivered to the President of United States asking him to terminate the mission. To the Japanese, Dr. Hiroaki Nakagawa was a national treasure and a celebrity. The Japanese government threatened to expose the U.S. government's plan to assassinate him by leaking their proof of the plot to the international press. The Japanese government warned that the release of the details would create an international incident, placing the credibility of the United States under fire.

Finally, under pressure, the White House ordered the cancellation of Hiro's assassination and granted him clear passage in U.S. air space. The CIA was also ordered to back off until a later opportunity presented itself.

Meanwhile Santa Clara Cuba, Hiro and General Abelardo González had a heated discussion about the new technology and security measures. Something drastic had to be done to protect the chip from cyber theft. Too many bad people wanted this powerful technology. The consequences could be devastating in the wrong hands.

Hiro knew that the general was a trustworthy man and that he would use the chip for good purposes. But Hiro was terrified that the general would be forced to release the technology to someone lacking in integrity, a sad consequence for technology and for researchers.

This is when Hiro decided to cease his secret research. It was time to move back to Hiroshima, Japan, with his family. He needed to protect his family and himself.

Before he left Cuba, Hiro promised the general that he would develop a new key security device for the Colbana-Nakajima-JPX009 chip. Without the accurate multiple key combinations, the chips would not operate properly. Also, if outside forces tried to manipulate the key combination, it was designed to lock down the entire CPU. Hiro agreed to do it. It took him almost three weeks working day and night on the project.

Hiro solved the problem of securing the chip by planting DNA mark-modified molecule codes inside the chip. This device needed a real human and his/her living tissue fingerprints to verify the key code and begin the program. Both the chip and the monitor needed the DNA molecules, blood type, and body temperature of the person for verification. This was necessary before the chip was operational. He implanted General Abelardo González as the user. He programmed codes matching the general's DNA molecules. The computer chip operated almost like an individual personality. It followed instructions like a human for its specific user. This was security at the highest level - tampering was not a possibility.

The Last Revolution

Only the original individual whose DNA molecules were programmed into the chip was able to access the computer. The general created a "DNA molecule surveillance chip monitoring center" in order to monitor all of the chips. This would eliminate cyber crime totally. This security system would give the chip safe passage for the future of mankind. The risk that this technology could get into the wrong hands was too great. That was impossible. Now, only the general had access to the system. Hiro handed one of the software to the general. This was the operational system he had developed for the new Colbana-Nakajima-JPX009 chips.

The general no longer had to use the archaic Russian system. They had the missing link. When Hiro placed the software into the general's hands, Hiro said, "This is my gift to Cuba. Congratulations! It's now up to you to use this technology for the good of mankind."

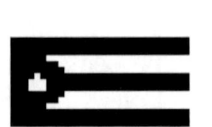

Chapter 66

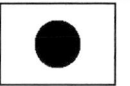

Hiro decided to relocate

with his wife and two daughters and stay for an extended period of time in his native home, Kure-city, in Hiroshima. Although Pedro would miss him, he was very pleased to hear of Hiro's decision to return to Japan. Pedro had been very concerned and uncomfortable with Hiro's involvement with Cuban intelligence. Pedro had always tried to look out for his friend, but now that was no longer possible. Cuban intelligence was way over his head.

Hiro also knew that he had taken risks by cooperating with Cuban intelligence. But since his involvement with the operation covert Spy, he had felt particularly uneasy and concerned for his own safety. Hiro was extremely worried that this might happen to him. He thought about the stories that people had told him about how people suddenly went missing. It had happened many times before, even to important military generals, such as army General Ochoa in 1989.

Commander Camilo Cienfuegos Gorriarán was one of the primary leaders of Fidel's revolution. On October 28, 1959 he mysteriously disappeared, leaving no trace. Several theories exist that instructions were given to eliminate him, but factual proof has ever been uncovered to explain what really happened.

Hiro decided that he must immediately leave the country. The next day he departed Cuba with his family for Japan. The Nakagawa had to leave without saying good-bye to many people, but they knew that one day they would return to Cuba and see their friends and family again. They left Pipo in charge of caring for their home and property.

Pedro drove them to the airport in Havana. He had always been a man of few words and this time was no different. Hiro and Pedro just looked at each other and shook hands. Their friendship transcended words.

As they parted Pedro said, "Take care of yourself, amigo."

Hiro smiled and answered, "Gracias, Pedro. You take care of yourself, too."

The Last Revolution

Dania quickly hugged Pedro and kissed him on the cheek saying, "Gracias Pedro, que te via bien!" She squeezed his hand and turned away from him to keep from crying. She didn't want to make a scene and upset the girls. As they boarded the plane, Hiro looked back to see Pedro waiting to see them board. It was an emotional moment for them all.

Hiro's family boarded the Lacsa DC-9, the Costa Rican Taca airliner. As it took off from Jose Martí. Airport in Havana, Dania and Hiro looked at one another and held hands. No words were necessary. As they took off, all eyes were tearful as they looked out the jet's windows saying good-bye to Cuba.

Their last sight of Cuba was filled with beautiful green palm trees, cattle in the fields and the nearby sugarcane farms. The sights became smaller and smaller as they lifted off into the sky. Finally Cuba disappeared.

Tears fell from Dania's cheeks. When Hiro and the girls saw this, it made them all weep. It was the first time that Dania and girls had ever been on an airplane. It was their first time to ever leave Cuba.

They were nervous in anticipation of what was ahead in Japan. They had only heard stories from Hiro about his home in the mountains. Hiro had prepared them for the intercontinental flight from Havana to Toronto and then on to Tokyo's Narita International Airport. From Tokyo, they would take the Shinkansen bullet train to Hiroshima. It would be a very long journey, but they all felt secure with Hiro's decision, especially Dania. She had been very worried about their safety in Cuba, so knew this was the right move. Besides, Cuba held painful memories for her. She convinced herself that she was ready to see the world and live abroad for awhile.

As Hiro and his family arrived at the Toronto airport, three members of the diplomatic staff from the Japanese Embassy in Ottawa, along with fifteen Royal Canadian secret agents, were waiting at the gate. They were there as security guards who would escort them safely to their next flight. Hiro, Dania and the children were in a daze, but safely boarded their final flight destined for Japan. It was an excruciating day and they still had a sixteen-hour trip ahead of them. They passed the time by sleeping and playing cards. They girls were excited yet pensive.

As they deplaned at Narita International Airport, security was tight. The Tokyo police deployed nearly twenty of its personnel for Hiro's security. No media were allowed due to security concerns. The family was safely escorted to the Shinkansen super bullet train. They were tired but couldn't sleep from the sensory overload. Dania and the girls stared at the people, their clothes, their actions and the funny Japanese language and writing they heard and saw everywhere. It was very different from what they knew in Cuba.

The bullet train was modern, sleek and very fast. The food and drinks were delicious but unusual to them. There were little rice cakes with seaweed and a small portion of savory meat and pickled vegetables. There were vegetables that were cut to look like flowers with pink sprinkles and sesame seeds on top. Each item was dainty and carefully cut. Each item was in its own small compartment in a box lunch. Instead of a fork and knife, two sticks were provided as utensils. There was tea to drink. Hiro said, "Boxed lunches are called *obento*."

Hiro continued, "The sticks are called "*hashi*." I will show you how to use them. This is *ban-cha* tea. Please try it." Dania and the girls were so hungry that they ate every bite. The *hashi* were difficult to control, so they used their fingers instead.

Yumiko said with her nose crinkled up, "Dad, I was really starving. I even ate that seaweed!" He laughed at her.

Hiro said, "You girls are perfect travelers. I am very proud of you." Soon another cart displaying sweet desserts, chocolates and candies appeared. Hiro let the girls pick a treat.

In a little while, Hiro told the girls to look out their windows. They saw a big, beautiful mountain. He announced, "This is Mt. Fuji. It is one of my favorite sites in Japan. It is actually a volcano." The girls were full of questions about volcanoes and Japan.

When they arrived in Hiroshima, the security guards accompanied them to another small local train. This train would take the family to Kure-city. Dania didn't complain once although she looked pale and tired. She was quiet for most of the trip keeping her thoughts to herself. They all looked out the window to see the homes and buildings. It was all so different from anything they had ever seen before. Finally, the journey that felt like it was taking forever ended.

The Last Revolution

At last the family arrived at Hiro's Mother's home where relatives were waiting. Hiro's sisters and their husbands and children were all there. The tiny house was full. Hiro's mother and sisters cried with happiness. They were overcome with joy and happiness. Hiro noticed how old his mother looked. It had been three years since he had last seen them.

They gave Dania, Yumiko, and Masako a warm introduction to Hiroshima. Hiro's mother and sister welcomed the family to their home and were overjoyed to see them. They had prepared many gifts. They gave the girls Japanese dolls carved from wood and painted with beautiful pink and red designs and flowers.

Dania was presented with a colorful kimono and sash. Hiro's Mother gave Dania a hair comb with hand-made silk flowers, pearls, and rhinestones encrusted on it. Dania and the children loved their presents and enjoyed getting to know their new family. Hiro's mother had prepared fish, soup, rice, and tempura vegetables. She made a special pink *mochi* with sweet bean paste inside.

Yumiko whispered to her dad, "I ate the seaweed again. I think I like it." He whispered something back to her. Then Yumiko said out loud, "*Oishi. Oishi. Domo Arigato!*" This meant delicious and thank you. Hiro's mother and sisters smiled and laughed because Yumiko was very cute.

Kure was most famous for being the location where the Yamato, the largest battleship ever, was built. The city was nestled between the Seto Inland Sea and a rugged mountain range. The inland sea was beautiful and looked like a big, expansive lake. It was a peaceful place with Shikoku and Kyushu seen on the distant horizon. There was a river running through the city to the ocean.

Kure had started as a sleepy fishing village in the late 1800's, but the industrial boom had brought shipbuilding to its docks. The town prospered and grew into a thriving port city. Because of its proximity to Hiroshima, this small village quickly became one of the Navy's top training academies and military shipbuilding cities in Japan. Kure-city was nestled under extremely high mountains. The flat land had been utilized for housing and commercial buildings. It was picturesque with scenic mountain views. The city was considered small in size with a population of 200,000. This made it the third largest city in Hiroshima prefecture, yet it had small-town charm and was well-maintained and clean.

The city center had good shopping and nice restaurants. There were beautiful parks and many beaches for tourists to visit. There was also a big library and an excellent school system. For Hiro, Kure was a perfect place to raise his family. He liked that it had retained its small town atmosphere while having all the amenities of any big city.

Kure was composed of many amalgamated villages and towns that grew together over the centuries. Kure was the oldest and original village so it naturally became the centerpiece of the city. The city was about thirty-five minutes southeast of Hiroshima by express trains and buses.

Today, Kure-city was a major international supplier of large cargo ships. However, most industry had relocated to bigger ports. All the heavy industry had moved to Korea and China because labor was cheaper, so few heavy industries remained in operation. The city was well past its peak, and its glory days were over. Progress was long gone, and the city had become quiet. The younger people had left for the big cities so the city was mainly occupied by senior citizens. But, that made it a very safe, easy-going, and secure place to live.

Nevertheless, Dania and the two children thought it was modern and beautiful. Meeting their Japanese family had been a dream comes true, and Kure was everything and more than they had expected. It was a thousand times bigger than either Rancho Veloz or Corralillo.

But, living in Japan was difficult. The family experienced immediate culture shock, and it took many days for Dania and the girls to adjust to Japanese living. The most difficult challenge, of course, was the language. The neighbors next door had a college student teacher living with them. Hiro asked her if she would tutor the entire family in speaking and learning Japanese. She was very sweet and came to their house every evening from 6 to 8:30 for private lessons. Little by little they grew accustomed to the changes.

Every day posed challenges, but everyone was friendly and helpful. Hiro also translated and helped Dania and the children understand the culture. Most of all Hiro and Dania were just happy that their daughters were safe. The girls loved their cousins and were introduced to other children in the

The Last Revolution

neighborhood. Hiro's family was like a unique commodity in this small neighborhood and the neighborhood children loved to play with them. Yumiko and Masako were enrolled in the local elementary school and within six months, they had completely adjusted to life in Japan.

Hiro's girls were able to learn Japanese quickly because of total immersion, and they were popular in school. They also joined many after-school clubs like *Kendo* and calligraphy. They were also asked to assist the English and Spanish clubs.

Yumiko had inherited a photographic memory from Hiro. For her, everything was easy. She already spoke excellent English which she had learned from Hiro, and she quickly learned Japanese. Now she was learning *Kanji* and writing. This was the most difficult part. Yumiko mastered the Japanese language while Masako was still struggling.

Yet, Masako was very pretty and outgoing like mom. She made many friends who helped her, and she loved art. She was a very creative child who liked Japanese cartoons and comic books. She joined an animation and drawing club, and from the beginning, was one of the best in the class.

Hiro began to teach his two daughters mathematics one hour every day. He was strict and taught them the Japanese way. Dania didn't like this method, because it was different from the Cuban way. But her two daughters seemed to love to study with their dad, and they were learning a lot together. He helped them advance their mathematical abilities rapidly, and the girls quickly rose to the top of their class. He taught them how to do mental calculations. Their teachers were impressed that the girls did not need calculators to solve equations.

Chapter 67

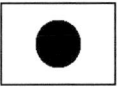

Hiro resumed teaching and consulting with the mathematics and computer science faculties at The University of Hiroshima. He was well-received and enjoyed reconnecting with his old colleagues and friends. Hiro was considered a legend of sorts there and was always treated with the highest respect. In his spare time, Hiro worked and researched the second phase of the implant for the war game implant that he had begun in Cuba. It was still premature, but he worked daily in the department's laboratory. There were many adjustments to be made.

Hiro decided to change the format to something completely different. The original was a Nintendo-based code, but he had a difficult time with it. So he began using his new neuro-electronic interfacing system language format. The general's neurons began to accept the information little by little. Over the next thirty days, Hiro continued to research and to put the final adjustments on his Sonic Cyclone software. He was finally able to manipulate the general's brain successfully. Since the general liked to play video games, Hiro knew he should implant his software into a video game format. Hiro knew the general loved the Japanese Ninja Series by Nintendo Wii.

Hiro began to study Japanese history. He went to the Hiroshima university library and researched the tactics of the Ninja in the fifteenth century. There were the Koga ninja from Shiga prefecture and Iga ninja from the Mie prefecture. The Iga School of Ninjitsu used the art of stealth and was the top school and training house in the feudal era.

There, ninjas learned how to make and use special tools, gadgets, and weapons with great skill to fight and to assassinate their targets. They were disciplined in the martial arts and were powerful warriors. They also had special diets because they had to learn to exist on very little food while in action because they roamed the fields and hid in trees and on rooftops for long periods of time until it was time to strike. Ninjas were pharmacology experts, making herbal remedies and medicines.

The Last Revolution

They used these techniques often to carry out their missions and to heal themselves.

Ninjas often disguised themselves as beggars, Buddhist priests, peddlers, or farmers, and even had night disguises which made them almost invisible. Ninjas had to sharpen their five senses of sight, smell, taste, touch, and sound, and learn to use their sixth sense of inner concentration and spiritual guidance to help them to be successful in their tasks. They turned the impossible into the possible and could eliminate targets secretly and swiftly. They were almost superhuman and fought with amazing force.

When Iga ninjas received orders to assassinate the Koga warlord, they found few opportunities to strike, as he was always guarded by many samurai. The only time the target was alone was when he used the toilet. The Saga ninja hid inside the foul hole called a honey-bucket. When the Koga warlord was taking care of his personal needs, the hidden ninja thrust his sword upward through the victim's rectum to his heart. Failure was not acceptable for ninjas; therefore, they often used unusual tactics to accomplish their missions in the least expected places.

Hiro smiled as he remembered all of this. Unfortunately Hiro wasn't a ninja he was only a scientist, but he could use his mind to find a way to eliminate Fidel. He knew he had to find a way to carry out his plan successfully, and he wasn't going to stop until the deed was done. He worked on formatting this information into his software.

It worked on the general's memory cells, but it was a complicated matter because the general was intelligent. It would be challenging to manipulate such a smart man, as Hiro had to bypass the general's strong will. Hiro needed to weaken the general's mind through outside stress so that he would have an easier time implanting the software. Since he couldn't do that, Hiro had to learn to implant even when the general was relaxed. At first, Hiro thought it would be "a piece of cake" because he had been able to duplicate the general's brain, but he was wrong. This was just the beginning.

Even though Hiro had learned how to implant his war game, new problems arose. He needed to learn how to activate his program from his remote location instantly. Hiro got a flash of genius. He knew how this could be done. The activation signal would have to be down-loaded through his morning correspondence with the general. To do this Hiro had to create a specialized web cam for the general. The web cam had advanced laser beam technology like the monitors at the Hotel Elquea in Cuba.

This way Hiro could manipulate the general through program codes and the laser beams via web cam. Hiro contacted the general and sent the special web cam through international special delivery. The general was excited to receive his new gift and set it up immediately. He couldn't wait to see Hiro daily during their correspondence.

General González and Hiro communicated every morning between 5 and 7. It was a perfect set up. Hiro was able to implant his war game while observing the general. This was all done while the general sat in front of the computer screen and web cam. The general had no idea that Hiro was implanting his war game into the general's memory during their visits.

Sometimes, the general's neurons rejected the software because his neurons were very complex. It was puzzling to Hiro, but he continued daily to implant the software. Throughout this ordeal, he taught the general about the Japanese *Bushido*. It was the ancient way of the warrior encompassing the code and philosophy of the Samurai. This way of life was based on loyalty, honor, self sacrifice, commitment, modesty, a sense of shame, justice, and bravery. The samurai were not interested in material gain and riches. Paramount to them was self respect, honor, and duty.

The samurai became fearless in battle against an enemy. Zen Buddhism heavily influenced *Bushido*. The warriors were taught to go within and became completely Zen during battle. This centered state of being gave them absolute focus. This state of mind helped them to remove thoughts that might interfere with them doing their best and erased their fear. The samurai were composed, quiet, disciplined, and mindful in everyday life.

Bushido required filial piety, absolute faithfulness, and trust. Additionally, the Japanese Shinto religion believed in ancestor worship. The samurai were completely dedicated to the Imperial family, and the emperor was considered to be a living God. The warriors pledged themselves to the Emperor, their daimyo or feudal overlord and to other higher ranking samurai.

The samurai also needed complete self-control, self-sacrifice and a stoic manner to be fully honored. A true

The Last Revolution

warrior had a composed body, mind and spirit which showed no signs of pain or passion. Many Cuban military soldiers had the same Japanese martial spirit existing among them.

The Cuban army had no idea of *Bushido* and was not taught about this ancient code, but in June of 1989, when General Ochoa Sanchez was to be executed, he requested that his executioners not cover his eyes with a blindfold. He was brave through the last seconds of his life. He was without fear of death. In *Bushido*, there was an honorable way to die which was considered a good death. The samurai didn't fear death because they believed in an afterlife and reincarnation.

Japanese *Bushido* also stressed that men who possessed these qualities were as accomplished in the world of the arts as in the world of martial skill and courage. This code was handed down to future generations in the oldest Japanese textbook, written in 712 AD. The code introduced the beauty of death.

Hiro taught these concepts to the general through computer code. The concept of death for honor was difficult to explain.

Seppuku or disembowelment and *hara-kiri* (*cutting* the stomach open with own knife) were considered an honorable way to kill one's self under certain circumstances. Hiro explained that the shame of being captured or dishonoring one's daimyo was reason for committing suicide Called *Jiketsu*. This was a typical example of beauty in death.

The guilty samurai would retain his honor by sacrificing himself and thereby neutralizing his weakness. The *Bushido* code was truly an attitude of proud invincibility and readiness to die for his leader and for his own honor. This martial tradition continues in one form or another even today.

Hiro sent the general information daily about important Japanese history and culture. The general was captivated by the topics. Hiro's program would work better if the general's brain was stressed, so he sent loads of information on Japan and the samurai culture daily. This information required a great deal of reading and study. The general's brain neurons reacted extremely well and received the program with ease. In just a few months, the general understood Japanese philosophy which was quite different from the Cuban way.

Hiro also focused on the samurai's *Bushido* in comparison with the Cuban revolutionary poet and philosopher,

Jose Martí. Martí. was a man of honor and conviction who lived life without fear.

He fled Cuba as a political dissident at the tender age of 17. He openly wrote and spoke out about the injustices of colonial rule by the Spanish in his country. He was formally educated in Spain and lived in Latin America and the U.S. until he was able to return to Cuba to lead the independence movement.

> White rose: poems by Jose Martí.
> *I cultivate a white rose*
> *in July as in January*
> *for the sincere friend*
> *who gives me his hand frankly.*
>
> *And for the cruel person who tears out*
> *the heart with which I live,*
> *I cultivate neither nettles nor thorns*
> *I cultivate a white rose.*

Sadly, he was killed at age 42 during the early part of the war. He gave his life in love and complete dedication to his motherland and his people. The Japanese would consider his passing an honorable death. Martí lived by similar codes as *Bushido,* and he left beautiful poems about liberty, honor, dedication, right action, and morality.

He spoke openly about the dangers of his island nation being controlled by other countries including the United States. He was completely dedicated to the freedom of the Caribbean islands. He believed that this was crucial for the security of Latin America, South America, the Carribean and the balance of power in this area of the world.

Hiro and the general both enjoyed their morning e-mails. They covered interesting subjects, and it was good to keep in contact. Hiro continued to research and study. This project was an extremely difficult task. Hiro began to have intellectual flashbacks from his intensive neurobiological research at Johns Hopkins. These thoughts would come in flashbacks and scattered passages.

Hiro's mind would race and suddenly there would be segment 5 page 22, ". . . necessary force or device and sensory

The Last Revolution

feed back trigger principle device for interface." Or a sentence from page 23, ". . . principal force that indicate with neural control command to trigger." Then he would see page 24, ". . . it helped technology similar to magnetic of digital as in the neurons synchronize much finer cellular solution." His photographic memory came in handy because he could instantly recall the information, but sometimes it came in scattered sentences which were distressing. Hiro was in full research mode and he was not able to relax because of it, but he continued to conduct his research and find as many options as possible.

Every code sent via the Internet to the general was received as a compressed binary code, including the neuro-electronic interfacing system. It was done via a device connecting the screen to the monitor and going directly into the brain's neuron. Hiro could then measure brain activity and program his software.

Hiro's war game consisted of five parts:

1. Bushido
2. The philosophy of Jose Martí
3. The Japanese Tosa dogs
4. Ayu fishing
5. Final target

When the game was completely downloaded to a subject's neurons, that person could recognize the last segment called final target. That phase had a specific individual in mind and if that successfully occurred during the implanting stage, then the game would reprogram itself and be completed within thirty-five days. Then, based on the subject or individual's natural intelligence, he or she would pursue further game play before beginning the first stage.

By Hiro's calculations, the implanting process took up to six months before it would be fully functional. Hiro finally discovered a key factor for activating his game. It was dependent on whether or not the general's true memory in his neurons would cooperate and be flexible and succumb to the game.

Nothing could be done to speed up this process, and it could not be manipulated by outside forces. Once the implantation stage was complete, then there was a period of waiting until the general's neurons reacted positively.

The reprogram activation must be voluntary and combined with the subject's own intelligence. The general was an excellent candidate, and he received the information better than Hiro had anticipated. The progress was sensational with the last two parts finally figured out, Hiro moved on to the final target. Then it was a wait for six months to see if activation of the war game was an entire success. It had been a long road with many challenges, but Hiro was in the home stretch. Hiro was anxious to see the fruit of his labor in action.

On August 6, 2006. Hiro took Dania and the children to *The Peace Park Memorial* in the heart of Hiroshima. It was in remembrance of all those who perished during the atomic bomb attacks on this same day back in 1945. At 8:15 a.m., the same time that the bombs were dropped, the peace bell rang and everyone in Japan stopped for one minute wherever they were and said a prayer for those who had perished and for the abolishment of atomic weapons. Thousands gathered in front of the *Genbaku dome* and the monument to pray for peace on earth.

The dome was all that remained of the original building that had stood in the center of the bomb blast. Yumiko and Masako had been to the memorial once before, but they were still compelled to ask Hiro many questions about what happened. Hiro tried to explain its meaning to them, but the girls still couldn't believe that this atrocity had really happened. So many lives had been lost and the beautiful city had been devastated in just seconds. The children also learned about the events that happened in Nagasaki. They were stunned and saddened. They also saw many people crying on this day which was unusual public sight in Japan.

But today was in honor of the atomic bomb victims and for the families who had suffered losses and hardships. There were many relatives there honoring their lost loved ones. It was an emotional and heartfelt gathering. The mayor of the city gave a speech honoring the memory of those lost.

Hiro's family spent the day walking and seeing the area. Hiro took them to one of his favorite *Okonomiyaki* restaurants for a late lunch. That night, lanterns were lit and floated down the Motoyasugawa River. Some of the victims had run to this very river seeking water as they were dying. It was a beautiful way of remembering those lives that had been lost. Dania, Hiro,

The Last Revolution

and the girls watched the lanterns float down the river. They were silent. They also thought about Cuba that night.

The leaves had turned colors in the beautiful autumn landscape. The Japanese maple trees were gorgeous hues of gold, orange and deep crimson red. It was one of the most colorful and scenic seasons in Japan, and Hiro, Dania and the girls loved to take walks in the local parks. There were special fall festivals called *matsuri*, celebrating the harvest. There were stalls with special foods, sweets, and fun things for the children.

The family enjoyed the festivals because it was a time to celebrate life and have fun. They were enjoying life in Kure city. The family was had assimilated well into the Japanese culture. They got along well with Hiro's family and felt a sense of community with new friends from the school, neighborhood and local area. They loved Japanese food and had ample time learn how to prepare authentic dishes with Sadayo and Reiko. Hiro always provided Dania and the girls with these unique opportunities so they could truly relish the Japanese culture and embrace his homeland. He wanted them to be happy and have an enjoyable cultural experience. He knew that one day they would return to Cuba, but this was their chance to soak up everything they could.

For Dania and the girls, this was their first time to experience a cold winter. They had never seen snow or ice on the streets, and they were not prepared for how cold Japan got in the winter months. It was new and exciting in this Asian winter wonderland. The girls loved playing in the snow and making snowballs and snowmen. Yumiko and Masako enjoyed Japanese living and by this time they spoke fluent Japanese. But Dania was still having a difficult time learning the language. This made it harder on her to adapt to living in Japan. She felt lonely during the winter with Hiro working and the girls at school. Sadayo was kind to her, but the winter months kept them stuck indoors and at home most of the time.

Everything was different from living in Cuba. Dania was treated like an instant celebrity wherever she went because of her dark skin and frizzy hair. She had a likable personality, and the people loved her. She had made many friends. But she felt homesick for Cuba.

When the family had first arrived in Japan, Hiro had taken Dania to his remote mountain village called *Jisheki*. This was Hiro's childhood home. It held a special place in his heart. It was amazing to see that the old Japanese home was still intact. It had been built so very long ago yet it remained sturdy and strong. Behind it were beautiful, steep mountains and a clear mountain stream. This is where Hiro used to fish for the Ayu and swim. It was his sacred spot and naturally beautiful, lush and fresh.

For him, it was the most gorgeous place on earth. Hiro taught Dania how to fish for Ayu. It took her much practice before she was able to hack properly. It was incredibly difficult to master. She had fun and was amused by Hiro's serious approach to fishing. He took her to a calm part of the stream which was like a pool with clear water.

Hiro said, "There is a real art to Ayu fishing. Watch and learn, woman!" As his back was turned, Dania pushed Hiro into the stream. He didn't know what had hit him. She laughed and screamed with delight. Hiro smiled. He put his hand out so she could pull him out of the water. When their hands touched, he pulled Dania right into the water with him. She screamed and laughed. He embraced her and kissed her tenderly. They went skinny dipping in the cool mountain stream. It was romantic and hidden. No one was around and they felt so free only wild snow monkey was watching. Their passion flowed and it was magical.

Afterwards, they stretched out on the bank in the sun. Hiro fished some more and Dania watched her man. It was the most fun they had had in a long time. It was good to be one with nature and away from the politics of the world. Every chance she got in private, she embraced Hiro and expressed her feelings. She was not used to hiding her affection, but it was not customary in Japan to kiss and hug in public. But they found time to steal away many private moments together.

Dania often remembered her mother and Pepe. She missed them so much. She wished they could see this place. She imagined how they would act here in Japan. What would they think of it?

Isabel would hug everyone whether they liked it or not. Dania laughed to think of it. But she always remembered her home in San Rafael near Sierra Morena and Rancho Veloz. Many times she became homesick and tears would come. For the first time, she understood what Hiro must have felt while living in Cuba. She wondered when they would return home. She thought of all the little ordinary things that she used to take for

The Last Revolution

granted. Now, she would do anything to be in Cuba again. Now that she was away, Cuba is the best she appreciated her home and country like she never had before.

Chapter 68

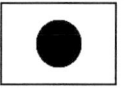

Dania took every opportunity to show Hiro her feelings. Being in Japan wasn't at all easy for her; it was so different here. She often found herself thinking of her mother and Pepe back in Cuba. What would they have thought about Japan if they had the chance to visit? She decided her musings were only normal; after all, she only had Hiro and the two girls here to occupy her. Sometimes, when she allowed her thoughts to stray, Dania became so homesick that her eyes filled with tears. Dania hid her weeping from everyone.

Now Dania understood first hand how truly alien Cuba must have seemed to Hiro, especially in the early years of his stay. The only thing that seemed to lessen his burden was the fact that at that time his emotions had been so frozen that perhaps the impact of culture shock had been softened. Dania, on the other hand, found fleeting thoughts of large family gatherings flashing through her mind, along with whiffs of goat barbecue and images of her mother combing her hair and encouraging her youthful dreams. The little ordinary things were what had made Cuba a place of great peace for her. Dania had never fully appreciated these things until now.

Hiro told Dania that he would only be able to be home for the week end because he was so busy at the university. She left him alone. Although she didn't know exactly what Hiro was working on, she understood the intensity of the work and its importance. She knew not to ask any questions.

Hiro was very busy working at the university. He was only home during the evenings and weekends. Recently, he had become quiet. He looked like he had a lot on his mind and he was always deep in thought. She knew this side of Hiro well and had seen it many times. She knew when he got reclusive and withdrawn that he was working on a big project. She knew it had to do with Cuba and Fidel, so she never asked any questions.

Hiro set up a home computer with Internet access for his family, but Dania never touched it. The computer reminded her

The Last Revolution

of the tragedy back in Sierra Morena. When she saw the computer, she had flashbacks about Isabel and Pepe on that fateful day. For the first several months she put a towel over the entire computer. She couldn't look at it.

But slowly the girls and Hiro helped Dania to overcome her anxiety. Hiro knew she just needed some time. He didn't push Dania and was thoughtful about her feelings. One day when she was ready, she asked him to teach her a little about the computer. He showed her how to operate the PC and how to use the key board. Little by little Dania got the hang of it. She liked accessing information on the Internet. She even found Spanish sites on Cuba.

Dania discovered a whole new world through the Internet that helped her when she felt isolated and home sick. She also helped her daughters access Internet sites that were useful for school reports. Dania learned many things and Hiro was proud of her new-found computer confidence. Dania got the hang of information technology and e-mail. She e-mailed her sister Lillian almost every day. They shared many stories and news across Internet traffic. There was also capability for special digital pictures. Dania was amazed and thought it was incredible that she could receive these pictures. Sometimes she even sent short videos over the net.

However, Hiro warned Dania and children that they should never discuss computer technology or political differences with Lillian because the Cuban government monitored Internet traffic and intercepted messages. The government had a special security watch on Internet traffic. When Dania communicated with Freddie's or General González's wife about what was going on in Cuba, they always said that there was nothing new.

The general sent Hiro a digital format video through the computer. It contained a speech dated January 16, 2006. The video was taken in Havana showing Fidel giving a speech to his fellow countrymen. Fidel began speaking at 5:00 p.m. on a sunny afternoon and didn't finish until it was very dark at 10:00 p.m. Even though Castro was older, he still had much vigor. It was a great speech, and he still had a strong vision for Cuba. His speech touched on many subjects, such as the economy, domestic issues, energy and international relations. Hiro had watched the speeches almost every weekend. Many people liked Fidel's speeches and viewed him as a father figure.

Fidel wanted to maintain the status quota in Cuba. From his viewpoint, this was best for everyone. It was insurance that retained family ties and promoted happiness. It was the best thing for the Cuban people. Castro did not want Cuba to become a country based on capitalism, because it would drastically change in the worst ways. Cuba with capitalism would become just like the rest of Latin America, which would be a sad day for Cubans. They would become selfish and greedy.

Dania could not watch the speeches. They awakened strong memories of her mother and Pepe. It hurt to watch. Most young people in Cuba were ready for a change. Aggressive white Cubans also had the same attitude toward freedom. The issues were complex to analyze. No system was a guarantee of a secure future. All systems had pluses and minuses. The Cuban people would have to decide which system they wanted to live under.

Chapter 69

The CIA had also intercepted Internet traffic proving that Hiro was corresponding with Cuba through secret encoded messages. They could not figure out the content of the communications. The CIA computer techs tried all their tricks but were unable to crack Hiro's secret code. In fact, the CIA computer technicians and professional hackers had never seen anything like this before. After weeks of work, they declared the code unbreakable. The chief said, "This guy's good. We've had our best minds working on cracking this for weeks, and they still can't touch him. His work is twenty years ahead of anything we've seen. We're going to have to enlist more help. Get an MIT or a Caltech computer scientist for us."

The CIA contacted MIT and due to the threat to national security, they assembled a team of scientists to work on cracking Hiro's code. But the team of scientists was not familiar with his technology. They had knowledge of DNA-based systems, but Hiro had created a system and language that operated outside of their scope of knowledge. Hiro also was working with his own hardware that did not exist in the public domain. For now, he was untouchable.

The CIA staff and technicians, as well as the government team of computer scientists, were tapped out and frustrated. They had spent weeks working on this project but still had nothing to show for their efforts. Hiro's device monitored brain activity through the computer screen so that he was able to outwit them by making adjustments in his compressed code.

The MIT scientists concluded it would take a very long time to actually crack through this code Most complicated interface format is MP00X they never have any publicity of any study before they knew some way connect with WAV, MP3, MP4, format MIT scientist conclude it will take very long process to actually crack through compressed code.

Back in Hiroshima Japan, Hiro continued corresponding with the general on a daily basis. The general's brain accepted code easily. Hiro had also implanted information on Eastern history and culture as well as the game strategy. Hiro's computer indicated that an intruder was trying to break in. But his anti-hacker software rejected and located the intruder within milliseconds. Hiro traced the interloper and found that it had originated from the CIA's supercomputer. He said, "Right on time!" And he smiled shaking his head at the screen. Hiro had to wrap up his project soon in case anyone detected his plan.

Hiro decided to finish the project by inviting General González to Japan. This way he could do the final fine adjustments on the general's brain neurons in person. Hiro suggested that the general come for a cultural visit so he could teach him the special technique of Ayu fishing. He also wanted to show him the impeccable form of the fighting Tosa dogs and talk to him about the final target as fine tuning. The general made a request to make a trip to Japan and told Hiro he would make the arrangements as soon as possible.

Meanwhile, Hiro arranged a secret meeting with a group of special CEO's. They were Japan's industrial giants. During their meeting, Hiro swore them to secrecy and mapped out his ideas for a future Cuba redesigned by them. He introduced the ideas of a Cuban rebuilding project for the country's infrastructure and industry. Hiro explained that when Cuba became a democratic and free country, having the inside track in the area of business would reap huge rewards for the Japanese.

Japan's involvement would also help Cuba by quickly catching them up to speed with the rest of the world with tremendous bottom line profits for everyone involved. It was the fast-changing world of politics, and if Japan didn't take the opportunity, someone else would.

Hiro had many secret meetings with the county's top executives. They were all on board and prepared to generate a change in Cuba. Hiro was busy planning the future of Cuba after Communism died with Fidel Castro.

Meanwhile, back in Santa Clara, General González requested permission to make an observation trip to Japan. He met with the Department of the Interior Minister who knew about Dr. Nakagawa and who had an interest in knowing more about technology and heavy industry in Japan. The general convinced the Minister of the Interior to approve his cultural observation trip. His main focus point would be to find out how Cuba could benefit from Japanese technology, modernization, and industrialization. The general was excited when he received

The Last Revolution

the green light for his trip. Fidel and Raúl were impressed with their latest technological acquisition. They recognized the capacity of the hi-tech Colbana-Nakajima-JPX008 chip and computer for their Army intelligence Center in Santa Clara.

They ordered an overhaul of the government's computer systems. The systems were dismantled and replaced by the new interface chip. Fidel and Raúl wanted to be completely integrated with the new Japanese technology. The Cuban military surveillance unit now had the ability to hack into the computer systems of many foreign governments for information. With their new technology, they succeeded on many of their attempts, but they still could not break into the CIA's magnetic supercomputer.

Back in Havana, Fidel and Raúl had central intelligence tapping and intercepting traffic on the general's and Freddie's home computers. Their purpose was to keep track of their own high-ranking officers and the possibility of espionage. They detected the unusual codes received by the general's computer from Japan. Even with the new Colbana- Nakajima chip and computer, the Cubans could not unscramble Hiro's sophisticated binary DNA-based compressed code using the new MP00X 008 format.

When Fidel and Raúl heard that the general had requested the trip to Japan, they said they could not allow him to leave the country because he was under investigation without his knowledge. Therefore, the Minister of the Department of the Interior had to put a hold status on the general's trip to Japan.

This hold threw a wrench into Hiro's plans, making him furious. The general was also annoyed because his requests had never been denied in the past. The general wondered if Fidel was planning to make him disappear like General Ochoa Sanchez had years earlier. Unknown to the general, because of Hiro's programming of his brain neurons, he had an overwhelming desire to visit Japan in person.

During the war in Angola, Cuba had deployed nearly 250,000 troops over a fifteen-year span into Africa. Supreme Division army General Arnaldo Ochoa Sanchez had become famous as a war hero and was credited with winning the war. This made General Sanchez an important figure in the Cuban government, but Fidel grew unsure of the independent minded general who diverted the public's attention with the island's mounting problems.

Sanchez was a war hero and popular with the people. General Sanchez had fulfilled his duty to his country and he was one of the best and brightest minds in the Cuban Army. Fidel was afraid of the general's personal ambition. Fidel wondered if General Sanchez was planning a coup to overthrow the government. Fidel felt threatened.

In 1998, Fidel saw his first opportunity to get rid of General Sanchez. There was widespread corruption in his unit with Colombian drug trafficking and smuggling. Charges by the CIA were sent to the U.S government and a federal prosecutor discovered there was indeed Cuban military involvement. Cuba had to drop trafficking as a result.

Fidel quickly took advantage of the situation for his own interests and arrested General Sanchez without any explanation. Fidel was known to act swiftly to eliminate any obstacles in his path. Fidel always took drastic measures to secure his own position of power. It was the exact same scenario when he was student at The University of Havana when he shot a rival student who had run against him in a school election.

Fidel ordered the execution of General Arnaldo Ochoa Sanchez by firing squad on July 13, 1989. Major Amodo Padron Trujilo and Commando Tony De La Guardia were also among those who faced the firing squad that day.

General Ochoa Sanchez was truly one of Cuba's finest warriors who was brave to the end. He died at the hands of his president and his compatriot. Fidel and General Sanchez had a long history together, but Fidel double-crossed him in the end.

General Sanchez was born in 1930 in Havana. His family farmed in the eastern mountains of Cuba. During the Batista era, he joined the July 26th Movement with Fidel. He eagerly pledged himself to the rebel army in the Sierra Maestro countryside fighting rank Camilo Cienfegos. He anticipated occupations of the Santa Clara in central Cuba with Che Guevara. It was the key battle in the Cuban revolution.

This battle covered nearly four weeks of intense fighting against Batista's government troops. It was the last battle of the Cuban revolutionary war. General Ochoa Sanchez was a brilliant fighter and he developed a superior combat tactic support by Che Guevara and his steady stream of soldiers. General Ochoa

The Last Revolution

Sanchez had distinguished himself from the rest due to his exceptional military tactics. He also took part in the fighting at The Bay of Pigs and the struggle against the bandit campaign during internal rebellions.

Sanchez was highly respected by his soldiers and by government officials. He became the best friend of Fidel's brother, Raúl Castro. Sanchez was made the Chief of Staff of the Cuban Army and took his position as next in line of command behind Raúl Castro Ruz.

Fidel also appointed General Sanchez Commander of the Cuban Expeditionary Forces in Ethiopia. His war strategies using lightning speed were successful against the Somalis. His brain worked like a computer chess game. Sanchez studied in the Frunza Academy in the Soviet Union where he learned to speak fluent Russian. Sanchez also became close to Gorbachev. Fidel was not impressed. At that time, General Abelardo González knew of the military's involvement in Columbian drug trafficking and the illegal exportation of many items from Africa including elephant tusks, diamonds, military supplies and hazardous materials. They had no choice but to look the other way because the Cuban military had huge resources pouring in from the illegal trafficking and the orders to participate in it were coming from the top.

The illegal activities were Fidel and Raúl Castro's idea. General Ochoa Sanchez was simply following orders from his high commander. Raúl used Cuban state-owned companies to direct the drug smuggling to the United States. General Abelardo González was ordered to complete several assignments as a special black market secret agent involving escorting drugs and other items to US waters on Cuban Navy boats. Many times he escaped from actually doing the assignment, but he was always involved with monitoring US satellite surveillance signals.

Sanchez helped with the technical aspects on these illegal assignments. At the time, he was the Major General, and he remembered on several occasions intercepting US surveillance signals in Africa. He suspected that Raúl Castro was directing the entire operation and financing military hardware with the profits. Times were tough financially and the resources of the Cuban armed forces were drained.

General Abelardo González knew very well what happened to his cohort. He knew that General Ochoa Sanchez's execution had taken place while he was serving in Western Angola dealing with Cuban intelligence surveillance. González was in charge of a unit that was working on unscrambling US spy satellite signals locating South African troops and tactics.

General González heard of Sanchez's execution via satellite communication after the fact. He was disheartened by the news because he knew General Ochoa Sanchez to be a fine man and an outstanding leader. He knew Sanchez had been framed, but there was nothing he could have done to save him. General González knew Fidel and what he was capable of, so this came as no surprise. Every Cuban feared Fidel, especially those in power.

Suddenly General González began to sweat and grew afraid of both Fidel and Raúl. They might be suspicious of his close contact with Hiro in Japan. Perhaps he was in more trouble than he thought from the communications. The general knew it was no time to panic. He had to wait it out and hope that he was not a target.

The general knew that Fidel was extremely interested in new industrialization. Japan and Cuba had a good relationship since 1929. After the revolution, Japan continued to co-operate with the government of Cuba by giving humanitarian aid. There was a good cultural exchange throughout this time, and the relationship with Japan's leaders and Fidel was positive.

Fidel visited Japan in 2003 and he enjoyed his trip immensely. Castro talked openly about how much he admired Japanese industrialization. But due to the ongoing problems between United States and Cuba, Japan had taken a back seat and continued to stand by without any major investment in the island nation. The Japanese were waiting for an opportunity to invest in Cuba. They knew that a new phase in the industrialization of Cuba was coming soon.

The general had always been extremely loyal to Fidel and Raúl. He was their golden boy and considered a part of the modern generation of Cuba's future. González had been handpicked as their youngest general because of his superb knowledge of computer technology. He was ambitious and had let his desire to be the Cuban Chief Army General be made known. Several days passed, and the general waited. He was interrogated and his answers lessened their suspicions. González had only formed a friendship with Hiro and their communications were benign. They were only discussing Japan, its history, and its rich culture.

The Cuban officials needed proof and the general asked Hiro to release the security code and open up the contents of their e-mails to government scrutiny. Hiro immediately edited out any parts of their correspondence that the Cuban government might find threatening. Then he sent the e-mails to the army Internet security. They were dated and proved to be harmless. The Cuban government asked that future correspondence remain open instead of encoded.

At this point, Hiro no longer needed to download his game, so he could comply with the request. They were not able to trace Hiro's location, but they could read the content. Hiro released the communications because he knew that if he didn't comply, the general might be imprisoned or worse.

Fidel and Raúl had no further reason to be suspicious of the general's intentions. In fact, the general came out looking interested in opening a new cultural door to Japan through Hiro and his connections. Fidel knew that the relationship with Hiro could be even more fruitful, so it was in their best interest to keep communications open. Since the general and Hiro were already good friends, Fidel allowed the cultural exchange to continue.

Shortly, the general was cleared by the Minister of the Interior and finally permitted to take his trip to Japan. General González was given approval for a journey of three weeks and was tasked to find out how Cuba could improve its educational curriculum in the areas of technology and industrialization. The general was accompanied by six Cuban federal secret agents led by the chief of secret agents, Ishmael Velázquez from Santa Clara.

Meanwhile, back at the CIA global surveillance office in Maryland, they still had not cracked any of the messages originating from Hiroshima, Japan, to the Cuban general. Hiro had used a highly complex system with a compressed secret code. He had the communications encrypted with information pertaining to Japanese literature, history and *Bushido*. It was Hiro's little game for those who tried to enter. He allowed them to think they had a chance of breaking this code if they knew enough about Japan. But in reality it had nothing to do with Japanese history or culture at all.

Micheal Kazuhiro Nishitani

It was a second generation of neuro-micro electronic interfacing system and no one had the technology that Hiro had created. No one could break his code and he knew it. But Hiro kept the techies busy trying. From an educational standpoint, it was a huge puzzle for the CIA technicians to solve. The government's team of MIT scientists and CIA technicians worked for months, but they were just like dogs chasing their tails. The CIA commander was growing more impatient and ordered the team to work faster, creating a pressure-cooker atmosphere at the CIA headquarters. Jobs were on the line.

Chapter 70

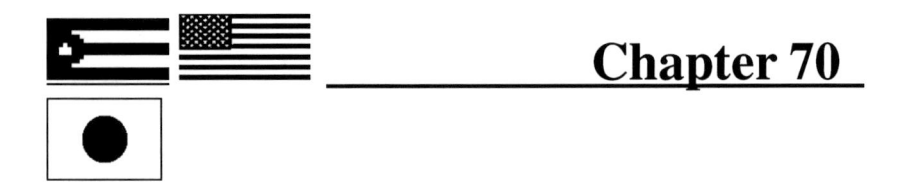

Back in San Rafael Cuba life had not changed much. Everything was the same except that Hiro's and Dania's old home was crumbling in the tropical climate. Pipo, Lillian, and Liana were living at the home and taking care of Hiro's vegetable garden and property. Pipo was keeping watch on Dania's sisters while she was away. They were growing up fast and were already young women. Before Dania had left town, she had given strict orders to Pipo that her sisters could not date any boys until she returned home. Dania had promised her mother to select good men as potential husbands for them so that her sisters would be well taken care of and happy.

Without Dania there, the two sisters had a very difficult time. Pipo tried his best to divert the girls' attention from the young suitors who congregated by inviting many relatives to keep the girls occupied. Pipo also had to scare the young men away who stopped by to talk to the girls. Pipo had to work very hard to shelter the girls and the girls remained innocent and secluded.

Pedro also missed Hiro very much. He remembered the fishing trips and driving around town together. He also remembered how Hiro had helped him with his carpentry work and their talks. Pipo knew that Hiro would return one day, but he wasn't sure when. He hoped that everything was working out for his friend in Japan. He hoped he would see Hiro and his family soon.

Sometimes Pedro ran into Freddie in Santa Clara. Freddie was very busy, but his wife Yorina showed Madeline the e-mails and pictures from Japan. She loved seeing pictures from a different culture. Freddie did not have a color printer or digital photo processor so they could not print copies of the photos. It was nice to see their friend's faces and to know how they were doing. Sometimes Pedro and his wife would stop by to visit Pipo's and Dania's sisters at Hiro's old home. Lillian shared Dania's e-mails and photos. Sometimes Dania would send short digital videos of places in Hiroshima and Kure-city. They enjoyed seeing the videos, but the pictures made them miss their friends.

Meanwhile, Freddie was busy building tourist hotels. There were many financial problems. Since the United States continued to tighten the rope around Fidel's neck using the trade embargo as the noose, finances were at an all time low.

The U.S. blocked relatives from visiting Cuba. The United States had changed their policy on visitation to once every three years. Before, visits had been allowed once a year and many American-Cubans returned home to visit loved ones and to spend U.S. dollars.

The American-Cubans support of their families back in Cuba was drastically reduced. It was very damaging to the Cuban economy because Cuba was dependent on the US dollars sent by Cuban relatives in United States. It had been the biggest revenue for the Cuban government. With the lack of resources, the government had problems importing food for the Cuban people. The people had to scramble to do the best they could in these hard times.

Many changes had occurred in the world since the Cuban revolution when Fidel had first taken control of the country. The world was now a fast-paced global community and many neighboring countries were no longer friendly. The politics of the Middle East had taken center stage and international politics focused on this hot bed of conflict and controversy. But the Cubans continued to isolate themselves.

The Cuban government had changed its monetary system and no longer operated on US currency circulating on the streets because of U.S. retaliation. The U.S. was tightening sanctions against Cuba and discontent was prevalent. Times were tough, and a wave of resentment and restlessness could be felt throughout the island.

The Cuban government changed its system so that only the Euro and other currency could equal the value of the Cuban Convertible tourist peso. The US dollar lost nearly twenty percent of its value when the system changed. To improve the economy, the government invented extra sources of revenue; but

The Last Revolution

even with this effort, the decline continued and tourist money got tighter.

Fidel could feel the pressure and he looked forward to visiting Venezuela. This was possibly his next ideal sanctuary and a new frontier to partner with Cuba. He frequently visited Venezuela to extend his ideology. Fidel had planned meticulously. He knew how to play the political card game very well.

The Venezuelan president, Hugo Chavez, had led a successful social-democratic government since he became president. This would not be a bad idea for Cuba at this stage in its political life. Hiro wondered how the transition would work. Hugo Chavez had changed Latin American history and its social-economic-system. Chavez was attempting to copy cat Fidel's model of leadership while using the democratic system to help the poor majority of Latin and South America. If Chavez could avoid becoming Communist, he could succeed. He knew in concept that the social-democratic government could work very smoothly in Latin America.

In contrast, Fidel's Cuba had very few friends and had been isolated for many years. This helped Fidel's regime survive, but in exchange, Fidel had missed the opportunity to become the big time leader of Central and South America. This enforced isolation of the Cuban people had caused them to suffer from the lack of connection to the world community.

But Fidel was known as the comeback kid who knew when it was time for something new. Castro remained a brilliant politician despite the deteriorating social and economic problems. Domestically, many Cuban people still considered him a grandfather figure.

Hiro had liked Fidel, too, until the problems that resulted in Pepe's and Isabel's deaths had occurred. Now Hiro despised the government that had murdered Dania's parents. Hiro thought, "How could they take such blessed and innocent lives? Isabel and Pepe were good people who loved their country and who loved Fidel."

Their deaths were still painful and fresh in his thoughts. Their deaths were unforgivable, and Hiro and Dania continued to be tormented by sad memories of the past. But for them, Cuba would always remain a beautiful and soulful place where the people were the true treasure Hiro and Dania knew that unless

Castro deposed Cuba would remain the same forever because Cuba was unique and there was no other place like it. The culture that had developed was special. The people were friendly and fun. It was a peaceful and slow-paced island. Cuba was the ideal country for happiness, if you were not interested in politics or business. The people were very content despite being poor. Compared to the standards of many other countries, though, Cuba was considered extremely poor But Cubans were intelligent, and the poverty in Cuba far exceeded the poverty in the United States.

At least in Cuba, nobody was left behind. They had something better than money. Actually, for nearly fifty years, Cubans had enjoyed a wonderful and easy-going lifestyle. Many did not realize what they had. But Hiro could.

Cubans had a much better life than the life he had in Japan when he was young. Life in Japan following WWII was much worse than life in Cuba today, but no one in Japan ever complained about their situation. Cubans always complained. Hiro wondered, "Why is that?" Perhaps, it was because of the background, heritage and culture of the Spanish conquest and colonialism. It was just a different culture from that of Japan.

Hiro never understood Cuban people. If they had wanted to change the government within twelve months, they could have. And they could get rid of Fidel if they really wanted to. But Cubans never did such things. They only had enough ambition to escape and jump into the water and head toward Miami. When they arrived in Miami and began to live in safety, they started demonstrating and protesting about Cuba. Hiro never understood why they did not do that in Havana? Demonstration in Miami was not accomplishing anything. He felt they were simply afraid and ran rather than stay and work for change within Cuba.

Hiro felt that any Japanese person would give their life for Japan and never try to escape from Japan to another country. The Japanese stayed in Japan to achieve goals for their country. The Cuban culture was a very different culture from that of Japan.

Freddie always said that Cubans were very passive. They just waited for someone to give them everything. They were losers if they only made noise from Miami. That would not change anything in Cuba, but just added to the frustration and

The Last Revolution

agony. Cubans worked very little and Cuba probably had the lowest productivity rate in the world. In contrast, most American-Cubans worked very hard to achieve their goals and to become financially secure in the United States. Why not in Cuba? Money must be the difference or is Cuban culture? There could be no other explanation. When one had money, there was no time to enjoy it. If people had plenty of time but no money, they were not happy. The Cuban people had chosen their destiny in 1958.

This choice was now a disaster but why not correct this mistake? No one in Cuba did anything but talk. The majority of Cubans liked Fidel's system and Hiro never heard a Cuban speak against Fidel. Basically, the difference was that Cubans who remained in Cuba just become Fidel's pets. Fidel was the only winner in Cuba.

If everyone had stayed in Cuba would it be different today? Hiro felt that would be not the case because Cuban people were very selfish. They did not understand sacrifice. Maybe this mentality developed because it was an immigrant society, unlike Japan. He now understood how the Taino and Arawak Indians must have felt. He could not imagine the sacrifices that had taken place in the early 1500s. Maybe Cuba had been cursed by the indigenous people who had been tortured, who had suffered, and who had disappeared nearly five hundred years ago. If the Cuban people believed in God, then they must pay for their sins. Hiro felt spiritual when he was surrounded by nature as he was in the Cuban country side. He felt a divine presence there.

Before Castro took over Cuba, seventy percent of the population consisted of peasants who were treated as slaves. One out of five babies died before the age of three. Mothers did not have milk or any kind of medicine. Less than twenty percent of the people were considered middle class. Ten percent of the population controlled Cuba and enjoyed wealth. In Havana, many rich housewives went to Miami for one day shopping trips. The rich lived lavish and jet set-style lives. Havana was considered the Las Vegas of the Caribbean, and it had been a decadent city with many tourists.

Corruption and bribery had been passed down through the generations originating with the Spanish. The Batista era was the worst because of interference by American big money.

When Fidel started the uprising, it was called the "peasant revolution". He had right idea and many poor people joined the revolution because they felt this new leader was their savior. Fidel had promised to share the wealth with the poor. Fidel's vision had designs no one will be left behind, no one will be rich or poor. Everything is divided equal among Cuban people. He fulfills his promise. That reason, Castro confiscated property and businesses from wealthy land owners.

In the meantime, the U.S. continued to pressure and squeeze Cuba, causing a financial famine. Fidel could not survive without financial support at that time. The only available help came from Communist USSR. At the peak of the cold war, Castro had visited Moscow and made the decision to join the ranks of Communism. There he announced officially that Cuba would now be a Communist-Socialist government.

Then he nationalized all the huge U.S. industries which controlled most Cuban resources and industry. Within three years, almost eighty percent of Cubans in business, professional and medical occupations had escaped to the U.S. and other destinations in Latin America.

In the meantime, the U.S. continued to pressure and squeeze Cuba, causing a financial famine. Fidel could not survive without financial support at that time. The only available help came from Communist USSR. At the peak of the cold war, Castro had visited Moscow and made the decision to join the ranks of Communism. There he announced officially that Cuba would now be a Communist-Socialist government. Then he nationalized all the huge U.S. industries which controlled most Cuban resources and industry.

Between 1958 to 1968, almost ninety percent of the upper and middle class Cubans abandoned Cuba for the U.S. and other Latin American countries.

Fidel's choice of the Communist regime turned out to be the best tool for him to use to control the people. It was a brilliant new take on Communism—Cuban style. Hiro had always admired Fidel's vision and his intelligence. Most poor Cubans had gotten what they were looking for, and they were glad to help Fidel eliminate all opposition. Castro didn't need machine guns for control. Weapons were never seen in public. Castro had built a superior system and continued to cleanse the country of dissidents.

The Last Revolution

Then the USSR disintegrated, diminishing financial aid to Cuba. After many sleepless nights, Fidel decided to open restricted tourism all over the island to remedy the deficit. Tourists could not mingle freely with the Cuban public and vice versa. If anyone disobeyed, they were charged with a crime. Only government employees could participate in the tourist business. To the average Cuban everything was off limits.

Fidel was a master card player and he always won. He was also a very energetic man with much charisma. He was known to give vigorous marathon speeches, never reading from a cue card. When he spoke, Fidel was so passionate and convincing that everyone gave him respect. Castro could easily begin a speech at 5 p.m. and continue until 10 p.m. It was no surprise that even at eighty years of age; he continued to be impressive and still believed in his dream. Hiro too admired Fidel so much. Life in Cuba after the revolution was a treasure. It was a time of peace and plenty. Still many complained and wanted to be "rescued."

By this time, in Tokyo,
Japanese Federal Secret agents were informed by the US government that Hiro might be involved in international computer crime. His computer at the University of Hiroshima was confiscated by look like Japanese undercover agents with two American-Japanese senior officers from Seattle undercover CIA agents.

The Prime Minister in Japan secretly sent personal messages to the President of the United States about Hiro's status. He explained that it was an isolated incident and asked the US to back off as it was a personal matter. The President of the United States intervened and told the head of the CIA not to execute Hiro as first planned. The President told them that Dr. Nakagawa was under his personal protection. The CIA chief had no other choice but to dismantle this operation. One young female agent, Laura Murphy, was placed in charge on stand by status in the US Embassy in Tokyo.

Hiro had been helping to increase technology education in Japan. Throughout his life, he had made extravagant lifetime commitments including large monetary donations to universities for mathematics, computer science, and engineering research. He also had given much personal time lecturing at universities and helping staff as a visiting professor. Many high-ranking Japanese government officials were his friends because of his achievement and gifts to the Japanese community.

Chapter 71

Few months later Back in Havana

The central intelligence's high-tech surveillance unit was working to recode the general's Internet correspondence. They were searching specifically for the artificial differential equalization compressed e-mails that had originated in Hiroshima and then been sent to Santa Clara. The team worked overtime, and they grew tense because they were having a very difficult time decoding the compressed coded e-mails. The chief of Intelligence and of the high-tech division requested that the Cuban government operation be suspended because they lacked information and had only limited technology to break this highly complicated compressed code. He reported to Fidel that most of the content contained educational theory and that no ulterior motive had been found.

Since the accident involving the infected monkey that had escaped from the Santa Clara Army research laboratory, General González and Hiro had become very close friends and had a meeting of the minds, so to speak. They both shared a common interest in the technical aspect of mathematics and computer science and enjoyed meeting to discuss these topics. As a result of their friendship, Cuba had obtained the new computer chip with the capability of hacking into the software of many countries via the Internet at almost no cost to Fidel.

Fidel had some idea about Hiro's presence in Cuba, but he was always suspicious of any foreigner. He had met Hiro once on a personal level about seven years ago through Freddie Diaz, Chief Deputy Minister of the Interior in Santa Clara's federal office within the University of Matanzs. The chance meeting had occurred when Fidel had gone to observe the construction of a new tourist site in North Central Cuba. At the time, Hiro had been giving a lecture seminar at the university.

Fidel remembered Hiro as a distinguished, intelligent individual. He thought this Japanese gentleman might have some information from the Far East that could benefit Cuba, especially in the areas of computer science and technology.

For the Cuban intelligence office, Hiro was a "new figure" and there was not much information in his file other than the mention that he was a well-respected professor of mathematical science. The file mentioned that Hiro was a genius in mathematics and highly regarded at the international level in mathematical strategy. Hiro was one of the few people who understood the language of numerical and electro-magnetic arithmetic.

The file also stated that he was a gentle and quiet man from Hiroshima, Japan, with no criminal history. It noted that while in Cuba, he had hijacked a satellite signal for his own personal use and had been jailed for the offense for seven days. However, all charges were dropped. The Japanese Embassy's information department verified that Dr. Nakagawa had no criminal history in Japan's federal police file. Dr. Nakagawa currently lived in Kure City near Hiroshima with his Cuban wife and two daughters. Cuban intelligence concluded for Fidel that Dr. Hiroaki Nakagawa was a "very gifted but harmless man from the Far East".

Since Hiro did not appear to be a threat, the Cuban intelligence staff was directed by a high-ranking Cuban officer to approve General González's observation trip to Japan. It would begin on June 20, 2007, and would include three weeks of official observation of various Japanese heavy industry installations, manufacturing companies, and high-tech conferences. The general would attend many technical seminars on information technology and a special high-tech computer exhibit. He was also allowed six days of personal time to explore Japan on his own. He requested an unofficial visit with Dr. Nakagawa at the University of Hiroshima. Since they were friends, the government granted this request. The Cuban intelligence office ceased all further investigation of General Abelardo González. His personal file was now closed, and his official trip was approved and finally accepted by Fidel himself.

The Cuban government requested that six federal secret agents accompany the general for security. Leading the team of agents was Freddie Diaz, the Deputy Chief of the Interior from Santa Clara's federal office. Freddie was chosen by Fidel himself because of his extensive background in Japanese culture and

The Last Revolution

language. Also, since Freddie spoke Japanese fluently, he would also serve as the general's official interrupter. As team leader, Freddie had full responsibility for all official trips to Japan and had to do much preparation for this journey. Freddie was excited about seeing Hiro again. It was a dream trip which mixed business with pleasure.

At the Cuban Embassy in Japan, a small Japanese woman by the name of Reiko Nagata was asked to be the personal translator for the general and his team. She was an official interpreter for the embassy, the chief assistant to the Ambassador, and fluent in many languages. She was also a likable and friendly woman and was asked to tour with the team extensively. Hector Ortiz, the Cuban Ambassador also spoke fluent Japanese, but he would not be available to accompany the team throughout the entire trip. Mrs. Nagata would fill in during his absences.

The staff at the Cuban embassy scrambled to coordinate this official visit from the Cuban Army General. They accommodated the general by giving him and his team office space on the third floor as well as living quarters. It was the first time this embassy had ever received such high ranking military officers on the premises. When Freddie had been in Japan many years earlier, he had stayed in the same location, but at that time the embassy was only a small house converted for commercial use. Since then, it had been remodeled into a modern five story building. The third floor of the embassy served as living quarters for the staff. The whole floor was decorated in a simple but elegant style.

Because Tokyo was extremely expensive, the Cubans could not afford the overhead for a larger embassy. The embassies of many smaller countries had been relocated to the outskirts of Tokyo for this reason. But since the Cubans and Japanese had a great relationship and a long history dating back to 1898 when the first Japanese immigrant came to the Cuban islands, the Japanese gave Cuba a desirable central location which had not changed in all these years. The address was 4-chome, Higashi-azabu Minato-ku. The Cuban Embassy was located in Higashi- azabu, Tokyo, and it had a long history at this location.

In Hiroshima, Hiro had been very busy organizing the trip for his visitors from Cuba. He was excited to be seeing his old friends. Hiro gathered together all the information they had requested and also informed many of his high ranking Japanese government friends and various industry executives of their visit. He set up many private meetings.

Hiro was willing to go to this trouble because he might need some serious help from his Cuban friends one day. All of his friends promised to stand by the three major Japanese conglomerates. These Japanese "Giants" offered many "observation field trips" and sent the general and his team invitations for special banquets. Hiro also contacted a dozen well known Japanese companies, and they promised to meet with the Cuban team. He even arranged to have them wined and dined. Hiro even arranged their transportation and accommodations. The expenses for the entire trip would be paid for by these corporations.

Hiro also contacted the Japanese Defense and Army through his government friends. They declined a visit and inspection of any kind. Hiro's government contact also mentioned that the US military had instructed them not to allow a military inspection by General González, and his entourage for security reasons. It was very unusual for a high-ranking Cuban Army general to visit another country for educational purposes. The CIA chief was suspicious and informed his people in Japan to keep a look out on the Cuban envoy and watch their every movement. He thought they might have a trick up their sleeves.

The US Embassy in Tokyo received a document indicating that the CIA's Central office in Langley, Virginia, had just broken the code for accessing Cuban intelligence. The Japanese Embassy in Havana also sent various immigration documents and official paper work.

The CIA file indicated the general's interested in technology and computer science in particular. It seemed to make sense that a trip to Japan to observe technology-based corporations for educational purposes would be beneficial to the Cubans. And it was not a personal, but an official visit to Japan. But in past years, when the Cuban military sent envoys overseas, they were always connected with a war mission or military aim. This was the first time Cuba had permitted such high ranking Cuban military general to visit Japan to learn about their technology and heavy industry. The US intelligence staff suspected that Cuba must be desperate for business and ways to

The Last Revolution

boost in their weak economy, especially if they sent their youngest and most computer savvy general.

The CIA report indicated that General González would also visit automobile and electrical corporations. And a special request to visit Nintendo Ltd. Japanese companies was granted. Nintendo officials were pleased to give a tour of their facilities and to allow the entourage to observe their factories and plants in Kyoto. The Cuban request was to see the technical and engineering aspects of the factories first and foremost.

At the CIA's office in the US embassy in Tokyo, agent Laura Murphy was informed directly from CIA headquarters in Langley of a new plan. Special unit CIA surveillance commando Patrick Davies ordered a special watch on the Cuban envoy. Ms. Murphy was to assemble a team to spy on the Cubans and to keep a log of their activities 24/7. They were looking for any suspicious activities.

Ms. Murphy had to scramble, but was quickly able to assign several Japanese undercover agents to the mission. She also sent one agent to Hiroshima and another to Kure City. She wanted watchers in those locations to keep their eyes on Dr. Hiroaki Nakagawa. They were on standby until General Abelardo González, arrived. She received orders only to observe the envoy and Dr. Nakagawa; there was to be no physical contact of any kind. This was due to an earlier agreement between the US and Japanese governments. Every act must be understood and agreed upon by both the President of the US and the Japanese Prime Minister.

The Japanese federal secret agent, Tokubetsu Keishi-cho, deployed 250 agents to monitor this mission in cooperation with the regular police unit. The staff was large because the government of Japan did not want any international incidents. Agent Laura Murphy presented her briefing on the assignment to the Japanese undercover agents with two American-Japanese senior officers from Seattle. There was no place for Caucasians on this assignment for obvious reasons. Everything had to look normal.

After much preparation, the details were finally in place. Agent Murphy got an urgent message from "Keishi-cho." He asked her to come to his office at The Japanese Federal Investigation Bureau for an immediate briefing on a special assignment. She ordered a taxi and headed to the bureau with two senior male agents.

The top man at the bureau was Koji Aki. He was a short but well-built man. He looked sturdy and serious and commanded everyone's full attention as he entered the briefing room. As Ms. Murphy walked in, Chief Aki stopped and motioned to some agents standing near the door. Four Japanese agents approached the Americans and handcuffed them. Chief Aki told the Americans, "You are under arrest for carrying unauthorized firearms."

Agent Murphy responded, "We are working in cooperation with your government. We carry firearms for our own protection because our assignment is very dangerous, and we must be prepared."

Chief Aki answered, "You must obey our laws while you are in Japan. You are only a private US citizen in our country. Your professional status has nothing to do with us. We do not officially recognize your position here. You are our counterpart and we wish to work with you, but no firearms are allowed." He spoke rapidly in stern Japanese. The four guards took the American's firearms and uncuffed them. Then the chief said, "Now, please take a seat."

The Japanese government had very strict orders to disarm all undercover American agents. Besides, they had had a secret tip reporting that the Americans were hiding three assassins believed to be part of the Cuban-American anti-Castro movement from Miami. The assassins were rumored to be hiding in Tokyo waiting for a chance to do a "hit" on the general. This information had come straight from the Cuban Interest Section in Washington D.C. to the Cuban Embassy in Japan.

"We take this threat very seriously," Chief Aki explained to agent Murphy.

Ms. Murphy said "I promise that all American undercover operations will be halted. We would like to offer technical assistance from our headquarters." The Japanese government had informed the CIA Global watch in Langley Virginia, about further cooperation regarding intruders from their Cuban-American files.

The Americans had agreed to three items: to assist the Japanese, to give them all information in the file, and to allow agent Murphy to be act as an observer with the Japanese Federal

The Last Revolution

Secret Service. She would also act as an official Japanese agent under these terms. Chief Aki accepted the agreement and terms. Ms. Murphy was now to be part of the Japanese team as an unarmed member.

All other undercover American agents were officially recalled from Hiroshima and assigned to the Tokyo office where they were to look for the Cuban-American insurgents. The American agents would be assisted by the Japanese government and were ordered to go to the surrounding prefectures and work along side the Tokyo Police Department. Chief Aki asked the US intelligence officers to avoid interaction with General Abelardo González, and his entourage.

Nearly 16,000 agents and Japanese police were on the hunt for the assassins from Miami, and they were caught within weeks. All three of the Cuban-American rebels were captured quickly. They were fish out of water because o their lack of Japanese language skills. This lack had made maneuvering inside Japan very difficult for them. The insurgents were extradited to the US for their crimes. Chief Aki was pleased with the way the mission was handled.

Back in Cuba in the Ville Clara province,

General González and his wife Marisa decided to hold a party to celebrate the approval of the trip to Japan. They had organized a barbecue cook out at The Hotel El Roca in Sagua la Grande for a select group of Hiro's friends and family members. Freddie was among those invited, but he was unable to attend because he was in Havana on official business. Freddie's wife Lourdes came to the party and told the group that her husband was not able to attend and was not due back until later the next day. Freddie had an important briefing with Fidel about the upcoming Japanese trip.

Pedro, Madeline, and their daughter Wendy drove up from Rancho Veloz to take part in the cookout. The guests were laden with items for the general to deliver to Hiro's family. Dania's sisters, Ileana and Liana, came and brought many letters from relatives and gifts of *caramelos de azucar hechos en casa*-homemade sugar candies. They also brought *dulces de guayaba hechos en casa*-homemade guava candy bars for Dania. They were Dania's favorite. For Hiro, they brought several pounds of home-grown coffee beans from their property.

They were special coffee beans that Dania's grandmother had planted when she was a little girl. Now those beans had grown into enormous coffee plants. There were nearly fifty of them in her garden.

There was nothing quite as good as fresh mountain grown coffee. And this was extra special coffee because it was grown in the familiar sweet home in San Rafael between Rancho Veloz and Sierra Morena. Pedro made a mahogany pencil holder for Hiro's desk. He had made it curved in the shape map of Rancho Veloz so Hiro would remember his family and friends there.

Everyone enjoyed this weekend, and it was a very peaceful gathering on the outskirts of the Sagua la Grande. Previously, Freddie had rented out this entire hotel for this weekend's event. Too bad Freddie was unable to attend himself. Everyone missed him.

The General loved the magnificent 380 degree panoramic from the hotel. The views were breathtaking. They represented Cuba at its finest.

Even though it was especially on this summer weekend, the nights were made comfortable by breezes from the Caribbean Sea. The night sky was gorgeous, and the distant view revealed a billion shining stars in the sky. It was the most beautiful evening in the universe.

In Hiroshima, Hiro had a very busy schedule. It had been almost five weeks since he finally received word of the 'go-ahead' decision regarding General González's trip to Japan. Hiro had sent many E-mails throughout the day and communicated with various organizations and industrial giants. He worked tirelessly to plan and map out all the meetings and educational technical briefings for the general.

Hiro knew that the general was there to learn as much as possible about various Japanese industries, especially the electronic and technology sectors. Hiro received confirmations from the Japanese corporation heads. They were eager for these meetings and even arranged elaborate luncheons and banquets. They were honored to host the general and Hiro. Hiro had quite a reputation and status due to his achievements.

Hiro wanted his Cuban friend to have the best possible trip to Japan. Hiro knew that he could gain access to the top level executives for the general, and he knew it would be the most

The Last Revolution

exciting trip of the general's entire life. Hiro wished that the general could feel what it was like to live in a free society. Perhaps one day it could be this way in Cuba. Hiro never openly discussed politics while living in Cuba, even with his close friend Freddie. In Cuba, people kept their political opinions secret.

In addition to the field trips to industrial sites, Hiro was informed by Cuban Ambassador Pedro Monzon that the general had requested to see a Tosa-dog fighting match. The general had also requested to go on a special fishing trip to Hiroshima alone with Hiro.

The Cuban Minister of the Interior allowed the fishing trip but rejected the general's request to go alone. He ordered that the general be accompanied by several Cuban security personnel. He instructed the guards that Hiro and the general were never to be left alone. The general would be under their protection at all times. The general was a very important figure within the Cuban government. He was also very popular among the Cuban people because he was the youngest Cuban general and was known as 'the high-tech' general.

In communications with the general, Hiro requested privacy for the last six days of his Japanese trip. Hiro need this time for the final stage of downloading his software game. This stage used ancient Japanese culture to input the war game. With the completion of this download, the final target would be revealed. Hiro had been waiting patiently for this moment. It all came down to perfect timing and precise techniques for the final fine tuning of his computer war game. The general's pre-existing memories blended with the war game's segments to influence the general's decision-making.

Hiro had been monitoring the general's brain activity through a neuroelectronic interfacing system using circuit sensor laser beams through the internet connection. This included a DNA molecule recognition device while at the same time measuring the general's brain activity as confirmation. Everything was working satisfactorily, and Hiro's project was almost completed.

Hiro had developed, researched, and tested the brain's various neurons and the volatile storm activity. Hiro was still a long way from turning his research into reality. Hiro knew that he could do it and tried to stay focused and calm. He believed in his idea and knew that his brainstorm had reached the maximum level. This made him feel very confident.

Hiro felt like a hunter whose final kill lurked just around the corner. Hiro had never mentioned his research to anyone, including his wife. But Dania knew that Hiro was working on something big. A good wife knew and understood her husband. And she quietly observed her husband's habits and movements. She dared not interfere or even ask; she only suspected that it was a plot to overthrow Castro and revenge her parents' deaths. She tried not to dwell on her suspicions.

The plan was already in motion and out of her control. Dania also did not want to let her mind run wild with too many ideas and thoughts because she might become afraid that something bad would happen to Hiro or her family. She had already lost too much. When these thoughts arose, Dania would take a deep breath and let them go. Dania tried to focus on the positive. She knew that her husband was no ordinary man. Dania trusted that what he was doing would be for the good of everyone. She knew her husband's heart.

Dania never bothered Hiro or asked too many questions. She did observe him with he wasn't looking. She saw that he was absorbed and removed from the present day to day activities. They had been in Japan for almost two years, and Hiro had often lived like a ghost in their home.

When Hiro became like this, something big was underfoot. She understood what going through Hiro's mind. Dania knew that something good was coming to Cuba. Hiro had mentioned the notion of a 'free and democratic' Cuba. She knew that when the time was right, he would tell her everything. For now, she just had to remain trusting and supportive.

Dania spent most of her time focused on the children and their lives in Japan. Dania remained busy and involved with her daughters' education and activities, including Japanese language lessons. Dania was very personable and after all this time in Japan, she began to make special friendships. Her life in Hiroshima was a very fruitful one. There were months of suffering and severe homesickness over that first two years, but she had finally moved into a joyous and contented stage.

But now, many good things were happening in her life. She took up sewing and began taking regular lessons from Hiro's mother. She had made Dania and the girls many clothes by hand,

The Last Revolution

and Dania loved them. She couldn't wait to learn this skill so each day she sat with Hiro's mother on the floor in her bedroom. They worked quietly together at a small square Japanese table next to the window.

Dania soon learned how to construct clothes for her daughters. She was proud because Hiro's mother new all the tricks for making the garments look beautiful and professionally made. Sewing had become one of her favorite hobbies. Dania found many other fun activities to partake in every week. There were no dull moments in her life as she prepared for the arrival of the Cuban entourage.

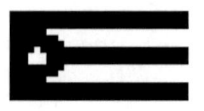

Chapter 72

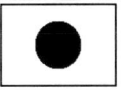

On June 20, 2007, at 3:30 p.m., an official Cuban Air liner from Cubaña touched down at Tokyo's Narita Airport. It was a Tupoel Tu-154 jet made by the Russians. The flight list included General Abelardo González, Freddie Diaz, the Deputy Minister Cuba's Department of the Interior; and a group of Cuban delegates. Among them were many university-level economic professors and development scholars. The Japanese Chief of the Department of Foreign Affairs, along with several top government high-ranking officials, stood waiting to greet and welcome the special envoy to Japan.

Representatives from the Japanese and international media scurried to the landing area to get good photos for their news reports. This was a newsworthy event because it was an extraordinary occasion. Never before had the government of Cuba sent an envoy of this sort to study and learn from the Japanese. The trip focused on an exchange of ideas between Cuba and Japan on economic and cultural issues. The Japanese media were excited to get their first look at Cuba's highest ranking military general and ministers. They had never seen them before today.

Absent from the spectacle were Japanese military personnel. However, many Japanese federal secret agents were assigned to monitor security. Among them were two CIA agents who had been sent to observe the arrival activities.

The general stepped off of the plane followed by Freddie Diaz and the rest of the group. After an official greeting, the group was led to a special limousine for transport to the Cuban Embassy. The entourage was accompanied by a security detail from the Tokyo Police Department. The visitors were taken directly to the Cuban Embassy in Minato-ku, the heart of downtown Tokyo. Everyone who saw the convoy coming down the street wondered who was riding in the limousine. People were peering out of their car windows to see what all the commotion was about. The general and his group were delighted

The Last Revolution

to see the interesting architecture and the densely populated modern high rise buildings. They were surprised to see how clean the streets and buildings were kept. There were also many unregulated electrical power lines. They ran in all directions. It was very different from Cuba.

At the Cuban Embassy, government employees were waiting to greet their special guests. They shook their hands and bowed. The Japanese custom was unusual to the Cuban eye. They were used to a firm handshake and a hug. The embassy staff rolled out the red carpet for the delegation. The general and his men were proud to receive this big welcome.

The official welcome was followed by a luxurious evening reception with many foods, drinks, and musical entertainment. The Cuban ambassador, Pedro Monzen, and his staff had been very busy for the past month preparing for their visitors. They had ordered special food for them and had delicious Cuban cuisine prepared by their best chefs. There were even Cuban beverages for the group. The ambassador wanted them to feel at home while they were visiting. He had tried to think ahead and take care of every detail. For most of the members of the delegation, it was their first trip to Japan.

Freddie was the only exception. He had lived in Japan many years ago, but he had not been back in a very long time. Freddie was eagerly awaiting the opportunity to return to this beloved country. Freddie had once been familiar with parts of Tokyo, but so much had changed over the years that he hardly recognized it. The city had developed at an extremely high rate, and there were many new modern facilities and many more high rise buildings than he remembered. There was even a new, above ground freeway. The other members of the group were astounded by the infrastructures and modernization. They almost could not believe what they were seeing.

Although, the city had changed, the culture itself was very much the same. Hiro had been invited for the ceremony at the Cuban Embassy, but he had declined the invitation. He wanted to greet the group when they arrived in Kyoto, Hiroshima in western Japan.

Hiro was still working on details for the event and the final schedule for the group's educational and cultural study. He was excited about the banquet with twenty CEOs from Japan's biggest industrial and technological conglomerates. He had organized not only a reception and banquet but also a panel of important speakers to discuss many topics. It was going to be a grand gathering, and Hiro knew his Cuban friends would be pleased.

Without involving politics, Hiro also arranged several mini-seminars with a dozen professors from University of Hiroshima. They would lecture on topics ranging from international economic development and the latest trends in science and mathematics to cutting edge computer science and technology. The lectures were to be held on the University of Hiroshima campus. University students were also able to attend, and the event was promoted as the 'Hiroshima Summit'. Dania was invited to accompany Hiro for this first time ever event.

As a Cuban citizen married to Hiro, Dania was very proud and excited. She hoped the team would take back as much information as possible and that what they learned would be used to promote a fruitful and successful economic recovery for Cuba. If used appropriately, the information could improve Cuba's poor economy and remedy Cuba's lack of technology.

Dania knew Hiro wanted the general and the team to see the future and what could be accomplished. Japan could be the catalyst to reinvigorate Cuba and to assist the poor majority. She was especially proud of her husband. Dania knew this was all possible because he had set the trip in motion. Hiro had gone to a lot of trouble calling upon his friends in high places for these favors. She knew her husband was a powerful and highly respected man in Japan based on the people who were stepping up to participate at his request.

Meanwhile, back in Havana, Fidel had his security detail monitoring every minute of the event. Freddie had been instructed as chief coordinator of this delegation to send intelligence reports every evening through the Cuban Embassy. He promptly reported the day's activities via the embassy's computer communications unit. Fidel and Raúl reviewed the reports with much satisfaction.

General Abelardo González and his delegation were overwhelmed by all the fanfare. They were not used to it, but it was exciting to be in Japan and to participate in this unique opportunity for a cultural exchange. The Japanese people were

The Last Revolution

kind and gracious to their guests. They were excellent hosts, and everything was taken care of with much attention to detail.

The food at the reception banquet was exquisite. There were many gourmet dishes with beautiful presentations. It was interesting to see how the Japanese prepared Cuban dishes. They did it with style and flair, and there was course after course followed by the most delicious desserts imaginable. All attendees all had a good time talking and eating. Cuban rum flowed and everyone relaxed and felt more at home by the minute. As the evening grew late, the delegation was escorted to their rooms upstairs in the embassy to rest after the enormous meal.

The accommodations were quite small but modern and very clean. They were contemporary Japanese accommodations with two small Japanese beds per room, a small cabinet for each person's clothing, and a Japanese style table next to the window for meals and work. There was a small bathroom and also a balcony which over-looked the city.

A multitude of bright lights could be seen from the balcony and windows. To the Cubans this was fantastic because they were not used to seeing so many lights burning all night long. They were fascinated with all the artistic neon lights and flashing signs with Japanese characters. They felt like they were on a different planet and a very colorful one at that. In Havana and Santa Clara, they did not have such lights because the country was concerned about conserving energy. The nights were dark in Cuba.

The visitors were assigned two men per room. Even Freddie and the general had to be roommates on this trip. There was also a large shared break room with a smoking lounge, coffee and snack station, and a computer and media room. Their offices were located down the hall on the same floor. Below on the first floor were the official embassy headquarters which were off limits to the delegation and were accessed only by selected embassy personnel and government officials. The embassy was small but very efficient and comfortable. The delegation spent their first night in Japan in comfort.

The Cubans spent a wonderful week touring the city's sights and industries including automobile plants, such as Honda and Toyota. Because of his interest in the Tokugawa Shogunate, General González had requested that the delegation visit *"Nikko,"* the resting place of one of Japan's most influential historical personalities. The mausoleum was a monument to Tokugawa Shogunate and Minamoto Yoritomo, Toyotomi Hideyoshi. It was a lavishly decorated shrine consisting of temples in beautiful natural surroundings the temples contained countless carved wooden statues. One of the most famous carvings was that of a cat who was believed to roam the grounds at night. General González paused for a moment of silence in front of Ieyasu tomb as a tribute to great warrior.

Many of the companies invited the group to elaborate dinners, receptions, and Tokyo's night life in *Roppongi*. For the general, Freddie, and the other Cuban delegates, they had never seen such a crowed place. There seemed to be millions of people walking around in this area. It was a Friday night, and the entire area was lit up like a firecracker. There were hundreds of neon lights and paper lanterns lighting up the area. Every inch of the district seemed to pulsate and glow.

There were countless restaurants, bars, discos, *karaoke* bars, and clubs everywhere they turned in the *Roppongi*. The visitors were also introduced to the infamous *pachinko* parlors. The Cubans tried their hand at this mixture of a ping pong and slot machine game. They didn't really understand the game, but they had a good laugh. The parlors were loud and smoky and decorated with bright colors. Freddie explained that they were really legalized gambling parlors for the masses. They were packed and obviously extremely popular with both men and women. As they walked with their corporate hosts, the entourage saw many places to drink, eat, and party along the long winding streets of Roppongi.

It was an incredible sight. The men were escorted to a popular jazz club. They were shown to an elegant room in the back of the famous night club. The corporation had arranged for this expensive private room just for their group. There were about twenty men there from both the Cuban delegation and the corporation. The general and Freddie were among them and were quite impressed with the club and the music. Soon, several beautiful Japanese hostesses entered and began talking to the men. The women explained that their corporate hosts had hired them to entertain the group.

It was a lavish evening of drinking and celebrating. The women poured the men's drinks and laughed and made witty conversation. They also offered to dance with the men—nothing

The Last Revolution

more risqué than that—these women were not prostitutes. The general was careful not to overindulge because he knew he had to be fresh in the morning for more sightseeing and meetings.

The general looked around and saw all of the very serious Japanese businessmen getting very drunk. It was interesting to see the CEOs of corporations getting inebriated to the point of not being able to stand up any longer. The general saw this cultural difference right away, but Freddie explained everything to him. In Cuba, men learned to hold their liquor and knew when to stop drinking. Here in Japan, it was customary for businessman to get drunk and act silly. This was one of the only times foolish behavior was acceptable. It was a common way for men to let their guard down and to relax and fraternize with their employees and co-workers without crossing the line. Many in the group stayed at the club until almost one in the morning.

The next day the group was taken sightseeing after their morning meetings at the famous *Meiji shrine*, the treasure museum, and *Yoyoji Park*. The general was awestruck by the beauty of the shrine and took time to stroll around the serene gardens and enjoy the splendor of the park. The Omotesando around the shrine was a famous cosmopolitan street lined with cafes, stores, and souvenir shops.

The men walked around Tokyo taking in the sights. Everything was new and unusual to them. There were so many differences that they felt they were in a different world. Even though they were high Cuban officials, they still had not experienced much outside of their own country. The Cuban delegation could not believe the prices. A cup of coffee cost nearly $10 in Tokyo, and a taxi cab ride cost a small fortune. There were many curious and funny things, too. The Cubans had never seen beer sold in vending machines. They all thought this was a great idea.

When the group went out on the town, the corporations paid for everything. The Cubans were grateful because prices were astronomical by their standards. The visitors were treated like kings on this trip; every evening there was a lavish affair. The trip to Tokyo was a success, and the time passed all too quickly for the Cubans. They were enjoying their visit and remained very busy participating in all of the events.

The general was very interested in the automobile industry, the high tech communications, and technology corporations. They were fascinating to him, and he spent as much time as possible meeting and touring the facilities. He remained longer at the tours and meetings than other members of the group, and Freddie always stayed behind with him translating the many questions and discussions for the general. The Japanese CEOs recognized that the general was a highly-motivated and intelligent man who was interested in knowing as much as possible about Japanese industrialization.

The CEOs found the general to be refreshing and sincere, and they tried their best to accommodate all of his concerns and questions. The meetings were intense but fruitful. Everyday was full of tours, meetings, and receptions. There was excitement in the air, and each day ended on a positive note. All of the people involved were exhausted but satisfied. Soon the Cubans loved Japanese beer even more than their favorite Cuban brand, Hatuey. The Cubans stayed up late drinking Japanese beers like *Kirin Iciban, Sapporo,* and *Asahi.* The cold beers were a treat at the end of each work day.

Back at CIA headquarters in Langley, Virginia, Chief Gates had just been informed by Commander Patrick Davis that the Cuban envoy was showing a tremendous interest in the high tech industry.

One of the reports indicated that a special seminar would be held in Hiroshima. It was being organized by Dr. Hiroaki Nakagawa. He had organized all of Japan's high tech experts to speak and lecture at this special technology summit for the general and the Cuban delegation. The report also indicated that the CIA would not be able to maneuver freely at this event. They had been restricted by their Japanese counterpart and were going to have a very difficult time conducting an investigation while this event was taking place.

The Japanese federal secret agents were seriously worried by the CIA's aggressive approach to surveillance. Chief Aki finally ordered the CIA to cease their undercover activities in Japan until the Cuban group returned home. Aki felt that this would be in the best interests of General González, and Dr. Nakagawa. The order to protect these two men came from the highest authority.

Japanese intelligence did not have confidence in their US counterparts. The Japanese had been alerted to the CIA's intention to eliminate the general and Hiro because both men would be the architects of Cuban cyber space surveillance technology and, as such, a threat to national security for the US.

At CIA headquarters, Chief Gates was frustrated and dissatisfied with these orders. He suggested to his commander that they approach the Director about swiftly putting their operation back into place. But Gates was informed that the White House had vetoed this notion and that they must cease and desist. There would be no negotiations with the government of Japan so there was no other option but to shut down the entire operation.

The CIA was only allowed to hijack and unscramble communications between Havana and Japan. They were also able to trace the computer traffic activity between Hiro and the general. The CIA chief sent a message to special agent Laura Murphy to remain on standby.

He also ordered additional personnel to be assigned to the code breaking unit. More man power was needed because the team had not yet broken the code. This was a big puzzle for the whole CIA team. They were very suspicious about communications between Cuba and Japan. They needed an answer. They had the best and brightest team assembled for this decoding task, and they still couldn't touch it. The chief was very inpatient and irritable as a result. Tensions were running high at the CIA offices.

The first portion of the Cuban delegations trip was an enormous success. There were no politics involved and only straight talk with professional economists, corporation executives, industry think tanks, academic scientists, and those in charge of leading Japan in the technology race. A tremendous amount of admiration emerged between the representatives of the two cultures. The participants left each day on a high from all the information and new ideas. They were learning so much, and they were very motivated about the new ideas.

Cuba was a nation desperately in need of restructuring. What the Japanese were teaching them was invaluable and gave them a glimpse into the future of Cuba. The members of the Cuban delegation felt as if Cuba had been left in the past. They exchanged many different scenarios for the future of culture, education, and industrialization in Cuba.

However, their Caribbean island nation was vastly different from its Pacific counterpart. They concluded by identifying the many obstacles that Cuba must first over come for a successful future. The summit participants agreed that a key to success for Cuba was the different cultures occupying the island.

The Japanese scholars gave their professional suggestions and a summary to the Cuban delegates. The scholars were uninterested in the political game taking place between Communism and capitalism. However, many of the Japanese industry heads were willing to help in any way possible.

The General was amazed that many of the Japanese heavy industries were actually made up many smaller "mom and pop" companies. They all worked together to become the finest conglomerate corporations in the world. He began to think that Cuba could adopt the same system. The possibility for this type of industry could function in Cuba if the obstacle of Cuban isolationism could be overcome. The "how" had yet to be figured out.

The United States continued to dictate Cuba's destiny, yet the Cuban government simply ignored US policy toward their country. They listened but did not take it seriously. Fidel used blockade for Cuba as a political bargaining tool. No other country was interested in helping Cuba because of the possibility of potential retaliation by the US. While the Cuban people continued to be isolated and suffering, Fidel continued to thrive The US thought the hardships caused by the sanctions of the blockade would force the Cubans to rise up against Fidel. But, in fact, the opposite was happening because Fidel used the blockade as the reason for the hardship and declining Cuban economy to promote his popularity and hatred toward the US.

This Japanese economic and educational summit made the general ponder and personally reassess many points about the Cuban political climate and its chances for real change. Everyday he found himself thinking and imagining how life would be different in Cuba if only certain changes were made.

Although, he had just left home only a few weeks ago, he had begun to develop a bad taste in his mouth. He also began to debate with himself about the social-Communist system and market economy. This trip was sparking his personal reawakening and an examination of his own beliefs. The general was pleasantly delighted and almost giddy as his mind was flooded with thoughts and ideas about how to overcome see the possibility for changes in Cuba within his own life time. For himself, it was an irritating feeling, like small piece of food wedged between his teeth. The general couldn't stop thinking about home sweet home.

Hiro had the correct target and the perfect plan for the general from day one. Hiro was the architect of the Cuban economic summit in Japan. The topics at the summit had been planned to stimulate the general's thought processes.

Since Hiro had been a faculty member at the University of Havana and was married to a Cuban citizen, he had special status at the Cuban Embassy. The Ambassador knew of his many his achievements as a mathematician and computer mathematic expert. Hiro was considered to be a brilliant professor and legend that was well-regarded. He had a good reputation, and it was well known that Hiro loved the Cuban people.

Nevertheless, without Hiro, the Cuban exchange with Japan would not have been possible. He had the connections and the resources and influence to make it happen. Hiro was able to coordinate the details in a relatively short time, and he knew that these corporate giants had enormous resources at their disposal. No other person could have planned such a large scale and elite gathering for the Cuban delegation. Hiro was the right person to bring it all together at the right time and at the right moment. The event was a huge success.

Finally, the group arrived in Hiroshima for the "high tech" summit involving major Japanese thinkers and players in the field. The original plan had been to have a small number of scientists participating; however, now twenty-nine universities were sending their best minds to the summit. It had become a high profile event consisting of open discussions and key speakers presenting new theories and inventions. They were there to speak about the latest in the world of technology and to present the most up-to-date information in the field.

Hiro was especially excited about this portion of the Cuban exchange because it dealt with his area of expertise. He was a friend or acquaintance of the scientists who were participating in the summit. Every year in Japan, the technology crowd met informally and exchanged new ideas, but it had never been this well-organized. Everyone knew one another at this level, and they were eager to participate when approached by Hiro. Many of the high tech corporations had donated resources for the event and to the participating universities. General González, Freddie, and the twenty-one professors and analysts from various universities throughout Cuba that had been studying technology were very excited to be attending this amazing event. They were eager for changes for their country. It was very difficult to get current information and news in Cuba so these scientists had a hunger for new ideas and technology forecasts. Suddenly in Japan, the Cubans, including the general, were inspired and buzzing with new ideas. This unique summit was a once in a lifetime opportunity.

As a result of Hiro's latest project, the Hiroshima Summit would become an annual event where scientists would discuss new research and theories that would lead Japan to possess the most highly developed technology in the world. Many other countries wanted to join this important event, but attendance was limited to Japanese university level science professors. Only Hiro's influence had allowed the Cubans to take part this year.

Hiro was already a legend in Japan, and he continued to teach, lecture, research, and give donations to various universities in Japan. Now, as the organizer and head of this major event, he enjoyed even more respect.

After the welcome, there were lectures on the latest in human-computer interfaces (vision, speech, and robotics), mobile applications (wireless and batteries), and progress in the classics of processing, storage, and networking. What only a few years ago had seemed like science fiction was now a reality in many cases.

The Japanese had developed many new innovations; this forum showcased them. Of special interest was a presentation of the ten most successful technology-based products expected to be developed by the year 2030. These included innovations in energy sources, such as the Quantum Digital Battery that would power whole cities for months; 4-D Digital Super Definition Television with super imaging and special 4-D effects; and human genome tracking, which could possibly eradicate certain cancers and the track progression of disease at a rapid rate.

There were interactive wireless pocket computers that would fax, phone, access the Internet, have television and radio, and store massive volumes of information. There were educational games and simulations that would help even the most computer illiterate student to improve, and computerized hybrid fuel vehicles. It was all about trends and the wave of the future. The general and the Cuban delegation were floored at the presentations. The Japanese also explained the future of DNA-based computer technology.

The summit was a four day extravaganza of presentations on the various innovations and technical aspects of these cutting edge devices. There were also various discussions and lectures on the future of technology. It was all mind-blowing for the Cubans. Every evening they attended special dinners in Hiroshima at big hotels and revisited the day's topics and ideas. These dinners gave them the opportunity to meet and speak personally with many of the Japanese professors from various universities.

Over dinner the invigorating discussions continued, and new ideas were exchanged. The Cuban scientists were in technology heaven; they had never dreamed they would have an opportunity to acquire such incredible information.

Chapter 73

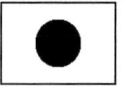

When the group from Cuba had

first arrived at the Hiroshima train station just days ago via the super express train from Kyoto, they found Hiro and Dania waiting for them. They had been sitting inside the waiting area at the station for quite a long time for their Cuban friends and guests to arrive. It had been two long years since Hiro and Dania had departed Cuba, and they missed the Cuban connection.

This connection was especially missed by Dania; she was still homesick from time to time and was impatient for their arrival. It would be almost like old times. The pair wondered if their old friends had changed much, and they were eager for news from back home. Soon the shrill sound of the Shinkansen train approached the tunnels. They stood up to greet the train.

As soon as Dania saw Freddie and the general debark, she showered them with big hugs and kisses on their cheeks. She couldn't stop herself as tears streamed from her eyes. She was crying for Cuba. The general and Freddie greeted her with loud Spanish in the quiet station. Hiro was all smiles, and he was touched by his wife's happiness. He also hugged Freddie and the general and shook their hands.

There were other Japanese people waiting for the group to arrive as well as local media who were waiting to capture a glimpse of the Cuban delegation on film. The Japanese were not used to seeing public displays of affection, especially from one of their own. They filmed Hiro as he hugged and laughed with his friends. The Cubans were loud and laughed openly in public which caused a small ruckus in the station. Hiro could have cared less about the media and was just happy to finally be standing with his old friends once more. This was quite an event at the Hiroshima train station.

The business men and students looked on as they headed off on their daily commute. For Hiro and Dania it was a heart felt reunion with two old friends. It was a beautiful scene as the media captured this special moment on camera.

The Last Revolution

As he had in Tokyo, Hiro used his political connections to make special arrangements with the various corporations in Hiroshima to share expenses for the Cuban delegation's visit to Hiroshima.

Many of the Cuban's stayed at The Royal Rihga Hotel. The accommodations were paid by some of the by the biggest corporations in Hiroshima like Mazda and Mitsubishi, Hitachi and Nakajima. The Royal Hotel was located in Hiroshima's central district which offered a stunning view of the Seto Inland Sea. The Cubans thought the hotel and view were magnificent, and they were excited to hear that they were staying nearby the famous Hiroshima Castle, The Peace Park Memorial, and the famous Itsukushima Shrine the visitors were also told not to miss the beautiful nature gardens. There were many places for sight seeing in the area, and they had many days to enjoy the city. But it had been a long day for them so they called it a night following dinner in the hotel's restaurant.

Everyday during their visit to Hiroshima, the general, Freddie, Hiro and Dania made time to sit together and chat like old times. There was much news from home, and they enjoyed recalling fond memories of the past. They also discussed current events and other topics of interest.

It was as if the two years since they had seen each other had evaporated. Dania loved being able to speak freely in Spanish again. It was something that she had taken for granted until her move to Japan. It was a pleasure for her to talk to other Cubans. When speaking in Japanese, Dania was restricted and had to think hard before she spoke. She often felt embarrassed at her poor Japanese so she kept quiet. It had been a long time since she had spoken to other Cubans. She still dreamed in Spanish and listened to Cuban salsa music.

At first her Spanish had a funny accent, but within a few minutes she had quickly adjusted. Soon Dania could not stop talking and smiling and laughing. Hiro was happy to see Dania like this again. It had been a long time.

Hiro was also eager to hear what Pedro was up to. Pedro was Hiro's closest friend in Cuba. Without him, he probably never would have met either Freddie or the general. Actually, it was because of Pedro that Hiro had met Dania. Pedro was like a brother to Hiro, and he had missed his dear friend.

The general and Freddie had seen Pedro about a week before they left for Havana. The general said, "Pedro was outside the Hotel El Roca attending a party with Madeline. We had a good talk and ate some wonderful barbecue at the cook out. Pedro is doing well, and things haven't changed too much."

Freddie added, "Pedro has been busy with his wood working. We have had Pedro and Madeline over for dinner at out house many times. He is a nice guy and so dependable. If I ever need anything, Pedro always offers to help me."

Hiro shook his head in agreement and said, "Yes that is true. Pedro is a very good man. Please tell him hello and that I am think about him often. I have many good memories of Pedro. I miss him lot." Dania also missed Pedro very much and told Freddie that she had many gifts to take back to Pedro and his family. Freddie said he would take them to Pedro when he returned to Cuba.

Dania quizzed Freddie, "How about my house. Have you seen my cousin?"

Freddie said, "Oh yes. I stop by periodically when I am on the way to Corralillo. The last time I was there was only three weeks ago. I am happy to report that everything is just like it was when you left it. Pipo is doing a good job, and he has a big vegetable garden. I saw many vegetables growing. He looks a like he knows something about gardening. He mast had green thumb?"

Dania smiled, "Oh yeas definite, did you see my dogs?"

Freddie shook his head, "Yes! Your dogs are mean! Your dogs were barking like crazy. He scared the shit out of me!" Everybody laughed.

Hiro started with several questions, "Tell me more about Pedro. How are Pedro's daughter and wife? You know his father and mother?"

Freddie said, "Pedro is very busy, and he still transports people to and from Havana. Lately, he has been very busy with his carpentry business. Pedro seems to work all the time leaving no time to enjoy life like when you were there. Pedro told me he misses you guys a lot, and he always mentions to me that his family is very well. But on a sad note, his grandmother who lived right next door passed away several months after you left Cuba. She was 98 so she had a good long life. Now his cousin and his wife have moved into her home. Do you remember them?"

The Last Revolution

Hiro scratched his head, "Yes, I remember Nancy and Craig. They have a son named Jorge and a daughter named Judi."

Freddie nodded, "Well, they are living next door now."

Hiro remembered Pedro's grandmother. She was very picky and complained every time Pedro parked his car near the house. She did not like him to parking so close to the house. Pedro always complained that he wanted to have a garage for just that reason. This talk of Pedro made Hiro really miss his old friend.

The conversation grew quiet as the friends enjoyed beers and tasty Japanese appetizers. There were so many different types to choose from. The general loved them all and thought that they were the best he'd ever eaten. He loved the seafood and sauces. Everyone enjoyed drinking and chatting. They used this time to get as much information about Cuba as possible.

They stayed up until almost midnight every night. The Japanese beer and sake flowed, and they had such a great time together talking up a storm. Inside the hotel was off limits to the Japanese and international media. Only Cuban TV and Cuban newspapers were allowed to be there. But the general's security had taken care of getting rid of them for now. The media were ordered to leave the general and his private party alone.

The general was watched and closely guarded by several Cuban secret agents. They were good and had their eyes on him every minute. Hiro had often observed this and thought they were similar to those small fish that live off the shark. The shark and the fish need each other to survive. The general had been used to living like this for many years so it didn't bother him anymore. With the exception of his army security guards, he had only brought two staff members along with him. He ordered them to work officially for eight hours a day. Evenings they were off duty. This way the general had time for a personal life and time alone. The general was usually with Freddie and Ishmael Velázquez, the Chief of Cuban Secret Intelligence. He also spent time with Oswardo Ramon, the Brigade General of Cuban Army Intelligence.

Food and drink were not the only things that the Cubans enjoyed. The technology conference was very successful and the presentations from the Japanese high tech industries were impressive to say the least. Many topics were covered in a short time. The Cuban delegation was both fascinated and overwhelmed. After four days of intensive lectures and discussions, it was time for the summit to come to an end. It was a complete success and everyone involved was highly satisfied with the results. They toasted Hiro and the many guests that had made this summit possible at a grand banquet at The University of Hiroshima on the last night.

The Japanese loved to celebrate. Hiro thanked all those who had volunteered their time and donated resources to make this event possible. Hiro was a humble man, but he made a good speech. He also thanked the Cuban delegation for their contributions and spoke briefly about his love of Cuba. The next morning, most of the Cuban delegates returned to Kyoto and Tokyo.

Meanwhile, Hiro had planned something unique for certain members of the delegation along with the CEOs of the industrial giants. The general and Chief Ishmael Velázquez had a special agreement with Freddie who agreed that Hiro's special plans would remain completely confidential. They wanted no official report to go to the Cuban central government or to Fidel Castro. Freddie understood and loyally agreed.

Hiro had arranged the best "Geisha girls" to entertain the six field secret agents and the two Army intelligent agents along with Brigade General Oswardo Ramon of the Army Intelligence. Those guys were responsible for keeping an eye on eight individuals as assigned by the general's order.

Soon many beautiful young Japanese Geisha girls arrived. They were highly trained and professional female entertainers. They performed traditional Japanese music and dance routines at banquets. The Geisha maintained purely above board relationships with the men. They wore extravagant kimonos and were beautifully made up and wore special hairdos. While they were not prostitutes, they were often mistaken for them by foreigners.

The younger women trainees were called maiko, and they were apprenticed to the more experienced geishas. They studied traditional Japanese music, songs, culture, dance, etiquette, world politics, history, and even business. They had to be able to hold a conversation with their male guests.

Sometimes a geisha had a patron with whom she was involved emotionally, economically, and sexually; however, these types of relationships were up to the geisha. A geisha was

The Last Revolution

considered a high class woman of good morals. They were consummate entertainers.

In the early era of the geisha, when most patrons were warlords or shoguns, Geisha Girls wore warrior-like outfits including large hats and decorative swords. During the Tokugawa period, many artistic changes in the areas of dancing and entertaining occurred in this ancient art form. Geisha wore their traditional hair in a bun or a uniform style with a single comb and two pins. At times they wore ornate hair combs which were usually given as gifts from their patrons. They also wore traditional elegant kimonos and beautiful white make-up that made them appear to be porcelain dolls. The makeup was a trademark of the geisha and distinguished them from other women. They were probably the only profession in Japan in which women were consistently ranked above the men in the profession. This is because geishas were allowed to work until a fairly old age. There was a very high value placed on the preservation of this traditional art form. It was a highly respected and valued part of Japanese tradition.

Chapter 74

While the security team for the general was off duty and being entertained by geisha, the general and Hiro had complete privacy. The Cuban chief secret agent, Ishmael Velázquez, understood the need for personal freedom so they decided to go to Tosa City for the famous "dog Sumo wrestling." This entertainment would be followed by a fishing trip to the remote mountain village of Jinseki.

It was going to be a week of pure personal freedom and relaxation for the first time in many years for the general and Ishmael Velázquez. To ensure that their time would be away from prying eyes, Velázquez manipulated the reports dispatched to Havana. He knew he had to keep things short and to the point so as not to give any indication that something was up. He knew just what to report and as long as he could keep everyone happy, he would receive plenty of extra resources for shopping and entertainment.

As further incentive, Velázquez had never forgotten that Hiro had played a major role in saving his only son. He thought about the terrible time when his child had been infected by the Ebola virus from a monkey bite several years ago. Velázquez was very pleased that he could now pay Hiro back. Besides, Japan was going to be a once in a lifetime experience for them all. Chances were that they would never return.

So the general, Freddie, Hiro, and Ishmael Velázquez packed a few belongings and headed to Shikoku Island to the famous Tosa prefecture. Tosa dog wrestling was legendary, and they were all eager to see these extraordinary animals. They traveled in style on a private jet provided by the Mitsubishi Corporation. Hiro had made arrangements with his personal connection there, and Mitsubishi was happy to provide for the Cuban general's travel needs. The flight was first class all the way providing the travelers with luxury service. The general asked Hiro to explain more about these fighting dogs. Hiro knew their history well.

The Last Revolution

Hiro began, "In Japan, the Tosa is considered a national treasure. Tosa is known as the Sumo wrestler of the dog world. They are not bred as domesticated home pets because they can be very dangerous. This type of dog is illegal in many countries because they are so deadly. But those Japanese who have raised one at home say that they are a loving and kind house pet although they can have a temper."

Hiro continued his explanation, "The dogs are a very athletic breed, but surprisingly agile. They are a large-sized breed with thick long tails and a thick coat. Usually, they are a reddish brown, but occasionally they are light black in color. They have a large broad head and a long squared off muzzle and facial features similar to the western Rhodesian ridgeback. Their jaws are like steel, and they can bite and bring down an opponent using massive force. They are a handsome breed of dog with little ears, small oval-shaped eyes, and a stately expression. They are an intelligent and courageous dog." The Cubans were fascinated and wanted to know more.

Hiro went on to explain, "The original Japanese Tosa dog originated in the sixteenth century during the Tokugawa Era in Japan. Back then, they were bred as a simple fighting dog. Over the centuries they continued to closely breed them with many local Kochi and other Shikoku dogs called Shiba- Inu. Later, they also bred them with western breeds such as the bull dog, mastiff, German pointer, Great Dane, and Bull Terrier. So the present day Tosa dogs developed over centuries of careful cross-breeding."

Hiro asked the Mitsubishi flight attendant to bring more drinks to his guests. He continued, "The Tosa is very brave, fearless, and bold. They are said to be attuned to their master's wishes and very sensitive to the tone of their master's voice. They are quiet, calm, and patient animals which are extremely protective and loyal. The Tosa has been bred strictly as a fierce wrestling dog. They fight silently and remain quiet and patient during their matches. They are extremely intelligent and do not require repetitious training."

Freddie interrupted, "Hiro, what are the matches like?"

Hiro smiled, "They are very exciting to watch. The rules of Tosa dog fighting were set in the last century and demanded that the dogs fight with strict silence and without cowering. They are majestic dogs, and they are relentless. The Tosa dog is a very rare breed, and they are the only wrestling dogs in the world so many people come to watch these special matches. Many Japanese have never had the chance to actually see such a dog, but everybody recognizes the famous Sumo dogs when they see their photo or see them on television. This fighting is a ritual which has a long history in the Japanese culture."

Hiro swallowed a sip of his beer and continued to tell his friends more. "These dogs are expertly-trained, and the fights are conducted under strict rules accompanied by holy rituals and processions. The dog fights should never be cruel or bloody, and they never end with the death of one of the animals. This is a strictly humane and regulated sport."

The general added, "Our bulls and chickens are not so lucky in the Latin and Spanish cultures. They fight to the death!"

Hiro shook his head, "Not here. These dogs are considered sacred animals and are held in high esteem."

Hiro went on to say, "The Tosa dog fighting is considered a ritual of the traditional sport of Sumo wrestling. Like men they try for a strong and quick victory. The fights are designed to last a short time, and the judgment is rendered based upon very technical results. The animal that meets the most criteria in the fight is declared the winner. The Tosa dog is carefully trained to hold their opponent down on the floor."

"They then dominate their opponent for more than three minutes. The winner, depending on the dog, can sometimes last for five minutes. It is very rare for a fight to last more than fifteen minutes. Any dog that turns its back to the opponent or moves back three steps when attacked is disqualified. These rules are strictly enforcement. Also, there is a rule that the dogs must be silent. If a dog whines or growls, it is declared the loser instantly. Even if a dog has successfully dominated his opponent and takes the other dog down to floor, if he growls or makes a noise, he is instantly disqualified. There is a thirty minute maximum for the match. After that time, the fight is called a draw. A rematch is then requested at a later time." The general and Ishmael Velázquez were all ears. They were amazed at what they were hearing. Nothing like this existed in Cuba.

Hiro added, "It is a highly regulated game. Dogs are graded using a hierarchy based on the number of points earned by each performance. Then at the end of tournament, the superior Tosa dog receives a recognition title, such as *Yokozuna* or champion. This is based on the famous ancient Japanese Sumo regulations. Dog fighting in Japan is considered illegal, as is gambling. But these special dog fights are considered an ancient cultural tradition so the national laws are bent and reinterpreted so that the sport can still exist. However, the number of matches are growing smaller and smaller because the nature of the event."

The general told the group that he had never seen any dog-fighting of any kind, but when he was young, he had seen many cock fights in Cuba. These events were considered illegal, but still continued to this date. Hiro heard about, but had never seen a cock fight, but the general added that they were bloody.

Hiro said, "Before the Tosa wrestling starts, the audience is informed and given an explanation of dog's origin and history and the fighting rules. The dogs sit right in the front row of the ring just like the men do during Sumo wrestling matches. The matches are always well-attended, and there are often several hundred people watching these fights. Even with all these spectators, when the match begins, everyone is completely silent. Usually the match is over within five minutes. It happens very quietly."

Freddie asked, "Hiro, how often do you come to these matches?"

Hiro answered, "It's been many years; I am not a regular spectator, but I do like the event. The last time I was here during a second match with a black Tosa against a reddish brown colored Tosa dog. They wrestled for nearly twenty-six minutes maintaining strict silence. Finally in the twenty-seventh minute the black dog growled, and the fight was over. The crowd went wild. It was a bloodless dog fight and yet so spectacular".

"It follows strict rules and showcases the nature and intelligence of the dog. It takes a special animal to become a grand *Yokozuna*. He must be the best and the brightest. The dog must execute his tactics with lightning speed. Then with great strength and power he works to achieve his goal by taking his opponent down to the floor as trained. This becomes an innate response for the dog. It is like a computer program that reacts in the dog's brain."

They couldn't wait to see the match now that they had learned so much about it from Hiro. The discussion about Tosa-dog fighting reminded the general of one of his favorite war hero's. The famous old Cuban General, Arnaldo Ochoa

Sanchez, was a brilliant war strategist and his planning and tactics were executed with lightning speed before the South African rebels could even detect anything.

In a flash, it was all over before they had time to figure out what was happening. Even the Russian General Pitove noticed his brilliant and intelligent war strategy. General Ochoa Sanchez had the same fighting spirit, like these brave Tosa dogs, like the sumo wrestler, and just like the samurai. When he was being executed by the Cuban fire squad he had no fear to speak of and didn't utter a word. He kneeled and looked the gunmen in the eyes. The Japanese and Cuban have this mentality of being an honorable brave warrior in common.

Freddie and Chief Ishmael Velázquez were impressed with the Tosa dog fighting, but they were more interested in their fighting techniques and their breeding efforts that dated back over many centuries.

They landed in Tosa. There was a driver waiting for to take them to Ko-chi where they were greeted by an officer from the Tosa dog association. The officer gave the group a long deep bow. By then, the Cuban's were well acquainted with this custom and automatically bowed back. He gave them a quick tour of the arena and explained to the general, Freddie, and Chief Ishmael Velázquez, the history, breeding methods, and techniques for training of the dogs. He confirmed what Hiro had just explained giving specific details. He concluded with a discussion about the exceptional silence and patient personality that had been bred into these dogs over time. He also explained in detail the rules enforced during the matches. The Tosa dog association seated them in special front row seats reserved for executives, corporate heads, and government officials.

The performance started promptly at 5:00 pm in the afternoon and soon, heated fighting began and went on until almost 10:00 pm. The general, Freddie, Hiro, and Ishmael Velázquez were wrapped up in the matches. They had to observe many fights before seeing and understanding the rules in motion. It took time to appreciate the dogs and their talents. They were amazed at the massive strength and silence of these animals. By the end of the evening, they were pumped up with excitement just as if they had been watching a football game, except they had to remain quiet. This was unique and new to them. After all

The Last Revolution

the exhibitors' dogs finished their matches, they sat in awe of the evening.

The general said, "Man, that was the most sweaty-handed excitement and stimulating mental fighting strategy I have seeing since the war in Angola. Amazing dogs!"

Freddie added, "That was a rare treat. Thank-you, Hiro."

Ishmael Velázquez shook his head, "I think this sport would be quite popular in Cuba, but no one would ever stay this quiet back at home." They all began to laugh because it was true.

There was an announcement that the evening's games had officially ended for the night. The Association of Tosa Sumo executives extended an invitation to the Cuban spectators. They accepted and went to a late night dinner with the local Tosa association at a good restaurant. There they were wined and dined with delicious regional Tosa dishes. This went on until the early hours of the morning. The Cuban guests and Hiro finally had to call it a night around 2:00 am. They were tired from their travels.

They left the restaurant and went to a traditional inn to sleep. The beds were futon-style and unique for the Cubans. Everyone agreed that it had been the most interesting evening spent on this trip yet. The general was impressed with the strategy and fighting technique of the animals that he had seen. As he stretched out on the futon, he thought about they way the dogs wrestled at lightning speed. They were strong and intelligent dogs which had no fear. It made him think of his career. He also remembered many war strategies in his career. His mind was racing. He had a tough time going to sleep.

Hiro's "game" was still continuing to download little by little but precisely into the general's memory. The seeds had been planted in the general's willing brain. Inside, the general was already beginning to question Castro's rule in Cuba. As a young boy, he had grown up with the belief that he would grow up free and strong and with harmony in the island nation that he and his family loved so much. After Castro took control everyone thought Cuba would become better. But sadly, his Cuba had never given any kind of chance to anyone on the island nation. There was always someone's ambition dictating the destiny and lives of the people; Castro's was no exception.

There was always some power hungry dictator exerting their perceptions and ideals over the people, even whether it was what they wanted or not. He had never wanted to leave or abandon his island home like many millions of Cubans had done in the early 1990s. He had watched as many friends and relative left for greener pastures in Miami. The general had thought people were crazy to abundant this tropical paradise.

The next day in the late afternoon everyone returned to the airport in East Hiroshima. There, a white mini bus limousine was waiting and to take everyone to Hiro's home in Kure-city. They drove on many winding roads up steep hills to get to Hiro's house. There, they were greeted by Dania and their two daughters. Hiro's mother's Japanese home was very small compared to their Cuban home. The house was immaculate. As they walked inside the house, there was an altar with a beautiful scroll written in Japanese calligraphy was they walked inside. There were sliding screen doors throughout the house.

Inside, the floors were covered with smooth Tatami mats. These were woven grass mats that were lined with a beautiful green silk design. The Cuban guests noticed them immediately and liked the look. The monsoon season in Japan resulted in tremendous humidity rising from the ground so to keep the houses fresh, air had to circulate better. With this in mind, the Japanese built smaller open rooms with sliding doors to the outside. They had built their homes in this way for many centuries until the arrival of modern technology came along. The older Japanese houses were different from the standard European-style home.

They were happy to be able to have this experience in such a different culture. Every place they had stayed previously had been built in the western style, except for the small inn in Tosa. They had never experienced living in an authentic family home.

The Japanese idea of living was completely different from a western-style dwelling. But his mother's home was considered to be much better living than the home in which he had grown up in the country. Hiro started to explain his childhood home in the remote mountain village. He told his guest that they would travel to his former mountain home tomorrow morning for fishing. They are all excited and couldn't wait to go fishing there. Hiro made it sound like a dream come true.

Dania made Cuban cuisine for them. It took her many days to find just the right ingredients, but she didn't mind the

The Last Revolution

extra work. To this group who had been away from Cuba for so long, it was a welcome feast. She cooked in the Creole-style that she had learned as girl from her mother. Isabel was always with her.

Hiro's family was also very helpful and made their house as comfortable as possible for their Cuban guests. Their visitors didn't understand the language, but they made attempts at communicating using gestures and body language. Somehow everyone seemed to understand one another.

Dania had given her daughter's a special job related to their guests. Masako and Yumiko were to serve as the official translators. They were proud to have been given this responsibility and took their assignment quite seriously. They were both smart and sweet, and for the Cuban men it was a source of entertainment. They had known the girls since they were very young, and now they seemed like mature teenagers. The general and Freddie understood how Hiro's mentality had developed because now they were experiencing Hiro's roots. They also saw that he came from a very closely knit family unit.

Many of the guest's conversations focused on the Tosa dogfight that they had recently witnessed. Dania and the girls were curious about them because they had never seen anything like them before. They had many long discussions about many topics as they sat in the traditional Japanese living room around the low table on the floor. They laughed and talked the entire evening.

Hiro spent some time describing the fishing village they would soon visit. Freddie and Chief Ishmael Velázquez checked their messages and received communications and received reports that the Cuban intelligence agents were having a terrific time shopping in city of Hiroshima. It was good news for them and a relief. This way they could relax with Hiro's family whose home was very comfortable and cozy. This was one thing the Japanese and Cuban homes had in common. The only thing missing at Hiro's home was an automobile. He had never bothered to drive a car while in Japan. He always used a chauffer.

Upstairs, there was a small office which had several computers and a High-tech laptop computer set up. There was a library containing books about Japanese history, literature, culture, samurai bushido, art, and technology. On the wall was a big photo of their home in San Rafael near Sierra Morena and the town of Rancho Veloz. There was also a small picture of Fidel when he was young man. For the Cuban guests it was a surprise to see these photos here in Japan. It was quite a contrast. They discussed that the Japanese and Cuban viewpoints had been very pleasant, but that Communism was the only problem.

The structure of the government of Japan was a social democratic government with help from many institutions. Japan had a great Communist nation right next door with China as its neighbor. The Japanese had a very difficult time understanding the communist government.

After the men finished their discussions, Hiro checked his computer for messages for Freddie and the general. The computer in Santa Clara, Cuba, was online. Hiro sent a message to stand by, and then he gave the general the computer chair. General González stayed online communicating with his wife for about an hour.   Then it was Freddie's turn online.

Dania had been sending e-mails to their guests families during their visit about what they were doing based on the schedule Hiro had made for them in Japan. Freddie and the general were very happy to be able to communicate with their wives and family back in Santa Clara. Freddie said, "I miss my home and my family, but everyone is doing okay. Nothing much new. Kids are all good. They want some souvenirs from Japan."

Dania asked, "What kind of souvenirs?"

Freddie said, "My wife wants something traditional and Japanese. Do you have any ideas?"

Dania said, "Oh, yes! How about a beautiful kimono and paper fan?"

Freddie replied, "She would love it. And my daughter Judi wants a new Japanese computer with a flat screen. Lalin wants new Nintendo games. And I need to get small things for my relatives!"

The general laughed and said, "I think our wives have been talking to each other. My wife gave me a list of things to buy, too. My wife wants Japanese sake, and I need to get her a kimono also. My son Alexander is also looking for a new Japanese Nintendo game. And my son Juan also wants a Japanese computer. I think my son and Freddie's Lalin have been talking to each other and have decided to ask for the same stuff.

The Last Revolution

This trip is going to be very expensive for me!" Both men started to laugh.

Chief Ishmael Velázquez smiled, "I have tried many times, but I cannot get a connection. But maybe that's lucky for me so I won't get orders for more souvenirs." They all three laughed. He added, "Well, may be I will try to connect before I go to sleep later."

Hiro said, "Hey, this is no trouble for me. Don't worry about the time." Ishmael thanked him.

Dania brought the men a tray with several beers. She placed it on the table with a small bowl of sweet and salty nori crackers to munch on. Everyone opened their beers and said, "Saludo." They also said it in Japanese saying, "Kampai." It was almost 6:00 pm in Kure- city. In Santa Clara it was just 9:00 am in the morning. Very few people in Santa Clara could communicate on the Internet. However, people who were high-ranking government officers or people who worked with foreign trading companies has email access. But there are very few in Santa Clara.

Sadly, for the average Cuban, using a computer and the Internet was off limits. They were shut off from modern technology and the world of global connection. Email connections were monitored by the Central Intelligence Department in Havana. And all Cubans who did have special access to the Internet knew what they could and could not say. It was the same with telephone conversations. They were never to discuss politics or anything related with government matters. Of course, Dania's two sisters knew how to use the computer. Dania demanded that her older sister Lillian be responsible for monitoring Liana's, her younger sister, Internet usage.

Dania told them both that Lillian must be present before the computer was turned on. Lillian must be there at all times to oversee what was happening until the computer was turned off. She made very strict rules for them to follow when they used the Internet. She wanted them to remain safe, and no one else was allowed to use the Internet except them. No talk or discussions about anything political with other people. Dania warned them that if they ever broke the rule, they could wind up in jail or worse. They both agreed and understood the trouble that would result from the government. Dania was willing to take the chance because they were good girls because that was the fastest way for Dania to communicate with them. It was a chance they had to take.

Then Hiro said, "Look, everyone! I already have a communication from my friend at a Tokyo trading company, and he can send me all those items and souvenirs. Just give me your lists and let me know by tomorrow morning. I can E-mail everything to him and then the items can be sent directly to Narita International Airport for your departure. Each boxes with have your name and the list of contents with a special paper from the Japanese trading company. This will make it very easy for you to pass through customs with this paper for the Japanese Export commission. I want to buy all the souvenirs as a gift from my family. It is my pleasure to welcome you to Japan, and it is an honor to be able to give gifts to your family form our family."

Dania added, "And if anybody refuses to accept Hiro's offer, we are going to have a heated discussion. You must let us do this."

The general, Ishmael, and Freddie finally accepted Hiro's generous offer. Freddie said, "Thank-you. We are going to accept your gift, but I must be informed of all our lists of personal souvenirs. I have to report everything to Cuban customs and the immigration department. Everything should be okay, and I am positive we will not have any trouble going through."

The general and Ishmael gave their personal gratitude to Hiro and Dania. Then Hiro asked, "Please give me your lists before bedtime tonight, and I will make special arrangements first thing tomorrow morning. It's getting very close to your departure time from Japan so the trading company will need several days to get the items and complete the special papers. I want to make contact with my friend in Tokyo to do this for me so don't forget." Dania got paper and pencils for them.

Hiro brought as many as eight Sake bottles out to show them and explained, "I bought these for you. This is very good Hiroshima sake. These brands are made right here locally and are very popular. They are sweet and smooth. Though each tastes a little different, they are all very good sakes." The Cubans smiled and looked at the bottles examining the beautiful labels and glass.

Hiro went on, "Good water is required to make premium sake, and we have good water in Hiroshima. Also, we grow excellent rice and have master brewers who use their knowledge and skills which are handed down from generation after generation to brew the best sake. There are many family-run companies that are several hundred years old. Hiroshima sakes are famous."

Freddie asked, "Tell us what you know about sake, Hiro." Hiro explained, "Well, I am no expert at the art of making sake. However, I have connections with one company. They explained many things to me. Some things I can share with you, and some things I simply can not reveal. The two most important ingredients are good rice and good water. Brewers take advantage of many types of natural waters. In Japan, our waters are some of the richest in the world. The rice that is used is not the same as the rice that we eat; it is specially cultivated for making sake. It has a large grain and low protein content."

He continued, "Sake is an alcoholic beverage that originated in Japan and is a cultural tradition. Scholars believe sake has been brewed since the 3rd century B.C. during the last of the Jomon Era. The original inhabitants of villages would chew the rice with millet and chestnuts. Then they would spit the mixture into tubs for fermenting. They would add water until a porridge-like substance formed. The concoction had good alcohol content and a delicate taste. This became the mash for sake. The enzymes from their mouths helped make the sugar." The Cuban's all made faces while listening to this part of Hiro's explanation.

Hiro laughed, "They don't do it like that now! They have developed special brewing methods and skills for over 500 years to make today's famous drink. There are even special sake institutes that the government created in the early 1900s that study sake and hold yearly competitions."

The general asked, "These days how is sake made?"

Hiro replied, "Well, the brewers ferment the polished rice with microorganisms or mold called koji, to make malt rice. Yeast mash or shobu is also added. The koji converts the starch in the rice to sugar. Then natural waters are added. The rice begins fermenting when yeast is added to this sugar. Then the mixture is pressed through a special mesh strain becoming like a pressed rice cake. This is called mash. After the mash is strained and collected, the liquid is filtered until a clear beverage is produced. Then it is pasteurized and bottled for aging."

The Cuban's continued to listen and were amazed at how rice and water and a few simple ingredients could make such a tasty drink. Dania entered from the kitchen holding a serving tray. She poured each of them some sake into tiny ceramic cups that were painted with special blue and brown designs. Hiro said, "Our custom is that we pour each other's sake. Not our own." They lifted their cups to make a toast, "Kampai! Saludos!" They all marveled at the sweet, rich flavor.

The general smiled and said loudly, "Hmmm! Good sake!"

Hiro continued his discussion on sake. "This process of sake brewing is considered a national treasure and is highly guarded. Companies never share information with each other. Everything is kept strictly confidential. Each brewery has its own special flavors and characteristics. All employees sign a confidentiality agreement to keep everything secret."

Freddie interrupted, "So, the final beverage that we are drinking is the definition of superb rice wine brewed from century old methods!"

Hiro smiled and nodded his head in agreement. Freddie picked up the bottle the label out loud, "Jinmai-sake. What does this mean?"

Hiro answered, "This means that it is made from pure and original techniques. They guarantee it."

Hiro said, "Obviously it is based on the same explanation! Everyone does not understand taste of sake."

Dania said, "I guess I'm dumb, but I don't understand the significance of the passage. At first I didn't like the taste of sake too much because it smelled like fingernail polish. It took a while to understand the quality of the beverage. You learn from experience, though to recognize the quality of the beverage. Now I like sake, and I actually love sweet Sake. Good sake is very expensive and can cost nearly $1,000 a bottle here. It's crazy but true."

Time passed and Dania insisted that the general open a special bottle of bubbly sake which was similar to champagne. Everybody was curious and couldn't wait to taste it. "Bubbly sake was a remarkable idea," Hiro added, "and good marketing. The Japanese public wanted something other than the traditional sake and this was it! It had a very dry taste but is not quite like champagne and yet not like sake either. They liked it." Hiro

The Last Revolution

said, "It is true that sake is very new product in Japan. It is called "Maboroshi no sake" meaning the beverage is "beyond imagination".

Freddie was curious and said, "Hiro it is true that the taste is incredible beyond imagination?"

Hiro said, "It is true because of price you pay and the special attention you give it when you drink it. I think it is just an incredible marketing gimmick." Then he added, "Well..? Maybe good it is a product made to impress other people I really think it is just a marketing technique, and I don't think I would actually purchase it to drink myself. I don't need impress anyone except my wife!"

Everybody was laughing. Dania opened the refrigerator and returned carrying a big black and silver labeled bottle on ice. Then Dania started singing, "Jajajajaja here it is! This is a Japanese beverage beyond imagination."

Hiro and Dania smiled as Freddie stood up and screamed, "Is this Maboroshi no sake?"

Dania said, "Saludos a todos Cubanos! Saludos a Fidel! Mierda" Everyone stood speechless and could not believe it was true.

The general said, "I know this is great gift and conversational piece. I was wondering if there was anyway we could get a case of this for Fidel."

Hiro answered, "No problem....and in that case, I will send Fidel something "beyond imagination," I'll get the best." Everyone agreed it was an excellent gift. Hopefully, Fidel would enjoy it.

Chapter 75

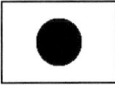

Early the next morning, Hiro and his company left on a limousine bus for their fishing trip in a remote mountain village in the Jinseki district. The trip took three hours on country highways. Along the way, the entourage passed many small towns. The scenery was interesting for everyone because they could see how different country life in Japan was compared to city life. The group was headed to Ueno, the small country village where Hiro had grown up nearly fifty years ago.

Ueno was in the district of Jinseki and in a central location in the Chugoku Mountains. It was a very remote village with a current population of less than twelve people in the whole village. The population was larger, numbering nearly sixty-five people, when Hiro was young. But Ueno remained a very peaceful and harmonious place where one could retreat to the natural world after the pace of Tokyo and other metropolitan areas.

Historical records showed that this district had begun in 615 A.D. Japanese and Korean transits traveled through Kyushu Island to Kyoto via this area. There were records tracing Hiro's family's genealogy to this area in the thirteenth century. The village was still very remote and had very few visitors. Hiro explained to the group that the only real visitors came to the nearby, newly developed golf course called Senyo-hara.

When Hiro was a school boy, all of the districts gathered together to participate in spring sporting events each year. Back then *Senyo-hara* had been just a mountain field with an elevation of nearly 1100 feet. On a clear day, one could see nearly a hundred miles away and the view was a stunning 360 degree panorama. *Senyo-hara* was on top of a volcanic mountain. There were no trees, just rolling grass fields that seemed to go on forever. At one time cows had grazed on the grass near the mouth of this ancient volcano. It had last erupted in 1650 but now was dormant.

The Last Revolution

As they drove into *Ueno village*, they saw ancient homes. The original structures were still standing although many had been abandoned by people who had left for the cities. Hiro told the group, "The youngest people in this village are seventy-two years of age. I know because two of them are my distant cousins. Sadly, within a couple of decades they will all be gone. Nature will reclaim this land, and it will become like it was before 615 A.D." For Hiro, his childhood home held a dear place in his heart. It was the place that he recalled in his memory every time he closed his eyes. He would always return to visit this village.

Hiro took them to the house where he had grown up. His cousins still lived there. Like all Japanese families, they handed down property to their first sons, and then on down the line. The house was unchanged. Only modern windows had been added since Hiro's time there; the rest was exactly the same.

The mountains were overgrown with dense green forest, and wild Japanese snow monkeys thrived in the rural area. Farmers could not control the monkeys to protect their produce. The monkeys stole or ate everything in sight.

There was no industry here. This was the last of the wide open spaces in Japan. The beautiful clear mountain stream and small river rapids still flowed just as they had many centuries ago. Hiro said quietly, "This is the land that time forgot."

Hiro's cousins and their friend walked out to greet the men. Hiro had sent word to them that they were coming for a fishing trip. The cousins' names were Shunji and Takatoshi. The older man with them had white hair and a very slender body shape. Hiro explained that he was their fishing guide. He introduced himself as Takao-san. He was a very good fisherman who would teach them special fishing techniques. Freddie and Ishmael were not going to fish but wanted to rest and watch the general and Hiro. They were happy to take it easy and do nothing for a change.

Hiro's cousins had access to old camping tents which they set up in front of the river bank near their home. They had placed old chairs and a sleeping bed, as well as various camping equipment, near the tents. Hiro thought his guests would be more comfortable in the tents than at the old home place. The home had a musty smell and lacked the amenities they were used to having. Perhaps his Cuban friends would not be comfortable in those conditions when they had access to very good tents.

Freddie and Chief Ishmael decided to remain in the tents and relax. Freddie was reading a book while Hiro and the general headed off to fish with Takao-san, the guide. There were several private uniformed Japanese state police present for security measures. Other than the police there was no one else around that day.

The sun was shining and there was absolute peace and quiet in the natural setting surrounding this quiet village. The travelers felt that they had nothing but time, just like in Rancho Veloz back in Cuba. For the general and Hiro, it was a true treat to be in this serene place. Hiro had rented a satellite telephone to communicate with the rest of the Cuban delegates. The Chief Ishmael had to stay in communication with the Cuban secret federal agents back at the hotel in Hiroshima.

Freddie and Chief Ishmael made contact before they joined the fishermen, and everything was under control. The general also had contacted the Cuban Embassy in Tokyo where he had spoken with Ambassador Hector Ortiz. He informed the general that everyone was enjoying their free time. The ambassador requested that they get together in three days for a dinner before leaving Tokyo for Havana.

Hiro hired a catering company who prepared meals for the group over the next three days. Since his cousins were elderly, he did not want to impose on them for meals. The company prepared the meals while Hiro's relatives who owned a catering business in the town of Yuki delivered the food to the fishing site. Yuki was located about 20 miles north of Ueno.

Hiro had rented his cousin's home for the three day trip because there were no hotels nearby. Since Yuki was even more remote than Ueno, the only option was to have the staff stay at his cousin's home. This was an agreeable arrangement for everyone. For Hiro's cousins, it was an exciting change to have company.

The catering company's staff was excellent at what they did. The two men and two women who made up the staff arrived at six am and left daily by eight pm. They prepared excellent meals and served good, cold beverages. They were professional and courteous.

This particular team had never before seen foreigners. At lunch time, Hiro's cousins returned to visit and to chat with Hiro. Freddie and Chief Ishmael Velázquez relaxed and enjoyed

The Last Revolution

reading and resting. They felt as if they had died and gone to a Japanese country heaven. They could do what ever they wanted, and time was on their side.

Upon the group's arrival in Ueno, Hiro and the general had gone straight to the river stream. It was so clear that they could see the Ayu swimming and feeding on the algae just off the rocks in the shallow areas. In the clear water rapids, they could see the Ayu swimming very swiftly. They were beautiful fish, constantly maneuvering and never standing still.

Ayu were a very hearty species. Their fishing guide, Takao-san, had been fishing in this area since he was eight-years-old. He was really a rice farmer who lived nearby but he had known Hiro when he was growing up in the area. Takao-san already had the equipment ready to show the general the special technique of Ayu-fishing.

As Freddie and Ishmael watched from the top of the river bank, they observed the old man's teaching techniques. Hiro said, "Unless you master this technique, you will never catch them. The Ayu are the fastest swimmers in the world."

The Ayu's behavior was extremely different from that of any other fish. They were territorial and each fish maintained its own territory on the river bed. They protected their 200 square foot area at any cost.

When an Ayu matured, it only fed on algae growing on the face of the stones. This made it extremely difficult to catch because bait would not work. Since their behavior was geared to aggressively protecting their territories, one had to know the Ayu's habits and use another Ayu as decoy bait. This provoked the fierce Ayu to attack the intruder who had entered the already claimed territory. They would attack the belly of the other fish with the aim of chasing the intruder away in order to protect their food supply. This was called tomozuri as the two fish hacked each other.

Takao-san showed the general step-by-step how it was done. Hiro acted as the translator. "First, you buy a license and then get some live Ayu for bait. All Ayu have a nose hole similar to other animals, but it is not used to breathe oxygen. We pierce the hole with a tiny nose ring into the live Ayu. Beneath the tail fin, you attach a trailing fish hook on a line called a *kakebari*. There were two, three, and four Ayu joined together on the barbless hooks so they were able to swim freely and naturally until weakened. You need a very long rod to guide the bait into the territory of the Ayu. The Ayu's instinct is to aggressively attack the bait Ayu to protect their territory."

"When the Ayu attack, they charge and ram the other bait fish's belly. The bait Ayu's response is to return the attack, and a big fight ensues. Because one has the rod with the bait Ayu, he is unable to escape and repeatedly attack to defend himself. He attacks again and again. Then, it is only a matter of time before the hook beneath the tail fin snags the attacker. They struggle to escape causing tremendous tension on the long rod. The rod line must be at a sixty-five degree angle against the rapids. The line needs to be at that tension so one can bring the captured Ayu into the fish net. The biggest challenge is to bring the Ayu to the net. It can be very difficult to land two fish using such a fine thread when both Ayu are struggling to escape."

"This part is thrilling and is the most exciting part of this fishing technique. Without this specific technique, you could never bring the Ayu to the fishing net. If the tension on the long rod is not correct angle, the Ayu can easily escape. The fish have a bright, white mouth and are uniquely-shaped. The fish have a very distinctive smell like watermelon. For this reason, the Japanese nicknamed them the fragrant fish. They are a very tasty fresh water fish. There is no other fish in the world quite like it. They have a glue-like texture to the touch and feel very slippery since they lack scales. They are beautiful creatures."

As time passed, the general got his first "hands on" lesson. At first, it was very difficult to control the Ayu, but Takao-san patiently taught him. Hiro translated between the two for about hour, and then everyone relaxed and became quiet. The general finally got the hang of the technique. Within a couple of hours, he had mastered the skills needed for this unique style of fishing.

Hiro fished about forty feet away. The general and Takao-san no longer needed a translator. They both seemed to be fishing very well together. Soon, the general was at the finish line. This was an enjoyable and excitement-filled moment. Hiro could see that he was struggling to land the fish into the net. Freddie and Ishmael sat on the banks and watched. They were taking pictures and video of this rare fishing event. Finally everyone was yelling and clapping for the general. He had his first Ayu fish in the net. He was so proud that his hand was shaking.

At noon, a young lady called them for lunch. A table with chairs had been set up near their tents. Lunch looked delicious. Hot Japanese noodles were being served. And a man had brought small kitchen equipment to prepare the fish they had just caught. Hiro, Takao-san, and the general cleaned their Ayu. The cook put the fish on sticks of bamboo and spread seasoning and salt all over them. Then he roasted them over a fire. Within a few minutes the fish were ready. The cooks had also prepared a vegetable salad with homemade country-style sauce.

Freddie said, "Oh boy! This is fantastic. This is the best fish I've eaten in a long time. It all tastes very good. I've never had such delicious freshwater fish."

Hiro added, "Ayu tastes very unusual, doesn't it?"

Chief Ishmael said, "Whoa! This is incredible. I never have tasted such good tasty fish before. I like the simple preparation, too. I am just wondering. Do you think we would be able to cultivate this fish in Cuba?"

Freddie said, "Yeah, maybe some place in Cuba where there are thick forests and cool mountains with abundant fresh water like here. Maybe in a place a wildlife sanctuary likes Topes de Collantes in Trinidad it would be possible. What do you think, Hiro?"

Hiro shook his head as he took his next bite, "I really don't know if it is possible in Cuba because the weather is so different. Cuba is the tropics, and I think Ayu need cooler mountain streams. I don't think they could survive in the warm temperatures." Hiro then switched to Japanese saying, "Takao-san what do you think?"

Takao-san sat quietly and thought. Then he said, "Ayu thrived naturally in their native habitat for thousands of years. Then during Japan's industrialization in the late 18th century, the natural waters became contaminated with agricultural chemicals. Also, many small dams were built, and the Ayu could not survive in the still water. They must have fast moving water and cool rapids. Ayu have to move constantly to breathe, and they feed on the fresh algae growth on the rocks. The Japanese wildlife agency took notice and set out to protect and cultivate the Ayu population that had died out. It took ten years of hard work, but finally they discovered how to cultivate the fish successfully."

"Now, about seventy percent of all Ayu are cultivated in fish hatcheries and released when they are juveniles for spawning. The fish are released in the late spring to early summer when they are only two to three inches. Then within two months, they grow to the adult size of six to seven inches. A few Ayu returned to the river mouth near the sea. I know this because I actually went to Okayama where there is a big Ayu fish hatchery facility. It is under contract with a private wildlife agency. It is a Japanese government affair." Hiro translated the conversation, and everyone enjoyed the educational session with Takao-san.

Next the cooks served Japanese yaki-soba noodles with many vegetables. There was hot rice and kabocha, a type of pumpkin. The entire meal featuring freshly caught Ayu was a hit. Everyone enjoyed the company and the good food in this peaceful, natural surrounding. This simple mountain village in Hiroshima was a place that made the men forget their problems and frustrations. It seemed far away from the rest of the world.

The general said, "It is great to live in touch with nature and to eat whatever nature brings. Today was fantastic! I am crazy about Ayu fishing. It reminds me of dogfights in the sky, but imagine that scenario in the water. It is very exciting, and you can control how they are going to attack when you learn how to control your bait Ayu. It was a wild chase at lightening fast speed. The fish were constantly moving. I could feel my fish fighting in the water. It was incredible!"

Freddie asked, "Was it difficult to bring your fish to your net?"

The general quickly answered, "Oh, yes! It was very difficult to keep consistent tension. That is critical because there is very fine thread on the fish line with the barbless hook on the fish. That could very easily come off so I had to work quickly and perfectly. It was thrilling, but I had to focus on my technique to be successful. I knew there was a fifty percent chance that I would lose the Ayu making my hard work worthless. It's challenging. I am just getting good at my technique. Maybe this afternoon or tomorrow I will have it down pat and do everything just right. Man, this is fantastic"

Hiro laughed and translated to Takao-san. Takao-san chuckled, too. Hiro said, "Oh. No! It's never just right. Ayu

The Last Revolution

fishing takes a lifetime to learn. Even Takao-san will tell you that!"

Takao-san added, "This technique takes many years to master. I have been fishing since I was eight, and I am still not perfect. You must have a certain tension on the line. As the Ayu move, you must change the angle of attack. It is constantly changing, and you must never ease up on the tension. If the tension changes even a little by the angle of the attack, the fish will get loose, and your Ayu is gone. Like the General mentioned, it is like a dogfight in the water. That description is a very good explanation. It made me think about Japanese fighter planes like the Mitsubishi Zero in the sky chasing American fighter planes during World War II. However, it was the opposite scenario because the killer happened to be the chaser rather than the invader struggling to escape." Takao-san used hand signs like an airplane dogfight to describe what he meant.

Then Hiro said, "What an incredible species. If only humans could master this behavior. I wonder how the first person discovered this fishing technique. He had to have been intelligent, and he must have observed the fish for many hours. It's such a unique and unusual way to fish, you know?" They all agreed. Hiro asked Takao-san, "Do you know when this Ayu fishing started?"

Takao-san replied, "Well, I really don't know, but when I went to that Ayu hatchery, one of the wildlife agents said that someone had seen an ancient Japanese book that indicated that the technique started around the twelfth century. At that time, they used silk thread as the line on a bamboo pole. The fish they described were similar to Ayu, but no one knows for sure." They talked until after dark. They all went to bed very tired from the day's events. They slept like babies in the comfortable futons inside the tents.

The next day the general, Takao-san, and Hiro continued to fish all afternoon. They were thrilled, and the general used many of the available techniques that Takao-san had shown him. He felt like he was finally getting the hang of Ayu hacking. The fish were constantly maneuvering and sometimes several groups of fish joined into the fight. That was especially exciting because the bait Ayu scrambled to escape. The general could feel the strong movement in his fishing rod. Then he had to be smart and try out many different fishing tactics. It was a great challenge that was also mentally stimulating.

While the Cubans were enjoying themselves, six police officers were on duty as the security measure. They were under the supervision of the Japanese federal secret agency. The villagers stayed away from them, but they did safe guard this place. At the same time, Chief Ishmael and Freddie took it easy and remained very comfortable. They didn't have any concerns for their personal security.

It was a peaceful time, and Freddie began to write his final report. Fidel and Raúl Castro wanted a report summarizing the trip. They wanted to know of his many observations and experiences. He needed some quiet time to compile the report, and this was the perfect place for doing it. Here, he could work uninterrupted and in serenity. Very few cars passed by, and there was almost no outside noise. There were no city sounds or sounds from modern mechanical machines. The only audible sounds were the soothing sounds of nature.

The general enjoyed this fantastic new hobby. He was a very good fisherman and stayed out all day long. Each night they gathered around the campfire. They enjoyed the beautiful night sky and the cool air. There were many insects chirping. After another delicious meal, they drank ice cold *Kirin, Iciban* beers. There was also a brand called *Sapporo*. They loved the taste of Japanese beer and decided it was much smoother than Cuban beer. Freddie asked Hiro if they could invite the Japanese security team over for a drink. Hiro said, "If they drink beer on the job, they will be fired immediately. The Japanese government is very strict and enforces its regulations. They cannot drink and socialize on the job." So Freddie asked the Japanese caterers and other villagers to join the campfire. They were friendly but very reserved. Hiro and Freddie translated for everyone. It was nice to mingle with the locals and connect with the villagers.

Early the next day they arose early and made coffee over the campfire. While the food was being prepared, the phone rang. It was Hector Ortiz, the Cuban ambassador from Tokyo. He called to give a briefing schedule for the next day and evening at the embassy. It was to be their last night in Japan before returning to Havana. He congratulated them on a successful trip. He had been informed by the Japanese industrial community that they would offer resources and technical support to the Cuban

The Last Revolution

government. This would, of course, depend on the Cuban political situation and negotiations with the government of Japan. Also, three of the industrial giants were involved in a joint venture to send donations of tons of rice to the Cuban people. The ambassador asked Freddie and the general to send a strong message to Fidel to ease the sanctions with the Japanese. He strongly urged them to communicate that Cuba needed Japanese technology and could learn a great deal from the Japanese to promote industrialization.

The ambassador continued to discuss this and further recommendations. He was concerned with diplomatic issues between the two countries since he had become the ambassador to Japan. He had worked with many Japanese companies and had suggested that Cuba urgently needed help in the area of technology. The alliance with Japan would help aid the failing economy in Cuba and assist in turning around a seriously deteriorating situation.

He also expressed that being the ambassador was a very difficult task. He could see many unfavorable objections with Cuba's political past. For the last five years, he had been very frustrated and hoped that this visit by the Cuban delegation would break the ice between the United States and Cuba. Freddie listened and continued to explain that it was almost impossible because Fidel's vision was set in stone. Fidel would never change his mind, and everybody must obey Fidel.

The general, Hiro, and Takao-san went down to the river one last time for Ayu fishing. It was their last day in the country, and the fishing had been very successful. It was a most beautiful day. By noon, the general had already caught six big fish. He was excited and totally addicted to the sport. Takao-san, the fishing guide, was constantly watching him and giving him the sign for "good fishing." Hiro was about fifty yards above the rapids. He had four beautiful fish and enjoyed this last day of his favorite past time as well.

Suddenly, the general saw four fish attacking his bait Ayu. He continued maneuvering for almost five minutes. Then he caught three fish on the hook. It was very rare to snare this many fish. Usually Takao-san was very serious, but when he saw this happening he, too, screamed with excitement. He could already see the three fish and their silver bellies reflecting in shallow water as they struggled to escape. He shouted in

Japanese for the general to change the fish line to a different angle of attack.

Instantly, he had a thought. It was like an inspiration and as if someone were manipulating his memory all of a sudden. It felt as if he was receiving orders, but he was conscious of it only for a moment. Suddenly, he threw down his fishing pole in the water rapids while his fish was still struggling to escape the three attackers.

Then he ran to Hiro about fifty yards away and grabbed his arm. He yelled, "What is going on? Why are you trying to manipulate my brain? Are you trying to brainwash me? What are you doing to me?"

Hiro wasn't surprised. He remained very calm and asked the general, "What is your target?"

The general grabbed his arm again very tightly. He had a glazed look in his eyes. He answered, "Fidel, his brother Raúl, and the Chief General. You want me to kill them. Correct?"

Hiro didn't say anything. He just nodded his head "yes" and remained calm and quiet.

The general yelled, "Look! I am second in command of the Cuban Army. I am not interested in doing such a thing. Hiroaki, listen to me! I am the next General in line to be Chief of the Cuban Army. In five years, when Chief General Hector Elias Garcia retires, I will be in charge. I am strongly loyal to Fidel and his brother. You are wrong, and I am ashamed to have a friend like you. I can report you to government of Cuba, and you will never be allowed to return to Cuba. And if you returned, you will be arrested, and Fidel will have a firing squad waiting to carry out your execution within twenty-four hours. This kind of crime against Fidel is treason and means immediate execution."

The general paused for a moment then added, "Look Hiro, I am willing not to mention this to anyone because of your achievements. You have been a great help, and you have connected us with many corporations for our government. But I am absolutely disgusted with you as a friend. You just pretended to be my friend when you were actually using me for your personal motives. Our friendship is over now. I am done with you after this moment. Please do not communicate with me again. You are a dangerous man! You are a mad man. I am very ashamed that I ever called you my friend." He turned and ran down the shallow water to the base camp where Freddie and

The Last Revolution

Ishmael Velázquez were writing reports. Suddenly, he jumped in front of them and demanded that they leave and return to the Cuban embassy in Tokyo right away.

Freddie and Ishmael were very surprised at the general's sudden action. The general insisted that they pack their personal belongings immediately. Meanwhile, Hiro was still fishing calmly. Takao-san didn't ask anything. They just watched in silence. Soon, the Cubans took off in the limousine bus for the city of Hiroshima. Once there, the general picked up his remaining staff and returned to Tokyo to the Cuban Embassy. In the bus, the general didn't utter a word. Freddie and Chief Ishmael just kept to themselves.

The general finally turned to them, "Forget everything that happened here. One day I will explain it to both of you. But until then, ask me no questions. Just disregard everything. Do you understand this order?" The men nodded.

Freddie remained quiet and wasn't allowed to say goodbye to his longtime friend, Hiro. This might be the last time he ever saw Hiro. He was very sad, and he wondered what had gone wrong between the two. He wondered if it was a political difference. He just couldn't understand what had happened. But he had promised not to ask the general questions and to keep his mouth shut. When they returned to the Cuban embassy in Tokyo, Ambassador Hector Ortiz noticed that Dr. Hiroaki Nakagawa was not among them as planned. He had wanted to thank him in person for his help and for making this all possible.

The general immediately offered the excuse that Dr. Nakagawa had been called away for something urgent. The Cuban delegation went ahead with their evening plans, but it was a tense evening for the general, Freddie, and Ishmael. They could not focus on the Ambassador and his dinner. Their minds were on the days' terrible event. The next day at six pm, they left Japan on a Cubaña Tupoel Tu-154 jet. They were all ready for take off. Their destination was Havana.

Chapter 76

Three months later Freddie was swamped and frustrated upon his return to Cuba from Japan. At least, he had enjoyed his vacation and the cultural experiences before his return home. There were numerous problems that had held up the construction of his Cuban tourist hotel project. This was largely due to lack of foreign funding and the sharp decline in Cuba's tourist industry due to recent US interference. The US was tightening sanctions along with other countries which meant more suffering for Cuba's already weak economy.

Most building projects in Cuba had been halted for the moment and placed on the back burner until further notice. Freddie had to scrap many projects to save on resources, and there was always massive corruption that made construction even more impossible. Freddie wasn't surprised but it made his job more frustrating and complicated. He had many important meetings and personal briefings with the central government to discuss the current hold-ups and delays in the schedule.

Freddie had met personally with Fidel and Raúl over a dozen times since his return from Japan. They were seeking alternative funding sources and discussing the possibility of seeking investors from Japan's corporate and government elite. Japan wanted to get involved, but only if Fidel would agree to some political changes in his agenda. Fidel scoffed at the notion and rejected it completely. Freddie could not push the issue.

Freddie had a very difficult time explaining the funding delays on the huge project being undertaken in a north central coast development. Fidel continued to insist on the construction of the new hotel development in Central Cuba even though resources were scarce. He insisted that Freddie make it work. Cuba depended on tourism, and this new hotel project would bring masses of foreigners to Cuba's northern shores. Freddie was under the gun and couldn't say "no" to Fidel.

Fidel also fantasized that Cuba could become a miniature computer technology force in the world with Japan's assistance and guidance. That would solve all of Cuba's economic woes,

The Last Revolution

and it could help bring down the evil US Empire once and for all. Fidel had devised a plan to begin setting up a department of computer technology for studying and planning of Cuba's future in technology.

Fidel understood that at the moment he had no other alternative because of the political situation in Cuba except to continue focusing on a new frontier with President Chavez of Venezuela. Fidel had maintained a strong relationship with him as Cuba suffered economic recession. Cuba had experienced zero growth for nearly five years, but the government continued to focus on a 3.5 percent growth expected.

General González was also covered up in work after his return from Japan. He tried not to think about Hiro and the incident, but it bothered him daily. He was plagued with paranoia and obsessive thoughts. Why had Hiro chosen him? What would happen? He knew that Hiro was capable of many things due to his extensive mathematical computer background, but he decided to put it out of his mind and to quit being paranoid. He had better things to think about and had to focus on the situation at hand.

Fidel wanted the general to change the entire government intelligence's computer system. He was given the task of upgrading the whole system using the Colbana–Nakajima JPX008 chip. It was a tremendous undertaking because Cuba didn't have an up-to-date technology facility to duplicate a large quantity of the chips. But Fidel didn't want to hear excuses of any kind. He wanted the general to "make it happen" and that was his sole objective.

The general knew with Fidel that he had to find a way. This made his life very difficult. The facility was only able to process a very small quantity of the chips so he had to plan construction of a new facility that could do the job Fidel expected. But with resources slim, it was very difficult. Fidel was also pressuring him to make it happen "yesterday," but to manufacture such a quantity of chips a large facility would be necessary and it would take many years and perhaps longer to design and build such a facility.

But with Cuba's present political situation it was nearly impossible to build such a facility. Freddie had also proposed help from Japan in his meetings with Fidel, but Castro was not willing to change his plan for Cuba's political future.

Fidel ranted saying, "How dare Japan expect this from him? I respect Japan and what they have accomplished, but they do not understand my vision." Therefore, Fidel looked toward Venezuela and South America for aid and support.

Because of Fidel's strong ties to the Venezuelan President, Hugo Chavez, millions of dollars poured into Cuba from a new trade agreement. The two leaders were political allies as well as trade partners.

Chavez sent crude petroleum and construction materials to Cuba as well as much needed food and clothing. The Venezuelan petroleum had solved the energy crisis so that now the people of Cuba had access to power twenty-four hours per day. The trade agreement had also brought a stable food source and resources for paving roads and highways. For the average Cuban citizen, this meant a better way of life.

In return, Fidel sent millions in medicine, medical equipment, and medical training into the poorest areas of Venezuela. Many Cuban doctors and health workers were also sent to help in cooperative programs.

He remembered when Hiro first arrived. At that time, there was no help from Venezuela. Cuba was suffering, and Rancho Veloz was crumbling. Electricity was available only a few hours per day. The people had to scramble to find food. At the worst times, dogs and cats would disappear. During hard times people had to survive in the countryside somehow. But now, Cuba has changed far better living condition then Hiro first step in to this island.

Freddie knew that Japan was a much wiser choice, but he could not argue the point with Fidel. It was just not done. General González left these meetings even more frustrated and concerned about Cuba's future. At age 81, Fidel was growing older, and the general knew that this could be a turning point for Cuba.

Ever since General González had returned form Japan, he had begun to have new ideas of his own. Cuba's political system needed many changes to align it with the rest of the world. He had begun to realize that a big political change was Cuba's only real way out of this hardship. He saw how the Cuban citizens were suffering, and he could see and feel the deeply ingrained desire for something better that now festered among the population. Under Castro, Cuba had a one party system: Castro's

The Last Revolution

communist party. But the generals knew there was no equality in this system. It was only tyranny covered up by rhetoric that it was "all for the people". They knew it was time for a two party or more system. It was time for Cuba's best and brightest to compete for the right to rule the country

González had been a member of the Communist Party since his youth and had always been a strong believer that every man was the equal of every other. He didn't believe in separation between the rich and the poor. His father had believed strongly in Fidel because of the corruption he had witnessed in the Batista government in the 40s and 50s. He had seen that because of widespread corruption, strong men could buy power at the expense of the poor who could not even afford to buy milk for their hungry babies. Many people starved or died for lack of proper medical care.

His grandfather also had been a strong believer in free enterprise, but after his grandfather's death his father watched as the Batista regime corrupted Cuba stealing everything in sight. He watched how bad politics and bad management had caused unrest throughout his life. So when Fidel came upon the scene spouting revolution, he supported him and his movement emphasized that Democracy would overwhelm the people, and the boy Abelardo believed what his father had taught him. After all, his father was an influential man who was deeply concerned about the welfare of the Cuban public. And his father had believed fervently that although Batista's system was flawed, it clearly was superior to the alternatives available in the 1950. Even as an adult, González, remembered that his grandfather and he had always compared the two systems of government long before he reached adulthood.

Since by then there was no other choice, he became a Communist so he could take advantage of the free education it offered him. He had wanted to focus on computer technology, but his father steered him toward the military academy in Havana. After finishing his computer studies at the University of Matanzas, he attended the Cuban Military Academy in Havana and became a captain in the Army technology surveillance unit. His entire military centered on technology and surveillance. He worked with the Cuban navy in Guantanamo and later with the Air Force in conjunction with communication spy units at the base in Pinar Del Rio.

Later González accompanied a secret unit to Angola, where his mission was to intercept and unscramble US military satellite signals. Based on what he learned, he directed the Cuban Army on the ground. That information led to many tactical successes so that when González returned to Cuba, he had risen rapidly to his the position of Lieutenant General of the Army Corps at the Santa Clara base.

In 1989 after General of Army Ochoa's execution, Santa Clara Army General Hector Elias Garcia became the General of Army directly under Raúl Castro Ruz. This opening resulted in promoting González, to General of the Cuban Army Corps.

González, was only thirty-three years old making him the youngest general ever in the Cuban Army. And his success was based almost entirely on his technological brilliance. Fidel loved to call him the "gift of the Cuban revolution" because he had helped so many Cuban youth achieve their educational goals through technology.

Soon González began to think that the political stance espoused by his family was a misinterpretation of man's ignorant use of authority for his own benefit. But he realized as well that the Communist system was equally wrong. He began to put two and two together and come up with much more than four. He began to understand the difference between true power and mere political theory.

The General had never lived under a democratic government, but his trip to Japan had made him open his mind to new possibilities and had made him wonder if some variation of the Japanese system of social democracy might be good for his island nation. He considered the big Japanese corporations as well as the mom and pop operations that could so easily be adapted in Cuba. He believed that the manufactured goods they created and distributed through a free market system were the only answer to the problems created by Fidel's own ignorant vision. He was convinced that Cuba's salvation lay in erasing the past and creating a new future for all Cuban citizens.

During the entire ten months since his return from Japan, González contemplated how to craft the governmental changes he felt were essential to the future of Cuba. Since his return from Hiroshima, memories of his childhood had flitted through his mind, sometimes resurfacing briefly, disappearing, and returning once again. At some point, his brain reprogrammed the Patriot

The Last Revolution

game without his conscious volition. At the same time, memories of his grandfather's teachings flooded in. Soon he was putting Hiro's idea of the Patriot game together in his thoughts. The five segments of the war game cycled through, seemingly reprogramming themselves until finally, the download was complete.

His brain had been altered to believe that a general must always obey his higher authority, swiftly executing all commands. No matter the cost, he must advance against the enemy. If he should fail in his mission, the general would lose all trust and authority. He must then die, but without the honor of a samurai. He applied these same five tenets to modern day warfare.

"The Last Revolution"

Segment 1 - Bushido: martial law, justice, and death for what one believed consisting of honor and the tactics of the samurai and their method of fighting
  • Pursued an absolute and lightning swift victory
* Advanced against the enemy, no matter the cost
* Was willing to sacrifice one's own life for one's beliefs

Segment 2 - Jose Martí: the philosophy of Jose Martí emphasizing his love for his country and for freedom
  • Pursued an absolute and lightning swift victory
* Supported liberty, justice, and the right to freedom of the individual
* Espoused ideals of democracy

Segment 3 - Tosa-dog Fighting: brilliant war tactics using lightning speed and silence
  • Pursued an absolute and lightning swift victory
 * used brilliant plans, intense training, and strategies to achieve victory

Segment 4 - Ayu Fishing: a skill and a technical tactic of the war game.

  • Used lightning speed to achieve victory
* Translated strategies into practical applications

* Simulated aerial dog fights which used air power as a tool to achieve victory

Segment 5 - Target

•Fidel Castro

Fidel Castro had been a strong leader ever since he had seized control from the Batista government and established Communism in Cuba with the financial support of the Soviet Union. Castro only used Soviet funds because he faced great difficulties in dealing with the United States which treated Cuba as a mere American colony.

Fidel realized that the only way he could escape the disasters brought on by the corruption of the previous regime was to refinance the country by developing a new economy and new markets for Cuban goods. While this was his original motive for linking his fortune with that of the Soviets, he soon realized that Communism was his salvation.

It was in fact the perfect system through which he could install himself as "dictator in residence." Castro's "Cuba vision" became the only show in town for fifty years. Communism must end and be replaced by Social-Democratic enterprise. The Japanese political model could be adopted perfectly in this island nation. Cuba would have the benefit of its US neighbor as an economic engine. Why should this opportunity be bypassed for the Cuban people?

Very quickly, González understood what his friend in Hiroshima had been trying to teach him through his "new Cuban vision" that cast the General himself as the savior of the island nation. As soon as he displayed Hiro's game scrip, the neurons in his brain gradually reprogrammed themselves within forty-eight hours. The General received the messages, and his brain began actively searching and analyzing his options for the future of Cuba.

He recalled that his grandfather had always spoken ill of Castro, saying that he had been a criminal to start with and would always remain a criminal. He said that Castro had hijacked Cuba, not for the benefit of the Cuban people, but for himself. He had been taught that the young Martí had been a true patriot who had envisioned a true and pure liberty for all. With all of these

The Last Revolution

ideas swirling around in his head, González began to envision sacrificing his own life for the good of his motherland. Dreams of a democratic Cuba filled his thoughts.

Chapter 77

April 25, 2008, ten pm, Santa Clara Cuba

In Hiroshima as Hiro awakened with coffee in hand, he began surfing the Internet to determine when the next summit meeting would be held at the University of Hiroshima. Twenty-seven university level computer scientists were scheduled to attend the meeting where many new ideas would be presented. Suddenly, Hiro's computer alerted him that it was receiving a coded message. The message was being sent from Al-G.@cubavision.cu.net. Hiro had been waiting to receive a message from González. It had been ten months since the general had left Hiroshima. When Hiro clicked on the message, he smiled as he read the text. He already knew what the message would say.

It usually only took about three months for Hiro's subjects to download the computer game into their neurons. Obviously, the general was a very intelligent man because he had been fighting the reprogramming taking place in his brain for ten months. Because of the general's passionate feelings for his Cuban homeland, he had sent his coded reply to Hiro immediately after his mind downloaded the game. The promptness of the reply indicated that the general appreciated and understood Hiro's passion for Cuba, too.

General González was concerned that the governments' financial setbacks following the revolution would make it difficult to feed the Cuban people. The general did not want to have to depend on handouts from US and Cuban-Americans for survival afterward. This would be a disaster for the Cuban people. Also, Hiro was convinced that the Japanese government and the team of Japanese industrial and corporate heads would move full speed ahead to aid Cuba and rescue its economy. He knew that Japan would seize the opportunity to step in and assist Cuba in its rebuilding efforts. They would do so without any strings attached. Hiro explained the plan to the general and

The Last Revolution

motivated him to imagine a free Cuba fulfilling its rightful place in the world as an island nation that was proud and productive.

Cuba had a great future ahead, and with Japan's help progress could begin immediately. The general and Hiro discussed the possibilities via Internet using Hiro's secret code. No one had successfully cracked the code, not even the CIA.

US government staff had resumed their attempts at breaking the code. While it had been difficult, they knew that they would crack the code eventually. It was only a matter of time, and Hiro was concerned that he might be running out of time.

April 15, 2008, Santa Clara, Cuba the general knew that his counterpart in the Air Force was the Ayu bait, but the timing had to be perfect. The general knew that the time had arrived when he received a message about an urgent meeting in Pinal Del Rio from the Chief of Command, Raúl Ruiz Castro. The chief had scheduled an inspection. Everyone predicted that the surprise inspection would happen within the two weeks.

The General was conducting inspections accompanied by Raúl Castro and General Hector Elias Garcia. They had been debating the purchase of forty-five new Russian MIG-31s and hardware. Fidel argued that they were not necessary against the threat of a US invasion of Cuba because the US had experienced an extremely tough time against Iraqi insurgents and the war in Afghanistan. Fidel felt that it would take the US many years to bring closure to these conflicts. Therefore, Cuba was not immediately in danger of invasion from their northern neighbor.

Fidel was against the acquisition of the new fighter jets. Although he liked the machines, the cost was forty-five million dollars each. Since the Cuban economy was in a decline, Fidel wanted to reign in all spending until the economy improved so as not to drain national resources. Even sugar productivity had continued to decline steadily and was at a record low for the decade.

But Raúl tried to convince Fidel otherwise. He believed that Cuba must have MIG-31s for defense against a possible US invasion. Raúl warned that the US would someday attempt to invade and take over the island. Therefore, Cuba must be prepared with protection and a means to fight the enemy so they met to inspect the current Cuban Air Force hardware. The inspection lasted three days.

On the second day of the inspection, they asked to view test flights and to see practice formations of their MIG-29 Fulcrums. These fighter jets were impressive, and the pilots were well-trained. Fidel was pleased, but he also learned about the capabilities of the new MIG-31s and the upgrades were many. On day three, Castro completed his personal inspection and called for a final meeting on Air Force hardware. There he discussed the need to review the Cuban national assembly budget. Fidel had to go before the committee to present the budget for the coming year, January 2009. He ordered the complete inspection of all Cuban hardware. He promised that he would release his final decision on whether or not Cuba would purchase 45 new MIG-31s very soon.

An intense and heated discussion occurred between Raúl and Fidel. Raúl urged his brother to consider the hardware because it was essential to secure the country. The US always had its eye on Cuba and would one day attempt to take the island.

Because of Cuba's strategic position, they were in a valuable location between North and South America. Raúl warned his brother of the consequences of allowing their Army and Army Air Force to fall behind. The MIGs were costly, but they were a necessary expenditure for the country's protection. Fidel listened to the opinions of his core team. Finally, he decided that he wanted a Cuban Army Air Force hardware inventory. Then he could give a definitive answer. Raúl immediately ordered General Enrique Hurtado Rodríguez to oversee the job. The jets needed adequate fuel supplies for testing, and Fidel wanted the full report within thirty days. The start date was set for July 1, 2008.

The Cuban Army Air Force had always been very small with the sole purpose of defending Cuba from hostile invaders. Currently, they were equipped with a MIG-23 that had been used to bring down two US Cessna planes in February, 1996. There was also an attack by the Bahamian's Coast Guard and the MIG-23 was once again used to sink the *HMBS Flaming* in 1980. There was very little use for tactics and for air defense against the United States. Usually, General Enrique Hurtado Rodríguez. allowed only twenty gallons of jet fuel to be in the fighters at all times. The reason the tanks were never full was to prevent defections by Cuba's own Air Force pilots.

The Last Revolution

Raúl ordered all hardware to be tested and maintenance reports within thirty days. He wanted detailed inspections to reassess their forces' power and ability to defend Cuba at a moments notice. He also requested that a full jet inventory be completed at the Pinar del Rio Air Force base.

Adequate jet fuel supply was requested and granted immediately. This was the first time a total inventory and inspection of this scale had ever been done. Fidel was having second thoughts about spending such huge resources on the new Mikoyan MIG-31s. "Foxhound" was a supersonic interceptor aircraft, and Russia's newest and most advanced high altitude interceptor.

This complete inventory, with full inspection and performance tests, would give him a precise answer on where they stood. It was an intense week and afterwards Fidel and Raúl and all the high-ranking generals returned to their posts General Garcia ordered General González to stay several days longer for some further official technical briefing with General Enrique Hurtado Rodríguez, for installation on the new Colbana-Nakajima JPX008 chip and updated new computer systems.

The two generals were long time friends who had worked together closely to achieve the great victory in Angola. They had much in common. They had both worked side-by-side in the high-tech surveillance unit in Angola, Ethiopia and were largely responsible for the Cuban's success.

Both men were highly decorated after the war in Angola and both became famous Four Star Generals in the Cuban Army. They were both young and loyal to Fidel. They were part of his small inner circle, but Fidel and Raúl never trusted anyone fully. The nature of Fidel was greedy and power hungry and they knew that they always had to be careful. Treachery lay around every corner. They made sure both men were closely watched by the Cuban secret service led by Ishmael Velázquez, Chief of Cuban Central Intelligence. Fidel always wanted to know what their motivation and intentions were, and he kept strict control over intelligence on his entire inner cabinet.

But over the long years, the general and Ishmael had become very good friends. So much so, that there were many incidents that Ishmael excused and didn't report. He maintained a protective watch over the general. But Ishmael was in a compromised situation because if Fidel and Raúl ever found out about his omissions, he would be imprisoned.

    General Rodríguez invited both Ishmael and the general to stay at his guest home during the two technical briefings and upgrade of the computer system. They could review much of the information at his home office. His wife Andréa would enjoy seeing their old friends so the general accepted.

    Ishmael was in a somber mood and replied, "That sounds fine, but first I must stop by my Cousin Juan Carlos house before joining you. He is very sick, and the doctor has told him that he only has a short time to live. I must visit. Does it matter what time I arrive at your house?"

    General Enrique Rodríguez answered politely, "Anytime is fine. Do you remember how to get to my home?"

    Ishmael said, "Oh yes, I remember where you live."

    Chief Ishmael's assistant asked if he could assist and serve as his replacement until he returned. But Ishmael declined and insisted that he would not be too long. Both generals left with a personal driver for the house. Upon reaching the white stucco house, Rodríguez. got out of the car and thanked and dismissed their aid. They would return to the base the next day at 01100 hours. The aide saluted both generals and left.

    The Rodríguez's home was a nice house by Cuban standards and had a pretty garden in the front and a fence around the property. The house was two stories high and was painted stark white and had a Spanish tile roof. It was an older home, but it had been well-maintained. As they entered the front door, they could smell a delicious scent in the room. Andréa was cooking a chicken dish. She was a well-mannered woman, about thirty - eight years old with light brown hair and tan skin. She was not particularly attractive and was on the plain-looking side, but she had a nice figure and was well-dressed. She also was kind and hospitable and had a pleasant demeanor.

    The general had not seen her in a long time and she welcomed them in with a cheerful greeting saying, "Well, hello there! It has been a very long time since I last saw you? How are your wife and children?"

    The general answered happily, "Everything is fine in Santa Clara. The kids are growing up too fast, and my wife is getting meaner every year. I think she is getting sick of me, don't you think so? Maybe I need a new wife?"

The Last Revolution

Andréa and Enrique both laughed at his humor. Andréa said, "You are still very funny."

He kidded back with a straight face saying, "No, I am not joking." Then he started laughing, too. Everybody knew then that he was just joking. They invited him to the patio and offered cold drinks. It was a humid evening, but the cold drink hit the spot. They sat talking and catching up on old times. They shared many old war stories and memories of years past. The general felt relaxed in their company.

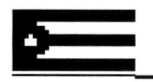

Chapter 78

Later in the evening, the general asked Enrique for a moment of his time for a very private conversation. Andréa understood and said she had some things to do upstairs. She brought them a small cooler containing cold drinks and beer and told them to call for her if they needed anything more.

General González became serious and asked, "Enrique, I would like to ask you some questions, and I want you to give me your honest opinion?"

Enrique said, "You know I have an open mind, and you know me very well. Go ahead and ask me?"

The general asked once again, "Enrique, this is very private business. Can you keep this discussion between you and me confidential?"

Enrique look, "Sounds like this is something serious. You have my complete discretion. What is up with you?"

The general wiped the sweat from his brow. He began, "I am getting very tired of the political game. I don't like what I see happening, and I have been thinking a lot about the country's state of affairs. What do you think? In what direction do you see Cuba really headed? Do you think Fidel will be able to last?"

Enrique responded, "Well…I really don't know what to say. You are asking something very complicated and difficult for me to answer. I have an opinion, but, well, I don't speak openly about these things. You should be careful, my friend. What you are asking and thinking is heading you in a precarious direction. It is fine and you can trust me, but you really need to be careful." The general looked visibly uncomfortable and did not say anymore. He thought that he had just made a great mistake by confiding in Enrique.

Then Enrique replied, "I know what you are asking. I want to be open with you too, but this has to stay between us. Do you understand?"

The general agreed. Enrique said, "I am right there with you in these thoughts. The state of the country is going south fast

The Last Revolution

and something needs to be done ASAP. Fidel is growing old, and Raúl is only concerned with the military and not his own people. Are we both crazy to speak so openly like this?"

"No, you and I both know many others feel this way, too. We have been silent for far too long. It is a shame that we are grown men who cannot speak the truth. We cannot say what is on our minds without severe penalties. I believe in a strong and proud Cuba, but I look around and people are depressed and lazy. Cubans are apathetic, and we have lost the vision for our future. What do you think about our future as Communists?"

Enrique said, "So far, things have not worked out as Fidel wanted, and the economy is shot to hell. I don't think we are going to survive like this much longer. Cuba has become more and more isolated from the rest of the world. We are falling behind, and we have very few prospects. Fidel is old, and Raúl is waiting for his turn to lead. You saw him this week. He was only concerned with acquiring the new Russian MIGs at any cost. We have taken a beating over the past decade. I am convinced that the Mikoyan MIG-31 Foxhound is already obsolete because the US is now replacing their F/A-18 Hornet, F19,s with F-22 Raptors."

"The Raptor is a super-sonic Stealth fighter that is virtually invisible to radar. There is no way we can match the gringos' superior power. You are second in command of the Cuban Army so you probably understand that we can't win against the gringos, but I can't say that to Raúl. He just won't listen."

González add "I know we need a change. And I am glad you and I are of the same opinion. I have been thinking the same thoughts, and since I returned from Japan, and I believe that Cuba needs to learn from the Japanese system. They have a strong market economy, and I think Fidel is crazy not to consider their help. He resists any change in his vision. Personally, Communism isn't working, and I think we should make the political changes toward a free enterprise system. The black market thrives, and the people want a better quality life. Fidel and Raúl have us all brainwashed with fear."

Enrique listened, but was very quiet then he said, "You make good points, but I think we had better stop talking about this topic. You never know who is listening, and Ishmael is due anytime. You know what will happen to us if we get caught talking about this stuff?"

The general leaned closer to Enrique, "We need change now. You and I can do it. No one else will ever take the risk. You know what we can do and what is possible. Look at what we achieved in Angola."

Enrique was getting concerned, "I can't risk Andréa's and my family's lives. It's not just me anymore. I have too much to lose to try anything. You are crazy to think about doing the same. You know people cannot be trusted, and Fidel and Raúl have spies everywhere."

"Look, stop thinking that way. Are you willing to die a slow death here? Fidel is draining the life blood out of this country. People are leaving for Miami everyday on pieces of wood."

Enrique said, "I will never escape from my problems. I have a good job and I love my family. It may not be much, but it is enough to take care of us for the rest of our lives. We can't change what Fidel has built overnight. Anyway, I am getting too old for thoughts of a new revolution. That is a pipe dream. I want to be with my family, and I want my security."

"You think you are secure? You have no freedom and your security depends on the good graces of Fidel. What happens if that runs out? Do you remember General Ochoa? He was Fidel's right arm next to Raúl. He fought for Cuba, and he was shot for it. Nothing is secure!"

Enrique was very uncomfortable at this point but replied, "All right, you've you're your point. I don't like what the United States is going to do if they gain control of this country. I would hate for that to happen. Japan is a good option; and if we can get away from this Communist poverty, we will get in trouble for financial bargaining. Cuban-Americans will come back and take over this entire island because they have the money. Exiled Cubans already have an agreement on who will control the Cuban economy. I read about this in the Cuban interior minister's report. I hate the Cuban-Americans. They will just return and control everything in sight, and we will become slaves to money. Fidel is correct about that. I don't want that kind of life. Fidel always said it would happen, and I do believe we must keep out all US Cubans. But it will not be allowed. If that happed

The Last Revolution

I will fights to Cuban-American until I died. Abe I am serious. You too right? That correct?"

"Look, whatever you and I decide will be the law. We could establish that Cuban-Americans who return to Cuba must live in the country for ten years before they can own a business. They may participate in politics, but they must have lived in the country continuously and for a minimum of thirty years. Otherwise, they cannot become a candidate for a political position."

"First, we must take care of the Cuban residents here. Those who fled to Miami have not given their life to our motherland. They simply abandoned this country for the protection of the US. But if they return, they must immigrate back here with some guidelines and rules. They must not be allowed to come here and take over. After all, we have given our blood, sweat, and tears for Cuba, not them. We can control this if we overthrow the Cuban Communists!"

Enrique asked, "Overthrow? And then what a true democracy?"

The general continued emphatically, "They are many political systems to consider. I think what the Americans did in Japan after WWII worked beautifully. We can adopt a similar system and make Cuba a social and democratic free country with reconstruction goals for our economy and nation. We are talking about progress! Communism doesn't work, but aspects of this system are good and may prevail. I envision it as a merging of the best of the current political systems for our new Cuba. Just as Hugo Chávez is achieving now, Japan already had done that almost 60 years ago" The general laughed. "I am a dreamer!"

Enrique smiled. "You are and your dreams are for a better life. I have those same dreams."

The general began again. "Ultimately, the Cuban people will speak for what they want. We must protect Cuba from political corruption and nurture the electoral system. That is the only way. The US model has produced a strong and stable democratic nation. The same cannot be said for many of our neighbors to the south."

Enrique and the general continued their intense discussion. Enrique brought out his humidor and offered the best of his cigars to his friend. The general chose a Montecristo White label #2 Torpedos. It was a beauty. Enrique said, "Impressive choice. I can tell a lot about a man from the choice of his cigars. And political reforms and opportunities for outside aid and investment will be answered in time. Cuba must create an equivalent of the US Senate or UK Parliament by voters. Incentives to get all Cubans to the polls can be put in place. Making the process accessible to everyone is the goal. This goes for the most educated to the poorest farmer."

Enrique questioned him, "Abe, what do you intend to do with any resistance movements and insurgents?"

The general leaped at the answer, "Enrique, military law will protect the state until the new government is past infancy. Our job will be to oversee the new Cuba through this critical stage. Between you and me and our intelligence teams, we will secure this and make sure no insurgents get in the way. A gun and arms law must be mandatory. The pubic may protest, but armed insurrection will not be tolerated. The trend of political corruption will end with Castro. Castro loyalists will be watched, but without their leader alive what do they have? Castro has had his day, and they will see that his vision died along with him. They will see that Castro has been a cancerous growth on the Cuban body. Castro is a cancer who has grown out of control. Once he is taken out, the body will heal and become strong again. Once the people get a taste of prosperity and a better life, they will forget Castro."

Enrique's family had always supported Castro, but in recent years they had grown apathetic toward him. His words seemed empty as they looked at their crumbling towns and empty lives. He knew what Abelardo was saying was the truth.

Enrique asked, "Abe, what about elitists who wish to control the country? That is South America's problem. Elitists make for bad politics."

The general responded, "We must educate the people and appoint an equal distribution of the population and oversee the process. Both the educated and the poor will be represented in this distribution. There will also be a socialized medical system. All people should have the right to good medical care in a society."

Enrique kept on with his questioning. Had his friend thought it all through, he wondered? Enrique added, "Abe, what about control of the resources and the infrastructure? What areas will the government still control?"

The Last Revolution

The general took a sip of his beer before answering. "A democratically elected committee consisting of Cuban citizens who have proven to be loyal, decent, educated, and hard working can work together to create laws to govern this process of dispersing resources and privatization. They must be approved by a vote from the country. Actually, I just had this same conversation with Dr. Hiroaki Nakagawa. We thought that all Cuban government assets could be divided up among the people in the true spirit of Communism. Then, with tenants of a social democracy, military, transportation, health care, hospitals, libraries, art collections, schools, agriculture, the postal services, etc. can be government-operated and owned. Heavy industry and banking will remain private with international and national corporations involved for investments and exchange."

"It will be modeled after a blend of modern day Japan, Sweden and France perhaps a blend of the social democratic model. We have never been a constitutional monarchy like Japan, but we can adopt similar aspects of their thriving system. Eventually, Cuba may even move toward a free market and capitalistic system like the US, but that will evolve over much time. But I see that ahead in Cuba's future."

Enrique was listening intently and frowned at the thought of Cuba turning into a miniature US. The general continued, "Assets that have been sold off can be used as stock for the Cuban stock market. But, Dr. Nakagawa and I both agreed that the initial wealth must be evenly dispersed like social security is in the US, among the Cuban citizens. They have stuck it out over this long haul and have suffered hardships for so many years. They deserve a piece of the pie. We must plant the seeds for freedom and change." Enrique agreed and thought this was appropriate.

"The resources must be reserved for the people and they must get their fair share of the wealth. I don't like the idea of a pure capitalistic Cuba, but I know we will need foreign and private investments. The Cuban government will have to regulate this system so that we are not exploited by the big G-8. Cuba is the gateway to South America, and they are all eager to have a foot in the door here. I also do not trust US intentions at all. Havana must never become a San Juan!" The general understood Enrique's concern.

The general was on a roll. The glimmer of light and excitement in his eyes was bright. This was something he felt passionately about, and he and Enrique knew that everything they were saying could be the future of Cuba which would become their children's future.

The general went on to say, "It could be done in many different ways. But it will be key for the new Cuban government to control the returning Cuban-Americans. They can become vested, but they must not take complete control any of businesses or government offices right away. They must earn them over time. When they do eventually climb up the ranks and own a business, they must hire Cuban workers and guarantee decent wages and insurance. There can be no exploitation of other Cubans for cheap labor."

"Cuba must not turn into another China or South East Asia. They are raping their own countrymen to line the pockets of foreign investors. It is a sad state of affairs as to what is going on there and in other parts of the world. We must protect the Cuban workers."

Enrique agreed and was pleased with the general's ideas. He had thought about these things himself many times over the years.

The general added, "We must make strict immigration laws, and the Cuban-Americans have to decide to have only one citizenship. They must choose between Cuba or the US, but not both. If they choose to become US citizens and have a US passport, they can come in as visitors, but they will not be able to have Cuban privileges. Those who return and want to become a Cuban citizen must abandon their other passport. Foreigners can have a business here, but they must pay high federal taxes. They cannot just come here and buy Cuba out. Those who choose to live here, well we can control everything and benefit. Anyway, these details can all be sorted out later by professional. Now, we must focus on the primary objective, correct?"

Enrique nodded as he drank his Cuban coffee. His mind was racing in many directions. This conversation was very stimulating and had created a reawakening within him. Enrique spoke again, "I feel better since you have explained things to me in more detail. And in jest he asked, "And tell me, will I still be a general in the Cuban army?"

The Last Revolution

González, laughed at his question. "Yes, my friend. Cuba needs you to lead the Army. You and I will oversee the Cuban Army as before, because if other greedy or radical politicians like Fidel are elected by the people, they will destroy the country completely. We will be in the same boat. But we will not interfere with the politics of the Cuban parliament. They must decide our destiny just like the Japanese parliament. But good leaders elected by democratic vote are necessary to make this plan succeed. The military must not interfere with government business. We are only here for the nation's security."

"What is most important is that someone decent who holds Cuba's best intentions in their heart leads the country. Our leader should be someone who has vision and strength who will help guide the country toward a free market economy and who will help us modernize and develop, perhaps even for a good decade or more. We may have to help lead until the country gets on its feet and can stand alone. Cuba will be in a very fragile state for the next few years, and we are vulnerable to takeovers from other governments and countries that have other interests here. Perhaps, you and I will help control the country until a good person is elected. Cuba must be protected so we will control the Army. We will be the transitional government until the people elect new leaders."

The general could see that the wheels in Enrique's head were turning. "Enrique, the situation will be totally different from anything you and I have ever seen before. We have lived in a dictatorship for so long that we have to get out of this brain-washed mentality and realize that all Cubans can work together to make the changes necessary for a new and stronger nation. We will be a team and family once again."

Enrique said, "I hear you, my friend but where do we begin? You know I have fantasized about this for years, but this is the first time I have ever realized it as an actual possibility. What do you see as a proper time frame for this plan?"

The general smiled, "Well, there is no need to rush into anything. Nothing this big happens overnight. It will take decades before Cuba will become settled. It can happen in the lifetime of our children if we begin now. The next five years will be a very critical time for our nation. We must act swiftly. We cannot afford another decade with Fidel or Raúl at the helm.

They are leading us to the rocky depths which would mean a sad future for our children and their children."

Enrique said, "So are you considering establishing a military government?"

"No, not at all. I am considering something similar to what the US and General McArthur set up in Japan right after WWII. That is probably the best model to adopt here in Cuba while we move toward a social democracy. The US did that very quickly and efficiently. We must get other governments to invest in Cuba, but not to control our destiny."

"Hiro explained that if we sell some industry to Japanese industrial giants, they will invest here in Cuba without trying to take over and run the country, not like the power hungry American gringo's. They would want to own us completely. And both Hiro and I believe the tourist or Real estate businesses might be a good investment as far as the Japanese are concerned. He explained that some industry will be very difficult because the world cannot compete with China's great manpower and cheap labor. But other industries like tourism, the service sectors, and light industry, pharmacy, and medical should be successful immediately."

Enrique said, "But the Cuban people will probably become slaves again. The Japanese government doesn't want to control Cuba like that. They are not interested in getting involved in our politics unlike the US. The Japanese only want to be involved commercially."

Enrique asked "Who is this guy Hiro? I think I met him once at the university in Pinar Del Rio. Isn't he a professor? Why do you feel like you can trust him so much?"

The general answered, "This is a man whom you will come to know very well. I trust him with my life. I met him in Santa Clara four years ago He is a Japanese mathematics professor with a long and impressive background in both computer science and mathematics. His new field of cutting-edge computer science and what he can do technologically speaking is almost endless. He is truly a genius, but he is also a very quiet and reserved Japanese man a humble individual. He moved to Cuba to learn more about the country then ended up falling in love with a Cuban woman and starting his family here in Rancho Veloz area. He has helped many people here, and he has become very dedicated to Cuba."

The Last Revolution

Enrique asked, "Sounds like a good man, but if he isn't Cuban, what does he have to do with all of this? I don't get it?"

"This is not just any friend. He is someone to be completely trusted, and I do not say this lightly. He is also well connected in Japan with links to the top of both government and heavy industry. He is also one of a handful of men in the entire world who can change computer technology as we know it. He helped invent the core of what we know and understand today. But his life took a dramatic change when he moved to Cuba. His heart is here. He is a friend to Cuba, and you must trust me on that. You know I trust only a handful of people. But this man will help us change Cuba, and we cannot do it without help. He made the cultural exchange to Japan possible, and he sent me a message via the Internet saying that he has already discussed our plans with the Japanese industrial giants. They can reprogram and retrain our country for modernization."

"Japan was once closed to the entire world, but after 1853 they opened up and now are one of the most powerful countries in the world. I certainly believe he is someone who can shape our destiny. No one else has even offered help and certainly not without greedy intentions."

Enrique asked "How can you communicate via the Internet? Fidel can detect any message before you ever get it. And what about Japan pre-and post 1853? Tell me more."

"Well, we are using a little secret weapon. Hiro created a special code to allow us to communicate undetected. It is impossible for the Cuban secret agency to crack this code anytime soon. Anyway, based on my study, Japan was a very fascinating, complex, and ancient culture. However, the country and economy was halted for nearly 300 years and put into deliberate hibernation by its military ruler. It is much like what is going on here in Cuba."

"But in 1853, the United States government forced Japan to re-open the country because US fleets had a lengthy voyage from Hawaii to China, and they needed to stop and re-supply in Japan. US post supply ports were needed because many seamen became sick with scurvy. Japan was in the perfect position for a supply stop because of its location between China and the US. But Japan was controlled by a group of Shogun, and the country was closed off from the rest of the world. They didn't allow foreigners, and they didn't permit anyone to leave island. They were completely isolated with a superior military dictator. Sound familiar?"

The general had Enrique's attention now. "Fidel is bad but not compared to the Japanese Shoguns. They were fierce military war lords with a strict code of honor which they lived by. They controlled Japan for nearly three centuries."

Enrique continued with his questions saying. "That is impressive. Three centuries? Please continue the history lesson."

"Japan was on the brink of self-destruction, like Cuba today, because of the enforced hibernation. But they were able to catch up with the rest of the world and had one of the strongest naval powers in the world. And you know of their history since WWII."

Enrique added, "That is interesting. I didn't know about Japanese's early history. Tell me all that you know. I need some catching up here, too!"

González continued to update Enrique on Japanese history from the 14th century to modern times. He talked for nearly two hours." Japan was at war with Russia from 1903-04. Within a very short time Japan built up their heavy industry. Forty years later they were at war with the US. Japan went to war with the United States because the US designated Japan as a "third world country." The Japanese were not going to stand for this so Japan became one of the world's top industrial nations. Even a small island country like Japan became a world leader. Now they are a member of the prestigious G-8. Japan was able to expand from having nothing to becoming a gigantic industrial and technological heavy hitter within a very short time. Japan has reached the top which is a very impressive achievement."

Enrique replied, "Look, Japan was a United States colony right?"

The general said quickly, "No! Are you serious? Japan is a market economy, and the United States is only the big engine for the financial and market economy. Without the United States, the whole world's economy would collapse. The world economy is like a big wheel of fortune. It is always moving buying and selling. Selling and buying. So, if you are trying to change the system, like Fidel did, it just doesn't work. It is beautiful in theory but not realistic, just a dream. Again, it just doesn't work. No system is perfect, but it is the driving machine of the world's economy, and we must work in harmony with it."

The Last Revolution

"We must join the ranks of free market economy it's the only system that is working. Cuba has become isolated since Castro. Fidel is a rogue dictator who is suffocating us. In the current situation, Cuba will continue to self-destruct little by little. And speaking of Japan, it was not until they opened up their country again that they began to catch up with the rest of the world. Then they became world leaders."

Enrique asked, "So when Cuba goes through the initial transition, who will control our island? The Cuban people will control this island like José Marti envisioned. Cuba must be absolutely free from greedy nations and dictators. No one person can control the government for more than five years. I think that is long enough, but all the Cuban people must decide what our destiny will be. I am talking about true elections. Something Castro would never allow. It his counties will as my county too Cuba belongs to all Cuban. You and I can see that no ballot tampering or fraud occurs, and we can help protect this process. The people will elect a president and a cabinet of leaders which will be made up of both men and women who possess the best and brightest minds in Cuba. The most important thing is that no one man's ambition will ever control our country again."

Enrique smiled, "Abe, You sound like a politician. Have you any ambitions to the lead the country?"

The general shook his head, "Hell no! I am not interested in leading this country. I am interesting in helping Cubans become independent and motivated. With everyone working hard again, we will enjoy our nation!"

Enrique became very quiet and still. There was no movement in his body language as he continued to think about Cuba's unknown future. He thought about the different scenarios and also that a coup would jeopardize his career as Cuban Army Air Force General. This scared him, but he continued listening to the general's ideas and plan. Enrique mentioned that he knew something about some hidden resources. The general asked, "What are you talking about? Money?"

Enrique said, "Abe, Fidel has ten billion dollars in a Swiss bank account. That is what I am talking about. Do you think we can access that money?"

The general answered, "Look, Fidel has money, but it is only to be used for an emergency, such as when Cuba gets in a money crunch. Then Fidel would use the funds to purchase food. If the Cuban people go hungry, then Fidel might lose his control over them. While ten billion dollars seems like a huge fortune, it is really nothing when it comes to government. Even if we could actually locate Fidel's money in Switzerland, it belongs to the Cuban people, not us. It is for everyone and should be used toward the reconstruction of our island. The changes will take many years, but it is possible if we can just make a start!"

Enrique was concerned and said, "Start? You mean you and I would start the revolution?"

The general replied, "Yes, the last revolution."

Enrique instantly froze and the general could see that he was nervous. But it had to be done and the general needed help to see it through. He trusted Enrique and knew that it would take strong and loyal men to see this mission to its conclusion. Both became very quiet in their thoughts. Many minutes passed as they sat outside. It was almost seven pm, and the sun was just setting in the west. They gazed out at the view and the peaceful and beautiful countryside of Pinar del Rio. The sunset was breathtaking and calmed them.

Then Enrique's wife Andréa called to her husband. He had a phone call from the Chief. He went kitchen to take the call. Andréa brought out more cold beer and talked with the general. She was interested in how his family was doing and about his children's education. They discussed school in Santa Clara. She also mentioned that she was going to see her family in Trinidad. They lived in Sancti Spritus. She was a sweet woman and very social. The general felt at ease with her. When Enrique returned there was a serious look about him.

His wife asked, "What is it. From the look on your face, I suspect bad news."

Enrique replied, "I do have bad news. Chief Ishmael phoned that his cousin Juan Carlos is getting worse. It doesn't look like he will make it thought the night. He is going to stay until tomorrow morning. He wants everyone to standby here until he returns. He is not sure what time he will be back tomorrow."

The general was visibly remorseful. "Ishmael must be taking this news very hard. I know Juan Carlos was his favorite cousin. They were very close growing up, and they are near the same age."

The Last Revolution

Andrés interrupted, "*Vía con dios*. We should all pray for them tonight." He closed his eyes and took a deep breath. He paused for a moment of silence and thought of Ishmael. He was a good person who had been a loyal friend for many years. He felt sorry for his friend's loss, but he did not pray. The general was not a man who attended church regularly, but he did have beliefs about God and was spiritual in his own way. But he did not believe in prayer. He believed in people.

At dinner they sat around chatting and catching up. It had been almost a year since they had last seen each other. Even though Cuba was a small island, work in the military had kept them isolated. The Cuban way was to spend the evening talking and talking for hours with a good cigar. They didn't rush meals, and quiet dinners with polite conversation were not the norm. Meals lingered on, and it was the enjoyment of the company of others that set the pace for the evening. There was always story telling and laughing. Andréa talked about her childhood home in Trinidad. The general was interested, but Enrique was quiet and deep in thought. He was thinking about a revolution.

His wife laughed and asked him, "Honey, you are a million miles away. You never act like this? What is bothering you? Are you thinking about Chief Ishmael's cousin who is dying?" Then she added coyly, "Or are you thinking about another woman?"

Enrique laughed at her joke. The general knew why he was so quiet, and his behavior wasn't related to Ishmael's cousin's declining health. He answered for Enrique, "I gave him some computer problem to think about. We have been having some technical problems in the new computer system back at the base. He is concentrating for me. Isn't that right?"

Enrique nodded putting his wife at ease. After dinner was finished, the general asked Andréa to keep this matter very private.

She answered, "What matter?"

The general was caught off guard by her words. She smiled and said quickly, "I am a general's wife after all.....you know I forget about everything as soon as I hear it." It was not the first time she had been around when "business" was being discussed. The general smiled back at her and thought about how many times his own wife had had to forget what she had just heard or at least pretend that she didn't know anything. He looked at Andréa, and they didn't have to say another word. They understood each other perfectly. After she cleaned the dinner table, she brought them a tray of cold beers and salty chips. She told them both goodnight and excused herself. It was getting late.

Chapter 79

Enrique walked outside with the general and sat in the comfortable chairs on the back patio. They opened their beers and toasted. They were eager to continue where they had left off. Enrique asked, "Well, how do we proceed?"

The general knew this was Enrique's way of saying that he was in. He was relieved and exhilarated all at once. This was the first step, and he had a trustworthy partner.

The general answered him. "You know it is not going to be easy. Fidel has his spies. We cannot end up like Ochoa."

Enrique said, "Ochoa waited too long and was found out. That's why he got into trouble. So we need to make our plan and move quickly."

Enrique was known to act very quickly. His motto was, "to strike while the iron was hot." The general, who was also very quick to act, was an equally a strong thinker. He never moved spontaneously; there was always a firm strategy behind his movement. Both were extremely intelligent men, and the goal was to execute the plan and stay alive while doing it. The general continued to speak of his well thought out plan. Enrique added to this and together they made quite a team. They decided that before the night was over that they would have a skeleton plan in place. They were not tired even though it was very late. They stayed awake on pure adrenaline. They felt that everything was possible. They believed they could execute this plan and free Cuba. For the first time in years, they had hope and more vitality than they could remember.

They renamed the war game from "The Last Revolution" to code name "Ayu". It would start with a surprise attack on Fidel Castro consisting of four waves within six hours, it would all be over. Castro would be gone that quickly. However, the one catch was Enrique's lack of know-how in the area of computer technology. He knew better than most people, but was not up-to-date, and there was no time to teach him. They had to find a way to bypass his inexperience in this area. So the general said, "Enrique, you are just going to have to trust me. I will send you full coded messages via computer and phone, and you must execute them without question." Enrique fully agreed to the plan.

Abelardo asked, "Enrique, are your best combat jets efficient enough to do the job within five hours?" Enrique reassured general that he could get enough fuel for the combat force and that his jets could do it. The Enrique planned four waves of attacks while the general would remain back at the station in Santa Clara. Once the combat jets did their jobs then he would finish the game personally. It was like old times for them. They were discussing the many tactical scenarios just like they had in Angola. Enrique revealed his four stages of attacks.

The first waves of jet fighters to be used were twenty MIG-23 Floggers. The Flogger was the most sophisticated Cuban fighter and could deliver bombs using precision accuracy. Additionally, the following MIGs would participate in the attack: Ten MIG 29 Fulcrums, ten MIG-19, and twenty MIG-21s. These MIGs would attack the fourteen residential houses of Fidel, Raúl, and Chief General Garcia. They moved so often in between these houses that no one could ever be sure where they were at any one time. Fidel never stayed in one place for very long.

The first wave would completely destroy and dismantle the military communications tower and the department of defense and its surrounding facilities. The first wave of bombing would include the Cuban secret service agency and all military communications systems including cellular phones, the communications tower for the security of Havana Harbor, and all airport communications. It would all take place in just one hour; this would accomplish sixty percent of the plan. The targets would be neutralized completely. Everything in a five mile radius around Fidel's personal transport helicopter would be left intact. They wanted Fidel alive until later. Then, the general would send in more jets consisting of five older MIG-21s, five Hoplites, twelve MiG-19SF and ten MIG-17s.

The second wave's main objective was to destroy additional re-enforcements that would be used for back up. The jet fleet would also bomb the fourteen residential homes of Fidel, Raúl and the Chief General. All military installations in Havana would be destroyed. But Fidel's transport helicopter was not to be touched yet.

The third wave was to re-arm the MIGs and refuel. Then the fleet of forty jets would continue to attack ground targets. They would continue to regroup and load more arms. They would then standby for the next order. Then, waves four and five would be more bombing of the same installations as needed. They would have to access the target with each fly by. The general would monitor it all by satellite phone from Santa Clara. Enrique proposed assisting with his air campaign by sending in extra ground forces for security. He discussed the idea of sending five thousand men to Havana and another five thousand to Pinar Del Rio at his Air Force base. Normally, there were less than two thousand ground troops stationed at the Air Force base on any given day. But Enrique suggested that an extra three thousand be put in place before the operation began.

But General González declined to send in any ground troops anywhere before the operation to prevent Fidel from suspecting a coup. Their moves had to remain undetected. He wanted to keep his troops on standby near Matanzas as Fidel had planned and instructed. They had to keep Fidel believing that everything was going as planned. But, they both agreed that they must strike Fidel the first chance they got.

Enrique said, "And what happens if we are not successful within five hours?"

"Look, by my calculations, it will be over in five hours. But, if something goes wrong you will regroup and standby. I will send one-third of my troops to support you. But that is just playing the war game. I will reinforce your position. Of course, if this scenario occurs, the revolution will be much longer than I anticipated. Let us plan for this, but focus on success!"

The general added, "No one knows exactly where Fidel and Raúl are staying. They are always moving. We only know how to reach them by emergency satellite phones until they schedule a meeting."

Enrique responded, "They have been living this way for the past forty-five years. They must be tired of it by now. Or very used to it!" the general interrupted. He added, "Since no one knows where to find Fidel, we will make him come to us."

Then Enrique said, "Hey look Abe! He hasn't come out and told us to please kill him."   Both men laughed hard.

General Gonzales continued, "I will then occupy Havana and take control of the surrounding cities, towns, and country side. I have faith that the Cuban people may help, but I cannot be one hundred percent sure. General Garcia has a strong hold, and I know he will fight. He still has nearly ten thousand troops under his control around the south side of the army base in Havana, but I have twice as many troops. I also know that many of his officers have been very unhappy because General Garcia is not taking care of his men. They have told me confidentially that he probably needs to retire. He's a tough old guy, but his methods are obsolete. He may come to fight, but he cannot win.

I know his brigade General Gustavo Valdez very well. We go way back to the Academy. I know for a fact that he will be with us, and he holds his troops' ear. He controls nearly five thousand men. I will brief him in private. Our objective will be to detect Fidel's and Raúl's location at a vulnerable moment and to move faster."

Enrique gave him a glance. "Otherwise, we are going to get our ass get kicked like General Ochoa, remember?" Enrique was also concerned about General Gerardo Rosales of the Third Division in Santiago de Cuba as well as the Cuban Navy and the Coast Guard Admiral under Sabasterico Santana.

To put his mind at ease the general said, "Santana is very intelligent, and he will be with us. I will persuade him. But, General Rosales might be a little tougher to convince. I have some ideas, though. I believe we can persuade him. I also believe that he can be bought."
Enrique asked, "Bought?"

The general responded, "He loves American baseball. If he joins us, we are going to agree to let him own an American baseball team in Havana. They will be named the "Havana Hatuey's."

Enrique laughed, "Abe! Is it that simple?"

The general was serious, "Yes it is. I know what brings a man joy. Besides, he will get very rich from it. Baseball and wealth are the way to Rosales's heart."

The general said, "I actually met with General Rosales not too long ago. We talked about Cuban politics, and he is not very happy about the Cuban economy and the future of Communism. He didn't speak against Fidel or the government, but I have a very strong idea about him. Do you remember when

The Last Revolution

his only sister left for Miami a few years ago? That was devastating to him, and he has been distraught over the separation. He told me he would do anything if his younger sister could return home. This will work to persuade him, too."

The general and Enrique talked the night away. Finally, they discussed the detailed plan for assassinating Castro. The general said, "You will begin by hand picking someone in your command whom you trust and whom you feel comfortable with. You will have to give them orders at a moments notice. Then you will start with a surprise attack on Havana. I will send troops to Havana to crush General Garcia's army. I will send more troops to surround Havana and to reinforce your position."

Then, the general leaned over and whispered the final plan to Enrique. It was for his ears only. Enrique was on the edge of his seat and his eyes grew wider as he responded, "Excellent idea!"

The general added, "Look! Never trust anybody else, and you will stay alive. If you don't, you will lose the entire game! You must trust me one hundred percent"

Enrique became very serious. He grew more uncomfortable as the details emerged during their discussion. Enrique asked, "It sounds to me like I am only going to be making noise. It's not actually fighting against Fidel, but the purpose is to get them to come to you?"

The general answered, "Exactly! We have to bring the wolf to the chicken coop. This revolution will be quick and fast. Remember, it will all be done within five hours from start to finish. If we miss any small detail, we are dead. We cannot miss the opportunity to neutralize Castro. Once we begin, there is no turning back. You must use your instincts, but I am the main force. From tonight on and for the first several weeks, we will work separately. Our men will go on thinking that they are preparing for the inspection and practice exercises. We will go with Fidel's timing. Then, at the last minute we will step in and hijack everything and go in for the final kill. Only a few select men who are our loyal followers will know the plan. But we must be very careful about whom we can trust. We will only get this one chance…..we know whom to trust. Remember to get all of your family members to the country side so they will remain safe."

Enrique asked, "Is this a coup d'etat or a revolution?"

The general retorted, "It is more than a coup....to end all of this with Fidel and begin with a new Cuba that's a revolution the last revolution!"

Enrique said, "Well, that's true because no one knows where Fidel stays at night. I hope we can finish in five hours. But it may take longer than we plan." They both continued to discuss things in great detail until they understood all aspects of the plan perfectly.

When they shook hands this night, they knew there was no turning back. They decided that there would be no other meeting or discussion about the patriot game. This was their first and last meeting. They didn't have other opportunities to meet due to work and they did not want to arouse suspicion. They could not risk taking notes or writing memos. They had to memorize the plan. It was a simple but strong plan. No information would be given to anyone, including their wives, family, or friends. "And you must do the same in your unit and wait to give the orders until the very last minute like the Japanese Tosa dog fights," added the general.

Enrique said, "What is a Tosa dog fight?"

The general said, "It is a traditional Japanese dog fight. They train the dogs to be silent, and they attack at lightning speed until the fiercest and most intelligent dog wins. If a sound is uttered the match is over. When I saw this in Japan, I was inspired. This is a brilliant strategy for us to use as well. Attack swiftly and silently The general continued to talk about his insights from his trip to Japan and from Dr. Nakagawa. They planned the entire war game in a single evening. It was just dawn when they finally decided to get some sleep.

The next morning at ten am two jeeps arrived at the house. It was the General's aide and Chief Ishmael Velázquez. The men knocked at the door. Andréa greeted them, saying "Good morning, gentlemen. I am afraid they are still sleeping. You know when it comes to technology they both get keyed up, and then they forget to sleep They had a very good time drinking and carrying on until late last night. Come in and let me make you some hot coffee and breakfast while I wake them up." They entered and sat in the living room. A few minutes later both the general and Enrique came out of their rooms to greet the new arrivals.

The Last Revolution

Chief Ishmael laughed, "You two look like shit! Too much rum? Looks like you need a few more hours of sleep!"

Enrique and the general gave each other a knowing glance. Enrique still looked bushed and swallowed some hot coffee before he answered them. "Yes, we had too much drink last night. I don't remember the last time we have been together. We talked all night."

The general chimed in, "Man, I also enjoyed talking and drinking with my old Angola buddy." They both turned to Ishmael. "How is your cousin? What happened to him?" the general asked.

Ishmael looked down. "Sadly, Juan Carlos passed away last night. He was a good man, but it was his time. I am going to stay with my relatives in Pinar del Rio for the funeral before retuning home to Santa Clara."

The general said, "I understand. I am deeply sorry." Enrique also extended his apologies and asked his wife to bring more coffee and food. He escorted the new arrivals to the outdoor patio where there was ample seating. There they began to discuss business. The Chief and Enrique talked about Fidel's inspection order coming up in July. Enrique explained that it was his responsibility to inspect the MIGs. He planned to bring all Cuban MIGs to his base. There he would inspect, test, and fly them with live ammunition. Then he would report to Fidel by the end of July. They continued to discuss the inspection of the Air Force hardware over breakfast. At noon they all returned to the Air Force base for further briefing on the inspection and final approval from Chief General Garcia.

In the afternoon, the general left by transport helicopter KA-50 for Santa Clara to the second division army base. He was ordered to return to his post by General Garcia. The inspection was to begin immediately. Fidel wanted to present the results to the Cuban assembly for the budget for the next five years. All Army and Air Force hardware were subject to inspection except for the Navy which had had their inspection six months earlier. The general normally checked the inventory every six months as part of his job so for him this was a fairly easy task. He always kept good records and was organized and very efficient. He could deploy troops within a short time. But besides the inspection, he was also responsible for reviewing new weapons for efficiency. He was also responsible for organizing his men, for implementing the plan, and for setting up security. There was much work to be done in a short time.

It was June 3, 2008, and back in Pinar Del Rio at the Army Air Force base, General Enrique Rodríguez was already beginning his part of the plan for code name "Ayu operation "Tosa". He had hand-picked three highly trusted members of this staff to form his team. He chose Major General Alejandro Llamas, a bright and trustworthy man who had worked with him for many years. His next pick was Major General Samuel Ruiz who was loyal to him and who would do anything for him. Finally, he selected his Chief of Operations Commander, Brigade General Gilberto Zepeda. Zepeda was one of his favorites whom he trusted implicitly. Enrique had selected these three men based on friendship, trust, and their great strength. He also understood how they felt about Cuba and knew that they would back this revolution. They all had suffered under Castro, and their families lived in poverty so he knew they would be ready to help in overthrowing Fidel. He waited until the right time and conducted a private with them.

Enrique felt a burning in the pit of his stomach much the same way he did before a battle. He told the men of the plan and spoke of the new Cuba waiting for all of them. As he predicted, after he finished all three men agreed wholeheartedly and pledged their absolute loyalty to General Rodríguez. They were ready to do what must be done to ensure a better life for their families and their countrymen. They all shook hands and were forbidden by Enrique to speak of the plan to anyone. They knew that from this point on, they could all be executed if anyone found out about their plans. He knew there were many spies in the field from Central Intelligence.

They realized the serious nature of the plot and knew that the plans must remain completely secret. The men started to cry from excitement and emotion. They, too, had thought about revolution and change, but today they knew they were making Cuban history together. They all had dreamed of a Democratic Free Cuba, and they pledged themselves to this mission. They were ordered to hold fast until further notice. The deed was done, and his team was in place.

On the same day back in Santa Clara, General González, was also selecting his team. He had thought about his choices for a very long time and knew who they would be from the

The Last Revolution

beginning. They were three officers whom he trusted above all. They were very special men who had pledged their loyalty to him a very long time ago and who would die for him if he asked them to. The first was Lieutenant General Diego Seville. The second was Major General Jose Santana. And the third was to be his operations commander, Major General Marros Rosas.

He called the three men together for a private meeting. They were very serious men, and they were not happy with the present state of their county or with the Cuban government. Over the years they had expressed to him how the country was deteriorating, and they were concerned about the continuing problems. They had each had tragedy strike their families due to the declining condition of Cuba.

These men were completely loyal to General González and had been under his wing since Angola. They loved the general because he was such a decent man, but they loved their country even more. They knew each other very well. The general met with them privately and began to explain the operation "Tosa" in detail.

They listened to the general without uttering a word. He gave a very emotional explanation along with his plan and he changed operation code name to "Tosa". He mentioned the hardships their families had suffered since Castro had come to power. They had lost many men and family members. After his moving speech, he asked for their support. The three patriots were honored to be a part of the plan for this revolution.

The four men embraced and promised to give their lives for Cuba if need be. They were emotionally charged after the general's speech and had tears in their eyes. They saluted their commander and pledged to keep the operation in strict confidence and secrecy. They would not speak a word of what they just heard. They were prepared to act when called upon. They knew their lives and their children's futures depended on it. They also knew that Cuba's independence from Castro was now within reach. Minutes after leaving his men, the general contacted his counterpart, General Enrique Rodríguez. He said one word "Ayu" and the date July 3, one am. The last revolution had begun.

Chapter 80

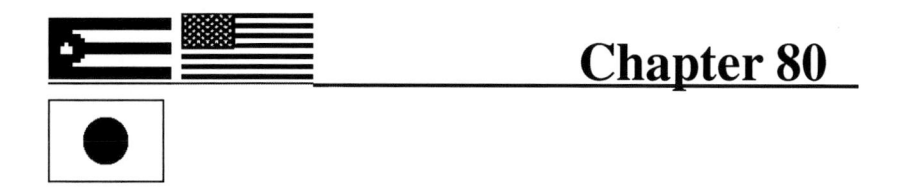

General Enrique Rodríguez

knew that this was his first and last chance to do the job. It was the perfect time to execute such a dangerous mission because of its coordination with the inspection. The jets would already be up in the air for testing and no one would suspect a thing. Both men were planning their logistical tactics in complete secrecy. They had to go over everything in their heads. Now the war game was finally being played out in real time.

General Rodríguez. Ordered Brigade General Gilberto Zepeda to complete surveillance on Lt. General Ricardo Lopez and his staff of twenty. When the signal was given, they would be rounded up, arrested temporarily, and placed in the Air Force jail for holding. General Lopez was a trouble maker and a threat. He was a second cousin of Raúl and Fidel and could not be trusted. He had to be detained at the proper time and fired from his post after the coup. He and his men would be required to hand over their weapons, and they would be detained until they could be escorted to the country side. After their release, they would remain under surveillance until the new government was in full working order. Political violence was always a threat and must be neutralized. They would be imprisoned if they organized and tried to stand in the way. This was the plan for all possible insurgents. They would be watched by intelligence agents, and they would not be given any opportunities for revenge.

Since this mission was extremely important, the patriots had to work very cautiously. Enrique used a special code name "Ayu." This was his signal to start the mission. Enrique had added two more officers to the inner circle: operational commander Major General Samuel Ruiz and Colonel Jesus Hidolgo to keep General González updated on mission readiness.

Back at the CIA Global watch in Langley Virginia, the team had intercepted months of communications between the Japanese scientist, Dr. Hiroaki Nakagawa, and Army Corps General González. Their messages had contained many

The Last Revolution

discussions on topics, such as Japan's history, industrialization, and the high tech industry. Some of the communications were coded and were unbreakable.

However, since the cultural trip taken to Japan by the Cuban delegation, the CIA had noted that Dr. Nakagawa had not contacted the general. But today after a long period of silence, the traffic had begun again. The general sent a coded E-mail message to Dr. Nakagawa containing just one word "Ayu." Dr. Nakagawa's response was coded using his unbreakable DNA-based computer.

This was highly frustrating to the CIA team. The CIA computer research team consisted of high tech hackers and researchers who had worked hard for two years trying to crack the code. They had not yet been successful, but they felt they were getting closer. They jumped on the new communications with renewed vigor after the long period of silence.

In Havana, the Federal Secret Surveillance Agency had been completely upgraded to the Colbana-Nakajima-JPX 008 technology. The Army intelligence technical team had organized a new section devoted to hijacking and hacking into various countries' computers. They had become very successful at it and were able to break into the US government's supercomputers. It was only a matter of time before they could access top secret information from the Pentagon and from CIA headquarters. They were also keeping a close watch on computer traffic between Dr. Hiroaki Nakagawa and General González. They intercepted many of the E-mails and saw that the content was on educational topics and programs, including industrial technical advice and forecasts. This was expected since the general had traveled to Japan for educational purposes, but Fidel still wanted strict tabs kept on the two. He was alerted that they had resumed coded contact.

Fidel was suspicious about the coded exchange. The team had been working furiously to unscramble the codes for the past three months, but they were too complicated. Cuban computer technology had been extremely poor until recently, but the code was still too complex for them to break. Unable to determine the meaning of their communications, Fidel grew frustrated and ordered that a spy be added to the mix. He wanted Brigade General of Cuban Intelligence, Oswaldo Ramon, to access the general's personal computer to try to break the code.

In addition, Raúl ordered Chief Cuban secret agent, Ishmael Velázquez in Santa Clara to keep a close watch on General González, from the Federal Secret Surveillance Agency (FSSA) information center. The FSSA was the equivalent of the Cuban FBI. They asked Velázquez because he was the top authority on the general.

They were concerned because the general was using special codes to communicate with Dr. Hiroaki Nakagawa. Ishmael Velázquez was concerned that his friend was under watch. This was never good, but he had to do his job. He went to the information center's data research room and asked Lt. Javier Perez to review the general's communications. Most were in standard computer language, but some paragraphs were completely coded in a different computer language. It was not a binary language or like anything they had ever seen before. The code was in a completely different format. They worked on trying to decode the message, but were unsuccessful. Chief Ishmael Velázquez was also puzzled by the secret contact.

When contacted about it by Raúl, Velázquez's reply was, "I was with them in Japan. They are both very good men and interested in technology. They are both interested in helping to industrialize Cuba. Dr. Hiroaki Nakagawa is very passionate about Cuba. He wanted to help us in any way he could.

When Raúl asked more about Dr. Nakagawa, Ishmael reassured him that he was a friend to Cuba and wanted to help the Cuban government as well as General González. Both men were extremely talented and highly educated individuals. Perhaps they were communicating through a new technology that could be used by Cuba as well. Ishmael defended his friend by saying, "As long as I have known González, he has been extremely loyal to Fidel. I honestly believe we don't have to worry about them. Perhaps they are testing a new computer language. They are not breaking any laws."

However, Lt. Javier Perez was not convinced. He suspected that there was something suspicious about this special code. Cuban government officials were free to use a personal computer and the Internet, but he wondered what message was hidden within the code. Chief Ishmael Velázquez was ordered by Raúl to work with his best technicians to break this code as soon as possible. He was also ordered to report to a higher authority, Fidel's top aide Roberto Cobarruvias.

The Last Revolution

Cobarruvias was a close friend of Freddie's. He called Freddie to get his opinion on the whole matter. Freddie immediately dismissed their suspicions. He protected his friends stating, "They must be trying out a new computer language. They are both technical wizards who like to dabble in computer languages. Just disregard the entire report." Roberto Cobarruvias listened to Freddie and did not forward any information to Fidel.

Freddie sent urgent word to the general asking him personally to stop testing this new computer language with Hiro. It was causing a huge controversy because he was involved with Cuban national security, and he cautioned that the suspicion was coming from the top. Freddie said that he would arrive from Havana at González's house this evening. They could talk more then. The general received the message and understood clearly that he was being investigated.

On June 21, 2008

At ten pm in Hiroshima, Hiro received a message from General González. The message informed Hiro that operation "Tosa" code name "Ayu" would start precisely at one am on July 3, 2008. Hiro replied giving technical advice and his recommendations. He would also work from Japan to descramble the commercial satellite telephone connections for the Cuban emergency line. He had already hacked into the key-code from the Globalstar located Mississauga, Ontario, in the Canada,

Globalstar had just purchased the commercial satellite telephone communication for all international units from AT&T the previous year. Hiro was successfully able to hack the many secret keys to temporarily dismantle service between the ground destinations to the satellite. From his home office in Japan, Hiro was able to use a remote device that implanted a connection in the satellite to Menu function in the main computer control facility at the Globalstar control center. He had planned the breach so well that they would never be able to detect any access by Hiroaki's computer. He reprogrammed the international satellite communications input filter and changed and re-routed the signal key for the Japanese satellite phone service.

Hiro could disconnect the global communications satellite with his special device. It would then alternatively send it to the Japanese JCSAT 9 communications satellite that was newly launched with a Zenith 3SL rocket. It was positioned at 132 degrees east longitude and overlapped the Canadian Global

Telecommunications service F3 satellite. Hiro then was able to reprogram the input device that resent the signal to the F3 satellite. The US would never detect Hiro's clever hijacking. Hiro made it possible that both generals had satellite communications activated while the rest of Cuba's satellite telecommunications service was halted temporarily from 12:30 am until 3:30 am. Communications service would resume 3:31am.

At that time, Enrique's and Abelard's communications would be terminated. Since 2003, Cuba had maintained special contracts with a commercial satellite company for usage and for the Cuban governments' emergency communications service. Cuba had a six channel line and forty-two commercial satellite telephones. This agreement was made possible via a contract through the Cuban Interest Section located in the Swiss Embassy in Washington D.C. Cuba had forged an agreement with the UN global communication treaty.

Hiro had already completed special software that would break the input and intercept the satellite communications signals. He tested his program successfully by temporarily pause communications.

He also hijacked output from the Japanese global communication DS-2000 satellite. It had been developed by Mitsubishi Electric in 2006. The DS-2000 was also used with the DRTS Kodama and the Superbird 7 communication satellites. Japan launched the newest generation of WINDS international communication global satellites in February of 2008.

It was owned by JTK commercial telephone company and the main control center was in Chiba near Tokyo. Japan now had the fastest version of the new generation of the Internet and telecommunications connections access in the world.

They were so fast that they had the capability to connect the two generals' satellite phones before they even heard a ring tone. They would have open communications during the war game. He urgently asked the general for both serial numbers from their receivers. He told the general that the information was necessary to dismantle the satellite signal temporarily. He reiterated the times saying service would be halted between 12:30 am to 3:30 am only. It would stress and confuse the targets and obscure ongoing operations on July 3, 2008.

The Last Revolution

The general agreed and was delighted to hear about the excellent communications tactic. He would get the receivers' serial numbers and pass the information along to his partner, General Rodríguez. He was also relieved to know that surveillance by the US CIA and Cuban intelligence would not be able to intercept their communications. It would all be done covertly throughout the take over.

It was the evening of June 21, and Freddie had just returned from Havana. He drove straight to the general's personal home. Freddie was exhausted after having a very frustrating meeting in Havana. He was also anxious to see the general and discuss what was going on with Hiro. He was concerned and knew that he would have to eventually report back to Cobarruvias with some facts. He wanted to urge them to stop so this matter would just die on the vine. He didn't want to see either one of his friends in trouble. Until now he had played it cool and had acted as if he thought nothing out of the ordinary was happening, but he was worried. He knew his friends were under the scope and that was never a good thing in Cuba.

The general's wife, Marisa, greeted him at the door and escorted him to the outdoor courtyard and patio. She was a kind and gracious woman. Marisa brought out drinks and refreshments. She had known Freddie and his family for many years.

Marisa said, "When Abe told me you were coming I decided to make a special dinner. I hope you like lobster with black beans and Panelela." Marisa knew Freddie loved home cooking.

Marisa, thank you so much. I always love your cooking. I have been eating junk in Havana all week. " Freddie was finally able to relax here. He was happy to have a good meal in the company of friends. But Freddie noticed that the general looked very tired and was not his normal, cheerful self. Immediately, he was suspicious that it had to do with Hiro and the computer code. But with Marisa around, he couldn't mention anything. He had to wait until they were alone. Thinking about what might be brewing made Freddie very uneasy.

The general began to tell Freddie about all the extra work the Army inspection was causing. He also told him that he was putting together a project with a Cuban computer technician to manufacture a replica of the Intel-Nakajima-JPX Chip. The general explained that he was having a very difficult time doing this. In fact, it was almost impossible to build. Fidel had insisted that the chip be replicated in one year, but it was next to impossible to locate the specific materials and silicone needed to do the job. Besides, the maker of the Nakajima chip and Intel were involved in a lawsuit that had been on-going for nearly three years. During this time, the Cuban government's computer science team had modified the chip's specifications so that the chip could be used commercially in the free trade world.

Marisa knew when the conversation reached a certain point that it was her cue to leave. She began to remove the dishes. But Freddie had not forgotten his manners and helped her carry everything to the kitchen. The general had so much on his mind that he could not share with Freddie. He thought about Fidel's plan to build a Cuban Silicon Valley close to the Santa Clara district. But it was an impossible dream in today's Cuba.

However, Fidel had very different ideas. For the time being, the general had to appear to just go along with the idea. He was ordered to work with Fidel's top aide, Roberto Cobarruvias, in Havana. He didn't trust him of computer technology. He had been sent abroad to study in England at Oxford. But the general had never liked Cobarruvias. He was greedy and smug and always brown nosing Fidel. Of course, he backed Fidel's unrealistic forecast for the Cuban Silicon Valley, but the general knew that the technology industry was an extreme challenge for Cuba because they had neither the financial backing nor the resources to make marketable items for distribution. With Cuba's political and economic climate, it was near impossible, but he kept his opinion to himself. Freddie walked back with another cold beer saying, "Abelardo that is one nice wife you have. I miss my wife. I am looking forward to some time with her. We are very lucky men, aren't we?"

When Freddie saw that the coast was clear and Marisa had gone to bed, he began to speak candidly to the general. "I got a call from Cobarruvias about you. You have to be careful, Abelardo. They suspect that you and Hiro are up to something. Your coded messages are seen as a threat to national security." The general knew very well that the government was taping his phone and Internet traffic.

Hiro had already warned him in early May the very first time they had sent an E-mail communication. But Hiro had

The Last Revolution

instructed the general in just what to say. The general was prepared for this moment. Hiro had already detected the use of the Tamotsu-JPX008 chip to trace the communications between the two men. It left a fingerprint-like trace through the Cuban federal secret surveillance agency's computer.

Hiro could monitor their computer traffic and filter out what he chose. He could break the information down into its original molecules through his DNA-based computer system. He also had the capability of tracing and pinpointing the exact global location via a built-in navigator-type option. No matter how much the chip was modified, the Nakajima-JPX008 serial number could never be removed from the original chip.

Freddie told the general that Fidel had made him his new Chief of Development for the Cuban Technology Department. Freddie accepted the new position and resigned as the Central and North Coast Tourist Development head. He had made many trips to Havana related to the new position. The new job came with a tremendous work load that took him away from his home, wife, and family in Santa Clara.

Freddie said, "Abe, whatever secret code Hiro is using could be of use to Fidel. Before long he is going to ask you to give us the technology. Any new inventions, languages, or innovations, etc. are extremely important for the Cuban government. Fidel sees dollar signs."

The general responded, "Fidel hasn't any idea about new technology. He wishes to scavenge from others and use Cubans as cheap labor to mass produce his new chip and technology." Freddie looked dismayed. He knew that this was Fidel's plan, but his hands were tied.

"Listen, Abe" he said, "stop using that code for your own sake. This is the only warning I can give you. If you want to stay in contact with Hiro, you must share the technology for new projects and new investors from the Japanese high-tech community with Cuba."

The general was quick with his comment, "So, the dog wants a bone?"

Freddie responded, "And you and I don't want to feel that dog's bite. He has sharp teeth." They laughed, but they both understood the seriousness of the situation.

Freddie told the general that he had been in touch with sources he had made during the cultural exchange in Japan. But he had not received any encouraging news from the Japanese technology community because of the mounting problems with the Cuban economy. He was hoping for investors, but they were not interested in getting involved in Cuba's political hot bed just yet. Also, the chip's on-going patent dispute between Intel and the Japanese company was holding everything up. Freddie expressed how frustrating this project was as the stand off continued.

The general knew that his friend Freddie was under pressure. Fidel was very impatient, and the general knew how badly he was counting on Japanese technology know-how and investment. So Fidel was turning the heat up on Freddie to pressure Ambassador Hector Ortiz at the Cuban Embassy in Japan for more contacts and information. The general knew that he was also under the microscope so he had to be careful around Freddie. They had been long time friends, but there was no telling what could happen if he was put under the gun by Fidel. Hiro had prepared him for this moment, and the general was ready to put on a good act.

He changed his demeanor almost immediately and began to ease Freddie's mind. "I understand your position, and it sounds frustrating. I will talk to Hiro and see what I can do. The code is an experimental, new computer language that Hiro is working on. Since he and I talk about computer science and technology, we often exchange ideas and he was testing his prototype out on me. It is still in its early stage and needs much work before release. All I know is that he is working on it with the computer science department at The University of Hiroshima, and it is an exciting new language. If successful, it could be the latest generation of computer languages and could change technology as we know it."

Freddie was relieved to hear this new, and it was as he had thought. He knew that his friends were not doing anything subversive. The general continued, "Very few people can understand this new phase of computer science using neuro-electronic interfacing systems. It will be the new generation of computer."

The general added, "Hiro and I were just messing around. I am like a guinea pig for the new language, but I can report that it doesn't work yet. Although, the Cuban government is not ready for this technology yet, I will try to convince Hiro to share it with Cuba when it is finalized. It, along with the chip, could produce the revenue that Fidel desires. Perhaps Hiro would be willing to help Cuba. After all, he is very passionate about our island nation. Hiro also mentioned returning to Cuba in a few months with his family. Maybe we can set up a meeting?"

Freddie looked pleased and felt optimistic for the first time in weeks. "Ahh! That's good news. I am dying to see Hiro. Please send him my regards and tell him that we must have a meeting upon his arrival." The general added, "As I said, Hiro's new computer language system is not fully-developed. I seriously think it will take another twelve months before it's functional. Since he is the inventor, there will not be a patent dispute. Perhaps we could make a special patent, borrow and nationalized his great invention. Perhaps there is a way to bring it to our government."

The general sweetened the pot a little more saying, "It could potentially mean a huge bottom line profit for our nation. I have a good feeling about this. After all, technology is a billion dollar business which could help Cuba take a seat in the modern world. Again, we can talk officially to Hiro when he arrives."

The general was very convincing. Freddie fell for it hook, line, and sinker. He was pleased to hear that Hiro was returning to Cuba. It had been a long time, and he missed his Japanese friend. He also needed Hiro's help with his new job. "I knew you were not using any new code against the government. But Fidel doesn't trust anyone. He always has to look over his shoulder."

The general remarked, "That is ridiculous! I have no agenda here and was just communicating with Hiro as I always have. However, thank you for the friendly warning. Perhaps it is time to stop communicating with Hiro for now."

Freddie scratched his head. "Wait! I can talk to them. May I have your approval to pass this information along to my superior? Actually, I will be glad to have some good news to report for a change."

The general had Freddie exactly where he wanted him and added, "Of course, tell him everything. I have nothing to hide."

Freddie spoke very seriously, "Abelardo, I just want to reassure you that you are my friend. I had your back when they came to me. They do not even know that I am here unless there are spies watching me.

The general nodded, "I know you are a very faithful friend. I appreciate your coming here to warn me. I know you are looking out for me." The general took another drink. He had convinced his good friend and knew this would buy him more time for implementing the war game. They began talking about something else as they rested on the patio chairs. It was a beautiful evening, and they took time to relax with the warm breeze.

The next day Freddie left for his office in Santa Clara. Once there and alone, he called Cobarruvias in Havana and explained everything about the new computer language being developed by Dr. Nakagawa in Japan. He explained that the general was just a test subject and that the language was still in development. It could be an exciting new breakthrough that could mean potential revenue for Cuba if they played their cards right. Freddie told him everything that the general had said. And he was happy to report that Dr. Nakagawa would be returning to Cuba in the next few months. The general would arrange an official meeting with Dr. Nakagawa.

Later that day, Cobarruvias phoned Freddie back. "I just had a briefing with Fidel. Tell the general to proceed with Dr. Nakagawa in the trials and tests via the Internet. He must also compile any and all information from Hiro and turn it over to you. Observations or insights from the general must be written and handed over to you also. But General González is to proceed with caution. Fidel is very interested in a personal meeting with Dr. Nakagawa when he returns to Cuba. Fidel wants to make sure that Dr. Nakagawa's intentions are friendly and that he has proof of this new language." Freddie understood and contacted the general with the requests.

Meanwhile, Fidel still had his reservations about Dr. Nakagawa, but he knew he needed his technology. He knew that this new language could be Cuba's trump card. Fidel had a thug mentality and knew that he would one day get his hands on this new generation of computer languages one way or another even if it meant kidnapping Dr. Nakagawa's children and wife for ransom.

Whatever had to be done would be done! Fidel ordered Major General Javier Perez of the Federal Secret Surveillance

The Last Revolution

Agency to continue to closely monitor their E-mail activity. He also wanted the tech team to continue working on cracking this code. He tasked his spies in Japan to keep a closer watch on Dr. Nakagawa and his family. Fidel wanted to know where they were at all times. Fidel didn't suspect any motives or immediate danger from Dr. Nakagawa.

This was Fidel's first mistake.

The general received confirmation that his plan had worked after the call from Freddie. He contacted Hiro using the code and told him that his plan had worked perfectly. They continued to communicate about the analytical portion of the war game tactics and game plan. Soon, Hiro told the general that things were getting risky using the Internet. The CIA headquarters were fast on their tails trying to crack the code. They were close, and Hiro expressed his concerns. Hiro tried frequent changes, but he was limited in what he could do at this point. However, his new computer language was so advanced that it was almost impossible to decode. There might be only two or three computer scientists in the entire world who were savvy enough to crack his neuro-electronic interfacing system DNA and molecular-based code.

Hiro suspected that the CIA might have recruited a computer expert from MIT for the team. He asked his old friend, Dr. Jon Katz, if he had heard or seen anything unusual. And indeed, Jon suspected that something out of the ordinary was taking place because many strange meetings had been held and several new people were working in the research department with Dr. Bernard Steinberg. He was the top man in the department, and this seemed odd to Jon. He wondered who those new researchers were, but it was none of this business so he didn't rock the boat. But it was possible that they were undercover CIA or government agents. Hiro knew that Dr. Steinberg was one of the only people capable in time of unraveling his code. He was a genius and a force unto himself. This made Hiro nervous, and he knew that if the CIA had Steinberg working for them that it was only a matter of time before they would be able to crack the code. Therefore, time was of the essence.

It was June 28, and Hiro had finalized the general's plan. The pair had planned the final details down to the exact minute. The tactics were clear and precise. Hiro's war game from concept to reality was in play, and it was all as he had originally intended. He went over every detail and felt confident that all would go as planned. He had the utmost confidence in the general's skills and war tactics, but Hiro's only concern was their communication via the Internet. Much incriminating information was traveling over the Internet, but it was for the time being protected by his program. But Hiro knew that it was only a matter of time before his code was cracked wide open. The clock was ticking and there was no room for mistakes.

Chapter 81

Back in Havana, Freddie was hard at

work on his assignment. His task was not an easy one because the Cuban economy continued to decline. Fewer and fewer Cuban-American visitors came from the United States. As a result, this caused an even greater set back for Cuba. They depended on tourism for their survival. Since the economy was going downhill fast with no end in sight, Freddie found it very difficult to secure funding from the government for anything.

Meanwhile General González continued to work on the new government venture for the Santa Clara Silicon Valley. He was overseeing the building of a computer chip manufacturing facility for the government. He also had a difficult time obtaining resources for the job from Havana.

Many materials had to be shipped from Canada. The US embargo created many problems and red tape. Humanitarian aid was fairly easy to obtain, but technology supplies were severely regulated and limited by the US government. The general had to continue to explain to Fidel's top aide, Roberto Cobarruvias, why he could not complete the facility. It was always the same story.

Meanwhile, the general thought about the war game non-stop. He planned and prepared in his spare time. He was frustrated and fed up with the government and could not wait to end this misery once and for all. Fidel had imposed an impossible drop dead date of forty-eight months to build the facility. Fidel had a vision that Cuba would be the "Technology Capital" for Latin and South America for the twenty-first century.

President Chavez told Fidel that his sources in Chile and Argentina had indicated that they were making good progress in developing the same industry. The very thought that other Lain American countries might achieve success in this effort before Cuba did caused Fidel to become extremely frustrated and angry. Hiro knew that Fidel would make one mistake by trusting a colleague.

Micheal Kazuhiro Nishitani

Back in Rancho Veloz, Pedro received a package from Hiroshima, Japan. It had been sent nearly four months earlier and was just now reaching his home. It was a Japanese wood working tool which had been reproduced from an old-fashioned tool. A letter from Hiro accompanied the package to Pedro that explained that many ancient Japanese carpenters had used this tool and that it was still being used today.

Hiro also mentioned in his letter to Pedro that he missed Rancho Veloz and his home in San Rafael near Sierra Morena. Hiro wished he could make a rocking chair again and go fishing in Rio San Pedro. He also missed going to the Hotel Elquea and the hot springs for retreats with his family and friends. He remembered his Cuban friend and his family and missed everyone. Hiro wanted to enjoy another goat barbeque, but he didn't say anything about when he would be returning.

Pedro could tell that Hiro was homesick for Cuba. Pedro thought about Hiro often and remembered all of their good times together just as if were just yesterday. He missed his incredible Japanese friend. Pedro and Hiro had forged a great friendship, one that they both would never forget. Every time Pedro went to Santa Clara, he stopped by Freddie's office. But he was never there anymore. The secretary told Pedro that Freddie was in Havana. A year had passed, and he had only seen Freddie twice. But Pedro stayed in the loop about Hiro through Dania's sister, Lillian. She communicated with Dania frequently via E-mail.

Every chance he could, Pedro went to hear the latest news. Every time he hoped that Lillian would tell him that they were returning, but that was never the case. Hiro and Dania did not know when they would return to Cuba. Everyone missed them, but they were happy to know that life was going well in Japan. It seemed like a different world and so far away. Pedro continued to drive his old brown 1956 Ford and, as always, spent most of his time working in the family wood working business. Life for Pedro had not changed much since Hiro's return to Japan.

The last sentence in Hiro's letter to Pedro read, "I miss you most of all. I have a great friend in Rancho Veloz." Hot tears fell from Pedro's eyes. Madeline was watching and she understood. She also missed Hiro.

Chapter 82

On June 25, 2008. In Santa Clara, General González ordered a war scenario as part of the on-going tests for the arms hardware inspection. He set it up as an exercise to practice defending Cuba during a mock US invasion near Havana and Matanzas involving 5000 Marines. He moved 12,000 Cuban Army soldiers into place. They prepared to intercept the enemy fully equipped. He set the date for the mobilization unit to test the war scenario in full on the evening of July 3. He planned for a night attack. In the scenario, the US Marine forces would land near the North coast of Havana and outside of Matanzas.

The general briefed his entire squad of commanders including Lt. General Diego Seville, Lt. Major General Joaquin Zamora, Major General Major General, Mario Rosas, and Lieutenant Colonel José Santana. Now they were ready for the final operation. It was a huge drill with precise ammunition tests to supply data for Fidel's report. The Santa Clara Army base was extremely busy and resembled a war zone.

A different kind of crisis was taking place about the same time in Japan. On June 28, back in Hiroshima, Japan, Hiro was on his way home from work when Dania called him on his cellular phone. Dania had just received an urgent E-mail from her sister Lillian. Their Aunt Dorita had suffered a serious heart attack. She was in the hospital recovering. Dania was in tears and wanted to return to Cuba to be with her in Nuevitas Camaguey as soon as possible. Her Aunt Dorita was her mother's only sister and Dania were very close to her. Dania desperately wanted to be with her in the hospital in Nuevitas.

Hiro rushed to get home. When he arrived, Dania ran to the door and buried her head on his shoulder. She couldn't stop crying. She felt so helpless and so far away from her family in Cuba. She expressed her love for her aunt and told Hiro that she must return home. Hiro tried to reassure her, and he wanted to read the E-mail himself. He couldn't think of anything else to say to Dania except, "Everything is going to be ok." But he didn't know this for sure. Dania showed him the message. As she reread the E-mail from her sister, she started crying again and screaming for help from God. Hiro didn't know what to do. His wife was hysterical.

Dania had always talked about her aunt as her second mother. Her Aunt Dorita had helped take care of her and her sisters when she was a young girl. They had lived on the outskirts of Nuevitas Camaguey. Dania had spent many summers there; it held a special place in her childhood memories.

Hiro just sat with her as she continued to cry. She wanted to return to Cuba and was getting very impatient and angry with Hiro. He asked Dania to send an E-mail telling Lillian that they would return in a few days. He would call the travel agent tomorrow to book flights for July 3 to Havana.

Finally Dania became quiet. She hugged him and wept on his shoulder. He could hear that her cries came from deep within her heart. She looked up at him and kissed him on the cheek. She had lived here in Hiroshima for almost two years, and she was very homesick. Hiro knew they must wait a few days because of the war game. The last revolution was on, and there were only two days before it would all play out. Everything was in place and running on schedule. He trusted the general and had complete confidence in his abilities. Dania didn't suspect anything. Hiro had not mentioned his plans to her because of security reasons. He was going to tell her when the time was right. That would be when the Japanese media started to report a war in Havana.

On June 30,

at the Army Air Force base in Pinar del Rio, General Enrique Hurtado Rodríguez called a private meeting to brief his team of six officers who would lead the simulation flights of the MIGs. Among them were his three hand-picks for the war game: Major General Llamas, Major General Ruiz, and Brigade General Zepeda. It had been over four weeks since his last meeting with his three-man revolution team.

They were standing by for his order to begin. They would be in control of nearly 150 various MIG fighter jets during the MIG performance tests at 0:100 hours on July 3. Their cover would be that they were testing the mechanical condition of the MIGs for Fidel's report. All of the MIG fighter jets were going to be lined up in operational formation on the ground ready for their

The Last Revolution

technical checks by the pilots, and then tested in air combat for their operational condition and limitations.

Fidel wanted all combat fighter jet data including night flying scenarios. He wanted to simulate a US air invasion. General Enrique Rodríguez had carefully organized his air defense team. The officers were ready for the upcoming testing and for the performance check during the night operation. They had spent weeks on this event and had gone through dozens of drills in preparation for the event. The scenarios included a huge ground invasion by the US Marines and a surprise attack by a squadron of US Air Force F-16 Falcon, F/A-18 Super Hornet fighter jets. These simulated drills were authorized by Chief General Garcia and Raúl and Fidel in Havana.

The general briefed the six officers. He carefully arranged his manpower with an available MIG fighter jet to do the job in six hours. He had stored huge quantities of jet fuel to be used during the drill. Everything had been approved by Fidel Castro himself. He had given his permission for the extra fuel to be used during the inspections. The general would make sure that his three-man team would have all the fuel they needed while the others had just enough to make their practice runs and to return to the base. Everything was going as planned, and the Air Force base was completely ready for the operation. No one suspected anything. The general and his men were ready. Everything was in order, and it was the perfect chance to begin the secret war games.

Their plan was already underway and both generals were filled with anticipation and hope that their plan would work. It had to. General Rodríguez meditated and went over everything in his mind. He could imagine the perfect execution of the war game. Now, all he had to do was to wait for the right moment to begin.

The plan was held in strict confidence by both generals and their team of loyal officers. General Rodríguez had sent his wife and family to Trinidad to visit her family. They would remain there until it was safe to return. Andréa didn't suspect anything when she said good bye to her husband, but Enrique couldn't help but hug her tightly saying. "I love you Andréa. Don't ever forget that," he whispered as he buried his head into her neck. He didn't want to let her go.   Andréa was surprised by his sudden emotional display and said, "I love you, too. You act as if I am going to be gone a long time."

He smiled, "You are a good woman, and I just wanted to tell you how I feel. I am going to miss you." But he knew this could be the last time he ever saw her. He yearned to tell her everything, and he ached inside. But he couldn't endanger her any further. It was too late for that. All he could do was to kiss her good bye and pretend as if everything were completely normal.

Andréa hugged him tightly and said her last good byes, "I'll see you soon, honey. I will call you tomorrow night." As she departed he thought about what could happen if the plan went bottom up. He would take his own life before being taken prisoner by Fidel. He hated to think that it could come to that, but he would not spend his last days being tortured in prison waiting to be executed by a firing squad. He tried to think of something else when he felt a burning in a pit of his stomach.

It was July 2 in Pinar del Rio

And General Rodríguez had been thinking all day about the war tactics. He had gone over the plan a thousand times in his mind. All hardware, supplies, manpower, and the target were rechecked many times. And each time, he took the opportunity to train himself and to review all details of the scenario personally so that the mission would run like clockwork. There could be no hesitation.

Timing was everything. All officers were on standby and believed that this was just a drill. Only his secret team of three commanders knew that it was for real. They were nervous but exhilarated. They never once spoke of the revolution to one another. Only knowing glances were exchanged. They knew that they were about to make history together. All they could do now was to be fully prepared and to wait for the order to attack the intruder in the night sky over Havana.

At four pm

Enrique called on his six officers. They were ordered to relax for the next four hours since all work had been completed. He wanted them rested so they could be fully energized for the exercise. He congratulated them, gave them a full salute, and dismissed them to their quarters. All MIGs were loaded with real bombs, missiles, and full ammunition. Fidel had never allowed them aboard before now, but he had permitted it to add reality to

The Last Revolution

the performance tests. They wanted to determine how much extra fuel consumption would be needed when their MIGs functioned at excess speeds with the weight of the bombs aboard so special permission was granted. Chief Genera Garcia and Raúl would be arriving from Havana in the morning. They wanted to be present for the day time intercept tests.

Brigade General José Santa Cruz had been in charge of overseeing strict security patrols on a twenty-four hour watch for the past week. He had 500 troops on call for security purposes. They were keeping an eye out for any suspicious activity on the grounds and around the MIGs. All men on the base were ordered to stay away from the MIGs and runways. Any unauthorized person found near the fighter jets would be shot on sight. There was always the threat of planes being hijacked by pilots and officers fleeing as political refugees to other Carribean nations or to Miami. Everything was set for the operation, and he was ready for his assignment.

Major General Samuel Luiz had been recommended by General Rodríguez because of his unwavering loyalty and because someone like him was needed to be the main ground operation coordinator. He ordered Major Ricardo Esparza to be the attack squadron leader and to take his orders directly from General Rodríguez.

At five pm back in the Havana

Lt. Colonel Perez of the Federal Secret Surveillance Agency was working overtime to break the secret computer code. At Fidel's request, he was monitoring all E-mail correspondence to General González from Dr. Nakagawa. Roberto Cobarruvias also suspected that Dr. Nakagawa and the general had a secret motive.

Cobarruvias also ordered Perez and his best men to use the chip to try and hack into the CIA's super computer. It was a long shot, but they had to use every possible avenue. He wanted to know if they had information on Dr. Nakagawa among other things.

The Army intelligence center in Santa Clara had been successful at hacking into some top secret CIA documents previously. But, since then, the CIA had changed their entrance keys. Perez was working on unscrambling them. The new Colbana-Nakajima JPX008 chip made that a viable possibility. It was just a matter of time and luck. If they could hack into the CIA super computer, then the sky was the limit.

At ten pm back at the base in Pinar del Rio, General Rodríguez called on one of his most trusted team members. He asked Brigadier General Alejandro Llamas to assist him in arresting Lieutenant General Lopez along with his commanders and officers. They were rounded up, stripped, and placed in jail cells until operation "Ayu" was over.

Lieutenant General Lopez and his men were completely shocked and stunned by this mutiny. They had not seen it coming. As Lopez entered the cell, he shouted to Enrique, "Tu eres un traidor! You are not going to get away with this. You have just dug your own graves!"

General Rodríguez had no intention of executing them. He just planned to keep them isolated to prevent any outside leaks. They would be escorted to the countryside and stripped of their military titles. They would be allowed to resume civilian life, but they would always be watched until the new government was fully established. If it were Fidel, he would have had them silenced for good. Fidel's policy was that all threats were neutralized either by execution or imprisonment. There were always accidents and people frequently went missing without a trace.

Chapter 83

Meanwhile, back at the Army Intelligence Center at the base in Santa Clara, General Abelardo González and his men arrested six officers including Brigade General Oswardo Ramon. General González had been spying on the intelligence center with special security software. He had found that Ramon was trying to send critical information to Havana. The security software, along with a hidden spy camera, was taking digital pictures every five minutes and showed all outgoing computer traffic. The general had detected unauthorized activity coming from Ramon, but the general had him arrested before it was too late.

Earlier, the general had issued a top secret order for the arrest of Brigadier General Sato and Lt. General Mantilla, along with 24 commanders, 125 other officers, and 150 enlisted men from the second brigade. All of these men were taken into custody because of their loyalty to Fidel Castro and his pro-Communist ideals. The arrests were necessary to prevent the men or officers from revealing any information they might have about the impending coup. They were stripped of all military clothing and put in military jails to await court-martials. A Cuban Communist military court-martial would have ordered immediate execution by firing squad, but General González wanted them to have a fair trial as would be expected in a free democratic society. Until that was possible, they would remain in the military jails.

At 10:30 pm

In Santa Clara, the general ordered Major General Diego Seville to order the entire Cuban army to prepare for the exercise mode. They must be alert and ready for combat. General Seville had personally selected twelve honorary guards who were loyal to the general. He repositioned his troops. As planned, he chose ten commanders to be put into position and gave them orders for their next assignment. He continued to regroup for his war tactics and covert plan. Three regiments from Matanzas were positioned east of Havana for night training exercise purposes and inventory inspections. This deployment was presumed to have been ordered and acknowledged by General Hector Elias Garcia, General of the Army under Fidel Castro.

General González continued to be very careful, and no one suspected anything. He planned every detail and knew he would never get a second chance to overthrow Fidel.

For a moment, he thought about his wife and children. He had already sent them to his in-laws' home in Nuevitas Camaguey. They thought they were leaving because their home needed a termite treatment. But his wife suspected that something very serious was up. His personality had changed in the last six months. He was preoccupied and busy in his home office. She asked him several times to tell her what was going on, but he could not. He thought about how unfair it was to keep his love in the dark, but it was for her protection. As she was leaving, she could feel that something was wrong. She looked at him for a sign or a word, but he just remained silent. He pictured her beautiful face and her last words, "Que te vaya bien mi Amor," God be with you, my love. Remember, I'll always love you." A tear fell down her cheek, and he gently wiped it away.

Major General Diego Seville had told the general that he had information that many American Marines might be coming ashore at 0100. General González agreed that this threat should be recognized as a real time combat scenario and gave orders to use live ammunition. The general told Seville that he had his complete confidence. Seville was silent for a moment but then accepted the task. He told the general that he would do whatever was necessary to complete the mission. The general ordered him to assemble the officers participating in the mission immediately at headquarters. He wanted to give them his final orders and his blessing.

Major General Diego Seville had told the general that he had information that many American Marines might be coming ashore at 0100. General González agreed that this threat should be recognized as a real time combat scenario and gave orders to use live ammunition. The general told Seville that he had his complete confidence. Seville was silent for a moment but then accepted the task. He told the general that he would do whatever was necessary to complete the mission. The general ordered him to assemble the officers participating in the mission

The Last Revolution

immediately at headquarters. He wanted to give them his final orders and his blessing.

At midnight

The general stood before his six trusted officers. They were Seville, Costello, Zamora, Cardona, Zapata, and Velasquez. First, he sent the signal to commence the war game to General Rodríguez at the base in Pinar del Rio. At precisely 12:30 am he would execute the first formation of the air raid called code name, "Ayu." He put his hand to his heart and asked for good luck. Then he ordered all of his officers to their assignments. "Good Luck, men. You've worked hard for this moment, and the time is at hand. Show me what you can do!" Everyone saluted the general.

At midnight

At the CIA headquarters' in Langley, Virginia, the research department finally broke Hiro's secret code. They could not believe what they were witnessing. It was all so clear. Suddenly, they could understand the communications between Hiro and the general. The computer screen displayed the correspondence translated into perfect English, and they could view what was being recorded at that very moment.

Commando Patrick Davis had just been informed of their success by the excited computer scientists in the research department. As he ran to the room, chaos had broken out. The computer scientists were recording the information as they yelled to one another. Davis was caught up in the commotion. He was trying to understand what had led to the breaking of the code. It was late, but the commotion had produced such high energy in the room that it seemed like noon at Grand Central Station. Chief Gates, Davis rushed into the computer room. He could not believe his eyes. The technician who had broken the code was trying his best to explain the details to him, but Davis was not listening.

At that moment, he was focused on the content of the E-mails. Was he seeing things correctly? His eyes followed the writing on the screen and he yelled, "My God, Cuba is on the brink of a revolution! Chief Gates, you'd better get the President on the phone immediately!"

They were all in total shock. Cracking the code itself was huge, but now to find out that Fidel was about to be overthrown within the hour was just unbelievable. Chief Gates screamed impatiently, "Hurry up…..come on!" A technician quickly handed him the red emergency phone to connect him to the White House.

"Mr. President, this is Chief Gates we have just cracked a top secret code indicating that a revolution is underway in Havana, Cuba. The order for execution is for 0100 Eastern Standard Time…..a little over an hour from now." The President asked him a few more questions, and then they disconnected.

The President immediately called the Vice-President and the entire cabinet. He ordered the Secretary of Defense to put the troops on high alert. He ordered all US vessels in the area on full standby status. He also ordered the Chief General at Guantanamo to place the base on high alert.

The Secretary of Defense also directed the Coast Guard to reposition its fleet in the off the coast of Florida toward Cuba. They would be in place so they could be ready to enter Cuban water within minutes, if necessary. The US Air Force was also ready to take part and was placed on high alert. Two thousand US Marines were airlifted to Guantanamo Bay. The US Armed Forces were streaming closer toward Cuban soil.

It was Three pm on July 4 {twelve am eastern standard time July 3}, Back in Kure city Japan In Hiroshima, Japan.

Hiro had been waiting for the past twenty-four hours at home. He was beside himself. He had received the start code from General González. It said simply "Ayu". Hiro bowed his head and paused for a moment of silence to say a Shinto prayer for safe passage and for success of the war game. He wished for good luck for all Cubans who participated in this historical event. When he opened his eyes, he entered the program to be executed. Hiro monitored every minute of the event via computer. He was printing out all communications between General González and General Enrique Hurtado Rodríguez.

Then there was a knock at the door. It was Dania calling, "Hiro, may I come in?"

He was surprised but did not hesitate. "Yes! Come in at once!" Than he picked up the computer print-out in Spanish and handed it to Dania to read. Her eyes grew wide. She was stunned. First she screamed; then she jumped up and down.

The Last Revolution

As she began to read further, tears of happiness streamed down her face. She said, "Oh my, God! I can't believe it. Freedom is on the way! We will be home soon." She wiped her face and began screaming again, "Oh my, God! Oh my, God!" Then she started to mumble a prayer calling on Orishas, a Santeria Saint from the old Yoruba tribes, to protect those fighting for Cuba's freedom.

Hiro said, "I must focus, but you can stay here." Hiro was very serious and did not utter a word as he continued to monitor the war game. Dania sat beside him and observed and read the information as it was printing. They sat on the edge of their seats waiting silently. Her hands were visibly shaking from excitement.

At midnight

In Pinar Del Rio, the 150 MIG fighter jets were armed with live bombs and air-to-surface AS-7 missiles and were ready for take off. The pilots formed a line inside the airport office to greet the General before their final boarding. He had recruited several loyal personal guards for security and had stationed them at the door. They were fully armed. He now had to take a big risk with his pilots. He knew them very well. They were a loyal bunch who had served him for years. He knew many of their families, and they respected him.

He general gave his pilots a full salute. They returned the salute. He said, "What I am about to ask of you will change your lives forever. I want you to listen carefully. You have been preparing for weeks for tonight's drill. But what if I told you this was not a drill? What if I told you this was real and that we are about to overthrow the Cuban communist government?" The men looked bewildered, but didn't say anything

"Gentlemen, I have selected you for this historic mission, but now it is up to you to accept it or to reject it. The fate of Cuba rests in our hands. It is time for change. You know it, and I know it! Fidel's time is over. Think of your families and your children. Cuba is dying under Castro's leadership. Tonight we can end that suffering. Tonight, is the beginning of a new Cuba! The beginning of progress, prosperity, and freedom! Everything is in place, and we are not alone. The men at Santa Clara and Santiago de Cuba are also with us. Tonight, we will strike our targets with real bombs and ammunition. Tonight Fidel and Raúl will be no more. If anyone disagrees, step aside now!"

There was dead silence from the pilots, only wide eyes and red faces. "You must choose your destiny tonight! Do you want a Democratic Free Cuba? If you choose to remain loyal to Fidel, step aside. You will not be harmed, only detained. I give you my word. Only those who use violence against us will perish."

The men were stunned. They were prepared for the drill simulating a US invasion, but never in their wildest dreams had they thought a revolution was underway. The pilots were very anxious at this point and just looked at the general. Many of the men had dreamed of this but never thought it would happen. They had waited and hoped for an opportunity to end Castro's oppressive regime. They were all forced to work for him, but they despised him. Every one of them had lost a family member or had suffered under Castro's rule over the years. Some had lost parents, siblings, grandparents, and friends. They all had felt the noose around their necks as the economy declined.

They were just waiting for Castro to die. Some of the pilots had thought about hijacking a jet and escaping to the US. They longed for a better life. They wanted out, but they were stuck because that would mean leaving their families behind. They had waited for this moment for so long. The men suddenly realized that the coup was their chance for freedom. All the pilots stood their ground and decided to fight for the revolution. They became vocal and cried out at the top of their lungs, "We are with you! Cuba libre! Democrática! Viva Cuba! Down with Castro!"

The general was also overcome with emotion. He could feel the energy in the room well up around him. It was incredible. They all shared a common thread in their feelings of injustice and oppression. At last, they could finally vocalize it their frustrations. They could taste freedom.

Chapter 84

Major Llamas began to highlight the target areas on the map of Havana quickly reviewing the locations of communication towers and equipment, telephone company towers, cellular wireless towers, and an anti-air missile installation. He then ordered a formation of forty-five MIGs forward to begin the first wave air attack. The pilots verified their specific target positions including all fourteen of Fidel's homes. Then the general ordered, "Attention, men! You must destroy every target on this list. Do not, and I repeat, do not destroy Fidel's presidential transport helicopter and keep out of the five block no-bombing area around the presidential helicopter." The general put a big red X on the position where Fidel's transport helicopter was last reported to be.

The general added, "More than likely, Fidel is in this area. Do not touch the helicopter!" He continued to review again with the squadron leaders and circled their targets. The men were buzzing around like bees to honey. They were visibly excited and anxious to be a part of this glorious mission.

At 12:15 pm

The general put his hands up, "Congratulations, gentlemen! The time is now. We are ready for the attack to begin. Tonight is the end of our oppression. Tonight we will give our children, our families, and our countrymen a chance to have better lives. It's time to live! I salute you, gentlemen. To our Motherland! Fight for Cuba! Fight for Freedom! Cuba Libre!"

The men shouted in unison, "Cuba Libre! Cuba Libre! Cuba Libre!"

Then Major General Llamas ordered no radio contact of any kind. He told them, "The code name, 'Tosa,' means to attack. There will be absolutely no communication allowed. You will maintain strict silence until after the second wave is completed. Just standby in silence until the next order is given. Take the next five minutes to be briefed by your squadron leader. Then it's time to begin the freedom fight!"

The pilots met with their squadron leaders and ended the meeting by embracing and shaking hands. They ran to their jets. The general felt full of confidence. He watched his men board their planes. The blasting sounds of jet thrusts were like music to his ears.

At 12:30 am,
the general gave the final order to Major General Llamas, and he ordered Brigadier General Fredric Alvares to execute operation "Ayu" Then he gave the signal to Commander Lieutenant Alex Morales. All forty-five MIGs assembled in formation for take off, and one-by-one they disappeared into the pitch black Caribbean night sky…destination Havana.

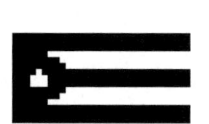

Chapter 85

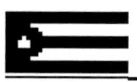

At 12:30 am, In Santa Clara,

a gray Jeep stopped in front of Freddie Diaz's home. Four MPs from the base knocked on his front door. Freddie and Yorina were in a deep sleep, but the banging startled them awake. Freddie jumped up and looked out the window to see who was causing this disturbance. When he saw the military Jeep, he instantly became concerned. He dressed in his robe and opened the door, "What is this about?"

The tall young man said, "Sir, I have orders to take you to see General González at headquarters immediately!"

Freddie nodded, "Ok, Let me get dressed. Wait here." Then he went back to the bedroom to change.

Yorina was wide awake now and very worried, "Freddie, what's wrong? It is almost midnight."

Freddie kissed her, "Nothing for you to be worried about. Please go back to sleep. I don't know when I will be back. But I will call you later." He gave her a kiss then left with the men.

As they drove to the base, Freddie asked, "What is going on? Did something happen?"

Both MPs were quiet and didn't answer him. They said nothing and just kept on driving straight to headquarters. As they entered the general's briefing room, Abelardo was standing with several of his generals briefing them with a map and board. The general stopped to greet Freddie and to shake hands. Freddie already suspected that something had gone awry with the inspection on Army hardware because men were running everywhere. The general took him aside and said, "Freddie, We are in a revolution. I am leading an operation to overthrow Fidel and his Communist government."

"We want a Democratic Free Cuba! By morning Fidel will be dead. Pinos Del Rio and Santiago de Cuba is also with us. Everything has been planned to coincide with the inspection. Right now we are taking Havana and Fidel by surprise. I want you to join us, but I will let your chose your own position. You are either with us or against us. If you are for Fidel, I will escort you to our jail in this compound. You will only be detained, not harmed. But you must make a fast decision, my friend. This revolution will be over within hours. We have been close friends for a very long time, but I had to keep things top secret until the last minute for security purposes. What is your decision?"

Freddie was stunned and speechless. He didn't know what to say at first.

The general said, "Speak up, my friend. I want to know where you stand."

Freddie rubbed his face and eyes with his hands. "I knew something was up last month when I was in Havana. But I didn't expect it to happen so fast. This is happening with lighting speed like the Japanese Tosa dog fighting. Tell me your plan!"

The general showed him the board and maps and began to brief him on his plan.

"General, I think we are going to succeed," said Freddie.

Then the general asked, "We?"

Freddie became very confident, "I will support our new government and do whatever needs to be done. What is my role in your plan?"

The general was relieved to hear this. "Freddie, I certainly need your help. You have been a high-ranking officer for so long, and you know how to lead. I need you to do what you know best."

Then his aide and another man entered the room. The general introduced Major General Joaquin Zamora to Freddie. The general told him, "Freddie, the General graduated from the University of Havana with a political science degree. He has an extensive work record and is responsible for transitional government affairs. You know everything there is to know. I want you to be the head architect of the new Cuban government's structure. You will be like a grand consultant. I am completely confident in you. Are you with me?"

Freddie felt really good about this plan and smiled, "It is certainly an honor, and I support you one-hundred percent. I will work with you toward success. I love Cuba, and it's about time that we had a new system. I am grateful to you for asking me to join you in this effort, and I trust your intelligence." Then Freddie saluted him.

The general asked, "I certainly trust your experience, but first I want you to think of your family. You must send them

The Last Revolution

somewhere safe until the revolution is over. I will get a military escort for your family to take them where you wish them to go."

Freddie answered, "I appreciate your thoughts about my family's needs. I left my car in my parking garage at my office last night. If your man can take my car to my wife Lourdes, I would certainly appreciate it."

The general was glad to assist, "Of course! Certainly. I will send my MP immediately, and he will escort your family to their destination."

The General replied strongly, "Freddie that is not good idea because military personal are already in the surrounding area and now hardware is everywhere. There is no electricity, no phone and we are forcing citizens to stay calm and keep off the highway. So, it's best for my MP to escort them to the outskirts of Corrallilo city limits. From there they can drive alone, and it will be a smooth and safe trip."

Both agreed and Freddie called his wife. Phone service in Santa Clara had not been interrupted. He explained briefly, and she understood. Then he left with Lt. Major General Zamora to discuss and plan for special government affairs. There was much to decide in a short time.

The three MPs caught Chief Ishmael Velázquez at his home, handcuffed him, and then arrested him. They took him to the general's headquarters.

As soon as they walked in, Ishmael saw Freddie. "Freddie, what are you doing here? What is happening? I am totally confused. Are we at war?"

The general answered him at Freddie's request. "Look, I don't have much time. Do you like our current Communist government or would you prefer for live and raise your family in a Democratic Free Cuba?"

Ishmael was caught off guard and looked confused. "General, what's going on?"

Freddie interrupted quickly, "We are taking over the government. This is Cuba's last revolution."

Ishmael was in shock. "What? Revolution? Who?"

Then the general asked him, "Tell me Ishmael, are you interested in joining our revolution against Fidel and his government or are you a Castro loyalist?"

Ishmael was silent and knew that he had to make a rapid choice. It was so fast. He needed to think, but there was no time.

Finally he said, "I have been a secret agent all my life. I did it for a job because my family had to eat?" Then he started to get really nervous, and his voice was shaking. He thought this was a set up, and maybe he was really going to be executed. Then the general ordered his MP to remove the hand cuffs.

The general explained to him, "Ishmael. You and I have known each other a very long time. We know each other's families. You and I have supported Fidel all our lives, but yet we have nothing to show for it. We live in fear, we have no freedom, and now our economy is shot to hell. Our children have no future under Fidel, and you know it. I have planned this revolution down to the smallest detail. I want you to join us. Fidel will be dead by morning, and a new government will begin. I know it seems like a dream, but I assure you this is very real. I am asking you to make a choice right now. Do you still support Fidel? Or are you going support the new Democratic Free Cuba. I need your help, but I will respect your decision, and you will not be harmed regardless of the decision that you make."

Ishmael had to sit down to think. All he could hear was the pounding of his own heart. He was trying to take in everything the general had just said. He knew how capable the general was and saw that an operation was in play. He thought of all the years he worked in distress under Fidel. He had worked in fear for his safety and for that of his family. Was this revolution for real? He knew it was. Finally he spoke saying, "I am in. I want to help organize the new law enforcement in your government. If you want me to assist, that is my specialty and what I got my degree in at the University of Havana, sir."

The general smiled and shook his hand. "I am honored that you wish to support us, and I want you to join Freddie in coming up with a strategy to get this new government off of the ground quickly and properly. There is much work to be done, and Cuba needs you!"

Freddie also shook his hand. He looked at his friend, "Can you believe it?" Ishmael was still in shock and shook his head. He was speechless for the first time in his life. All three men had worked together for so many years. By now, they understood everything about each other. It would be a busy night for all of them.

Lt. Major General Zamora asked Freddie and Ishmael to come with him to a special government affairs meeting room.

The Last Revolution

This would be a historical meeting, and one for the record books. In spite of the seriousness of the occasion, the general felt calm. He had a good team assembled and knew that they would do what was right for Cuba. They were extremely good and loyal government employees. They had never had a choice before. Now they would.

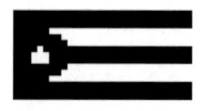

Chapter 86

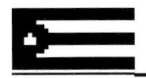

12:45 am Back in Havana

Lt. Colonel Perez of the Federal Secret Surveillance Agency made a special arrangement with Fidel to spy on General González. He headed a secret intelligent unit and put Brigade General Maria Ramiro Medina of Central Intelligence, in charge. She was responsible for leading the entire operation. They had worked to break into the CIA's supercomputer for quite some time.

The Cubans hardware had been updated with the Colbana-NakajimaJPX009 chip so it was only a matter of time. They worked around the clock, and today they had made a big breakthrough with their data. They knew they were close, and she ordered the entire staff to work overtime tonight.

They had a very busy night ahead of them. They knew that the military was engaged in a simulation of an enormous scale, but they had not been given any details. Her spies were in place near the general, but nothing out of the ordinary was happening. Suddenly her top agent informed her, "General Medina, we are reporting a large formation of Cuban MIGs streaming over the Havana area. They are headed due east. This is very unusual for a simulation." General Medina ordered, "Get Lt. Colonel Perez on the phone now!"

She spoke to him at once about the MIG formation and her concern. He told her, "Never mind. They are authorized. We have a report from the Air Force that they are doing a night drill between Havana and Pinar Del Rio. Everything is fine." She also informed him that they were in the final stages of breaking the code. They hoped to be inside the CIA's supercomputer by midnight, and all personnel were on standby. Perez expressed his appreciation and said that he would wait for the call. He wanted her spies to maintain round-the-clock surveillance on General González.

Within minutes of disconnecting the call, Perez received an urgent message from his team at the Cuban Central Intelligence Computer Laboratory. They had successfully broken

The Last Revolution

the first key to the CIA's supercomputer. They had five more to go.

Perez was immediately airlifted to the lab. He arrived at 12:55 am. The lab technicians were going crazy. Everything came together at the exact moment of his arrival. The computer hackers on the team immediately plugged into the Cuban Affairs Department. As they entered their system, they were suddenly privy to all data including top secret documents. Then they hacked into the current files. They were all amazed that they were looking at the CIA's files on Cuba. Perez ordered his men to access all information regarding Dr. Nakagawa. Perez was peering at the monitor while speed reading through the sketch.

A brief biographical sketch of Dr. Nakagawa was immediately
 requested.

Name
Dr. Hiroaki Nakagawa
General Information
Born in 1942 in Fukuyama in the Hiroshima Prefecture of

Japan. Known as father of computer science.
Discontinued his research in 1995 and returned to his native

Japan.

Education
B.A. in 1962 from University Hiroshima (Japan)
Master's and Ph.D. in 1966 from MIT (US)

Areas of Expertise
Specializes in understanding the language of calculating electromagnetic
mathematics.
Expert in hardware and software.

Research topics led to development of:
Artificial intelligence used to create memory chips
Internet
Computer games (Nintendo)

Micheal Kazuhiro Nishitani

Mouse and window operation system
Anti-virus software
Digital images (digital camera and digital audio player)
Neuro-electronic interface system (currently theory)

Since he left the Silicone Valley in 1995, he returned to Hiroshima where he became an honorary professor. Then on March 18, 1995, he left Hiroshima for Havana Cuba. He stayed on a cultural exchange visa as a visiting professor of mathematical science for The University of Havana where he conducted seminars for staff.

He lived in Rancho Veloz, Cuba and married Dania Altamirano Hernandez in October 1996. They had two children born in 1997 and 1998. Then in June 2004, he entered the U.S. port of Boston. He stayed four weeks, then traveled to Hiroshima, Japan. He stayed five months in Japan and then returned to Cuba, where he remains.

As Perez read Hiro's bio, his jaw dropped open, and he shouted, "My God! That son of a bitch! I didn't know that Hiro was a computer scientist. Woooo……..! An incredible accomplishment! Man this guy is impressive! He is one of the fathers of computer science! Fidel is going to want to see all of this. This man could develop all of our technology!"

Perez tried to use his SAT phone, but the line was dead so he used his cellular phone instead. Normally the use of wireless phones was prohibited for relaying top secret information, but under the circumstances, Perez's first priority was to inform his boss. After all, they had just hacked into the CIA's veins.

Perez called Roberto Cobarruvias. He alerted him that the emergency line was down and requested that Cobarruvias come to the lab immediately. It was of the utmost importance. Suddenly, Perez was able to see the CIA's current computer traffic in the Cuban sector on the display. He was in the middle of a sentence when suddenly his face turned white. He almost fell out of the chair as he read the message. It was an urgent memo to the US President George T. Bingham which had been sent 11:55 pm:

"President Bingham, our information and sources indicate that a coup de etat is underway in the Republic of Cuba.

The Last Revolution

A revolution is planned for precisely 01:00 am on July 3, 2008, in Havana. We strongly recommend that the Atlantic US Naval fleet and the US Marines along the southern coast be repositioned and put on high alert status. All Air Force and armed forces also should be alerted. Gitmo must be placed on code red immediately."

Lt. Colonel Perez was stunned. His entire his body began to tremble. He looked at his watch, and it was 12:59 am. By this time, Cobarruvias was yelling at him on the phone. Lt. Colonel Perez! Are you all right? What is going on?" But Perez could not hear him. He was frozen. He couldn't utter a word. Suddenly, a huge explosion hit the building.

Smoke and fire engulfed the lab. Perez thought he had died; but when he opened his eyes, he saw that he was still alive. There was a loud ringing in his ears. He was in shock. He looked around, and many of the team lay dead. People were scrambling to get out of the building. Perez somehow managed to get to his feet. The lab was on the ground floor. He used a chair to break the remaining glass from a window and jumped out and stumbled toward the parking lot. All the cars were burning, and there was sparking from the explosion. Black smoke and the smell of propane gas surrounded him. Men were shouting in the distance. There was an Army vehicle just a few feet away. The driver was dead, but the jeep was still running. He dragged the driver's body out of the jeep and vaulted into the driver's seat. He floored the accelerator as he sped from the parking lot. He had to tell Fidel's brother Raúl who was back at the office of the Ministry of Interior in *Vedado* what was happening.

In the sky, MIGs were streaming in low flying formation. He could hear the blasting sound of the jet thrusts above him. Perez drove like a bat out of hell. He had to get to Raúl and warn the others. He was just seventy-five yards from his office when suddenly a blast obliterated the entire building. The Ministry of Defense was no more! He was horrified. Fires, burning debris, and smoke were everywhere. Through the smoke he could see people moving and screaming. Above the inferno, he could see many MIGs flying. Havana was a war zone! Perez's heart was pumping so fast that he thought he was going to explode. He forced himself to breathe. He began to think, "Why is this happening? Where is Fidel? What has happened to the Cuban Defense system?"

He could hear no activity. There was no retaliation of any kind taking place anywhere. As the smoke cleared, he looked around and almost all of the buildings in the defense complex had been leveled or were on fire. Everywhere he looked there was devastation. It was an unimaginable sight. He thought, "It must be the gringo Americans! Where is Fidel?"

Meanwhile, General Rodríguez's men targeted only the military installations and the military communications facility. They hit the military's anti-gun installation and its anti-missile site. They also hit the wireless tower and the telephone facility in Havana. As he drove toward the city he could see only two areas burning. He was relieved to see that most of Havana looked untouched. But there was no electricity anywhere. People had rushed into the streets and chaos reigned. It was very difficult to drive because people were scattering in every direction.

Several weeks before, the Cuban Defense Department had reported through the news media that there would be a big night drill involving Cuban fighter jets. They reported that it was just a simulation, and it would take place from July 1 through July 31. But the people were never told about bombs being part of the exercise. They were afraid and knew that something serious had happened. The Havana sky was full of MIGs flying at low altitudes. It appeared that there were hundreds of fighter jets flying overhead. It seemed like Havana was under attack.

As Perez drove through the crowd he could hear people screaming that this was a surprise attack by the US. Many were screaming for joy that the Americans finally had come to rescue them. Everyone assumed that the jets flying above must be American Air Force fighters. They had never seen anything like this before. They had never seen MIGs flying over Havana. It was like a scene from a war movie. The streets were dark due to the absence of lights, and chaos was everywhere. People were yelling and shouting.

Chapter 87

Suddenly, there was a huge explosion nearby. As Perez drove, an object from the street stuck his car causing him to veer out of control and smash into a pole. The hood was dented and the engine was smoking. His shoulder began to bleed. Not far in the distance a MIG dropped a bomb on the cellular communication tower, and the explosion looked like fire works. People nearby were also hit. There were people screaming and running. Two women stopped to help him out of the jeep. They escorted him inside their home and cleaned his left shoulder. They wrapped t-shirts around his arm to make a tourniquet. Perez was bleeding very badly.

There was no electricity so the house was dark except for some small candles they had lit. As the older woman checked his arm she said, "Your cuts are not too deep. It looks all right to me. The bleeding is slowing down. Keep your arm up and the tourniquet tight. You are very lucky." The woman moved the candle closer and saw his uniform.

She asked, "What's going on? Is America invading Cuba?"

He answered her, "I don't know anything. I don't know who that is up there. I suspect it is the US, but it was a surprise attack." He moved to get up and asked, "Do you have a telephone?"

She tried to help him up. "Yes, please come into my kitchen!"

Perez scrambled to get to the kitchen and grabbed the telephone, but there was no dial tone. He tapped the receiver several times, but the phone was dead. He asked, "Was your phone working before?" She confirmed that it was.

Perez figured that communications were out all over Havana because his cellular was not working either. He didn't know what to do, but he knew that he had to find a way to communicate with his superiors. He thanked the women and left. His jeep was totaled, and the streets were now filled with people. His only chance was to run on foot. He knew the city well and, although he was in severe pain, he had to get to someone. The defense department was about two miles away.

He ran for what seemed like an eternity, but he made it. Finally, he reached the Department of Defense. But as he approached he could see that the building was completely destroyed, and there were no signs of personnel. He walked through the entry gate and up to the entrance of the building. Outside, he found the body of Roberto Cobarruvias. A huge concrete block from the blast that destroyed the building lay across his bloody body. Perez checked for a pulse, but Cobarruvias was dead.

Suddenly another huge explosion hit the communications tower. All Perez could see was smoke and debris. A huge piece of metal fell near him. There was a military vehicle nearby. He broke the window and reaching inside managed to get the door open. He was injured and dazed, but he reached for the satellite phone and tried to call emergency. The line was dead.

Perez could see Roberto Cobarruvias' old Mercedes parked across the lot. He removed the keys from his boss's body and ran to the car. It would not start. He saw that the battery was missing. Everyone was running, and the frenzy surrounded him.

By 1:45 am
Back at the Pinar Del Rio Army Air Force base, General Rodríguez was receiving streams of data. There was information coming in from Major General Llamas. He reported, "The first wave formation destroyed eighty percent of Fidel's communications as well as his military installations and facilities. We have also attacked eight of his fourteen presidential homes. We still need to attack four more of his residential facilities on the second wave. There has been no confirmation regarding Fidel's and Raúl's exact position. We have had only one report that his helicopter was undamaged."

Major General Llamas repeatedly warned all of his pilots not to target or destroy anything in a five block radius of Fidel's personal helicopter. He gave strict orders which all of the pilots understood. Lt. Major Claro Diaz flew over Fidel's chopper and confirmed that it was on the ground and intact. He also conformed that several of Fidel's security personnel were nearby. Diaz reported, "We have twenty-three MIGs ready for take off, sir."

The Last Revolution

General Rodríguez thought quietly for a moment. He asked Brigadier General Fredric Alvares what the jet fuel situation was. He wanted to determine if there were any in-coming coming troops or retaliation forces present. Lt. Major Ricardo Esparza reported, "Sir, my pilots have reported that ground forces are moving ten miles west of Matanzs. Aren't those General Gonzalez's forces moving toward Havana?"

Just then, the door banged opened and Major General Alejandro Llamas rushed in with a frightened look on his face. He was very serious and said, "General! I just received a report from the communications unit. Lt. Major Ricardo Esparza confirmed that General Gonzalez is loyal to Fidel and is sending 10,000 troops by 0800 hours from Santa Clara, Sir!"

Rodríguez said, "In that case, those must be his forces located just twenty-five miles this side of Matanzas. Why is he reinforcing Matanzas?"

He became instantly rigid and concerned and said, "So that means we are fighting alone with no support from the army? General González has been set up, we got fucked."

Enrique became still and replied, "Look, there is no radio communication. I want to know every move that General González's main makes. Let's hope Fidel doesn't try to escape to another country like Venezuela, for instance. If that happens, we are going to have a tough time doing anything. He will use his politics to join forces with them and try to reclaim control of the Cuban government. Then we will never get rid of Communism. If that happens on a mass scale, we are finished. We already have an agreement with General González, and I trust him. He is simply pretending to be loyal to Fidel because it is a game. He must make Fidel believe that he will come and save him until he gets Fidel right where he wants him to be. Then when that happens….. the war game can end and so will Fidel! Look, everything has been planned in detail, and we must follow his command. Has the second air battalion left yet?"

Because of the lack of communication, Enrique began to doubt his tactics. Major General Llamas responded, "Sir, the second attack squadron is already out there. The first wave of MIGs should be touching down any second to reload and to refuel. They will leave around 0500 after the fourth wave of the air attack has ended."

Micheal Kazuhiro Nishitani

The general had received a report indicating that none of his jets were damaged. Every single MIG had returned safely. He ordered that the first wave of planes be gassed up as soon as they had landed. The second wave was on standby, and the third attack would be halted until 0330 hours for 60 minutes because they were running out of ammunition and jet fuel. Lamas added, "We must finish Fidel off before morning, sir."

General Rodríguez ordered the second air wave. Four jets were to do a fly over to access damage done by the attack and report back. He ordered that all pilots keep away from Fidel's helicopter. Between 3:00 am and 4:00 am he ordered a break, saying "There should no more attacks for that hour. We need to conserve energy."

Llamas asked, "Sir, why are we keeping Fidel's helicopter intact? He might escape by sea or air to Venezuela."

Enrique responded, "That is good thinking, but if anyone tries to escape from this island, we will shoot to kill. General González is already in place, and I trust his instincts." He smiled, but didn't offer any details. He then ordered, "Prepare for the next move and tell me about the morale of the troops?"

One of the other generals replied, "The overall morale is very good, sir. They are ready for this fight. They all stand behind a Democratic Free Cuba, and everyone here sends you tremendous support from my company."

Llamas asked, "What are we going to do after 0600 when we have no more fuel and no more ammunition? Are we going to have to fight on the ground? If General González doesn't help like he supposed to, we will get our asses kicked."

Enrique responded quickly, "Don't worry! General González will tell us the answer before morning. You have to trust him. Now, I want an assessment of damages. Send out several more reconnaissance patrols. I want a complete report by 0300 hours." Everybody saluted him and returned to their posts. Enrique thought to himself, "We might get in big trouble if the Army cannot help us. Maybe I am getting set up by Abelardo to demolish the entire Cuban Air Force." General Rodríguez then sent an order to conserve jet fuel for security.

Chapter 88

It was 3:35 am, In Pinar Del Rio. General Enrique Rodríguez continued to get information from the Air Force commander. They repeatedly reported that they had heard that the second Army Corps would be deployed by 0800 and was headed to Pinar Del Rio. He thought, "If this is true, they will wipe us out. Ten thousand well-trained troops led by General González will be too much for us to handle."

Even his three generals were concerned and nervous about the report given by the Air Force commander. As soon as General Rodríguez ordered the next assignment, he went back to his command post. The general announced, "I want a moment of silence please. No one is to enter my office. I want to be alone for the next ten minutes!"

The aide saluted him and said, "Yes, sir!"

Enrique sat in his chair looking over the map. He was sweating and began to feel a moment of confusion. A seed of doubt was growing in his mind about General González's intentions. He could not communicate with him for another hour. He had to wait until 0400 hours. But he remembered that the general had told him that he would just have to trust him. Their lives depended on it. Enrique wanted to trust his opinion because they had shared a strong friendship for many years. The general had never let him down before; why would he now?

But his commander had reported that the general was still loyal to Fidel. This was one part of the plan that Abelardo had not clarified with him during their discussions. This is what made him doubt his friend. He was confused about his motives. He pulled open a desk drawer, removed a flask of rum, and took a long pull from the flask. He thought long and hard. He began to have flashbacks of his conversations last May with Abelardo. Then he began to think of his many experiences with him over the past twenty years. He had to go with his gut instinct, and they were telling him to trust his friend. General González had always come through and kept this word. He was also a genius.

He let his doubts go and decided to stick exactly to the general's plan.

With this settled in his mind, Enrique opened his humidor and removed a Romeo y Juliet. Although his hands were shaking, he cut it and slowly placed the cigar in his mouth. He lit the lighter, held it near the end of the cigar, and inhaled slowly. Ahh! The sweet flavor and nicotine worked its magic, and he finally relaxed.   At last his hands stopped shaking.

At 3:30 am

General González had grown uneasy because he had not yet received confirmation about Fidel, Raúl and General Garcia's where about. It was completely dark and silent since satellite communications had been disrupted. The last time he had made contact with Raúl was at 10:30 last night during a brief five minute conversation. Nothing was mentioned about their location or where they had been staying since the black out when all civilian and military communications had been completely shut down. All of the Havana area, except for their satellite emergency phone, was also down.

The General's first three regiment were near Havana. There was a communications data plane over the night sky of the city that could communicate using limited lines. Two and a half hours had passed since the last revolution had begun and still there was no final word on Fidel. He began to get very concerned. His plan was to be completed within five hours after the operation began. Time was of the essence.

Right about that time, Air Force radio communications were restored to a limited number of select channels by a special communications company from the Pinar Del Rio Army Air Force base. The general was in his first round of communications with General González, but he refused to talk and remained silent.   It was 2:30 am. He had received a report from reconnaissance that all fourteen of Fidel's personal residences and compounds had been destroyed completely. Also, all civilian and military communications facilities and power in Havana were out.

But they wondered about Fidel's and Raúl's whereabouts. They still had not heard anything from either one of them. Since all of Havana was unable to communicate, they both began to get concerned.   Could Fidel have escaped to another country or was

The Last Revolution

he in some safe hiding place? If that was the case, the last revolution would take a lot longer than he had planned for. It would be a case-by-case scenario. The general started to plan for a longer war scenario. He said to Major General Samuel Luiz, "Damn communications black out! Look, if you see anything unusual, report to me immediately."

5, 30 pm July 4 (July 3; 2, 30 am eastern standard time), Back in Kure city Japan,

Hiro had miscalculated the three global communications satellite's maintenance schedule set ups. He didn't realize it until communications were disrupted on his home computer in Hiroshima. It was going to take some time to put all three satellite schedules together and reprogram them. Cracking the complicated maintenance code was similar to solving a Rubik's Cube puzzle. The input codes were always a challenge because they were based on the individual's style who wrote the code.

Hiro was very concerned that this interruption would affect the critical timing of his war game. While he remained very calm outwardly, his fingers were on fire. His brain worked like a computer, searching for the special key-code to bypass the system. It didn't take him long to reprogram and reconnect all three global communication satellites with the correct input and key. But he was still unable to tune into the correct transponders. He was under pressure to find the key in a short amount of time so he had to work at a lightening fast pace. Time was running out.

Previously, he had researched a global satellite computer with a bio-mathematical graphic layout. This valuable information helped him to find the correct input code so he was able to bypass maintenance for the third transponder as key. He used the South Korean Koreasat 5 Satellite, "dubbed Mugunghwa," which was equipped with a super high frequency band, including four super Ka-band transponders. It was also located at a perfect position at the site of the Earth's fastest rotation, with the lowest latitudes at the Equator. It was located at a longitude of one hundred fifty-four degrees west which overlapped the Canadian Anik F3 satellite and the Japanese N-SAT-110 and JCSAT-11 satellites. So, all were able to connect to the transponders beams as one unit. Finally, Hiro programmed the entire system to go undetected by the CIA global stealth spy satellite.

Even for Hiro, a highly knowledgeable computer master, he was sweating after this intense moment. Dania sat silently glued to the screen. This was the first time she watched him work like this. She was amazed at how her husband's brain worked. Finally, his program was functioning correctly and communication resumed as normal. Hiro mumbled as he rubbed his hands together Hiro took a breath and smiled.

Oslo for Hiro, he had something different in mind. Upon returning to Hiroshima, he had invented the Magnum Stealth Laser Dot Gun or MSLDG. Its nickname was appropriately North Korean Missile Taepodong. Hiro had based the "gun" on the Japanese global spy satellite lens that could pinpoint an individual's location exactly using a specialized heat-seeking laser and magnetic DNA Helix These molecules encode a detailed for made up blueprints of cell mark. This DNA-based mark was called the Halting Stimulation Response System. With it, Hiro could closely monitor Fidel's and Raul's locations by monitoring their DNA with infrared sensors and scans for any given time. This monitoring combined with the global positioning navigational system allowed Hiro to track them around the globe. Hiro could monitor their every movement directly from Japan.

It was a miraculous invention that could be used by every government on earth, as well as any terrorist organization, but Hiro was only interested in tracking Fidel. He knew the potential for both good and evil if this invention were to get into the wrong hands. Hiro decided to use it for this mission and not to reveal this discovery to the world.

At 3:30 am
Both generals were finally able to make satellite contact. The general took a moment to give Enrique a briefing regarding his concerns about Fidel's position. He ordered him to reassess and change the second phase of the plan for the revolution. General González started to tell Enrique that if they couldn't locate Fidel, then their plan would need to run longer, perhaps even over the next six months. Whatever it took, Enrique was to completely cut off all in bound and out bound sea, land, and air traffic for the next sixty days. All vehicles and cars would be

The Last Revolution

searched. All farms and villages would be searched. A hefty reward would be offered for any information about the whereabouts of Fidel and Raúl. There was to be a complete lock down of Cuba. No one could come into or go out of the country until further notice.

General Enrique Hurtado Rodríguez became relaxed. His face immediately changed back to its normal color. He had made the right choice in trusting his friend. Everything was in order.

It was 3:45 am

In Washington D.C. Normally, it was quiet at this time of the morning at the White House, but tonight there was tight security and a wealth of activity taking place. President Bingham's aides and his select cabinet members and secretaries had arrived and had been attending an intense meeting since midnight. Their sources in Havana were unable to communicate because communications were down. Communications from Guantanamo had been intercepted so they were unable to make contact. Everything was in an uproar. All they had to go on was the CIA's information about Ayu and the time and place. They knew who was involved in Ayu's planning and the objective was to kill Castro, but they had no other information. The President was furious about the communications break down. He ordered that a spy plane be sent in immediately. The President lost his patience and shouted, "This is not acceptable! We cannot be left in the dark. What the hell is Ayu?"

Two U2 spy planes were fueled and sent in to collect information. They began to monitor the troops' movement. A US spy satellite was beaming in to intercept communications. They scrambled to get information without success. The President was frustrated and he began to scream at the Chief of Staff of the Army, Navy and Air Force for news, but there was none. US intelligence tried to get live action information, but they were locked out. The President ordered everyone to stand by.

The Secretary of State called the Cuban Embassy, but there was no answer. He had his aides used the emergency phone to try and contact the Cuban Interest Section's residence. Finally, he reached Ambassador Rodolfo Ponce. He asked the US representatives not to interfere and explained that Cuba was participating in a large scale military exercise. He explained that it was only a drill which had been ordered by Castro and planned for the month of July. All communications were down as a consequence. Ponce informed them that only the military had detailed information about the event, and he knew nothing more. Ponce had tried to call the US to notify them about the July exercise, but the information had been lost in a sea of bureaucratic red tape.

The Secretary of States reported back to the President after his conversation with Ponce. The President was not satisfied with this report and demanded more information immediately. The lack of information made him feel desperate and out of control. The greatest power in the world was now impotent. The Cuban Interest Section did not have any further information about this military exercise.

The White House security adviser was very frustrated due to the lack of sufficient information. They needed access to their spies and open communication lines, but they had none. The CIA was also working to unscramble any information from Cuba, but they had encountered only complete silence for the last three hours.

3:35AM, July 3, 2008, Pinar Del Rio Army Air Force Base

Suddenly, Major general Ricardo Esparza received an urgent message that two private, unauthorized jets had managed to take off from Havana International Airport. They were headed due south at approximately 150 knots and at an altitude of 29,000 feet on a course aimed southeast of Cuba. General Rodríguez received the urgent update. He knew it was Fidel escaping the island and heading to Caracas, Venezuela. He ordered four MIG 29s to confront them and force them to land. If they ignored the warning, then he ordered that they be shot down over the island of Isla de la Juventud.

The second attack squadron leader, Lt. Major Claro Díaz got the order from the general to engage and intercept the jet with a four MIG team. Within twelve minutes the MIGs were on their way to that part of Cuba in a line formation sortie group. They locked onto the jet and maneuvered into position around it. The two private jets raced to get out of Cuban air space. Lt. Major Díaz warned the jets to return immediately to the nearest Cuban Coast Guard air base at Isla de la Juventud but there was no response.

The Last Revolution

The Lt. Major warned them both again saying, "Attention! This is Cuban Air Force Lt. Major Claro Díaz. You are unauthorized to fly and are ordered to land immediately at the Cuban Coast Guard base at Isla de la Juventud. Do you understand? Over."

Finally, after a long pause one of the jets answered. A man responded, "I am president of the National Assembly, Minister Miguel Luis Aragón, Lt. Major! We request safe passage, and we are approaching the international border. You don't have jurisdiction over us. You wouldn't violate the Geneva Convention's treaty. You must return to your Air Force base!"

Díaz asked, "Negative! Do you have President Fidel Castro aboard, sir?"

The pilot responded, "Negative. We do not have Fidel or Raúl Castro on board. I repeat, we are on the international border, and you have no jurisdiction here."

Lt. Major Díaz shouted, "You are ordered to land your jets immediately, and we will escort you to the nearby Coast Guard base, sir. Turn on course 160. If you do not turn around peacefully, then we will force a landing. Those are our orders." The Lt. Major warned them fervently. He waited for their response. Thy completely ignored the warning.

The Lt. Major said sternly, "If you do not turn immediately, we will be forced to fire upon you. This is your final warning!"

Within minutes the Lt. Major ordered his two MIGs to fire two intermediate air-to-air heat-seeking R-73 missiles. As the jets were hit, they looked like two giant balls of fire. They were in flames as they spiraled downward from the dark Caribbean night sky. The Lt. Major cautiously assessed the incident and reconfirmed that the two jets were down. He reported to Pinar Del Rio Air Force base. They were to wait for the Coast Guard to arrive on the scene of the crash, and then terminate their mission and return to base. A Cuban Coast Guard Frigates and fleet rescue team was already on their way and would arrive at the site within minutes.

They found the body of Minister Miguel Luis Aragón, dead in the water. Sadly, his wife and two children, and four other family members had perished in the crash. There were no survivors. As the Coast Guard lights shined all around the sea where the plane went down, US dollars were floating everywhere in the water. It was an incredible sight. They couldn't believe how much money was in the water. The second jet was not carrying any passengers, but instead was full of money. But it was already sinking. Nothing could be salvaged. It was determined later that Aragón had stolen several hundred million dollars and was headed to Venezuela. General Rodríguez immediately reported all the facts related to this incident to General González.

González warned, "Enrique, Fidel didn't get out in the first wave, but he will have many other opportunities to escape until we have secured Havana International Airport by the morning. Although, we are not one hundred percent sure that he has not already escaped, we don't have any sightings or confirmation. So we are assuming that he is still alive and in the country. I am ordering the Coast Guard and Navy Admiral Gustavo Pedro Terre to send an additional research team immediately to the crash site to salvage more evidence."

The general was still convinced that Fidel was somewhere in Havana. He remained very cautious and ordered his troops to stand by but not to enter the city of Havana yet. He continued to deploy them nearby. And he sent his undercover surveillance unit to detect any kind of movement of Cuban government officials, especially Fidel and Raúl. He urged his men to seek out their whereabouts. Then he decided to change his tactic at the last minute. It was going to be different than the previous plan. He informed General Rodríguez of this change.

Over two hours had passed and there still no word on Fidel's location. The general had confidence in his new plan. He knew that Fidel couldn't hide much longer. He halted air sorties for one hour and put the jets on stand by status.

Chapter 89

At 3:45am after a long pause of silence, Fidel's senior aide, Porfiro Amesquil, was on the emergency satellite phone. Finally, he was able to get a successful connection to General González. Fidel got on the phone. He was in hiding in a secret underground bunker. The MIG jet bombardment had temporarily come to a halt, and there was quiet in Havana.

General González asked Fidel, "Sir, are you alright? We have been concerned about your safety, sir!"

Fidel sounded very alarmed and answered, "Damn Gringos! They are invading us. But we are going to kick their ass again. They never learn. What is your situation there Abe?"

The general responded, "Gringos?"

Fidel was speaking very loudly and was very upset, "Look! God-damned gringos are all over Havana bombing us. The streets of Havana are in chaos!"

Then the general said, "Sir! We are not being attacked by the Americans. This is an act of war and rebellion by our own Cuban Army Air Force in Pinar Del Rio, Sir!"

8Fidel became very quiet, "That is impossible!" The general said, "Sir, can you hear me? Sir, the connection is not good….. It is very hard to hear you, Sir." Fidel yelled, "Are you sure you mean the Cuban Air Force?"

General González said, "Yes, sir. At the moment the US is not involved, but that may change later, sir. But if that happens, we are ready for the gringos, sir!"

Fidel was struck with panic. He was very angry and could not believe his own army was revolting. But then, his voice returned to normal and he asked, "What about the other generals? What information do you have at the present time? Abe, what are your tactics so far?"

General Gonzalez replied, "Sir, all of the generals are loyal and with us. We are not sure who is responsible for the break down in communications from Santa Clara to the Army

Air Force base. We are completely cut off from all communications from Havana. At 0100 hours I ordered all three regiments of ground troops to the Pinar Del Rio base. As soon as they reach the base, they will attack the insurgents. We believe they only have two thousand troops. By my calculations, our two regiments will be there by early morning, and they will be ready to attack by 0800 hours. We will crush them, sir. We are very concerned your safety. What are your orders, sir?"

Fidel was talking to Raúl in the back ground. He said, "Here in Havana it's chaos. Those pigs are everywhere. General Garcia is on the way here any minute! We are just leaving the bunker."

The general could hear Fidel briefing Raúl. Then Fidel yelled to General Garcia. Suddenly, Garcia got on the phone, "Abe what is the situation at your command post?"

The general said, "Here everything is normal. Sir, we had a report earlier that Havana was under siege by MIGs. They are believed to be from our Air Force. We believe there is an uprising and a military coup d'etat occurring. We have sent our first regiment to secure the Havana area. We are already sending four regiment, twelve battalions composed of ten thousand men to the western Army base at Pinar Del Rio. We have information that they only have two thousand ground troops. I think we will neutralize them within forty-eight hours. Please give me any other assignments, sir!" Garcia briefed Fidel and Raúl.

The Raúl got on the phone, and his voice was harsh and upset, "Damn Enrique! That traitor! You did right by sending the regiment. They are going to destroy Enrique and his men. God-damn it! When they catch him, we are going to skin him alive and hang that traitor upside down and drag his body all around the streets of Havana so all Cuban pigs can see him. The general was silent as he listened to Raúl's tirade.

Raúl asked, "Abe how long is it going to take to neutralize that son-of-a-bitch?"

The general answered quickly and very confidently, "Sir, we have been completely out of contact due to the blackout for the last three hours. We expect to begin the attack around 0800 hours. Then my troops will crush the rebellion within forty-eight hours, sir!" Raúl continued to consult with Fidel and General Garcia.

The Last Revolution

"Look, Abe send your troops in to attack as soon as possible. Do not wait! We think it's probably best that we to move to Santa Clara for safety. Here in Havana there is mass hysteria."

Fidel took the phone, "We are on the way to Santa Clara. We need an escort by air and ground!"

General González said, "Yes sir Give me your location, and I will send you a helicopter escort within thirty minutes sir!"

Raúl said, "The Mi-8 Presidential helicopter is operational. We only have one attack helicopter, a KA-50 to escort us, but it has only enough fuel to get us half way. We don't have any access to a fuel supply here right now.

The general interrupted, "I can send more fuel right away sir!"

Then Raúl yelled, "No! We don't have enough time; we need get out of here immediately. Listen, we only need to make a rendezvous point half way where there is no MIG activity. Send your escort to five miles due east of Pedro Betancourt, to the south side Army chopper port. Do you understand me?"

The general had to contain himself. He now had a location point for Fidel. Quickly he said, "Yes sir! The rendezvous escort point is five miles due east of Pedro Betancourt on the south side of town at the Army Corps of Engineer's R- 4 heliport. Is this correct, sir?"

Fidel said, "That's correct. We are on our way now!"

The satellite phone was still on and Fidel was listening. General González was giving orders very loudly to Lt. Major General Diego Seville saying, "Send eight KA-50 Werewolf attack choppers immediately to the south side of town five miles due east of Pedro Betancourt to the south side Army Corps point Right now. Stand by for further instructions!" Then the general said, "The escort will be there by 0410 hours. Keep a safe distance and watch out for MIGs."

General Garcia got on the line, "Do you have air-to-air defense missiles activated in the choppers?"

General González answered, "Sir, my KA-50 Werewolf attack choppers are equipped with six R-27-10 lamo intermediate range air-to-air heat-seeking missiles and four dogfight medium range R-73 missiles for fighting MIGs before they can see us. We don't have access to any MIG-23s, but we have six operational MIG-19s. At the Cienfuegos Naval Base there are equipped six air-to-air heat-seeking missiles, but they were supposed to be moved to the base at Pinar Del Rio for tomorrow morning's test. But due to mechanical problems with their transportation, they halted the departure date. But the MIGs are there and ready to go, sir!

General Garcia said, "Six MIG-19SUs? They are old, and their technology is no match against the MIG-29s, but some air coverage for our escort is better than no coverage."

General González answered, "Sir, I will send them over to Havana right now least you have the High-altitude interceptors. I will send them with my top gunners. If any MIG-29s attack, at least you will have some air defense against the rebels. That is the best I can do to protect your escort to Santa Clara. I can also send some ground troops for back up, sir!"

General Garcia ordered, "Is your gunship ready?"

General González answered confidently, "Yes, sir! They are completely armed with ten missiles on each chopper, and they are already on the way to the rendezvous escort point, sir."

Garcia responded, "OK, that will do. Over and out!"

Fidel, Raúl, General Garcia along with six personal body guards boarded the large Russian-made Mi-8 presidential helicopter. It took off into the sky above Havana. Along side of it was their single KA-50 with two gunners for escort. They were headed to the rendezvous point. The choppers hovered low and flew over buildings and tree tops trying to pass unnoticed by any MIGs and to stay near the ground in case of the need for an emergency landing.

At the same time, the six MIG-21s had already left the Cienfuegos Naval Base headed toward Havana. They were ordered to shoot any jets sighted over Havana. General González ordered complete silence for security reasons, and no communications until the job was done. He needed confirmation before any mission on the air.

Chapter 90

At 0350 hours

At CIA headquarters in Langley, Virginia, a US spy satellite surveillance unit intercepted a communication between Fidel and General González. They immediately phoned the emergency line at the White House. They relayed the information to the Secretary of Defense to give to the President.

The message contained Fidel's last communication to González, and details about the evacuation mission to the Santa Clara Army base. He was told of the fifteen thousand ground troops being sent to the Havana area to secure the capital, and the other ten thousand en route to Pinar Del Rio to neutralize the Western Army rebels. This would bring an end to the revolution within the next twelve to twenty-four hours.

There was already an emergency meeting taking place in the situation room as President George Tiffany Bingham assembled his staff. Present were the Vice President, the Secretary of Defense, the Secretary of State, the Joint Chiefs, the CIA Director, and several White House cabinet security advisors.

President Bingham told them, "We need to decide whether or not to invade Cuba. The 4th of July is our Independence Day, and it might just become Cuba's, too! We can provide support to the rebels at the Pinar Del Rio Army and Air Force bases. They want Fidel ousted, and we can help them. They want change, and we can assist them. The time is ripe for democracy in Cuba. Besides, we need to take the scope off of the Iraqi crisis for the moment. God sakes; we are taking a lot of heat about it. This is something that will inspire the American citizens. They will see that under my watch, evil can be defeated and democracy will reign." It was a golden opportunity, and the entire group was energized with ideas.

Vice President Dick A. Burnett commented, "It's been the best chance to gain control of Cuba since 1965. You know Mr. President; it would be a great victory. This would be a great moment for us in history! We help the Cuban Air Force, and then we take control….it's perfect. We can finally neutralize Fidel."

The White House cabinet security advisors Michael Danielson interrupted, "Mr. President, I think US involvement in Cuba is a mistake. We are in over our heads in Iraq. The Cuban crisis is long over. We don't need to control Cuba now. We have our foot there at Guantanamo."

The President thought about this and said, "I am not interested in sending any more young men to their deaths. We have taken a big loss in Iraq."

The Secretary of Defense and the Vice President interrupted, "We don't agree sir. Involvement in Cuba is entirely different from Iraq. There is a momentous opportunity here. Cuba wants Fidel out, and they need our assistance. Within forty-eight hours we could have control of Cuba, Mr. President!"

The defense secretary Donald Albertson added, "Mr. Burnett had a good point. I think America is ready this time. And this could be a quick victory. Iraq is going to take more time. Cuba is ready. All Cuban-Americans have been for this waiting this sensational news. We will not have another chance. It would be a great mistake to pass up this opportunity."

They reviewed the current information coming from the CIA and from Havana. The President thought for a moment and said, "I thought General González was in cahoots with General Rodríguez. Now, we hear from Havana that González is going to attack Rodríguez?"

Vice President Burnett added, "What the hell is going on? Which is it?"

Donald responded, "Dick, apparently he is loyal to Fidel. That is what we do know, and he has always been highly trusted by Fidel. Damn CIA! They never have their shit right. Look what happened in Iraq with Saddam. I don't know if I can ever fully trust another CIA report."

Lisa Oates, the Secretary of State added her opinion, "Gentlemen, permit me to say something on the matter. I think our best avenue is to work with the CIA to try and intercept General Rodríguez's current emergency satellite phone communications. In a very short time we could help him, and he could permit us to land at his Air Force base with US invasion forces."

Dick said, "We definitely need to go in, George. What is your assessment, Donnell?"

The Last Revolution

Donnell was reading reports and commented, "I already discussed this with Chief of Staff, General Baker. He told me he would be able to neutralize the entire Cuban Army and Air Force within four days. He is standing by in his office. Mr. President, all you need to do is say the word."

The President said, "Get Baker on the line. I want to hear what he has to say." The security adviser called the Pentagon.

The Chief of Staff was on the other line. "Sir, I am on standby. I have been briefed about the present condition in Cuba, sir!"

Donald said, "General, what do you propose we do? If we give the order, you and your troops will have to end this thing in Cuba within forty-eight hours and occupy Havana and the surrounding Air Force and Army bases. Are you capable of doing this on such short notice?"

General Baker said, "Sir, at the present time it is not possible to occupy and invade Cuba, sir." Everyone was surprised to hear General Baker's opinion.

President Bingham asked, "General, tell me why you do not think we can achieve our objective? What do you feel is the best strategy?"

General Baker cleared his throat, "Sir, I recommend to mobilize and cut off traffic between the east and west access to Havana. Send more troops to western Pinar Del Rio and reinforce the Air Force general. We could send our Air Force planes there and completely cut off Havana from all inbound air and sea traffic. I believe a complete blockade is necessary. Fidel would have to face a mob made up of the people of Cuba. If they decided his fate, I think they would chose to oust him. This way it comes from within Cuba and is not forced by us."

Dick said, "George, the Army will get Fidel. What do you think, Mr. President?"

He answered calmly, "I don't know for sure. Dick, what do you propose?"

"You are the President of United States. You are going to have to make the decision on this one. You know what I think. Your dad and I worked on similar situations in the past with Grenada and Panama. I think Cuba is no different. Fidel is not a threat. Their economy is weak, and the people no longer support him."

The President said firmly, "What is your educated guess

on tactics?"

Dick responded, "I think we go in as quickly as possible and cut off the sections of Cuba as recommended by General Baker. That would be the eastern province and the western Air Force base. Then we attack the central division. We will encounter tough resistance because General González is an experienced soldier, and I think we are ready and could probably do the job with ten thousand soldiers within one week. If we are lucky, we could take over within forty-eight hours depending on the situation."

Lisa added, "As we have all mentioned, Fidel is old and has fallen behind the times. He is a relic, and the people are waiting for a new direction. Mr. President, Cuba is a valuable asset for us within the Caribbean and is the gateway to South America. I recommend you move on this quickly."

Donald said, "Mr. President, if you give me the authority, I promise to hand you Cuba on a silver platter. It will bring glory to this administration. America needs to feel we are doing something positive. To deliver the Cubans out of the hands of a tyrannical dictator like Castro would be phenomenal. Not to mention having control of Cuba for strategic purposes is a worthy asset.

The President took a sip of his water and closed his eyes. He was silent for a moment. "All right, we will go in like Dick said. I... a... a...you know." Then all three members grew quiet and looked each other.

Then Dick asked, "General Baker you said it was impossible to invade Cuba now. What do you mean by that?"

General Baker was still on the line and answered, "Sir, I will invade by 0800 Eastern Standard Time. First, I will send in one thousand US Marine recon units to western Cuba Then I will support the Cuban general by sending in two thousand Para Marine Airborne and five hundred Navy Seals to gain control of the coast. They will cut off Havana from the west and make it secure—a neutral zone. Then the Air Force can deliver supplies to the Pinar del Rio Air Force base. I think this will do the job. My men are well-trained and have practiced a similar scenario in past drills."

President Bingham asked, "What about the Army?"

General Baker fervently replied, "Sir, Mr. President, we don't have many good troops here. What we have here is a bare

The Last Revolution

minimal housecleaning staff. They are good men, but I am afraid we could not guarantee a victory. We need highly trained professional combat soldiers who have been well seasoned. Currently, they are all in Iraq. Right now, sir, the Army reserve troops are more a peacetime, voluntary Army. But, if I could bring back some good soldiers from Iraq," he hesitated, "I don't think now is the right time. That is just not possible, sir. If we take men for Cuba and have more insurgent uprisings in Iraq, we will have a big mess on our hands. I recommend that we don't spread ourselves too thin. We are just doing the bare minimum in Iraq with our best troops, sir."

Dick was upset and the intensity of this voice was audible to everyone, "You mean to tell me that you don't have enough back up troops here in the US for our own protection, let alone to support and to invade Cuba?"

The general answered, "Yes, sir, more and more troops have been deployed to Iraq, sir. All we have is a barebones crew for national security purposes and the reserves."

Dick was speechless and frustrated to hear this. "How can this be?" he asked.

General Baker announced, "We only have US Army rotation personnel available, and they will be deployed to Iraq as soon as their thirty day leaves are up. I can send that rotation army to Cuba, but I can only promise five thousand men. That is the maximum I can spare."

The President asked, "General, do you think five thousand US soldiers can get the job done? Are they prepared to deal with the Cuban Army?" The President was still undecided.

The general said confidently, "Five thousand soldiers are not enough. I will get an additional eight thousand Marines from Iraq, but it will take six days to transport them here. The Cuban Air Force General must also agree to allow us to use their Air Force base because we going use C-5-A maybe as many as 25 around the clock. Sir, are we trying to occupy Cuba? I have only enough re-enforcements to help neutralize the current situation and assist the Air Force General, not for an occupation. They will have to come up with Cuban military manpower for a big fight. For an occupation, sir, we would need almost our entire Army division! It is impossible, sir!"

Dick said, "We need a draft!" Everyone at the table looked at one another.

Donald voiced his concerns, "Two wars simultaneously? Damn Iraq! We should have never gotten involved there. Mr. President, the American people are not going to have a draft for Cuba or Iraq. Talk about a big mess, you are going to have one right here on American soil while the world looks on. You cannot do it, George! It's political suicide for all of us, as well." The President looked at his team, but he remained very quiet and his face showed concern and confusion.

Lisa looked at the others, "I'm sure this war would not be like Iraq because the people of Cuba are ready. They will join our troops for a freedom fight. The 4th of July is the perfect date to rally the American people. They will be behind a movement for Cuban Independence as they are patriotic about our own history. Sir, the Cuban-Americans can volunteer to participate in this fight. Then we can put a Cuban-American in office as President. I don't think this is as complicated as you all are making it."

Donald said, "Well, I am with Lisa. I think we can handle this—no problem. We don't need to occupy Cuba; we only need to help the Cubans to liberate it from Fidel and then back a Cuban-American for President of Cuba or whatever they decide to call their new leader. That is the key."

The President asked General Baker, "How can we contact General Rodríguez?"

Lisa answered for the General Baker, "Well…the CIA is working on reaching his satellite emergency phone now! We will tap in and discuss the plan with him within an hour. We will know where we stand by 6:00 am."

Dick said, "All right, as soon as the CIA contacts General Rodríguez, Donald can begin a dialogue with him. Let Lisa negotiate since this is her area of expertise." Donald looked around the table and was very candid, "Well, ladies and gentlemen. Are we all on board? As they say back where I am from, I think it's time to shit, or it's time to get off of the pot!"

Then President Bingham quietly said, "Well, I ah…guess that is the plan. I ah…I'll order…ah the invasion of Cuba." But he wasn't very convincing, and he still looked deep in thought.

Donald took the lead, "Mr. President that's great! We will go in at 0800 hours. General Baker, put whatever troops you have ready on stand-by. Get your Army rotation troops back in

The Last Revolution

the saddle. We will need the additional Marines to fly back home and suit up for Havana."

General Baker was quick to answer, "Yes, sir!" Donald continued to give directions, "Dick, we are going to need to get the American-Cubans rallied. Your people take care of that. Have them narrow down the top three political candidates for possible Cuban presidency who are tight with us!"

He looked at Lisa, "The press will be waiting for an official statement. Get your spin doctors to give them a patriotic sound bite to digest at the right time. We have to get the American people on board. Contact your sources and get footage of Fidel and the images of how Cuba has declined in the past decade on the tube. I want that run 24/7. Also, get your team and the CIA to get us hooked up with the Cuban General ASAP!"

President Bingham glanced at everyone and looked confident for the first time during the entire meeting, "All right, I'll authorize the intervention at 7:45 am. What Kennedy didn't finish….I will."

Just then his secretary interrupted, "Sir, George Sr. is on the red line."

The President said, "Are we through?" They all stood up, shook hands, and left the Oval office.

The United States assembled all military personal and moved adequate hardware to Guantanamo and the coast of Florida. The United States invasion force was transported to Guantanamo. War was eminent. The US Navy and Coast Guard were headed toward Cuban waters for their final positions. The CIA continued to intercept satellite telephone signals, but it was very quiet and there was no communication for nearly three and a half hours. The preparation for the media machine to advertise the war and convince the American population that Cuba needed US intervention was in high gear. The US forces were on standby.

Chapter 91

At 3:30 am back at the Army base in Santa Clara Twelve young, uniformed honor guard soldiers were lining up at the helicopter port at the Santa Clara army Corps base security compound. They were armed with blank bullets in their A Type 2 AK-47s. General González and Lt. Major General Diego Seville entered the port. Lt. Tomaz Nunes was in charge of the honor guards. First he saluted the two generals, and then the entire group saluted the two high commanders. General González said, "At ease, men."

The general began to talk very seriously, "Brothers, I am proud to have you as comrades in the Cuban Army. Each of you is very important to me! We are countrymen and share the same love of Cuba. That is why we are here. What I am about to tell you is from my heart. I want you to listen very carefully! We have been prisoners in our own country. Fidel and his brother have taken Cuba hostage."

"We were once a thriving country, and now our countrymen have to scramble for food and basic necessities on the black market. We have no hope for the future. All of us have suffered losses, and we are afraid to even speak what is on our minds. If we speak out, we are afraid of imprisonment or death by Fidel. We have had no voice for too long."

"Tonight, we can end that together. Tonight, I call upon you to free Cuba from its shackles. We do not need a master. We are not slaves. We are free men! We need equality and democracy. We need a say in our lives, our government, and in the future of our families and children. We need to take our power back! Today is the beginning of a new era, and you are about to make history tonight. Within thirty minutes and with your cooperation, Cuba will be free from tyranny and Fidel. His vision is obsolete and has run Cuba into the ground. Fidel will never step down and give the people back the power to make necessary changes toward progress. Raúl will take over, and it will be more of the same. They rule with an iron fist. Tonight I ask you to free Cuba. If you are with me—stand. If you are not, put down your weapons. You will be detained, but unharmed. This, I promise." The twelve soldiers were silent. They were very serious and frozen from the words uttered during the general's surprise speech.

The general ordered, "Men, if you are in agreement. Salute me, and we will make history together. Cuba libre!" Slowly, each of the honor guards began to show their solidarity and salute him. For the general, it was a beautiful moment. The faces of the young men were priceless. He could see their look of excitement at the thought of a new Cuba, but they were well-trained and continued to look ahead in silence. They were all connected in the dream for a better life and a free Cuba.

Finally, the last soldier dropped his AK-47 on the floor. His hands were visibly shaking. He slowly raised his hand in salute to the general and cried out, *"Viva Cuba!"* The energy was tense in the port. All the men were moved by the moment. They began to yell in unison, *"Viva Cuba! Viva Cuba! Cuba Libre!"* Many of the men were estatic with smiles and expressions of excitement. Some had tears in their eyes. But they were all ready for the last revolution.

That moment hit the general hard. It was like a boulder striking his chest and knocking the wind out of him. He had a lump in his throat, and then tears fell from his eyes. It was the first time he had ever allowed himself to show his true emotions to his men. For his entire career and for most of his adult life, he had had to suppress his emotions and feelings. But at this intense moment, he was overcome by the reaction of these young men. They were young—aged eighteen to twenty-three. They were the future of Cuba. He looked into their eyes and knew that anything was possible. After tonight, their world would forever be changed.

Lt. Major General Diego Seville and Lt. Tomas Nunes saluted each other in silence. Then they handed out boxes of live ammunition to the men. Nunes briefed them and told them what to do. The young soldiers were nervous yet humble. As they loaded their weapons, they knew exactly what to do. No one said a word.

At 4:00 am

On July 3, at the Santa Clara Army base, the air-to-air heat seeking missiles were fully-armed in the Werewolf KA-50 Russian-made attack gunship choppers. The eight chopper escort team met Fidel's helicopter. Then they made contact and left together at precisely 4:00 am. As they left the rendezvous point, General González watched all communications between the choppers and the Santa Clara Army base. Lt. Major General Diego Seville reported everything to the general. That half an hour seemed to last an eternity. The heart of every man involved was pounding. They thought about Fidel. They thought about the future. They thought about their wives, their children, and their families. They were ready and waiting.

Finally, Seville announced, "General, sir! The choppers have left the rendezvous point at Pedro Betancourt. They are due to arrive within thirty minutes. The presidential choppers are carrying Fidel, Raúl, and General Garcia. With them are Fidel's body guards and personnel. His body guards are heavily armed sir." The General ordered Major General Seville to bring the twelve honorary guards to meet him at the end of the official red carpet.

The general also stationed fifty extra soldiers as backup security. Major General Marros Rosas was in charge of this security force which had already been briefed by the general. It was their job to make sure that if the twelve guards missed Fidel, they would finish the job. They were to also eliminate Fidel's personal body guards and personnel as soon as Fidel was down. None of Fidel's men were to be left standing. They would all witness the sensational and historical event.

At 4:30 am

As the eight choppers neared the heliport, everything looked very normal. The port was on full alert due to the emergency situation. The helicopter KA-50 commander, Lt. Martin Naranjo communicated with the Santa Clara Army communications tower. The first of the helicopters lined up in preparation for landing in the air space above the E2 heliport.

The twelve honor guards were prepared and waiting. At precisely 4:35 am, the ground crew directed the helicopter traffic as normal. Fidel's team didn't suspect a thing, nor did they seem at all suspicious that something could be wrong. Fidel, Raúl, and the Chief General's helicopter touched down first. Then, eight attack gun ships touched down. The ground crew was waiting.

They opened the door and assisted Fidel Castro, Raúl Ruz Castro, and Army General Hector Elias Garcia to the ground. A

The Last Revolution

team of elite and heavily-armed bodyguards rushed out and surrounded Fidel who looked old and tired. The Army ground crew directed them to the lighted red carpet.

Fidel always insisted on an official reception whenever he arrived anywhere. General González stood waiting. As Fidel approached him, the general looked into his eyes. Fidel looked relieved to see his favorite young general and smiled at him. Fidel saluted him. The general saluted Fidel for the last time and stepped back. That was the signal.

Suddenly, the guards took aim. In rapid succession, they fired their rifles. Fidel, Raúl, and General Garcia were killed instantly. Bullets from the highly accurate marksmen went straight into the heads of the three men. The great Cuban dictator, Fidel Castro, was dead by the hand of his youngest and most trusted general.

Raúl and General Garcia lay on the ground next to Fidel. Blood drenched the red carpet. There was no sign of movement. Before any of Fidel's team had time to lift their guns to fire, the twelve guards and the fifty-man back up team was in position and shot multiple rounds in a second wave of gunfire. It was a storm of bullets. Nothing and no one could have survived it. Men in green military uniforms fell down around the helicopter near their deceased leader. Fidel Castro's once elite staff now lay dead on the ground.

There was a long, tense pause of silence. The general was awestruck. He would never forget this moment. Fidel's end had come and with it the fall of Communism for Cuba was inevitable. The team of honor guards dropped their guns and began hugging and walking around chanting, *"Viva Cuba! Viva Cuba! Cuba Libre!"* Everyone in the Army compound started singing the Cuban National Anthem.

It was a surreal moment. A great outcry of exploding emotion surrounded the base. The last revolution had finally come to an end in Santa Clara which ironically was the same place where just fifty-two years earlier, Fidel's last revolutionary battle had ended on December 1958.

Epilogue

General Abelardo González'
After the last revolution was implemented, General Abelardo González' continued as the commander of the military for two years to prevent chaos from overtaking Cuba. After the election of a new Cuban president, he resigned from the military and became the head of the Santa Clara Technology Center (SCTC) which was similar to Silicon Valley, Cuban style.

The general's SCTC began manufacturing a PC neuro-electronic, micro-electronic interfacing system (DNA-based) super-high speed chip developed by Hiro. The company was sold to Intel Corp. for $150 billion. With his wealth, the general endowed a high-tech department at the university in Cuba for promising low-income students. González and Hiro serve as consultants to the program.

General González's two sons attended graduate school at MIT and Caltech, respectively, taking full advantage of their father's financial success in the capitalistic Democratic Free Cuba. They followed in the footsteps of rich Cuban children who, prior to Castro's takeover, received higher education in the US.

The former general discovered that it was a struggle to be successful financially under the constraints of capitalism. While the general mastered the system quickly, he longed for the days under Fidel when his life was free from financial pressures.
González' began to reaccredit Fidel's vision for Cuba and realized his revolution had destroyed a dream world.

Freddie Alvarez Díaz.
Freddie was actively involved in designing the transitional government of the new Democratic Free Cuba. Many wanted him to run for president, but he declined the nomination.

Freddie entered the tourist business through a joint venture with a Canadian and Japanese corporation. With funding from the corporation and his connections, he built a four-star hotel and a luxurious retirement complex in central Cuba. The business was later sold to the US real estate conglomerate, Crye-Leike, for an unspecified amount.

The Last Revolution

Freddie's two daughters also took full advantage of his success under the capitalistic system. Their interest in technology led them to attend graduate school at the University of Tokyo and Princeton, respectively.

Enrique Hurtado Rodríguez.

After the new government formed, the General continued to command the Air Force with General González'. When González retired, he became the Chief of Staff to the Cuban Military under the Democratic Free government. He moved to Havana work with the Department of Defense and was head of the entire Cuban Armed Forces.

Five years later, he retired and returned to civilian life and moved to a small village, Tops de Collantes near Trinidad. There he lived with his wife Andrea and her family.

He purchased a huge government co-op coffee plantation and poured his savings into this company and supporting the local community and his family. Hiro and Abelardo remained close friends and supported his business endeavors. He became a successful coffee entrepreneur on the world market.

But he missed the military life, at times he had nothing but time of his hands. He was living the dream life that Fidel had sought to create, that was rare in the world.

Aimee Gomez Menendez

Soon after the revolution, Aimee moved to Las Vegas; however, she missed her tropical island and returned to Havana. When a Venezuelan media concern purchased the Cuban government's TV Broadcasting Corporation, Aimee rose through the ranks to become president of company. She also started a new woman's magazine called, *Prenza, La Cubana* which enjoyed huge success.

Aimee is single and continues to live in Havana. She remembers her old life when money was scarce but time was abundant.

Hiroaki Nakagawa and Dania Altamirano Hernández

Dania and Hiro remained happily married. She managed Hiro's assets. Dania later died from complications from surgery to remove a malignant brain tumor. Hiro returned to his native Hiroshima, Japan.

Micheal Kazuhiro Nishitani

Hiro's daughters: Yumiko Adriana and Masako Alexandra
Hiro's two daughters attended Harvard. Masako's interest in technology led her to attend graduate school at MIT. Yumiko returned to Hiroshima, Japan, and attended graduate school at the University of Hiroshima. She completed medical school and became a heart surgeon. Yumiko speaks three languages fluently and lives in Japan.

Pedro Gomez Perlayo
After the revolution, Pedro continued to work as a carpenter. Freddie asked him to supervise the construction of his hotel and retirement community. Pedro became Freddie's right arm until Freddie sold the business to Crye-Leike. Then Crye-Leike hired Pedro as a special consultant. Pedro still lives in the Rancho Veloz area.

Pedro's daughter Wendy became a pediatrician after attending University of Miami followed by medical school at Johns Hopkins.

Piyo and Pipo Requeiro Hernández
Piyo ended his Army career as a captain. His life has not changed much since the last revolution. He is still living in the same apartment and struggling to survive in Democratic Free Cuba. His white wife died from pneumonia because Piyo had no money to buy medicine. Hiro did not find out that the medicine was needed until it was too late to save her.

Pipo lives in Hiro's old home where he raises hogs to supply pork to tourist hotels. He struggles financially and is broke with huge debts.

Pipo's life has not changed since Cuba became a free Democratic country. He became the housekeeper in Hiro's new home. Pipo still lives in the same house with his Cuban common law wife. They have one son named Sierra Morena. Pipo misses the old Cuban government's welfare system and remembers that time as the 'good old days'. Both Piyo and Pipo miss the welfare system under the old Cuban government and remember when all of their needs were provided for and when they had time on their hands.

When Hiro purchased a huge ranch near Hotel La Roca, he built a compound consisting of eight houses for members of

The Last Revolution

Dania's family. Hiro covered all of their expenses in exchange for their working for their cousin, Dania and her family. Piyo became Hiro's chauffeur.

Even though the system of government had changed in Cuba, Dania's family, like the majority of Cubans, just replaced Communism with a return to the way of life in Cuba before 1959.

Micheal Kazuhiro Nishitani

Biographical sketch of Hiroaki Nakagawa

Hiroaki was born in Fukuyama in the Hiroshima Prefecture in Japan in 1942. He received his B.A. from the University of Hiroshima (Japan) in 1962 and earned his Master's and Ph.D. degrees in mathematics from M.I.T. in the United States in 1966.

Hiro's research included understanding the languages layout numerical sequent. He formalized procedures related to binary code. He studied electrical and integrated circuit analysis and the computer languages used by engineers and scientist to understand the computer world. In addition, he studied and created the primary model of the first electromagnetic which stored various computer languages and led to the field knows as aurora, discovery of artificial intelligence that scientists used to create the memory chips. Hiro invented the theory of arithmetical layout for hardware or software, he is expert both.

Also, Hiro discovered the multiple systems or single socket that enabled an integrated circuit system to send communicated signal to various high-speed systems computer this theory later became a milestone that we know as the Internet. While still at M.I.T., Hiro created the first computer game. This became the incredibly popular Nintendo game.

In 1968, he discovered the first window in a computer circuitry system. This allowed various programs to be projected onto a screen through the use of a small tool described as Nezumi (mouse). That discovery evolved into advanced high-speed sequence which enabled easy access to files.

Hacking became a popular past time while Hiro was at M.I.T. Hiro's research led to the ultimate surveillance security software with digital sources which enabled control of all incoming computer traffic. By studying incoming traffic, Hiro synchronized the binary system of electric circuit that prevented control of binary numerical code dysfunctions that protect artificially created binary phenomena which protect the microprocessor and hard drive from incoming digital code activity. The currently used anti-virus software developed from this finding. Later his studies improved various computer programs for business purposes.

Hiroaki researched various application files and new facets of an advanced digitalized and compressed file system

The Last Revolution

which becomes the MP3.WAV MP00X created new format on digital signal. Later he reassembled the digitalized high-speed storages he had created to store compressed digital images based on his studies. This discovery later became the digital file system for the digital camera and the digital audio player.

His final discovery resulted in a new generation of the neuroelectronic interfacing system which is an interfacing system between neuron cell, and the computer which has remained only a theory.

Hiro was considered to be the father of computer science. He discontinued his research in 1995 and returned to his native Japan.

In 2003, his ultimate discovery, digital artificial chemical violence duplicated the brain's memory system and implanted the duplicate in the brain stem initiating a new phase of computer science in Cuba. In 2008, because of the outcomes of using this system, Hiro received honorary citizenship from the newly formed government of the Democratic Free Cuba.

Up to now, the nature of memory function in the brain is not clarified. This has remained only a theory. But we can imagine and describe this as a part of novel.

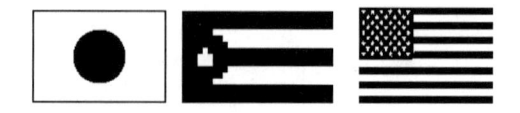

Micheal Kazuhiro Nishitani

The Last Revolution

401922

Made in the USA